I0585083

George William Cox

The Mythology of the Aryan Nations in Two Volumes

Vol. 1

George William Cox

The Mythology of the Aryan Nations in Two Volumes
Vol. 1

ISBN/EAN: 9783742851048

Manufactured in Europe, USA, Canada, Australia, Japa

Cover: Foto ©Andreas Hilbeck / pixelio.de

Manufactured and distributed by brebook publishing software
(www.brebook.com)

George William Cox

The Mythology of the Aryan Nations in Two Volumes

ARYAN MYTHOLOGY.

VOL. I.

LONDON: PRINTED BY
SPOTTISWOODE AND CO., NEW-STREET SQUARE
AND PARLIAMENT STREET

THE MYTHOLOGY

OF

THE ARYAN NATIONS.

BY

GEORGE W. COX, M.A.

LATE SCHOLAR OF TRINITY COLLEGE,
OXFORD.

IN TWO VOLUMES.

VOL. I.

LONDON:

LONGMANS, GREEN, AND CO.

1870.

All rights reserved.

PREFACE.

WITH a deep consciousness of its shortcomings, but with a confidence not less deep in the security of the foundations laid by the Science of Comparative Mythology, I submit to the judgment of all whose desire it is to ascertain the truth of facts in every field of inquiry a work on a subject as vast as it is important. The history of mythology is, in a sense far beyond that in which we may apply the words to the later developements of religious systems, the history of the human mind ; and the analysis which lays bare the origin and nature of Iranian dualism, and traces the influence of that dualism on the thought and philosophy of other lands, must indefinitely affect our conclusions on many subjects which may not appear to be directly connected with it.

For myself I confess candidly, and with a feeling of gratitude which lapse of time certainly has not weakened, that Professor Max Müller's Essay on Comparative Mythology first opened to me thirteen years ago a path through a labyrinth which, up to that time, had seemed as repulsive as it was intricate. I well remember the feeling of delight awakened by his analysis of the myths examined in that essay, of which it is but bare justice to say that by it the ground which it traversed was for the first time effectually broken for English scholars, and the fact established that the myths of a nation are as legitimate a subject for scientific investigation as any other phenomena. The delight which this investigation has never ceased to impart is strictly the satisfaction which the astronomer or the geologist feels in the ascertainment of new facts : and I have written throughout under a constant sense of the paramount duty of simply and plainly speaking the truth.

Of one fact, the importance of which if it be well ascertained can scarcely be exaggerated, I venture to claim the discovery. I am not aware that the great writers who have traced the wonderful parallelisms in the myths of the Aryan world have asserted that the epic poems of the Aryan nations are simply different versions of one and the same story, and that this story has its origin in the phenomena of the natural world, and the course of the day and the year. This position is, in my belief, established by an amount of evidence which not long hence will probably be regarded as excessive. At the least I have no fear that it will fail to carry conviction to all who will weigh the facts without prejudice or partiality, who will carefully survey the whole evidence produced before they form a definite judgment, and who will fairly estimate the cumulative proof of the fact that the mythology of the Vedic and Homeric poets contains the germs, and in most instances more than the germs, of almost all the stories of Teutonic, Scandinavian, and Celtic folk-lore. This common stock of materials, which supplements the evidence of language for the ultimate affinity of all the Aryan nations, has been moulded into an infinite variety of shapes by the story-tellers of Greeks and Latins, of Persians and Englishmen, of the ancient and modern Hindus, of Germans and Norwegians, Icelanders, Danes, Frenchmen, and Spaniards. On this common foundation the epic poets of these scattered and long-separated children of one primitive family have raised their magnificent fabrics or their cumbrous structures. Nay, from this common source they have derived even the most subtle distinctions of feature and character for their portraits of the actors in the great drama which in some one or more of its many scenes is the theme of all Aryan national poetry.

Momentous as this conclusion must be, it is one which seems to me to be strictly involved in the facts registered by all comparative mythologists; and while I wish to claim for myself no more than the honesty which refuses to adopt the statements of others without testing their accuracy, I may feel a legitimate confidence in the assurance that in all important points I am supported by the authority of such writers as Grimm, Max Müller, Bréal, Kuhn, Preller, Welcker, H. H. Wilson, Cornewall Lewis, Grote, and Thirlwall.

If in the task of establishing the physical origin of Aryan myths the same facts have been in some instances adduced more than once, I must plead not merely the necessity of the case, but the reiterated assertions of writers who seem to regard the proclamation of their views as of itself conclusive. The broad statement, for example, that Hermes is primarily and strictly a god of commerce, and of the subtlety and trickery which commerce is on this hypothesis supposed to require, makes it necessary at every step, and at the cost of repetitions which would otherwise be needless, to point out the true character of this divine harper.

In the wide field of inquiry on which I have entered in these volumes, I need scarcely say that I have very much more to learn, and that I shall receive with gratitude the suggestions of those who may wish to aid me in the task. Many portions of the subject are at present little more than sketched out : and of these I hope that I may be enabled to supply the details hereafter. The evidence thus far examined justifies the assurance that these details will not affect the main conclusions already arrived at.

Some of the pages in the First Book have appeared in articles contributed by me to the ' Edinburgh,' the ' Fortnightly,' and the ' Saturday ' Reviews ; and I have to thank the editors for the permission to make use of them.

The Greek names in this work are given as nearly as possible in their Greek forms. On this point I need only say that Mr. Gladstone, who, standing even then almost alone, retained in his earlier work on ' Homer and the Homeric Age ' their Latin equivalents, has in his ' Juventus Mundi ' adopted the method which may now be regarded as universally accepted.

I have retained the word Aryan as a name for the tribes or races akin to Greeks and Teutons in Europe and in Asia. Objections have been lately urged against its use, on the ground that only Hindus and Persians spoke of themselves as Aryas : and the tracing of this name to Ireland Mr. Peile regards as very uncertain. To him the word appears also to mean not 'ploughmen,' but 'fitting, worthy, noble.' If it be so, the title becomes the more suitable as a designation for the peoples who certainly have never called themselves Indo-Germanic.

But however sure may be the foundations of the science of Comparative Mythology, and however sound its framework, the measure in which its conclusions are received must depend largely on the acceptance or rejection of its method in the philological works chiefly used in our schools and universities. Hence, in acknowledging thankfully the great improvement of the last over the previous editions of the Greek Lexicon of Dr. Liddell and Dr. Scott in the etymology of mythological names, I express a feeling shared doubtless by all who wish to see a wide and fertile field thoroughly explored. The recognition of the principle that Greek names must be interpreted either by cognate forms in kindred languages, or by reference to the common source from which all these forms spring, is the one condition without which it is useless to look for any real progress in this branch of philology; and this principle is here fully recognised. The student is now told that he must compare the Greek Charites with 'the Sanskrit Haritas, the coursers of the sun,' and that both received their name from a root *ghar*, to shine, or glisten. Zeus is referred to the Sanskrit Dyaus, the brilliant being, Ouranos to Varuṇa, and Erinys to Saranyû. It is only to be regretted that the method has not been carried out more systematically. In all doubtful cases a Lexicographer is fully justified in keeping silence: but the affinity of Arês and the Latin

Mars with the Sanskrit Maruts, the Greek Moliôn, the
Teutonic Miölnir, and of Athênê with the Sanskrit
Ahanâ and Dahanâ and the Greek Daphnê, is as well
established as that of Erinys and Saranyû, of Ouranos
and Varuṇa.   Yet under Arês we read that it is 'akin
to ἄρρην, ἄρσην, as Lat. Mars to *mas*, perhaps also to
ἥρως, Lat. vir;' under Athênê we are referred to ἀνθέω,
where it is said that ' ανθ is the root of ἄνθος, perhaps
also of 'Αθήνη and ἀνήνοθε.'   But to the Comparative
Mythologist the acceptance of his method will more
than atone for the few blemishes still remaining in a
great work, which must determine the character of
English scholarship.

   I have said that the task of analysing and comparing
the myths of the Aryan nations has opened to me a
source of unqualified delight.   I feel bound to avow
the conviction that it has done more.   It has removed
not a few perplexities ; it has solved not a few difficulties which press hard on many thinkers.   It has
raised and strengthened my faith in the goodness of
God ; it has justified the wisdom which has chosen to
educate mankind through impressions produced by the
phenomena of the outward world.

March 8, 1870.

CONTENTS

OF

THE FIRST VOLUME.

BOOK I.

CHAPTER I.

POPULAR THEORIES ON THE ORIGIN AND GROWTH OF MYTHOLOGY.

CHAPTER V.

GREEK CONCEPTIONS OF MYTHICAL TRADITION.

CHAPTER VI.

GREEK NOTIONS RESPECTING THE MORAL ASPECT OF MYTHOLOGY.

CHAPTER VII.

THEORY OF GREEK MYTHOLOGY AS AN ECLECTIC SYSTEM.

CHAPTER VIII.

THE DIFFUSION OF MYTHS.

CHAPTER IX.

MODERN EUEMERISM.

CHAPTER X.

THE CHARACTER OF GREEK DYNASTIC AND POPULAR LEGENDS IN RELATION TO TRIBAL AND NATIONAL NAMES.

CHAPTER XI.

MYTHICAL PHRASES FURNISHING THE MATERIALS OF THE HOMERIC POEMS.

CHAPTER XII.

MYTHICAL PHRASES FURNISHING MATERIALS FOR THE TEUTONIC EPIC POEMS, AND THE LEGENDS OF ARTHUR AND ROLAND.

BOOK II.

CHAPTER I.

THE ETHEREAL HEAVENS.

SECTION I.—DYAUS.

SECTION II.—VARUNA AND MITRA.

SECTION III.—INDRA.

SECTION IV.—BRAHMA.

CHAPTER II.

THE LIGHT.

THE MYTHOLOGY

OF

THE ARYAN NATIONS.

BOOK I.

CHAPTER I.

POPULAR THEORIES ON THE ORIGIN AND GROWTH
OF MYTHOLOGY.

WE cannot examine the words by which we express our
thoughts and our wants, or compare the stories which English children hear in their nurseries with the folk-talk of
Germany and Norway, without speedily becoming aware that
the inquiry on which we have entered must carry us back to
the very infancy of mankind. We have undertaken the
investigation of fact, and we must follow the track into which
the search for facts has brought us. If we have been accus-
tomed to think that the race of men started in their great
career with matured powers and with a speech capable of
expressing high spiritual conceptions, we cannot deny the
gravity of the issue, when a science which professes to resolve
this language into its ultimate elements, asserts that for a
period of indefinite length human speech expressed mere
bodily sensations, and that it was confined to such expressions, because no higher thoughts had yet been awakened in
the mind. But unless we choose to take refuge in assumptions, we must regard the question as strictly and simply a
matter of fact: and all that we have to do, is to examine

impartially the conditions of the problem, with the determination of evading no conclusion to which the evidence of
fact may lead us.

The nature of the problem to be solved.
This problem is sufficiently startling, on whatever portion
of the subject we may first fix our minds.   The earliest literature, whether of the Hindu or the Greek, points in the
direction to which the analysis of language seems to guide
us.   In both alike we find a genuine belief in a living Power,
to whom men stand in the relation of children to a father;
but in both, this faith struggles to find utterance in names
denoting purely sensuous objects, and thus furnishing the
germ of a sensuous mythology.   Hence the developement of
religious faith and of a true theology would go on side by
side with the growth of an indiscriminate anthropomorphism,
until the contrast became so violent as to call forth the indignant protests of men like Sokrates and Pindar, Euripides
and Plato.   Yet this contrast, as throwing us back upon the
analysis of words, has enabled us to unlock the doors before
which the most earnest seekers of ancient times groped in
vain, and to trace almost from their very source all the
streams of human thought.

Condition of society in the Greek heroic age.
This antagonism reached its highest point among the
Hellenic tribes.   From this point therefore we may most
reasonably work back to that indefinitely earlier condition
of thought in which 'the first attempts only were being
made at expressing the simplest conceptions by means of a
language most simple, most sensuous, and most unwieldy.' [1]
The Iliad and Odyssey exhibit a state of society which has
long since emerged from mere brutishness and barbarism.
It has its fixed order and its recognised gradations, a system
of law with judges to administer it, and a public opinion
which sets itself against some faults and vices not amenable
to legal penalties.   It brings before us men who, if they
retain, in their occasional ferocity, treachery, and malice,
characteristics which belong to the savage, yet recognise the
majesty of law and submit themselves to its government—
who are obedient, yet not servile—who care for other than
mere brute forces, who recognise the value of wise words and

---

[1] Max Müller, *Chips from a German Workshop*, vol. i. p. 354.

prudent counsels, and in the right of uttering them give the earnest of a yet higher and more developed freedom.[1] It shows to us men who, if they regard all as enemies until by an outward covenant they have been made their friends, yet own the sanctity of an oath and acknowledge the duty of executing true judgment between man and man; who, if they are fierce in fight, yet abhor mutilation, torture, and unseemly insult, and are willing to recognise merit in an enemy not less readily than in a friend. Above all, it tells us of men who in their home life are honest and truthful, who make no pretension of despising human sympathy and setting lightly by kindness, gentleness, and love. If here and there we get glimpses of a charity which seeks a wider range,[2] yet the love of wife and children and brethren is the rule and not the exception; and everywhere, in striking contrast with Athenian society in the days of Perikles and Aspasia, we see men and women mingling together in equal and pure companionship, free alike from the arrogance and servility of Oriental empires, and from the horrible vices which, if even then in germ, were not matured till the so-called heroic ages had long passed away.[3]

But these epic poems tell us also of gods, some of whom at least had all the vices and few of the virtues of their worshippers. They tell us of a supreme ruler and father

Character of 'Homeric' mythology.

[1] It cannot, of course, be maintained that this freedom was more than in its germ. The king has his Boulê or Council, where he listens to the chieftains whose judgment nevertheless he can override. There is also the Agora, where the people hear the decisions of their rulers on questions of state, and in which justice is administered. The case of Thersites is barely consistent with an acknowledged right of opposition, while the complaints of the Hesiodic poet show that an unjust verdict could easily be obtained. But it was everything that a people should acknowledge Zeus to be the author of law—

δικασπόλοι ... θέμιστας
πρὸς Διὸς εἰρύαται.   *Il.* i. 238.

and allow the superiority of mind over matter even in their chieftains. Mr. Grote has brought out the imperfections

of the Homeric society both in discussion and in the administration of justice (*History of Greece*, ii. 90-101). Mr. Gladstone presents the picture in a more favourable light (*Homer and the Homeric Age*, ii. 122, &c.).

[2] It is the praise of the wealthy Axylos (who is slain by Diomêdês) that

φίλος ἦν ἀνθρώποισιν·
πάντας γὰρ φιλέεσκεν ὁδῷ ἔπι οἰκία
ναίων.   *Il.* vi. 14.

[3] To this, more than to any other cause, were owing even the political disasters of later Greek history. It may, perhaps, be said with truth that the evil did not exist in the Homeric age, but the canker had eaten very deeply into the heart of society before the days of Thucydides and Sokrates. For its results see Thirlwall's *History of Greece*, viii. ch. lxvi.

of gods and men who had not always sat upon his throne, of other gods deposed and smitten down to dark and desolate regions, of feuds and factions, of lying and perjury, of ferocious cruelty and unmeasured revenge. They tell us of gods who delight in sensual enjoyments and care for little more than the fat of rams and goats, of gods who own no check to their passions, and recognise no law against impurity and lust. And even those gods who rise to a far higher ideal exhibit characters the most variable and actions the most inconsistent. The same being is at different times, nay, almost at the same time, just and iniquitous, truthful and false, temperate and debauched.

Contrast between mythological and religious belief.
As describing the origin and attributes of the gods, the whole series of Greek myths may be said to form a theology; and with the character of the people, this theology stands out in marked contrast. It is impossible for us to determine precisely the extent to which this mythical theology was believed, because it is not in our power to throw ourselves back wholly into their condition of thought; but if the absence of all doubt or reflection constitute faith, then their faith was given to the whole cycle of fables which make up the chronicles of their gods. But if we look to its influence on their thoughts at times when the human heart is stirred to its depths, we can scarcely say that this huge fabric of mythology challenged any belief at all: and thus we must draw a sharp line of severance between their theology and their religion, if we use religion in the sense attached to the word by Locke or Newton, Milton or Butler. If the poet recounts the loves of Zeus, the jealousies of Hêrê, the feuds and the factions in Olympos, it is equally certain that Achilleus does not pray to a sensual and lying god who owns no law for himself and cannot be a law for man. The contrast is heightened if we turn to the poems known as the Hesiodic. If the poet narrates a theogony which incurred the detestation or disgust of Pindar and of Plato, he tells us also of a Divine King who is a perfectly upright judge, and loves those who are clear of hand and pure of heart.[1] If he

[1] The identity of authorship for the Hesiodic *Theogony* and the *Works and* Days is very doubtful: but the question is immaterial. Both poems exhibit the

tells of horrible banquets to which the more fastidious faith
of the lyric poet refuses to give credence,[1] he bids all to
follow after justice, because the gods spend their time, not
in feasting, but in watching the ways and works of men.[2]
If Æschylos in one drama depicts the arrogant tyranny of
Zeus as a usurper and an upstart, if the reiterated conviction
of the prophetic Titan is that the new god shall fall, yet in
others he looks up to the same Zeus (if indeed it be the
same),[3] as the avenger of successful wrong, the vindicator of a
righteous law whose power and goodness are alike eternal.
If for Sophokles the old mythology had not lost its charm,
if he too might tell of the lawless loves and the wild licence
of Zeus and other gods, yet his heart is fixed on higher
realities, on that purity of word and deed which has its
birth, not on earth, but in heaven, and of which the imperishable law is realised and consummated in a God as holy
and everlasting.[4]

sentiment of the same age, or of times
separated by no long interval; and in
the latter poem the action of Zeus in
the legend of Pandora, (which is also
related in the *Theogony*) is utterly
unlike that of the Zeus who figures in
all the didactic portions of the work.

[1] ἐμοὶ δ' ἄπορα γαστρίμαρ-
γον μακάρων τιν' εἰπεῖν· ἀφίσταμαι.
PINDAR, *Olymp.* i. 82.

Pindar's objection is a moral one;
but Herodotos proceeded to reject on
physical grounds the legend which told
of the founding of the Dodonaian oracle,
(ii. 57), as well as some of the exploits
of Herakles (ii. 45.) It was, however,
a moral reason which led him practically to disbelieve the whole story of
Helen's sojourn at Troy, (ii. 120). See
also Grote, *History of Greece*, part i.
ch. xv.

[2] *Works and Days*, 247-253.

[3] Ζεὺς ὅστις ποτ' ἐστίν.
Agamemnon, 160.

[4] *Oid. Tyr.* 863-871. The objection
that comparative mythology, while it
explains the Greek myths, fails 'to
explain the Greek religion, or to explain
how the mythology and the religion got
mixed up together,' turns on the meaning
of words. In one sense, their mythology
was at once their theology and their
religion; but if we regard religion as a

rule of life based on a conscious submission to Divine Will and Law as
being absolutely righteous, and if we
ask how far the Greek had such a rule,
we enter on a question of the gravest
moment, which it is too much the
practice of the present day summarily
to dismiss. The acknowledged dislike
which some felt for at least part of their
theology, can be explained only by their
knowledge of a higher law. But if it
be maintained that the sense or the
sentiment, which lay at the root of this
dislike, is either some relic of earlier
and purer knowledge—in other words,
of an original common revelation—'or
else a wonderful exercise of man's own
reflective power,' we may reply that this
is not the only alternative left open to
us. When St. Paul speaks of Gentiles
as being by nature a law to themselves,
he uses the word *nature* in a sense
which implicitly denies that they obtained a knowledge of this law by a
mere exercise of their reflective powers,
and which implies that God had in all
countries and ages left a witness of
himself in the hearts of men as well as
in the outward world. Surely we who
acknowledge that all holy desires, all
good counsels, and all just works proceed
directly from God, may well believe that
the religious sense which led Pindar to
reject some mythical tales, and Sokrates

The lyric
and tragic
poets were
conscious
of this
contrast.

It would be difficult to discover a more marvellous combination of seemingly inexplicable contradictions, of belief in the history of gods utterly distinct from the faith which guided the practice of men, of an immoral and impure theology with a condition of society which it would be monstrous to regard as utterly and brutally depraved. Yet, in some way or other, this repulsive system, from which heathen poets and philosophers learnt gradually to shrink scarcely less than ourselves, had come into being, had been systematized into a scheme more or less coherent, and imposed upon the people as so much genuine history. What this origin and growth was, is (strange as it may appear) one of the most momentous questions which we can put to ourselves, for on its answer must depend our conclusions on the

to insist on a moral standard of which our common practice falls sadly short, was the direct work of the Spirit of God. Language is as much the gift of God, whether according to the popular notion man spoke articulately from the first, or, as the analysis of language seems to show, acquired the power of speech through a slow and painful discipline; nor would many venture to say that we learnt to walk or to judge by sight or touch through powers originally acquired by ourselves. If then, whatever of truth the Greek poets possessed came from God, that truth would continue to grow, even while they spoke of the Divine Being under a name which had originally signified the sky. If Comparative Mythology brings before us a time during which men appear at first to have little consciousness of a personal Maker of the Visible World, it may also show us how out of the darkness of their earlier thoughts they were led to feel that there was a Power—independent of all things, yet pervading all things— with which they had to do, and that this Power was righteous and good. But the Greek who like Xenophanes (Max Müller, Chips from a German Workshop, i. 366), had this feeling and was conscious of it, would still speak of that Power as Zeus; nor has Christianity itself banished from its language names which come from the myth-making ages. The Romance and Teutonic names for God remain what they were before the growth of Christianity; they

have merely acquired another connotation.

If, then, we wish to have a true idea of Greek religion in the highest sense of the word, we must patiently gather all the detached sentences bearing on the subject which are scattered throughout the wide field of their literature; but without going over the ground traversed by M. Maury, (Les Religions de la Grèce antique), the inquiry may practically be brought into a narrow compass. We have abundant evidence that the religion of the Greeks, like our own, was a trust 'in an all-wise, all-powerful, eternal Being, the Ruler of the world, whom we approach in prayer and meditation, to whom we commit all our cares, and whose presence we feel not only in the outward world, but also in the warning voice within our hearts.' It is in this sense that Augustine speaks of the Christian religion as existing among the ancients; but Professor Max Müller, who rightly lays great stress on this remark (Chips from a German Workshop, i. xi.), has also pointed out the little regard which Augustine paid to his own doctrine. 'Through the whole of St. Augustine's work, and through all the works of earlier Christian divines, as far as I can judge, there runs the same spirit of hostility, blinding them to all that may be good and true and sacred, and magnifying all that is bad, false, and corrupt in the ancient religions of mankind.' (Lectures on Language, second series. x. 421.)

conditions of human life during the infancy of mankind. If
the fragmentary narratives, which were gradually arranged
into one gigantic system, were the work of a single age or of
several generations who devoted themselves to their fabrication, then never has there been seen in the annals of
mankind an impurity more loathsome, an appetite more
thoroughly depraved, a moral sense more hopelessly blunted,
than in those who framed the mythology of the Greek or the
Hindu. Of the answers which have been given to this
question, it can be no light matter to determine which furnishes the most adequate solution.

The method which Mr. Grote, in his 'History of Greece,'[1] Historical
has adopted for the examination of Greek legend, appears significa-
rather to avoid the difficulty than to grapple with it. There Greek
is unquestionably much personification in their mythology; mytho-
there is also undoubtedly a good deal of allegory; but logy.
neither allegory nor personification will furnish a real explanation of the whole. It may be true to say that Ouranos,
Nyx, Hypnos, and Oneiros are persons in the Hesiodic
Theogony, although it is probably erroneous to say that they
are just as much persons as Zeus or Apollôn; and the supposition is certainly inadmissible 'that these legends could all
be traced by means of allegory into a coherent body of physical doctrine.'[2] But there are beyond doubt many things
even in the Hesiodic Theogony which have at least no human
personality;[3] nor does the assertion of personality, whether
of Zeus or Herakles or Apollôn, in the least degree account
for the shape which the narrative of their deeds assumes, or
for the contradictory aspects in which they are brought
before us. It does not in any way explain why Zeus and
Herakles should have so many earthly loves, and why in
every land there should be those who claim descent from
them, or why there should be so much of resemblance and of
difference between Phoibos and Helios, Gaia and Dêmêtêr,
Nereus and Poseidôn. But Mr. Grote was examining the
mythology of Greece as an historian of outward facts, not as

---

[1] Part i. ch. i.-xvi.
[2] Grote, *History of Greece*, part i.
ch. i. See also Mure, *Critical History
of Greek Literature*, i. 104; Milman,

History of Christianity, i. 13, &c.
[3] For instance, οὐρέα μακρά.—*Theog* .
129

BOOK
I.

one who is tracing out the history of the human mind ; and from this point of view he is justified in simply examining the legends, and then dismissing them as the picture 'of a past which never was present.' To this expression Professor Max Müller takes great exception, and especially protests against Mr. Grote's assertion of 'the uselessness of digging for a supposed basis of truth' in the myths of the Greek world.[1] But although it appears certain that the Greek mythology points to an actual and not an imaginary past, a past which must have for us a deep and abiding interest, it would yet seem that Professor Müller has misinterpreted the words of Mr. Grote, who by 'truth' means the verification of actual occurrences, and by a real past means a past of whose events we can give an authentic narrative.[2] In this sense, to assert the truth of the lives and adventures of Zeus and Herakles, after stripping away from them the clothing of the supernatural, is to fall back on the system of Euêmeros, and to raise a building without foundation. But it is obvious that this method leaves the origin of this theology and the question of its contradictions, and still more of its impurity and grossness, just where it found them. It carries us no further back than the legends themselves, while it fails to remove the reproach which heathen apologists and Christian controversialists alike assumed or admitted to be true.[3]

Conflicting views as to its origin.

Two theories only appear to attempt a philosophical analysis of this vast system. While one repudiates the imputation of a deliberate fabrication of impurities, the other asserts as strongly the wilful moral corruption exhibited in the theogonic narratives of the Greeks. In the inconsistent

---

[1] 'Comparative Mythology,' *Chips from a German Workshop,* ii. 1, 67, 84.
[2] From this point of view it is impossible to deny the truth of Mr. Grote's statement, when, speaking of the Northern Eddas, he says that 'the more thoroughly this old Teutonic story has been traced and compared in its various transformations and accompaniments, the less can any well-established connection be made out for it with authentic historical names or events.' *History of Greece,* part i. ch. xviii. It is strange that having thus swept away its historical character, he should not have seen that there *must* be some reason for that singular agreement between Teutonic and Greek mythology, which, at the least, he partially discerns, and that the 'remarkable analogy' presented by the *Völsunga Saga* 'with many points of Grecian mythical narrative' is a fact to be accounted for.
[3] Grote, *History of Greece,* part i. ch. xvii.

and repulsive adventures of Zeus or Herakles, it sees the perversion of high and mysterious doctrines originally imparted to man, and discerns in the gradations of the Olympian hierarchy vestiges of the most mysterious doctrines embraced in the whole compass of Christian teaching. By this theory all that is contradictory, immoral, or disgusting in Greek mythology is the direct result of human sinfulness and rebellion, and resolves itself into the distortion of a divine revelation imparted to Adam immediately after the Fall.

There are few subjects on which it would be more rash to give or withhold assent to any statement without the clearest definition of terms. We may admit the truth of Bishop Butler's assertion that the analogy of nature furnishes no presumption against a revelation when man was first placed upon the earth;[1] but it is obvious that they who agree in asserting the fact of such a revelation may yet have widely different conceptions of its nature and extent. And although it is easy to see the place which Butler's statement holds in the general connection of his argument, it is not so easy to ascertain what on this point his own judgment may have been. Human feeling recoils instinctively from any notion that the Being who placed man in the world ever left him wholly to himself; but the repudiation of such an idea in no way determines the amount of knowledge imparted to him at the first. Nations have been found, and still exist, whose languages contain not a single word expressive of divinity, and into whose mind the idea of God or of any religion seems never to have entered.[2] If it be hard to measure the depth of degradation to which the Abipones, the Bushman, and the Australian may have fallen, it is impossible to believe that the struggles of men like Sokrates and Plato after truth had no connection with a guiding and controlling power. If in the former we discern the evidence

---

[1] *Analogy*, part ii. ch. ii. § 2.

[2] 'Penafiel, a Jesuit theologian, declared that there were many Indians, who, on being asked whether during the whole course of their lives they ever thought of God, replied *No, never.*' Max

Müller, *History of Sanskrit Literature*, 538. It is a miserable fact that this condition of thought finds a parallel among certain sections of Englishmen. See also Farrar, *Chapters on Language*, iv. 45.

of wilful corruption, we must recognise in the latter the vigorous growth of a mind and spirit which seeks to obey the law of its constitution.[1] In Bishop Butler's philosophy, the reason of man is the Divine Reason dwelling in him; the voice of his conscience is the word of God. That these gifts involved a revelation of divine truth, it is impossible to deny; but whether this is all that he meant by the assertion of an original revelation, the Analogy does not enable us to determine with precision. He does, however, assert that the question of the extent of that revelation is to be considered 'as a common question of fact;' and too great a stress cannot be laid on these words.[2]

Extent of original revelation.
No such charge of ambiguity can be brought against the view which Mr. Gladstone has maintained in his elaborate work on 'Homer and the Homeric Age.' In his judgment, all that is evil in Greek mythology is the result not of a natural and inevitable process, when words used originally in one sense came unconsciously to be employed in another, but of a systematic corruption of very sacred and very mysterious doctrines. These corruptions have, in his opinion, grown up not around what are generally called the first principles of natural religion, but around dogmas of which the images, so vouchsafed, were realised in a long subsequent dispensation. In the mythology of the Hellenic race he sees a vast fabric, wonderfully systematized, yet in some parts ill-cemented and incongruous, on the composition of which his theory seems to throw a full and unexpected light. In it he hears the key-note of a strain whose music had been long forgotten and misunderstood, but whose harmony would never of itself have entered into mortal mind. It could not be supplied by invention, for 'invention cannot absolutely create, it can only work on what it finds already provided to hand.'[3] Rejecting altogether the position that 'the basis of the Greek mythology is laid in the deification of the powers of nature,'[4] he holds that under corrupted forms it presents the old Theistic and Messianic traditions,[5]

---

[1] Butler, *Sermons*, ii. 'On Human Nature.'
[2] *Analogy*, part ii. ch. ii. § 2.
[3] *Homer and the Homeric Age*, ii. 9.
[4] *Ibid*. 10.   [5] *Ibid*. 12.

that by a primitive tradition, if not by a direct command, it upheld the ordinance of sacrifice;[1] that its course was from light to darkness, from purity to uncleanness.[2] Its starting point was 'the idea of a Being infinite in power and intelligence, and though perfectly good, yet good by an unchangeable internal determination of character, and not by the constraint of an external law.'[3] But the idea of goodness can be retained only by a sound moral sense; the notion of power is substituted when that sense is corrupted by sin.[4] But sin has no such immediate action on the intellect. Hence the power and wisdom of the Homeric Gods is great and lofty, while their moral standard is indefinitely low.[5] But the knowledge of the Divine Existence roused the desire to know also where He dwelt; and, in the mighty agencies and sublime objects of creation in which they fancied that they saw Him, Mr. Gladstone discerns the germs of that nature-worship which was ingrafted on the true religion originally imparted to mankind.[6] This religion involved (i), the Unity and Supremacy of the Godhead; (ii), a combination with this Unity, of a Trinity in which the several persons are in some way of coequal honour; (iii), a Redeemer from the curse of death, invested with full humanity, who should finally establish the divine kingdom; (iv), a Wisdom, personal and divine, which founded and sustains the world; (v), the connection of the Redeemer with man by descent from the woman. With this was joined the revelation of the Evil One, as a tempting power among men, and the leader of rebellious angels who had for disobedience been hurled from their thrones in heaven.[7]

---

[1] *Homer and the Homeric Age*, ii. 15.
[2] *Ibid.* 17: 'The stream darkened more and more as it got further from the source.'
[3] *Ibid.* 18. [4] *Ibid.* 19. [5] *Ibid.* 20.
[6] *Ibid.* 31.
[7] *Ibid.* 42. This theory, put forth ten years ago, has been received with no great favour; but nothing less than the repudiation of it by Mr. Gladstone himself could justify our passing it by in silence, when our purpose is to show that the problem can be solved only by the method of comparative mythology. But far from retracting this hypothesis, Mr.

Gladstone has propounded it again in his parting address to the University of Edinburgh (1865), and more recently with certain modifications in his volume entitled *Juventus Mundi* (1868). These modifications will be noticed in their several places; but as his last work is intended to embody the greater part of the results at which he arrived in his *Homeric Studies*, and as his theory of the origin of Greek mythology remains substantially what it was before, I have not thought it necessary to alter the text which was written long before the publication of *Juventus Mundi*. Indeed,

BOOK
I.

Its alleged perversion by the Greeks,

Putting aside the question how far these ideas may reflect the thought of later ages, we must admit with Mr. Gladstone that from this shadowing forth of the great dogmas of the Trinity the next step might be into Polytheism, and from that of the Incarnation into anthropomorphism or the reflection of humanity upon the supernatural world.[1] This true theology, in the hands of the Greeks, was perverted into a Trinity of the three sons of Kronos: Zeus, Hades, and Poseidôn. The tradition of the Redeemer is represented by Apollôn; the Divine Wisdom is embodied in Athênê;[2] and Lêtô, their mother, stands in the place of the woman from whom the Deliverer was to descend. The traditions of the Evil One were still further obscured. Evil, as acting by violence, was represented most conspicuously in the Titans and giants—as tempting by deceit, in the Atê of Homer, while lastly, the covenant of the rainbow reappears in Iris.[3]

as shown in the attributes of their Gods.

For these primitive traditions, which are delivered to us 'either in the ancient or the more recent books of the Bible,'[4] Mr. Gladstone alleges the corroborative evidence furnished by the Jewish illustrative writings during or after the captivity in Babylon.[5] These writings bear witness to the extraordinary elevation of the Messiah, and to the introduction of the female principle into Deity, which the Greeks adopted not as a metaphysical conception, but with a view to the family order among immortals.[6] Thus in the Greek Athênê and Apollôn respectively he distinguishes the attributes assigned by the Jews to the Messiah and to Wisdom— the attributes of sonship and primogeniture, of light, of mediation, of miraculous operation, of conquest over the Evil One, and of the liberation of the dead from the power of hell, together with 'an assemblage of the most winning and endearing moral qualities.'[7]

System of secondaries.

This theory Mr. Gladstone has traced with great minuteness and ingenuity through the tangled skein of Greek mythology. The original idea he finds disintegrated, and a

the slightness of the modification which his theory has undergone, renders it perhaps even more necessary to exhibit clearly the dilemmas and difficulties involved in this theory, if carried out to

its logical results.
[1] *Homer and the Homeric Age*, ii. 43.
[2] *Ibid.* 44.   [3] *Ibid.* 45.   [4] *Ibid.* 48.
[5] *Ibid.* 50.   [6] *Ibid.* 51.   [7] *Ibid.* 53.

system of secondaries is the necessary consequence. Far
above all are exalted Apollôn and Athênê, in their personal
purity[1] yet more than in their power, in their immediate
action,[2] in their harmony with the will of the Supreme
King, and in the fact that they alone, among the deities of
a second generation, are admitted to equal honour with the
Kronid brothers, if not even to higher.[3] But some of their
attributes are transferred to other beings, who are simply
embodiments of the attribute so transferred and of no other.
Thus Athênê is attended by Hermes, Ares, Themis, and
Hephaistos; Apollôn by Paiêôn and the Muses;[4] as, similarly, we have in Gaia a weaker impersonation of Dêmêtêr,
and Nereus as representing simply the watery realm of
Poseidôn. In Lêtô, their mother, is shadowed forth the
woman whose seed was to bruise the head of the serpent;
for Lêtô herself has scarcely any definite office in the Homeric
theology, and she remains, from any view except this one, an
anomaly in mythological belief.[5] But the traditions which
relate to the under-world, which is the realm of Hades, are
not less full than those which tell us of the heavenly order
of Olympos. Amidst some little confusion, Mr. Gladstone
discerns a substantial correspondence with divine revelation,
and finds in the Homeric poems the place of bliss destined
finally for the good, the place of torment inhabited by the
Evil One and his comrades, and the intermediate abode for
departed spirits, whether of the good or the evil.[6] But while
the prevalence of sacrifice attests the strength of primitive
tradition, of the Sabbatical institution there is no trace.[7] It
was an ordinance ' too highly spiritual to survive the rude
shocks and necessities of earthly life.'

Of the other deities some owe their existence to invention, Inventive,
which has been busy in depraving and debasing the idea as distin-guished
even of those which are traditive.[8] Thus Hêrê was invented from tra-
because Zeus must not live alone, and Rhea because he must ditive,
deities.
have a mother; and a whole mass of human adventure and
of human passion without human recognition of law is

---

[1] *Homer and the Homeric Age,* ii.
87-107.
[2] *Ibid.* 89-93. [3] *Ibid.* 57.
[4] *Ibid.* 61.
[5] *Ibid.* 170.
[6] *Ibid.* 173.
[7] *Ibid.* 152.
[8] *Ibid.* 171, 172.

BOOK
I.

Nature of
the doc-
trines per-
verted in
Greek my-
thology.

heaped up round almost every deity (except the two who stand out unsullied in their purity and goodness), not, however, without occasional protests from the poet who had not yet become familiar with the deification of vicious passion.[1]

Thus, on the hypothesis of Mr. Gladstone, Greek mythology is no distortion of primary truths which first dawn on the mind of a child or are imparted to it, and which, it might have been supposed, would form the substance of divine truth granted to man during the infancy of his race. It is the corruption of recondite and mysterious dogmas which were not to become facts for hundreds or thousands of years, of doctrines which the speculations of Jewish rabbis may have drawn into greater prominence, but which form the groundwork of Christian theology. Zeus, the licentious tyrant, the perjured deceiver, the fierce hater, the lover of revelry and banqueting, who boasts of his immunity from all restraint and law, is the representative of the Infinite and Eternal Father. He with Hades and Poseidôn represents the Christian Trinity; but Hades represents also the power of darkness, and Poseidôn shares the attributes of God with those of the devil,[2] while all are children of the dethroned Kronos, in whom again the evil power finds an impersonation.[3] When we survey the whole mass of mythological legend, when we spread out before us the lives of Zeus and his attendant gods (scarcely excepting even Athênê and Apollôn), we stand aghast at the boldness of an impiety which has perhaps never had its parallel. The antediluvian records of the Old Testament bring before us a horrible picture of brute violence, resulting possibly from a deification of human will, which, it would seem, left no room for any theology whatever; but this is an astounding parody which would seem to be

[1] *Homer and the Homeric Age*, ii. 270.
[2] *Ibid*. 164; see also *National Review*, July 1858, 53, &c.
[3] *Ibid*. 207. Writing some months before the publication of Mr. Gladstone's work on Homer, Professor Max Müller had remarked that 'among the lowest tribes of Africa and America we hardly find anything more hideous and revolting,' than the stories told of Kronos and his offspring. 'It seems blasphemy,' he adds, 'to consider these fables of the heathen world as corrupted and misinterpreted fragments of a divine revelation once granted to the whole race of mankind.' 'Comparative Mythology:' *Chips from a German Workshop*, ii. 13. But the disposition so frequently shown at present to explain the growth of mythology by bold assumptions renders it necessary to examine arguments which might otherwise be passed by in silence.

founded not on dim foreshadowings of a true revelation, but CHAP.
on the dogmatic statements of the Athanasian Creed. That I.
a theology thus wilfully falsified should be found with a
people not utterly demoralised, but exhibiting on the whole
a social condition of great promise and a moral standard
rising constantly higher, is a phenomenon, if possible, still
more astonishing. On the supposition that Greek mythology
was a corrupted religious system, it must, to whatever extent,
have supplied a rule of faith and practice, and the actions
and character of the gods must have furnished a justification
for the excesses of human passion. That no such justification
is alleged, and that the whole system seems to exercise no
influence either on their standard of morality or their common
practice, are signs which might appear to warrant the presumption that this mythology was not the object of a moral
belief. The whole question, viewed in this light, is so utterly
perplexing, and apparently so much at variance with the
conditions of Homeric society, that we are driven to examine
more strictly the evidence on which the hypothesis rests.
We remember that we are dealing not with a theme for
philosophical speculation, but with a common question of
fact,[1] and that Mr. Gladstone assumes not only that there
was a primitive revelation, but that it set forth certain
dogmas. With these assumptions the phenomena of mythology must be made to fit: a genuine historical method
excludes all assumptions whatsoever.

If, however, hypothesis is to be admitted, then it must be Attributes
granted that the attributes and functions of the Hellenic of Athênê
and
gods have seldom been analysed with greater force, clearness, Apollón.
and skill; nor can it be denied that Mr. Gladstone's hypothesis, as in the case of Lêtô, furnishes a plausible explanation
of some things which appear anomalous.[2] But it introduces
the necessity of interpreting mythology so as to square with
a preconceived system, and involves a temptation to lessen

[1] See p. 10.
[2] Mr. Gladstone (*Homer, &c.* ii. 155),
dwells much on the indistinct colouring
which is thrown over Lêtô, and which
leaves her 'wholly functionless, wholly
inactive,' and 'without a purpose,' except
in so far as she is the mother of Phoibos.

But this is precisely the relation in
which the mythical Night stood to the
Day which was to be born of her. It
was impossible that the original idea
could be developed into a much more
definite personality.

BOOK
I.
or to pass over difficulties which appear to militate against it. The Homeric legends are not so consistent as for such a purpose would seem desirable, and there are the gravest reasons for not inferring from the silence of the poet that he was ignorant of other versions than those which he has chosen to adopt.[1] On the supposition that Athênê and Apollôn represent severally the Divine Redeemer and the Divine Wisdom, their relation of will to the Supreme Father becomes a point of cardinal interest and importance. But when Mr. Gladstone asserts that, 'although Athênê goes all lengths in thwarting Jupiter' in the Iliad,[2] 'yet her aim is to give effect to a design so unequivocally approved in Olympus, that Jupiter himself has been constrained to give way to it,' he places too far in the background certain other Homeric incidents which imply a direct contrariety of will. No weaker term can rightly characterise that abortive conspiracy to bind Zeus, in which she is the accomplice of Hêrê and Poseidôn. In this plot, the deliverance comes not from Apollôn, whose office it is to be 'the defender and deliverer of heaven and the other immortals,' but from Thetis, the silver-footed nymph of the sea;[3] and by her wise counsels Zeus wins the victory over one who is with himself a member of the traditive Trinity. The same legend qualifies another statement, that Athênê and Apollôn are never foiled, defeated,

<hr/>

[1] See Chapter IX. of this book.
[2] Gladstone's Homer, &c. ii. 70.
[3] Ibid. 72. This conspiracy is mentioned more than once by Mr. Gladstone, (75, 182): but he mentions it, not as a drawback on the traditive character of Athênê, but as showing first that Zeus himself might be assailed, and secondly that his majesty remained nevertheless substantially unimpaired. Yet a reference to it, as bearing on the moral conception of Athênê, would seem to be indispensable; and this reference Mr. Gladstone has supplied in Juventus Mundi, p. 273. He here states that 'we have in the case of Apollo an uniform identity of will with the chief god, and in the case of Athênê only an exceptional departure from it.' The admission is important; and with it we must couple other traditions, to be noticed hereafter, which

we have not the slightest warrant for regarding as the growth of ages later than those in which our Iliad and Odyssey assumed their present form. In fact, the admission seems fatal to the theory; nor can it be said that 'the case of Apollo stands alone as an exhibition of entire unbroken harmony with the will of Zeus, which in all things he regards.'—P. 272. In the myths of Asklêpios and Admêtos he draws on himself the wrath and the vengeance of Zeus for slaying the Kyklôpes as a requital for the death of his son, the Healer; and we are fully justified in laying stress on this fact, until it can be proved that any one myth must necessarily be regarded as of earlier growth than another, merely because it happens to be found in our Iliad and Odyssey.

or outwitted by any other of the gods;[1] for Athênê here is foiled by Thetis. Elsewhere we have Apollôn,[2] like Poseidôn, cheated by Laomedôn whom he had served, and finding a more congenial master, but yet a master, in Admêtos;[3] while the parentage of the three Kronid brothers[4] and the double character of Poseidôn[5] stand forth as the most astounding contradictions of all.

There are other legends which represent Athênê in a light inconsistent with the personification of the Divine Wisdom. In the tale of Pandora, at the instigation of Zeus she takes part in the plot which results in the increased wickedness and misery of man;[6] in that of Prometheus, she aids in the theft of fire from heaven against the will of Zeus, while one version represents her as acting thus, not from feelings of friendship, but from the passion of love. These legends are not found in our Homer, but it is impossible to prove that the poet was unacquainted with them. He makes no reference to some myths, which are at once among the oldest and the most beautiful; and he certainly knew of the dethronement of Kronos, as well as of factions in the new dynasty of the gods.[7]

But if the theory of religious perversion, apart from its moral difficulties, involves some serious contradictions, it altogether fails to explain why the mythology of the Greeks assumed many of its peculiar and perhaps most striking features. It does not show us why some of the gods should

Margin notes: CHAP. I. — Relations of will between Zeus and Athênê. — Peculiar forms of Greek mythology.

---

[1] Gladstone, *Homer, &c.*, ii. 74.
[2] *Ibid.* 75.
[3] *Ibid.* 81. If these legends are strictly developements from old mythical phrases, the meaning of which was only in part remembered, there remains no difficulty whatever in such statements. In these there is reflected upon Apollôn an idea derived from the toiling sun, which is brought out in its fulness in the adventures of Herakles and Bellerophôn. Mr. Gladstone lays stress on the relation of Apollôn and Artemis to Death (p. 103), and holds that here we are on very sacred ground (p. 104) the traces, namely, 'of One who, as an all-conquering King, was to be terrible and destructive to his enemies, but who was also, on behalf of mankind, to take away the sting from death, and to

change its iron band for a thread of silken slumber.' The question is further examined p. 123 etc.: but the myths developed from phrases which spoke originally of the beneficent and destructive power of the sun's rays and heat perfectly explain every such attribute, whether in Apollôn or Artemis.
[4] Gladstone, *Homer*, ii. 162.
[5] *Ibid.* 206.
[6] Hesiod, *Theogon.*, 573; *Works and Days*, 63.
[7] Similarly, the *Iliad* says nothing about the death of Achilleus: yet the poet is aware that his life is to be short.

μῆτερ, ἐπεί μ' ἔτεκές γε μινυνθάδιόν περ ἐόντα

is the frequent reproach of Achilleus to his mother Thetis.

be represented pure, others as in part or altogether immoral : it does not tell us why Zeus and Herakles should be coarse and sensual, rather than Athênê and Apollôn; it does not explain why Apollôn is made to serve Admêtos, why Herakles bears the yoke of Eurystheus, and Bellerophôn that of the Kilikian king. It fails to show why Herakles should appear as the type of self-restraint and sensuality, of labour and sluggishness, why names so similar in meaning as Lykâôn, Helios and Phaethôn, should be attached to beings whose mythical history is so different. If for these and other anomalies there is a method of interpretation which gives a clear and simple explanation, which shows how such anomalies crept into being, and why their growth was inevitable— if this method serves also as a key, not merely to the mythology of Greece, but to that of the whole Aryan race, nay, even to a wider system still, a presumption at least is furnished, that the simpler method may after all be the truest.

Yet more, the hypothesis of a corrupted revelation involves some further consequences, which have a material bearing on the question. That which is so perverted cannot become clearer and more definite in the very process of corrupt developement. Not only must the positive truths, imparted at the first, undergo distortion, but the ideas involved in them must become weaker and weaker. If the Unity of God formed one of those primitive truths, then the personality and the power of Zeus would be more distinct and real in the earliest times than in the later. The ideas of the Trinity, of the Redeemer, and of the Divine Wisdom, would be more prominent in those first stages of belief in the case of a people who confessedly were not sustained by new or continued revelations. The personality of a Divine Wisdom is not a dogma which men in a thoroughly rude society could reason out for themselves; and if it formed part of an original revelation, the lapse of time would tend to weaken, not to strengthen it. If, again, this corrupting process had for its cause a moral corruption going on in the hearts and lives of men, then this corruption would be intensified in proportion to the degree in which the original revelation was overlaid.[1]

---

[1] The same argument seems to be of force against the supposition that a revelation so extensive as that assumed by Mr. Gladstone preceded the age

In the Hellenic mythology, this process is reversed. Even as it appears in the poems which we call Homeric, it must have undergone a developement of centuries ; but if it is impossible to measure, by any reference to an older Greek literature, the personality and attributes of each god as compared with the conceptions of a previous age, it is obvious that the general tone of feeling and action, and the popular standard of morality had not been debased with the growth of their mythology. Whether the Hesiodic poems belong to a later period than our Iliad and Odyssey is a question into which it is unnecessary here to enter: but it must be admitted that if their theology is more systematised, and their theogony more repulsive, their morality and philosophy is immeasurably higher and more true. The latter may not exhibit the same heroic strength, they may betray a querulous spirit not unlike that of the Jewish preacher; but they display a conviction of the perfect justice and equity of the Divine Being, and an appreciation of goodness, as being equally the duty and the interest of mankind,[1] which we could scarcely desire to have strengthened.[2] With the growth of a mythology and its more systematic arrangement the perception of moral truth has become more keen and intense; and the same age which listened to the book of the generations of Zeus, Kronos, and Aphroditê, learnt wisdom from the pensive precepts of the ' Works and Days.'

whose language gave birth to the later Aryan mythology. For a revelation so corrupted implies a gradual degeneration into coarseness, sensuality, even brutishness ; but the mind of that early' time, as exhibited to us in their language, is childish or infantile, but not brutish ; and it is not easy to see how from a period in which they had sensualised and debased a high revelation men could emerge into a state of simple and childish wonder, altogether distinct from either idolatry or impurity, and in which their notions as to the life of nature were as indefinite and unformed as their ideas respecting their own personality.

[1] See especially the striking analogy of the broad and narrow ways leading respectively to ruin and happiness (*Works and Days*, 285-290). It is not pretended that this morality, many of the precepts of which seem almost echoes from the Sermon on the Mount, was handed down from an original revelation. If then, in this respect, the course was from the lesser to the greater, the progress could be the work only of the Spirit of God ; and the downward course of their mythology from a positive revelation appears therefore the more mysterious and perplexing.

[2] The Hesiodic *Works and Days* seem to exhibit, along with some decline of physical energy, a sensitiveness of temperament to which the idea of overbearing arrogance and wanton insult threw a dark colouring over the whole course of human life. With such a feeling the mind may easily pass into a morbid condition.

BOOK
I.

Compari-
son of the
Homeric
with the
Vedic my-
thology.

It is perhaps difficult to determine how far the characters of Phoibos and Athênê have been drawn out and systematised by the genius and moral instinct of the poet himself. We have no evidence, in any extant literature, of the precise state in which he found the national mythology; but it seems unlikely that he had what may be termed a theological authority for every statement which he makes and every attribute which he assigns to the one or the other. It is certain that Athênê once conspired against the freedom of Zeus ;[1] but we cannot tell how far the poet himself intensified the general harmony of her will to that of the King of gods and men, nor can we forget that Ushas is as dear to gods and men as Athênê herself, and that Ushas is undeniably nothing but the morning. But language has furnished evidence, which it is impossible to resist, of the gradual process which imparted to these mythical deities both their personality and their attributes. The literature of another branch of the same Aryan race exhibits a mythology whose substantial identity with that of the Greeks it is impossible to dispute; but in that mythology beings, whose personality in the Homeric poems is sharply drawn and whose attributes are strictly defined, are still dim and shadowy. Even the great Olympian king has not received the passions and appetites, and certainly not the form of man. Nay, in that older mythology their persons and their attributes are alike interchangeable. That which among the Greeks we find as a highly developed and complicated system, is elsewhere a mere mass of floating legend, nay, almost of mere mythical phrases, without plan or cohesion. This difference, at first sight so perplexing, may itself enable us to discover the great secret of the origin and growth of all mythology: but the fact remains indisputable that in the Veda, to use the words of Professor Max Müller, 'the whole nature of these so-called gods is still transparent, their first conception in many cases clearly perceptible. There are as yet no genealogies, no settled marriages between gods and goddesses. The father is sometimes the son, the brother is the husband, and she who in one hymn is the mother is in another the wife. As the

[1] *Iliad*, i. 400.

conceptions of the poet vary, so varies the nature of these gods. Nowhere is the wide distance which separates the ancient poems of India from the most ancient literature of Greece more clearly felt than when we compare the growing myths of the Veda with the full-grown and decayed myths on which the poetry of Homer is founded.'[1] But the unformed mythology of the Veda followed in its own land a course analogous to that of the mythology of Greece. There was the same systematic developement, with this difference, that in India the process was urged on by a powerful sacerdotal order who found their interest in the expansion of the old belief. In the earlier Vedas there is no predominant priesthood, and only the faintest indications of caste ; there are no temples, no public worship, and, as it would seem, no images of the gods; and (what is of immeasurably greater importance in reference to the mythological creed of the Homeric poets) there are, in the words of Horace Wilson, ' no indications of a triad, the creating, preserving, and destroying power. Brahma does not appear as a deity, and Vishnu, although named, has nothing in common with the Vishnu of the Puranas : no allusion occurs to his Avataras. . . . . These differences are palpable, and so far from the Vedas being the

[1] ' Comparative Mythology,' *Chips from a German Workshop*, ii. 75. This flexible nature of the earliest myths explains some apparent contradictions in the Homeric mythology. To my conclusion that some of the most striking features in the character of Paris are reproduced in Meleagros and Achilleus, Professor Max Müller has taken exception on the ground that ' if the germ of the *Iliad* is the battle between the solar and nocturnal powers, Paris surely belongs to the latter.'—*Lectures on Language*, second series, xi. I venture to think that in this instance Professor Max Müller has answered his own objection. As the seducer of Helen, Paris represents the treacherous night; but he is also the fated hero doomed to bring ruin on his kinsfolk, while he is further known as Alexandros, the helper of men. Hence in this aspect of his character, a number of images which describe the solar heroes have been grouped around his person, while the leading idea embodied in him is that of the dark thief which steals away the twilight. It may be added that the very words which Professor Max Müller quotes to show that ' he whose destiny it is to kill Achillos in the *Western Gates* could hardly have been himself of solar or vernal lineage,' would also prove that Phoibos Apollôn belonged to the ranks of the powers of night, for the death of Achilleus is brought about by him no less than by Paris. Paris, however, is not of solar or vernal lineage. He is essentially the deceiver who draws away the golden-haired Helen in his dusky dwelling; and all that I would urge is that when the poet described him as a warrior, he naturally employed imagery with which the solar heroes had made him familiar, and wove into the tale the incidents which make up the myth of Oinônô and which recur in the stories of Sigurd and of Theseus, of Kephalos and of Herakles. The subject will be further treated in its proper place.

basis of the existing system, they completely overturn it.' [1]
The comparison is scarcely less fatal to the mythological
Trinity of the Greeks.

Methods of
determin-
ing the
extent of
primitive
revelation.

We come at length to the question of fact. What was the
measure of divine truth imparted to man on his creation, or
immediately after the fall, and under what forms was it conveyed? If, when stated thus, the question should be one
which we cannot absolutely determine, we may yet ask, was
it a revelation as explicit and extensive as Mr. Gladstone
represents it to have been? To allege the rabbinical traditions and speculations of comparatively recent times [2] as
evidence for the latent meaning of Greek mythology, is to
treat the subject in a way which would simply make any
solution of the problem impossible. The force of a current,
when its stream has been divided, will not tell us much about
the course or depth of kindred streams which have branched
off in other directions. Accordingly, although later traditions
appear to be blended in his idea of the primitive belief, [3] Mr.
Gladstone rightly insists that the Homeric mythology must,
if his hypothesis be correct, show the vestiges of a traditional
knowledge 'derived from the epoch when the covenant of
God with man, and the promise of a Messiah, had not yet
fallen within the contracted forms of Judaism for shelter,' [4]
and that these traditions must 'carry upon them the mark
of belonging to the religion which the Book of Genesis
represents as brought by our first parents from Paradise and
as delivered by them to their immediate descendants in
general.' [5] Thus the era of the division of races is the latest
limit to which we can bring down a common tradition for all
mankind; and for that tradition we are confined to the first
eleven chapters of the book of Genesis.

Evidence
of the
Book of
Genesis.

From these chapters we must derive our proof that our
first parents and their immediate descendants possessed the
idea of an Infinite Being whose perfect goodness arose, not

[1] Professor H. H. Wilson, in the
Edinburgh Review for October 1860,
No. CCXXVIII. p. 382 ; and Vishnu
Purana, p. ii., where he emphatically
denies that the old Vedic religion was
idolatrous. His remarks on the general
character of the Vedic religion deserve the
deepest attention. They seem entirely
to subvert the hypothesis which Mr.
Gladstone has maintained.
[2] Gladstone, Homer, &c. ii. 50.
[3] Ibid. 48.   [4] Ibid. 3.   [5] Ibid. 4.

from external restraints, but from an unchangeable internal determination of character[1]—of a Trinity of Co-equal Persons in the Divine Unity—of a Redeemer who should hereafter assume their nature and deliver from death and sin—of a Divine Wisdom which was with God from the beginning, and of an Evil One, who, having fallen from his throne in heaven, had now become an antagonistic power, tempting men to their destruction.[2]

Whether these early chapters may contain this theological scheme by just and legitimate inference, whether the words there written may contain the earnest and the warrant of the full Christian revelation, are questions with which we are not here concerned. It is not a question of doctrine or belief or theological analysis. It is a simple question of fact which must determine whether various races of mankind were or were not guilty of wilful perversion of high and mysterious doctrines. Here, if anywhere, that purification of the intellect would seem to be needed, the lack of which tends to a substitution of traditional teaching or association for an impartial sifting of evidence.[3] There was a time when these early records formed the whole literature of the people; and, to adopt Mr. Gladstone's expression, it would not be 'safe to make any large assumption respecting a traditional knowledge of any parts of early revelation' beyond what those records actually contain.[4] Taken wholly by themselves, and not interpreted by the light thrown on them by the thought and belief of later ages, these records tell us of man as being (in some sense not explicitly defined) made in the Divine image and likeness—of one positive prohibition, the violation of which was to be followed by immediate death—of a subtle beast which tempts the woman to disobey the command, and of a sense of shame which follows the transgression. They tell us of flight and hiding when the man hears the voice of God walking in the garden in the cool of the day—of an attempt to transfer the blame from the man to the woman,

marginal note: Its character.

---

[1] Gladstone, *Homer, &c.* ii. 18.
[2] *Ibid.* 42.
[3] The necessity of such a process in all questions of fact will scarcely be disputed, and the present would seem to fall strictly under this class. See Grote, *History of Greece*, part ii. ch. lxviii. vol. viii. p. 617, &c.
[4] Gladstone, *Homer, &c.* ii. 40.

from the woman to the serpent—of a sentence of humiliation passed upon the latter, with the warning that its head should be bruised by the woman's seed—of a life of toil and labour for the former, ending with a return to the dust from which he had been made. Besides this, they tell us briefly that after some generations men began to call upon the name of the Lord; that in the course of time they sank (with but one exception) into brute lust and violence; and that on the renovation of the earth men were made answerable for each other's blood, and received the token of the rainbow as a warrant for the future permanence of the course of nature. But of any revelation before the fall, beyond a command to till the garden and to abstain from the fruit of a particular tree, these records give not the slightest indication.

Limits of that evidence.

If the doctrines which, in Mr. Gladstone's belief, made up the primitive revelation, are contained in these chapters, it is, he admits, by a dim and feeble foreshadowing.[1] They tell us nothing of God in the perfection of His nature, or of a Unity of Three Persons in the Godhead. They tell us of a subtle serpent, not of a fallen angel, of the seed of the woman as bruising that serpent's head, not of a Divine Redeemer delivering from sin and spiritual death. Still less do they tell us of a Divine Wisdom, of an institution of sacrifice,[2] or of a spiritual communion in prayer as existing from the first between man and God. All these doctrines may be legitimate deductions; but if to us the record itself gives only mysterious glimpses of a future fuller revelation, if to us these inferences from its contents are the result of careful comparison with the later books of the Old Testament, if even to us their harmony with the belief of prophets and righteous men of later ages seems clear only because we have been taught to regard it as clear, then what evidence have we that in the time of which the third chapter of Genesis speaks to us, our parents had a full apprehension of what

---

[1] Gladstone, *Homer, &c.* ii. 39.

[2] The fact of offerings is obviously very different from an ordinance commanding such offerings. The former may exist without the latter. Nor is there the slightest intimation that the offering of Cain was rejected because it was not one of blood; its rejection is made to depend, not on the quality of the oblation, but on the moral condition of him who brings it.

even to us apart from later associations would be faint and shadowy? For if on the revelation made to them the vast mass of Greek mythology grew up as a corrupt incrustation, they must have received these truths not in their germ but in full dogmatic statement. It is difficult to understand how such a statement would have been to them anything more than a dead unmeaning formula, waiting to be quickened into life by the breath of a later revelation or by the evidence of later facts.

If, again, there is any one lesson which may be drawn before others from the character of the Old Testament records, it is that ideas, dim and feeble at first, acquire gradually strength and consistency, that the clearness of revelation is increased as the stream widens, and that all positive belief is the result of years and generations of discipline. But in some mysterious way, while the course of the Jewish people was from the lesser to the greater, they in whose hands the Homeric theology was moulded started with a fulness of doctrinal knowledge which was not attained by the former until a long series of centuries had passed away.

Course of revelation in the Old Testament.

If, further, an acceptance of the records of the book of Genesis involves no assumption of the previous existence of traditions or doctrines not mentioned in those records, it frees us not less from the necessity of supposing that in all but the Jewish world a process was going on directly contrary to that under which the Israelites were being trained. But while we assent to Mr. Gladstone's remark on the ease with which these foreshadowings of the Trinity and of Redemption might pass into polytheism and anthropomorphism, it would scarcely argue a spirit of irreverence if we asked why doctrinal statements should have been given which the receivers could not understand, and which under these conditions rendered such a transition not merely likely but inevitable.

Greek corruption of revelation.

There is an instinctive reluctance to accept any theory which heightens human depravity and corruption, unless there are weighty reasons for doing so.[1] And, unquestion-

Necessity of accounting for the character of Greek mythology.

---

[1] For the mass of facts which seem to negative the hypothesis of degenera-tion see Sir J. Lubbock's *Prehistoric Times,* second edition, 1869.

BOOK
I.

ably, on the hypothesis which has just been examined, the mythology of the Greeks exhibits an instance of wilful and profane perversion, to which perhaps we can find no parallel. But the character of that mythology still remains when we have rejected this supposition. We have still before us the chronicles or legends of gods who not merely eat and drink and sleep, but display the working of the vilest of human passions. Some process, therefore, either conscious or unconscious, must have brought about a result so perplexing ; and if even for conscious invention there must have been some groundwork, much more must this be the case if we take up an alternative which even less admits the exercise of a creative faculty.

Conditions
of the
inquiry.

If then, apart from the controversies which have gathered round the documents which compose the book of Genesis, we gain from the earliest Jewish records no knowledge of the mode in which mythology was developed, it is clear that, if the question is ever to be answered, we must seek the evidence in the history of language and of ancient civilisation. If both alike seem to carry us back to a time in which the condition of man resembled most nearly that of an infant, we can but accept the evidence of facts, so far as those facts are ascertained and understood. The results of archæological researches may not be flattering to human vanity. They may reveal a coarse brutality from which during a long series of ages man rose in the struggle for existence to some notion of order and law. They may disclose a state of society in which a hard apathy and a stupid terror seemed to render all intellectual growth impossible, and in which a religion of fear found its universal expression in human sacrifices.[1]   Yet the

[1] If the theories which make language the necessary adjunct and outcome of thought must be abandoned as inconsistent with known facts, if we must face the conclusion that man speaks not because he thinks, but because he wishes to share his thoughts with others, and hence that words are wholly arbitrary and conventional signs without the slightest essential relation to the things signified, no reason for surprise remains if human ideas of God and of the service due to him should be found to exhibit the same process of slow and painful developement from the first faint dawn of intelligence. The conclusion must, indeed, be proved: but its establishment no more calls into question the Divine Education of the world, than the slowness with which infants learn to walk proves that our powers of motion originate in ourselves; and certainly the evidence both of archæology and language, so far as it has gone, tends more and more to exhibit mankind in their primæval condition as passing

picture, if it be gloomy, introduces no new difficulties beside those with which philosophers or theologians have to contend already in their attempts to explain the phenomena of the material or moral world. The fact that there has been growth, the fact that out of such poor elements there has been developed a knowledge of the relations in which men stand to each other and of the consequences which flow from these relations, is of itself the evidence that at all times and in all places the Divine Spirit has been teaching and educating the children of men, that always and everywhere God has been doing the work of which we now see darkly but a very small part, and of which hereafter we shall better understand the nature and purpose.

If then the mythology of the Aryan nations is to be studied to good purpose, the process applied to their legends must be strictly scientific. In every Aryan land we have a vast mass of stories, some preserved in great epic poems, some in the pages of mythographers or historians, some in tragic, lyric, or comic poetry, and some again only in the oral tradition or folklore of the people. All these, it is clear, must be submitted to that method of comparison and differences by which inductive science has achieved its greatest triumphs. Not a step must be taken on mere conjecture: not a single result must be anticipated by ingenious hypothesis. For the reason of their existence we must search, not in our own moral convictions, or in those of ancient Greeks or Romans, but in the substance and materials of the myths themselves. We must deal with their incidents and their names. We must group the former according to their points of likeness and difference ; we must seek to interpret the latter by the principles which have been established and accepted as the laws of philological analysis. It becomes therefore unnecessary to notice at

Allegorical interpretation of myths.

through forms and stages of thought in which the adoption of human sacrifices universally would inevitably mark an important stage. This subject has been treated by Mr. E. B. Tylor in his *History of Early Civilisation*, with a vigour and impartiality which justify the hope that he may hereafter fill up the outlines of his masterly sketch. The developement of the doctrine of sacrifice has been traced with singular clearness and force by Dr. Kalisch, *Historical and Critical Commentary on the Old Testament*, Leviticus, part i. See also the article 'Sacrifice' in the *Dictionary of Science, Literature and Art.*

length any of those hypotheses or assumptions which resolve
the Aryan myths into allegories, or explain them as expressions of high truth in theology, morality, or art. It would
scarcely be necessary to notice such theories at all, were it
not that they are from time to time revived by writers who
from their manifest earnestness and sincerity, and from the
great good which they have done, may fairly claim to be
heard. It may, however, be enough to take some of these
theories, and to show that they are not true to the features
of the myths which they profess to explain, and that interpretations which twist some of the incidents and names of a
story and ignore others, while they treat each tale as standing by itself, cannot be regarded as trustworthy.

Lord
Bacon's
method.
In the opinion of Lord Bacon, the story of the Sphinx was
'an elegant and instructive fable,' 'invented to represent
science, especially as joined with practice.' His reason for
so thinking was that 'science may without absurdity be
called a monster, being strangely gazed at and admired by
the ignorant and unskilful.' The composite figure of the
Sphinx indicates 'the vast variety of subjects that science
considers'; the female countenance attributed to her denotes
the 'gay appearance' of science and her 'volubility of
speech.' Her wings show that 'the sciences and their in-
ventions must fly about in a moment, for knowledge, like
light communicated from one torch to another, is presently
caught and copiously diffused.' Her sharp and hooked
talons are 'the axioms and arguments of science,' which
'enter the mind, lay hold of it, fix it down, and keep it from
moving and slipping away.' She is placed on a crag over-
looking the Theban city, because 'all science seems placed on
high, as it were on the tops of mountains that are hard to
climb.' Like her, 'science is said to beset the highways,
because, through all the journey and peregrination of human
life, there is matter and occasion offered of contemplation.'
If the riddles which the Sphinx receives from the Muses
bring with them trouble and disaster, it is because 'practice
urges and impels to action, choice, and determination,' and
thus questions of science 'become torturing, severe, and
trying, and unless solved and interpreted, strangely perplex

and harass the human mind, rend it every way, and perfectly tear it to pieces.' The fable, in Bacon's judgment, adds with the 'utmost elegance,' 'that, when Sphinx was conquered, her carcass was laid upon an ass; for there is nothing so subtle and abstruse but, after being once made plain, intelligible, and common, it may be received by the lowest capacity.' But he feels himself bound not to omit that ' Sphinx was conquered by a lame man and impotent in his feet, for men usually make too much haste to the solution of Sphinx's riddles; whence it happens that, she prevailing, their minds are rather racked and torn by disputes than invested with command by works and effects.'

A large number of the Greek myths are made by Lord Bacon to yield 'wisdom' of this kind, and it is quite possible that the same process might be applied with equal success to all Greek, or even all Aryan myths. Such interpretations certainly tend to show how great our debt of gratitude must be to a set of mysterious philosophers, prophets, or politicians, who, living before there were any constitutions, alliances, confederacies, and diplomacy, furnished in the form of amusing stories a complete code for the guidance of kings, members of parliament, cabinet ministers, and ambassadors. It would be unfair to grudge to these interpretations the praise of cleverness and ingenuity; but the happy turns which they sometimes exhibit are more than counterbalanced by misrepresentations of the myths themselves. The comparison of the claws and talons of the Sphinx to the axioms and arguments of science may be both amusing and instructive; but the ass which carries her carcass is seemingly a creature of his own imagining, and Oidipous was neither lame nor impotent in his feet when he came to the final conflict. The reason, also, by which Bacon accounts for this fact, would be an argument for making Oidipous not ·the conqueror, but only another of the victims of the Sphinx.

Its consequences.

But, ingenious as Bacon's interpretations may have been, they were emphatically unscientific. To him these Greek stories were isolated or detached fables, whose growth it was superfluous to trace, and to each of which he might attach

Such interpretations unscientific.

any explanation which might seem best to fit or to give most significance to its leading incidents. In short, they were things with regard to which he saw no need of following rules which in all the processes of science and in all matters of fact he would have held to be indispensable. Had he followed these rules, he might, even without a knowledge of the language or the myths of other cognate tribes, have seen that the Hellenic legend of Oidipous and the Sphinx could not be judged of rightly apart from a comparison with other tales. He would have seen that Oidipous was not the only child exposed on a mountain side, or rescued by a shepherd, or doomed to slay his father or grandsire, and to conquer a snake, dragon, or other monster. He would have seen that these beings, with features more or less resembling each other in all the stories, were yet each spoken of under a different name, that the Sphinx of the Theban myth became the Python or Echidna, the Gorgon or Minotaur or Chimaira or Hydra of another, and that these names must be accounted for not less than the incidents of the tale. He might have perceived that the names in some or many of these legends bore a certain analogy to each other, and that as the names could not be the result of accident, the explanation which would account for the myth must account also for them, and that short of this result no interpretation could be accepted as adequate. The discovery that Bacon's mode of extracting from myths the 'wisdom of the ancients' is thoroughly un-scientific, releases us from any further duty of examining in detail either his explanations or even others, urged by more recent writers, which may resemble them in theory or method.

CHAPTER II.

THE RELATION OF MYTHOLOGY TO LANGUAGE.

THE analysis of language has fully justified the anticipation of Locke, that 'if we could trace them to their sources, we should find in all languages the names which stand for things that fall not under our senses to have had their first rise from sensible ideas.' So thoroughly, indeed, has this conjecture been verified, that the assertion is fast passing into the number of trite and hackneyed sayings; and though the interest and vast importance of the fact remains, few are now tempted to question the conclusion that every word employed to express the highest theological or metaphysical conceptions at first denoted mere sensuous perception. '*Spiritus*,' says Professor Max Müller 'is certainly derived from a verb *spirare*, which means to draw breath. The same applies to *animus*. *Animus*, the mind, as Cicero says, is so called from *anima*, air. The root is *an*, which in Sanskrit means to blow, and which has given rise to the Sanskrit and Greek words for wind *an-ila* and *án-emos*. Thus the Greek *thymos*, the soul, comes from *thyein*, to rush, to move violently, the Sanskrit *dhu*, to shake. From *dhu*, we have in Sanskrit, *dhúli*, dust, which comes from the same root, and 'dhúma,' smoke, the Latin *fumus*. In Greek the same root supplied *thýella*, storm-wind, and *thymós*, the soul, as the seat of the passions. Plato guesses correctly when he says (Crat. p. 419) that *thymós*, soul, is so called ἀπὸ τῆς θύσεως καὶ ζέσεως τῆς ψυχῆς.' It is the same with the word *soul*. 'Soul is the Gothic *saivala*, and this is clearly related to another Gothic word, *saivs*, which means the sea. The sea was called *saivs* from a root *si* or *siv*, the Greek *seió*, to shake; it

CHAP. II.

Origin of abstract words.

---

¹ *Lectures on Language*, 2nd series, viii. 343.

BOOK
I.

Expansive
power of
sensuous
words.

meant the tossed-about water in contradistinction to stag-
nant or running water. The soul being called *saivala*, we
see that it was originally conceived by the Teutonic nations
as a sea within, heaving up and down with every breath,
and reflecting heaven and earth on the mirror of the deep.'[1]
If to these primæval sensuous words we are indebted for
all the wealth of human language, these words must necessarily have possessed an almost boundless power of expansion.
A single instance will amply suffice to prove this fact. The
old root which expressed the idea of crushing, grinding, or
pounding has given birth not only to its direct representatives
the Greek μύλη, the Latin *mola*, the Irish *meile*, and the
English *mill* and *meal*; but it may be traced through a vast
number of words between the meaning of which there is no
obvious connection. In the Greek μάρναμαι, to fight, the
root has acquired that metaphorical meaning which is
brought out more clearly in its intransitive forms. In these
it embodies naturally the ideas of decay, softening, or destruction; and so it furnished a name for man, as subject to
disease and death, the *morbus* and *mors* of the Latins. If
again man was βροτὸς or *mortal*, the gods were ἄμβροτοι, and
drank of the amrita cup of immortality.[2] The grinding away
of time was expressed in the Latin *mora*, and in the French
demeurer, while the idea of dead water is perhaps seen in
mare, *mer*, the sea. The root was fruitful in proper names.
The Greeks had their gigantic Moliones, or Pounders, while
the Norseman spoke of the hammer of Thor Miölnir. So,
again, the huge Aloadai derived their name from ἀλωή, the
threshing-floor, a word belonging to the same root, as ἄλευρον,
corn, existed in the form μάλευρον. From the same source
came the Sanskrit Maruts, or Storms, the Latin Mars, the
Slavonic Morana, and the Greek ἄρης and ἀρετή. But the
root passes into other shades of meaning. Under the form
marj or *mraj*, it gave birth to the Greek μέλγω, the Latin
mulgeo and *mulceo*, the English *milk* (all meaning, originally,
to stroke); and in these words, as well as in the Greek βλάξ,
μαλακός, μαλθάσσω, the Latin *marcidus* and *mollis*, the Greek

---

[1] *Lectures on Language*, 2nd series ix. See also *Dictionary of Science*, &c.
s.v. *Soul*.   [2] Southey, *Curse of Kehama*, xxiv. 10.

μέλι, and Latin *mel*, it passed into the ideas of softness, sweetness, languor, and decay. From the notion of melting the transition was easy to that of desiring or yearning, and we find it, accordingly, in this sense, in the Greek μελεδώνη and ἔλδομαι (which may on good ground be traced to an older μέλδομαι), and finally, in ἐλπίς, hope. Not less strange, yet not less evident, is the passage of the root *jan* from its original force of making or producing (as shown in the Sanskrit *janas*, the Greek γένος, γονεύς, and γονός, the English *kin*; in the Sanskrit *janaka*, the Teutonic *könig*, the English *king*, in γυνή, and *queen*, and *quean*) to the abstract idea of knowing, as seen in the Sanskrit *jnâ*, the Greek γνῶναι, the Latin *gnosco*, the English *know*. The close relationship of the two ideas is best seen in the Teutonic *kann* (can) and *kenne* (ken).[1]

The facts which the growth of these words bring before us are in the strictest sense historical. The later meanings presuppose the earlier significations, and the stages are reached in a chronological as well as a philosophical order, while the several developements mark an advance of human thought, and a change in the conditions of human society. From the highest conceptions of the profoundest thinkers, we are carried back step by step to the rudest notions of an intellect slowly and painfully awakening into consciousness; and we realise the several phases of primæval life, as vividly as if they had been recorded by contemporary chroniclers. But if the process invests the study of words with a significance which it is impossible to overrate, it completely strips the subject of its mystery. No room is left for theories which traced the origin of speech to a faculty no longer possessed by mankind,[2] when the analysis of words exhibits from the beginning the working of the same unvarying laws.[3] If the words denoting purely spiritual ideas are all evolved from roots expressing mere sensuous perceptions, if these

CHAP. II.

Origin of language.

[1] Max Müller, *Lectures on Language*, second series, vii.; *Chips*, ii. 257.
[2] Max Müller, *Lectures on Language*, first series, 370, *et seq.*
[3] Whitney, *On Language and the Study of Language*, passim. Mr. Whit-

ney has carried to its logical results the proposition that man was born, not with speech, but simply with the capacity for speech. His whole book is an earnest and able defence of all the conclusions involved in this proposition.

words are thus confessedly accidental or arbitrary or conventional signs, without any essential or necessary relation to
the notions signified, although they are a necessary growth
from the original verbal stem, the real question at issue is
set at rest. The sensations expressed in these primary words
are felt by infants, by the deaf and dumb, by brute animals,
as well as by speaking men; they might therefore, rather
they must, have been felt by man before he made the first
attempt to acquaint his comrade with the thoughts which
were passing in his own mind. The word was needed not to
enable him to realise the perception for himself; but to give
him the power of awakening the same idea in another. It
mattered not, therefore, what sound conveyed the thought,
so long as the signal or message was understood; and thus,
where at the outset all was arbitrary, there might be many
signs for the same object or the same idea. The notions
which, as we have seen, found expression in words derived
from the roots MR or ML, might have been denoted as
easily by words derived from the stem GR. And in fact the
latter has been scarcely less fertile than the former. To it
we owe the words which denote the grating and grinding
sound of things rubbed forcibly against each other, the grain
which serves as grist for the mill, the gravel which the digger
scrapes up as he delves his grave, the groan of pain, the
grunt of indolence, the scribbling of the child and the delicate engraving of a Bewick or an Albert Durer.[1] We see,
further, that words drawn from imitations of natural sounds
have furnished names for impressions made on other senses
besides that of hearing, and that a presumption is thus
furnished for the similar origin of all words whatsoever.

Immo-
bility of
savage
races.
It may seem a poor foundation for a fabric so magnificent
as the language of civilised mankind;[2] but whatever belief
may be entertained of the first beginnings of articulate

[1] To this list may be added the
name for corn as ground or crushed, in
the Scottish *girnel*, the Lithuanian
girnos, the Gothic *quairnus*, our *quern*.
Max Müller, 'Comparative Mythology,'
Chips from a German Workshop, ii. 43.
[2] 'Never in the history of man has
there been a new language. What does

that mean? Neither more nor less than
that in speaking as we do, we are using
the same materials, however broken up,
crushed, and put together anew, which
were handled by the first speaker, i.e.
the first real ancestor of 'our race.'—
Max Müller, *Chips*, ii. 255.

speech, the gradual growth of language from its earliest CHAP. elements is disputed by none; and the examination of our II. own language carries us back to a condition of thought not many degrees higher than that of tribes which we regard as sunk in hopeless barbarism. Yet that this difference of degree involved in this instance a difference of kind is proved by the very fact that the one class of men has risen indefinitely in the scale of being, while the other exhibits no power whether of self-culture or of imitation. These are facts which, like other physical facts, we cannot gainsay, although we may not be called on to determine the further question of the unity or plurality of the human race.[1] The point with which we are more immediately concerned, is the light thrown by the history of words on the social and political history of the race, and on the consequences which followed the disruption or separation of tribes speaking dialects more or less closely akin.

[1] Mr. Farrar, *Chapters on Language*, iv. 42, &c., lays great stress on the immobility of savage races and their inherent and insuperable incapacity for education. As directed against the notion that the creation of man in a state of infancy is inconsistent with the goodness of God, his argument seems to be unanswerable. It is surely not more difficult to believe that the first stage of human existence exhibited the closest analogy to that of childhood, than it is to believe that God would now 'suffer the existence of thousands who are doomed throughout life to a helpless and hopeless imbecility, and that for no fault of their own.' Nor can we well misapprehend Mr. Farrar's meaning when, after mentioning the Yamparico, 'who speaks a sort of gibberish like the growling of a dog, and lives on roots, crickets, and several buglike insects;' the Veddahs of Ceylon, 'who have gutturals and grimaces instead of language, who have no God, no idea of time and distance, no name for hours, days, months and years, and who cannot count beyond five on their fingers,' he adds, 'These beings, we presume, no one will deny, are men with ordinary human souls:' p. 45. The primæval man was certainly not in a worse condition than these miserable races; yet Mr. Farrar ends his chapter with the assertion 'that Man is a very

much nobler and more exalted animal than the shivering and naked savage whose squalid and ghastly relics are exhumed from Danish kjökken-möddings, and glacial deposits, and the stalactite flooring of freshly opened caves,' p. 56. In other words, these primæval beings were not men with ordinary human souls; and hence the Veddahs, the Banaks, Dokos and the rest, are likewise not men with ordinary human souls. There could not well be a more complete contradiction. We may the more regret this inaccurate language, because it tends to keep up mischievous distinctions on grounds which may turn out to be purely fictitious, while the real question whether these primæval races were direct ancestors of the Aryan and Semitic nations, is really unaffected by such suppositions. The question of affinity, like that of an original revelation, is simply one of fact, and cannot be determined by our belief. So far as the evidence carries him, Mr. Farrar is quite justified in avowing his opinion that the men who have left their ghastly relics in kitchen-middens were not our ancestors, but he is not justified in denying to them the title of men and the possession of ordinary human souls, unless he denies it to existing races of savages, and to idiots.

D 2

Historical
results of
the ana-
lysis of
language.

It can never be too often repeated that the facts laid bare in the course of philological inquiry are as strictly historical as any which are recorded of the campaigns of Hannibal, Wellington, or Napoleon. The words possessed in common by different Aryan languages point to the fact that these now separated tribes once dwelt together as a single people, while a comparison of these common words with others peculiar to the several dialects furnishes evidence of the material condition of the yet undivided race. Thus, from the identity of words connected with peaceful occupations as contrasted with the varying terms for war and hunting, Professor Max Müller gathers 'that all the Aryan nations had led a long life of peace before they separated, and that their language acquired individuality and nationality as each colony started in search of new homes, new generations forming new terms connected with the warlike and adventurous life of their onward migrations.'[1] But these new terms were evolved from the common stock of verbal stems, and the readiness with which these roots lent themselves to new shades of meaning would not only render it easier to express thoughts already needing utterance, but would itself be a fruitful source of new ideas and notions. This process would be, in fact, a multiplication of living images and objects, for all names in the earliest stages of language were either masculine or feminine, 'neuters being of later growth, and distinguishable chiefly in the nominative.' Thus the forms of language would tend to keep up a condition of thought analogous to that of infants; and the conscious life of all natural objects, inferred at first from the consciousness of personality in the speaker or thinker, would become an article of belief sanctioned by the paramount authority of names, and all descriptions of phenomena would bring before them the actions of conscious beings. Man would thus be

[1] So again from the fact that in Sanskrit, Greek, and Gothic, 'I know' is expressed by a perfect, meaning originally 'I have perceived,' Professor Max Müller infers that 'this fashion or idiom had become permanent before the Greeks separated from the Hindus, before the Hindus became unintelligible to the Germans.' Such facts, he insists, teach us lessons more important than all the traditions put together, which the inhabitants of India, Greece and Germany, have preserved of their earliest migrations, and of the foundations of their empires, ascribed to their gods, or to the sons of their gods and heroines.' —Chips, ii. 252.

living in a magic circle, in which words would strengthen an CHAP.
illusion inseparable from the intellectual condition of child- II.
hood. Yet we can scarcely fail to see the necessity of his
being left to ascertain the truth or falsehood of his impressions by the patient observation of facts, if he was ever
to attain to a real knowledge and a true method for its
attainment—if, in other words, he was to have an education,
such as the wisest teacher would bestow upon a child. Ages
may have been needed to carry him forward a single step in
the upward course; but the question of time can throw no
doubt on the source from which the impulse came. The
advance made, whether quick or slow, would be as much the
work of God as the existence of man in the class of mam-
malia. Until it can be shown that our powers of sensation
and motion are self-originated, the developement of a higher
idea from a sensuous conception must be ascribed to the
Divine Spirit, as truly as the noblest thought which can be
embraced by the human mind. Hence each stage in the
growth of language marks the formation of new wants, new
ideas, and new relations. ' It was an event in the history of
man,' says Professor Max Müller, ' when the ideas of father,
mother, brother, sister, husband, wife, were first conceived
and first uttered. It was a new era when the numerals from
one to ten had been framed, and when words like law, right,
duty, generosity, love, had been added to the dictionary of
man. It was a revelation, the greatest of all revelations,
when the conception of a Creator, a Ruler, a Father of man,
when the name of God was for the first time uttered in this
world.' [1]

In that primæval time, therefore, after he had learnt to Earliest
express his bodily feelings in articulate sounds, but before he conditions
of thought.

[1] Max Müller, *Lectures on Language*,
second series, vii. 308; *History of Sanskrit Literature*, 528, *et seq.* After tracing
the evolution of a moral and spiritual
meaning from myths originally purely
physical, M. Baudry concludes, ' Le
sentiment moral et religieux n'existait
qu'implicitement dans le naturalisme
primitif. L'idée du Dieu créateur, père
des hommes, aimant le bien et menant
la création vers ce but final, n'apparaît
pas nettement dans la mythologie origin-
aire et ne s'en dégagea que peu-à-peu.
Quoique l'Inde ait été plus tard le pays
par excellence de la théologie, le Rig-
Véda ne contient de théologie que dans
ses parties les moins anciennes. Il en
faut prendre son parti; la métaphysique,
la morale elle-même en tant qu'elle
arrive à se formuler, sont des fruits du
développement intellectuel et non des
souvenirs d'une antique sagesse.'—*De
l'Interprétation Mythologique*, 30.

had risen to any definite conception of a Divine Being, man could interpret the world around him through the medium of his own sensations. It was thus impossible that he could fail to attribute sensations like his own to every object on which his eyes rested in the material universe. His notions about things external to himself would be the direct result of his psychological condition; and for their utterance he would have in language an instrument of boundless power.

CHAPTER III.

THE SOURCE OF MYTHICAL SPEECH.

If the analysis of language and the researches of antiquarians bring before us, in the earliest annals of mankind, a state of society which bears to our own a resemblance not greater than that of infancy to mature manhood, we shall scarcely realise that primæval condition of thought except by studying closely the mind of children. Stubborn facts disclose as the prominent characteristics of that early time the selfishness and violence, the cruelty and slavishness of savages; yet the mode in which they regarded the external world became a source of inexhaustible beauty, a fountain of the most exquisite and touching poetry. So true to nature and so lovely are the forms into which their language passed, as they spoke of the manifold phases of the changing year; so deep is the tenderness with which they describe the death of the sun-stricken dew, the brief career of the short-lived sun, and the agony of the earth-mother mourning for her summer-child, that we are tempted to reflect back upon the speakers the purity and truthfulness of their words. If the theory of a corrupted revelation as the origin of mythology imputes to whole nations a gross and wilful profanity which consciously travesties the holiest things, the simplicity of thought which belongs to the earliest myths presents, as some have urged, a picture of primæval humanity too fair and flattering.

No deep insight into the language and ways of children is needed to dispel such a fancy as this. The child who will speak of the dawn and the twilight as the Achaian spoke of Prokris and Eôs will also be cruel or false or cunning. There is no reason why man in his earliest state should not express his sorrow when the bright being who had gladdened

him with his radiance dies in the evening, or feel a real joy
when he rises again in the morning, and yet be selfish or
oppressive or cruel in his dealings with his fellows. His
mental condition determined the character of his language,
and that condition exhibits in him, as in children now, the
working of a feeling which endows all outward things with a
life not unlike his own. Of the several objects which met
his eye he had no positive knowledge, whether of their
origin, their nature, or their properties. But he had life,
and therefore all things else must have life also. He was
under no necessity of personifying them, for he had for himself no distinctions between consciousness and personality.
He knew nothing of the conditions of his own life or of any
other, and therefore all things on the earth or in the heavens
were invested with the same vague idea of existence. The
sun, the moon, the stars, the ground on which he trod, the
clouds, storms, and lightnings were all living beings; could
he help thinking that, like himself, they were conscious
beings also?[1] His very words would, by an inevitable necessity, express this conviction. His language would admit
no single expression from which the attribute of life was
excluded, while it would vary the forms of that life with
unerring instinct. Every object would be a living reality,

[1] In his most able and interesting
preface to the edition of Warton's
History of English Poetry, 1824, Mr.
Richard Price lays great stress on this
tendency, from which he holds that
even advanced forms of society are by
no means free. 'It is difficult,' he
remarks 'to conceive any period of
human existence, where the disposition
to indulge in these illusions of fancy
has not been a leading characteristic of
the mind. The infancy of society, as
the first in the order of time, also affords
some circumstances highly favourable to
the developement of this faculty. In
such a state, the secret and invisible
bands which connect the human race
with the animal and vegetable creation,
are either felt more forcibly in an age
of conventional refinement, or are more
frequently presented to the imagination.
Man regards himself then but as the first
link in the chain of animate and inanimate
nature, as the associate and fellow of all
that exists around him, rather than as
a separate being of a distinct and superior order. His attention is arrested by
the lifeless or breathing objects of his
daily intercourse, not merely as they
contribute to his numerous wants and
pleasures, but as they exhibit any
affinity or more remote analogy with
the mysterious properties of his being.
Subject to the same laws of life and
death, of procreation and decay, or
partially endowed with the same passions,
sympathies, and propensities, the speech-
less companion of his toil and amuse-
ment, the forest in which he resides,
or the plant which flourishes beneath
his care, are to him but varied types of
his own intricate organisation. In the
exterior form of these, the faithful record
of his senses forbids any material
change; but the internal structure,
which is wholly removed from the view,
may be fashioned and constituted at
pleasure.'—26.

and every word a speaking picture. For him there would be
no bare recurrence of days and seasons, but each morning
the dawn would drive her bright flocks to the blue pastures
of heaven before the birth of the lord of day from the toiling
womb of night. Round the living progress of the new-born
sun there would be grouped a lavish imagery, expressive of
the most intense sympathy with what we term the operation
of material forces, and not less expressive of the utter absence
of even the faintest knowledge. Life would be an alternation
of joy and sorrow, of terror and relief; for every evening the
dawn would return leading her bright flocks, and the short-
lived sun would die. Years might pass, or ages, before his
rising again would establish even the weakest analogy ; but
in the meanwhile man would mourn for his death, as for the
loss of one who might never return. For every aspect of the
material world he would have ready some life-giving expression ; and those aspects would be scarcely less varied
than his words. The same object would at different times,
or under different conditions, awaken the most opposite or inconsistent conceptions. But these conceptions and the words
which expressed them would exist side by side without producing the slightest consciousness of their incongruity ; nor
is it easy to determine the exact order in which they might
arise. The sun would awaken both mournful and inspiriting
ideas, ideas of victory and defeat, of toil and premature death.
He would be the Titan, strangling the serpents of the night
before he drove his chariot up the sky ; and he would also be
the being who, worn down by unwilling labour undergone
for men, sinks wearied into the arms of the mother who bare
him in the morning. Other images would not be wanting ;
the dawn and the dew and the violet clouds would be not
less real and living than the sun. In his rising from the
east he would quit the fair dawn, whom he should see no more
till his labour drew towards its close. And not less would he
love and be loved by the dew and by the morning herself,
while to both his life would be fatal as his fiery car rose
higher in the sky. So would man speak of all other things
also ; of the thunder and the earthquake and the storm, not
less than of summer and winter. But it would be no per-

BOOK
I.
sonification, and still less would it be an allegory or metaphor.
It would be to him a veritable reality, which he examined
and analysed as little as he reflected on himself. It would
be a sentiment and a belief, but in no sense a religion.

Primary myths.
In these spontaneous utterances of thoughts awakened by
outward phenomena, we have the source of the myths which
must be regarded as *primary*. But it is obvious that such
myths would be produced only so long as the words employed were used in their original meaning. While men
were conscious of describing only the departure of the sun
when they said ' Endymion sleeps,' the myth had not passed
beyond its first stage; but if once the meaning of the word
were either in part or wholly forgotten, the creation of a
new personality under this name would become inevitable,
and the change would be rendered both more certain and
more rapid by the very wealth of words which they lavished
on the sights and objects which most impressed their imagination. A thousand phrases would be used to describe the
action of the beneficent or consuming sun, of the gentle or
awful night, of the playful or furious wind : and every word
or phrase became the germ of a new story, as soon as the
mind lost its hold on the original force of the name.[1]

Secondary myths.
Thus in the Polyonymy which was the result of the earliest
form of human thought, we have the germ of the great epics
of later times, and of the countless legends which make up
the rich stores of mythical tradition. There was no bound
or limit to the images suggested by the sun in his ever
varying aspects ; and for every one of these aspects they
would have a fitting expression, nor could human memory
retain the exact meaning of all these phrases when the men
who used them had been scattered from their original home.
Old epithets would now become the names of new beings,
and the legends so framed would constitute the class of
secondary myths. But in all this there would be no disease

[1] ' That Titanic assurance with which
we say, the sun *must* rise, was unknown
to the early worshippers of nature, or if
they also began to feel the regularity
with which the sun and the other stars
perform their daily labour, they still
thought of free beings kept in temporary
servitude, chained for a time, and bound
to obey a higher will, but sure to rise,
like Herakles, to a higher glory at the
end of their labours.'—Max Müller,
' Comparative Mythology,' *Chips, &c.,*
ii. 96.

of language. The failure would be that of memory alone,— a failure inevitable, yet not to be regretted, when we think of the rich harvest of beauty which the poets of many ages and many lands have reaped from these half-remembered words.[1]

CHAP.
III.

It mattered little, then, of what object or phenomenon they might happen to speak. It might be the soft morning light or the fearful storm-cloud, the wind or the thunder. In each case there would be Polyonymy, the employment of many names to denote the same thing. In each case, their words would express truthfully the impressions which the phenomena left on their senses, and their truthfulness would impart to their language an undying beauty; but the most fruitful source of mythical phrases would be found undoubtedly in the daily or yearly course of the lord of day. In the thought of these early ages the sun was the child of night, or darkness; the dawn came before he was born, and died as he rose in the heavens. He strangled the serpents of the night; he went forth like a bridegroom out of his chamber, and like a giant to run his course. He had to do battle with clouds and storms. Sometimes his light grew dim under their gloomy veil, and the children of men shuddered at the wrath of the hidden sun. Sometimes his ray broke forth only, after brief splendour, to sink beneath a deeper darkness; sometimes he burst forth at the end of his course, trampling on the clouds which had dimmed his

Polyonomy, as affecting the growth of mythology.

[1] In his *Lectures on Language*, second series, 358, Professor Max Müller asserts that 'whenever any word, that was at first new metaphorically, is new without a clear conception of the steps that led to its original metaphorical meaning, there is danger of mythology; whenever those steps are forgotten and artificial steps put in their places, we have mythology, or, if I may so, we have diseased language, whether that language refers to religious or secular interests.' The mythology thus produced he terms the bane of antiquity. This view is opposed by M. Baudry in his able paper, *De l'Interprétation Mythologique*. After quoting the sentence just cited, he adds, 'Voilà le langage accusé de maladie et de révolte, fort injustement à notre avis, car la faute n'est qu'aux défaillances de la mémoire, qui a gardé le mot mais oublié le sens. Ce mal arrive tantôt pour un mot, tantôt pour une figure symbolique dont on a perdu la clef. Mais parce qu'une représentation mal comprise d'un évêque debout devant des catéchumènes plongés dans la cuve baptismale a donné lieu à la légende de saint Nicholas ressuscitant les enfants, en faut-il conclure aussi que la sculpture était malade ?' But after all there is no real antagonism between the view taken by Professor Max Müller and that of M. Baudry. With the former, mythology arises when the steps which led to a metaphor are *forgotten*; in other words, from a failure of memory, not from disease in language.

brilliance and bathing his pathway with blood. Sometimes, beneath mountains of clouds and vapours, he plunged into the leaden sea. Sometimes he looked benignly on the face of his mother or his bride who came to greet him at his journey's end. Sometimes he was the lord of heaven and of light, irresistible in his divine strength; sometimes he toiled for others, not for himself, in a hard, unwilling servitude. His light and heat might give life or destroy it. His chariot might scorch the regions over which it passed; his flaming fire might burn up all who dared to look with prying eyes into his dazzling treasure-house. He might be the child destined to slay his parents, or to be united at the last in an unspeakable peace to the bright dawn who for brief space had gladdened his path in the morning. He might be the friend of the children of men, and the remorseless foe of those powers of darkness who had stolen away his bride. He might be a warrior whose eye strikes terror into his enemies, or a wise chieftain skilled in deep and hidden knowledge. Sometimes he might appear as a glorious being doomed to an early death, which no power could avert or delay. Sometimes grievous hardships and desperate conflicts might be followed by a longer season of serene repose. Wherever he went, men might welcome him in love, or shrink from him in fear and anguish. He would have many brides in many lands, and his offspring would assume aspects beautiful, strange, or horrible. His course might be brilliant and beneficent, or gloomy, sullen, and capricious. As compelled to toil for others, he would be said to fight in quarrels not his own; or he might for a time withhold the aid of an arm which no enemy could withstand. He might be the destroyer of all whom he loved, he might slay the dawn with his kindling rays, he might scorch the fruits who were his children; he might woo the deep blue sky, the bride of heaven itself, and an inevitable doom might bind his limbs on the blazing wheel for ever and ever. Nor in this crowd of phrases, all of which have borne their part in the formation of mythology, is there one which could not be used naturally by ourselves to describe the phenomena of the outward world, and there is scarcely one perhaps, which has

not thus been used by our own poets. There is a beauty in
them, which can never grow old or lose its charm. Poets
of all ages recur to them instinctively in times of the deepest
grief or the greatest joy; but, in the words of Professor Max
Müller, ' it is impossible to enter fully into the thoughts and
feelings which passed through the minds of the early poets
when they formed names for that far east from whence even
the early dawn, the sun, the day, their own life seemed to
spring. A new life flashed up every morning before their
eyes, and the fresh breezes of the dawn reached them like
greetings wafted across the golden threshold of the sky from
the distant lands beyond the mountains, beyond the clouds,
beyond the dawn, beyond the immortal sea which brought
us hither! The dawn seemed to them to open golden gates
for the sun to pass in triumph; and while those gates were
open, their eyes and their minds strove, in their childish
way, to pierce beyond the limits of this finite world. That
silent aspect wakened in the human mind the conception of
the Infinite, the Immortal, the Divine; and the names of
dawn became naturally the names of higher powers.' [1]

But in truth we need not go back to that early time for
evidence of the fact that language such as this comes naturally to mankind. Abstract names are the result of long
thought and effort, and they are never congenial to the
mass of men. They belong to a dialect which can never be
spoken by poets, for on such unsubstantial food poetry must
starve and die. Some of us may know now that there is
nothing in natural phenomena which has any positive relation with the impressions produced on our minds, that
the difference between the temperatures of Baiæ and Nova
Zembla is simply the difference of a few degrees more or less
of solar heat, as indicated by Reaumur or Fahrenheit; that
the beautiful tints of morning and evening are being produced every moment, and that they are mere results of the
inclination which the earth at a particular moment may
have to the sun. We may know that the whispering breeze
and the roaring storm are merely air moving with different
degrees of force, that there is no generic difference between ice

Use of abstract and concrete names.

---

[1] *Lectures on Language,* second series, p. 500.

and water, between fluids and solids, between heat and cold.
What if this knowledge were extended to all? Would it be
a gain if the language of men and women, boys and girls,
were brought into strict agreement with scientific facts, and
exhibit the exactness of technical definitions? The question
is superfluous, for so long as mankind remain what they are,
such things are impossible. In one sense, the glorious hues
which spread over the heavens at sunrise and sundown, the
breeze and the hurricane, are to us nothing. The phenomena
of the outward world take no notice of us. Shall it then be
said that there is not One who does take note of the impressions which the sights or the sounds of nature make
upon our minds? Must we not recognise the feelings which
those phenomena irresistibly evoke in us as not less facts
than the phenomena themselves? We cannot rid ourselves
of these impressions. They are part of us; they grow with
our growth, and it is best for us if they receive a wholesome
culture. Modern science may show that our feelings are
merely relative; but there is still that within us which
answers to the mental condition from which the mythical
language of our forefathers sprang. It is impossible for us to
look on the changes of day and night, of light and darkness,
of summer and winter, with the passionless equanimity
which our philosophy requires; and he who from a mountain
summit looks down in solitude on the long shadows as they
creep over the earth, while the sun sinks down into the
purple mists which deaden and enshroud his splendours, cannot shake off the feeling that he is looking on the conscious
struggle of departing life. He is wiser if he does not
attempt to shake it off. The peasant who still thinks that
he hears the soft music of the piper of Hameln, as the leaves
of the wood rustle in the summer air, will be none the better
if he parts with this feeling for some cold technical expression. The result of real science is to enable us to distinguish
between our impressions and the facts or phenomena which
produce them, whenever it may be necessary to do so; but
beyond this, science will never need to make any trespass on
the domain of the poet and the condition of thought which

finds its natural expression in the phrases that once grew up into a mythology.[1]

CHAP.
III.

Myths
arising
from the
use of
equivocal
words.

To the primary myths which spring from phrases employed in their original meaning to express the phenomena of the outward world, and to the secondary myths which arose from a partial or complete forgetfulness of that meaning, must be added a third class, which came into existence from the use of equivocal words. If, as the tribes and families of men diverged from common centres, there was always a danger that words expressing sensuous ideas might be petrified into personal appellatives, there was also the more imminent danger that they might be confounded with other words most nearly resembling them in sound. The result would be, in grammatical phrase, false etymology: the practical consequence would be the growth of a mythology. Many of the tales belonging to the most complicated mythical systems arose simply from the misinterpretation of common words. From a root which meant to *shine*, the Seven Shiners received their name; possibly or probably to the same roots belongs the name of the Golden Bear (ἄκρτος and *ursa*), as the Germans gave to the lion the title of Goldfusz; and thus, when the epithet had, by some tribes, been confined to the Bear, the Seven Shiners were transformed first into seven bears, then into one with Arktouros (Arcturus) for their bearward. In India, too, the meaning of riksha was forgotten; but instead of referring the word to bears, they confounded it with *rishi*, and the Seven Stars became the abode of the Seven Poets or Sages, who enter the ark with Menu (Minos), and reappear as the Seven Wise Men of Hellas, and the Seven Champions of Christendom. The same lot, it would seem, befell another name for this constellation. They who spoke of the seven *triones* had long forgotten that their fathers spoke of the stars as *taras* (staras) or strewers of light, and converted the bearward into Boötes, the ploughman, while the Teutonic nations, unconscious that they had retained the old root in their word *stern* or *star*, likewise embodied a false etymology

[1] See further Max Müller, 'Comparative Mythology,' *Chips*, ii. 96.

[2] *Lectures on Language*, second series, 303.

in wagons or wains. But when we turn to the Arkadian
tale, that Kallistô, the mother of the eponymous hero Arkas,
was changed into a bear by the jealousy of Hêrê, and imprisoned in the constellation, we find ourselves in that
boundless region of mythology, the scenes of which are
sometimes so exquisitely fair, sometimes so gloomy, hideous,
and repulsive. The root *vah*, to convey (the Latin *veho*), gave
a name to the horse, to the flame of fire, and to the rays of
the sun. The magic wand of metaphor, without which
there can be no growth or expansion of language, soon
changed the rays of the sun into horses. But these horses,
vahni, had yet another epithet, *Harit*, which signified at first
the brilliance produced by fat and ointment. Like the Greek
words σιγαλόεις and λιπαρός, applied to things anointed with
lard or oil, *ghritá-prishthâh* (glittering with fat) furnished
a title for the horses (or flames) of Agni, *ignis*, the fire.
Thus the Harits became the immortal steeds who bear the
chariot of Indra across the sky and the car of Achilleus over
the plains of Ilion. The Greek carried away the name at an
earlier stage; and the Charites, retaining simply the qualities of grace and brightness, became the lovely beings who,
with Himeros and the Muses, charm earth and heaven with
their song. But before the Hesiodic theogony had defined
their numbers and fixed their attributes, Charis remained a
mere name of Aphroditê, the radiant dawn who springs from
the sea before the rising of the sun. Still, though even at
that early time Aphroditê was the goddess of sensuous
beauty and love, she was yet, with a strange adherence to
the old meaning of her name, known as Enalia and Pontia,
the child of the sea foam. For yet another title which she
bore they could but frame a tale that Argynnis, the beloved
of Agamemnon, had died at Kephisos. Yet that title,
identified with the Sanskrit *arjuni*, spoke simply of dazzling
loveliness. By a similar process of metaphor, the rays of
the sun were changed into golden hair, into spears and
lances, and robes of light. From the shoulders of Phoibos
Lykêgenês, the light-born, flow the sacred locks over which
no razor might pass. On the head of Nisos, as on that of

[1] See further Max Müller, *Rig Veda Sanhitâ*, vol. i. p. 26.

Samson,[1] they become a Palladion invested with a mysterious power. From Helios, the sun, who can scorch as well as warm, comes the robe of Medeia, which reappears in the poisoned garments of Deianeira. Under the form of spears and arrows the rays of the sun are seen in almost every page of all Aryan mythology. They are the invincible darts of Phoibos, Achilleus, and Meleagros, of Heraklês and Theseus, of Artemis, Perseus, and Bellerophôn, the poisoned arrows which Philoktêtês and Odysseus, the model, as some will have it, of Hellenic character, scruple not to use.

Thus the disintegration of the primary myths would be insured by the wealth of synonyms which the earliest form of human thought had brought into existence. If the Greek mythographers had been conscious that Kephalos and Prokris meant only the sun and the dew, the legend would have continued to belong to the same class with the myths of Indra and his cloud-enemy Vritra. As it is, it stands midway between these primary legends and the later tales which sprung up when the meaning of such names as Lykâôn, Korônis, and Sarpêdôn had been wholly forgotten. The form of thought which looked on all sensible phenomena as endowed with a conscious life, found utterance in a multiplicity of names for the same object, and each of these names became or might become the groundwork of a new myth, as in process of time they were confounded with words which most nearly resembled them in sound.

[1] Dean Stanley (*Lectures on the Jewish Church,* i. 368) points out the likeness between the features of Samson and those of Heraklês.

CHAPTER IV.

THE DEVELOPEMENT OF MYTHOLOGY.

BOOK I.

Elasticity of mythical speech.

WHEN in the Vedic songs we read of Indra, the sun-god, as fighting with Vritra, the dark power who imprisons the rain in the storm cloud, or with Ahi, the throttling snake, or as pursuing the beautiful Dahanâ, of the dawn as the mother or the bride of the sun, or of the sun as slaying the dark parent from whom he has sprung, we feel at once, that in such language we have an instrument of wonderful elasticity, that the form of thought which finds its natural utterance in such expressions must be capable of accommodating itself to every place and every climate, and that it would have as much room for its exercise among the frozen mountains of the North, as under the most smiling sky and genial sun. But the time during which this mythical speech was the common language of mankind, would be a period of transition, in which the idea of existence would be sooner or later expanded into that of personality. Probably before this change had taken place, the yet unbroken Aryan family would be scattered to seek new homes in distant lands; and the gradual change of language, which that dispersion rendered inevitable, would involve a more momentous change in their belief. They would carry away with them the old words and expressions; but these would now be associated with new ideas, or else be imperfectly or wrongly understood. Henceforth, the words which had denoted the sun and moon would denote not merely living things but living persons. From personification to deification the steps would be but few; and the process of disintegration would at once furnish the materials for a vast fabric of mythology. All the expressions which had attached a living force to natural objects would remain as the description of personal and anthropomorphous gods. Every word would become an attribute, and all ideas once grouped round a single object would branch off into distinct personifications. The sun had been the lord of light, the driver of the chariot of the day; he had toiled and laboured for the sons of men, and sunk down to rest, after a hard battle, in the evening. But now the lord of light would be Phoibos Apollôn, while Helios would remain enthroned in his fiery chariot, and his toils and labours and death-struggles would be transferred to Heraklês. The violet clouds which greet his rising and his setting would now be represented by herds of cows which feed in earthly pastures. There would be other expressions which would still remain as floating phrases, not attached to any definite deities. These would gradually be converted into incidents in the life of heroes, and be woven at length into systematic narratives. Finally, these gods or heroes, and the incidents of their mythical career, would receive each ' a local habitation and a name.' These would remain as genuine history, when the origin and meaning of the words had been either wholly or in part forgotten.

But in such a process as this, it is manifest that the men amongst whom it sprang up would not be responsible for the form which it might assume. Words, applied at first simply to outward objects or phenomena, would become the names of personal gods; and the phrases which described those objects would then be transferred to what were now deities to be adored. But it would not follow that a form of thought which might apply, not only without harm but with a marvellous beauty, to things if living yet not personal, would bear translation into the conditions of human life. If in the older speech, the heaven was wedded to the earth, which returned his love with a prodigal fertility, in the later time the name of the heaven would be the name of a god, and that god would necessarily be earthly and sensual. But this developement of a mythology, much of which would inevitably be immoral and even repulsive, would not necessarily exercise a similar debasing influence on the morality and practice of the people. It had started with being a sentiment, not a religion,—a personal conviction, but not a moral belief;

BOOK
I.

and the real object of the heart's adoration would remain not less distinct from the creations of mythology than it had been before. Nay, it might be that, with any given people, the tone of thought and the character of society might be more and more raised, even while the incongruous mythological fabric assumed more stupendous proportions. But the first condition of thought, which regarded every object in creation, would have *in itself* only two possible developements. It must issue either in an anthropomorphous polytheism, or in a degrading fetish worship.[1] The character of the people would in each case determine whether the result for them should be an idolatrous terror of inanimate things, or the multiplication of deities with human forms and human passions, mingling with men, and sharing their partialities and their feuds.

Evidence
of this
develope-
ment far-
nished by
the Rig-
Veda.

For the proofs of these assertions, we shall look in vain to the earliest Hellenic literature. But the Vedic poems furnish indisputable evidence, that such as this was the origin and growth of Greek and Teutonic mythology. In these poems, the names of many, perhaps of most, of the Greek gods, indicate natural objects which, if endued with life, have not been reduced to human personality. In them Daphnê is still simply the morning twilight ushering in the splendour of the new-born sun ; the cattle of Hêlios there are still the light-coloured clouds which the dawn leads out into the fields of the sky. There the idea of Heraklês has not been separated from the image of the toiling and struggling sun, and the glory of the life-giving Hêlios has not been transferred to the god of Delos and Pytho. In the Vedas the myths of Endymion, of Kephalos and Prokris, Orpheus and Eurydikê, are exhibited in the form of detached mythical phrases, which furnished for each their germ.[2] The analysis may be extended indefinitely : but the conclusion can only be, that in the Vedic language we have the foundation, not only of the glowing legends of Hellas, but of the dark and sombre

---

[1] In the growth of a higher belief and a purer morality by the side and in spite of the popular mythology, we can see only the operation of the Divine Spirit on the mind and heart of men.

[2] See the analysis of these myths in Professor Max Müller's essay on 'Comparative Mythology,' *Chips from a German Workshop*, vol. ii.

mythology of the Scandinavian and the Teuton. Both alike have grown up chiefly from names which have been grouped around the sun ; but the former has been grounded on those expressions which describe the recurrence of day and night, the latter on the great tragedy of nature in the alternation of summer and winter.

CHAP.
IV.

Of this vast mass of solar myths, some have emerged into independent legends, others have furnished the groundwork of whole epics, others have remained simply as floating tales whose intrinsic beauty no poet has wedded to his verse. Whether the whole may be classified in order of priority, may be doubtful ; but the strong presumption would be, that those which have not been systematised into coherent narratives are the oldest, as not having sufficiently lost their original meaning. At the least, they exhibit to us the substance of mythology in its earliest form. Thus the legends of Kephalos and Prokris, of Daphnê, Narkissos, and Endymiôn, have come down to us in a less artificial form than that of Heraklês, while the myth of Heraklês has been arrested at a less advanced stage than those of Zeus and Apollôn. But all alike can be translated back into mythical expressions, and most of these expressions are found in the Vedas with their strict mythical meaning. The marvellous exuberance of this early language, and the wealth of its synonyms, may well excite astonishment as we watch its divergence into such myths as those of Kephalos and Endymiôn, Heraklês, Daphnê, the Pythian and Delian Apollôn, Phaethôn and Meleagros, Memnôn and Bellerophôn.

Relative age of Greek myths.

That the form of thought which found utterance in mythical language would lead to the accumulation of a vast number of names for the same object, we have already seen ; and so clearly does the mythology of the Aryan nations exhibit the working of this process, that the task of tracing it through the several legends of which it is composed becomes almost a superfluous work. It seems impossible not to see that when the language of mythology was the ordinary speech of daily life, the night laboured and heaved with the birth of the coming day, and that his toil and labour is reproduced in the Homeric hymn, in which Lêtô, the power

Solar myths.

of forgetfulness and sleep, gives birth to the lord of light in Delos. His coming was preceded by the pale twilight, who, in mythical times, drove his cows to their pastures; but in the Odyssey his herds feed at Tainaron or in Thrinakia far away, where Phaethousa and Lampetiê, the bright and gleaming daughters of Neaira, the early morning, tend them at the rising and the setting of the sun. The old mythical feeling is strikingly manifest throughout the whole legend, not merely in the names and office of the wife and children of Helios, but in the delight with which he gazes on his cattle at the beginning and the close of his daily course, and in the indignation which prompts him, when they are slain, to hide his light in the regions of the dead. But the sun loves not only the clouds, but the dawn who is their leader; and so the dawn comes before us as followed by him, and flying from his love, or else as returning it. The former phrase ('the dawn flies from the sun') is embodied in the legend of . Daphnê, who flies from her lover and vanishes away as he seeks to embrace her. In the tale of Orpheus she appears, under the name of Eurydikê, as the bride of the sun, loved by him and returning his love, yet falling a victim to it, for whether to Daphnê or Eurydikê the brightness of his glance is fatal as he rises higher in the heaven. The same feeling is manifest under a form, if possible, more intense, in the tale of Kephalos and Prokris. 'The sun loves the dew,' was the old mythical phrase; and it is reproduced in the love of Kephalos (the head of the sun) for Prokris, the glittering dewdrop. But 'the morning loves the sun.' Eôs seeks to win Kephalos for herself; and her jealousy of Prokris is at once explained. But again the dewdrops each reflect the sun, and Prokris becomes faithless to her lover, while she grants him her love under a new disguise; and finally, when her fault has been atoned, she dies by the spear of Artemis (the fiery ray), with which the sun unwittingly strikes her down. It is the old tale of Daphnê and Eurydikê: and Kephalos goes mourning on his solitary journey, labouring not for himself, but for men who need his help,[1] until he sinks to sleep beneath the western sea.

[1] In this legend he goes to the aid of Amphitryon; but such details might, of course, be varied at will, so long as the movements are still to westward.

But, as we have seen, the sun may be spoken of as either beneficent or destructive, as toiling for the good of men or as slaying them. Sometimes he may sink to rest in quietness and peace, while the moon comes to give him her greeting of love; or he may die after a battle with the struggling clouds, leaving a solitary line of blood-red light behind him. So in the Hellenic legend, Phoibos cannot rest in his birth-place of Lykia or Delos; he must wander far westwards over many lands, through the fair vale of Telphoussa, to his western home in Delphi. There the mighty power of his rays is shown in the death of the great dragon, whose body is left to rot at Pytho.[1] Yet it was strange that the sun, whose influence was commonly for life and gladness, should sometimes vex and slay the sons of men; and so the tale went that plague and pestilence came when Phaethon had taken the place of Helios, and vainly sought to guide aright his fire-breathing horses. So again the legend of Meleagros exhibits only the capricious action of the sun, and the alternations of light and shade are expressed in the sudden exploits and moody sullenness of the hero; but his life is bound up with the torch of day, the burning brand, and when its last spark flickers out the life of the hero is ended. More commonly, however, he is the mighty one labouring on and finally worn out by an unselfish toil, struggling in his hard task for a being who is not worthy of the great and costly sacrifice. So Phoibos Apollôn, with his kinsman Heraklês, serves the Trojan Laomedôn; and so he dwells as a bondman in the house of Admêtos. So likewise, as Belle-rophontes, he encounters fearful peril at the bidding of a treacherous host, and dies, like Sarpêdôn and Memnôn, in a quarrel which is not his own. But nowhere is his unutterable toil and scanty reward brought out so prominently as in the whole legend, or rather the mass of unconnected legend, which is gathered round the person of Heraklês. Doomed before his birth to be the slave of a weak and cruel master, he strangles, while yet in his cradle, the serpents of the night,

---

[1] We have here only a reproduction of the snakes which are killed by Hera-klês, and the serpent which stings Eury-dikê. It reappears in Norse myths as the serpent Fafnir, and carries us to the throttling snake, who, as Vritra, is smitten by the spear of Indra.

which stung to death the fair Eurydikê. His toils begin. His limbs are endued with an irresistible power, and he has a soul which knows no fear. He may use this power for good or for evil, and his choice for good furnishes the groundwork for the apologue of Prodikos. Other legends there were which perverted this idea; and in these he is exhibited under gross, uncouth, or repulsive forms. But he goes upon his way, and is hurried on through many lands. In all he has mighty works to do, and he fails in none. The remembrance of Iolê may linger in his memory, but there are others who claim his love in the days of his strength and power, and it would seem as though he had forgotten the daughter of Eurytos. But his time draws towards its close: the beautiful maiden, whose face had gladdened him long ago, returns to cheer him in the evening of his life. With her comes the poisoned robe (the mantle of cloud), which he strives in vain to tear away from his bleeding limbs. In a deeper and redder stream flows the life-blood, till, after a convulsive struggle, the strife is closed in the dead silence of night.

Repulsive developements of solar legends.
But it is in the case of Heraklês that the perfect truth of the old mythical language gave rise more especially to that apparently strange and perplexing meaning which repelled and disgusted even the poets and philosophers of Greece. Pindar refuses to believe that any god could be a sensualist or a cannibal; he might in the same spirit have rejected the tales which impute something of meanness or cowardice to the brave and high-souled Heraklês. For Heraklês fights with poisoned arrows, and leaves them as his bequest to Philoktêtês. But the poisoned arrows are the piercing rays which burn in the tropical noon-day, and they reappear as well in the poisoned robe of Deianeira as in that which the Kolchian Medeia professes to have received from her kinsman Hêlios.

Origin of these developements.
A deeper mythical meaning, however, underlies and accounts for the immorality and licence which was introduced into the transmuted legend of Heraklês. The sun looks down on the earth, and the earth answers to his loving glance by her teeming and inexhaustible fertility. In every

land she yields her special harvest of fruits and flowers, of corn and wine and oil. Her children are countless, but all spring up under the eye of the sun as he journeys through the wide heaven. It is easy to see what must be the result when the sun is transmuted into the human, yet god-like, Heraklês, and how repulsive that myth must become which, in its primitive form, only told how

> The sunlight clasps the earth,
> And the moonbeams kiss the sea.[1]

The same explanation removés the mystery of the even greater degradation to which the Hellenic mythology reduces Zeus himself, the supreme father of gods and men. He who should be the very type of all purity and goodness becomes the very embodiment of headstrong lust and passion, while the holiness of the lord of life and light is transferred to Apollôn and his virgin sister, Athênê. The difficulty is but slight. Zeus, the Vedic Dyaus, is but another form of Ouranos, the veiling heaven or sky; and again, as in the words of our own poet, who sings how

> Nothing in the world is single,
> All things by a law divine
> In another's being mingle,

and how

> The mountains kiss high heaven,

so Ouranos looked down on Gaia, and brooded over her in his deep, unfailing, life-giving love. But these are phrases which will not bear translation into the conditions of human life, without degrading the spiritual god into a being who boasts of his unbounded and shameless licence.

The same process which insured this degradation insured at the same time the local boundaries which were assigned to mythical heroes or their mythical exploits. When the adventures of Zeus assumed something like consistency, the original meaning of his name was less and less remembered, until his birthplace was fixed in a Cretan cave, and his throne raised on a Thessalian hill. So Apollôn was born in Lykia or in Delos, and dwelt at Patara or Pytho. So Endymiôn had his tomb in Elis, or slept his long sleep on

Tendency to localise mythical incidents.

---

[1] Shelley, *Love's Philosophy.*

the hill of Latmos. So Kephalos first met Prokris on the Hymettian heights, and fell from the Leukadian cape into the Western Sea. So, as she wandered westward in search of her lost child, Têlephassa (a name which, like those of Phaethousa, Lampetiê, and Brynhild, tells its own tale), sank to sleep on the Thessalian plain in the evening.

Vitality of the mythopœic faculty.
Yet although much was forgotten, and much also, it may be, lost for ever, the form of thought which produced the old mythical language had not altogether died away. Showing itself sometimes in directly allegorical statement of historical fact, sometimes in similar descriptions of natural objects or of the incidents of common life, it still threw the halo of a living reality over everything of which it spoke. So the flight of Kaunos from Miletos to Lykia, and the sorrow of the sister whom he had left behind, figured the migration of colonists from the one land to the other. So in the Hesiodic Theogony, Nyx (night) is the mother of Hypnos, (sleep,) and Oneiros, (dream,) of Eris, (strife,) and Apatê, (deceit,) and Mômos, (blame,) where we speak merely of sleeping and dreaming, and of evil deeds wrought in secrecy and darkness.[1]

Constant demand for new mythical narratives.
If again, the mythology of the Homeric poets, as handed down to us, points to an age long anterior to their own, yet the mythopœic faculty still exerted itself, if not in the invention of myths altogether new, yet in the embellishment and expansion of the old. It was not easy to satisfy the appetite of an imaginative age which had no canon of historical criticism, and which constantly craved its fitting food. It was not easy to exhaust the vein opened in almost every mythical theme. The sun as toiling and suffering, the sky as brooding over and cherishing the earth, the light as gladdening and purifying all visible things, would suggest an infinity of details illustrating each original idea. The multiplication of miracles and marvels stimulated the desire for more ; and new labours were invented for Heraklês, new loves for Zeus, as easily as their forefathers uttered the words to which the myths of Zeus and Heraklês owed their existence. The mere fact of their human personification

[1] Max Müller, 'Comparative Mythology,' *Chips from a German Workshop,* ii. 64, *et seq.*

insured the growth of innumerable fictions. If Zeus had CHAP. IV. the form and the passions of men, then the conditions of his life must be assimilated to theirs. He must have wife and children, he must have father and mother. The latter must be no less divine than himself; but as he is enthroned above them, they must belong to a dynasty which he has over-thrown. Their defeat must have been preceded by a long and fierce struggle. Mighty beings of gigantic force must have fought on each side in that tremendous conflict; but the victory must belong to the side which, to brute force, added wise forethought and prudent counsel.[1] Here there would be the foundation for that marvellous supernatural machinery of which we have some indications in the Iliad, and which is drawn out with such careful detail in the Hesiodic Theogony. But Zeus, to whom there were children born in every land, must have his queen; and the jealousy of Hêrê against Iô, or Semelê, or Alkmênê would follow as a necessary consequence. The subject might be indefinitely expanded, and each subject would of itself suggest others; but there was no fear that the poet should weary the patience of his hearers, if only his additions, whether of incident or detail, did not violate the laws of mythological credibility. Nothing must be related of Heraklês which was repugnant to the fundamental idea of his toil and suffering for a master weaker than himself; nothing must be told of Athênê which would rather call up associations of the laughter-loving Aphroditê.

And, finally, there would be a constant and irresistible temptation to sever historical incidents and characters from the world of reality, and bear them into the cloudland of my-thology. Round every hero who, after great promise, died in the spring-time of his life, or on whom the yoke of an unworthy tyrant lay heavy, would be grouped words and ex-pressions which belonged to the myth of the brilliant yet quickly dying sun. The tale of Achilleus and Meleagros may be entirely mythical; but even if it be in part the story of men who really lived and suffered, that story has been so inter-woven with images borrowed from the myths of a bygone age,

Transmu-tation of names really historical.

---

[1] Hence the mythical Prometheus.

BOOK
I.

Ground-
work of
the mytho-
logy of
Northern
Europe.

as to conceal for ever any fragments of history which may lie beneath them. Names apparently historical have been introduced into the Nibelungen Lied which are not to be found in the Edda. The great Theodoric at Verona is transmuted into Dietrich of Bern; while Siegbert, the Austrasian king, and the infamous Brunehault[1] have taken the place of Sigurd and Brynhild.

But if the mythical phrases which gave birth to the legends of Heraklês, Endymion, and Orpheus, of Phaethôn, Meleagros, and Bellerophontes, spoke of the daily course of the sun, there were others which told of alternating seasons. For the character of mythical speech must necessarily be modified, and its very phrases suggested by the outward features and phenomena of the country. The speech of the tropics, and still more, of the happy zone which lies beyond its scorching heat, would tell rather of brilliance than of gloom, of life rather than decay, of constant renovation rather than prolonged lethargy. But in the frost-bound regions of the North, the speech of the people would, with a peculiar intensity of feeling, dwell on the tragedy of nature. It would speak not so much of the daily death of the sun (for the recurrence of day and night in other lands would bring no darkness to these), but of the deadly sleep of the earth, when the powers of frost and snow had vanquished the brilliant king. It would speak, not of Eôs rising from the Titan's couch, or of Hêlios sinking wearied into his golden cup behind the sea, but of treasures stolen from the earth and buried in her hidden depths beyond the sight and reach of man. It would tell of a fair maiden, wrapped in a dreamless slumber, from which the touch of one brave knight alone could rouse her; it would sing of her rescue, her betrothal,

---

[1] In this instance 'the coincidence between myth and history is so great that it has induced some Euhemeristic critics to derive the whole legend of the Nibelunge from Austrasian history, and to make the murder of Siegbert by Brunehault the basis of the murder of Sifrit or Sigurd by Brynhild. Fortunately it is easier to answer these German than the old Greek Euhemerists, for we find in contemporary history that Jor- nandes, who wrote his history at least twenty years before the death of the Austrasian Siegbert, knew already the daughter of the mythic Sigurd, Swan- hild, who was born, according to the Edda, after the murder of his father, and afterwards killed by Jörmunrek, whom the poem has again historicised in Hermanricus, a Gothic king of the fourth century.'—Max Müller, 'Compa- rative Mythology,' Chips, &c. vol. ii. 112.

and her desertion, as the sun, who brought back the spring, forsook her for the gay and wanton summer. It would go on to frame tales of strife and jealousy, ending in the death of the bright hero; it would speak of the bride whom he has forsaken as going up to die upon his funeral pile. This woful tragedy, whose long sorrow called forth a deep and intense sympathy which we, perhaps, can scarcely realise, is faintly indicated in the beautiful hymn to Dêmêtêr; but winter, in the bright Hellenic land, assumed a form too fair to leave any deep impression of gloom and death on the popular mythology. The face of nature suggested there the simple tale which speaks of Persephonê as stolen away, but brought back to her mother by a covenant insuring to her a longer sojourn on the bright earth than in the shadowy kingdom of Hades. But how completely the tragedy, to which this hymn points, forms the groundwork of the Volsung myth and of the Edda into which it was expanded, to what an extent it has suggested the most minute details of the great epics of the North, Professor Max Müller has shown, with a force and clearness which leaves no room for doubt.[1] Like Achilleus, Sifrit or Sigurd can be wounded only in one spot, as the bright sun of summer cannot grow dim till it is pierced by the thorn of winter. Like Phoibos, who smites the dragon at Pytho, the Northern hero slays the serpent

[1] 'Comparative Mythology,' p. 108, &c. The story of Sigurd and Brynhild comes up again in the legends of Ragnar and Thora, and again of Ragnar and Aslauga. Like Brynhild, Thora with the earth's treasure is guarded by a dragon whose coils encircle her castle; and only the man who slays the dragon can win her for his bride. But Ragnar Lodbrog, who so wins her, is still the son of Sigurd. Thora dies, and Ragnar at length woos the beautiful Kraka, whom, however, he is on the point of deserting for the daughter of Osten, when Kraka reveals herself as the child of Sigurd and Brynhild. The myth has been weakened in its extension; but the half consciousness of its origin is betrayed in the very names and incidents of the story, even as, in the *Iliad*, the tears which Eôs sheds on the death of Memnôn are 'morning dew.' See Thorpe's *Northern Mythology*, vol. i. pp. 108, 113. Mr. Thorpe is aware of the resemblance of the Northern mythology to that of the Greeks, but he seems scarcely to have understood its extent. In his explanations he inclines (vol. i. p. 122, &c.) to the opinion that real historical events have given rise to myths, a conclusion which Mr. Grote refuses to admit. But his method throws no light on the cause of these resemblances between the mythological systems of nations utterly severed from one another; still less does it show why they should in each case assume their particular form, and why it is that they could have assumed no other. In this Teutonic story Sigurd and Ragnar are each unfaithful to their betrothed brides: in the Welsh legend the faithlessness of Guenevere to Arthur reproduces the desertion of Menelaos by Helen, who finds her Lancelot in Paris.

BOOK I.

Fafnir, and wins back the treasure of the Niflungar, while he rouses Brynhild from her long slumber.[1] This treasure is the power of vegetation, which has been lulled to sleep by the mists and clouds of winter; the seeds which refuse to grow while Dêmêtêr sorrows for her child Persephonê. The desertion of Brynhild is the advance of spring into summer; and from it follows of necessity the hatred of Brynhild for Gudrun, who has stolen away the love of Sigurd.[2] A dark doom presses heavily on him, darker and more woful than that which weighed down the toiling Heraklês; for the labour of Heraklês issued always in victory, but Sigurd must win his own wife Brynhild only to hand her over to Gunnar. The sun must deliver the bright spring, whom he had wooed and won, to the gloomy powers of cold and darkness. Gudrun only remains; but though outwardly she is fair and bright, she is of kin to the wintry beings, for the late summer is more closely allied to death than to life. Yet Gunnar, her brother, cannot rest; the wrath of the cold has been roused, and he resolves to slay the bright and beautiful Sigurd. The deed is done by Gunnar's brethren—the cloud, the wind, and the storm; and Brynhild, filled again with her early love, lies down to die with him who had forsaken her.[3]

[1] The same myth, as we might expect, forms the subject of several of the 'Sculptured Stones' of Scotland. 'The legend of a dragon holding a maiden in thrall until he is slain by a valiant knight, occurs more than once.'—Burton, *History of Scotland*, vol. i. p. 150.

[2] It is but another form of the jealousy of Eôs and Prokris. It finds its most tender expression in the grief of Oinônê for the treachery of Paris.

[3] Mr. Dasent, who has very ably traced the intimate connection of the mythological systems of the Aryan race, seems, like Mr. Gladstone, to attribute their repulsive aspects to a moral cause. His reasons, however, are very different. The incessant display of the Hellenic and Teutonic gods he attributes to a consciousness on the part of their worshippers that they were *subjective*, and hence non-substantial. He contrasts rightly the 'restlessness' of a false religion, 'when brought face to face with the quiet dignity and majesty of the' true; but his instances appear to be scarcely in point. The manifestations of Moloch, Chemosh, and Milcom, may originate in such a feeling; but we cannot at once assign a moral and a mythological origin to those of Zeus and Odin, Thor and Vishnu. If Zeus and Odin were once the heaven or the sky, then their human personification must, as we have seen, be followed by the developement of their special mythical attributes and history, and could have been followed by no others. The idea of the mighty sun toiling for weak and worthless men would inevitably be developed into the strong Heraklês, brave or coarse, grave or even comic, virtuous or immoral.' The adventures of Zeus may be 'tinged with all the lust and guile which the wickedness of the natural man, planted on a hot-bed of iniquity, is capable of conceiving;' but we shall scarcely trace them to a religious perversion, if we accept the conclusions which a comparison of Greek mythology with the earliest Vedic literature forces upon us. The main

Phrases similar to those which gave birth to the legends of the Volsungs and the Nibelungs lie at the root of the epics to which Greek genius has imparted such wonderful consistency and beauty. Yet it can scarcely be too often repeated, that these poets adopted as much of the popular mythology as suited their purpose, and no more. If casual expressions throughout these poems leave no room to doubt that they knew of wars among the heavenly beings, of the dethronement of Kronos, the good service and the hard recompense of Promêtheus, and the early death of Achilleus, it appears not less manifest, that the idea of Oinônê and of her relations to Paris could not have dawned for the first time on the mind of a later age. It was not part of the poet's design to furnish a complete mythology; and the Iliad exhibits only that process of disintegration which was per-

difference between the adventures of Odin and Zeus is that, while those of the latter are chiefly erotic, the former involve the exhibition of gigantic physical strength,—a distinction at once accounted for by differences of soil and climate.—See Dasent, *Popular Tales from the Norse*, Introduction, p. lix.

Whether the Beast epic of the North had, or had not, its origin in a Nature-worship, Mr. Dasent appears to include in the various Beast epics of the Aryan races some instances which seem not to belong to them. Thus, as illustrating the transformation of men into beasts, he mentions Europê and her bull, Leda and her swan—(*Popular Tales*, p. cxix). If it be an illustration, it accounts for all such transformations: but it does so in a way which is completely subversive of any hypothesis of Nature-worship. Such myths may all be traced to mere forgetfulness of the original meaning of words. In the Vedas the image of a bull is very commonly employed as expressing the power and speed of the sun, and this image reappears in the bull which bears Europê, the broad spreading light, to the Western land. Thus also, as we have seen, the seven shiners become seven bears, and the seven stars are converted into wains. A similar confusion between words so nearly alike in sound and origin as λευκός, *shining*, and λύκος, *a wolf*, so named from the glossiness of its coat, produced the myth that Lykaon and

his children were turned into wolves, and probably laid the foundations of a superstition which has, from time to time, raged with disastrous fury. See Lecky, *History of the Rise and Influence of Rationalism in Europe*, vol. i. ch. i., and the article ' Witchcraft,' in the *Dictionary of Science, Literature, and Art*. But if the terrible delusion of Lykanthropy arose from the mere use of an equivocal word, we cannot cite such legends as evidence in favour of Dr. Dasent's hypothesis of a primæval belief that ' men under certain conditions could take the shape of animals.' That this belief prevailed in the time of Herodotos, cannot be denied ; but in the *Iliad* and *Odyssey* the power of assuming different forms is reserved to the gods only. A distinction may, however, be fairly drawn between the involuntary transformations of men in Norse mythology, and the genuine Beast epic, which accurately describes the relations of brute animals with one another, and of which Dr. Dasent speaks as ' full of the liveliest traits of nature.' But this very fact seems to prove conclusively, that this Beast epic never had anything to do with Nature-worship. The Egyptian who worshipped Apis was not likely to appreciate most keenly the character of the animal whom he reverenced. Had Norsemen ever worshipped bulls, bears, and wolves, they would not have drawn their portraits with such nice discrimination.

petually multiplying new tales and new beings from the old mythical language. In no instance, perhaps, is this process brought out with greater clearness than in that of Paris. This son of Priam, as leading away the beautiful Helen from the far west and hiding her through ten long years in his secret chambers, represents the dark power which steals the light from the western sky, and sustains a ten-hours' conflict before he will yield her up again. Paris thus is Paṇi, the dark thief of the Vedic songs, who hides the bright cattle of Indra in his dismal caves; in other words, he is Vritra, the veiling enemy, and Ahi, the throttling serpent of night. Such is he in his relations to Menelaos and the children of the Sun, who come to reclaim the lost Helen. But among his own people Paris is the most prominent actor in the great drama which ends in the fall of Ilion. He is beautiful, he is brave, and he is fated to bring ruin on his parents. In these characteristics he resembled Perseus, Têlephos, Oidipous, and Theseus; and at once the mass of floating phrases, which were always at hand to furnish germs for new myths, fastened on Paris until the idea which had called him into being is well nigh lost to sight. It is impossible to read the story of Paris as given by Apollodoros without perceiving the double character thus assigned to the seducer of Helen. His name, Alexandros, may certainly have borne at first a meaning quite opposite to that which it afterwards assumed; but the modification of his character had already been effected when Paris was described as the helper of men.[1] Henceforth the story assigns to him attributes which cannot be explained by the idea of Night. Doomed to destroy his parents, the babe is exposed on the slopes of Ida, like Oidipous on the slopes of Kithairôn, as the rays of the newly risen sun rest level on the mountain side. The child is nourished by a bear, but the bear carries us at once to the legend of the Seven Stars, and to the confusion of the name of the sun-god with that of the wolf. He grows up beautiful in form; and if his love is

[1] According to Apollodoros, vol. iii. 11, 5, he is so named as aiding the herdsmen, or more strictly, the flocks, against robbers. But it is possible that word itself might have been used to describe him as the enemy of man, as ἀλεξίκακος denotes one who keeps off evil, and ἀλεξίγαμος signifies one who shuns or keeps off marriage.

sensual, so also in many myths is that of Herakles.[1] If, again, after the seduction of Helen, his former bravery gives place to sullen or effeminate inaction, this feature only marks more curiously the affinity between the later conception of Paris, and the original idea of Meleagros and Achilleus. If he is capricious, so are they; and each sits burnishing his golden armour in his tent or his secret chamber, making ready for the fight, yet doing nothing. If, again, it is by the weapon of Paris that Achilleus is to fall in the western gates,[2] the arrow which slays Paris is drawn from the quiver of Herakles. But with the fatal wound comes back the love of Paris for the lost Oinônê; and not less forgiving than Prokris to the faithless Kephalos, Oinônê stands before him. With a soft and tender grief she gazes on the face which had once filled the whole earth for her with beauty. She sees his life-blood flowing away; but though she is of the bright race of the gods, and though she has the power of the soft evening time to soothe the woes of mortal men, she cannot heal the poisoned wound which is slaying Paris as the deadly mistletoe slew the bright and beautiful Baldur. But with the death of him who once was called Alexandros, the light of her life is gone. Paris rests in the sleep of death, and Oinônê lies down to die by his side.[3]

---

[1] The term γυναιμανής, as applied to Paris, only translates in a somewhat strengthened form a common epithet of Indra and Krishna, who, like the sons of Priam, are 'the lovers of the girls,' 'the husbands of the brides.' The idea would not fail to assume a sensual aspect when the actors of the tale were invested with human personality.

[2] Professor Max Müller, under the impression that I had sought 'to show that Paris belongs to the class of bright solar heroes,' lays stress on this fact, as pointing to an opposite conclusion. 'If the germ of the *Iliad*,' he adds 'is the battle between the solar and nocturnal powers, Paris surely belongs to the latter, and he whose destiny it is to kill Achilles in the *western gates*,

ἤματι τῷ ὅτε κέν σε Πάρις καὶ Φοῖβος
'Απόλλων
ἐσθλὸν ἐόντ' ὀλέσωσιν ἐνὶ Σκαιῇσι πύλῃσιν,

could hardly have been himself of solar or "vernal lineage."'—*Lectures on Lan-

guage*, second series, ch. xi. But this passage of the *Iliad* would, if taken with this strictness, reduce Phoibos himself to the ranks of the dark powers; nor must it be forgotten that in the great conflict the lord of life and light takes part with Hektor and his followers against the bright and short-lived Achilleus. The original idea of Paris is certainly not solar: but as he comes before us in the *Iliad*, he exhibits many features which belong to purely solar heroes, and which went far to transmute his character in later mythology.

[3] The parallelism seems complete, while, if we bear in mind the flexible character of the earliest mythical gods, on which Mr. H. H. Wilson and Mr. Max Müller have both laid great stress, there is very little to perplex us in this modification in the character of the seducer. This process, which must inevitably follow the disintegration of myths, is seen in the germ in the double

The Iliad is, in short, the Volsung tale, as wrought out by the poets of a bright and fertile land.[1] Yet, if the harsh climate of the north modified the Norse mythology, it also moulded indefinitely the national character, and the two acted and reacted on each other. Bred up to fight with nature in a constant battle for existence, the Northman became fearless, honest, and truthful, ready to smite and ready to forgive, shrinking not from pain himself and careless of inflicting it on others. Witnessing everywhere the struggle of conflicting forces, he was tempted to look on life as a field for warfare, and to own no law for those who were

meaning attached to the name of Orthros, who, as representing Vritra, would be the enemy of gods and men, while, as embodying the idea of daybreak, he might readily assume the benignant aspect of solar heroes. And, finally, the idea of treachery is as naturally suggested by the course of the sun, as the idea of his beneficence, his toil, his conflicts, and his early death. The sun forsakes the dawn for the glare of noonday, or the fair and blushing spring for the more brilliant and flaunting summer: and thus far the Trojan Paris is simply the counterpart of Sigurd or of Theseus.

[1] The Hellenic myths can no longer be regarded as exponents of abstract physical truths or theories. There can be no doubt that (whatever appearance of such a system may have been imparted to it by the priests), the supposition does not apply with more force even to Egyptian mythology. In Egypt, as well as in Greece and Northern Europe, we have again the solar legend. The spring was the time of festival, the autumn of fast and mourning. It would almost seem as though the Egyptian myths were in this respect more closely akin to those of Northern than of Southern Europe.— See Milman, *History of Christianity*, vol. i. p. 13. Compare also the Surtr of the Icelandic mythology, Dasent's 'Norsemen in Iceland,' *Oxford Essays* for 1858, p. 198.

The groundwork of the *Volsunga Saga*, of the tales of Helen, Alkestis, Sarpédôn, and Memnon, reappears in the legends and the worship of Adonis. The origin of the myth is in this case self-evident, while the grossness of the forms which it has assumed, shows the

degree to which such legends may either influence or be modified by national characteristics or the physical conditions of a country. Even in their worst aspects, Zeus and Odin retain some majesty and manly power; but in the legend of Adonis, the idea of the sun as calling the earth back to life has been sensualised to a degree far beyond the sensuousness of Greek or Teutonic mythology. In fact, the image of Dêmêtêr has passed by a very easy transmutation into that of Aphrodité: but there not only remains the early death of Adonis, but it is assigned to the very cause which cuts short the life of Achilleus, Sigurd, Baldur, and Meleagros. The boar's tusk, which reappears in the myth of Odysseus, is but the thorn of winter and the poisoned robe of Herakles; and accordingly there were versions which affirmed that it was Apollôn who, in the form of a boar, killed the darling of Aphrodité. The division of time also varies. In some legends the covenant is the same as that which is made with Dêmêtêr for Persephonê. In others, he remains four months with Hades, four with Aphrodité, while the remaining four, being at his own disposal, he chooses to spend with the latter. But the myth had been not merely corrupted: it was poisoned by the touch of oriental sensuality. In the *Volsung* tale, Sigurd dies as pure as lives the Hellenic Phoibos: in the eastern myth, from Adonis springs Priapos. The mourning of the women for Tammuz might well rouse the righteous indignation of the Hebrew prophet. The hymn of Dêmêtêr would have called from him a rebuke less severe.

not bound with him in ties of blood and friendship. Hence there was impressed on him a stern and fierce character, exaggerated not unfrequently into a gross and brutal cruelty; and his national songs reflected the repulsive not less than the fairer aspect of his disposition. In the Volsung tale, as in the later epics, there is much of feud, jealousy, and bloodshed, much which to the mind of a less tumultuous age must be simply distasteful or even horrible. To what extent this may be owing to their own character it may perhaps be difficult to determine with precision; yet it would seem rash to lay to their charge the special kinds of evil dealing of which we read in their great national legends. Mr. Dasent, who accounts for the immoral or repulsive details of Greek mythology entirely on moral and religious grounds, has consistently assigned a purpose not less didactic to the mythology of the North. In the Volsung tale he sees simply men and women, whose history had never grown out of conditions not belonging to human life. It speaks to him of love and hate, of 'all that can foster passion or beget revenge. Ill-assorted marriages . . . envyings, jealousies, hatreds, murders, all the works of the natural man, combine together to form that marvellous story which begins with a curse, the curse of ill-gotten gold; and ends with a curse, a widow's curse, which drags down all on whom it falls, and even her own flesh and blood, to a certain doom.'[1] This picture of mythology, the composition of which has been so strangely and fully laid bare by comparative mythologists, is no fair representation of the Northman. It is not easy to believe that the relations between Sigurd and Gunnar were (even rarely) realised in the actual life of the Norwegian or the Icelander. But, in his eagerness to defend their domestic morality, Mr. Dasent appears to be hurried into something like injustice to the society of the Greek heroic ages. These ages, to him, are polished and false,[2] a period in which woman was a toy, whereas she was a helpmeet to the Teuton, a time in which men lacked in general the feelings of natural affection. If the words refer to a later age, the

---

[1] *Popular Tales from the Norse*, introduction, lxi.   [2] *Ibid.* lxxiv.

comparison is scarcely relevant; and of the Homeric society the picture is scarcely true. The feelings of friendship are even exaggerated in Achilleus; the pure freedom of domestic equality is brought out with winning lustre in Nausikaâ and Penelopê. But whether with the Greek or the Northman, all judgment is premature until we have decided whether we are or are not dealing with legends which, whether in whole or in part, have sprung from the mythical expressions of a forgotten language. We can draw no inference from the actions of Zeus or Herakles as to the character of the Greeks; we cannot take the fatal quarrels of Brynhild, Gunnar, and Sigurd, as any evidence of the character of the Northman.

Special characteristics of Greek mythology.
Living in a land of icebound fjords and desolate fells, hearing the mournful wail of the waving pine-branches, looking on the stern strife of frost and fire, witnessing year by year the death of the short-lived summer, the Northman was inured to sombre if not gloomy thought, to the rugged independence of the country as opposed to the artificial society of a town. His own sternness was but the reflection of the land in which he lived; and it was reflected, in its turn, in the tales which he told, whether of the heroes or the gods. The Greek, dwelling in sunnier regions, where the interchange of summer and winter brought with it no feelings of overpowering gloom, exhibited in his words and songs the happiness which he experienced in himself. Caring less, perhaps, to hold communion with the silent mountains and the heaving sea, he was drawn to the life of cities, where he could share his joys and sorrows with his kinsmen. The earth was his mother: the gods who dwelt on Olympos had the likeness of men without their pains or their doom of death. There Zeus sat on his golden throne, and beside him was the glorious Apollôn, not the deified man,[1] but the sun-god invested with a human personality. But (with whatever

---

[1] The common mythology of the whole Aryan race goes against the supposition that Apollôn and Athênê owe their existence to man-worship and woman-worship respectively. Athênê, originally nothing more than the dawn, was to the Greek an embodiment of moral and intellectual greatness. The absence or deterioration of the former converts Athênê into the Kolchian Medeia. The latter type, when still further degraded, becomes the Latin Canidia, a close approximation to the ordinary witch of modern superstition.

modifications caused by climate and circumstances) both
were inheritors of a common mythology, which with much
that was beautiful and good united also much that was
repulsive and immoral.[1] Both, from the ordinary speech of
their common forefathers, had framed a number of legends
which had their gross and impure aspects, but for the grossness of which they were not (as we have seen), and they could
not be, responsible.

But if the mythology of the Greeks is in substance and in
developement the same as that of the North, they differed
widely in their later history. That of the Greeks passed
through the stages of growth, maturity, and decay, without
any violent external repression.[2] The mythical language of
the earliest age had supplied them with an inexhaustible
fountain of legendary narrative; and the tales so framed
had received an implicit belief, which, though intense and
unquestioning, could scarcely be called religious, and in no
sense could be regarded as moral. And just because the
belief accorded to it was not moral, the time came gradually
when thoughtful men rose through earnest effort (rather, we
would say, through Divine guidance) to the conviction
of higher and clearer truth. If even the Greek of the
Heroic age found in his mythology neither a rule of life
nor the ideal of that Deity whom in his heart he really

CHAP.
IV.

Full deve-
lope.
ment
of Greek
mytho-
logy.

[1] In his analysis of the *Volsung* tale, Mr. Dasent very ably traces the marks left by the national character on the Norse mythology; but he scarcely brings into sufficient prominence the fact that after all it was only modification, not invention. Sigurd is the very reverse of the orientalised Adonis; but the intermediate link is supplied by the Hellenic Phoibos. In describing Sigurd, Mr. Dasent, perhaps unconsciously, falls into the Homeric phrases which speak of the glorious sun-god. His beautiful limbs, his golden hair, the piercing eye of which none dared to meet the gaze, are all characteristics of the Homeric Apollôn. To these are undoubtedly added the hardier virtues of the North, which may to us make the picture more attractive, and which appear in some degree to soften in Mr. Dasent's eyes the harshness and extreme intricacy of the Northern mythology. The

sequence of motives and incidents is such as might well perplex or even baffle the reader. It is impossible to know what is coming. The ordinary conditions of society wholly fail to explain the actions and purposes of the chief actors in the story, and we are left at a loss to know how such a tangled web of inscrutable adventures could ever have been woven by the fancy of man. The key to the mythology of Greece also unlocks that of the North. The mystery is substantially explained; but the discovery involves the conclusion that the groundwork of the story is not peculiar to the Norse, and that its special forms of cause and effect do not therefore represent the ordinary motives and conditions of their social life.

[2] Grote, *History of Greece*, part i. ch. xvii.

worshipped, still less would this be the case with the poets
and philosophers of later times. To Æschylos, Zeus was
the mere name[1] of a god whose actions were not those of the
son of Kronos; to Sophokles it made no difference whether
he were called Zeus or by any other name, as long as he
might retain the conviction of His eternity and His righteousness.[2] If from his own moral perception Pindar refused to
credit charges of gluttony or unnatural crime against the
gods, no violent shock was given to the popular belief; and
even Sokrates might teach the strictest responsibility of
man to a perfectly impartial judge, even while he spoke of
the mythical tribunal of Minos, Rhadamanthys, and Aiakos.[3]
He was accused indeed of introducing new gods. This
charge he denied, and with truth: but in no sense whatever
was he a worshipper of the Olympian Zeus, or of the Phoibos
who smote the Pythian dragon.

Arrested
growth of
Northern
mytho-
logy.
As compared with the Greek, the mythology of Northern
Europe was arrested almost in its middle growth. After a
fierce struggle, Christianity was forced upon the reluctant
Northmen long before poets could rise among them to whom
the sensuality or ferocity of their mythology would be repulsive or revolting, long before philosophers could have
evolved a body of moral belief, by the side of which the
popular mythology might continue peacefully to exist. By a
sudden revolution, Odin and the Æsir, the deities of the North,
were hurled from their ancient thrones, before the dread
Twilight of the Gods[4] had come. Henceforth they could
only be regarded either as men or as devils. The former
alternative made Odin a descendant of Noah;[5] by the latter,
the celestial hierarchy became malignant spirits riding on
the stormcloud and the whirlwind. If these gods had sometimes been beneficent before, they were never beneficent now.
All that was beautiful and good in the older belief had been

[1] *Agamemnon*, 160.
[2] *Oid. Tyr.* 903.
[3] Plato, *Gorgias*, lxxx.
[4] This idea Mr. Dasent seems to
regard exclusively as a characteristic
of Teutonic mythology. (*Popular Tales
of the Norse*, introduction, lvii. lxxv.)

It seems to be embodied in the Æschylean legend of Prometheus, although
other versions accounted for his deliverance without the deposition of Zeus.
[5] Grote, *History of Greece*, vol. i.
p. 264.

transferred to the Christian ideas of chivalry and saintliness, which furnished a boundless field and inexhaustible nourishment for the most exuberant inventive faculty.[1] The demons of Hesiod were the spirits of the good who had died the painless death of the Golden Age; but even in heathen times they were gradually invested with a malignant character.[2] With Thor and Odin the transmutation was more rapid and complete; and Frigga and Freya became beings full of a wisdom and power which they used only for evil. The same character passed to those who were, or professed to be, their votaries; and the assumption of an unlawful knowledge paved the way for that persecution of a fictitious witchcraft which has stamped an indelible disgrace on mediæval Christendom.[3]

So marvellous is that chronicle of heathen mythology, as it lies spread out before us in the light of the ancient speech, marvellous not only as showing how nations, utterly severed from each other, preserved their common inheritance, but as laying bare that early condition of thought without which mythology could never have had a being. Yet, if it has much to astonish us, it has nothing to bewilder or even to perplex, for the simultaneous developement of the same myths by countless tribes unknown to each other would be a marvel too vast even for the greediest credulity to swallow—a standing miracle without purpose and without meaning. To the earliest records of Aryan literature is due the discovery that the vehement accusations of Christian controversialists and the timid explanations of heathen apolo-

CHAP IV.

Light thrown on both by the Vedic hymns.

---

[1] Grote, *History of Greece*, vol. i. p. 628. M. de Montalembert's History, *Les Moines d' Occident*, is a storehouse of legends belonging to the ideal of saintliness. He appears, however, to treat some of them rather in the spirit of Euêmeros. See *Edinburgh Review*, No. ccxxxii., Oct. 1861, p. 399.

[2] Grote, *History of Greece*, i. 96.

[3] See Mr. Dasent's sketch of the origin and developement of the modern ideas of witchcraft, *Popular Tales from the Norse*, introduction, p. cvii., &c , and the more detailed account of Mr. Lecky, in his *History of the Rise and Influence of Rationalism in Europe*, vol. i., ch. i.

Some valuable remarks on this subject may be found in Mr. Price's preface to Warton's *History of English Poetry*. (P. 57). It was this idea of a knowledge gained unlawfully from evil spirits which, far more perhaps than a habit of submission to church authority, impeded or repressed all researches in physical science. Gerbert of Ravenna (Sylvester II.) and Roger Bacon alike acquired the reputation of dabbling in diabolical lore. In the time of Galileo, the accusers confined themselves to the simple charge of an unlawful use of human intellect.

gists were alike unfounded,[1] that the impersonations of the old mythology had no substantial existence, and that the mythical narratives which grew up around them were not wrought out by a vile and corrupt imagination deliberately profaning the deposit of a revealed truth which it was hopeless that they should understand. To the language of the early Vedic hymns we owe our knowledge that the developement of such a mythology was inevitable, and that the phrases of that early speech, when their original meaning was once forgotten or misapprehended, would give rise to just those coarse, sensual, and immoral images, from which the purer feeling of later times would instinctively recoil.

Step by step this analysis of mythology leads us back to what would seem to be the earliest condition of the human mind, and from that onwards through the mythopœic age to the philosophy of historical Greece. On the general character of its course there can be no doubt, nor is the question materially affected by the hypothesis that a period of pure monotheism intervened between the earliest time and that which multiplied the mythical inhabitants of Asgard or Olympos.[2] In one sense the supposition may be true: in another it might be truer to say that the monotheism so attained never died away. It was impossible that any real fetish worship could arise while man had not arranged his first conceptions with regard to the nature of all material things, or even to his own. If from the consciousness of his own existence he attributed the same existence to all outward objects, he did so, as we have seen, without drawing any distinctions between consciousness and personality. The idea of their divinity in any sense would be an inference, not a sensation; and the analysis of language, which shows that all predicative words are the expression of general ideas, does not show us that the human mind was immediately exercised by any train of connected reasoning. If, however, this earliest state was not followed by one which invested outward things with a personal life, if in some way men

---

[1] Grote, *History of Greece*, part i. ch. i. p. 15.
[2] Dasent, *Norse Tales*, introduction,

p. lxvii. Max Müller, 'Semitic Monotheism:' *Chips from a German Workshop*, vol. i.

could believe in a malignant yet unconscious and nonsentient power residing in stones and rocks, there would at once be developed a fetish worship, the most degrading and the most hopeless, which, if expanded at all, could issue only in a polytheism of devils. Yet even here some faint perceptions might remain of moral qualities, unless we believe that the Divine likeness might be wholly blotted out; but is it possible to account for the loathsome earthliness of some forms of heathenism, except by the hypothesis that on them the idea of Deity has never dawned? If, however, when gradually awakened, the consciousness of their own personality might lead others to attribute the same personal life to outward objects, the deification of these objects or powers would not follow as an immediate or even as a necessary consequence. For a long time they might scarcely be conscious of the degree to which they personified them; or they might continue to look upon them as beings condemned to the same life of toil and trouble with themselves. Such a thought, it is obvious, might lead at once to the idea of One (distinct from all that they saw or heard), who ordained this life of labour; and the conviction of a Supreme God, the Maker of all things, might take possession of the mind.[1] But it is not less clear that such a conviction would not necessarily affect their ideas as to what they saw in the world around them. The Sun in all his various aspects, the Morning, the Evening, and the Night, might become more and more personal, even while the belief in a God exalted high above all might continue to gain strength. In other words, the foundation of their moral belief would at once be distinct from the foundation of their future mythology. Still, except to the thoughtful few, the personality of the great objects of the natural world would be more and more exalted, even while it assumed more and more a strictly human form. The result would be a polytheism of anthropomorphous gods, in which the chief divini-

---

[1] This state might also easily pass into Eastern dualism. The developement of the Hellenic mind was more wholesome. The prevalence of evil never led it to regard evil as co-ordinate with good. For the parallel growth of Hebrew idolatry with that of the purer religion of Jehovah, see Kalisch, *Historical and Critical Commentary on the Old Testament*, 'Leviticus,' part i. ch. xxiii. p. 380.

ties would be the heaven and the sun.[1] To the former, as covering and shielding all things, would be assigned those attributes which almost make us look on the Olympian Zeus and the Teutonic Alfadir as faint reflections of him who has made and loves mankind.[2] But neither for the majesty of Zeus or Odin, nor for the unsullied purity of Phoibos Apollôn, of Athênê, or of Artemis, need we look further than to mythical phrases, which spoke once of Dyaus, Varuṇa, or Indra.

So might a mythology the most intricate and a moral belief entirely independent of it, go on side by side. For the former had not sprung up from any religious conviction ; and the latter might advance beyond the stage of infancy, before the corruption of the true mythical speech led to the multiplication of mythological narratives. In the absence of any historical sense or any written literature, these tales would be eagerly welcomed and disseminated without a doubt of their truth. But the national character might exhibit many good and noble qualities, even while that of its greatest mythical heroes stood indefinitely lower. The moody sullenness, the implacable passion, and the ferocious cruelty of Achilleus ; the capricious jealousy, idleness, and activity of Meleagros, are well-nigh incredible ; nor is there any evidence either that those qualities were common amongst the Greeks in the heroic age, or that they attracted any great admiration or esteem. It can be no subject of regret to learn that they were as little responsible for the moral standard of Achilleus and Meleagros as for that of Zeus and Herakles, and that the idea of each originated as little with them as the conception of Odin and Baldur, of Sigurd and Gunnar, originated in the mind of the Teuton. So might the Spirit of God work in the human heart, even while a vast fabric of mythology was assuming proportions more and more colossal and systematic ; so, in spite of sensual gods, the thought of whom made the poet shudder,

---

[1] It is easy also to see how a substantial conviction of the Divine Unity might co-exist with the worship of his manifestation under the image of fire, the Vedic Agni, Ignis. This is again a belief founded on the sun as the all-seeing eye of day.

[2] Dasent, 'Norseman in Iceland,' *Oxford Essays* for 1858, p. 187.

might the real faith both of the poet and his hearers in an unseen Father continue substantially unshaken. So, while he cared not to avow any disbelief in mythical stories of Niobê or Promêtheus, Sokrates might tell of One who made men and watches over them for their good, and by the aid of that unseen God strive to keep his hands clean and his heart pure.

CHAPTER V.

GREEK CONCEPTIONS OF MYTHICAL TRADITION.

BOOK I.

Gradual assignment of an historical character to mythical beings.

THE exuberant growth of myths from a few roots expressing originally mere bodily sensations or wants is almost less astonishing than the inability of the several Aryan nations to see through the thin disguise which differences of name and local colouring had thrown over legends identical in all essential characteristics. In India, the old phrases retained in a high degree their primitive significance; but then these phrases remained comparatively barren stocks. In the West, where their meaning was more or less forgotten, the several sayings gave birth to independent legends which were all regarded as genuine and veracious history. The names Theseus, Perseus, Oidipous, had all been mere epithets of one and the same being; but when they ceased to be mere appellatives, these creations of mythical speech were regarded not only as different persons, but as beings in no way connected with each other. Political alliances were made, and nationals quarrels excited or appeased, by appeals to the exploits or the crimes of mythical heroes. The Persian King, before setting foot on European soil, secured, it is said, the neutrality of Argos by claiming a national affinity with the son of Danaê.[1] On the eve of the fight at Plataiai, the Tegeatans did not scruple to waste precious moments in support of a claim founded on the exploits of the fabulous Echemos, while the Athenians held that they rebutted this claim by bringing up their ancient kindness to the banished Herakleidai.[2] The tale of Othryades was regarded by Sparta and Argos as a sufficient ground for

[1] Herod. vii. 150. [2] Ibid. ix. 26, 27.

inserting a special article into a treaty made during the Peloponnesian war.[1]

But if they were thus convinced of their historical truth, they felt still more certain that the legends of one staté or city were essentially distinct from those of another. The Athenian was sure that the tales which he had heard of Erechtheus or Theseus had nothing in common with the legends of Argos, Thebes, or Pherai, beyond those incidents of local intercourse which were acknowledged by the narrative. The Arkadian, when he told the tale of Zeus and Kallistô, never supposed that it was repeated by the Thessalian in the story of Phoibos and Korônis. Perseus, Kadmos, Iasôn, Achilleus, moved each in their own circle, and had left behind them a history seemingly as distinct as that of Athens and Sparta from the days of Pausanias and Themistocles.

This conviction was a dream. But it has its parallel in the scornful assurance with which the British soldier would even now repudiate all affinity with the Hindu whom he holds in subjection. They who can see a little further know that this kindred is a fact too stubborn to be denied, while they perceive also that the national traditions of Hellênes, of Dorians and Ionians, with the political legends of Athenians, Thebans, Thessalians, Spartans, Argives, move in the same charmed circle, and revolve more or less closely round the same magic point. The great family legend of the Perseids is as magnificent a subject for an epic as that of the wrongs and woes of Helen. Its incidents are not less marvellous, its action is scarcely less complicated. Like the tale of Troy, it forms a coherent whole, and exhibits an equal freshness of local life and colouring. It serves, therefore, the more completely to prove the extent to which the Hellenic local legends sprung up from a common source, and to furnish the means of detecting the common element in isolated traditions with which they may seem to be not even remotely connected.

To the citizen of the Peloponnesian Argos the mere name

Marginal notes:
CHAP. V.

Each clan or tribe regarded its own traditions as distinct from any other.

This belief was wholly without foundation.

Connection between

---

[1] Thucyd. v. 41. Sir G. C. Lewis accepts the groundwork of the legend as historical. *Credibility of early Roman History*, ii. 515.

BOOK
I.

the legends
of Argos,
Thebes,
and
Athens.

of Perseus sufficed as a conclusive mark, separating him from all who traced their origin to Theseus or to Kadmos. Yet his designation as a destroyer of noxious things linked the son of Danaê at once with other heroes of Greek mythology. If Perseus won or deserved his name because he slew the deadly Gorgon or the Libyan sea-monster, Phoibos Apollôn had also killed the mighty serpent Python, and Hipponoös received his title Bellerophontes as the slayer of the fearful Belleros. It was the arbitrary sentence of the cruel and cowardly Polydektes which sent Perseus on his weary errand to the caves of the Graiai and the Gorgons; but it was no less the relentless hatred of the mean and false Eurystheus which made the life of the high-souled Herakles a long series of unrequited labours. Nay, Apollôn himself was driven forth to serve as a bondman in the house of the kindly Admêtos, and, with Herakles, to look in vain for a recompense from the treacherous Laomedôn. If, in doing the bidding of the Seriphian king, Perseus encountered overwhelming dangers, Theseus surmounted perils not less appalling for the same reason and from the same motives, while his victory over the Minotauros only repeats the slaughter of the Libyan dragon by Perseus. Thus, then, as unwilling workers, as destroyers of unclean or hurtful things, Perseus, Theseus, Hipponoös and Herakles are expressions of the same idea. If, again, his name as the child of the golden shower points to the splendour of his birth, so also Phoibos springs to light, in Delos or in Lykia, while the gloomy prison-house or cave in which, like Zeus or Krishna, he is born, has its parallel in the sleep or death of Night, which is the parent of the Delphian god. If it is the hope and the boast of Perseus that before his life's labour is done he will bring back Danaê to the home which she had left when he was a babe, so also Herakles meets at the close of his toils the maiden whom he had wooed while his life was in its morning. From the island in the Eastern sea Perseus journeys through many lands to the dark home of the Graiai in the far west; but Herakles also wanders from Argos to the distant gardens of the Hesperides, Hipponoös is driven from Lykia, the land of light, and dies on the shore of the western sea, while Kephalos seeks in the Leukadian gulf the love which he had lost in Attica. In his attack on the Gorgon maiden, Perseus is armed with the sword which slays everything on which it falls; but Apollôn is also the invincible Chrysâôr, and Artemis carries the unerring spear which is fatal to the guileless Prokris and the less innocent Korônis or Kallistô. On the golden sandals Perseus moves through the air quicker than a dream; but the golden chariot also bears Helios and Phaethon across the blue vault of heaven, and when Achilleus tries his armour, it bears him aloft like a bird upon the wing.[1] After slaying the sea-dragon, Perseus wins Andromeda; after killing the Minotauros Theseus wins Ariadnê. In unselfishness of character, and in the determination to face rather than to shrink from danger, there is no difference between Perseus and Theseus, until the latter returns from Crete; or again between Perseus and Bellerophontês. Perseus is the strongest and the most active among the people in all manly exercises. So, too, none can vie with Apollôn in the use of the bow, and the children of Niobê fall not less surely than the Pythian dragon. If, again, Perseus is the child of a mother of whom we know little more than the name, gentle, patient, and long-enduring, the same neutral colouring is seen in Iokastê in the Theban legend of Oidipous; in Lêtô, who gives birth to Apollôn in Delos; and in Alkmênê, from whom is born the mightiest of heroes, Herakles. The life of Perseus closes in darkness. He has slain his grandfather, and he has not the heart to remain in his ancient home; but Kephalos also cannot abide at Athens after he has unwittingly slain Prokris, or Herakles in Kalydôn after slaying the boy Eunomos, and each departs to die elsewhere.

Without going further, we have here no very insufficient evidence, if we sought to prove a close connection, or even a complete identity, between Perseus, Bellerophôn, Theseus, Kephalos, Herakles, and Apollôn. If we cease to confine ourselves to a single legend, the coincidences might be indefinitely multiplied, while any other legend may be submitted to the same treatment which has just been applied to that of

Identity of the tribal legends.

---

[1] *Iliad.* xix. 386.

Perseus. If Kephalos, having won the love of Prokris, is obliged to leave her for a time, Apollôn in like manner is constrained to desert Korônis. If Prokris yields her affection to one whom she almost believes to be Kephalos, the guilt of Korônis is not many shades deeper; while both are alike smitten by the fatal spear of Artemis. In the legends of Thebes, Athens, Argos, and other cities, we find the strange yet common dread of parents who look on their children as their future destroyers. Thus Oidipous is cast forth to die on the slopes of Kithairôn, as Paris is abandoned on those of Ida or Arthur to the mysterious Merlin, while Perseus is entrusted to the mercy of the deep sea. Nay, the legends interchange the method by which the parents seek the death of their children; for there were tales which narrated that Oidipous was shut up in an ark which was washed ashore at Sikyôn.[1] In every case the child grows up beautiful, brave, and strong. Like Apollôn, Bellerophôn, and Herakles, they are all slayers of monsters. The son of the gloomy Laios returns to destroy the dreaded Sphinx, as Perseus slays the Gorgon, and the Minotauros falls by the sword of Theseus. They have other features in common. The fears of their parents are in all cases realised. Akrisios and Laios are killed by Perseus and Oidipous, as Romulus and Cyrus bring ruin on Amulius and Astyages.[2] All of them love fair maidens and are somewhat prone to forsake them; and after doing marvellous things, they return to the maiden whom they loved at the beginning of their career, or to the mother from whom they had been parted long ago. Herakles finds Iolê by his funeral pile on Oita, while in the myth which has invested his character with a solar colouring Oinônê cheers Paris in his last hour on Ida.

[1] In this version of the myth he is a son of Euryklein, a name which belongs to the same class with Euryganeia, Eurydikê, Eurymedê, etc. In the same way Dionysos, who, in the Theban legend, was born amid the blaze of the lightning which destroyed his mother, is in the Lakonian story placed in a chest with his mother and carried to Brasiai, where Semêlê was found dead. Paus. ii. 24, § 3.

[2] This illustration must not be regarded as banishing Cyrus wholly to the domain of mythology, although it seems sufficiently to prove that to the person of the historical Cyrus, as to that of Charles the Great, a mass of floating mythology has attached itself, and that, from such traditions we cannot be said to derive any part of our historical knowledge. The conclusions which these facts seem to force upon us are given elsewhere. (Ch. ix.)

Still more significantly, Oidipous marries Iokastê (the con- CHAP. V. nection of the name with that of Iolê is manifest),[1] and the unwitting sin thus committed becomes the starting-point of a more highly-complicated history.

Wonderful, again, as is the seeming variety of action and incident in these legends, the recurrence of the same imagery, freshened by ingenious modifications, is not less remarkable. If Heraklês begins his career of marvels by strangling the serpents who have twined round his limbs, the youthful Apollôn slays the huge snake Pytho, and Perseus smites the snaky haired Medousa. The serpents, in their turn, win the victory when Eurydikê falls a victim on the banks of the Hebros, or assume a more kindly form in the legends of Iamos and Melampous.[2] The former they shelter in the thickets, because, as with Perseus, Oidipous, Romulus, and Cyrus, his kinsfolk seek his death, while to Melampous,

The imagery of these legends.

---

[1] The violet or purple colour can be traced through a large number of Greek mythical names. Iolaos is the son of Iphiklês, the twin-brother of Heraklês, (*Scut. Her.* 74). Through Epaphos and Danaos, the line of Heraklês is traced back to Iô, in whose story is brought out the favourite image of the bull, as a figure of Indra or the sun. The names of Iasion, whom Dêmêtêr loved, and Zeus slew, of Iasô, the daughter of Asklêpios, and Iason, were referred to the idea of healing (Ἰασις); but Æschylos derived Lykios, as an epithet of Apollôn, from the destruction of wolves,

Λύκει' ἄναξ, Λύκειος γενοῦ
στρατῷ δαίῳ.   *Theb.* 145,

and thus unconsciously explained not only the transformation of Lykaôn into a wolf, but the origin of the superstition of Lykanthropy. See note 3, p. 62. In short, the Greek poets were far more frequently wrong than right in accounting for mythical names; and thus the names Iason, Iolaos, and the rest, may, so far as their belief is concerned, have had the same origin with that of Iamos, which is directly referred to the violet beds under which he was hidden by the Drakontes, who, in the myth of Iason bear the chariot of Medeia. There remain some epithets, as Ieios, and Iacchos, both of which are commonly referred to the cry ἰή, an explanation supported by

the known connection of words denoting sound and colour. About these it may be rash to speak positively, although the opinion of Greek writers is not worth much, and Iacchos may be another form of *Bacchus,* which Dr. Latham connects with the Slavonic *bog,* our bogy and Puck, the Welsh Pwcca, &c.—Johnson, *English Dictionary,* s.v. *Bogy.*

[2] In the Gaelic story of Fearchus Leigh (Campbell, *Tales of the West Highlands,* ii. 362) the snake is boiled in a pot, round which paper is wrapped to prevent the steam from escaping. 'But he had not made all straight when the water began to boil, and the steam began to come out at one place. 'Well, Farquhar saw this, and thought he would push the paper down round the thing; so he put his finger to the bit, and then his finger into his mouth, for it was wet with the bree. 'So he knew everything, and the eyes of his mind were opened.' Farquhar now sets up for a doctor; but the old myth of Asklêpios must still be fulfilled in him. 'Farquhar the physician never came to be Farquhar the king, for he had an ill-wisher that poisoned him, and he died.' The poison represents the thunder-bolt of Zeus in the Greek story, and the ill-wisher is Zeus himself.

by cleansing his ears, they impart a new power, so that he may understand the voices and the song of birds. The spotless white bull bears Európê across the waters of the sea: the glistening ram soars through the air with the children of Nephelê, or the mist. Phaethousa and Lampetiô drive the cattle of Helios to their pastures, and Hermes steals the herds of Apollôn when he is scarce an hour old. The cattle in their turn assume an unkindly aspect. The Minotauros plagues the Cretans, the Marathonian bull ravages the fields of Attica. The former is killed by the child of the golden shower, the latter by the son of Aithra, the pure air.

Signifi-
cance of
the names
employed
in Greek
legends.
The very names occurring in these tribal legends have a significance which the Greek language itself interprets, whenever they tell us of the great heroes whose lives run so strangely in the same magic groove. Oidipous loves Iokastê, as Heraklês loves Iolê; but he is also the husband of Euryganeia, who spreads the light over the broad sky. The names of Phaethon, of Phaethousa and Lampetiô, the children of Neaira, tell their own tales. In the obscure mythology of Tegea, when the name of Heraklês is introduced, the maiden whom he chooses is Augê, the brilliant.[1] She too, like Danaê, is driven away by the terror of her father, and in the far eastern land becomes the mother of Têlephos, who, like Oidipous and Paris, is exposed on the rough hill-side, and whose office as the bringer of light is seen again in the name of Têlephassa, the mother of Európê. So, again, when the genealogy of Phthia is to be mingled with that of Elis, it is Protogeneia (the earliest dawn) who becomes the mother of Aethlios (the toiling and struggling sun), who is the father of Endymiôn, the tired sun at his setting, in whose child Eurydikê we see again the morrow's light restored to its former brightness.[2]

Opinions
of Greek
Thus in the marvellous tales which recounted the mighty

<hr>

[1] Paus. viii. 4, 6; Grote, *History of Greece*, vol. i. p. 240.
[2] Paus. v. 12. Aethlios is the husband of Kalykê, the night. By some canon of probability, better known to himself than to others, Pausanias chooses to marry Endymiôn to Asterodia, rather than to Selênê, as the mother of his fifty children. He was making a

distinction without a difference. Mr. Grote gives the several versions of the myth (*History of Greece*, i. 188 &c.): but he is probably mistaken in supposing that the names Aethlios and Endymiôn are of late introduction, although their connection with the Olympic games undoubtedly was.

deeds of Perseus and Heraklês the people of Argos saw a coherent whole,—the chronicle of the great actions which distinguished the founders of their state from those of any other. Yet the tale of Perseus, and still more that of Heraklês, is re-echoed in the Attic legends of Theseus; and even more significant is the fact of their utter unconsciousness that the life of Perseus is, in all its essential features, repeated in that of his great descendant Heraklês, through whose career the *epos* of Argos is twisted into a complicated chain with that of Attica. The conclusion is forced upon us that the Greeks knew no more about the historical facts possibly underlying these traditions than they knew about the names which occurred in them. We see at once that Athenians, Thebans, Argives, Spartans, regarded as independent narratives tales which are merely modified versions of the same story. Hence their convictions furnish not even the faintest presumption that the actors in the great dynastic legends ever had any historical existence, or that the myths themselves point to any historical facts.

CHAPTER VI.

BOOK
I.

Coarse
development of
certain
mythical
phrases.

THE method, which has enabled us to compare the story of
the Iliad with the Volsung Tale or the epic of Firdusi, tends
to show that, in many instances at least, even the grossest
myths arose from phrases which were truthful and therefore
beautiful descriptions of phenomena. But it has also shown
us that these phrases, when translated into the conditions of
human life and morality, would inevitably give rise to precisely those tales which, related boldly and nakedly, must
appear coarse, repulsive, or disgusting. Nor can it be
denied, that if children or grown men are only to cram
their memories with a thousand tales which speak of Oidipous as marrying his mother, of Tantalos as roasting his own
son, of Lykaôn as placing a meal of human flesh before Zeus,
of Hephaistos as defiling Athênê, of Heraklês as a creature of
unbounded and indiscriminate lust, it must be in every way
better to remain ignorant of such things in spite of all the
allusions of poets and the suggestions of painters and sculp-
tors. If we are to know only these incidents or details, (and
the works which do not avowedly adopt the method of comparative mythology attempt nothing more,) the knowledge
must be simply unwholesome.

Protests of
Greek
writers.

It is no wonder that a mythology which still drives some
critics to desperate shifts in their efforts to account for such
strange developements, and which the Greek shared with
barbarians, whose minds he despised and whose language he
could not understand, should perplex and baffle the poets
and philosophers of Hellas. Some little suspicion they had
of the meaning of a few mythical names and phrases : how

the vast majority of them had come into being, they could have no idea. Still less, therefore, could they surmise that these names themselves had given rise to the tales which charmed, bewildered, or horrified them. They knew that Zeus sometimes meant the sky; they knew that Selênê must be the moon; they half fancied that Enдymion must be the sleeping sun: but they did not know why Zeus and Heraklês must have many loves in many lands, why Kronos should maim his father Ouranos and swallow his own children, why Tantalos should place the limbs of his son on the banquet table of the gods, why Oidipous should marry his mother and bring unimaginable woes on her, on himself, and on his children. From all these horrors their moral sense shrank with an instinctive aversion. The Zeus whom they worshipped was the all-seeing ruler and the all-righteous judge. In him there was no passion and no shadow of turning. He was the fountain of all truth and goodness, from which could flow nothing impure or foul. How then should he be envious or jealous, capricious, lustful, and treacherous? The contradiction was glaring, and some among them had trenchant methods of dealing with it. Later philosophers condemned in a mass the glorious epics which bear the name of Homer: later poets contented themselves with rejecting every legend which was distasteful to their moral sense. Plato would give no place to Homer in his ideal commonwealth: Euripides, like Homeric heroes, could tell Zeus to his face, that he and his kinsfolk had done fearful things, or when he cast aside his mythological faith, could assert unequivocally,

> If the gods do aught unseemly,
> Then they are not gods at all.[1]

The power of resting content without seeking to account for this portentous growth of an immoral theology seems

Limits of their knowledge.

---

[1] Fragm., *Belleroph.* 300. It can scarcely be denied that, from his own point of view, 'Plato was right in warning the guardians of his ideal polity against the danger to youth, if they were permitted to receive the Homeric tales concerning the gods and heroes either as true descriptions of deity, or as examples of human conduct.' Some remarks on the connection of this subject with that of modern education may be found in Mr. H. B. Wilson's *Introduction to the Examination of Prevalent Opinions of Inspiration* (1861), p. xv.

BOOK
I.

to be reserved for modern minds. Examining this subject at greater length, Mr. Max Müller remarks that the Greeks 'would not have been Greeks, if they had not perceived that the whole of their mythology presented a problem that required a solution at the hand of a philosopher.' But, however great their efforts might be to explain its origin, the same causes which prevented them from discovering the affinity of their own language with that of Persians, Thrakians, or Italians, must have placed insuperable barriers in their way; and thus they were the more tempted to accept a compromise, which saved them from antagonism with 'some of the most venerable institutions' of their country.[1]

Explanation of the seeming immorality of Aryan mythology.

But if the examination of the most complicated epic poetry discloses precisely the frame-work which we find even in the most fragmentary legends,[2] if Theseus and Sigurd,

[1] *Lectures on Language*, second series, ix.

[2] It is impossible to determine the aid which Comparative Mythology might have received from the lost poems of the so-called epic cycle. There can, however, be little doubt, that they would have made still more evident the truth of facts which, even without them, seem to be indisputably established. We might also, with their aid, have been better able to measure exactly the knowledge which the poets of the *Iliad* and *Odyssey* had of legends which they have not mentioned or have treated only incidentally. The epic poem, which had for its subject simply the capture of Oichalia by Herakles, the Danais, the Europia, might have added to our knowledge of the materials with which all these poems were built up. The *Iliad* and *Odyssey* have assumed in our eyes more than their fair proportions, from the mere fact that they alone have survived unhurt the wear and tear of ages. Whether our *Iliad* and *Odyssey* are really the poems which were known under those titles to the Attic historians and tragedians is a graver question, which these lost epic poems would have aided us in answering, and which must be examined by the aid of such materials and evidence as we have at our disposal. That the fact of their transmission to the present day is not to be explained on the ground of their manifest supe-

riority to the lost poems, is at once clear, when we remember that the great Athenian poets deliberately drew the characters and incidents of their dramas from poems which we called cyclic, in preference to those which we regard as alone deserving to be called Homeric. The so-called Orphic hymns consist almost entirely of invocations to the various beings with which the old mythical language peopled the visible world, followed by a string of epithets which were held to be applicable to them. Almost every one of these epithets may be made the germ of a mythical tale. Thus the hymn to Protogonos (whose counterpart is Protogoneia) hails him as born from the egg (of night), and having the face of a bull (Indra), as Phanes the brilliant, and Antauges (Antigoné), reflecting the light of the Sun (vi.). Helios (viii.) is Paian, the healer, merging into the idea of Asklêpios; he is also Zeus, a relic of the interchangeable character of the earlier Vedic gods, the moon being also still male and female (ix.). Heraklês (xii.) is the father of Time, benignant and everlasting, producing and devouring all things, yet helping all, wearing the dawn and the night round his head. Adonis (lvi.) dwells partly in Tartaros and partly on Olympos. The rays of the sun and moon cannot come without the Charites, the Harits or glistening horses of Indra (lx.). Asklêpios is Paian the healer as well as Helios, and he has

Phoibos and Achilleus, Odysseus, Oidipous, and Perseus CHAP VI are, though different, yet the same,—if their adventures or their times of inaction are simply the fruit of an inevitable process going on in all kindred languages, all charges of immorality founded on the character of these adventures fall completely to the ground. It is simply impossible to believe that the great Athenian poets were descended from a people who, some centuries earlier, had deliberately sat down to invent loathsome or ridiculous fictions about the gods whom they worshipped and the heroes whom they revered. To the mind of Æschylos there was a depth of almost inexpiable guilt in the sacrifice of Iphigeneia. The imagination of Sophokles was oppressed by the unconscious incest of Oidipous and all its frightful consequences, while Pindar turned aside with contemptuous indignation from the stories which told of gods devouring their own offspring. But we, to whom the tale of Kronos points to the Time which consumes the years to which it has given birth,—we, for whom the early doom of the virgin Iphigeneia, caused by the wrath of Artemis, is a mere reflection of the lot which pressed alike on Dahanâ and Daphnê, on Iolê, and Brynhild, and Oinônê,—we, who can read in the woeful tale of Iokastê the return of the lord of day, the slayer of the Sphinx and of the Python, to the mother who had borne him in the morning, must feel, that if Greeks or Northmen who told of such things are to be condemned, they must be condemned on other grounds and not because in Achilleus or Sigurd or Odysseus they have given us pictures of obstinate inaction or brutal revenge. Possibly, to some among those old poets, the real nature of the tales which they were telling was not so completely hidden as we may deem. It is not easy to think that the writer of the Hymn to Hermes knew nothing of the key which was to unlock all its secrets. The very form of their language would warrant us in saying much more. But the words of Kumârila prove, that among the Eastern Aryans the real character of their mythology had not been forgotten. He,

---

Health as his spotless bride. The date of these hymns is a matter of little moment. To whatever age they may belong, they lay bare not a few of the stages in the mythopœic poems.

too, had to listen to complaints like those which Pindar and Plato bring against the follies or the vices of the gods. His answer is ready.

'It is fabled that Prajâpati, the Lord of Creation, did violence to his daughter. But what does it mean? Prajâpati, the Lord of Creation, is a name of the sun; and he is called so because he protects all creatures. His daughter Ushas is the dawn. And when it is said that he was in love with her, this only means that, at sunrise, the sun runs after the dawn, the dawn being at the same time called the daughter of the sun, becauses she rises when he approaches. In the same manner, if it is said that Indra was the seducer of Ahalyâ, this does not imply that the god Indra committed such a crime; but Indra means the sun, and Ahalyâ the night; and as the night is seduced and ruined by the sun of the morning, therefore is Indra called the paramour of Ahalyâ.'[1]

The morality of Hesiod.
It is the legend of Oidipous and Iokastê, one of the most awful and, in some aspects, the most repulsive in the wide range of Greek mythology.[2] If the real nature of this tale is laid bare before us, we may at once assure ourselves that these stories are not the fruit of depraved imaginations and brutal lives. There is no longer any mystery in the strange combination of repulsive legends with a sensitive morality in the Hesiodic poems of the 'Works and Days.' We cease to wonder, that the same poet who has recounted the tale of Pandora should tell us that the eye of God is in every place, watching the evil and the good;[3] that the duty of man is to

[1] Max Müller, *History of Sanskrit Literature*, p. 530. Muir, *Sanskrit Texts*, part iv. ch. i. sect. 2.

[2] Nothing can exceed the coarseness of the legend of Erichthonios as given by Apollodoros, iii. 14, 6. It is, however, nothing more than a strange jumble of images which are found scattered through a hundred legends, and which may be translated into the following phrases :--
The Dawn stands before the Sun, and asks him for his armour.
The face of the Dawn charms the Sun, who seeks to embrace her.

The Dawn flies from the Sun, and a soft shower falls on the Earth as his piercing rays shoot across the sky after her departing form.
From the soft shower springs the Summer with its fruits.
The Dawn would make the Summer immortal, and entrusts the Summer to the care of the Dew.
The serpents of night lie coiled round the Summer in the morning.
The sisters of the Dew are slain by the Dawn.
[3] *Works and Days*, 252, 253, 265.

avoid the smooth road to evil,[1] and to choose the strait path of good, which, rough at the first, becomes easy to those who walk in it.[2]

CHAP.
VI.

[1] *Works and Days*, 286.
[2]   μακρὸς δὲ καὶ ὄρθιος οἶμος ἐπ' αὐτὴν
καὶ τρηχὺς τὸ πρῶτον. ἐπὴν δ' εἰς ἄκρον ἵκηαι,
ῥηιδίη δὴ ἔπειτα πέλει, χαλεπή περ ἐοῦσα.—*Ib.* 288.

CHAPTER VII.

BOOK.
I.
───
Reproduction of the same myth under different forms.

FEW who have considered the subject at all will be disposed to deny that the Argive legends which relate the exploits of Perseus might well be expanded into a longer poem than the Iliad. We have, therefore, the less reason to be surprised if the Iliad itself, on examination, is found to relate part only of a more extended legend, or to exhibit under a different colouring modified versions of a single story. If in the mythology of Argos alone we have the ideal of Perseus recurring in the tale of Heraklês, there is the less reason for wonder if the Hellenic Achilleus is but the counterpart of the Lykian Sarpêdôn and Memnôn, the son of Eôs,—nay, if the character of Achilleus recurs in that of other Achaian heroes. The Iliad, or rather, as Mr. Grote would say, the Achillêis,[1] sings of the wrath of the Phthiotic chieftain, who is also the child of the sea-goddess Thetis, and this wrath is followed by a time of gloomy and sullen inaction. The glorious hero, the lightning of whose countenance struck terror into his enemies, hangs up his weapons and hides his face. The sun has passed behind the veil of the storm-cloud. The expression is literally forced from us: we cannot withhold the metaphor. But so was it with the men of Kalydôn while Meleagros lay sullen and angry in his secret chamber with his beautiful wife Kleopatra. So complete is the identity of the two characters, so thoroughly does it rebuke his moody anger, that the episode of Meleagros is recited at length by Phoinix, in the hope that it may appease the fury of Achilleus.[2] But the issue with both is the same. Meleagros comes forth at last

---

[1] *History of Greece,* ii. 236.   [2] *Iliad,* ix. 529-599.

to the aid of his people, and Achilleus, after a long struggle, makes up his quarrel with Agamemnon to avenge the death of Patroklos. Both again are doomed, after their time of obstinate inaction, to an early and violent death, preceded by a brief outburst of their former splendour. That such was to be the lot of his great hero, the Homeric poet knew well; but, ignorant though he may have been of the source of the materials of which he made such splendid use, he chose, with a poetical instinct rarely surpassed, to close his tale when Achilleus grants the prayer of Priam, and yields to him the body of his dead son, Hektor.

If, however, resemblances of detail are not wanting to show that Eastern and Western legends have in the Iliad been blended together, it would follow that such a blending of the mythology of different cities or countries must issue in a highly complicated story. But it is obvious, at the same time, that no historical inferences can be drawn from the mere fact of such a complication. Rightly convinced that the tale of Troy, with its marvellously vivid details and astonishing incidents, must have some foundation, Bishop Thirlwall is disposed to refer it to some great expedition in which the chieftains of Western Hellas were combined against an Asiatic power ruling in Ilion.[1] The evidence of such a fact may possibly be found in isolated statements contained in the Iliad, but scarcely in the plot of the story. If it may be assumed, from the form of the prophecy of Poseidôn, that

No historical conclusions can be drawn from the complications so caused.

[1] *History of Greece.* vol. i. ch. v. Dr. Thirlwall is struck by the contrast of the futile efforts of Agamemnon and his host with the success of Heraklês in his attack on Troy during the reign of Laomedon. He makes some plausible historical conjectures to account for this difference. But the tale explains itself. Heraklês is a transformation of the invincible sun-god, and his might therefore beats down every enemy, when the actual moment for conflict has come. But Agamemnon and his host must wait ten years before they can be permitted to storm the citadel of Ilion. They are the children of the sun, seeking through the weary hours of darkness the beautiful light, which after sundown was taken away from the western sky. They can do nothing, therefore, in spite of their numbers, until at the fated hour Achilleus comes forth to help them. Such, at least, is the burden of the *Achilléis.* The interpolated *Iliad* was the result of a patriotic feeling struggling against the laws of mythical speech. Dr. Thirlwall sees clearly that the abduction of Helen may have been 'a theme for poetry originally independent of the Trojan war,' and he rightly insists that the tale of the war, 'even if unfounded, must still have had some adequate occasion and motive.' This is indisputable: but hypotheses connecting it with Greek colonies in Asia prove nothing; the comparison of Greek legends among themselves and with the systems of mythology explains all.

princes claiming descent from Aineias ruled in the poet's time in the Troad,[1] no light is thrown by it on the existence of that chief, or on the reality of the Trojan war. The ruins of Tiryns attest to a certain extent the truthfulness of Homeric description in the catalogue of the contending forces;[2] the walls of Mykênai bear out the statement that it was once the seat of a powerful dynasty, but archæological evidence tells us nothing of Perseids or of Pelopids.

Substantial identity of Greek and Norse mythology.

But if we can trace this recurrence of the same ideal in different heroes and of the same imagery in the recital of their adventures in Hellenic mythology alone, the marvel is intensified a thousandfold when we compare this mythology with the ancient legends of Northern Europe or of the far-distant East. There is scarcely an incident in the lives of the great Greek heroes which cannot be traced out in the wide field of Teutonic or Scandinavian tradition; and the complicated action of the Iliad, or rather of the whole legend of which the Iliad forms a part, is reproduced in the Edda and the lays of the Volsungs and the Nibelungs. It may seem almost superfluous, and yet the persistency of traditional opinion makes it necessary, to repeat, that if the Greek tales tell us of serpent-slayers and of destroyers of noxious monsters, the legends of the ice-bound North also sing of heroes who slay the dragons that lie coiled round sleeping maidens. If the former recite the labours of Heraklês and speak of the bondage of Apollôn, Sifrit and Sigurd are not less doomed to a life of labour for others, not for themselves. If Heraklês alone can rescue Hesionê from a like doom with Andromeda, or bring back Alkêstis from the land of Hades, it is Sigurd only who can slay the serpent Fafnir, and Ragnar Lodbrog alone who can deliver Thora from the Dragon's grasp. If, at the end of his course, Heraklês once more sees his early love; if Oinônê comes again to Paris in his death hour, so

---

[1] *Iliad*, xx. 307, 308. It is, after all, the merest inference.—Grote, *History of Greece*, i. 428.

[2] It must, however, be remembered, that alleged archæological evidence must not be accepted in every case without question. It is now asserted that 'Offa's dyke' is a natural work, and Offa himself is thus carried suspiciously near the cloudland of mythology. The supposed canal of Xerxes, at the base of mount Athos, has shared the same fate; and the suspicion of Juvenal, x. 74, that the story was a myth has thus been unexpectedly verified. Offa's dyke and the canal of Xerxes are, in short, not more artificial than Fingal's Cave or the Giant's Causeway.

Brynhild lies down to die with Sigurd who had forsaken her. If Achilleus and Baldur can only be wounded in a single spot, Isfendiyar in the Persian epic can be killed only by the thorn thrown into his eye by Rustem. If the tale of Perseus is repeated in the career of Herakles, the legend of Ragnar Lodbrog is also a mere echo of the nobler story which told of the sun-bright Sigurd. It is scarcely necessary to enter into more minute detail. The chief features of Hellenic mythology may be traced in the mythical system of all the Aryan nations.

But at this point we encounter a difficulty which, if not removed, must prove fatal to the method which Comparative Mythology applies to the legends of the East and West. If that science has guided us to any measure of the truth, it has taught us something not merely of the growth of tales which recount the actions of deified heroes, but of the conceptions from which sprang the highest deities of Olympos— Artemis, Dêmêtêr, Apollôn, and Zeus himself. It has identified Phoibos with Helios, Herakles, Perseus, Theseus, Oidipous, and many others. It has traced the several aspects of his character through the phases presented in the legends of Theseus, Kephalos, Daphnê, Endymiôn, Bellerophontes, and Meleagros. It has taught us that he is the child of Zeus and Lêtô, while the maiden Persephonê is sprung from Zeus and Dêmêtêr. It tells us of Ouranos looking down on Gaia, and of Gaia returning the love of Ouranos by her unbounded fertility. It speaks of the toiling sun, visiting all the regions of the earth as he ascends or goes down the slope of heaven, and of earth as yielding to him her fruits wherever his light may exercise its beneficent power. It speaks of Zeus as the son or the husband of Gaia, and of the tears which fell in raindrops from the sky when he mourned for the death of his son Sarpêdôn. It seems to tell us, then, of a mythological or religious system which, simple at the first, became at the last excessively complicated, and further that this system was the result not of philosophical generalisations, but of the consciousness of an exuberant life which was extended from man to every object which he beheld in the visible creation. It seems to show that once upon a time, while the ancestors of European nations and tribes were still comparatively united, man had uttered as the simple phrases of every day speech sayings which became afterwards the groundwork of elaborate religious systems; that once upon a time they spoke of the dawn coming from the chambers of the night, while the night herself was struggling with the birth of the brilliant sun; that the new-born sun saw and loved and pursued the dawn, which vanished at his touch. It seems to teach us that from such phrases, which, slightly varied, were expanded into the tales of Kephalos and Prokris, of Korônis and Apollôn, grew finally the more definite personalities of Zeus and Phoibos, of Lêtô and Daphnê, of Artemis and Herakles. Hence, whatever in the Greek religious systems there was of direct anthropomorphism or of a fetish nature-worship would be the result of later thought and of attempts to arrive at philosophical abstractions, and not the maimed and distorted relics of a higher knowledge once possessed but now only not forgotten.

Theory of
Dr.
Döllinger
on the
origin of
Greek my-
thology.
If the theory which makes the growth of Greek mythology from the first a philosophical process can be established, then the results of Comparative Mythology must be abandoned as of no value, and we must be content to look on the points of resemblance between Greek, Teutonic, Scandinavian, and Eastern legends as a problem utterly beyond our powers to solve or even to grapple with. In any case it is a question of evidence; and the objections, which seem to be conclusive against the hypothesis of an original dogmatic revelation, of such a kind at least as that of which Mr. Gladstone speaks, have been considered already. But Dr. Döllinger's position[1] lies open to no charges of fanciful extravagance; it needs, therefore, to be the more carefully examined, as professing to be a legitimate deduction from the state of religion, or rather of religious *cultus*, among the Greeks in historical times. This state was, in the opinion of Dr. Döllinger, the result of an attempt to reduce a variety of conflicting systems and notions into one harmonious whole. In it were mingled the mysticism of Egypt and the orgiastic ritualism of the East, with the rude nature-worship of the older and less

[1] *The Gentile and the Jew in the Courts of the Temple of Christ*, book ii.

civilised ages ; and his purpose is to trace the several ideas
so amalgamated to their original sources. With this view
he is obliged to assume that in his primæval innocence man
was enabled 'to conceive of the Divinity as a pure, spiritual,
supernatural, and infinite being, distinct from the world and
exalted above it.' The loss of this conception, and the
yearning for something in its place, led to the deification of
material nature, which 'unfolded herself to man's nature as
a boundless demesne, wherein was confined an unfathomable
plenitude of powers, incommensurable and incalculable, and
of energies not to be overcome.' With this was developed a
sympathy for naturalism, 'and thus man, deeper and deeper
in the spells of his enchantress, and drawn downwards by
their weight, had his moral consciousness overcast in proportion, and gave the fuller rein to impulses which were
merely physical.'[1] This deification of natural powers led,
as Dr. Döllinger believes, first of all to the worship of the
elements—of ether as the vault of heaven ; of the earth as its
opposite ; of fire as the warming and nourishing, the consuming and destroying power ; of water as the element of
moisture separated from that of earth. To this succeeded
astrolatry in the East, and geolatry in the West, where the
idea of the earth as a susceptible and productive agent led
to the distinction of male and female divinities. But the
actual Greek religion of the heroic and later ages was a
blending of the several notions derived from supplanted
races—Leleges and Karians, Thrakians and Pelasgians—
together with importations from Asia and Egypt.[2] Thus
Gaia and Helios, Zeus and Hêrê, belong to the Pelasgic
stock, while Poseidon was introduced by Karian and Phœnician visitors of the coasts of Hellas.[3] Pallas Athênê was
also Pelasgian, as a goddess of nature and the elements.
Apollôn, likewise Pelasgian, 'has so many features in common
with Athênê, that in many respects one might call him an
Athênê of the male species.' Artemis was in continental
Greece Pelasgian, while at Ephesos she exhibits an Asiatic
character, and becomes 'a sort of Pantheistic deity.' From

[1] *The Gentile and the Jew in the Courts of the Temple of Christ,* vol. i. p. 66.
[2] *Ibid.* p. 68.   [3] *Ibid.* p. 80.

the Pêlasgians also came Hestia, Hermes, and Aphroditê; but Arês was the god of the Thrakian race, 'which, having penetrated into Bœotia and the Peloponnese, took his worship along with them.' Of the rest, Dêmêtêr was Pelasgic, Hephaistos came from the Thrakians of Lemnos, and Dionysos from the more distant East; while Hades was almost an afterthought, not much worshipped, and not greatly cared for by the people.[1]

The picture drawn by Dr. Döllinger of the great Olympian deities may in all its particulars be strictly true. It is possible or probable that ideas utterly foreign to the Greek mind may have been imported from Phrygia, Phœnicia, or Egypt, and that the worship so developed may have embodied philosophical conceptions of nature and of the powers at work in it. But the question which calls for an answer cannot be determined by the most masterly portraiture of the great gods of Olympos: and Dr. Döllinger's hypothesis does not enable us to answer it. It starts on an assumption for which we have no evidence; and all the evidence furnished by the book of Genesis and still more all that is furnished by the study of language, militates against the idea that man started originally with a conception of God, 'as a pure, spiritual, supernatural, and infinite being, distinct from the world, and exalted above it.' How soon he might have risen to this conception, had his lot been different from what it has been, it is impossible to say: but if we are to argue simply from statements before us, we may affirm that men were from the first conscious of the existence of a Being more powerful than themselves, whom they were bound to obey, but we can scarcely maintain more. This sense of duty, and still more the sense of shame following on the violation of it, would show that the groundwork of that relation was the goodness and justice of the Being with whom they had to do. But in this conviction there was nothing to determine their ideas in the objects and phenomena of the natural world. Feeling a conscious life in himself, man would, until corrected by experience, attribute the same conscious life to everything he saw or felt. The sun and moon, the cloud and

[1] *The Gentile and the Jew in the Courts of the Temple of Christ*, 93.

the wind, would be living beings not less than himself; but CHAP. VII.
he could not embody them in anthropomorphic forms so long
as the names by which he spoke of them retained their
real meaning. Still less could he start with a primary worship of the elements until he had learnt to regard as abstractions the objects or powers which, it would seem, he looked
upon only as living beings. Three ways lay before him.
He might, like Abraham in the old Arabian legend,[1] be led
by the rising and setting of the sun and stars to the conviction that they were simply passive instruments in the hands
of an almighty and righteous God ; or he might, as he forgot
his old language, invest with an anthropomorphic life the
deities with which he peopled the whole visible creation ; or,
lastly, he might bow down crushed beneath the dead weight
of nature, and yield himself a living slave to a loathsome
and degrading fetishism. Of these three courses the first
was chosen by the Hebrew people, and even by them feebly
and fitfully ;[2] the second was followed by the tribes of the
Hellenic stock ; the third has been rejected by every portion
of the great Aryan family of nations. These, as they journeyed
from their ancient home, carried with them the old language
and the old morality ; but the measure in which they forgot
the meaning of proper names would determine the extent to
which new gods would be called into existence. This developement, as the result, primarily, of a corruption of language, would not be in the strictest sense, a religion, and the
moral sense of the worshipper would not be darkened in proportion to the number of the gods whom he venerated. Dr.
Döllinger's hypothesis, not less than the theory of Mr. Gladstone, would require a continually increasing degradation ;
but the history of language, apart from the growth of Aryan
epic poetry, furnishes conclusive evidence against any such
idea. There is no evidence that the Greeks of the seventh
or sixth centuries before the Christian era had their 'moral

[1] Milman, *History of the Jews,* book i.
[2] In truth, when we speak of the monotheistic faith of the Jewish people, we speak of their faith of their teachers. All the evidence at our command seems to show that at least down to the time of the Babylonish captivity the main body of the people was incurably poly-theistic. 'The history even of the Jews,' says Professor Max Müller 'is made up of an almost uninterrupted series of relapses into polytheism.' 'Semitic Monotheism,' *Chips, &c.* i. 365.

BOOK
I.

consciousness more overcast' than the Greeks of the tenth or twelfth; there is much to lead us to the contrary conclusion.

Historical speculations of Dr. Döllinger.

But Dr. Döllinger's theory requires him to deal with Karians, Leleges, and Pelasgians; and the chain of his argument becomes weakest where it should have the greatest strength. His speculations may be masterly, and his conclusions forcible; but we lack the means of determining their truth. Mr. Grote, in his History of Greece, hesitates to speak of any events as historical facts before the first recorded Olympiad, i.e. 776 B.C. Sir Cornewall Lewis regards the researches of scholars respecting the primitive history of the Hellenic or Italian tribes as ' not less unreal than the speculations concerning judicial astrology, or the discovery of the philosopher's stone and the elixir of life.'[1] Dr. Döllinger must have evidence not accessible to either of these writers, to warrant the assertion that the chief seats of the Pelasgians were Arkadia, Argolis, and Perrhoibia, and that the immigration of the Doric and Aiolic races took place precisely in the year 1104 B.C.[2]

They leave the real difficulties of Greek mythology unexplained.

His analysis thus leaves the Greek mythology, as he found it, a strange and perplexing riddle. It omits all notice of the marvellous likeness between Greek and Scandinavian legends; it does not even attempt to explain why each Greek god should have certain special attributes and not others. It does not tell us why Herakles, and Perseus, and Bellerophôn, and Apollôn should all be made to serve creatures meaner and weaker than themselves,—why Herakles and Zeus should have a thousand earthly loves, and Artemis and Athênê, according to some legends, have none. Still less does it explain why the character of Herakles and Hermes should sometimes assume a comic aspect, which is never allowed to weaken the serious majesty of Athênê, Dêmêtêr, or Apollôn.

[1] *Credibility of Early Roman History*, i. 297.
[2] *Jew and Gentile, &c.*, vol. i. pp. 68, 74.

CHAPTER VIII.

IF in the legends of any people we find a number of names which explain themselves, if further the exploits of the gods or heroes who bear these names are in strict accordance with those meanings, then at once we are warranted in conjecturing that other names in the same legends not yet interpreted may be of the same nature, while at the same time a basis is furnished for classifying the several stories. If further we find that in the traditions of different Aryan tribes, or even of the same tribe, the same characters reappear with no other difference than that of title and local colouring, the inference is justified that a search into the mythical stores of all the Aryan tribes would disclose the same phenomenon. If here too our conjectures are verified, it will be impossible to withstand the conclusion that these tribes must have started from a common centre, and that from their ancient home they must have carried away, if not the developed myth, yet the quickened germ from which might spring leaves and fruits varying in form and hue according to the soil to which it should be committed, and the climate under which the plant might reach maturity. These variations in the names, it may be, of all the actors, as well as in the minor details of their career, would prove, in exact proportion to the fidelity with which the essential type was preserved, that this germ was furnished by the every day speech of the people, or, in other words, by their way of regarding the phenomena of the outward world. If these facts are established, two important consequences follow: I. The hypothesis of any conscious borrowing or adaptation of myths on a large scale by one tribe from another after their separation from the common home becomes untenable, unless we assume an amount of intercourse between them far in excess of any for which we have the evidence of history; and the clearest proof of direct importation in the case of any given story or fable which does not belong to the genuine mythology of a people fails to throw any suspicion on the latter. II. The process of analysis and comparison will have deprived these legends of all claim to the character of historical traditions; and even if it were maintained in the last resort that the myth as brought from the common home grew up from some historical fact or facts, still no such title can be made out for the same incidents when we find them repeated in the same order and with the same issue in different ages and different lands. If in the primæval home there was a war brought about by the carrying off of a beautiful woman, a strife between two chieftains, and a time of inaction for the hero of the story followed by his signal victory and his early death, then unquestionably these incidents, with a hundred others common to the background of these legends, did not repeat themselves at Ilion and Delphoi, in Ithaka and Norway, in Lykia and Iran.

. The Greek mythology of itself explains the nature of this common element.
This is the goal to which we must be brought if the track be of this kind; and the matter may perhaps be soonest brought to an issue if we take the most complicated myths of the Hellenic tribes as our starting point. We can scarcely read the legends of Herakles and Dêmêtêr, of Theseus, Kadmos, Perseus, and a host of other mythical heroes, without feeling that a few simple phrases might well have supplied the germ for the most intricate of these traditions. Every incident in the myth of the Eleusinian Dêmêtêr may be accounted for, if only men once said (with the conviction that the things of which they spoke had a conscious life), ' The earth mourns for the dead summer. The summer lies shut up in the prison of Hades, the unseen '—or, as in the language of the Northman, ' She sleeps in the land of the Niflungs, the cold mists, guarded by the serpent Fafnir; and the dwarf Andvari keeps watch over her buried treasures.' The tale of Endymion seems to speak for itself; ' The moon comes to gaze on her beloved, the sun, as he lies

down to sleep in the evening.' In the story of Niobê, we seem to see the sun in his scorching power, consuming those who dare to face his dazzling brightness; in that of Orpheus, we seem to hear his lamentation for the beautiful evening which has been stung by the serpent of the night, and which he brings back to life only to lose her at the gates of day. In the myth of Eurôpê we have the journey of the sun from the far East to the Western land, until Têlephassa, the far-shining, sinks down wearied on the Thessalian plain. Still more transparent appear the tales of Kephalos and Daphnê. Prokris, even in the mouth of the Greek, is still the child of Hersê, the dew : Eôs is still the morning, Kephalos still the head of the bright sun. In Daphnê we seem to behold the dawn flying from her lover and shrinking before his splendour. In the Homeric Hymn, Lêtô, the night, dark and still as death, promises that Phoibos shall long abide in Delos, the bright land. Doubtless she made the same promise to Lykians, Argives, Arkadians, Athenians, and all others who called themselves the children of the light; but the sun cannot tarry, and in spite of her plighted word he hastens onward to slay the serpent of darkness. In Herakles we see the sun in other guise, loving and beloved wherever he goes, seeking to benefit the sons of men, yet sometimes harming them in the exuberance of his boisterous strength. In the tale of Althaia we read the sentence that the bright sun must die when the torch of day is burnt out. In Phaethon we seem to see the plague of drought which made men say 'Surely another, who cannot guide the horses, is driving the chariot of the sun.' The beautiful herds, which the bright and glistening daughters of early morning feed in the pastures of Thrinakia, seem to tell us of the violet-coloured clouds which the dawn spreads over the fields of the blue sky. In Bellerophon, as in Perseus, Theseus, Phoibos, and Herakles, we find again the burden laid on the sun, who must toil for others, although the forms of that toil may vary. Perseus goes to the dwelling of the Graiai, as men might have said, 'The sun has departed to the land of the pale gloaming.' When Perseus slays Medousa, the sun has killed the night in its solemn and death-like beauty, while the wild pursuit of the immortal Gorgons seems to be the chase of Darkness after the bright Sun who, with his golden sandals, just escapes their grasp as he soars into the peaceful morning sky, the Hyperborean gardens, which sorrow, strife, and death can never enter. In the death of Akrisios we have the old tale which comes up in many another legend, where Oidipous and Theseus mourn that they have unwittingly slain their fathers.

The Norse mythology points in precisely the same direction.
If the Greek legends by themselves thus exhibit, or seem to exhibit, their ancient framework, the Norse tradition points with at the least equal clearness in the same direction. If any now can be found to assert that the one set of legends were copied from the other, he not only maintains a theory which, in Dr. Dasent's words, 'hangs on a single thread,' [1] but he displays a credulity which needs not to shrink from the avowal that the whole of the Arabian Nights' Entertainments is a genuine and veracious history. The wildest prejudice can scarcely shelter itself behind these treacherous and crumbling barriers, although it may urge that, whether in Teutonic or in Greek mythology, the dawn, the evening, and the night, the toiling and capricious sun, are already persons with human forms and a fixed local habitation. But even this position would be greatly strained. Mr. Grote himself allows that what he terms allegory is one of the constituent elements of Greek mythology.[2] But even if we admit the objection in its full force, we lack but a single link to complete the chain of evidence and turn an overwhelming probability into fact. Have we any records of that old time in which men spoke as Greek and Norse myths seem to tell us that they spoke? Have we any actual relics of that speech in which men talked of Daphnê as chased by Phoibos, even while Daphnê was still a common name of the dawn, and Phoibos meant simply the sun?

The missing link is supplied in the older Vedic poems.
The Vedic hymns of the Mantra period stand forth to give us the answer, but they do so only to exhibit a fresh marvel. While they show to us the speech which was afterwards petrified into the forms of Greek and Norse mythology, they

[1] *Popular Tales from the Norse*, introduction, p. xliii.
[2] *History of Greece*, vol. i. p. 2.

point to a still earlier time, of which no record has come down, and of which we can have no further evidence than that which is furnished by the laws which determine the growth of language. Even in the Mantra period, the earliest in all Sanskrit, and therefore (as exhibiting the earliest form of thought) the oldest in all human literature,[1] the whole grammar is definitely fixed, and religious belief has assumed the character of a creed. And if in them man has not lived long enough to trace analogies and arrive at some idea of an order of nature, he has grown into the strongest conviction that behind all the forms which come before his eyes there is a Being, unseen and all-powerful, whose bidding is done throughout the wide creation, and to whom men may draw nigh as children to a father.

CHAP. VIII.

When, therefore, in these hymns, Kephalos, Prokris, Hermes, Daphnê, Zeus, Ouranos, stand forth as simple names for the sun, the dew, the wind, the dawn, the heaven and the sky, each recognised as such, yet each endowed with the most perfect consciousness, we feel that the great riddle of mythology is solved, and that we no longer lack the key which shall disclose its most hidden treasures. When we hear the people saying, 'Our friend the sun is dead. Will he rise? Will the dawn come back again?' we see the death of Herakles, and the weary waiting while Lêtô struggles with the birth of Phoibos. When on the return of day we hear the cry—

The key to all Aryan mythology.

'Rise! our life, our spirit is come back, the darkness is gone, the light draws near!'

—we are carried at once to the Homeric hymn, and we hear the joyous shout of all the gods when Phoibos springs to life and light on Delos.[2] The tale of Urvasî and Purûravas [3] (these are still the morning and the sun) is the tale of Orpheus and Eurydikê. Purûravas, in his dreary search,

---

[1] Max Müller, *History of Sanskrit Literature*, pp. 528, 557.

[2] ἐκ δ' ἔθορε πρὸ φόωσδε· θεαὶ δ' ὀλόλυξαν ἅπασαι.
Hymn to Apollo, 119.

[3] In the essay on Comparative Mythology, Professor Max Müller has given not only the older forms of this myth,

but a minute analysis of the play of Kalidâsa on this subject. This poem is very instructive, as showing that the character of the Homeric Achilleus adheres as closely to the original idea as do those of Urvasî and Purûravas in the later poetry of Kalidâsa.

hears the voice of Urvasi saying 'I am gone like the first of the dawns; I am hard to be caught, like the wind.' · Yet she will come back to him at the close of the night, and a son, bright and beaming, shall be born to them. Varuna is still the wide heaven, the god ' who can be seen by all; ' the lord of the whole earth: but in him we recognise at once the Greek Ouranos, who looks lovingly on Gaia from his throne in the sky. Yet more, we read the praises of Indra, and his great exploit is that

' He has struck the daughter of Dyaus (Zeus), a woman difficult to vanquish—

' Yes, even the daughter of Dyaus, the magnified, the Dawn, thou, O Indra, a great hero hast ground to pieces.

' The Dawn rushed off from her crushed car, fearing that Indra, the bull, might strike her.

' This her car lay there, well ground to pieces : she went far away.'

The treatment is rude, but we have here not merely the whole story of Daphnê, but the germ of that of Eurôpê borne by the same bull across the sea. More commonly, however, the dawn is spoken of as bright, fair, and loving, the joy of all who behold her.

' She shines upon us like a young wife, rousing every living being to go to his work.

' She rose up, spreading far and wide (Euryganeia, Eurydikê), and moving towards every one. She grew in brightness, wearing her brilliant garment. The mother of the cows (the morning clouds, the Homeric herds of the sun), the leader of the days, she shone gold-coloured, lovely to behold.

' She, the fortunate, who brings the eye of the god (Kephalos, or the one-eyed Odin), who leads the white and lovely steed (of the sun), the Dawn was seen revealed by her rays ; with brilliant treasures she follows every one.

' Shine for us with thy best rays, thou bright Dawn, thou who lengthenest our life, thou the love of all, who givest us food, who givest us wealth in cows, horses, and chariots.

' Thou, daughter of the sky (Dyaus, Zeus), thou high-born Dawn, give us riches high and wide.' [1]

[1] Max Müller, *History of Sanskrit Literature*, p. 551,

Still more remarkable, as exhibiting the germs of the ideas which find their embodiment in the Hellenic Athênê and the Latin Minerva, is the following hymn.

'The wise priests celebrate with hymns the divine, bright-charioted expanded Dawn; worshipped with holy worship, purple-tinted, radiant, leading on the sun.

'The lovely Dawn, arousing man, goes before the Sun, preparing practicable paths, riding in a spacious chariot; expanding everywhere she diffuses light at the commencement of the days.

'Harnessing the purple oxen to her car, unwearied she renders riches perpetual; a goddess praised of many, and cherished by all, she shines manifesting the paths that lead to good.

'Lucidly white is she, occupying the two (regions, the upper and middle firmament), and manifesting her person from the East: she traverses the path of the sun, as if knowing (his course), and harms not the quarters of the horizon.

'Exhibiting her person like a well-attired female, she stands before our eyes (gracefully) inclining like (a woman who has been) bathing (Aphroditê Anadyomenê). Dispersing the hostile glooms, Ushas, the daughter of heaven, comes with radiance.

'Ushas, the daughter of heaven, tending to the West, puts forth her beauty like a (well-dressed) woman; bestowing precious treasures on the offerer of adoration, she, ever youthful, brings back the light as of old.'[1]

We can but wonder at the marvellous exuberance of language, almost every expression of which may manifestly serve as the germ of a mythical tale. We say, 'The fire burns, the wood crackles and smokes.' They said, Germs of mythical tales.

'Neighing like a horse that is greedy for food, it steps out from the strong prison: then the wind blows after his blast: thy path, O Agni (Ignis), is dark at once.'

The Latin carried with him the name of the Hindu Fire-god to little purpose. In the hands of the Greek similar phrases on the searching breath of the wind grew up into Truthfulness of mythical description.

[1] H. H. Wilson, *Rig Veda Sanhita*, vol. iii. p. 369.

the legend of Hermes. Nor can it be said that the instinct of the Greek was less true than that of the old Vedic poet to the sights of the natural world. If we recur with feelings of undiminished pleasure to the touching truthfulness of the language which tells of the Dawn as the bright being whom age cannot touch, although she makes men old, who thinks on the dwellings of men and shines on the small and great, we feel also that the 'Homeric' poet, even while he spoke of a god in human form born in Delos, was not less true to the original character of the being of whom he sang. He thought of the sun rising in a cloudless heaven, and he told how the nymphs bathed the lord of the golden sword in pure water, and wrapped him in a spotless robe.[1] Still, although the stress of the hymn lies wholly on the promise of Leto that her child shall have his chief home in Delos, the poet feels that Delos alone can never be his home, and so he sang how Apollôn went from island to island, watching the ways and works of men; how he loved the tall sea-cliffs, and every jutting headland, and the rivers which hasten to the broad sea, even though he came back with ever fresh delight to his native Delos.[2]

Ground-work of Aryan my-thology. Thus the great mystery of Greek as of other mythology is dispelled like mist from the mountain-side at the rising of the sun. All that is beautiful in it is invested with a purer radiance, while much, if not all, that is gross and coarse in it is refined, or else its grossness is traced to an origin which reflects no disgrace on those who framed or handed down the tale. Thus, with the keynote ringing in our ears, we can catch at once every strain that belongs to the ancient harmony, although it may be heard amid the din of many discordant voices. The groundwork of Greek mythology was

---

[1] ἔνθα σε, ἦιε Φοῖβε, θεαὶ λοῦον ὕδατι
καλῷ
ἁγνῶς καὶ καθαρῶς· σπάρξαν δ' ἐν
φάρεϊ λευκῷ
λεπτῷ νηγατέῳ.
       Hymn to Apollo, 120.
This is the white and glistening robe in which Cyrus and Arthur are wrapped, when they are carried away from the house in which they were born.

[2] Αὐτὸς δ', ἀργυρότοξε, ἄναξ, ἑκατηβόλ'
Ἄπολλον,

ἄλλοτε μέν τ' ἐπὶ Κύνθου ἐβήσαο
ταιπαλόεντος,
ἄλλοτε δ' αὖ νήσους τε καὶ ἀνέρας
ἠλάσκαζες·
πᾶσαι δὲ σκοπιαί τε φίλαι καὶ
πρώονες ἄκροι
ὑψηλῶν ὀρίων, ποταμοί θ' ἅλαδε
προρέοντες·
ἀλλὰ σύ Δήλῳ, Φοῖβε, μάλιστ' ἐπιτέρ-
πεαι ἦτορ.—*Hymn to Apollo*, 140.

the ordinary speech which told of the interchange of day and night, of summer and winter; but into the superstructure there may have been introduced any amount of local or personal detail, any number of ideas and notions imported from foreign philosophical or religious systems. The extent of such importations is probably far less than is generally imagined; but however this may be, the original matter may still be traced, even where it exists only in isolated fragments. The bull which bears Europê away from Kadmos (Kedem, the East),[1] is the same from which the dawn flies in the Vedic hymn. The robe with which Medeia poisons the daughter of Kreôn was a gift from Helios, the burning sun, and is seen again as the poisoned robe which Deianeira sends to the absent Herakles, as the deadly arrow by which Philoktetes mortally wounds the Trojan Paris, as the golden fleece taken from the ram which bears away the children of (Nephelê) the mist, as the sword which Aigeus leaves under the stone for Theseus, the son of Aithra, the pure air; as the spear of Artemis which never misses its mark; as the sword of Perseus which slays all on whom it may fall; as the unerring weapons of Meleagros; as the fatal lance which Achilleus alone can wield. The serpents of night or of winter occur in almost every tale, under aspects friendly or unkind. The dragon sleeps coiled round Brynhild or Aslauga, as the snakes seek to strangle the infant Herakles or sting the beautiful Eurydikê. If the power of the sun's rays is set forth under such different forms, their beauty is signified by the golden locks of Phoibos, over which no razor has ever passed;[2] by the flowing hair which streams from the head of Kephalos, and falls over the shoulders of Perseus and Bellerophon. They serve also sometimes as a sort of Palladion, and the shearing of the single golden lock which grew on the top of his head leaves Nisos, the Megarian

---

[1] Niebuhr, (in his *Lectures on Ancient History*, vol. i. p. 239) sees that the tale points to the East; but from the words Kadmos and Hunna as occurring in the Boiotian dialect only ho is perfectly convinced of the 'Phœnician origin of Thebes.' The identity of the name Melikertes (in the myth of Inô) with the Syrian Melkarth and Moloch, can scarcely be questioned.

[2] Φοῖβος ἀκερσεκόμης (*Iliad*, xx. 39), a significant epithet, which of itself would suffice to give birth to such a legend as that of Nisos and Skylla. The shearing of the locks of the sun must be followed by darkness and ruin.

king, powerless as the shorn Samson in the arms of the
Philistines. In many of the legends these images are mingled
together, or recur under modified forms. In the tale of
Althaia there is not only the torch of day which measures
the life of Meleagros, but the weapons of the chieftain which
no enemy may withstand. In that of Bellerophôn there are
the same invincible weapons, while the horrible Chimaira
answers to the boar of Kalydon, or to that of Erymanthos
which fell by the arm of Herakles.

Greek
dynastic
legends.
If the greater number of Greek legends have thus been
reduced to their primitive elements, the touch of the same
wand will lay open others which may seem to have been
fashioned on quite another model. Even the dynastic legends
of Thebes will not resist the method which has disclosed so
many secrets. For most other tales the work is done. There
is absolutely nothing left for further analysis in the stories
of Orpheus and Eurydikê, of Kephalos and Prokris, of Selênê
and Endymion, Niobê and Lêtô, Dêmêtêr and Persephonê,
Kadmos and Eurôpê, Daphnê and Apollôn. Not an incident
remains unexplained in the legends of Herakles, of Althaia
and the burning brand, of Phaethôn, Memnôn, and Bellerophôn. If there are bypaths in the stories of Ariadnê,
Medeia, Semelê, Prometheus, or of the cows of the Sun in
the Odyssey, they have been followed up to the point from
which they all diverge.

Growth of
popular
traditions.
If then in the vast mass of stories which make up the
mythology of the Aryan nations there seems to be evidence
showing that in some cases the legend has been brought by
direct importation from the East to the West or from West
to East, the presumption of conscious borrowing cannot with
any fairness be extended to any tales for which such evidence
is not forthcoming. The great epic poems of the Aryan race
sprung into existence in the ages which followed the dispersion of the tribes, and during which all intercourse between
them was an impossibility; yet these epic poems exhibit an
identical framework, with resemblances in detail which even
defy the influences of climate and scenery. But many of the
actors in these great dramas reappear in the popular stories
of the Aryan tribes, with subtle points of likeness and dif-

ference, which can be accounted for by conscious borrowing only on the supposition that the traditions of one country were as intimately known to the people of another country as the traditions of many, if not most, of the Aryan nations are now known to us through the long toil and vast researches of comparative mythologists, aided by the mighty machinery of the printing press. In truth, the more that we examine this hypothesis of importation as affecting the general stock of mythical tradition in any country, the more scanty and less conclusive will the evidence appear; and in the issue we shall find ourselves driven practically to reject it altogether, or to suppose that the impulse of borrowing amounted to a universal and irresistible mania. The dynastic legends of Thebes do but reproduce those of Argos; the legends of both alike do but repeat the career of Achilleus or of Sigurd; and the great heroes of these tales reappear as the Boots and the disguised beggar of Teutonic and Hindu folklore. The supposition of any deliberate borrowing attributes to Greeks, Teutons, Scandinavians, and Hindus, a poverty of invention not less amazing than their skill in destroying the evidence of the theft, and wearing borrowed plumage as with an inborn grace. Unless we are prepared to say that the borrowing was wholesale, and to determine the source of this exhaustless store of wealth, it is more prudent and more philosophical to admit that in every country the myths which have their roots in phrases relating to physical phenomena have been kept alive by independent tradition from the times of the first dispersion.

But if the story of Achilleus, as told in the Iliad, is only another form of the legend which relates the career of the Ithakan chief in the Odyssey; if this tale reappears in the Saga of the Volsungs and the Nibelungen Lied, in the epical cycles of Arthur and Charlemagne, in the lay of Beowulf and the Shahnameh of Firdusi, and if further all these streams of popular poetry can be traced back to a common source in phrases which described the sights and sounds of the outward world, the resemblances thus traced are nevertheless by no means so astonishing as the likeness which runs through a vast number of the popular tales of Germany and Scandinavia, of Greece and Rome, of Persia and Hindustan. On the hypothesis of a form of thought which attributed conscious life to all physical objects, we must at once admit that the growth of a vast number of cognate legends was inevitable. Nor is there anything bewildering in the fact, that phrases which denoted at first the death of the dawn, or her desertion by the sun as he rose in the heavens, or the stealing away of the evening light by the powers of darkness, should give birth to the legends of Helen and Guenevere, of Brynhild and Gudrun, of Paris and of Lancelot, of Achilleus and Sigurd. All that this theory involves is that certain races of mankind, or certain tribes of the same race, were separated from each other while their language still invested all sensible things with a personal life, and that when the meaning of the old words was either wholly or in part forgotten, the phenomena of the earth and the heavens reappeared as beings human or divine, and the Pani, or Night, which sought to lure Saramâ, the Dawn, into his dismal cave, became the Paris who beguiled Helen to Troy, and the Lancelot who 'corrupted the faith of the wife of Arthur.

Legends
not resolv-
able into
phrases re-
lating to
physical
pheno-
mena.

The wonder becomes greater when from the necessary outgrowth of certain conditions of thought and speech we turn to popular stories which cannot be brought within this class of epical legends, and which yet exhibit, in spite of differences of detail and local colouring, a closeness of re- semblance which establishes their substantial identity. If, among the stories which Hindu, Persian, Greek, or Teutonic mothers recounted to their children, we find tales which turn on the same incidents, and in their most delicate touches betray the influence of precisely the same feelings, we must conclude either that these legends were passed from the one tribe or clan to the other, or that before these tribes separated from their common home they not only possessed in mythical phrases relating to physical phenomena the germs of the future epics of Europe and Asia, but had framed a number of stories which cannot be traced back to such phrases, which seem to point rather to a storehouse of moral proverbs, and which cannot be accounted for on any hypothesis of conscious borrowing by one distinct people from another. It would, indeed, be safer to affirm of any given story that it has not been thus borrowed than to say that it cannot be traced back to the one source from which have sprung the great epic poems of the world. The story of the Master Thief is a case in point. It looks at first sight as though it had nothing to do with the legends of the great Norse or Hellenic heroes, and the resemblance of some of its incidents to those of a story told in the Hitopadesa suggests the conclusion that it found its way into Europe through the Arabic translation known as the Kalila and Dimna. Professor Max Müller plainly avowing this belief, says that 'the story of the Master Thief is told in the Hitopadesa.'[1] The Sanskrit tale is that of the Brahman who, on hearing from three thieves in succession that the goat which he carried on his back was a dog, throws the animal down and leaves it as a booty for the rogues who had hit upon this mode of cheating him. 'The gist of the story,' adds Professor Müller, 'is that a man will believe almost anything, if he is told the same by three different people.' But, while a far greater resemblance to the Egyptian tale is exhibited by the Hindu version of the Master Thief as told by Somadeva Bhatta, presently to be noticed, it may fairly be asked whether this is either the story or the moral of the European 'Master Thief.' In the Teutonic version we find no incidents resembling those of the Sanskrit tale. The Norse story exhibits some points of likeness, together with differences which rather force us to think that it cannot have been suggested by the Eastern fable. In the latter the Brahman is directly deceived by others; in the Norse legend the peasant deceives himself, and the moral seems to be, not that a man can be brought to believe anything if he hears it asserted by several seemingly independent witnesses, but that experience is thrown away on one who will put his hand into the fire after he has been burnt. In the Norse tale, the farmer intends to drive one of his three oxen to market, and the youth, who is a postulant for the novitiate in the worshipful order of thieves, is told that his desire shall be granted if he can steal this ox on the road, without the owner's knowledge and without doing him

[1] *Chips from a German Workshop*, ii. 229.

any harm. The lad accordingly puts a silver-buckled shoe in the way. The man admires it, but passes on without picking it up, as an odd shoe would be of little use. Presently he sees before him the same shoe, which the thief, having run by another way, has again cast on the road, and tying up his ox hastens back to pick up the fellow, while the lad goes away with the beast. Determined to test him further, the fraternity tell the boy that he shall be as good as any one of them if, under the same conditions, he can steal the second ox, which the man was now driving to market. As he goes along, the peasant sees a lad hung under the armpits to a tree, but passes on with little concern until he sees as he supposes another lad in the same position on another tree. Still not caring to give any help, he plods onwards until the thief hangs himself up for the third time on his road. The man, thinking that he is bewitched, resolves to go back and see whether the other two still hang where he saw them, and the ox which he leaves tied up is the second sacrifice. The thieves now tell the youth that if he can steal the third ox he shall be their master. So he places himself in a thicket, and as the man draws near with his last beast, imitates the bellowing of cattle; and the peasant, his wits even more flustered than before, hurries away to catch the lost oxen, leaving his third animal a prey to the thief.[1] At this point the resemblance of the Norse to the Brahman story ceases; but the career of the Master Thief is as yet scarcely begun. He has yet to overreach the society over which he now presides. The thieves set out to see whether they cannot do something surpassing all that he had done; and the lad, taking advantage of their absence to drive the three oxen into the road to the great delight of their owner, who sees them return to the farm, carries off all the precious things which formed the common store of the robbers. Thus far the Norse story agrees in its main features with the Scottish tale of the Shifty Lad,[2] although even here the points of difference are so great as to preclude the idea that the one was derived from the other. The sequel of the Norse tale is

[1] Dasent, Norse Tales, 'The Master Thief,' 268.

[2] Campbell, Popular Tales of the West Highlands, vol. i. p. 320.

substantially the same as the Teutonic story of the Master Thief. This story has, therefore, really nothing to do with the fable of the Brahman and the goat, and it may fairly be doubted whether, on the supposition that the idea was gained from the Hitopadesa, ' nothing was easier than to invent the three variations which we find in the Norse Master Thief' and the Shifty Lad of Highland tradition. Professor Max Müller adds that ' the case would be different if the same story occurred in Herodotos.'

' At the time of Herodotos,' he continues, ' the translations of the Hitopadesa had not yet reached Europe, and we should be obliged to include the Master Thief within the most primitive stock of Aryan lore. But there is nothing in the story of the two sons of the architect who robbed the treasury of Rhampsinitos which turns on the trick of the Master Thief. There were thieves, more or less clever, in Egypt as well as in India, and some of their stratagems were possibly the same at all times. But there is a keen and well-defined humour in the story of the Brahman and his deference to public opinion. Of this there is no trace in the anecdote told by Herodotos. That anecdote deals with mere matter of fact, whether imaginary or historical. The story of Rhampsinitos did enter into the popular literature of Europe, but through a different channel. We find it in the ' Gesta Romanorum,' where Octavianus has taken the place of Rhampsinitos, and we can hardly doubt that there it came originally from Herodotos.'[1] But what are really the facts of the case? The evidence which proves that the Herodotean story was reproduced in the ' Gesta Romanorum ' cannot be taken as of itself establishing the same origin for the Norse, the Teutonic, and the Irish legend. The incident of the Brahman and the goat may be left on one side, as only distantly resembling a very subordinate part of the Norse version; but the real story of the Master Thief's career is precisely the story of the architect's son in the legend of Rhampsinitos. The possible affinity of thievish stratagems in all countries can scarcely account for a series of extraor-

The legend of Rhampsinitos.

[1] *Chips from a German Workshop*, ii. 231.

dinary incidents and astounding tricks following each other
in the same order, although utterly different in their outward garb and colouring. Strangely enough, the Highland
version, which agrees with the Norse tale in making the
young thief cheat his master, agrees most closely with the
Egyptian myth.[1] In the latter, the younger of the two sons
who have learnt from their father the secret of entering the
treasure-house is caught in a trap placed there by the
king, when he found his gold and jewels dwindling away.
At his own request the elder brother cuts off his head, and
the king, astounded at finding a headless body, bids his
guards to impale it on a wall, with strict charge to bring
before him anyone whom they might hear mourning for
the dead man. The mother, seeing her son's body thus
exposed, threatens to tell the king everything unless the
body is brought safely home to her. Loading some asses
with skins full of wine, the elder son, as he approaches the
guard, loosens the string of two or three wine skins, and
the soldiers, rushing up at the sight of wine trickling on
the ground, try to soothe the seemingly distracted owner,
while they solace themselves by the liquor which they catch
in their cups, until at length, overcoming the young man's
reluctance, they sit down with him, and drink themselves to
sleep. The dead body is then taken away by the brother,
who, hearing of the new device by which the king pro-
posed to catch him, crowns his exploits by cheating the
king's daughter, and leaving a dead man's hand in hers.
His marriage with the princess follows, and he is held in

[1] The groundwork of the *Arabian
Nights'* story of the Forty Thieves is
manifestly the same, but the likeness
to the legend of Rhampsinitos is not
nearly so close. Here, however, as in
the Egyptian tale, we have two brothers,
who become possessed of the secret of a
treasure-house. The king is replaced
by the forty thieves; but it may be
noted that Herodotos speaks of the
wealth of Rhampsinitos as amassed by
extortion if not by direct robbery. Here
also one of the brothers is unlucky;
but although he is found alive in the
cave, the thieves are none the wiser,
as he is immediately killed. Here too
the body is nailed up against the wall,
but it is within the cave; and it is
taken away by the other brother, who is
impelled to this task, not by the mother
of the dead man, but by his wife. The
thieves are not less perplexed than
Rhampsinitos when they find that the
body has been removed, and that thus
some one else is possessed of their secret.
The spell which opens the cave connects
the Arabian story with the vast mass
of legends turning on substances which
have the power of splitting rocks, and
which Mr. Gould has resolved into
phrases descriptive of the action of
lightning.—*Curious Myths of the Middle
Ages*, second series, 'Schamir.'

honour as the cleverest man of the cleverest people in the world.[1]

This story in some of its leading features agrees closely with the Adventure of the Mason, related by Washington Irving in his 'Tales of the Alhambra.' Probably Irving himself knew nothing of the story of Rhampsinitos, and certainly was unacquainted with the Tales of the Master Thief and his followers. Still a Spanish legend must be regarded with some suspicion. In this case it must at least be admitted that the traces of direct borrowing have been as skilfully hidden as if the changes in the story had been the work of Hermes or the Master Thief himself. Here the king is turned into a priest, who is so far wiser than Rhampsinitos that he guards against the .knowledge of the mason by keeping him blindfolded from the time of his leaving home to his return, except while he is actually at work preparing the treasure-chamber. In this case, then, the mason knows the secret of the hidden wealth, but cannot tell in what house it is stored up. The priest dies: but not only have his riches vanished, but his ghost haunts the house, and no one will become its tenant till the landlord chances to betake himself to the poor mason, who declares that he is 'not to be frightened by the devil himself, even though he should come in the shape of a big bag of money.' When he is led to the house, he finds that it is the very one in which he had worked for the priest, and discreetly keeps the secret to himself, till, like the Egyptian architect, he reveals it on his deathbed to his son.

The Hindu version of the story of Rhampsinitos is less ingenious than this Spanish story, and is in every way inferior to the well-pointed legend of Herodotos. It is related by Somadeva Bhatta of Cashmir in his 'Ocean of the Streams of Narrative,' a professed abridgement of the still older collection called the Vrihat Kathâ. In this tale the elder of the two thieves simply makes a hole through the wall (which would at once betray their mode of entrance) in order to reach the chamber in which the king has placed not only his treasures but his daughter. He remains with her too long, and being

CHAP. VIII.

The story of the Poor Mason.

The story of Karpara and Gata.

---

[1] Herodotos, ii. 121, &c.; *Tales of Ancient Greece*, 385.

caught in the morning, is hanged, but not before he has by signs bidden his brother Gata to carry off and save the princess. Gata therefore on the next night enters the chamber of the princess, who readily agrees to fly with him. The body of Karpara is then exposed, in order to catch the surviving malefactor, who tricks them much after the fashion of the Egyptian story, the chief difference being that Gata burns the body of his brother Karpara, for whom he contrives to perform the necessary amount of mourning by dashing on the ground a karpara, or pot of rice, and then bewailing his loss by the words, 'Alas for my precious Karpara,'—words which the guards of course apply to the broken pipkin, and not to the dead thief. The story winds up with a proclamation from the king, promising half his realm to the magician who has done all this: but the princess bids him beware, and Gata goes away with her to another country.[1]

The story of Trophonios and Agamêdês.

The mason's secret is much more closely reproduced in the story which Pausanias tells of Trophonios and Agamêdês, the builders of the temple of Phoibos, after he had slain the dragon at Delphoi. These two builders also raise the treasury of Hyrieus, placing one of the stones so that they could remove it from the outside. Hyrieus, astonished at the lessening of his wealth, sets a snare, in which Agamêdês is caught, and Trophonios cuts off his head to save him from torture and himself from discovery. The latter precaution seems unnecessary, since Pausanias adds that the earth opened and received Trophonios as in the myth of Amphiaraos.

The Shifty Lad.

In the Scottish story the Shifty Lad goes through his apprenticeship not among a company of thieves, but under the sole charge of the Black Rogue, of whom he rids himself by getting him to try the pleasant sensation of being hung by the neck. The trick answers to that of the Norse thief, but

[1] See Mr. Cowell's Paper 'On the Hindu Version of the Story of Rhampsinitos,' in the *Journal of Philology*, No. I. p. 66. The imprisonment of the king's daughter in the treasure-chamber can scarcely fail to remind us of Brynhild within her flaming walls; and thus the myth seems to exhibit an affinity to the legends which tell of unsuccessful attempts to rescue the imprisoned maiden, who is finally won only by the peerless knight or irresistible warrior who can leap the hedge of spears or cross the fiery barrier. See also book ii. ch. viii. sect. 2.

the mode of effecting it differs widely. Having disposed of his master, he engages himself to a carpenter whom he persuades to break into the king's storehouse. The advice of the Seanagal whom the king consults is that a hogshead of soft pitch should be placed near the entrance. The wright, again making the venture, sinks into the pitch, and the Shifty Lad, stepping in on his shoulders, takes as much as he can carry, and then sweeping off his master's head, leaves the body in the hogshead. Again the Seanagal is consulted, and his answer is ' that they should set the trunk aloft on the points of the spears of the soldiers, to be carried from town to town, to see if they could find any one at all that would take sorrow for it.' As they pass by the wright's house, his wife screams, but the Shifty Lad cutting himself with an adze leads the captain of the guard to think that the cry was caused by sorrow at his own hurt. The body is then by the king's order hung on a tree, the guard being ordered to seize any one who should venture to take it down. The lad, driving before him a horse loaded with two kegs of whisky, approaches the soldiers 'as though he wished to pass them stealthily, and when they catch the horse's bridle, he runs off, leaving the men to drink themselves to sleep, and then returning takes away the wright's body. This exploit is followed by others which occur in no other version: but the final scene is a feast, at which, according to the Seanagal's prediction, the Shifty Lad asks the king's daughter to dance. The Seanagal upon this puts a black mark upon him, but the lad, like Morgiana, in the story of 'Ali Baba and the Forty Thieves,' discovering the mark, puts another on the Seanagal, and on twenty other men besides him. The king is then advised to say that the man who had done every trick that had been done must be exceedingly clever, and that if he would come forward and give himself up, he should have the princess for his wife. All the marked men accordingly claim the prize; and the craft of the Shifty Lad is once more called into practice, to secure the maiden for himself.[1] Mr. Campbell, who relates

[1] The theft of treasure by a clever rogue occurs in the story of the Travels of Dummling, who is Boots under another name. Compare also Grimm's stories of ' The Four Accomplished Brothers,' ' The Rogue and his Master,' and of the ' Young Giant.' In the latter tale Hermes takes more the form

this story, gives full weight to the suggestion that the incidents in which it resembles the version of Herodotos may 'have been spread amongst the people by those members of their families who study the classics at the Scotch Universities,' but he adds with good reason, that if the resemblances to other stories not classical are to be accounted for in the same way, it must be supposed 'that these books have all been read at some time so widely in Scotland as to have become known to the labouring population who speak Gaelic, and so long ago as to have been forgotten by the instructed who speak English and study foreign languages.'[1]

In the Norse and Teutonic versions it seems impossible not to see the most striking incident of the Egyptian tale in a connection and under forms which force on us the conclusion that they are not related to each other in any other way than by their growth from a common root. In these versions the king is represented by a goodhumoured squire who makes himself merry over the successful devices of the Master Thief, as he accomplishes the several tasks imposed upon him. These tasks taken separately are much the same in each, but the difference of order indicates that no one was regarded at the first as essentially more difficult than another. In none of them, however, does the humour of the story turn on the force of public opinion. The whole point lies in the utter inability of any one to guard against the thief, even when they know that they are going to be robbed and have themselves pointed out the object to be stolen. Here, as in the stories of Rhampsinitos and the Shifty Lad, the means for achieving one of the tasks is wine : but the thief has to take away not the dead body of a man, but a living horse, on which sits a groom, or, as in the Norse tale, twelve horses, each with a rider guarding them. The disguise assumed by the thief is the dress of a beggar-woman, and her wine, which in the German story is power-

---

of the Maruts, or Crushers ; and the myth of the Molionids is re-enacted with singular exactness. The young giant brings up from the water a huge mill-stone which he places round his neck, and so keeps watch all night. He is assailed by evil demons, but he returns every blow with interest — a

description which reminds us of the Hesiodic narrative of the toil of Hermes the whole night through. The only reward which he asks is the pleasure of kicking his master, who is sent spinning into the air and is never more seen.

[1] *Tales of the West Highlands*, i. 352.

fully drugged, soon puts the guards to sleep as soundly as the soldiers of the Egyptian king. In this version the thief swings the rider, saddle and all, in the air by ropes tied to the rafters of the stable; in the Norse tale, the twelve grooms find themselves astride the beams in the morning. The theft of the sheet and ring from the persons of the squire and his wife is an incident not found in either the Egyptian or the Scottish stories; but the trick practised on the priest occurs again in the Hindu tale of the nautch-girl Champa Ranee, under a disguise which cannot hide the common source from which the stories have come down to us, while it leaves no room for the notion that the one version has been suggested by the other.

But in truth the supposition is in this case wholly uncalled for. The story of the Master Thief was told in Europe, probably ages before the Homeric poems were put together, certainly ages before Herodotos heard the story of the Egyptian treasure-house. In all the versions of the tale the thief is a young and slender youth, despised sometimes for his seeming weakness, never credited with his full craft and strength. No power can withhold him from doing aught on which he has set his mind : no human eye can trace the path by which he conveys away his booty. It is the story of the child Hermes, and even under the most uncouth disguise it has lost but little either of its truthfulness or its humour. Bolts and bars are no defence against him; yet the babe whom Phoibos can shake in his arms is the mighty marauder who has driven off all his oxen from Pieria. When his work is done, he looks not much like one who needs to be dreaded; and the soft whistling sound which closes his defence wakes a smile on the face of Phoibos,[1] as the Teutonic squire laughs on finding himself tricked in the northern story. In each case the robber is exalted to the same high dignity.

'Well, friend,' said Apollôn with a smile, ' thou wilt break into many a house, I see, and thy followers after thee;

The Hellenic Master Thief.

---

[1] This is precisely reproduced by Horace in his well-known ode, with an incident which is not mentioned in the Homeric hymn, but is in close agreement with the spirit of the Norse tale :

Te boves olim nisi reddidisses
Per dolum amotas, puerum minaci
Voce dum terret, viduus pharetra
    Risit Apollo.   *Carm.* i. x.

and thy fancy for beef will set many a herdsman grieving. But come down from the cradle, or this sleep will be thy last. Only this honour can I promise thee, to be called the Master Thief for ever.'[1]

The thief in the northern stories marries the squire's daughter, as the architect's son marries the daughter of Rhampsinitos. The marriage represents the compact made between Phoibos the all-seeing and Hermes the sweet singer. In this peaceful alliance with the squire the Teutonic tale leaves him; but there are other sides to the character of the Master Thief, and each of these describes with singular fidelity the action and power of air in motion. He is the child breathing softly in the cradle, he is the giant rooting up trees in his fury. No living thing can resist the witchery of his harping. As he draws nigh, life is wakened where before he came there had been stillness as of the dead. With him comes joy or sorrow, health or the pestilence. His lyre is the harp of Orpheus, and it discourses the music of the Vedic Ribhus, or of the Finnic Wäinämöinen, the son of Ilmatar, the daughter of the Air,[2] whose singing draws the sun and moon from heaven. The beasts of the field come to hear him, like the clouds which gather in the sky when the wind blows; the trees move along his track when he comes in his sterner moods. Nothing can remain still when he pipes. The leaf must wave on the hill-side, the Jew must dance in the thorn-bush, while the music lasts.[3] He is the

---

[1] τοῦτο γὰρ οὖν καὶ ἔπειτα μετ' ἀθανά-
τοις γέρας ἕξεις,
ΑΡΧΟΣ ΦΗΛΗΤΕΩΝ κεκλήσεαι ἥματα
πάντα.—*Hymn to Hermes*, 292.
This may, I think, be considered demonstrable evidence that the story of the Master Thief belongs to the class of myths which Professor Max Müller calls organic, as being legends 'which were known to the primeval Aryan race, before it broke up into Hindus, Greeks, Romans, Germans, and Celts,' all stories imported in later times from one literature into another being secondary or inorganic. The number of stories belonging to the latter class is probably much smaller than is generally supposed

[2] As Hermes is one of the fire-

making or fire bringing gods, so Wäinämöinen catches the fish that has swallowed the fire, which, struck by Ukko, the lord of the air, from the new sun and moon, has fallen into the sea.

[3] This story of 'The Jew among the Thorns,' in Grimm's *Household Tales*, is reproduced under a hundred forms; but in few or none of these can it be maintained with any show of reason that one has been deliberately adapted from another. The fiddle which makes the Jew dance is reproduced in the form of a stick in 'The Lad who went to the North Wind,' (Dasent, *Norse Tales*, 263). The stick is of course the gift of the wind, just as Hermes gives the harp to Phoibos. In the German story the Jew is made to yield up his purse to the

Erlking, whose mysterious harmony is heard by the child nestled in his father's arms.[1] He is the piper of Hameln,[2] who drives away the noisome rats, but who also draws the children of the town happy and joyous to the blue river, where they leave all griefs behind them, as gently as the Homeric Psychopompos guides the souls across the waters of Lethe. But in all his offices he retains his character of searching subtlety. The barred gates of the unseen land cannot stay the harping breeze, whether he comes as Orpheus or Wäinämöinen: and his curious searching into every nook and cranny, his mocking laugh at those who come to see the mischief wrought by him, are reproduced under a strange disguise in Paul Pry and peeping Tom of Coventry. Nay, the Hindu deity Rudra, the 'bountiful,' the 'gracious,' the god 'with braided hair' (the streaming vapours), the 'thousand quivered,' appears sometimes in an aspect scarcely more dignified. Like Hermes and the Shifty Lad, he too is 'the lord of thieves, the robber, the cheater, the deceiver, the lord of pilferers and robbers.'[3]

Thus, then, in the story of the Master Thief, the idea of any lateral transmission becomes inadmissible. But as this tale in all its modifications can be traced back to phrases denoting physical phenomena, we have yet to see whether there are other tales which apparently cannot be resolved into such expressions, and for which the idea of any such borrowing is equally untenable or superfluous. If any such stories are forthcoming, we cannot avoid the conclusion that before the several branches of the Aryan race separated from their common home, they not only had in their language the germs of all future mythological systems, but carried with them as nursery tales a number of stories not evolved from

Limits to the hypothesis of conscious borrowing.

---

fiddler, who, when brought to trial, excuses himself by a quibble like that of Hermes. He had not robbed any one: the Jew gave the money of his own free will. Hermes is a very truthful person and knows not how to tell a lie.

[1] 'Hörest du nicht
Was Erlenkönig mir leiso verspricht?'
                        Goethe.

[2] The magic pipe or lyre reappears in the legend of 'The Rose of the Alhambra,' where it is applied with great humour to cure the mad freak of Philip V.—Irving's Alhambra.

[3] Muir, Sanskrit Texts, part iv. ch. iii. section vii. Slightly altered, the story of Godiva in Coventry is told again in the tale of Allah-ud-deen, who sees through a crevice the king's daughter on her way to the bath, when it is death for any one to be seen abroad or to be found looking on her.

phrases descriptive of natural phenomena, the ideas of which were impressed on their minds not less firmly than the more strictly mythical words and phrases were impressed on their memories. These stories were, however, little more than outlines, for it cannot be too often repeated that even in the tales which exhibit the closest likeness in their most developed forms, the points of difference in detail and colouring are so striking as to leave no room for doubt that the Aryan tribes carried away with them for these stories no rigid types to which they were compelled to adhere with Egyptian slavishness, but living ideas which each tribe might from time to time clothe in a different garb. How these ideas were furnished is a question which it may be by no means as easy to answer as it is to resolve the life of Achilleus and Meleagros into the daily course of the sun through the heavens. It becomes therefore of the utmost importance in such an inquiry as this, to bring together and compare the popular traditions of nations whose geographical positions show that their parting when they left the common home was for them a final separation. No one could have the hardihood to maintain that the countrymen of Herman had access to the pages of Pausanias, or that the soldiers of Varus had in their childhood listened to stories borrowed from the epic of Wäinämöinen. Yet the children's tales gathered during the last half-century have established the general affinity of the folk-lore of Greeks, Romans, Germans and Scandinavians, and a likeness not less astonishing runs through the popular tales of these races and those of the Hindu.[1] In India, as in Germany, old women, who doubtless thought themselves fit for nothing, have preserved to us a series of exquisite legends which pour a flood of light on the early history of the human mind. The Hindu child is still roused and soothed by the stories of the sweet Star-Lady and the lovely Queen of the Five Flowers, just as the young German and Norseman used to listen to the tale of

---

[1] *Old Deccan Days*, a series of tales taken down from the dictation of Anna Liberata de Souza, and translated by Miss Frere. The stories are of great importance; but their value is inde- finitely enhanced if, as the translator assures us, they are given precisely as they came from the lips of the narrator, without additions or embellishments.

the beautiful Briar-rose sleeping in death-like stillness until the kiss of the pure Knight rouses her from her slumber. We are clearly debtors to the old women for the preservation of thousands of lovely and touching legends which have never found their way into epic poetry. Had it not been for the grandmothers of Hellas, we should in all likelihood never have heard of the grief of Dêmêtêr, as she sank down by the fountain in Eleusis, or of the woe of Telephassa, which ended as she sank to rest on the Thessalian plain in the evening. Schools in Athens, Thebes, or Argos, doubtless did their inevitable destructive work; but we can as little doubt that many an Athenian mother pointed on the slopes of Hymettos to the spot where the glistening form of Prokris first met the eye of Kephalos as he stepped forth on the shore, and the young Delian learnt to be proud of the rugged island, where the nymphs bathed the infant Phoibos in pure water and swathed him in broad golden bands. Clearly we have to thank old crones for the story of Narkissos who died for love of his own fair face, and of Selênê gazing on Endymion as he slept on the hill of Latmos.

Among these Hindu tales we find a large class of stories which have little or nothing in common with the epic poems of the Aryan nations, but which exhibit a series of incidents in striking parallelism with those of the corresponding Teutonic versions. These incidents are in themselves so strange, and the result is brought about by turns so unexpected, that the idea of their independent developement among separated tribes who had carried away with them nothing but some proverbial sayings as the groundwork of these stories becomes a wild extravagance. Whatever the consequences may be, the conclusion seems irresistible that these stories had been wrought out into some detail, while these tribes or nations still continued to form a single people; and if these tales can scarcely be resolved into phrases denoting physical phenomena, they are perhaps more wonderful even than the epic poems, the growth of which from common germs would be inevitable if the theory of comparative mythologists be regarded as established. The resemblances between these stories may perhaps bring down the

BOOK I.

time of separation to a comparatively late period; but the geographical position of Hindu and German tribes must still throw that time back to an indefinitely distant past; and close as the parallelism may be, the differences of detail and colouring are such that we cannot suppose these Aryan emigrants to have carried away with them to their new abodes more than the leading incidents grafted on the leading idea. The fidelity with which the Hindu and the German tales adhere to this framework is indeed astonishing.

The story of the Dog and the Sparrow.

One of the most remarkable of these coincidences is furnished by the story of the 'Dog and the Sparrow,' in Grimm's collection, as compared with an episode in the 'Wanderings of Vicram Maharajah.' In both a bird vows to bring about the ruin of a human being; in both the bird is the helper and avenger of the innocent against wanton injury, and in both the destruction of the guilty is the result of their own voluntary acts. There are other points of likeness, the significance of which is heightened by points of singularly subtle difference. In the German story, the sparrow is offended because a carter, not heeding the warning which she had given him, drove his waggon over a dog which she had saved from starving.

'You have killed my brother, the dog,' she said, 'and that shall cost you your horses and your cart.'

'Horses and cart, indeed,' said the carrier. 'What harm can you do to me?' and he drove on.

But presently the sparrow contrived to force out the cork from the bunghole of one of the casks in the waggon, and all the wine ran out on the ground. 'Ah me! I am a poor man now,' cried the carter, when he saw it. 'Not poor enough yet,' said the sparrow, as she perched on the head of one of the horses, and picked out his eye. The carter in his rage took up his hatchet to kill the bird, but instead of it, he hit his horse, which fell down dead. So it fared with the second cask and the two remaining horses. Leaving his waggon on the road, the carter found his way home, and bemoaned to his wife the loss of his wine and his beasts.

'Ah my husband,' she replied, 'and what a wicked bird has come to this house; she has brought with her all the birds in the world, and there they sit among our corn, and are eating every ear of it.'

'Ah me, I am poorer than ever,' said the man, as he beheld the havoc. 'Still not poor enough, carrier; it shall cost you your life,' said the bird as she flew away. By and by the sparrow appeared at the window-sill, and uttered the same words, and the carrier, hurling his axe at it, broke the window-frame in two. Every other piece of furniture in the house was demolished as he vainly attempted to hit the bird. At length he caught her, and his wife asked if she should kill her.

'No,' said he, 'that were too merciful; she shall die much more horribly, for I will eat her alive.' So saying, he swallowed her whole; but she began to flutter about in his stomach, and presently came again into his mouth, and cried out, 'Carrier, it shall cost you your life.'

Thereupon the man handed the axe to his wife, saying, 'Kill me the wretch dead in my mouth.' His wife took it, and aimed a blow, but missing her mark struck her husband on the head and killed him. Then the sparrow flew away and was never seen there again.[1]

In the Hindoo story the bird is a parrot, and the dog's place is taken by a poor woodcutter, from whom a dancing-girl attempts to extort a large sum of money by deliberate falsehood. The girl thus represents the carter, and at once the framework of the tale is provided; but the method by which the sparrow wreaks her vengeance on the man is thoroughly awkward and unartistic when compared with the simple scheme which brings about the ruin of the nautch-woman. She, like the carrier, is rich; but she cannot resist the temptation of making more money by charging the wood-cutter with the dowry which she said that he had promised to pay on marrying her, the promise and the marriage being

The story of the Nautch-girl and the Parrot.

[1] This last incident is clearly the same as that which brings about the death of the bald carpenter, who being attacked by a mosquito called his son to drive it away. The son aiming a blow at the insect, splits his father's head with the axe. This story from the Pankatantra Professor Max Müller (*Chips &c.* ii. 232) identifies with the fable in Phædrus, of the bald man who, trying to kill a gnat, gives himself a severe blow in the face, and he attributes it, therefore, to some old Aryan proverb. The German story of the carter has certainly all the appearance of a more independent growth.

alike purely imaginary. The rajah, being called to give judgement in the case, determines to abide by the decision of a parrot famed for his wisdom, and belonging to a merchant in the town. When the woodcutter had given his version of the matter, the parrot bade Champa Ranee, the nautch-girl, tell her story. After hearing it, he asked where the house was to which her husband had taken her. 'Far away in the jungles,' was the reply. 'And how long ago?' The day was named, and twenty witnesses proved that Champa was at the time in the city. The parrot then gave judgement for the woodcutter against the nautch-girl, as the sparrow had befriended the dog against the carter. Great was the praise bestowed on the wise parrot, but the incensed nautch-girl said, 'Be assured I will get you in my power, and when I do, I will bite off your head.'

Then follows the vow of the parrot, answering to the oath of the sparrow; but he has no need to repeat it.

'Try your worst, madam,' said he, 'but in return I tell you this; I will live to make you a beggar. Your house shall be by your own orders laid even with the ground, and you for grief and rage shall kill yourself.'

Time goes on, and the nautch-girl, summoned to the merchant's house, dances so well that he asks her to name her own reward; and the price which she demands is the parrot. Taking the bird home, she ordered her servants to cook it for her supper, first cutting off its head and bringing it to be grilled, that she might eat it before tasting any other dish. The parrot is accordingly plucked, but while the servant goes to fetch water wherein to boil him, the bird, who had pretended to be dead and thus escaped having his neck wrung, slipped into a hole let into the wall for carrying off the kitchen sewage. In this dilemma the maid grilled a chicken's head, and placed it before Champa Ranee, who, as she eat it, said,

'Ah! pretty Polly, so here is the end of you. This is the brain that thought so cunningly and devised my overthrow; this the tongue that spoke against me; this is the throat through which came the threatening words. Ha! ha! who is right now, I wonder?'

With some little fear the parrot heard her words, for the loss of his wing feathers had left him unable to fly; but at length he contrived to find his way to a neighbouring temple, and to perch behind the idol. It was the favourite god of Champa Ranee, who, in her abject fear of death, had long besought him to translate her to heaven without the process of dying. So when she next came to offer her wonted supplication, the parrot spoke, and the nautch-girl at once took its words for the utterances of the god.

'Champa Ranee, nautch-girl, your prayer is heard, this is what you must do; sell all you possess, and give the money to the poor, and you must also give money to all your servants and dismiss them. Level also your house to the ground, that you may be wholly separated from earth. Then you will be fit for heaven, and you may come, having done all I command you, on this day week to this place, and you shall be transported thither body and soul.' [1]

The infatuated woman does as she is bidden, and after destroying her house and giving away all her goods, she returns to the temple, attended by a vast train of men and

---

[1] This incident recurs in the Norse version of the Master Thief. Here, however, there is no real bird, but only the thief disguised as a bird, nor are the victims of the trick actually killed, but they are grievously mauled, and are robbed as effectually as the nautch-girl. What is more to the point is, that the property is in each case abandoned by an act of their own free will. Having undertaken to cheat the priest and his clerk, the thief 'dressed himself up like a bird, threw a great white sheet over his body, took the wings of a goose and tied them to his back, and so climbed up into a great maple which stood in the priest's garden, and when the priest came home in the evening the youth began to bawl out, 'Father Lawrence, father Lawrence,'—for that was the priest's name, 'Who is that calling me,' said the priest. 'I am an angel,' said the Master Thief. 'sent from God to let you know that you shall be taken up alive into heaven for your piety's sake. Next Monday night you must hold yourself ready for the journey, for I shall come then to fetch you in a sack; and all your gold and your silver and all that you have of this world's goods you must lay together in a heap in your dining-room.' Well, Father Lawrence fell on his knees before the angel and thanked him; and the very next day he preached a farewell sermon and gave it out how there had come down an angel unto the big maple in his garden, who had told him that he was to be taken up alive into heaven for his piety's sake, and he preached and made such a touching discourse that all who were at church wept, both young and old.'—Dasent, Norse Tales, 'Master Thief.' Here, as in the Hindu story, the time is fixed, and the farewell sermon answers to the invitations sent out by Champa Ranee to all her friends that they should come and witness her ascension. Another priest is deceived in the admirable Gaelic story of the 'Son of the Scottish Yeoman who stole the Bishop's Horse and Daughter, and the Bishop Himself.' See also Mr. Campbell's excellent remarks on this story, Tales of the West Highlands, ii. 263.

women whom she had invited to be witnesses of her glori-
fication.

As they waited, a fluttering of little wings was heard, and
a parrot flew over Champa Ranee's head, calling out,
'Nautch-girl, nautch-girl, what have you done?' Champa
Ranee recognised the voice as Vicram's: he went on, 'Will
you go. body and soul to heaven? Have you forgotten Polly's
words?'

Champa Ranee rushed into the temple, and falling on her
knees before the idol, cried out, 'Gracious Power, I have
done all as you commanded; let your words come true;
save me, take me to heaven.'

But the parrot above her cried, 'Good bye, Champa
Ranee, good bye; you ate a chicken's head, not mine.
Where is your house now? Where are your servants and
all your possessions? Have my words come true, think you,
or yours?'

Then the woman saw all, and in her rage and despair,
cursing her own folly, she fell violently down on the floor of
the temple, and, dashing her head against the stone, killed
herself.[1]

Origin
and growth
of these
stories.
It is impossible to question the real identity of these two
stories, and incredible that the one could have been invented
apart from the other, or that the German and the Hindu
tale are respectively developements merely from the same
leading idea. This idea is that beings of no repute may be
avengers of successful wrongdoers, or to put it in the language of St. Paul, that the weak things of the earth may be
chosen to confound the strong, and foolish things to confound
the wise. But it was impossible that this leading idea
should of itself suggest to a Hindu and a Teuton that the
avenger should be a bird, that the wrongdoer should punish
himself, and should seal his doom by swallowing his per-
secutor or by at least thinking that he was devouring him.
There is no room here for the argument which Professor
Max Müller characterises as sneaking when applied even to
fables which are common to all the members of the Aryan

[1] Frere, *Old Deccan Days*, p. 127.

family.[1] A series of incidents such as these could never have [CHAP. VIII.]
been thought out by two brains working apart from each
other; and we are driven to admit that at least the
machinery by which the result was to be brought about had
been devised before the separation, or to maintain that the
story has in the one case or in the other been imported
bodily. Probably no instance could be adduced in which a
borrowed story differs so widely from the original. In all
cases of adaptation the borrower either improves upon the
idea or weakens it. Here both the stories exhibit equally
clear tokens of vigorous and independent growth.[2]

But the story of the nautch-girl is only one incident in a
larger drama. The bird of the German tale is a common
sparrow; the parrot which brings about the death of Champa
Ranee is nothing less than the Maharajah Vicram, who has

The stories of Vicram and Hermotimos.

---

[1] *Chips from a German Workshop,* ii. 233.

[2] It is scarcely an exaggeration to say that there is scarcely one important feature of the Hindu popular stories which are not to be found in those of Germany and Scandinavia, and which are not repeated in Celtic traditions. In each case the story is the same, yet not the same, and the main question becomes one rather of historical than of philological evidence. The substantial identity of the tales is indisputable; and if the fact be that these stories were in the possession of Germans and Norwegians, Irishmen and Scottish Highlanders, long before any systematic attempt was made to commit to writing and publish the folklore of Europe, the further conclusion is also involved that these stories do not owe their diffusion to book-learning; and assuredly the commercial intercourse which would account for them implies an amount and a frequency of communication beyond that of the most stirring and enterprising nations of the present day. Mr. Campbell, in his invaluable collection of *Popular Tales of the West Highlands,* dismisses the hypothesis as wholly untenable. Of the notion that these Highland traditions may have sprung up since the publication of Grimm's and Dasent's collections of German and Norse tales, he asserts that a manuscript lent to him by the translator proves that the stories were

known in Scotland before these translations were made public (vol. i. p. xlvi), and adds, reasonably enough, that 'when all the narrators agree in saying that they have known these stories all their lives, and when the variation is so marked, the resemblance is rather to be attributed to common origin than to books' (*ib.* xlviii). More definitely he asserts, 'After working for a year and weighing all the evidence that has come in my way, I have come to agree with those who hold that popular tales are generally pure traditions' (*ib.* 227). The care with which he has examined the large body of Celtic traditions, gives his judgement the greatest weight, and fully justifies his conclusion that 'popular tales are woven together in a network which seems to pervade the world, and to be fastened to everything in it. Tradition, books, history, and mythology hang together; no sooner has the net been freed from one snag, and a mesh gained, than another mesh is discovered; and so, unless many hands combine, the net and the contents will never be brought to shore' (*ib.* 229). It is not a little startling to find that the so-called classical mythology of the Greeks, in which the myth of Psyche was supposed to be almost the only popular tale accidentally preserved to us, contains the germs, and more than the germs, of nearly every story in the popular traditions of Germany, Norway, India, and Scotland.

received from the god of wisdom the power of transporting
his soul into any other body, while by an antidote he keeps
his own body from corruption. And here we are brought to
a parallelism which cannot be accounted for on any theory
of mediæval importation. The story of Vicram is essentially
the story of Hermotimos of Klazomenai, whose soul wanders
at will through space, while his body remains undecayed at
home, until his wife, tired out by his repeated desertions,
burns his body while he is away, and thus effectually prevents
his resuming his proper form. A popular Deccan tale, which
is also told by Pliny and Lucian, must have existed, if only in
a rudimentary state, while ·Greeks and Hindus still lived as
a single people. But a genuine humour, of which we have
little more than a faint germ in the Greek legend, runs
through the Hindu story. In both the wife is vexed by the
frequent absence of her husband : but the real fun of the
Deccan tale rises from the complications produced by the
carpenter's son, who overhears the god Gunputti as he
teaches Vicram the mystic words which enable him to pass
from his own body into another ; but as he could not see
the antidote which Vicram received to keep his tenantless
body from decay, the carpenter's son was but half enlightened.
No sooner, however, had Vicram transferred his soul to the
parrot's body, than the carpenter's son entered the body of
Vicram, and the work of corruption began in his own. The
pseudo-rajah is at once detected by the Wuzeer Butti, who
stands to Vicram in the relation of Patroklos to Achilleus,
or of Theseus to Peirithoös, and who recommends the whole
court to show a cold shoulder to the impostor, and make his
sojourn in Vicram's body as unpleasant as possible. Worn
out at last with waiting, Butti sets off to search for his friend,
and by good luck is one of the throng assembled to witness
the ascension of Champa Ranee. Butti recognises his friend,
and at once puts him into safe keeping in a cage. On
reaching home it became necessary to get the carpenter's
son out of Vicram's body, and the Wuzeer, foreseeing that
this would be no easy task, proposes a butting match between
two rams, the one belonging to himself, the other to the
pseudo-rajah. Butti accordingly submits his own ram to a

training, which greatly hardens his horns; and so when the fight began, the pretended rajah, seeing to his vexation that his favourite was getting the worst in the battle, transported his soul into the ram's body, to add to its strength and reso- lution. No sooner was this done, than Vicram left the parrot's body and re-entered his own, and Butti, slaying the defeated ram, put an end to the life of the carpenter's son, by leaving him no body in which to take up his abode. But fresh troubles were in store for Butti; and these troubles take us back to the legends of Brynhild and Persephonê, of Tammuz, Adonis, and Osiris. Not yet cured of his wandering propensities, Vicram goes to sleep in a jungle with his mouth open, into which creeps a cobra who refuses to be dislodged —the deadly snake of winter and darkness, which stings the beautiful Eurydikê, and lies coiled around the maiden on the glistening heath. The rajah, in his intolerable misery, leaves his home, just as Persephonê is taken away from Dêmêtêr, and Butti seeks him in vain for twelve years (the ten years of the struggle at Ilion), as he roams in the disguise of a fakeer. Meanwhile, the beautiful Buccoulee, who had recog- nised her destined husband under his squalid rags as Eury- kleia recognises Odysseus, had succeeded in freeing Vicram from his tormentor, and thus all three returned to the long forsaken Anar Ranee. But before we examine incidents which take us into the more strictly mythical regions of . Aryan folk-lore, it is necessary to show how large is that class of stories to which the tale of the Dancing Girl and the Woodcutter belongs. There are some which are even more remarkable for their agreement in the general scheme with thorough divergence in detail.

In the story entitled, 'The Table, the Ass, and the Stick' in Grimm's collection, a goat, whose appetite cannot be satisfied, brings a tailor into grievous trouble by leading him to drive his three sons away from their home on groundless charges. At last, finding that he had been cheated, he scourges the goat, which makes the best of its way from his dwelling. Meanwhile, the three sons had each been learning a trade, and each received his reward. To the eldest son was given a table, which at the words 'Cover thyself,' at once presented a magnificent banquet; the second received a donkey, which on hearing the word 'Bricklebrit' rained down gold pieces,[1] and both were deprived of their gifts by a thievish innkeeper, to whom they had in succession revealed their secret. On reaching home, the eldest son, boasting to his father of his inexhaustible table, was discomfited by finding that some common table had been put in its place; and the second in like manner, in making trial of his ass, found himself in possession of a very ordinary donkey. But the youngest son had not yet returned, and to him they sent word of the scurvy behaviour of the innkeeper. When the time of the third son's departure came, his master gave him a sack, adding 'In it there lies a stick.' The young man took the sack as a thing that might do him good service, but asked why he should take the stick, as it only made the sack heavier to carry. The stick, however, was endowed with the power of jumping out of the sack and belabouring any one against whom its owner had a grudge. Thus armed, the youth went cheerfully to the house of the innkeeper, who, thinking that the sack must certainly contain treasure, tried to take it from the young man's pillow while he slept. But he had reckoned without his host. The stick hears the fatal word, and at once falls without mercy on the thief, who roars out that he will surrender the table and the ass. Thus

[1] This donkey is, in fact, Midas, at whose touch everything turns to gold — a myth which reappears in the Irish tradition of Lavra Loingsech, who had horse's ears, as Midas had those of an ass. The reeds betrayed the secret in the case of Midas; the barber of Lavra whispered the secret in the Irish story to a willow; the willow was cut down, and the harp made of the wood murmured 'Lavra Loingsech has horse's ears.' (Fergusson, *The Irish before the Conquest*.) The horse and the ass doubtless represent the Harits of Hindu mythology; the production of gold (the golden light) by the sun or the dawn recurs again and again in Aryan legends. In Grimm's story of the 'Three Little Men in the Wood,' the kindly dawn-child shares her bread with the dwarfs, who, as in the Volsung tale, guard the treasures of the earth, and in return they grant to her the power of becoming more beautiful every day, and that a piece of gold shall fall out of her mouth every word that she speaks. But she has a stepsister, the winter, who, not having her kindly feelings, refuses to share her bread with the dwarfs, who decree that she shall grow more ugly every day, and that toads shall spring from her mouth whenever she speaks. This is the story of 'Bushy Bride' in Dasent's *Norse Tales*. The dawn-children reappear in the story of Hansel and Grethel, who, wandering into the forest (of night or winter), come upon a house with windows made of clear sugar (ice), where they fall into the power of a witch (Hades), who, like the dwarfs, guards the hoard of treasure. The old witch is destroyed by Grethel after the fashion of the cannibal in the Zulu tale. (Max Müller, *Chips*, ii. 214.)

the three gifts reach the tailor's house.[1] As for the goat, whose head the tailor had shaven, it ran into a fox's house, where a bee stung its bald pate, and it rushed out, never to be heard of again.

In the Deccan tale we have a jackal and a barber in the place of the goat and the tailor: and the mischief is done, not by leading the barber to expel his children, but by cheating him of the fruits of his garden. The parallel, however, is not confined to the fact of the false pretences; the barber retaliates, like the tailor, and inflicts a severe wound on the jackal. As before, in the German story, the goat is a goat; but the jackal is a transformed rajah, none other in short than the Beast who is wedded to Beauty and the monster who becomes the husband of Psyche, and thus even this story lies within the magic circle of strictly mythical tradition. But before he wins his bride, the jackal-rajah is reduced to sore straits, and his adventures give occasion for some sharp satire on Hindu popular theology. Coming across a bullock's carcass, the jackal eats his way into it, while the sun so contracts the hide that he finds himself unable to get out. Fearing to be killed if discovered, or to be buried alive if he escaped notice, the jackal, on the approach of the scavengers, cries out, 'Take care, good people, how you touch me, for I am a great saint.' The mahars in terror ask him who he is, and what he wants. ' I,' answered the jackal, 'am a very holy saint. I am also the god of your village, and I am very angry with you, because you never worship me nor bring me offerings.' ' O my lord,' they cried, ' what offerings will please you? Tell us only, and we will bring you whatever you like.' 'Good,' said the jackal; 'then you must fetch hither plenty of rice, plenty of flowers, and a nice fat chicken: place them as an offering beside me, and pour a great deal of water over them, as you do at your most solemn feasts, and then I will forgive you your sins.' The wetting, of course, splits the dry bullock's skin, and the jackal, jumping out, runs with the chicken in his mouth to the jungle. When again he was

[1] The Norse story of 'The Lad who went to the North Wind' turns on the same machinery.

nearly starved, he heard a Brahman bewailing his poverty, and declaring that if a dog or a jackal were to offer to marry one of his daughters, he should have her—an eagerness in complete contrast with the reluctance of the merchant who is obliged to surrender his child to the beast. The jackal takes him at his word, and leads his wife away to a splendid subterranean palace, where she finds that each night the jackal lays aside his skin, and becomes a beautiful young man. Soon the Brahman comes to the jackal's cave to see how his child gets on; but just as he is about to enter, the jackal stops him, and, learning his wants, gives him a melon, the seeds of which will bring him some money. A neighbour, admiring the fruit produced from these seeds, buys some from the Brahman's wife, and finding that they are full of diamonds, pearls and rubies, purchases the whole stock, until the Brahman himself opens a small withered melon, and learns how he has been overreached. In vain he asks restitution from the woman who has bought them; she knows nothing of any miraculous melons, and a jeweller to whom he takes the jewels from the withered melon, accuses him of having stolen the gems from his shop, and impounds them all. Again the Brahman betakes himself to the jackal, who, seeing the uselessness of giving him gold or jewels, brings him out a jar which is always full of good things.[1] The Brahman now lived in luxury; but another Brahman informed the rajah of the royal style in which his once poorer neighbour feasted, and the rajah appropriated the jar for his own special use. When once again he carried this story of his wrongs to his son-in-law, the jackal gave him another jar, within which was a rope and a stick, which would perform their work of chastisement as soon as the jar was opened. Uncovering the jar while he was alone, the Brahman had cause to repent his rashness, for every bone in his body was left aching. With this personal experience of the powers of the stick, the Brahman generously invited the rajah and his brother

[1] This jar is, of course, the horn of Amaltheia, the napkin of Rhydderch, the never-failing table of the Ethiopians, the cup of the Malee's wife in the Hindu legend; but the countless forms assumed by the mysterious vessel which serves as the source of life and wealth will be more fitly examined when we come to analyse the myth of the divine ship Argo. See the section on the Vivifying Sun. Book II. ch. ii.

Brahman to come and test the virtues of his new gift; and a belabouring as hearty as that which the wicked innkeeper received in the German tale made them yield up the dinner-making jar. The same wholesome measure led to the recovery of the precious stones from the jeweller, and the melons from the woman who had bought them. It only remained now, by burning the enchanted rajah's jackal-skin, the lion-skin of Herakles, to transform him permanently into the most splendid prince ever seen on earth.[1]

The independent growth of these tales from a common framework is still more conclusively proved by the fact that the agreement of the Norse with the Hindu legend is far more close and striking than the likeness which it bears to the German story. In the Norse version we have not three brothers, but one lad, who represents the Brahman; and in the Norse and Hindu stories alike, the being who does the wrong is the one who bestows the three mysterious gifts. The goat in the German version is simply mischievous: in the Norse tale, the North Wind, which blows away the poor woman's meal, bestows on her son the banquet-making cloth, the money-coining ram, and the magic stick.[2] The jackal and the cloth are thus alike endowed with the mysterious power of the Teutonic Wish. This power is exhibited under a thousand forms, among which cups, horns, jars, and basins hold the most conspicuous place, and point to the earliest symbol used for the expression of the idea.

The points of likeness and difference between the Hindu story of Punchkin and the Norse tale of the 'Giant who had no Heart in his Body' are perhaps still more striking. In the former a rajah has seven daughters, whose mother dies while they are still children, and a stepmother so persecutes them

---

[1] In the mythology of Northern Europe the lion-skin becomes a bear-sack, and thus, according to the story of Porphyry, Zalmoxis, the mythical legislator of the Getai, was a Berserkr, as having been clothed in a bearskin as soon as he was born. Probably the explanation is about as trustworthy as that which traces the name Tritogeneia to a Cretan word trito, meaning head. The other form of the name, Zamolxis,

has been supposed (Nork, _heal-Wörterbuch_, s.v.) to point to mulgeo, mulceo, and thus to denote the wizard or the sorcerer. The story of his remaining hidden for years in a cave, and then reappearing among the Getai, is merely another form of the myths of Perse-phone, Adonis, Baldur, Osiris, and other deities of the waxing and waning year.

[2] Dasent, _Tales from the Norse_, xciv. cxli. 266.

that they make their escape. In the jungle they are found by the seven sons of a neighbouring king, who are hunting; and each takes one of the princesses as a wife, the handsomest of course marrying the youngest. After a brief time of happiness, the eldest prince sets off on a journey, and does not return. His six brothers follow him, and are seen no more. After this, as Balna, the youngest princess, rocks her babe in his cradle, a fakeer makes his appearance, and having vainly asked her to marry him, transforms her into a dog, and leads her away. As he grows older, Balna's son learns how his parents and uncles have disappeared, and resolves to go in search of them. His aunts beseech him not to do so; but the youth feels sure that he will bring them all back, and at length he finds his way to the house of a gardener, whose wife, on hearing his story, tells him that his father and uncles have all been turned into stone by the great magician Punchkin, who keeps Balna herself imprisoned in a high tower because she will not marry him. To aid him in his task, the gardener's wife disguises him in her daughter's dress, and gives him a basket of flowers as a present for the captive princess. Thus arrayed, the youth is admitted to her presence, and while none are looking, he makes himself known to his mother by means of a ring which she had left on his finger before the sorcerer stole her away. But the rescue of the seven princes seemed to be as far off as ever, and the young man suggests that Balna should now change her tactics, and by playing the part of Delilah to Samson, find out where his power lies, and whether he is subject to death. The device is successful, and the sorcerer betrays the secret.

'Far away, far away, hundreds of thousands of miles away from this, there lies a desolate country covered with thick jungle. In the midst of the jungle grows a circle of palm trees, and in the centre of the jungle stand six jars full of water, piled one above another; below the sixth jar is a small cage which contains a little green parrot; on the life of the parrot depends my life, and if the parrot is killed I must die.'[1]

[1] In the Gaelic story of the 'Young King of Eassidh Ruadh,' which contains   this story, this puzzle is thus put. 'There is a great flagstone under the

But this keep is guarded by myriads of evil demons, and Balna tries hard to dissuade her son from the venture. He is resolute, and he finds true helpers in some eagles whose young he saves by killing a large serpent which was making its way to their nest. The parent birds give him their young to be his servants, and the eaglets, crossing their wings, bear him through the air to the spot where the six water jars are standing. In an instant he upsets the jar, and snatching the parrot from his cage, rolls him up in his cloak. The magician in his dismay at seeing the parrot in the youth's hands yields to every demand made by him, and not only the seven princes but all his other victims are restored to life — a magnificent array of kings, courtiers, officers, and servants.[1] Still the magician prayed to have his parrot given to him.

'Then the boy took hold of the parrot, and tore off one of his wings, and when he did so, the magician's right arm fell off.

'Punchkin then stretched out his left arm, crying, "Give me my parrot." The prince pulled off the parrot's second wing and the magician's left arm tumbled off.

'"Give me my parrot," cried he, and fell on his knees. The prince pulled off the parrot's right leg, the magician's right leg fell off; the prince pulled off the parrot's left leg, down fell the magician's left.

'Nothing remained of him save the limbless body and the head; but still he rolled his eyes, and cried, "Give me my parrot!" "Take your parrot then," cried the boy; and with that he wrung the bird's neck, and threw it at the magician, and as he did so, Punchkin twisted round, and with a fearful groan he died.'

threshold. There is a wether under the flag. There is a duck in the wether's belly, and an egg in the belly of the duck, and it is in the egg that my soul is.'

[1] This portion of the story is found in the *Arabian Nights'* tale of 'The two Sisters who were jealous of their Younger Sister.' Here also the enchantments are overcome by gaining possession of a bird, and the malignant demons who guard it are represented by dismal cries and jeering voices which assail all who attempt the task. The bird, as in the Hindu tale, is won by the youngest of the family, but it is the princess Parizade disguised as a man who performs the exploit, having, like Odysseus, as he approached the Seiren's land, filled her ears with cloth. Nor is the bird less mighty than the magician, although he is not killed off in the same way.

In its key-note and its leading incidents this story is precisely parallel to the Norse tale of the ' Giant who had no Heart in his Body.' Here, as in the Deccan legend, there is a king who has seven sons, but instead of all seven being sent to hunt or woo, the youngest is left at home; and the rajah whose children they marry has six daughters, not seven. This younger brother who stays at home is the Boots of European folk-lore, a being of infinitely varied character, and a subject of the highest interest for all who wish to know whence the Aryan nations obtained the materials for their epic poems. Seemingly weak and often despised, he has keener wit and more resolute will than all who are opposed to him. Slander and obloquy are to him as nothing, for he knows that in the end his truth shall be made clear in the sight of all men. In Dr. Dasent's words, ' There he sits idle whilst all work; there he lies with that deep irony of conscious power which knows its time must one day come, and meantime can afford to wait. When that time comes, he girds himself to the feat amidst the scoff and scorn of his flesh and blood ; but even then, after he has done some great deed, he conceals it, returns to his ashes, and again sits idly by the kitchen fire, dirty, lazy, despised, until the time for final recognition comes, and then his dirt and rags fall off—he stands out in all the majesty of his royal robes, and is acknowledged once for all a king.'[1] We see him in a thousand forms. He is the Herakles on whom the mean

[1] Dasent, *Norse Tales*, cliv. Some of the stories told of Boots are very significant. Among the most noteworthy is Grimm's story of 'One who travelled to learn what shivering meant.' The stupid boy in this tale shows marvellous strength of arm, but he is no more able to shiver than the sun. At midnight he is still quick with the heat of fire, which cannot be cooled even by contact with the dead. Like Sigurd, he recovers the treasures in the robber's keeping, and he learns to shiver only when his bride pours over him at night a pail of water full of fish—in other words, when Helios plunges into the sea as Endymion. Elsewhere, he is not only the wanderer or vagabond, but the discharged soldier, or the strolling player, who is really the king Thrushbeard in the German story, who tames the pride of the princess as Indra subdues Dahanâ ; or he is the countryman who cheats the Jew in the story of the 'Good Bargain.' He is the young king of Easaidh Ruadh in the Scottish story, who gets for the giant the Glaive of Light (Excalibur, or the spear of Achilleus), and who rides a dun filly, gifted like the horse Xanthos with the power of speech. He is the ' bald rough-skinned gillie' of the smithy in the Highland tale of ' The Brown Bear of the Green Glen,' on whose head the mysterious bird alights to point him out as the father of the dawn-child. In the story of the 'Three Soldiers' in the same collection, he is the poor soldier who is wheedled of his three wish-gifts, but recovering them in the end is seen in his native majesty.

Eurystheus delights to pour contempt; he is Cinderella sitting in the dust, while her sisters flaunt their finery abroad;
he is the Oidipous who knows nothing,[1] yet reads the mysterious riddle of the Sphinx; he is the Phoibos who serves in
the house of Admêtos and the palace of Laomedon; he is the
Psyche who seeks her lost love almost in despair, and yet
with the hope still living in her that her search shall not be
unsuccessful; above all, he is the Ithakan chief, clothed in
beggar's rags, flouted by the suitors, putting forth his strength
for one moment to crush the insolent Arnaios, then sitting
down humbly on the threshold,[2] recognised only by an old
nurse and his dog, waiting patiently till the time comes that
he shall bend the unerring bow and having slain his enemies
appear once more in glorious garb by the side of a wife as
radiant in beauty as when he left her years ago for a long
and a hard warfare far away. Nay, he even becomes an
idiot, but even in this his greatest humiliation the memory
of his true greatness is never forgotten. Thus the Gaelic
' Lay of the Great Fool' relates the

> Tale of wonder, that was heard without lie,
> Of the idiot to whom hosts yield,
> A haughty son who yields not to arms,
> Whose name was the mighty fool.

> The might of the world he had seized
> In his hands, and it was no rude deed;
> It was not the strength of his blade or shield,
> But that the mightiest was in his grasp.[3]

He becomes, of course, the husband of Helen,

> The mighty fool is his name.
> And his wife is the young Fairfine;
> The men of the world are at his beck,
> And the yielding to him was mine;

and the Helen of the story has, of course, her Paris. The
fool goes to sleep, and as he slumbers a Gruagach gives her a
kiss, and like Helen ' the lady was not ill-pleased that he
came.' But his coming is for evil luck, and the deceiver shall
be well repaid when the fool comes to take vengeance.

> Still will I give my vows,
> Though thou thinkest much of thy speech;
> When comes the Gruagach of the tissue cloak,
> He will repay thee for his wife's kiss.

---

[1] ὁ μηδὲν εἰδὼς Οἰδίπους.
    Sophokles, Oid. Tyr. 397.
[2] Odyssey, xviii. 110.
[3] Campbell, Tales of the West High-
    lands, iii. 164.

BOOK
I.

Mythical
repetitious
and com-
binations.

Boots then acts the part of Balna's son in the Hindu story, while the sorcerer reappears in the Norse tale as a giant, who turns the six princes and their wives into stone. The incident is by no means peculiar to this tale, and the examples already adduced would alone warrant the assertion that the whole mass of folk-lore in every country may be resolved into an endless series of repetitions, combinations, and adaptations of a few leading ideas or of their developements, all sufficiently resembling each other to leave no doubts of their fundamental identity, yet so unlike in outward garb and colouring, so thoroughly natural and vigorous under all their changes, as to leave no room for any other supposition than that of a perfectly independent growth from one common stem. If speaking of the marvels wrought by musical genius, Dr. Newman could say, 'There are seven notes in the scale; make them thirteen, yet how slender an outfit for so vast an enterprise,'[1] we may well feel the same astonishment as we see the mighty harvest of mythical lore which a few seeds have yielded, and begin to understand how it is that ideas so repeated, disguised, or travestied never lost their charm, but find us as ready to listen when they are brought before us for the hundredth time in a new dress, as when we first made acquaintance with them.

Agency of
boasts in
these
stories.

In the modified machinery of the Norse tale, the remonstrances addressed to Balna's son in the Hindu story are here addressed to Boots, whose kindness to the brute creatures who become his friends is drawn out in the more full detail characteristic of Western legends. The Hindu hero helps eagles only; Boots succours a raven, a salmon, and a wolf, and the latter having devoured his horse bears him on

---

[1] *University Sermons*, p. 348. In there two stories the Magician Punchkin and the Heartless Giant are manifestly only other forms of the dark beings, the Panis, who steal away the bright treasures, whether cows, maidens, or youths, from the gleaming west. In each case there is a long search for them; and as Troy cannot fall without Achilleus, so here there is only one who can achieve the exploit of rescuing the beings who have been turned into stone, as Niobé is hardened into rock. The youthful son of Balna in his disguise is the womanlike Theseus, Dionysos, or Achilleus. Balna herself imprisoned in the tower with the sorcerer whom she hates is Helen shut up in Ilion with the seducer whom she loathes; and as Helen calls herself the dog-faced, so Balna is transformed into a dog when Punchkin leads her away. The eagles whose young he saves, like the heroes of so many popular tales, are the bright clouds who bear off little Surya Bai to the nest on the tree top.

its back with the speed of light to the house of the giant
who has turned his brothers into stone.[1] Then he finds, not
his mother, like Balna's son, but the beautiful princess who
is to be his bride, and who promises to find out, if she can,
where the giant keeps his heart, for, wherever it be, it is not
in his body. The colloquies which lead at length to the true
answer exhibit the giant in the more kindly and rollicking
character frequently bestowed on trolls, dwarfs, elves, and
demons, in the mythology of the Western Aryans. The
final answer corresponds precisely to that of Punchkin. 'Far,
far away in a lake lies an island; on that island stands a
church; in that church is a well; in that well swims a duck;
in that duck there is an egg; and in that egg there lies
my heart, you darling.' His darling takes a tender farewell
of Boots, who sets off on the wolf's back, to solve, as in the
Eastern tale, the mystery of the water and the bird. The
wolf takes him to the island; but the church keys hang high
on the steeple, and the raven is now brought in to perform
an office analogous to that of the young eaglets in the Deccan
legend. At last, by the salmon's help, the egg is brought
from the bottom of the well where the duck had dropped it.

'Then the wolf told him to squeeze the egg, and as soon
as ever he squeezed it, the giant screamed out.

' " Squeeze it again," said the wolf; and when the prince
did so, the giant screamed still more piteously, and begged
and prayed so prettily to be spared, saying he would do all

---

[1] The constant agency of wolves and
foxes in the German stories at once
suggests a comparison with the Myrmidons whom the Homeric poet so elabo-
rately likens to wolves, with Phoibos
himself as the wolf-god of Æschylos,
and with the jackal princes of eastern
story. In Grimm's story of 'The Two
Brothers,' the animals succoured are
the hare, fox, wolf, and lion, and they
each, as in the Hindu tale, offer their
young as ministers to the hero who has
spared their lives. In the beautiful
legend of the Golden Bird, the youngest
brother and the fox whom by his kindness he secures as his ally, alike represent the disguised chieftain of Ithaka,
and the rajahs of the Hindu stories.
The disguise in which the youngest

brother returns home is put on by himself. He has exchanged clothes with a
beggar; the fox is of course enchanted,
and can only be freed by destroying the
body in which he is imprisoned. But
this idea of enchantment would inevitably be suggested by the magic power
of Athênê in seaming the face of Odysseus with the wrinkles of a squalid
old age, while the Christianised Northman would convert Athênê herself into
a witch. In this story the mere presence
of the disguised youth, who was supposed
to be murdered, just as the suitors supposed Odysseus to be dead, makes the
golden bird begin to sing, the golden
horse begin to eat, and the beautiful
maiden to cease weeping. The meaning
is obvious.

that the prince wished if he would only not squeeze his heart in two.

' "Tell him if he will restore to life again your six brothers and their brides, you will spare his life," said the wolf. Yes, the giant was ready to do that, and he turned the six brothers into king's sons again, and their brides into king's daughters.

' "Now squeeze the egg in two," said the wolf. So Boots squeezed the egg to pieces, and the giant burst at once.'

The Two Brothers.
If the morality of myths be a fair matter for comparison, the Eastern story has here the advantage. Balna's son makes no definite promise to the magician; but a parallel to Punchkin, almost closer than that of the giant, is furnished in Grimm's story of the Two Brothers, where a witch is forced to restore all her victims to life. ' The old witch took a twig[1] and changed the stones back to what they were, and immediately his brother and the beasts stood before the huntsman, as well as many merchants, workpeople and shepherds, who, delighted with their freedom, returned home; but the twin brothers,[2] when they saw each other again, kissed and embraced and were very glad.'[3]

Influence of written literature on Folklore.
The supposition that these stories have been transmitted laterally is tenable only on the further hypothesis, that in every Aryan land, from Eastern India to the Highlands of Scotland, the folk-lore of the country has had its character determined by the literature of written books, that in every land men have handled the stories introduced from other countries with the deliberate purpose of modifying and adapting them, and that they have done their work in such a way as sometimes to leave scarcely a resemblance, at other times scarcely to effect the smallest change. In no other range of literature has any such result ever been achieved. In these stories we have narratives which have confessedly been received in the crudest form, if the fable of the Brahman and the goat is to be taken as the original of the Master Thief, and which have been worked up with marvellous vigour and

[1] The rod of Kirkè. The persons changed into stones represent the companions of Eurylochos. They are petrified only because they cannot resist the allurements or temptations of the place.
[2] The Dioskouroi, or the Asvins.
[3] See also Campbell's *Tales of the West Highlands*, i. 103.

under indefinitely varied forms, not by the scholars who imported the volumes of the Kalila and Dimna, or the Exploits
of the Romans, but by unknown men among the people.
The tales have been circulated for the most part only among
those who have no books, and many if not most of them have
been made known only of late years for the first time to the
antiquarians and philologists who have devoted their lives
to hunting them out. How then do we find in Teutonic or
Hindu stories not merely incidents which specially characterise the story of Odysseus, but almost the very words in
which they are related in the Odyssey? The task of analysing and comparing these legends is not a light one even for
those who have all the appliances of books and the aid of a
body of men working with them for the same end. Yet old
men and old women reproduce in India and Germany, in Norway, in Scotland, and in Ireland, the most subtle turns of
thought and expression, and an endless series of complicated
narratives, in which the order of incidents and the words of
the speakers are preserved with a fidelity nowhere paralleled in the oral tradition of historical events. It may
safely be said that no series of stories introduced in the form
of translations from other languages could ever thus have
filtered down into the lowest strata of society, and thence
have sprung up again, like Antaios, with greater energy and
heightened beauty, and 'nursery tales are generally the last
things to be adopted by one nation from another.'[1] But it
is not safe to assume on the part of Highland peasants or
Hindu nurses a familiarity with the epical literature of the
Homeric or Vedic poets; and hence the production of actual
evidence in any given race for the independent growth of
popular stories may be received as throwing fresh light on
questions already practically solved, but can scarcely be regarded as indispensable. It can scarcely be necessary to
prove that the tale of the Three Snake Leaves was not
derived by the old German storytellers from the pages of
Pausanias, or that Beauty and the Beast was not suggested by
Appuleius. There is nothing therefore which needs to
surprise us in the fact that stories already familiar to the

[1] Max Müller, *Chips*, ii. 216.

The stories
of King
Putraka,
and the
Three
Princesses
of White-
land.

western Aryans have been brought to us in their eastern versions only as yesterday.

Among such tales is the story, cited by Dr. Dasent, of King Putraka, who wandering among the Vindhya mountains finds two men quarreling for the possession of a bowl, a staff, and a pair of shoes, and induces them to determine by running a race whose these things shall be. No sooner have they started than Putraka puts on the shoes, which give the power of flight, and vanishes with the staff and bowl also. The story, which in this form has only recently been made known in Europe through the translation of the tales of Somadeva, is merely another version of the old Norse legend of the Three Princesses of Whiteland, in which three brothers fight for a hundred years about a hat, a cloak, and a pair of boots, until a king, passing by, prevails on them to let him try the things, and putting them on, wishes himself away. The incident, Dr. Dasent adds, is found in Wallachian and Tartar stories,[1] while the three gifts come again in the stories already cited, of the Table, the Ass, and the Stick, the Lad that went to the North Wind, and the Hindu tale of the Brahman, the Jackal, and the Barber. But the gifts themselves are found everywhere. The shoes are the sandals of Hermes, the seven-leagued boots of Jack the Giant Killer;[2] the hat is the helmet of Hades, the Tarn-Kappe of the Nibelungen Lied;[3] in the staff we have the rod of Kirkê, and in the bowl that emblem of fertility and life which meets us at every turn, from the holy vessel

---

[1] It occurs also in the German legend of 'The King of the Golden Mountain.' In the story of Gyges (Plato, *Pol.* 360), this power of making the wearer invisible resides in a ring, which he discovers far beneath the surface of the earth. This ring enables him to corrupt the wife of Kandaules, and so to become master of the Lydian kingdom; and thus it belongs to the number of mysterious rings which represent the Hindu Yoni. See also the Gaelic tale of 'Conal Crovi.' Campbell, i. 133. The triple power of wish is invested in the stone given by the dwarf to Thorston. Keightley, *Fairy Mythology*, 71.

[2] The ladder by which Jack ascends

to heaven is not peculiar to this story. It is possibly only another form of the Bridge of Heimdall. 'Mr. Tylor,' says Professor Max Müller, 'aptly compares the [Mandan] fable of the vine and the fat woman with the story of Jack and the Bean Stalk, and he brings other stories from Malay and Polynesian districts embodying the same idea. Among the different ways by which it was thought possible to ascend from earth to heaven, Mr. Tylor mentions the rank spear-grass, a rope or thong, a spider's web, a ladder of iron or gold, a column of smoke, or the rainbow.' *Chips,* ii. 268.

[3] *Il.* v. 845.

which only the pure knight or the innocent maiden may touch, to the horseshoe which is nailed for good luck's sake to the wall. These things have not been imported into Western mythology by any translations of the folk-lore of the East, for they were as well known in the days of Perikles as they are in our own; and thus in cases where there appears to be evidence of conscious adaptation the borrowing must be regarded rather as an exceptional fact than as furnishing any presumption against stories for which no such evidence is forthcoming. It will never be supposed that the imagery and even the language of the old Greek epics could be as familiarly known to the Hindu peasantry as to the countrymen of Herodotos: and hence the greater the resemblance between the popular stories of Greeks, Germans, and Hindus, the less room is there for any hypothesis of direct borrowing or adaptation. Such theories do but create and multiply difficulties; the real evidence points only to that fountain of mythical language from which have flowed all the streams of Aryan epic poetry, streams so varied in their character, yet agreeing so closely in their elements. The substantial identity of stories told in Italy, Norway, and India can but prove that the treasure-house of mythology was more abundantly filled before the dispersion of the Aryan tribes than we had taken it to be.

Probably no two stories furnish more convincing evidence of the extent to which the folk-lore of the Aryan tribes was developed, while they still lived as a single people, than that which we find in the German legend of Faithful John and the Deccan story of Rama and Luxman, who reflect the Rama and Laxmana of Purana legends. A comparison of these legends clearly shows that at least the following framework must have been devised before Hindus and Germans started on the long migration which was to lead the one to the regions of the Ganges and the Indus, and the other to the countries watered by the Rhine and the Elbe. Even in those early days the story must have run that a king had seen the likeness of a maiden whose beauty made him faint with love; that he could not be withheld from seeking her; that his faithful friend went with him and helped him to win his bride; that certain wise birds predicted that the trusty friend should save his master from three great dangers, but that his mode of rescuing him should seem to show that he loved his master's wife; that for his self-sacrifice he should be turned into a stone, and should be restored to life only by the agency of an innocent child. That two men in two distant countries knowing nothing of each other could hit upon such a series of incidents as these, none probably will have the hardihood to maintain. Still less can any dream of urging that Hindus and Germans agreed together to adopt each the specific differences of their respective versions. In the German story the prince's passion for the beautiful maiden is caused by the sight of her portrait in a gallery of his father's palace, into which the trusty John had been strictly charged not to let the young man enter.[1] Having once seen it, he cannot be withheld from going to seek her, and with his friend he embarks as a merchant in a ship laden with all manner of costly goods which may tempt the maiden's taste or curiosity. The scheme succeeds; but while the princess is making her purchases the Faithful John orders all sail to be set, and the ship is far at sea when the maiden turns to go home. At once we recognise the form in which Herodotos at the outset of his history has recorded the story of Iô, and are tempted to think that Herodotos did not in this instance invent his own rationalistic explanation of a miraculous story, but has adopted a version of the myth current in his own day. The comparative freedom from supernatural in-

---

[1] This is substantially the Rabbinical story of 'The Broken Oath,' the difference being that the young man is already in Fairy Land, and finds in the forbidden chamber, not the picture, but the maiden herself. The sequel of this story exhibits the maiden as the Fairy Queen, who lays the man under a pledge to remain with her. After a while he feels a yearning to return to his earthly home. He is suffered to do so on pledging his word that he will come back. But the pledge redeemed without murmuring by Thomas of Ercildoune is set at nought by the hero of this tale. The forsaken fairy carries the case before the Rabbis, who decide that he must go back; but on his persistent refusal, she beseeches him to suffer her to take leave of him and to embrace him. 'He replied that she might, and as soon as she embraced him, she drew out his soul, and he died.' Thus far the story runs like that of Fouqué's Undine; but in the sequel the insensibility of the Jew to the ludicrous is shown in the words put into the mouth of the fairy, who leaves her son Solomon in the keeping of the Rabbis, assuring them that he will pass examinations satisfactorily. Keightley, *Fairy Mythology*, 505.

cidents would of course determine his choice. The next scene in the drama is a colloquy between three crows, whose language Faithful John understands, and who foretell three great dangers impending over the prince, who can be saved only at the cost of his preserver. On his reaching shore a fox-coloured horse would spring towards him, which, on his mounting it, would carry him off for ever from his bride. No one can save him except by shooting the horse, but if any one does it and tells the king, he will be turned into stone from the toe to the knee. If the horse be killed, the prince will none the more keep his bride, for a bridal shirt will lie on a dish, woven seemingly of gold and silver, but composed really of sulphur and pitch, and if he puts it on it will burn him to his bones and marrow. Whoever takes the shirt with his gloved hand and casts it into the fire may save the prince; but if he knows and tells him, he will be turned to stone from his knee to his heart. Nor is the prince more safe even if the shirt be burnt, for during the dance which follows the wedding the queen will suddenly turn pale and fall as if dead, and unless some one takes three drops of blood from her right breast she will die. But whoever knows and tells it shall be turned to stone from the crown of his head to the toes of his feet. The friend resolves to be faithful at all hazards, and all things turn out as the crows had foretold; but the king, misconstruing the act of his friend in taking blood from his wife, orders him to be led to prison. At the scaffold he explains his motives, but the act of revelation seals his doom; and while the king intreats for forgiveness the trusty servant is turned into stone. In an agony of grief the king has the figure placed near his bed, and vainly prays for the power of restoring him to life. Years pass on; twin sons are born to him, and one day, as he gives utterance to the longing of his heart, the statue says that it can be brought back to life if the king will cut off the heads of the twins and sprinkle the statue with their blood. The servant is restored to life, and when he places the children's heads on their bodies they spring up and play as merrily as ever.

In truth and tenderness of feeling this story falls far short of the Deccan tale, in which the prince Rama sees the image of his future bride, not in a picture, but in a dream. Having won her by the aid of Luxman, he is soon after attacked by the home-sickness which is common to the heroes of most of these tales, and which finds its highest expression in the history of Odysseus. During the journey, which answers to the voyage of the king with Faithful John, Luxman, who, like John, understands the speech of birds, hears two owls talking in a tree overhead, and learns from them that three great perils await his master and his bride. The first will be from a rotten branch of a banyan-tree, from the fall of which Luxman will just save them by dragging them forcibly away; the next will be from an insecure arch, and the third from a cobra. This serpent, they said, Luxman would kill with his sword.

‘But a drop of the cobra’s blood shall fall on her forehead. The wuzeer will not care to wipe off the blood with his hands, but shall instead cover his face with a cloth, that he may lick it off with his tongue; but for this the rajah will be angry with him, and his reproaches will turn this poor wuzeer into stone.

‘ “Will he always remain stone?” asked the lady owl. “Not for ever,” answered the husband, “but for eight long years he will remain so.” “And what then?” demanded she. “Then,” answered the other, “when the young rajah and ranee have a baby, it shall come to pass that one day the child shall be playing on the floor, and, to help itself along, shall clasp hold of the stony figure, and at that baby’s touch the wuzeer will come to life again.” ’

As in the German tale, everything turns out in accordance with the predictions of the birds. When, therefore, Luxman saw the cobra creep towards the queen, he knew that his life must be forfeited for his devotion, and so he took from the folds of his dress the record of the owl’s talk and of his former life, and, having laid it beside the sleeping king, killed the cobra. The rajah, of course, starts up just as his friend is licking the blood from his wife’s forehead, and, drawing the same inference with the German prince, overwhelms him with reproaches.

'The rajah had buried his face in his hands: he looked up, he turned to the wuzeer; but from him came neither answer nor reply. He had become a senseless stone. Then Rama for the first time perceived the roll of paper which Luxman had laid beside him; and when he read in it of what Luxman had been to him from boyhood, and of the end, his bitter grief broke through all bounds, and falling at the feet of the statue, he clasped its stony knees and wept aloud.'

Eight years passed on, and at length the child was born. A few months more, and in trying to walk, it 'stretched out its tiny hands and caught hold of the foot of the statue. The wuzeer instantly came back to life, and stooping down seized the little baby, who had rescued him, in his arms and kissed it.' [1]

There is something more quiet and touching in the silent record of Luxman which stands in the place of Faithful John's confession at the scaffold, as well as in the doom which is made to depend on the reproaches of his friend rather than on the mere mechanical act of giving utterance to certain words. But the Hindu legend and the German story alike possess a higher interest in the links which connect them, like most of the popular stories already noticed, with the magnificent epic to which we give the name of Homer, with the songs of the Volsungs and Nibelungs, with the mythical cycle of Arthur and Charlemagne, and the Persian Rustem. The bridal shirt of sulphur and pitch, which outwardly seemed a tissue of gold and silver, carries us at once from the story of Faithful John to the myth of

[1] The calamity which overtakes Luxman and Faithful John is seen in an earlier and less developed form in the German story of the Frog Prince. Here the faithful friend is overwhelmed with grief because his master is turned into a frog. But this transformation is merely the sinking of the sun into the western waters (see note 3, p. 166), and the time of his absence answers to the charmed sleep of Endymion. Trusty Henry is so grieved at the loss that he binds three iron bands round his heart, for fear it should break with grief and sorrow. When the Frog Prince sets out with his bride in the morning, the iron bands break and Trusty Henry is set free. This is the stony sleep of Luxman, brought on by grief, and broken only by the light touch of early morning, there represented by the innocent child of Rama.

Deïaneira and the poisoned coat which put an end to the career of Herakles. We enter again the charmed circle, where one and the same idea assumes a thousand different forms, where we can trace clearly the process by which one change led to another, but where any one disregarding the points of connection must fail to discern their sequence, origin, and meaning. In the legend of Deïaneira, as in that of Iasôn and Glaukê, the coat or shirt is laden with destruction even for Herakles. It represents, in fact, ' the clouds which rise from the waters and surround the sun like a dark raiment.' This robe Herakles tries to tear off, but the ' fiery mists embrace him, and are mingled with the parting rays of the sun, and the dying hero is seen through the scattered clouds of the sky, tearing his own body to pieces, till at last his bright form is consumed in a general conflagration.' [1] In the story of Medeia this robe is the gift of Helios, which imparts a marvellous wisdom to the daughter of the Kolchian king. It is the gleaming dress which reappears in story after story of Hindu folk-lore. ' That young rajah's wife,' people said, ' has the most beautiful saree we ever saw : it shines like the sun, and dazzles our eyes. We have no saree half so beautiful.' It is the golden fleece of the ram which bears away the children of the Mist (Nephelê) to the Eastern land. In other words, it is the light of Phoibos, the splendour of Helios, the rays or spears of the gleaming Sun. As such, it is identified with the sword of Apollo the Chrysâôr, with the sword which Aigeus leaves to be discovered by Theseus under the broad stone, with the good sword Gram which Odin left in the tree trunk for Volsung to draw out and wield, with the lion's skin of Herakles, with the jackal's skin worn by the enchanted rajahs of Hindu story, with the spear of Achilleus and the deadly arrows of Philoktêtês, with the invincible sword of Perseus and the sandals which bear him through the air like a dream, with the magic shoes in the story of King Patraka and of the Lad who went to the North Wind, with the spear of Artemis and the unerring darts of Meleagros. Whether under the guise of spears or fleece or arrows, it is the golden hair on the head of Phoibos

[1] Max Müller, *Chips from a German Workshop*, ii. 89.

Akersekomês, which no razor has ever touched. It is the wonderful carpet of Solomon, which figures in the Arabian Nights as the vehicle for relieving distressed lovers from their difficulties,[1] and bears away the Princess Aldegonda by the side of the Pilgrim of Love in the exquisite legend of the Alhambra.

· This story is, indeed, only a more beautiful form of the German and Hindu tales. Here, as in the other legends, special care is taken to guard the young prince against the dangers of love, and the lad grows up contentedly under the care of the sage Eben Bonabben, until he discovers that he wants something which speaks more to the heart than algebra. Like Balna in the tower or Helen in Ilion, he is prisoned in a palace from which he cannot get forth ; but the sage Bonabben has taught him the language of birds, and when the joyous time of spring comes round, he learns from a dove that love is 'the torment of one, the felicity of two, the strife and enmity of three.' The dove does more. She tells him of a beautiful maiden, far away in a delightful garden by the banks of the stream from which Arethousa, Daphnê, Athênê, Aphroditê, all are born ; but the garden is surrounded by high walls, within which none were permitted to enter. Here the dove's story, which answers to the picture seen in the German tale and the dream of Rama, connects the legends with the myths of Brynhild, Surya Bai, and other imprisoned damsels, whom one brave knight alone is destined to rescue. Once again the dove returns, but it is only to die at the feet of Ahmed, who finds under her wing the picture seen by the prince in the German story. Where to seek the maiden he knows not ; but the arrow of love is within his heart, and he cannot tarry. The princess too, to whom the dove had carried the message of Ahmed, is yearning to see him ; but she is surrounded by a troop of suitors as numerous as those which gather round Penelopê, and she must appear at a great tournament (the fight at Ilion) which is to decide who shall be her husband. But Ahmed, like Achilleus after the death of Patroklos, is unarmed ; how then can he think of encountering the valiant warriors who are hastening to the

[1] The story of Prince Ahmed and Pari Banou.

Marginal notes: CHAP. VIII. — The Pilgrim of Love.

contest? In this dilemma he is aided by an owl (the white
bird of Athênê), who tells him of a cavern (the cave in which
Zeus, Mithra, and Krishna alike are born) 'in one of the wildest
recesses of those rocky cliffs which rise around Toledo; none
but the mousing eye of an owl or an antiquary could have
discovered the entrance to it. A sepulchral lamp of everlasting oil shed a solemn light through the place. On an
iron table in the centre of the cavern lay the magic armour;
against it leaned the lance, and beside it stood an Arabian
steed, caparisoned for the field, but motionless as a statue.
The armour was bright and unsullied as it had gleamed in
days of old; the steed in as good condition as if just from
the pasture, and when Ahmed laid his hand upon his neck,
he pawed the ground and gave a loud neigh of joy that
shook the walls of the cavern.' Here we have not only the
magic armour and weapons of Achilleus, but the steed which
never grows old, and against which no human power can
stand. Probably Washington Irving, as he told the story
with infinite zest, thought little of the stories of Boots or of
Odysseus: but although Ahmed appears in splendid panoply
and mounted on a magnificent war-horse, yet he is as inso-
lently scouted by the suitors of Aldegonda as the Ithakan
chieftain in his beggar's dress was reviled by the suitors of
Penelopê. But the same retribution is in store for both.
Ahmed bears the irresistible weapons of Odysseus. No sooner
is the first blow struck against the Pilgrim of Love (for
Ahmed again like Odysseus and Herakles must be a wanderer) than the marvellous powers of the steed are seen.
'At the first touch of the magic lance the brawny scoffer
was tilted from his saddle. Here the prince would have
paused; but, alas! he had to deal with a demoniac horse
and armour—once in action nothing could control them.
The Arabian steed charged into the thickest of the throng;
the lance overturned everything that presented; the gentle
prince was carried pell-mell about the field, strewing it with
high and low, gentle and simple, and grieving at his own
involuntary exploits. The king stormed and raged at this
outrage on his subjects and his guests. He ordered out all
his guards—they were unhorsed as fast as they came up.

The king threw off his robes, grasped buckler and lance, and rode forth to awe the stranger with the presence of majesty itself. Alas! majesty fared no better than the vulgar—the steed and lance were no respecters of persons: to the dismay of Ahmed, he was borne full tilt against the king, and in a moment the royal heels were in the air, and the crown was rolling in the dust.' It could not be otherwise. The suitors must all fall when once the arrow has sped from the bow of Odysseus; but although the Ithakan chief was earnest in his revenge, the involuntary exploits of Ahmed are matched by many an involuntary deed of Herakles or Oidipous or Perseus. That the horse of Ahmed belongs to the same stock with the steeds of Indra it is impossible to doubt as we read the words of the Vedic poet :—

'These thy horses, excellent Vayu, strong of limb, youthful and full of vigour, bear thee through the space between heaven and earth, growing in bulk, strong as oxen; they are not lost in the firmament, but hold on their speed, unretarded by *reviling*; difficult are they to be arrested as the beams of the Sun.'[1] .

The incidents which follow present the same astonishing accordance with old Greek or Hindu traditions. No sooner has the sun reached the meridian than 'the magic spell resumed its power; the Arabian steed scoured across the plain, leaped the barrier, plunged into the Tagus, swam its raging current, bore the prince breathless and amazed to the cavern, and resumed his station like a statue beside the iron table.' The spell is, in fact, none other than that which sends the stone of Sisyphos rolling down the hill as soon as it has reached the summit; the Tagus is the old ocean stream into which Helios sinks at eventide, and the cave is the dark abode from which the wandering Sun had started in the morning, and to which he must come back at night. But further, Ahmed appears in the sequel as Paiêôn, the healer. Aldegonda is sick with love for the beautiful prince who has gladdened her eyes but for a few brief moments. In vain do hosts of physicians seek to cure her. The power to do so rests with Ahmed only, and the owl, coming to his aid as

[1] *Rig Veda Sanhita*, H. H. Wilson, vol. ii. p. 51.

zealously as Athênê Glaukopis (the owl-eyed or bright-
faced) to that of Odysseus, advises him to ask as his reward
the carpet of Solomon, on which he soars away with Aldegonda, like the children of Nephelê on the Golden Fleece.
The force of these astonishing parallelisms is certainly not
weakened by any suggestion that some of these incidents
may be found in legends of the Arabian Nights. The enchanted horse reappears in the Dapplegrim of Grimm's
German stories, in the steed which carries the Widow's Son
in the Norse tales, and the marvellous horse of Highland
tradition.[1]   In a burlesque aspect, it is the astonishing horse
in the Spanish story of Governor Munco,[2] who is outwitted
by the old soldier precisely as the Sultan of Cashmere is
outwitted by the possessor of the Enchanted Horse in the
Arabian Nights story.

The sleep
or death
of Sum-
mer.
In the Hindu story, as in the Spanish tale, the bride of
Rama is won after an exploit which in its turn carries us
away to the deeds of Hellenic or Teutonic heroes.   When
the prince tells Luxman of the peerless beauty whom he has
seen in his dream, his friend tells him that the princess lives
far away in a glass palace.[3]   'Round this palace runs a large
river, and round the river is a garden of flowers.   Round
the garden are four thick groves of trees.   The princess is
twenty-four years old, but she is not married, for she has
determined only to marry whoever can jump across the river
and greet her in her crystal palace; and though many
thousand kings have assayed to do so, they have all perished
miserably in the attempt, having either been drowned in the
river or broken their necks by falling.'   The frequent recurrence of this idea in these Hindu tales might of itself lead
any one who knew nothing of the subject previously to doubt
whether such images could refer to any actual facts in the
history of any given man or woman.   In the story of Rama
it has lost much of its old significance.   The death-like cold
of a northern winter gives place to the mere notion of solitude
and seclusion.   Running streams and luxuriant gardens show

[1] Campbell, *Tales of the West High-*
lands, 'The Young King of Easaidh
Ruadh.'
[2] Washington Irving, *Tales of the*
Alhambra.
[3] The glass or marble of the Hindu
tale answers to the ice of the Norse
legends.

that the myth has been long transferred to a more genial climate; but it is scarcely necessary to say that the changes in the story indefinitely enhance its value, so long as the idea remains the same. In some form or other this idea may be said to run through almost all these legends. In the story of ' Brave Seventee Bai ' it assumes a form more closely akin to the imagery of Teutonic mythology; and there we find a princess who declares that she will marry no one who has not leaped over her bath, which ' has high marble walls all round, with a hedge of spikes at the top of the walls.' In the story of Vicram Maharajah the parents of Anar Rance ' had caused her garden to be hedged round with seven hedges made of bayonets, so that none could go in nor out; and they had published a decree that none should marry her but he who could enter the garden and gather the three pomegranates on which she and her maids slept.' So, too, Panch Phul Ranee, the lovely Queen of the Five Flowers, ' dwelt in a little house, round which were seven wide ditches, and seven great hedges made of spears.' The seven hedges are, however, nothing more than the sevenfold coils of the dragon of the Glistening Heath, who lies twined round the beautiful Brynhild. But the maiden of the Teutonic tale is sunk in sleep which rather resembles death than life, just as Dêmêtêr mourned as if for the death of Persephonê while her child sojourned in the dark kingdom of Hades. This idea is reproduced with wonderful fidelity in the story of Little Surya Bai, and the cause of her death is modified in a hundred legends both of the East and the West. The little maiden is high up in the eagle's nest fast asleep, when an evil demon or Rakshas seeks to gain admission to her, and while vainly striving to force an entrance leaves one of his finger-nails sticking in the crack of the door. When on the following morning the maiden opened the doors of her dwelling to look down on the world below, the sharp claw ran into her hand, and immediately she fell dead. The powers of winter, which had thus far sought in vain to wound her, have at length won the victory; and at once we pass to other versions of the same myth, which tell us of Eurydikê stung to death by the hidden serpent, of Sifrit smitten by Hagene (the Thorn), of Isfendiyar slain by the thorn or arrow of Rustem, of Achilleus vulnerable only in his heel, of Brynhild enfolded within the dragon's coils, of Meleagros dying as the torch of doom is burnt out, of Baldur the brave and pure smitten by the fatal mistletoe, of the sweet Briar Rose plunged in her slumber of a hundred years.

The idea that all these myths have been deliberately transferred from Hindus or Persians to Greeks, Germans, and Norsemen may be dismissed as a wild dream.[1] Yet of their substantial identity in spite of all points of difference and under all the disguises thrown over them by individual fancies and local influences, there can be no question. The keynote of any one of the Deccan stories is the keynote of almost all; and this keynote runs practically through the great body of tales gathered from Germany, Scandinavia, Ireland, and Scotland. It is found again everywhere in the mythology of the Greeks, whether in the legends which have furnished the materials for their magnificent epics, or have been immortalised in the dramas of their great tragedians, or have remained buried in the pages of mythographers like Pausanias or Diodoros. If then all these tales have some historical foundation, they must relate to events which took place before the dispersion of the Aryan tribes from their original home. If the war at Troy took place at all, as the Homeric poets have narrated it, it is, to say the least, strange that precisely the same struggle, for precisely the same reasons, and with the same results, should have been waged in Norway and Germany, in Wales and Persia. The question must be more fully examined presently; but unless we are to adopt the hypothesis of conscious borrowing in its most exaggerated form, the dream of a historical Ilion and a historical Carduel must fade away before the astonishing multitude of legends which comparative mythologists have

[1] Of these stories, taken as a class, Professor Max Müller says 'that the elements or seeds of these fairy tales belong to the period that preceded the dispersion of the Aryan race; that the same people who, in their migrations to the north and the south, carried along with them the names of the sun and the dawn, and their belief in the bright gods of heaven, possessed in their very language, in their mythological and proverbial phraseology, the more or less developed germs, that were sure to grow up into the same or very similar plants on every soil and under every sky.'—*Chips*, ii. 226.

traced to phrases descriptive of physical phenomena. At the least it must be admitted that the evidence seems to point in this direction. To take these stories after any system, and arrange their materials methodically, is almost an impossible task. The expressions or incidents worked into these legends are like the few notes of the scale from which great musicians have created each his own world, or like the few roots of language which denoted at first only the most prominent objects and processes of nature and the merest bodily wants, but out of which has grown the wealth of words which feed the countless streams of human thought. In one story we may find a series of incidents briefly touched, which elsewhere have been expanded into a hundred tales, while the incidents themselves are presented in the countless combinations suggested by an exuberant fancy. The outlines of the tales, when these have been carefully analysed, are simple enough; but they are certainly not outlines which could have been suggested by incidents in the common life of mankind. Maidens do not fall for months or years into deathlike trances, from which the touch of one brave man alone can rouse them. Dragons are not coiled round golden treasures or beautiful women on glistening heaths. Princes do not everywhere abandon their wives as soon as they have married them, to return at length in squalid disguise and smite their foes with invincible weapons. Steeds which speak and which cannot die do not draw the chariots of mortal chiefs, nor do the lives of human kings exhibit everywhere the same incidents in the same sequence. Yet every fresh addition made to our stores of popular tradition does but bring before us new phases of those old forms of which mankind, we may boldly say, will never grow weary. The golden slipper of Cinderella is the slipper of Rhodôpis, which an eagle carries off and drops into the lap of the Egyptian king as he sits on his seat of judgement at Memphis.[1] This slipper reappears in the beautiful Deccan story of Sodewa Bai, and leads of course to the same issue as in the legends of Cinderella and Rhodôpis. The dragon of the Glistening Heath represents the seven-headed cobra of the Hindu story,

[1] Ælian, *V. H.* xiii. 33; Strabo, xvii. p. 808.

and in the legend of Brave Seventee Bai the beautiful Bryn-hild becomes his daughter, just as the bright Phoibos is the child of the sombre Leto. In the Greek myth dragons of another kind draw the chariot of Medeia, the child of the sun, or impart mysterious wisdom to Iamos and Melampous, as the cobras do to Muchie Lal. That the heroes of Greek and Teutonic legends in almost every case are separated from, or abandon, the women whom they have wooed or loved is well known; and the rajahs and princes of these Hindu stories are subjected to the same lot with Herakles and Odysseus, Oidipous and Sigurd, Kephalos and Prokris, Paris and Oinônê. Generally the newly-married prince feels a yearning to see his father and his mother once more, and, like Odysseus, pines until he can set his face homewards. Sometimes he takes his wife, sometimes he goes alone; but in one way or another he is kept away from her for years, and reappears like Odysseus in the squalid garb of a beggar.

Charms or spells in the Odyssey and in Hindu stories.
Curiously enough, in these Hindu stories the detention of the wandering prince or king is caused by one of those charms or spells which Odysseus in his wanderings discreetly avoids. The Lotos-eaters and their magic fruit reappear in the nautch-people or conjurors, whom the rajah who has married Panch Phul Ranee, the Lady of the Five Flowers, asks for rice and fire. The woman whom he addresses immediately brings them. ' But before she gave them to him, she and her companions threw on them a certain powder, containing a very potent charm; and no sooner did the rajah receive them than he forgot about his wife and little child, his journey and all that had ever happened to him in his life before: such was the peculiar property of the powder. And when the conjuror said to him, "Why should you go away? Stay with us and be one of us," he willingly consented.'[1] Unless the translator has designedly modified the language of the Deccan tale-teller (and in the absence of any admission to this effect we cannot

[1] This forgetfulness of his first love on the part of the solar hero is brought about in many of the German stories by his allowing his parents to kiss him on one side of his face, or on his lips. In the Gaelic story of the Battle of the Birds neither man nor other creature is to kiss him, and the mischief is done by his greyhound, who recognises him as Argos knows Odysseus. Campbell, i. 34.

suppose this), we may fairly quote the words as almost a paraphrase from the Odyssey:—

> τῶν δ' ὅτ τις λωτοῖο φάγοι μελιηδέα καρπόν,
> οὐκ ἔτ' ἀπαγγεῖλαι πάλιν ἤθελεν οὐδὲ νέεσθαι,
> ἀλλ' αὐτοῦ βούλοντο μετ' ἀνδράσι Λωτοφάγοισιν
> λωτὸν ἐρεπτόμενοι μενέμεν νόστου τε λαθέσθαι.[1]

The nautch-woman here has also the character of Kirkê, and the charm represents the φάρμακα λυγρά which turn the companions of Eurylochos into swine, while Kirkê's wand is wielded by the sorcerers who are compelled to restore to life the victims whom they had turned into stone, and by the Rakshas from whom Ramchundra, in the story of Truth's Triumph, seeks to learn its uses. 'The rod,' she replies, 'has many supernatural powers; for instance, by simply uttering your wish, and waving it in the air, you can conjure up a mountain, a river, or a forest, in a moment of time.' At length the wanderer is found; but Panch Phul Ranee and Seventee Bai have the insight of Eurykleia, and discern his true majesty beneath the fakeer's garb.[2] 'The rajah came

---

[1] *Od.* ix. 97.

[2] This garment of humiliation appears in almost innumerable legends. In the German story of the Golden Bird the prince puts it on when, on approaching his father's house, he is told that his brothers are plotting his death. In the tale of the Knapsack, the Hat, and the Horn, the wanderer who comes in with a coat torn to rags has a knapsack from which he can produce any number of men, and a horn (the horn of the Maruts) at whose blast the strongest walls fall down. He thus takes on his enemies a vengeance precisely like that of Odysseus, and for the same reason. In the story of the Golden Goose, Dummling, the hero who never fails in any exploit, is despised for his wretched appearance. In that of the Gold Child the brilliant hero comes before the king in the guise of a humble bear-hunter. The tale of the King of the Golden Mountain repeats the story of King Putraka, and shows the Gold Child in a shepherd's rugged frock. Elsewhere he is seen as the poor miller's son (the Miller's Son and the Cat), and he becomes a discharged soldier in the story of 'The Boots made of Buffalo Leather.' The beggar reappears in the Norse tale of Hacon Grizzlebeard, the Thrushbeard of Grimm's collection, while Boots, who grovels in the ashes, is the royal youth who rides up the mountain of ice in the story of the Princess on the Glass Hill. In another, Shortshanks, who by himself destroys all the Trolls opposed to him, is a reflection of Odysseus, not only in his vengeance, but in his bodily form. Odysseus is Shortshanks when compared with Menelaos (*Iliad* iii. 210-11). In the tale of the Best Wish (Dasont), Boots carries with him in the magic tap the horn of Amaltheia, and is seen again as a tattered beggar in the story of the Widow's Son. In the legend of Big Bird Dan he is the wandering sailor, who, like Odysseus, is tossed, worn and naked, on the Phaiakian shore; in that of Soria Moria Castle (a tale in which the Sun seeks for the Dawn, the reverso of the Psyché story) he is Halvor who grubs among the ashes—the connection with fire and light being never forgotten in these stories, for these ashes are always living embers. The adventure of Halvor is for the recovery of a Helen, who has been stolen away by a Troll; but no sooner is the Ilion or stronghold of the robber demolished than, like Odysseus, he begins to feel an irresistible

BOOK
I.

towards them so changed that not even his own mother knew him; no one recognised him but his wife. For eighteen years he had been among the nautch-people; his hair was rough, his beard untrimmed, his face thin and worn, sunburnt, and wrinkled, and his dress was a rough common blanket.' Can we possibly help thinking of the wanderer, who in his beggar's dress reveals himself to the swineherd—

ἔνδον μὲν δὴ ὅδ' αὐτὸς ἐγώ, κακὰ πολλὰ μογήσας,
ἤλυθον εἰκοστῷ ἔτεῖ ἐς πατρίδα γαῖαν.¹

or of his disguise, when Athênê

ξανθὰς ἐκ κεφαλῆς ὄλεσε τρίχας, ἀμφὶ δὲ δέρμα
πάντεσσιν μελέεσσι παλαιοῦ θῆκε γέροντος,
κνύζωσεν δέ οἱ ὄσσε πάρος περικαλλέ' ἐόντε·
ἀμφὶ δέ μιν ῥάκος ἄλλο κακὸν βάλεν ἠδὲ χιτῶνα
ῥωγαλέα ῥυπόωντα, κακῷ μεμορυγμένα καπνῷ.²

and lastly of his recognition by his old nurse when she saw the wound made by the bite of the boar who slew Adonis? So in the Vengeance of Chandra we see the punishment of the suitors by Odysseus, an incident still further travestied in Grimm's legend of the King of the Golden Mountain. So too as we read of the body of Chundun Rajah, which remained undecayed though he had been dead many months, or of Sodewa Bai, who a month after her death looked as lovely as on the night on which she died, we are reminded of the bodies of Patroklos³ and of Hektor⁴ which Aphroditê or Apollôn anointed with ambrosial oil, and guarded day and night from all unseemly things.

The Snake
Leaves.

But though the doom of which Achilleus mournfully complained to Thetis lies on all or almost all of these bright beings, they cannot be held in the grasp of the dark power which has laid them low. Briar-Rose and Surya Bai start from their slumbers at the magic touch of the lover's hand, and even when all hope seemed to be lost, wise beasts provide an antidote which will bring back life to the dead. In the story of Panch Phul Rance these beneficent physicians are jackals, who converse together like the owls of Luxman or

longing to see his father and his home once more.
    The story of Shortshanks is told in the Gaelic tale of the Sea-Maiden,

Campbell, i. 101.
¹ Od. xvi. 207, xxi. 208.
² Ibid. xiii. 435, xvi. 175.
³ Il. xix. 32.   ⁴ Ib. xxiv. 20.

the crows in the tale of Faithful John. 'Do you see this
tree?' says the jackal to his wife. 'Well, if its leaves were
crushed, and a little of the juice put into the rajah's two ears
and upon his upper lip, and some upon his temples also, and
some upon the spear-wound in his side, he would come to
life again, and be as well as ever.' These leaves reappear in
Grimm's story of the Three Snake Leaves, in which the
snakes play the part of the jackals. In this tale a prince is
buried alive with his dead wife, and seeing a snake approaching her body, he cuts it in three pieces. Presently another
snake, crawling from the corner, saw the other lying dead,
and going away soon returned with three green leaves in its
mouth; then, laying the parts of the body together, so as to
join, it put one leaf on each wound, and the dead snake was
alive again. The prince applying the leaves to his wife's
body restores her also to life. The following are the words
of Apollodoros in relating the story, also told by Ælian, of
Glaukos and Polyidos:—'When Minos said that he must
bring Glaukos to life, Polyidos was shut up with the dead
body; and, being sorely perplexed, he saw a dragon approach
the corpse. This he killed with a stone, and another dragon
came, and, seeing the first one dead, went away, and brought
some grass, which it placed on the body of the other, which
immediately rose up. Polyidos, having beheld this with
astonishment, put the same grass on the body of Glaukos,
and restored him to life.'[1]

These magic leaves become a root in the German story of The Two
the Two Brothers, a tale in which a vast number of solar Brothers.
myths have been rolled together. The two brothers, 'as like
one another as two drops of water,' are the Dioskouroi and
the Asvins, or the other twin deities which run through so
large a portion of the Aryan mythology. They are also the

[1] Apollodoros, iii. 3, 1. Mr. Gould, referring to this story as introduced in Fouqué's 'Sir Elidoc,' places these flowers or leaves in the large class of things which have the power of restoring life, or splitting rocks, or opening the earth and revealing hidden treasures. The snake leaves represent in short the worms or stones which shatter rocks, the sesame which opens the robbers' cave, and finally the vulgar hand of glory, which, when set on fire, aids the treasure-seeker in his search. All these fables Mr. Gould refers to one and the same object—lightning; and thus a multitude of popular stories again resolve themselves into phrases origin-ally denoting merely physical pheno-mena. *Curious Myths of the Middle Ages*, second series, p. 145, &c.

Babes in the Wood, although it is their father himself who,
at the bidding of his rich brother, thrusts them forth from
their home, because a piece of gold falls from the mouth of
each every morning. They are saved by a huntsman, who
makes them marksmen as expert as Kastor and Polydeukes.
When at length they set out on their adventures, the huntsman gives them a knife, telling them that if, in case of separation, they would stick it into a tree by the wayside, he who
came back to it might learn from the brightness or the rusting
of the blade whether the other is alive and well. If the tale
thus leads us to the innumerable stories which turn on sympathetic trees, gems, and stones, it is not less noteworthy as
bringing before us almost all the brute animals, whose names
were once used as names of the sun. The two brothers lift
their weapons to shoot a hare, which, begging for life,
promises to give up two leverets. The hare is suffered to go
free, and the huntsmen also spare the leverets, which follow
them. The same thing happens with a fox, wolf, bear, and
lion, and thus the youths journey, attended each by five
beasts, until they part, having fixed the knife into the trunk
of a tree. The younger, like Perseus, comes to a town where
all is grief and sorrow because the king's daughter is to be
given up on the morrow to be devoured by a dragon on the
summit of the dragon's mountain. Like Theseus and Sigurd,
the young man becomes possessed of a sword buried beneath
a great stone, and, like Perseus, he delivers the maiden by
slaying the dragon. Then on the mountain-top the youth
rests with the princess, having charged his beasts to keep
watch, lest any one should surprise them. But the victory
of the sun is followed by the sleep of winter, and the lion,
overcome with drowsiness, hands over his charge to the bear,
the bear to the wolf, the wolf to the fox, the fox to the hare,
until all are still. The Marshal of the kingdom, who here
plays the part of Paris, now ascends the mountain, and,
cutting off the young man's head, leads away the princess,
whom, as the dragon-slayer, he claims as his bride. At
length the sleep of the lion is broken by the sting of a bee,
and the beast rousing the bear asks the reason of his failing
to keep watch. The charge is passed from one beast to the

other, until the hare, unable to utter a word in its defence,
begs for mercy, as knowing where to find a root which, like
the snake leaves, shall restore their master to life. A year has
passed away, and the young man, again approaching the town
where the princess lived, finds it full of merriment, because
she is going on the morrow to be married to the Marshal.
But the time of his humiliation is now past. The huntsman
in his humble hostel declares to the landlord that he will
this day eat of the king's bread, meat, vegetables, and
sweetmeats, and drink of his finest wine. These are severally brought to him by the five beasts, and the princess, thus
learning that her lover is not dead, advises the king to send
for the master of these animals. The youth refuses to come
unless the king sends for him a royal equipage, and then,
arrayed in royal robes, he goes to the palace, where he convicts
the Marshal of his treachery by exhibiting the dragon's tongues
which he had cut off and preserved in a handkerchief bestowed on him by the princess, and by showing the necklace, of
which she had given a portion to each of his beasts, and
which is, in fact, the necklace of Freya and the Kestos or
cestus of Aphrodite. But the tale is not told out yet, and it
enters on another cycle of the sun's career. The youth is no
sooner married to the princess than, like Odysseus or Sigurd,
he is separated from her. Following a white doe into a forest,
he is there deceived by a witch, at whose bidding he touches
his beasts with a twig, and turns them into stones, and is then
changed into a stone himself. Just at this time the younger
brother returns to the place where the knife, now partially
covered with rust, remained fixed in the tree. He becomes,
of course, as in the myth of Baldur, the avenger of his
brother, and the witch undergoes the doom of Punchkin or of
the Giant who had no heart in his body; but when he tells the
younger brother that even his wife had taken him to be her
husband, and admitted him into her chamber, the latter cuts
off the elder's head. The magic root is again brought into
use, and he learns how faithful his brother had been when
his wife asks him why, on the two previous nights, he had
placed a sword in the bed between them. The story thus, in

M 2

BOOK
1.

Myths of
the Night,
the Moon,
and the
Stars.

its last incident, runs into the tales of Sigurd and the Arabian Allah-ud-deen.[1]

If we sought to prove the absolute identity of the great mass of Hindu, Greek, Norse, and German legends, we surely need go no further. Yet there are other points of likeness, at least as striking as any that have been already noticed, between the stories which in the East and West alike relate to the phenomena of night. In the Hindu tale the disguised wife of Logedas Rajah finds Tara Bai on a gold and ivory throne. 'She was tall and of a commanding aspect. Her black hair was bound by long strings of pearls, her dress was of fine-spun gold, and round her waist was clasped a zone of restless, throbbing, light-giving diamonds. Her neck and her arms were covered with a profusion of costly jewels, but brighter than all shone her bright eyes, which looked full of gentle majesty.' But Tara Bai is the star (boy) child, or maiden, the Asteropaios of the Iliad, of whom the Greek myth said only that he was the tallest of all their men, and that he was slain after fierce fight by Achilleus, whom he had wounded.[2] Elsewhere she reappears as Polydeukes, the glittering twin brother of Kastor, and more particularly as the fairy Melusina, who is married to Raymond of Toulouse. This beautiful being, who has a fish's tail, as representing the moon which rises and sets in the sea, vanishes away when her full form is seen by her husband.[3] In another phase she is Kalypsô, the beautiful night which veils the sun from mortal eyes in her chamber flashing with a thousand stars, and lulls to sleep the man of many griefs and wanderings.[4] Lastly, she is St. Ursula, with her eleven thousand virgins (the myriad stars), whom Cardinal Wiseman, in a spirit worthy of Herodotos, transforms into a company, or

[1] The Norse tale of Shortshanks (Dasent) is made up in great part of the materials of this story.
[2] Il. xxi. 166, &c.
[3] The name Melusina is identified by Mr. Gould with that of the Babylonian Mylitta, the Syrian moon-goddess.— Curious Myths of the Middle Ages, second series, 'Melusina.'
  Mr. Gould, in his delightful chapter on this subject, connects Melusina, as first seen close to a fountain, with the Vedic Apsaras, or water-maidens, of Vedic mythology, and the swan maidens of Teutonic legend. She thus belongs to the race of Naiads, Nixies, and Elves, the latter name denoting a running stream, as the Elbe, the Alpheios. The fish's or serpent's tail is not peculiar to Melusina, and her attributes are also shared with the Assyrian fish-gods, and the Hellenic Proteus.
[4] Od. v. 60, &c.

rather two companies, of English ladies, martyred by the
Huns at Cologne, but whose mythical home is on Horselberg, where the faithful Eckhart is doomed to keep his weary
watch. Labouring on in his painful rationalism, Cardinal
Wiseman tells us of one form of the legend which mentions
a marriage-contract, made with the father of St. Ursula, a very
powerful king, how it was arranged that she should have
eleven companions, and each of these a thousand followers.'[1]
There are thus twelve, in addition to the eleven thousand
attendants, and these twelve reappear in the Hindu tales,
sometimes in dark, sometimes in lustrous forms, as the
twelve hours of the day or night, or the twelve moons of the
lunar year. Thus in the story of Truth's Triumph a rajah
has twelve wives, but no children. At length he marries
Guzra Bai, the flower girl, who bears him a hundred sons
and one daughter; and the sequel of the tale relates the
result of their jealousy against these children and their
mother. Their treacherous dealing is at last exposed, and
they suffer the fate of all like personages in the German and
Norse tales.

There is, in fact, no end to the many phases assumed by
the struggle of these fairy beings, which is the warfare
between light and darkness. But the bright beings always
conquer in the end, and return like Persephonê from the
abode of Hades to gladden the heart of the Mater Dolorosa.[2]
The child in the Deccan stories appears not only as Guzra
Bai, but as Panch Phul Ranee, as Surya Bai, as the wife of
Muchie Lal, the fish or frog-sun.[3] All these women are the

The battle of light and darkness.

[1] *Essays on Religion and Literature,* edited by Abp. Manning (1865), p. 252.
[2] Grote, *History of Greece,* i. 55.
[3] The frog prince or princess is only one of the thousand personifications of names denoting originally the phenomena of day and night. As carrying the morning light from the east to the west, the sun is the bull bearing Európê from the purple land (Phoinikia); and the same changes which converted the Seven Shiners into the Seven Sages, or the Seven Sleepers of Ephesus, or the Seven Champions of Christendom, or the Seven Bears, transformed the sun into a wolf, a boar, a lion, a swan. As resting on

the horizon in 'the morning,' he is Apollôn swathed by the water-maidens in golden bands, or the wounded and forsaken Oidipous; as lingering again on the water's edge before he vanishes from sight, he is the frog squatting on the water, a homely image of Endymion and Narkissos. In this aspect the sun is himself an apsara, or water-maiden; and thus the Sanskrit Bheki is a beautiful girl, whom a king wins to be his wife on the condition that he is not to let her see a drop of water. Of course the king one day forgets his promise, shows her water, and Bheki vanishes. This is the counterpart to

BOOK
I.

daughters of a gardener or a milkwoman, in whom we see the image of Dêmêtêr, the bountiful earth, who lavishes on her children her treasures of fruits, milk, and flowers. In her hand she holds her mystic cup, into which falls the ripe mango, which is her child transformed, as the ripe fruit falls on the earth. This cup, again, is the horn of Amaltheia, the table of the Ethiopians, of which Herodotos speaks as laden continually with all good things, the cup into which Helios sinks each night when his course is run, the modios of Serapis, the ivory ewer containing the book of Solomon's occult knowledge, which Rehoboam placed in his father's tomb, the magic oil-bowl or lamp of Allah-ud-deen, and finally the San-Greal which furnishes to the knights of Arthur's round table as splendid a banquet as their hearts can desire.

Character
of Aryan
folklore.

It is scarcely necessary to go further. If we do, we shall only be confronted by the same astonishing parallelism which is exhibited by the several versions of the stories already cited. The hypothesis of conscious borrowing is either superfluous or dangerous. It is unnecessary, if adduced to

the legend of Melusina, who also dies if seen in the water. The sun and moon must alike sink when they reach the western sea. 'This story,' says Professor Max Müller, 'was known at the time when Kapila wrote his philosophical aphorisms in India, for it is there quoted as an illustration. But long before Kapila, the story of Bheki must have grown up gradually, beginning with a short saying about the sun—such as that Bheki, the sun, will die at the sight of water, as we should say that the sun will set when it approaches the water from which it rose in the morning.'— *Chips from a German Workshop*, ii. 248. In the Teutonic version, the change of the sun into the form of a frog is the result of enchantment; but the story of the Frog Prince has more than one point of interest. The frog is compelled to jump into the fountain, out of which only the youngest daughter of the king has the power of drawing him. These daughters again are the companions of Ursula; the daughters of the rajah who are jealous of their youngest sister; the hours of the night, sombre in their beauty, and envious of the youngest and

the fairest of all the hours, the hour of the dawn, which alone can bring the frog prince out of the pond. In the German story the enchantment can be ended only by the death of the frog; but this answers to the burning of the enchanted rajah's jackal skin in the Hindu tale. The sun leaping fully armed into the heaven as Chrysâôr might well be another being from the infant whom the nymphs swathe with golden bands in his gleaming cradle. The warrior comes to life on the death of the child, and the frog on being dashed against the wall becomes a beautiful prince. Of course he takes away his bride, 'early in the morning as soon as the sun rose, in a carriage drawn by eight white horses with ostrich feathers on their heads, and golden bridles,' the Harits who draw the car of Indra, the glistening steeds of Helios, the undying horses who are yoked to the chariot of Achilleus. But with Achilleus comes Patroklos; and as Luxman attends on Rama, so 'Trusty Henry' who comes with the carriage of the Frog Prince, represents the Faithful John of the Teutonic legend. (See note [1], p. 149.)

explain the distant or vague resemblances in one story, while they who so apply it admit that it cannot account for the far more striking points of likeness seen in many others. It is dangerous because it may lead us to infer an amount of intercourse between the separated Aryan tribes for which we shall vainly seek any actual evidence. It is inadequate, because in a vast number of instances the point to be explained is not a similarity of ideas, but a substantial identity in the method of working them out, extending to the most unexpected devices and the subtlest turns of thought and expression. That the great mass of popular tradition has been thus imported from the East into the West, or from the West into the East, has never been maintained; and any such theory would rest on the assumption that the folklore of a country may be created by a few scholars sitting over their books, and deliberately determining the form in which their stories shall be presented to the people. It would be safer to affirm, and easier to prove, that no popular stories have thus found their way from learned men to the common people. The ear of the people has in all ages been dead to the charming of the scholars, charm they never so wisely. Bookmen may, if they please, take up and adapt the stories of the people; but the legend of ' the Carter, the Dog, and the Sparrow' would never have found its way into the nurseries of German peasants if written by Grimm himself in imitation of some other Aryan tale. The importation of one or two stories by means of written books is therefore a matter of very slight moment, so long as it is admitted that legends, displaying the most astonishing parallelism in the most distant countries of Europe and Asia, cannot be traced to any intercourse of the tribes subsequent to their dispersion from a common home. We thus have before us a vast mass of myths, fables, legends, stories, or by whatever name they are to be called, some in a form not much advanced beyond the proverbial saying which was their kernel, others existing apparently only as nursery tales, others containing the germs of the great epics of the Eastern and the Western world. All these may be placed together in one class, as springing from phrases which at first denoted

physical phenomena ; and enough has perhaps been already
said to show that this class includes a very large proportion
of strictly popular stories which seem at first sight to be in
no way connected with epical mythology. There remain
the comparatively few stories which seem to have had their
origin in proverbs or adages ; and it is, of course, possible
that some or all of these may belong to those more recent
times when men had attained to some notion of the order of
a moral world, to some idea of law and duty. But it is impossible not to see that some at least of these stories turn on
notions suggested by the older mythical speech. The dog
and the parrot in the stories of the Carter and the Nautch-
girl are weak things which bring down the pride of those
who oppress the helpless; but this is simply the character
and the office of Boots in Teutonic stories, and Boots and
Cinderella, Oidipous and Herakles, alike represent the sun,
who, weak and powerless as he starts on his course, is at
length victorious over all his enemies. The phenomena of
nature present analogies to the order of the moral world,
which are perhaps closer than theologians have imagined.
If the words which we use to denote the most abstract ideas
were at first mere names of sensible things,[1] the phrases
which described the processes of nature must be capable of
receiving a moral meaning. The story of the sun starting
in weakness and ending in victory, waging a long warfare
against darkness, clouds, and storms, and scattering them all
in the end, is the story of all heroism, of all patient self-
sacrifice, of all Christian devotion. There is, therefore,
nothing to surprise us if the phrases which we use with a
spiritual meaning, and the proverbs in which we sum up
our spiritual experience, should have been suggested by the
very phenomena which furnished the groundwork of Aryan
epic poetry. The tendency of physical science is to resolve
complex agencies into a single force : the science of language
seems to be doing the same work for the words and the
thoughts of men.

Historical
value of
But the story of the heroes of Teutonic and Hindu folk-
lore, the stories of Boots and Cinderella, of Logedas Rajah,

[1] See p. 31, &c.

and Surya Bai, are the story also of Achilleus and Oidipous, CHAP
of Perseus and Theseus, of Helen and Odysseus, of Baldur VIII.
and Rustem and Sigurd. Everywhere there is the search Aryan
for the bright maiden who has been stolen away, everywhere popular
traditions.
the long struggle to recover her. The war of Ilion has been
fought out in every Aryan land. Either, then, the historical
facts which lie at the root of the narrative of the Iliad took
place before the dispersion of the Aryan tribes from their
common home, or they are facts which belong to the beautiful cloudland, where the misty Ilion 'rises into towers' at
early dawn. In either case the attempts recently made to
exhibit the war in the plains of Troy to the south of the
Hellespont as an historical reality are rendered plausible
only by ignoring the real point at issue.

CHAPTER IX.

MODERN EUEMERISM.

The Method of Euêmeros.
WHATEVER may have been the sins of Euêmeros against truth and honesty, his method aimed simply at the extraction of historical facts from the legends of his country by stripping them altogether of their supernatural character, and rejecting all the impossible or improbable incidents related in them. Making no pretence of access to documents more trustworthy than the sources from which the poets had drawn their inspiration, he claimed to be regarded as a historian, merely because, after depriving him of all divine powers, he left Zeus a mortal man, who, for benefits done to his fellows, was worshipped as a god.[1]

Its results.
Although in more recent times this system has been eagerly adopted and obstinately maintained, Euêmeros was not popular among his countrymen. To them the process which reduced the gods to the level of mankind seemed to resolve itself into mere atheism. Still, except as applying his method to the stories of the gods as well as to the legends

---

[1] For a detailed account of Euêmeros, see Grote, *History of Greece*, part i. ch. xvi. His method has been reproduced in all its completeness or nakedness in the article on Mythology inserted in the *Encyclopædia Britannica*. Having told us that 'the adventures of Jupiter, Juno, Mercury, Apollo, Diana, Minerva or Pallas, Venus, Bacchus, Ceres, Proserpine, Pluto, Neptune, and the other descendants and coadjutors of the ambitious family of the Titans, furnish by far the greatest part of the mythology of Greece,' the writer with prodigious assurance adds, 'They left Phœnicia, we think, in the days of Moses; they settled in Crete, a large and fertile island; from this region they made their way into Greece.' There they introduced art, religion, law, custom, polity, and good order; but, oddly enough, in spite of all these wholesome and sobering influences, the Greeks remained a 'deluded rabble, who insisted on paying them divine honours.' The mere enunciation of such absurdities is disgraceful in any work which professes to speak to educated readers, and would deserve even a severer condemnation if addressed to the unlearned. But it is altogether inexcusable, in an article to which are affixed references to the works of Grimm, K. O. Müller, Max Müller, Hermann, and others. For the amusing Euemerism of the Abbé Banier, see Max Müller, *Lectures*, second series, 400.

·of the epical heroes, he gave no cause of offence which had
not already been given by Herodotos and Thucydides. To
the historian of the Persian war the legends of Iô and
Eurôpê, of Medeia and Helen, were valuable simply as
supplying links in the chain of human causes which led to
that great struggle. For this purpose he either availed
himself of the least improbable versions of these myths
current in his own day, or he placed the myths, full as they
were of dragons and speaking heifers, into the crucible of
probabilities, and was rewarded with a residuum of plausible
fiction which would have gladdened the heart of De Foe.
This method, as applied by Thucydides to the story of the
Trojan war, produces results which make it difficult to believe
that his knowledge of that strife was obtained only from the
poems which told of the wrongs and woes of Helen. Yet so
it is. Although in these poems their career was inwoven
into the whole fabric of the narrative, Helen is gone, and
Paris and Achilleus; Hektôr and Sarpêdôn have vanished,
with Memnôn and Athênê and Aphroditê; and there remains
only a. chieftain who undertakes the expedition not at all to
rescue a woman who may never have existed, and a war
which lasted ten years, not because Zeus so willed it,[1] but
because want of men made it necessary that part of the
forces should betake themselves to tilling the ground and
raising crops on the Thrakian Chersonesos, while the rest
carried on the siege.[2]

That such a method should find favour at the present day
with writers who have made themselves in any degree acquainted with the results of comparative grammar is indeed
astonishing. Argynnis and Phoroneus, Brisêis and Achilleus,
Paris and Helen, names of persons in Hellenic legend, are in
the earliest songs of the Aryan family found still in their
original application as names of the morning, of the sun, or
of darkness; and as it is with these, so is it also with Ker-
beros and the Charites, with Orthros, with Varuṇa, and Zeus
himself. That these names and these tales could have over-
run the world from chance, or that the incidents which they
relate could have a distinct historical foundation in a series

Its antagonism with the science of language.

[1] *Iliad*, ii. 328.   [2] Thucyd. i. 9-11.

of incidents occurring in the same sequence and with the same results in every Aryan land, are positions which few would now venture to maintain; yet such were the theories which attempted, with some show of reason, to account for their origin and diffusion before the sciences of comparative grammar and mythology came into being. There can scarcely be a greater extravagance of credulity than that which frames an infinite series of the most astounding miracles in the vain effort to solve mysteries which must all be opened by one and the same key, or by none. No absurdity needs to startle us if we are ready to believe that four or five independent writers could describe a series of events in exactly the same words; [1] it is, if possible, even more absurd to suppose that tribes, savage and civilised, many of them utterly unknown to each other, should hit upon the same stories, should disfigure them by the same indecencies, should atone for these blots by the same images of touching pathos and grace and beauty. Yet some such demand is made on our powers of belief by a writer who holds that 'they who literally accept Scripture cannot afford to, ridicule mythology,' and who, looking about for traces of an historical character in Greek mythical tradition, concludes that 'there are the fairest reasons for supposing that Hercules was not an allegorical hero, typical of ideal prowess, endurance, and physical strength; but a real man, who, living in very remote times, and in some part of the world where the land was infested with savage beasts and perhaps the sea with pirates, earned the gratitude of a defenceless people by clearing earth and sea of monsters, as a remarkably uniform tradition ascribes to him. The Cyclopes were probably a race of pastoral and metal-working people from the East, characterised by their rounder faces, whence

[1] In the supposed case of a number of special correspondents sending home to English journals accounts of a battle or a campaign, the narrative of which was in all nearly word for word the same in several passages, Mr. Froude says that, 'were the writers themselves, with their closest friends and companions, to swear that there had been no intercommunication, and no story pre-existing of which they had made use, and that each had written *bonâ fide* from his own original observation, an English jury would sooner believe the whole party perjured than persuade themselves that so extraordinary a coincidence could have occurred.'—*Short Studies on Great Subjects*, i. 246.

It is enough to say that the application of any such hypothesis of independent origination to the mythology of the Aryan nations involves difficulties, if possible, still more stupendous.

arose the story of their one eye.' In the myth of Atlas, the CHAP.'
same writer thinks it 'impossible to doubt that we have a IX.
tradition of the Garden of Eden.' If it be said that these
traditions are common to many nations, he is ready with the
reply that the real Herakles or the real Theseus lived very
long ago, and that the other nations got these, as they got
most of their mythical heroes, from the Etruscans. We find
'Adrastus, Tydeus, Odysseus, Meleagros, Polydeuces, written
Atresthc, Tute, Utwye, Melacre, Pultuke; and similarly Agamemnon, Thetis, Perseus, Polynices, Telephus, represented by
Achmien, Thethis, Pharse, Phulnike, Thelaphe. So Apollo
is Apulu, Hercules is Ercule, Alexander is Elchentre.' It
might as well be said that English names are French in
their origin because London and Dover are written Londres
and Douvres, and Sir Humphry Davy has been designated
'Sromfredévé.' It can scarcely be maintained with serious-
ness that that which is only in part obscure, and elsewhere
is wonderfully luminous, can be illustrated by what is utterly
dark. These names in their Etruscan dress have absolutely
no meaning; in their Greek form most of them are transparent. · But when Achilleus is found in Greek and Aharyu in
Sanskrit tradition, when Brisêis reappears as the child of Brisaya, Helen as Saramâ, Ouranos as Varuṇa, Orthros as Vritra,
and when the meaning of these names is perfectly plain, we
are forced to the conclusion that no explanation can be
received which does not apply to Greek, Sanskrit, and Teutonic names alike. It would be more reasonable, failing this,
to fall back upon the ingenious theory by which Lord Bacon,
in his 'Wisdom of the Ancients,' converted the whole cycle
of Greek legend into wholesome advice for princes, cabinet
ministers, and heads of families.[1]

[1] *Home and Foreign Review*, No. VII.
p. 111, 1864. It is possible, and even
likely, that the distinguished critic whose
well-known initials appended to this
article make it unnecessary to keep up
any disguise may have modified or
rejected these conclusions. It is unnecessary to say that among modern
thinkers none can be found actuated by
a more earnest and single-minded desire
to ascertain the truth of facts without
regard to any secondary considerations

than Mr. Paley. If he has examined
the question since the time when his
article appeared in the *Home and
Foreign Review*, he will probably have
seen, with Professor Max Müller
(*Lectures on the Science of Language*,
second series, ix.), that we cannot
accept any etymology for a Greek name
which is not equally applicable to the
corresponding terms in Sanskrit and
Latin.

BOOK
I.

The
science of
language
in its
bearing
on history.
But the science which traces both the names of Greek mythical heroes and the incidents in their career to the earlier forms in which their original signification becomes . apparent, completely strips of all historical character the localised wars of Troy or Thebes, and the traditions which speak of Kolchis as the scene of the exploits of Iasôn. It is possible that there may have been a war undertaken to avenge the wrongs of an earthly Helen; that this war lasted ten years, and that ten years more were spent by the chiefs in their return homewards; that the chief incident in this war was the quarrel of the greatest of all the heroes with a mean-spirited king, a quarrel in which a truce of gloomy inaction is followed by the magnificent victory and early death of the hero. But if such a war took place, it must be carried back to a time preceding the dispersion of the Aryan tribes from their original home, and its scene can be placed neither in the land of the Five Streams, nor on the plains of the Asiatic Troy, not in Germany or Norway or Wales. The comparison of the Aryan languages sufficiently establishes these con-clusions; but the denial of any historical character to the general narrative of the Trojan war, as given whether by the Attic tragedians or by our so-called Homeric poems (be these earlier or later than the days of Æschylos and Sophokles), makes it a matter of justice to examine patiently and im-partially the arguments and alleged facts adduced by those who still maintain the positions of Euêmeros with regard to the story told in all its supernatural detail in the Iliad, and pared down to the plausible prosiness of Robinson Crusoe by Thucydides.

At the outset it may be safely affirmed that undue stress has been laid on the Wolfian theory respecting the origin and structure of the Iliad as affecting the attitude of historical critics at the present day towards the momentous topic of Homeric credibility. There is really no ground for the notion that doubts as to the historical credibility of the poems to which we give the name of Homer can be entertained only by those who accept the position of Wolf and his followers. The Wolfian theory, to speak briefly, maintains that the Iliad is made up of a number of songs which existed at first

as detached poems, and which were handed down from gene- CHAP.
ration to generation by a school of rhapsodists or professional IX.
minstrels. It was not, therefore, the work of any one man,
and possibly not even of any one age. This conclusion is
grounded partly on the absence of writing at and long after
the time when these poems first came into existence, and in
part on the incoherence and contradictions which an examination of the poems brings prominently into view. It follows
that there was no one author of the Iliad, or in other words,
that Homer is a name, not a person. This hypothesis has
found its extreme expression in the 'Klein-lieder Theorie' of
Köchly.

But if this notion were exploded utterly,[1] the real question The real
at issue would probably be in no degree affected. Thus, question at
issue.
although Mr. Grote may have affirmed that 'Homer is no
individual man, but the divine or heroic father of the gentle
Homerids,'[2] he nowhere argues from this statement as a pre-
miss, while he is careful to add that the Odyssey is indubitably one poem·written by one man, and that the Iliad in its
present form, although it contains an Ilias and an Achilléis
combined, is probably the work of one and the same poet,
who pieced together two compositions which he had wrought
out for two different purposes. If we further take his conclusion, that the Odyssey in all likelihood was not composed
by the author of the Iliad, even then we have only two, or
at the utmost only three poets, to whom we are indebted for
the great Greek epics which have been handed down to us.
Whether these conclusions are hasty or extravagant, whether

[1] At present it cannot be regarded as
exploded at all. Dr. Latham's words
have here great weight:—'The Wolfian
doctrine of the rhapsodic character of
the Homeric poems, had the existing
state of knowledge been sufficient for
the criticism, would scarcely have been
paradox. As it was, it dealt with the
Iliad and Odyssey as ordinary epics,
comparing them only with those of
Virgil, Tasso, Ariosto, Camoens, Er-
cilla, and Milton: epics of which the
single-handed authorship was a patent
historical event, as clear as that of the
authorship of Falconer's Shipwreck or
Glover's Leonidas. The fact that was

either not recognised or not promul-
gated was, the essentially rhapsodic
character of all known poems belonging
to that stage of civilisation to which the
Homeric compositions are referred.
With the recognition of this, the method, as the details, of the criticism
wants changing; and it is not so much
a question whether the facts in the
structure of two wonderful poems justify
the hypothesis that they arose out of the
agglutination of rhapsodies, but whether
there is even a presumption against their
having done so.'—Nationalities of Europe,
i. 207.
[2] History of Greece, part i. ch. xxi.

they run counter to the evidence of facts or are opposed to common sense, it is clear that the poems are not invested with more of a historical character because we hold that they are the work of three or two authors, or of one. Such a result is impossible, unless we can prove that the poet (or poets) lived in or near to the time of which the history is professedly narrated, and if his (or their) statements are borne out by other contemporary writers. If the story which the poet relates had come down from a period remote even in his day—if its general character, both in the causes and the sequence of incidents, exhibits a close resemblance to the traditions of distant countries with which the Hellenic tribes could not possibly have had any intercourse—if the very names of the actors and the deeds attributed to them are found in the legends of other lands or other ages—we are obviously just where we were before, so far as the attainment of historical fact is concerned, even when we have succeeded in proving that there was only one Homer, and that he was born at Smyrna. Whether we believe in twenty Homers or in one is, in one sense, a matter of supreme indifference in comparison with the inquiry which is to determine whether the events recorded in the poems are to be considered historical.

Residuum of historical fact in the Iliad. On such a subject as this all reference to consequences is out of place, and of itself suffices to show that we are not actuated wholly and solely by a disinterested and unswerving resolution to reach, so far as may be in our power, the truth of facts. The question must be treated altogether as one of evidence only, and no pain which we may feel at the possible necessity of parting with old associations should have the slightest weight with us. Even if we had to abandon a rich inheritance of poetical beauty; the sacrifice ought to be cheerfully made. The fear that any such sacrifice will be demanded of us is idle and groundless; but for those who deny the historical credibility of the Iliad or Odyssey it is necessary to know how much of real history their opponents suppose these poems to contain. Happily, this question is answered with most satisfactory clearness by the latest and the most strenuous of the champions of the traditional theory.

In the belief of Mr. Blackie, the residuum of fact is, it seems, this: 'That there was a kingdom of Priam, wealthy and powerful, on the coast of the Dardanelles; that there was a great naval expedition undertaken against this Asiatic dynasty by the combined forces of the European Greeks and some of the Asiatic islanders, under the leadership of Agamemnon, king of Mycenæ; that there was a real Achilles, chief of a warlike clan in the Thessalian Phthiotis, and a real quarrel betwixt him and the general-in-chief of the Hellenic armament; that this quarrel brought about the most disastrous results to the Greek host, in the first place, and had nearly caused the failure of the expedition; but that afterwards, a reconciliation having been effected, a series of brilliant achievements followed, which issued soon after in the capture of the great Asiatic capital.' [1]

If this outline of Homeric history were placed before one who had never heard of Homer, and if he were further told that the outline is the picture, what would be his reply? Must he not say, ' You do not ask me to believe much, and indeed you have only sketched out some incidents of not uncommon occurrence; I suppose, however, that you have obtained them from some narrative which gives no ground for calling its trustworthiness into question, and which is corroborated by the testimony of competent witnesses. In other words, you have doubtless gained this knowledge precisely in the same way as I have learnt that some eight hundred years ago there was a great struggle which ended in the death of the English king at Hastings, and the forced election of William the Norman in his place?'

The admission that he must look for nothing of the kind, and that the process by which these historical results are obtained is of a wholly different nature, would probably cause him some perplexity, and might possibly waken in him a vague feeling of distrust. If he were possessed of the critical faculty, and still more, if he had any acquaintance with the applications of the laws of evidence to alleged facts

The test of Homeric credibility.

Results of this test.

---

[1] Blackie, *Homer and the Iliad.* Mr. Blackie does not point out with the same clearness the precise historical residuum of the Odyssey, although that poem has an important bearing on the theory which he so zealously upholds.

of the present day, he would naturally begin to examine with some care the statements brought before him, and the grounds on which they rest. The examination would be followed by unfeigned astonishment, for he would find himself asked to believe in political struggles between conflicting empires on the authority of a narrative in which from first to last there is not a semblance of political motive, and where, instead of a chain of causation like that which obtains in ordinary life, there is throughout a thaumaturgic plot in which gods and men are inextricably mingled together. He is introduced to a struggle which lasts ten years, because so it had been ordained of Zeus according to the sign of the snake and the sparrows, and which is brought about and turns solely on the theft of the Spartan Helen by Paris, once or otherwise called Alexandros. Apart from this, there is absolutely no motive for the war, nor without it is there anything left of the story. It is of the very essence of the narrative that Paris, who has deserted Oinônê, the child of the stream Kebrên, and before whom Hêrê, Athênê, and Aphroditê had appeared as claimants for the golden apple, steals from Sparta the beautiful sister of the Dioskouroi; that the chiefs are summoned together for no other purpose than to avenge her woes and wrongs; that Achilleus, the son of the sea-nymph Thetis, the wielder of invincible weapons and the lord of undying horses, goes to fight in a quarrel which is not his own; that his wrath is roused because he is robbed of the maiden Brisêis, and that thenceforth he takes no part in the strife until his friend Patroklos has been slain; that then he puts on the new armour which Thetis brings to him from the anvil of Hephaistos, and goes forth to win the victory. The details are throughout of the same nature; Achilleus sees and converses with Athênê; Aphroditê is wounded by Diomêdês, and Sleep and Death bear away the lifeless Sarpêdôn on their noiseless wings to the far-off land of light.[1]

By what standard, then, or by what tests is this story to

[1] 'The contents of the two great poems of Homer are . . . of an entirely mythic character. They treat divers series of legends which stand in close uninterrupted concatenation, and only here and there take notice of others lying apart from this connection: these series are, moreover, so handled as to form each a rounded-off and complete whole.'—K. O. Müller, *Introduction to a Scientific Mythology*, p. 24.

be judged, and how are we to measure its historical value ?
Mr. Blackie pauses in some vehement denunciations of
modern sceptical tendencies, to refer us to Sir Cornewall
Lewis's volumes on the Credibility of Early Roman History,
'a work distinguished by all that comprehensiveness of plan,
massive architecture, and substantial workmanship, so characteristic of its author.' The reader who is unacquainted
with the book might well suppose, from the absence of all
other reference to it, that on the whole it bears out Mr.
Blackie's method of dealing with the Homeric poems. He
would again be perplexed at finding there a merciless de-
molition of all his theories and all his conclusions. But at
the least he would be under no doubt as to Sir Cornewall
Lewis's meaning, and he would find principles laid down
which claim to be of universal application, and which must
be false if exceptions are to be admitted. 'It seems to be
often believed,' says Sir G. C. Lewis, 'and at all events it is
perpetually assumed in practice, that historical evidence is
different in its nature from other sorts of evidence. Until
this error is effectually extirpated, all historical researches
must lead to uncertain results. Historical evidence, like
judicial evidence, is founded on the testimony of credible
witnesses. Unless, therefore, a historical account can be
traced by probable proof to the testimony of contemporaries,
the first condition of historical credibility fails.'

How then would a British jury deal with a charge brought
against the chief of one Scottish clan of murdering the chief
of another clan, in feuds which, if now unknown, were
familiar enough not many generations ago ? What if the
witnesses came forward to say that even before his birth the
slain chief had been marked as the future destroyer of his
kinsfolk; that deserting his own wife, he had requited the
hospitality of the accused by carrying off his young bride;
that thence had sprung a feud between their clans, which
the seanagals or soothsayers had said should last for ten
years; that before the final conflict, in which the aggressor
was slain, strange sights were seen in the heavens, and
strange sounds were heard in the air; that in the battle
itself the progenitors of the clans had been seen fighting

Their ap-
plication in
English
courts of
justice.

n 2

BOOK
I.

with the warriors of flesh and blood, and that by the death of the betrayer, according to the ancient tokens, the wrong had been at length atoned? According to the theory which finds a real historical residuum in the Iliad, the verdict ought to be one of guilty; for, although certain parts, nay, indeed all parts, of the story were in one sense incredible, yet 'the materials, so far as they assume the human and narrative form, are in their root and scope historical materials;'[1] and therefore as there must be some foundation for the tale, it may be fairly concluded that the one chief had killed the other, although there was strong reason for thinking that the cause and duration of the quarrel were not at all what they had been represented to be. This, however, could make no difference, for so long as the existence of a feud had been shown, it really mattered very little how it had been brought about, or whether either chief had a wife at all.

Application to Homeric history.

This process, which we laugh at as midsummer madness when applied to recent incidents, becomes, it seems, not only legitimate but indispensable, when we have to deal with legends which have flowed down the sea of tradition through centuries or even millenniums. No injustice is done to Mr. Blackie in thus putting the matter.[2] It is his own

[1] Blackie, *Homer and the Iliad.*

[2] It can scarcely be necessary to say that the arguments of the Edinburgh Professor of Greek are here cited, only because they are the most recent, and probably the most able, exposition of the traditional theories.

The Euemeristic method, for so it may be most conveniently termed, has been applied to the unwieldy Hindu epic, the Mahâbhârata, by Professor Lassen and Mr. Wheeler. The results obtained are sufficiently contradictory. The poem, or collection of poems, is as full of supernatural or impossible incidents as the *Iliad* or the *Odyssey*, or any other Aryan epic; but the main story turns on a struggle between the Kauravas and the Pândavas, as fierce and protracted as the warfare between the Trojans and Achaians, while the return of the Pândavas to the inheritance of which they had been deprived presents in many of its incidents a tolerably close

parallel to the return of the Herakleids. Many of the marvels in the poem are met with also in Greek and Teutonic tradition. Arjuna, the child of the sun, is wedded to a serpent princess, as in the story of Herakles and Echidna, or of Raymond of Toulouse and Melusina. To get at the *caput mortuum* of history supposed to be contained in the poem, all these wonders are of course to be rejected. Thus far both critics are agreed: but for all practical purposes here the agreement ends. Professor Lassen looks on the chief actors in the drama not as real persons, but only as symbolical representations of conditions and events in the early history of India. Thus the polyandric marriage of Draupadi would point to the five tribes of the people of Pânchâla, and the whole poem would exhibit the subjugation of the aboriginal inhabitants by the Aryan invaders. Accepting this view of the purport of the poem, Mr. Wheeler, in

assertion that ' whether the treacherous abduction of the fair Helen was the real cause of the Trojan War or not, is a matter of the smallest moment. That there were such abductions in those times, and in those parts of the world, is only too certain.' It might well be thought that the writer of these words had before him some irrefragable evidence of this fact; but the reader who is here referred ' particularly (to) what Herodotus says in the well-known Introduction to his History,' is doomed to a fresh surprise. If he is approaching the subject for the first time, he will read a perfectly probable, although somewhat dull, story of a young lady of Argos who went down to buy wares from a Phenician merchant-ship, and either with or against her own will was carried off by the captain. The refusal of the Phenicians to make reparation leads to retaliation, and the Argive chiefs steal away Europê, the daughter of the Tyrian king. Thus far the game was equal, for neither side would make amends; but some time afterwards the quarrel was renewed by the Greeks who took Medeia from Kolchis, and thus led to the seduction of Helen by Paris. Thus was brought about the expedition of Troy, in requital of which Xerxes invaded Europe, leaving it to Alexander the Great to clear off old scores at Issos and Arbela. On turning to what are called the original authorities for these events, the much-suffering reader would find that the young Argive lady was one of the many loves of Zeus, who changed her into a heifer; that in this form, chased by the gad-fly of Hêrê, she wandered over mountains and deserts, until she came to the desolate crags where Prometheus was paying the penalty for his love of man; that the Phenician maiden is the sister of Kadmos the dragon-slayer, and is borne on the back of the white bull across the western waters ; that the daughter of the Kolchian

his *History of India*, looks on the five husbands of Draupadî as contemporary princes, and regards her polyandric marriage as a historical incident in the lives of these five men. It is obvious that both these conclusions cannot be accepted, and as no valid reasons can be given for preferring either, we are bound to reject both. It is enough to say that the gleanings of Professor Lassen and Mr. Wheeler are no more the story of the Mahâbhârata than the Trojan war of the Euemerists is the Trojan war of our *Iliad* and *Odyssey*, or of the great lyric and tragic poets of Greece. See the *Westminster Review*, April, 1868, p. 406, &c.; Max Müller, *Sanskrit Literature*, p. 46, &c.

king is the wise woman, who enables Iasôn to overcome the fire-breathing bulls after destroying the offspring of the dragon's teeth, who is carried through the air in her dragon chariot, and who possesses the death-dealing robe of Helios. If on being thus brought into the regions of cloudland, the reader asks whether Herodotos had not before him some evidence different in kind from that which has come down to us, or from that which is given in his Introduction, the answer is that he obtained his very prosaic and likely story from precisely those legends and those legends only, with which we are scarcely less familiar than he was.

The value of the historical residuum in the Iliad.   The result then is briefly this, that Mr. Blackie has before him a singularly circumstantial and complicated narrative, in which the motives of the actors and their exploits are detailed with the most minute care, and in which no distinction whatever is drawn between one kind of causation and another. This narrative he reduces to the merest *caput mortuum*. The causes of the war, the general character of the struggle, the plans and objects of the combatants, all vanish. Nothing remains but the bare fact that there was a quarrel of some kind or other; and the conclusion forced upon us is this,—that in all traditional narratives which involve thaumaturgic action, or which exhibit a causation different from that which we see at work in the world around us, the historical residuum, according to Mr. Blackie, must be sought by rejecting all motives and incidents which transcend the course of ordinary experience. All such things are the mere husk or shell, of no consequence whatever, as long as we admit the naked fact which is supposed to lie beneath. This is, in truth, to lay down a canon in comparison with which the Wolfian hypothesis becomes weak and almost pointless; and they who commit themselves to this position must take the consequences which cannot fail to follow the application of these principles to all records whatsoever.

Difficulties involved in the traditional view.   At once, then, two questions may be asked : (1) Why, if we are thus to pick and choose, should we accept precisely the fare which Mr. Blackie puts before us, neither more nor less ? (2) Why should we affirm the historical reality of the residuum, merely because we decline formally to deny its existence? If the story of Jack the Giant-Killer be clipped and pared as the traditionalists have pared down the 'tale of Troy divine,' the beanstalk-ladder to heaven, the giant, and the giant's wife, all go into thin air together, and there remains only some valiant John who overcomes and punishes some tyrant or oppressor. Giants do not exist, and beanstalk-ladders to the moon conflict with the theory of gravitation. Yet it is not easy to see why out of such wealth of materials we should retain so little, or why, in the latter case, we should not say boldly and candidly that we do not believe any part of the story. This was the straightforward and manly course adopted by the poet when he said emphatically,

οὐκ ἔστ' ἔτυμος λόγος οὗτος,
οὐδ' ἔβας ἐν νηυσὶν εὐσέλμοις,
οὐδ' ἵκεο πέργαμα Τροίας.

That whole nations should fight year after year for the sake of one woman, and that the Trojans should allow their city to be beleaguered when her surrender would have set everything straight at once, was to Herodotos simply incredible, and therefore he caught eagerly at the version which said that Helen, instead of being at Troy, was detained at the court of Proteus, King of Egypt.[1] The same disbelief of the Homeric legend led Thucydides quietly to ignore Helen, to substitute a political for a personal motive in the case of Agamemnon, and to account for the length of the war by the alleged fact that from lack of numbers the Achaians were driven to divide their forces, some betaking themselves to agriculture in the Chersonesos, and others to piracy, while the rest maintained the siege of Ilion. All that can be said on this point is, that the scepticism of Thucydides is far less than that of the modern Euemerists. 'If the great historian,' says Mr. Grote, 'could permit himself thus to amend the legend in so many points, we might have ima-

---

[1] Herodotos, i. 112. This Proteus, however, is simply the wise man of the sea, the fish-god of Ninevites and Philistines.—*Od.* iv. 385, &c. On this narrative in Herodotos Sir Cornewall Lewis remarks that 'much of what is called Egyptian history has evidently been borrowed from Greek mythology.' —*Astronomy of the Ancients*, ch. vi. sect. viii.

gined that a simpler course would have been to include the duration of the siege among the list of poetical exaggerations, and to affirm that the real siege had lasted only one year instead of ten. But it seems that the ten years' duration was so capital a feature in the ancient tale, that no critic ventured to meddle with it.'[1] If with Mr. Blackie we set aside even the abduction of Helen as a matter of not the slightest importance, we may very reasonably set aside the period assigned to the war; but having gone so far, why should we not at once adopt the version of Dion Chrysostom, which gives an account of the war diametrically opposed to that of the Iliad, representing Paris as the lawful husband of Helen, and Achilleus as slain by Hektôr, while the Greeks retire, disgraced and baffled, without taking Troy? It is hard to see why the residuum of modern Euemerists should be preferred to that of a Greek writer certainly much nearer to the time when the events took place, if they ever took place at all. The ruins of Mykênai and Tiryns, even if they attest the fidelity of Homeric epithets, and the existence of an ancient and powerful state in the Peloponnesos,[2] cannot of themselves prove that the kings or chiefs of those cities were successful in all their expeditions, and

[1] *History of Greece*, part i. ch. xv.

[2] With the geographical accuracy of the Homeric poets of the *Iliad* and *Odyssey* we are only indirectly concerned. If the epithets so freely inserted in the Catalogue and elsewhere themselves point to poems of which portions have been absorbed into our *Homer*, the composite character of these poems is still further established, and a fresh difficulty placed in the way of those who claim for them a definite historical value. And it may be fairly urged that a great deal too much has been made of this supposed exactness of description. The reviewer of Mr. Gladstone's *Homeric Studies*, in the *Edinburgh Review* for October 1858, p. 511, boldly avers that of any personal acquaintance on the part of the poet with the interior of Northern Greece, or the Peloponnesos, or many even of the principal islands, there is no evidence beyond that of the epithets by which places are described, and especially in the Catalogue; and in support of this position quotes the words of Mr. Clark, who, in his *Peloponnesus*, p. 206, asserts that 'Sometimes the story and the language are in strict accordance with the observed facts of geography and topography; sometimes in striking contradiction.' Mr. Clark adds the explanation of this fact. 'Each city has its own heroes and legends, and own bards to celebrate them. A multitude of smaller epics have been absorbed in the *Iliad* and the *Odyssey*, and the epithets attached inalienably to this city and that, are among the relics of those perished songs: and the audience required no more.' This is as far advanced as the scepticism of Köchly, while the reviewer's conclusion (that the author of the *Iliad* was well acquainted with the region round Troy and with parts of the Egean coast, and that the author of the *Odyssey* was personally familiar with the western side) implicitly denies the common authorship of the two poems which seems to be conceded by Mr. Grote.

therefore that they did not fail at Ilion. The reality of the struggle is unaffected by the victory or the defeat of Agamemnon. If it be urged that the West ultimately achieved a supremacy, it does not follow that the fall of Ilion was the beginning, any more than that it was the consummation of their triumphs.

But not only does Mr. Blackie (and here it must be re-peated that his arguments are cited only as the latest and perhaps the most able defence of the conservative theory) misrepresent or keep out of sight the real position taken upon such subjects by the most rigorous historical critics in this country: he also uses ambiguous words in defining his own conclusions, or substitutes in later passages expressions which alter or take away the force of statements previously made. In one page we are told that the Homeric narrative sets forth some historical facts, as in the passage already quoted,[1] one of these facts being that Achilleus had a real quarrel with the general-in-chief of the Hellenic armaments.[2] In another, the facts resolve themselves into impressions which the facts may have left on the minds of the poets, but which, far from being in accordance with the incidents as they actually occurred, may, he admits, be altogether at variance with them.[3] In another, the quarrel itself of Achilleus fades away like every other feature of the story, for 'whether we suppose Agamemnon and Achilles, the representatives of southern and northern Greece, to have actually set out together in the same expedition, or to be the distinct captains of two separate armaments confounded in the popular imagination, so far as the essentials of history are concerned, both the men and the facts remain.'[4]

Can anything be more amazing? We are told first that the quarrel and the subsequent reconciliation of the two chiefs form an essential part of the history of the Iliad, and next, that it really makes no difference if we suppose that the king and the hero never met at all. This is, in truth, to blow hot and to blow cold from the same mouth; and all that we can do is to oppose a determined front to such

Eueme-ristic methods of dealing with the Homeric narratives.

Their irre-concilable results.

---

[1] *Homer and the Iliad*, vol. i. p. 177.   [2] *Ibid.* i. 31.
[3] *Ibid.* i. 33.   [4] *Ibid.* i. 79.

arbitrary demands on our credulity, or to surrender ourselves
bound hand and foot to a despot who is to dictate to us from
moment to moment the essentials, as he is pleased to term
them, of historical tradition. We have a right to ask not
only what we are to receive as facts of history, but also by
what method these facts are ascertained. If the method be
worth anything, its working must be regular, and its application ought to yield the same results in every hand; but
we have already seen that the system (if it can be called
such) followed by the Euemerists has produced one version
of the Trojan war by Thucydides, another by Stesichoros
and Herodotos, another by Dion Chrysostom, and two more
by Mr. Blackie; every one of these being irreconcilable with
the rest. If we choose anyone of these summaries of historical residues at the expense of the others, what is this
but to cheat ourselves with the conceit of knowledge without
the reality?

Value of
traditional
impres-
sions.
But although it is impossible to grapple with canons of
interpretation so supple and elastic, it is possible to show
that they cannot be applied except on the basis of pure
assumption. The broad statement that the Iliad gives us an
account of certain incidents which really took place, resolves
itself in other passages into the assertion that the oral tradition of a people may, after hundreds or even thousands of
years, 'be more true to the real character of the fact than
the written testimony of this or that contemporary witness.'
But a fact is one thing, and the impression produced by a
fact is another; and if the impression leads to the ascription
of an historical character to incidents which confessedly
never took place, then it is certain that we cannot from this
impression derive any historical knowledge. We can only
suppose that the impression was caused by something we
know not what, and cannot say when or how, unless we have
authentic contemporary narratives to explain it; but even in
this our knowledge is derived (and too great a stress cannot
be laid on this fact) wholly from the historical document,
and not from the floating popular tradition. That this is so
will be made clear by examining those very instances which
Mr. Blackie brings forward in support of a different con-

clusion. The first is the tradition which points out the
summit of a flat-topped conical hill near Scarborough as the
spot where Cromwell encamped during the siege of the castle
in the great rebellion. 'This,' he tells us, 'is the tradition
of the place. But on looking at the topographical authorities, we learn from Parliamentary papers that Cromwell
was not there at the period implied, and in fact never could
have been there, as at that time he was conducting military
operations in another part of the country. Here is a plain
case of local and oral tradition at issue with authentic
written evidence; but what points does the issue touch?
Only this, that at the siege of a particular castle, at a certain
date in the great civil war, the future head of the great
English commonwealth and virtual king of the British empire was not bodily present. This, however, is a comparatively small matter; the triple fact remains, that there was a
great civil war in England between the Crown and the Com-
mons at the time specified; that in this war the castle of
Scarborough was an object of contention between the parties;
and that in the same war a man called Oliver Cromwell was
one of the principal generals of the popular party.'[1] Here
the tradition relates to a time for which we have confessedly
the most ample and minute contemporary information in
written documents: but we must suppose that our whole
knowledge of the great struggle in the time of Charles I. is
derived from the Scarborough tradition, before we can have
the slightest warrant for comparing it with the Homeric
story. How would the case stand then? It would simply
assert an incident to be a fact which, as it so happens, we
know to be not a fact, and we should have a vague idea of
some contest without knowing anything about its causes, its
character, or its issue. All that can be said is that, as it so
happens, the known history of the time enables us to account
for the impression, but that from the impression itself we
derive no historical knowledge whatever. It is the same
with the next alleged instance of the two women, M'Lachlan
and Wilson, who are said to have been exposed on the beach,
and drowned at the mouth of the Bladnoch water.'[2] In this

---

[1] *Homer and the Iliad.* [2] *Ibid.*

case Mr. Blackie thinks it more likely that certain legal documents may have been lost than that the sentence was not carried out; but even admitting that the women were reprieved, he thinks that nothing more is disproved than the fact that they were drowned, ' not that there was no intention to drown them, not that the act of drowning them, if carried out, was not in harmony with the whole character of the government by whose minions they had been condemned.' Here again we are thoroughly acquainted with the character of the government from other sources; but if we were confined to the tradition or to others like it, we should have before us only a string of incidents, none of which took place, while we should be left to guess the causes which led to such false impressions. But history is not a field for conjecture, however ingenious.

Nor is it more reasonable to dismiss the Carolingian epic cycle as worth little, because in its ultimate form we see 'that wanton play of fancy, and that intentional defiance of all probability' which makes Ariosto useful to the student of Homer only 'as presenting the greatest possible contrast.'[1] The reality of this contrast is a mere assumption which, as we have seen, was denied by Stesichoros, Herodotos, and Dion Chrysostom. The very pith and marrow of the Iliad lies in the detention of Helen at Troy while the ten years' siege went on; and so great, and so thoroughly intentional in their eyes was this defiance of probability, that they altogether denied the fact. But the Carolingian legends, like the Scarborough tradition, relate to a time for which we have contemporary historical information; and in support of the story of Roland, who fell at Roncesvalles, the statement of Eginhard has been adduced that in a battle with the Basques there was slain, along with others, ' Hruodlandus Britannici limitis præfectus.' It is therefore argued that we may expect to find in the Trojan legend about the same amount of truth which the Carolingian myth is supposed to contain. The answer to this is, that apart from the words of Eginhard we could not affirm the death of Roland as a fact, although we could not in terms deny it. But the slender

[1] *Homer and the Iliad*, i. 55.

trust to be reposed even in the names preserved by popular tradition is brought out prominently by the remarkable song of Attabiscar.[1] In this song (which seems to relate to the fight at Roncesvalles, although the place is named Ibañeta), the Frank king mentioned in it is called Carloman.

> Fly, ye who have the strength: fly, ye who have horses:
> Fly, King Carloman, with thy sable plumes and scarlet mantle.

This, as Grimm and Michelet have supposed, was the real name of Charles during his lifetime, Carolus Magnus being merely the Latinised form of Carloman. But as Charles had a brother named Carloman, who survived his father Pippin three years, it is possible that the Basque poet may have confused the names of the two brothers, although Carloman died seven years before the fight of Roncesvalles. But for the crucial instance of the fallacious nature of popular tradition we are forced back upon the Nibelungen Lied, which tells us of Gunther, the Burgundian king, conquered by the Huns of Attila, and relates the murder of Siegbert, king of Austrasia, who defeated the Huns. From independent contemporary historians we know that these persons actually lived, and these deeds were actually done. The conclusion, that here we may really separate the historical element from the fictitious, seems at first sight irresistible. Yet every one of these incidents and almost all the names are found, as we have already seen, in the older Saga of the Volsungs. We can measure, therefore, the value to be assigned to the statement that 'the general character of this Teutonic epic is distinctly historical.'[3] The true facts are these. We have in the later poem the names which are supposed to denote Siegbert, Brunhilt, Attila, Gunther, Swanhild, while in the older lay we have Sigurd, Brynhild, Atli, Gunnar, Swanhild; the incidents recorded of each being in both cases the same. It is unnecessary here to urge that the Volsung story of Sigurd, Brynhild, and Gudrun is precisely the same as the story of Paris, Helen, and Oinônê, and many others in the Greek cycle, for even without this parallelism, close as it seems to be, we see beyond all possibility of doubt that our

---

[1] Michel, *Le Pays Basque*, p. 236.   [2] See page 60.
[3] Blackie, *Homer and the Iliad.*

knowledge of the supposed Austrasian actors in the Nibelung
song is in no way derived from that poem, and that in attempting to separate the historical from the mythical elements we are only following a will of the wisp. Far, therefore, from furnishing any warrant for the conclusion that
there was a real Agamemnon and a real Achilleus, the great
German epic justifies a strong suspicion even of the names
which are embodied in the oral traditions of a people. Far
from being able to extract any history from the Nibelung
tale, we should even be wrong in thinking that the legend
reflected the history of the age of Attila, Theodoric, and
Gundicar. The names and incidents alike recede into the
beautiful cloudland, where they mingle with the parallel
legends of Agamemnon and Odysseus, of Isfendiyar and
Feridun; and the distinction which some have sought to
establish between quasi-historical myths, as those of the
Trojan and Carolingian cycle, and those which, like those
of Herakles and Perseus, are termed quasi-theological, falls
to the ground, or at the least, becomes for all practical purposes worthless.[1] If we know that Hruodland died at Roncesvalles, it is only because we happen to have for that fact
the testimony of the contemporary Eginhard; and the same
contemporary evidence shows that the popular tradition is
wrong in the very substance of the story which takes the
great Karl himself as a crusader to the Holy Land. But the
more ancient epics of the Aryan nations cannot be checked
by any such contemporary history; and the results as applied to the Carolingian myths is not sufficiently encouraging to justify our regretting that the process is in the case
of the Trojan legends impossible. All the stories stand, in
short, on the same level.[2] The myth of Herakles enters into
the so-called history of Laomedontian Troy as much as that
of Agamemnon into the annals of the Troy of Priam; and
there is no reason why the capture of the city by Herakles
should not be as historical as its overthrow by the confede-
rated Achaians. The quasi-theological myth of Herakles is

---

[1] *Fortnightly Review*, No. XXIV.   Max Müller, *Lectures on Language,*
May 1, 1866.   second series, 399.
[2] Grote, *History of Greece,* i. 636.

thus also quasi-historical; and from both alike it is impossible to reap any harvest of historical facts.

In reality, we have to go back to first principles. Sir Cornewall Lewis has laid down certain canons of credibility which are at the least intelligible, and which are exclusively acted on in English courts.[1] The modern Euemerist lays down none: and even in cases where he abandons existing incidents as given in the popular tradition, even where he admits that the legends contradict each other or themselves, even where he puts aside, as matters of no importance, the cardinal facts on which they turn, he yet insists on retaining what he calls the central fact, and on maintaining the general truth of popular impressions, while he imparts to that fact and to those impressions the particular form which may best suit his present purpose. All that can be said is, that the application of such principles to alleged facts of the present day would issue in the total collapse of justice, and set up a reign of universal terror. Where narratives or chronological schemes, of whatever kind, or of whatever age, contradict themselves or each other, we are bound, according to Sir Cornewall Lewis,[2] to reject them all, unless we have good grounds for adopting one to the exclusion of the rest. A mere isolated name, and a bare fact, can be of no use to us. If the Homeric poems (and to this, after all, even Mr. Blackie finds himself reduced) tell us no more than that there was a king named Agamemnon, and a chief called Achilleus, who may never have been at Troy, (for Cromwell was not at Scarborough), and that there was also a struggle of some sort, although we know not what, at Ilion, we have before us a barren statement of which we can make nothing. Such a war may be matched with that Arabian invasion which, according to Assyrian tradition, cut short the so-called Chaldean empire. Of this invasion Mr. Rawlinson admits that he can say but little. 'Indeed, we do not possess any distinct statement that it was by force of arms the Arabians imposed their yoke on the Chaldean people. The brief

---

[1] *Credibility of Early Roman History,* vol. i. ch. iv. See also *Dictionary of Science, Literature, and Art,* article 'Historical Credibility.'

[2] *Astronomy of the Ancients,* p. 348.

summary of Berosus's narrative preserved to us in Eusebius does but say that after the Chaldean dynasty which held the throne for 458 years, there followed a dynasty of nine Arab kings, who ruled for 245 years. Still, as we can scarcely suppose that the proud and high-spirited Chaldeans would have submitted to a yoke so entirely foreign as that of Arabs must have been, without a struggle, it seems necessary to presume a contest wherein the native Hamitic race was attacked by a foreign Semitic stock, and overpowered so as to be forced to accept a change of rulers. Thus, then, the Chaldean kingdom perished.'[1] Certainly, if ever there was such a kingdom, it may have so fallen; but to say that it did so, is the purest guess-work; and it may be enough to quote the words of the 'Edinburgh Review,'[2] on a like reconstruction of English history, after the narrative has been lost. 'The dynasty of the Stuarts,' it may then be said, 'seems to have given four kings to England, and many more to Scotland, when it was expelled by Dutch invaders. Of this invasion we have no details. Indeed, it is not distinctly stated that the Dutch yoke was imposed by force of arms upon the English people. Still, we can scarcely think that proud and high-spirited Englishmen would submit to so foreign a nation as the Dutch without a struggle, especially when we have reason for thinking that a rebellion, headed by one who called himself Duke of Monmouth, was vigorously put down not long before. It seems necessary, then, to presume a contest in which the native English population was attacked and overpowered by the men of Holland. Thus, then, the Stuart dynasty perished.' The conjecture would in this instance be utterly false, although no objection on the score of improbability could be urged against it. In such a case, a genuine historian would simply suspend his judgment. He would not deny that there was a Stuart dynasty, or that it was expelled : he would only decline to lay down any conclusions on the subject, adding that the alleged facts, thus standing bare and isolated, could have for him no use. This is all that the most sceptical of critics have affirmed in the

[1] Rawlinson, *Ancient Eastern Monarchies*, vol. i. p. 223.
[2] January 1867, p. 140.

case of the Homeric and early Roman traditions; and it is
a mere misrepresentation to speak of them as denying the
possible occurrence of some contest on the plains of the Helles-
pontian Troy. Like them, the modern Euemerists reject all
the marvellous and supernatural incidents, and the mingling
of gods and men. The cause and character of the war, its
duration, and the mode in which it was carried on, they regard
as points of very slight consequence; and having thus destroyed
the whole story, they come forward with surprising assurance
to demand our acceptance of a residue of fact which by some
divining process they have discovered to be historical. When
Sir Cornewall Lewis dismisses the accounts of the Decemviral
legislation at Rome as involved in inextricable confusion, he
does not deny the existence of Decemvirs; he merely says that
the narratives which have come down to us are self-contra-
dictory from beginning to end, and untrustworthy in all
their particulars. In like manner, of such a Trojan war as
that in which the Euemerists would have us believe, 'without Helen, without Amazons, without Ethiopians under the
beautiful son of Eos, without the wooden horse,' nay, as they
admit, perhaps without a quarrel between Agamemnon and
Achilleus, and possibly without even their presence in the
Argive camp, Mr. Grote only says that 'as the possibility of
it cannot be denied, so neither can the reality of it be
affirmed.' One step further we may, however, take. Whatever struggle may have taken place within fifty miles of the
southern shores of the Sea of Marmora, that struggle is not
the subject of the Homeric poems. History does not repeat
itself with monotonous uniformity in every country; and
the story of Helen and Achilleus is the subject of the popular
traditions in every Aryan land. If then the conflict, a few
scenes of which are described in our Iliad, belongs to the
history of men and women of like passions with ourselves,
this conflict arose out of events which happened before the
separation of the Aryan nations from their common home.
To convert a bare possibility of this sort into an historical
fact is indeed to build a house on sand; and while we are
wasting time on this worthless task, the early language of the
Aryan peoples points to that real conflict in the daily and

yearly drama of the outward world which must strike the deepest chords of the human heart, so long as men continue to be what they are.

But the question must be carried still further into that domain of Hellenic tradition which is supposed to be the border land between mythology and history, and to exhibit a larger amount of fact than of fiction. The inquiry may not be wholly new: but if, in spite of all that has been said by those who maintain the unity of the Iliad and the Odyssey and attribute to their narratives a historical character, their opponents are not satisfied, it is clear that the question cannot be regarded as settled, unless dogmatic assertion on the one side is to overbear the patient statement of facts on the other. If the conclusions of the modern Euemerists are to be received, then, on the faith of a supposed general consent of critics through a long series of centuries, we are bound to believe that the events of which the Homeric poets sang were historical incidents which materially affected the later history of the Greeks, in spite of all contradictions in the narrative, and in spite of all other difficulties which the literature whether of the Greeks or of any other people may force on our attention. If we are not as yet told that, the historical foundation of the legends being established, we are bound to receive all the marvellous details of the picture with a ready acquiescence, still the method by which the upholders of the so-called Homeric history seek to sustain these conclusions may well appal the sober seekers after truth, who see the havoc thus made in those canons of evidence which should guide the statesman and the judge not less than the scholar. When we have before us narratives full of extraordinary incidents and exhibiting throughout a supernatural machinery, when we see further that these narratives contradict themselves on vital points, it is our duty, it seems, not to reject those narratives, but to pare away all that is miraculous or hard to believe, and then to regard the naked outline as fact. It cannot be too often or too earnestly repeated, that by any such method the ascertainment of the truth of facts becomes impossible. The Euemerists charge their opponents with robbing us of large treasures of in-

herited belief;[1] but it is not too much to say that their own
criticism is far more unsettling and destructive, and that it
tends to blunt that instinct of truthfulness, and that impartial determination to seek truth only, without which all
criticism is worse than worthless. If we are to hold with
Mr. Blackie in one place that ' there was a real kingdom of
Priam on the coast of the Dardanelles, and a real expedition of
the western Greeks against this kingdom,' with a real Achilleus, and ' a real quarrel between him and the general-in-chief of
the Hellenic armament,' and in another, that the impressions
left by the facts on the minds of the poets might be ' altogether at variance with the incidents as they occurred,' while
in a third we are to admit that the historical character of
the legend is not affected, even though Agamemnon and
Achilleus may never have met at all, and no Helen may have
existed to give cause to the war, then it is clear that all freedom of judgment is gone. But no one can submit to be thus
bound, who believes that his powers of thought are given to
him as a sacred trust, and that, unless he seeks to know facts
as they are, he is chargeable with the guilt of wilfully blinding himself. It matters not how great may be the array of
authorities on the other side; he dares not to give his assent
to these conclusions, if facts in his judgment contradict or
appear to contradict them. To profess a belief in the proposition that the Iliad and Odyssey moulded the intellectual
life of the Greeks from a time long preceding that of Herodotos and Thucydides, would be to him an act of sheer dis-
honesty, if he is not convinced that the proposition is true ;
and if, after a careful survey of the field, he still retains his
doubts, he is bound to state his reasons, and thus to do what he
can towards solving the problem. The attitude of all critics
towards this subject ought to be that of patient seekers after
truth, who are quite prepared to receive any conclusions to
which the evidence may lead them. If we wish only to
ascertain facts, we shall be ready to believe indifferently that
the Iliad and Odyssey were composed by one poet or by
twenty; that they were written within a few years or many
centuries after the incidents which they profess to record ;

[1] Blackie. *Iliad.* i

that their narratives are partly historical or wholly mythical, if only the propositions are irrefragably established. But whatever be the result, the statement of the grounds of doubt calls for gratitude rather than blame, and the tone adopted by some who have lately taken part in these discussions is a matter, to say the least, of very grave regret. Thus in the book which he is pleased to call the 'Life of Homer,' Mr. Valetta has ridiculed those who range themselves on the side of Lachman, Köchly, or Mr. Grote, as overshooting their mark, one condemning one third, another another, and a third the remaining third of the twenty-four books of the Iliad. Such assertions can gain at best but a temporary advantage. None who go beneath the surface of the question can fail to see that the critics thus censured do not reject each a different portion of the Iliad; that the attribution of the first book of the Iliad to one poet, and of the second book to another, is really no condemnation whatever, and that Mr. Grote at all events regards the Iliad as made up of only two poems, both of which he believes to be the work of the same poet. In fact, the points on which these critics fasten are not in each case different. The same difficulties have forced themselves on the attention of all, and some of the most strenuous asserters of Homeric unity are not slow in acknowledging their force. Even Mr. Blackie admits that Homer composed the Iliad 'in piece-meal,' and strung his songs together 'with a distinct know-ledge that they would be used only in separate parts,' and that 'not only the separate materials, but the general scheme of the Iliad existed in the Hellenic mind before Homer.'[1] It is hard to see how this position differs materially from that of the writer in the Edinburgh Review, who, while maintaining the unitarian hypothesis, asserts that 'the text was handed down in fragments from remote antiquity, that those fragments were cast and recast, stitched together, unstitched again, handled by uncritical and unscrupulous compilers in every possible way.'[2] Like Mr. Blackie, Colonel Mure allows

---

[1] Blackie, *Iliad*. i. 206, 222.
[2] No. ccxx. October 1858, p. 503. It is unnecessary to enter at length into the question relating to the unity of the

Odyssey. As Mr. Grote insists, it is impossible to shut our eyes to the unity of plan which pervades this poem. In the *Iliad* we look in vain for any such

that 'the circumstances under which the texts were transmitted, render it next to impossible but that their original
purity must have suffered,'[1] and that Homer was probably
'indebted to previous traditions for the original sketches of
his principal heroes.'[2] Bishop Thirlwall, while he refused to
commit himself to any positive conclusion on the subject,
saw long ago, with his usual sagacity, that the unity of
Homer, even if universally conceded, would add little or
nothing to the value of the Iliad or Odyssey as historical
records. In his words, ' the kind of history for which Homer
invoked the aid of the Muses to strengthen his memory was
not chiefly valued as a recital of real events,' and ' if in detached passages the poet sometimes appears to be relating
with the naked simplicity of truth, we cannot ascribe any
higher authority to these episodes than to the rest of the
poem.' With a singular anticipation of the course into which
the discussion has now drifted, he adds that ' the campaigns
of Nestor, the wars of Calydon, the expeditions of Achilles,
probably appear less poetical than the battles before Troy,
only because they stand in the background of the picture,
and were perhaps transferred to it from other legends in
which, occupying a different place, they were exhibited in a
more marvellous and poetical shape.'[3] Thus, in Bishop
Thirlwall's judgment, every incident nakedly recorded in the
Iliad received its full clothing of the supernatural in other
epic poems now lost; and since to incidents so clothed no
credit is to be given, the tissue of wonders in which all are
involved puts completely out of sight any possibly historical
incidents on which they may have been founded, and makes
them for us as though they had never been. This emphatic
verdict scatters to the wind all inferences respecting the age
of Homer drawn from the silence of the Homeric poems as
to the return of the Herakleids. These inferences involve the

unity, and are forced to strange shifts
in order to establish a continuous unity
of any kind. But on the other hand it
is impossible to prove that no parts of
the *Odyssey* ever existed in the form of
separate lays. The tale of the death of
Achilleus points to a different conclusion,
and this may also be said of the longer

lay of Demodokos and of the episode of
the solar herds in Thrinakia, as well as
of many other incidents of the poem.
[1] *Critical History of Greek Literature*, book ii. ch. iv. § 4.
[2] *Ibid.* book ii. ch. iv. § 5.
[3] *History of Greece*, vol. i. ch v.

BOOK I.

assumption that the return of the Herakleids was a cause of such thorough change in the Greek dynasties as well as in Asia Minor, that if the poet had written after that event, his language must have exhibited some knowledge of its results. The argument is commonly urged by writers who further assume that Homer wrote within a generation or two of the Trojan war,[1] and that Thucydides has assigned the right date for the conquest of Peloponnesos by the Herakleids. Thus the whole Iliad, as we have it now, was composed within eighty years at furthest from the fall of Ilion, and perhaps much earlier. Here then we are enabled to measure at once the value of that ancient tradition which, it is said, no Greek author of note has disputed or doubted, when it is submitted to the fast and loose method of critics who maintain the unity of Homer. The whole character of the tradition is essentially changed, if in one statement the poet is a contemporary writer, and in another is separated by a vast interval of time from the events which he professes to describe. In the one view, the composition of the Iliad within eighty years after the recovery of Helen is indispensable to the historical authority of Homer. According to the other, which is adopted by Thucydides, Homer lived ‘a very long time’ after the Trojan war;[2] while the poet, who may surely be allowed to tell his own tale, clearly speaks of the actors in his great drama as belonging to an order of men no longer seen upon the earth.[3] The special pleading of Mr. Gladstone limits the meaning of the phrase to a period of at most forty or fifty years. Few, probably, will attach much weight to the argument. All that Nestor says in the passage on which Mr. Gladstone[4] relies for the truth of his interpretation, is that none then living could fight as Perithoös and other heroes had fought in the days of his youth.[5] In all

[1] Gladstone, *Homer and the Homeric Age*, i. 37.

[2] Thuc. i. 3. The contradiction cannot be laid to the charge of Thucydides, who clearly regarded Homer as living at a time long subsequent to the return of the Herakleids. A statement so clear can scarcely be set aside with consistency by critics who are eager on all possible occasions to shelter themselves under ‘the authority of the ancients.’

To Thucydides the absence of all reference to the Herakleid conquests in our *Iliad* and *Odyssey* (if he ever saw those poems), involved no sort of necessity for supposing that the poet lived before the so-called Dorian settlement of the Peloponnesos.

[3] *Il.* v. 304.

[4] *Homer and the Homeric Age*, i. 37.

[5] *Il.* i. 272.

the other passages where a like phrase occurs, the poet in his .own person ascribes to Aias, or Hektor, or Aineias the power of hurling boulders, scarcely to be lifted by two men, as easily as a child might throw a pebble.[1] The change of which Nestor speaks is only one of degree. The poet, had he lived in times so close to the events which he relates, would rather have gloried in the exploits of his own kinsmen, and allowed their fame to shed some portion of its lustre on his living countrymen.

But if the alleged event which is called the return of the Herakleids led, as we are told, to such thorough changes in the (historical) dynasties of Eastern and Western Greece, and if this event, the belief of Thucydides to the contrary notwithstanding, occurred within a century after the fall of Troy, and if the Iliad and Odyssey, as we now have them, were composed in the interval between these two events, the upholders of Homeric unity have fairly established their position. What then is the value of the traditions which relate this so-called historical event? In plain speech, they are narratives which exhibit a singular parallelism with other incidents in the mythical history of Hellas, and from which the residuum of historical fact, if it can be extracted at all, must be extracted by the same method which Thucydides, Herodotos, Dion Chrysostom and the modern Euemerists apply to the story of Troy, namely, by stripping off the whole clothing of the supernatural which has been thrown around them, and by ingenious conjectural arrangement of the little that then remains. In truth, argument here becomes really superfluous. It may be fairly said, and it should be said at once, that the most vehement defenders of the historical character of the Iliad have themselves acknowledged that we can get nothing out of it which deserves the name of history. The whole thaumaturgy of the poem they shatter at a blow: and although we are told in one breath that there was a real expedition from Mykênai to Troy, with a real Achilleus and a real Agamemnon, whose quarrel was an actual fact, we are told in another that Agamemnon and Achilleus may have been leaders of successive expeditions

---

[1] *Il.* xii. 383, 449 ; xx. 287.

and may never have met at all, and that there may, there-fore, have been no quarrel and no Helen to give cause for the war. This, according to their own admissions, is no caricature, and hence it may be said that the critics who are represented by Mr. Blackie have torn to shreds the historical character of the Iliad. Bishop Thirlwall, while he accepts the fact of some war as the basis of the story, has dealt not less cruelly with the narrative. He has swept away all belief in the detailed narratives of the Iliad and the Odyssey, while his statements that the incidents cursorily noticed in these poems were exhibited in full mythical garb in other epics destroy all belief in the remainder. It must therefore be emphatically repeated that on the historical character of the Trojan war, the unitarians are in substan-tial agreement with their antagonists. There may have been a war at Ilion on the Propontis : but as we cannot deny, so we cannot say that there was, and about it we know nothing.

Do we know anything more about the return of the Hera-kleids? Mr. Grote, it is true, asserts that at this point we pass, as if touched by the wand of a magician, from mythical to historical Greece.[1] But he connects the myth with the subsequent historical distribution of the Greek states, only because it happens to come latest in order of sequence, and the story itself he at once banishes to the region of myths. The traditions again are contradictory, and Bishop Thirlwall especially notes that, while one version represents Pamphylos and Dymas as falling in the expedition by which their countrymen made themselves masters of the Peloponnesos, another speaks of Pamphylos as still living in the second generation after the conquest. If then we say that in Greece, when it becomes historical, we find a certain ar-rangement of Dorian, Ionian, and other tribes, but that we know nothing of the events which led to it, our conclusion is simply that of Dr. Thirlwall, and Dr. Thirlwall is commonly regarded as free from the scepticism of Mr. Grote. ‘It is much less probable,’ in his judgment, ‘that the origin of the Dorian tribes, as of all similar political forms which a nation has assumed in the earliest period of existence, should have

[1] *History of Greece*, part i. ch. xviii. § 1.

been distinctly remembered, than that it should have been forgotten, and have then been attributed to imaginary persons.'[1] Have we then any adequate grounds for believing that there was any historical reconquest of the Peloponnesos by the Herakleids? Mr. Grote, who accepts the fact, although he rejects the legends which profess to account for it, urges that no doubt is expressed about it even by the best historians of antiquity, and that 'Thucydides accepts it as a single and literal event, having its assignable date, and carrying at one blow the acquisition of Peloponnesos.'[2] But no one has shown more forcibly than Mr. Grote himself the utter worthlessness of the method of Thucydides when applied to the Trojan war, which also has its assignable date, for Thucydides marks it as preceding the return of the Herakleids by eighty years. When, again, Thucydides sets down the expulsion of the Boiotians from the Thessalian Arnê as an event occurring sixty years after the war at Troy, Mr. Grote rejects his statement summarily, on the ground that he 'only followed one amongst a variety of discrepant legends,.none of which there were any means of verifying.'[3] But this remark applies with equal force to the traditions of the return of the Herakleids, and it has been well said that 'the tendency of the Greeks in the historic age to assign definite dates to uncertain events was very likely to lead them into statements not chronologically correct,'[4] and that the dates assigned by Thucydides, for example, to the various immigrations into Sicily 'must surely be received with great caution.' They are, at the least, as trustworthy as the tabulated results of Chaldæan and Assyrian chronology by M. Gutschmid and Mr. Rawlinson; and they all rest alike on the shifting sands of ingenious conjecture.[5] The last argument of Mr. Grote for the historical return of the Herakleids has been refuted by Sir Cornewall Lewis. This event, if it be an event, does not lead us at once from mythical to historical Greece. The whole history of Athens for many centuries later either is a blank,

[1] Thirlwall. *Greece*, i. 257.
[2] *History of Greece*, part i. ch. xviii. § 1.
[3] *Ibid.* § 2.
[4] F. A. Paley, 'The Iliad of Homer,' (in the *Bibliotheca Classica*), introd. xix.
[5] *Edinburgh Review*, January 1867, p. 128.

or exhibits a series of fables; and the conclusion is that 'it seems quite impossible to fix any one period for the commencement of authentic history in all the different Greek states.' Of the string of dates assigned to the various alleged immigrations from Western Hellas, some may possibly be correct; but 'how far these dates are authentic, we have little means of judging, but the colonial legends connected with the early foundations are for the most part fabulous.' It follows that 'a connected account of the affairs of the principal Greek States begins about a century before the birth of Herodotus, and that a continuous narrative of the principal transactions is carried on from the time of Crœsus and Cyrus, when the Ionic Greeks first became subject to the Lydian and Persian kings. As soon as we ascend beyond the memory of the generation which preceded Herodotus and his contemporaries, we find the chronology uncertain, the order of events confused, and the narrative interspersed with legend and fable. As we mount higher the uncertainty increases, until at last the light of history is almost quenched, and we find ourselves in nearly total darkness.'[1] To this region of the Graiai and the Gorgons we must, therefore, assign the return of the Herakleids, with all the incidents which are said to have preceded it, and not a few which are said to have followed it. If any real facts underlie the tradition—if any names of real Achaian or Hellenic chieftains have been preserved in it, we cannot separate them from the fictions beneath which they are buried. To us they are lost beyond recall: and for us, therefore, the tales of Troy and of the return of the Herakleids are not history, and cannot possess any historical value.[2]

[1] *Credibility of Early Roman History*, ch. xiv. § 18.

[2] Unless it can be shown that we have better historical information for the so-called Aiolic migration than we have for the Herakleid conquests, the Aiolic migration ceases to be for us a fact from which we can reason to any conclusions respecting the *Iliad* or the *Odyssey*. These poems know nothing of individual eponymoi named Hellén, Ion, or Achaios, and Aiolos is mentioned simply as a son of Hippotas, dwelling in the island Aiolia (*Odyssey*, x. 2). Hence Mr. Grote (*History of Greece*, part i. ch. vi.) infers that Aiolos is older in the legend than Hellén and the rest. Yet Hellas in these poems is a well-defined though small district, while of Aiolians and Ionians it can scarcely be said that they have any local habitation. It is, therefore, labour lost to make attempts to determine whether these two poems are to be regarded as Ionic or Aiolic.

Here, then, the inquiry ends so far as it belongs to the province of historical credibility; and it must never be forgotten that the negative conclusions thus reached are the result of mere historical criticism, and that they can in no way be affected by the failure of any theories which may

We have no more means for ascertaining this point than we have for writing the history of the inhabitants of Jupiter; and to ask with the writer in the *Quarterly Review* (October 1868, p. 445), how the same body of poems can be Aiolic in its original materials, the theatre of its action, and the interests to which it was first addressed, and Ionic in its ultimate form and language, is to entangle ourselves in difficulties which exist only in our own imaginations.

It may be remarked that the Quarterly reviewer, who professes to take the conservative position, is quite as destructive in his criticism as Mr. Blackie. With him the name Homeros can hardly mean anything but 'fitted together, harmonious,' and Homer, like Eumolpos or Daidalos, is 'the personification of an art, and the eponymous ancestor of an hereditary guild.' The reviewer, having thus destroyed the personality of Homer, assumes that the *Iliad* and *Odyssey* are the first of a long series of once familiar poems (*ibid.* p. 450), the latter being the so-called cyclic poems, which are extensions from the *Iliad*, and took that poem as their basis and model. This priority of the *Iliad* and *Odyssey* in point of time to the other poems of the epic cycle is asserted repeatedly. It is enough to say that there is no sort of proof that these poems are later than our Homer, or that they were in any sense extensions of it. The fact, admitted by the reviewer, that the tragic poets followed the cyclic stories, is proof of their wide difference from the legends of the *Iliad* or the *Odyssey*. But according to Colonel Mure all these poems were immeasurably inferior to the *Odyssey*; why then did Æschylos and Sophokles always follow them? The reviewer adopts the answer of Aristotle, that the *Iliad* and *Odyssey* possessed too much unity and completeness in themselves, that they were, in short, already too dramatic to be made a quarry of subjects for the stage (*ibid.* p. 468). Whatever authority the judgment of Aristotle may carry with it on facts which he had himself ascertained, it would be a plain breach of truthfulness to refrain from saying that these assertions are both false and absurd. The *Iliad* and the *Odyssey* are very mines of tragic subjects, and we might as reasonably accept his monstrous dictum dividing all mankind into φύσει ἄρχοντες and φύσει δοῦλοι as justifying the perpetuation of slavery. To Mr. Paley's conclusion that the tragedians followed 'the more savage old epics which had none of the virtue, the chastity, the gentle humanity that have made our *Iliad* and *Odyssey* the admired of all subsequent ages,' the reviewer replies by saying that 'scholars have usually attributed this difference to the exigencies of the stage.' It is well, perhaps, to know that a certain amount of savagery, brutality, and impurity are necessary requirements of the stage: but unfortunately this theory, while it might explain the popularity of the drama of Charles the Second's time, fails to account for the greater purity of the drama of Shakspeare. But in fact it is impossible to maintain that tragedians in any age could be driven to choose anything lower than the highest models, or that poets like Æschylos and Sophokles would of their own will select the coarser-grained and ruder material. The very thought is a slander on our common humanity; and we can but wonder at the shifts to which critics are driven who will not put aside old prejudices and associations, and confine themselves resolutely to the examination of facts. With the Quarterly reviewer the wonder becomes the greater, because he maintains that 'the *Iliad* represents not the beginning, but the culmination of a great school of poetry' (*ibid.* p. 471). It was, therefore, in his power to say that the tragic poets drew their materials from these earlier poems; but it is unfortunate that no such earlier poems are anywhere spoken of or referred to, and the so-called cyclics cannot be both older and later than the *Iliad* and the *Odyssey*. If this is all that can be said, the battle of the Euemerists and traditionists is lost.

profess to account for the origin and growth of these traditions, although the fact that their historical character has
been disproved already must tend to strengthen any theory
which gives a consistent explanation of the whole, and which
rests on a comparison of these traditions with the myths of
other countries. 'The siege of Troy is,' in Professor Max
Müller's words, ' a repetition of the daily siege of the East by
the solar powers that every evening are robbed of their
brightest treasures in the West.' [1] Few—probably none—
will venture to deny that the stealing of the bright clouds of
evening by the dark powers, the weary search for them
through the long night, the battle with the robbers as the
darkness is driven away by the advancing chariot of the lord
of light, are favourite subjects with the poets to whom we
owe the earliest Vedic songs. How far the names occurring
in this most ancient Hindu literature are found in Hellenic
legends, how far the incidents connected with these names
are reproduced in the so-called Homeric poems, may be
gathered in some measure from what has been said already.
But whether the old Vedic hymns contain the germ of the
Iliad and Odyssey, or whether they do not, it seems impossible to shut our eyes to the fact that the whole mythical
history of Hellas exhibits an alternation of movements from
the West to the East, and from the East back to the West
again, as regular as the swayings of a pendulum. In each
case either something bright is taken away, and the heroes
who have been robbed, return with the prize which, after a
long struggle, they have regained; or the heroes themselves
are driven from their home eastward, and thence return to
claim their rightful heritage. The first loss is that of the
Golden Fleece; and the chieftains led by Iason set forth in
the speaking ship on their perilous voyage to the shores of
Kolchis. Before the fleece can be regained there are fearful
tasks to be done : but the aid of the wise Medeia enables
Iasôn to tame the fire-breathing bulls, and to turn against
each other the children of the dragon's teeth. Then follows
the journey homeward, in which Medeia again saves them
from the vengeance of Aiêtês, and Iasôn reigns gloriously in

[1] *Lectures on the Science of Language*, second series, p. 471.

Iolkos after his long wanderings are ended. This tale is repeated again in the story of the wrongs and woes of Helen. She, too, is stolen, like the Golden Fleece, from the western land, and carried far away towards the gates of the morning, and a second time the Achaian heroes are gathered together to avenge the disgrace, and to bring back the peerless queen whom they have lost. Here again is the weary voyage, lengthened by the wrath of the gods, and the perilous warfare which must precede the ruin of Ilion. But the aid of Athênê, answering to that of Medeia, wins the victory at last for Achilleus, and then follow again the wanderings of the heroes as they return each to his home in the far west. Here, too, the help of Athênê, when her first anger has passed away, supports Odysseus on his toilsome pilgrimage, and beats down his enemies beneath his feet. With the scene in which Odysseus and Penelope appear in all the splendour of their youthful beauty after the fall of the suitors, the second westward movement comes to an end. But the enmity which darkened the life of Herakles continued to cast its shadow over his children; and if we follow the mythographers, we have before us, in a series many times repeated, the expulsion of the Herakleids and their attempts to return and take possession of their inheritance.[1]

[1] The writer in the *Quarterly Review* (October, 1868), whose arguments on the age of the *Iliad* and *Odyssey* have been already noticed (note 2, p. 202), admits that Comparative Mythology may perhaps furnish a complete answer to the question, What are the germs or outlines out of which the Trojan story was formed? (p. 453). Declining to enter into this subject generally, he asserts that 'Even without going out of the narrower circle of Greek tradition we may derive valuable suggestions from the comparative method,' and adds that 'the main incidents of the *Iliad*—the abduction of Helen, the anger of Achilles, the taking of Troy—are found repeated, with slight modifications, in the mythology of other parts of Greece. Theseus, like Paris, carried off Helen, and the Dioscuri led an expedition into Attica for her recovery, which exhibits on a smaller scale the essential features of the expedition of Agamemnon. Another tradition, ap-

parently Messenian, represented her as carried off by the twin heroes Idas and Lynkeus. Again, the anger of Achilles finds an almost perfect parallel in that of Meleager, as told in the ninth book of the *Iliad*. Finally, the taking of Troy is an exploit of Hercules as well as of Agamemnon.' The inference from these coincidences is that 'the incidents of the *Iliad* are not a mere distortion of actual events, but originally and properly mythical: that the myth is the primary and essential, the history only the secondary and accidental ingredient.' Unfortunately these secondary ingredients (if there were any such) are so buried beneath the former as to be lost beyond recovery. The reviewer has, therefore, only to account for the shape assumed by the *Iliad* story, and his answer is, 'First, the personality of Achilles, as it was conceived by the primitive tradition, must have exerted in itself an overpowering attraction on the story. Se-

The so-called Dorian migration is the last in the long series of movements from east to west. The legends which profess to relate its history have doubtless lost in great degree the freshness and charm of the myths which had gathered round the fair-haired Helen and the wise Medeia. This poverty may arise from their comparative nearness to an historical age, and from the intermixture of real incidents on which the floating myths of earlier times had fastened themselves. That this may have occurred again and again is a matter not of mere conjecture, but of certainty, although the fact of the intermixture furnishes, as we have seen, no ground of hope for those who seek for history in mythology. Unless they are known to us from contemporary writers, the real events, whatever they may have been, are disguised, distorted, and blotted out as effectually as the stoutest trees in American forests are killed by the parasitical plants which clamber up their sides. But, meagre as these later myths may be, the ideas and incidents of the older legends not unfrequently reappear in them. The disasters which befall the Herakleid leaders before they gain a footing in the Peloponnesos answer to the troubles and losses which Odysseus undergoes on his homeward voyage. The story of the soothsayer Karnos, whose death draws down on them the wrath of Apollôn, carries us to the legend of Chryses in the tale of Troy: and the three sons of Hyllos answer to the three sons of Arkas in the Arkadian stories, and to the three sons of Mannus in the mythology of the Teutonic tribes. Whether the eastward migrations, which are described as the consequences of the return of the Herakleids, represent

condly, the incident of a wrathful inactivity must have been felt to be peculiarly fit to be the turning-point of a long poem. This fitness appears to consist in the facility which it offered for the addition of episodes, celebrating the other national heroes of the different Greek states' (*ib.* p. 464). But to the first of these points the reviewer has himself replied that Achilleus in the earlier tradition is Meleagros, that the wrath of the one is the wrath of the other. The second assertion assumes that one and the same poet sate down and composed the *Iliad* as we have it.

from one end to the other. If the books to which Mr. Grote gives the distinguishing name of *Ilias* were inserted into an older or an independent Achilleis, this prior fitness is converted into a mere accident. In any case we cannot assume in such an inquiry as this that the poem was composed at the first in its present form, *i.e.* with a book recounting the causes of the wrath of Achilleus, followed by others relating the exploits of various heroes who stand forth in his place, and by a sequel which narrates the reconciliation and victory of the Phthiotic chieftain.

any real events, we cannot tell, although we cannot in terms CHAP. IX. deny it; but the fact remains that they are movements eastward, corresponding in many of their features to other movements which are said to have preceded them. All that can be said further about these legends as a whole is that 'matter of fact (if any there be), is so intimately combined with its accompaniments of fiction as to be undistinguishable without the aid of extrinsic evidence;'[1] and no such evidence is forthcoming. The pendulum which had marked the lapse of the mythopœic ages is here arrested in its even beat. The mighty stream, which had brought down on its waters the great epical inheritance of mankind, is lost in the sands of the barren centuries which intervene between the legend-making age and the period of genuine contemporary history.

Thus, then, we have before us a cycle of legends many Materials of epical tradition. times recurring, with differences of local colouring, but with a general agreement in essential features. The search for a stolen treasure, and the homeward return either of the conquerors who have smitten the robbers, or of the heroes who come to claim their rightful kingdom, form the burden of all. In other words, we are brought back to the favourite theme of the Vedic poets—to the hymns which tell us of the Sun-god robbed of his cows in the west, of the mission of Saramâ to discover the fastnesses where the thieves have hidden them, of their resistance until Indra draws nigh with his irresistible spear, of his great vengeance and his beneficent victory. Carrying us back yet one step further, these legends, it must be repeated, resolve themselves into phrases which once described, with a force and vividness never surpassed, the several phenomena of the earth and the heavens. The stream is thus traced to its fountain-head, and at once we are enabled to account for the beauty and majesty, the grossness and unseemliness, of the great body of legends which make up the genuine mythology of the world. The charge of monotony which has by some been adduced in summary condemnation of the method and results of comparative mythology, may be urged with as much and as little reason against the life of man. If there is monotony in the thought

[1] Grote, *History of Greece*, part i. ch. xviii § 2.

of the daily toil of the sun for beings weaker than himself—
of his wrath as he hides his face behind the dark cloud, of
his vengeance as he tramples on the vapours which crowd
around him at his setting, of the doom which severs him
from the dawn at the beginning of his journey to restore her
at its close—there is monotony also in the bare record of
birth and love and toil and death, to which all human life
may be pared down. But where there are eyes to see and
hearts to feel, there is equally life in both; and we are
driven to admit that the real marvel would be, not the
multiplication of magnificent epics, but the absence of these
epics from a soil on which the seeds had been so lavishly
scattered; not the production of characters differing from and
resembling each other—as those of Meleagros and Achilleus,
of Hektor and Paris, of Herakles and Theseus, of Perseus
and Apollôn, of Athênê and Danaê, of Helen and Iô and
Medeia—but the absence of such beings from the common
stories of the people.

Materials
of the
poems
commonly
called
Homeric. The historical character of the Argonautic, the Trojan,
and the Herakleid legends has been swept away; and Comparative Mythology steps in to account for the nature, growth,
and extent of the materials which the Homeric or other poets
found ready to their hands. That they worked on some
materials provided by ancient tradition, is allowed by all;[1]
and the admission involves momentous consequences. The
earliest mythical phrases tell us of a hero whose chariot is
drawn by undying horses, and who is armed with an unerring
spear; who is doomed to toil for beings meaner than himself,
or to die an early death after fighting in a quarrel which is
not his own; who must be parted from the woman to whom
he has given his heart, to be united to her again only when
his days are drawing to an end; in whom may be seen
strange alternations of energy and inaction, of vindictiveness
and generosity; who, after a long struggle, and just when he
seemed to be finally conquered, scatters his enemies on every
side, and sinks, when the battle is ended, into a serene and
deep repose. The outline is but vague, but it involves all the
essential features in the careers of Achilleus and Odysseus,

[1] Gladstone, *Homer and the Homeric Age*, ii. 9.

of Meleagros and Herakles, of Perseus, Theseus, and Bellerophôn; and not only of these, but of the great heroes of the
lays of the Volsungs and the Nibelungs, of the romance of
Arthur, and the epic of Firdusi. In some cases the very
names are the same, as well as the incidents; in others they
translate each other. There is thus the closest parallelism
between the great epics of the Hellenic and Teutonic tribes,
of the Persians and the Hindus; and thus also the narrative
of the Trojan war is not only divested of all local historical
character, but finds its place as one among the many versions
of the tale which relates the career of the great mythical
heroes of all lands. At once, then, we are brought round to
the conclusion (which Dr. Thirlwall had reached by another
path) that a source so rich in mythical elements must yield
an abundant harvest of great epic poems, and that our Iliad
and Odyssey must be but a very small part of the inheritance
left by the mythopœic ages, even if this conclusion were not
supported by the general testimony of ancient writers and
the phenomena of Greek literature. These great epics, at
whatever time they may have been brought into their present
shape, are but two epics which were not the most popular
(even if they were known) during the most flourishing period
of Greek literature. They are but varying forms of the wide-
spread tradition which has come down from a source common
to all the tribes of the Aryan race. A purely historical
inquiry stripped them of all historical character; a philosophical analysis has resolved their materials into the earliest
utterances of human thought, when man first became capable
of putting into words the impressions made on his mind by
the phenomena of the outward world.

The method by which these results have been obtained
must be either wholly rejected, or carefully followed without
the slightest regard to consequences, unless it can be shown
in special instances and by tangible evidence to be unsound.
The expression of vague fears either is thrown away or does
mischief, by encouraging an unscientific fashion of looking
at a subject which must be handled systematically or not at
all. Nothing can be clearer than that if the name Zeus is
confessedly another form of Dyaus, Ouranos of Varuṇa, Azi-

dahaka of Zohâk, the method which has yielded these results
must be applied to all names, nay, to all words; and that, in
all instances where the laws which govern the method are
not violated, the result must be admitted as established.
The child who can swim may dread to plunge into a stream,
because he thinks that the water may be beyond his depth ;
the dogmatist may hesitate to admit conclusions which he
cannot refute, because he fears that they may lead to other conclusions subversive of his traditional belief; but such evasions
are unworthy of men who seek only to know the truth of facts.
It is no longer possible for any who allow that Dyaus must
be Zeus and Ouranos must be Varuna, to ask with any consistency why the Greek Charites should be the Vedic Harits, or .
Eros the Sanskrit Arvat. In either case it is a mere question
of fact, and the answer is that the words are etymologically
identical, and that Charis and Erinys can no more be explained by any Greek word than can Zeus or Ouranos. No
room is left for captious questions which ask why, though
Apollôn be certainly the sun, all other mythical heroes should
represent the sun also. It has probably never been thought,
and certainly never been said, that all the actors in the great
epic dramas of the Hellenic and Teutonic tribes, of the
Persians and Hindoos, are solar heroes. Such a statement
would strike at the very root of Comparative Mythology,
which teaches that the mythical treasures of the Aryan race
have been derived from phrases expressing the genuine feelings
of mankind about all that they saw, felt, or heard in the world
around them. Assuredly neither Odysseus, Herakles, Oidipous, nor any other can be the sun, unless their names, their
general character, and their special features, carry us to this
conclusion. Whether they do so or not can be determined
only by the analysis and comparison of the legends. To
those who hold that the Greek γένος and the old English cyn
are the same, the identity of Aeshma-Daêva and Asmodeus,
of Ormuzd and Ahura-mazdâo, of Arbhu and Orpheus, of
Orthros and Vritra, cannot possibly be a matter of faith.
The identification must stand or fall, as it fulfils or violates
the canons which determine that the Greek θυγάτηρ and the
German tochter represent the English daughter, the Sanskrit

duhitar, and the Persian *docht*. It is absurd to make exceptions unless some philological law has been broken. It
is not less unreasonable to draw distinctions between the
sciences of Comparative Philology and Comparative Mythology on the ground that in the one case the phenomena of
language are made to explain themselves, in the other case
they are made to explain something quite different. The
meaning of this objection is that Comparative Mythology
brings before us a struggle between Phoibos and Python,
Indra and Vritra, Sigurd and Fafnir, Achilleus and Paris, ·
Oidipous and the Sphinx, Ormuzd and Ahriman, and from
the character of the struggle between Indra and Vritra, and
again between Ormuzd and Ahriman, infers that a myth,
purely physical in the land of the Five Streams, assumed a
moral and spiritual meaning in Persia, and, as indicating the
fight between the co-ordinate powers of good and evil, gave
birth to the dualism which from that time to the present
has exercised so mighty an influence throughout the East
and the West. Language has thus been made to explain a
very difficult problem in moral philosophy, which is something quite different from language; and such an office as this
is never, it is urged, discharged by Comparative Philology.
The former, therefore, must be regarded with greater suspicion than the latter. Here again we are dealing with a
mere matter of fact, and we find at once that the objection
brought against the one science applies with equal force to
the other. Words cognate to our *ear* are found in the Greek,
Teutonic, and Indian dialects, the inference being that the
plough was known to the ancestors of Hindus, Greeks, and
Teutons, while they still lived together as a single people.
Here, then, language is made to throw light on the history
of agriculture; and we must therefore infer either that agriculture is the same thing as language, or that the distinction
is wholly baseless. In the Aryan names for father, brother,
sister, daughter, we have the proof that the words existed
for an indefinite length of time before they assumed the
meanings which we now assign to them, and we are forced
to conclude that the recognition of family relations was not
the first step in the history of mankind. Here, then, lan-

guage is made to throw light on the growth of morality;
and unless we say that morality and language are the same
thing, it follows that in both these sciences language is made
to explain something different from itself, and that no distinction can on this ground be drawn between them.[1]

Assumed
early
popularity
of our
Iliad and
Odyssey.
There is more of plausibility than of truth in the words
of Mr. Gladstone, that ' he who seems to impeach the knowledge and judgment of all former ages, himself runs but an
evil chance, and is likely to be found guilty of ignorance and
folly.'[2] Verdicts unanimously given and obstinately upheld
are not always just; and in the great battle for the ascertainment of fact, and more especially in the struggle against
false methods, one man is not unfrequently called upon to
face the world, unsupported by any of his own age. For hundreds if not for thousands of years, the world was convinced
of the reality of witchcraft; the belief is now denounced
on all sides as a gross and deadly delusion. Aristarchos of
Samos opposed his heliocentric theory of the universe to all
others;[3] but many a century had yet to pass before that
theory superseded the Ptolemaic. In truth, nothing is
gained by appeals to majorities or to parties, or by hyper-
bolical laudation of poems ancient or modern. Whatever
may be the beauty or the magnificence of Homeric or any

[1] The remark is, in fact, less applicable to the science of mythology than to
that of language. The former throws a
wonderful light on the first thoughts
awakened by all sensible objects in the
human mind; but this is only one fact,
however astonishing may be the results
obtained from it. The mere analysis of
language yields a vast residuum of historical facts known with as much certainty as if they had come down to us
on the clearest contemporaneous testimony. No small portion of Professor
Max Müllor's great essay on Comparative Mythology is occupied with such il-
lustrations; and the facts so discovered
are of the greatest moment. Thus the
comparison of the Lithuanian wiesz-
patis, a lord, with the Sanskrit vis-patis,
shows that before the dispersion of the
Aryan tribes there was 'not only a
nicely-organised family life, but the
family began to be absorbed by the
state, and here again conventional titles

had been fixed, and were handed down
perhaps two thousand years before the
title of Cæsar was heard of.' Even
more remarkable is the certainty with
which the difference of Aryan names for
wild beasts and weapons of war, contrasted with the similarity of their
peaceful names, shows that the great
Aryan family ' had led a long life of
peace before they separated.' A similar
analysis proves that although they were
well acquainted with river navigation,
the undispersed Aryan tribes had not
yet seen the sea. How far this early
state stretches back it is impossible to
determine; but the interval which separates the dispersion of these tribes from
the dawn of contemporary history is
probably far greater than we are generally disposed to imagine.
[2] Gladstone, Homer, &c. i. 2.
[3] Sir G. C. Lewis, Astronomy of the
Ancients, ch. iii. sect. xii.; Edinburgh
Review, July 1862, p. 94.

other poetry, this beauty and magnificence will still remain, whether it be the work of one man or of a hundred men, of one age or of many. Exaggerated theories, springing from exaggerated praises, have wrapped the whole field of Homeric inquiry in mists, out of which we cannot easily find our way; and statements are boldly made, and unhesitatingly accepted, without the faintest misgiving that, after all, facts may point in quite another direction. In Colonel Mure's opinion, the poems known to us as the Iliad and Odyssey were 'the acknowledged standard or digest, as it were, of early national history, geography, and mythology.' [1] With a generalisation still more sweeping, Baron Bunsen assures us that 'the Iliad and Odyssey, especially the former, are the canon regulating the Hellenic mental developement in all things spiritual, in faith and custom, worship and religion, civil and domestic life, poetry, art, science. Homer is not only the earliest poet, but the father of all succeeding poets. The Iliad is the sacred groundwork of lyrical poetry no less than of the drama.' [2]

These are either very important facts or very great delusions; and to accept them without rigid scrutiny must lead to widespread and fatal mischief. Our business is simply with the evidence on which these conclusions are said to be based, and all impartial and unprejudiced thinkers owe a debt of gratitude to Mr. Paley for his masterly analysis of this evidence, and for the single-minded honesty which has led him to discuss this question in a book intended especially for young scholars. [3] The cry raised against the unsettlement

---

[1] *History of Greek Literature*, book ii. ch. ii. § 5.

[2] *God in History*, book iv. ch. viii.

[3] 'The Iliad of Homer.' *Bibliotheca Classica*, introduction; see also Mr. Paley's paper on 'The Comparatively late date and the Composite Character of our Iliad and Odyssey,' in the *Transactions of the Cambridge Philosophical Society*, vol. xi. part ii. For our present purpose, the inquiry as to the date and composition of our *Iliad* and *Odyssey* must be confined to its negative results. If it be shown that these poems were not known or not popular among the Greeks of the age of Herodotos and

Thucydides, the positive assertions of Colonel Mure and Baron Bunsen fall to the ground; and it follows that these poems, as we have them, were not the work of a poet earlier than Pindar—in other words, not of the Pindaric or Æschylean Homer. Who the author or rather compiler of our *Iliad* and *Odyssey* may have been, we are not concerned to inquire. The task of Bentley was done when he had proved that the epistles of Phalaris were not written by Phalaris. To the comparative mythologist the ascertainment of this point is a matter of indifference. The materials of the *Iliad* and the *Odyssey* were no more

of their minds is both disingenuous and irrelevant. If the
Iliad and Odyssey really moulded the mental life of Greek
lyric and dramatic poets, the fact must be as clear as the
sun at noonday; and counter-statements can but serve to
establish that fact more firmly. But, in the first place, the
composers of our Iliad and Odyssey do not speak of themselves as the first poets. Not only do they tell us of bards
who had won their fame at an earlier time, but the Odyssey[1]
shows that an account of the wrath of Achilleus, wholly
different from that which we have in the Iliad, was both
current and popular. 'If it does not show this,' adds Mr.
Paley, 'it at least shows that there were other ballads on
Trojan affairs in existence before the Odyssey was composed
or compiled.'[2] Colonel Mure naturally lays great stress on
the alleged familiarity of later poets with our Iliad and
Odyssey;[3] and if Baron Bunsen's statement has any measure
of truth, the Attic drama must be steeped in the sentiment,
if not in the language, of our Iliad and Odyssey. But in
fact, 'although two Greek plays, and two only, are taken
directly,—the one from our Iliad, the other from our Odyssey
—the allusions to these poems are singularly few, and those
few often uncertain, in the writers previous to the time of
Plato.'[4] Nay, although these earlier writers speak not unfrequently of Homeric poems and Homeric subjects, we find
in far the larger number of instances, that the epithet is
applied to poems which no longer exist, or to subjects which
are not treated in our Iliad or Odyssey.[5] 'Out of at least

invented by any compiler of these
poems after the close of the Peloponnesian war, than they were invented
by our Homer four hundred years
before Herodotos. The only sacrifice
to be made is that of the ingenious
reasoning which pretends to account
for the alleged degradation of Homeric
characters as shown by the contrast
between the Helen and Odysseus of our
Iliad and Odyssey and the same personages as painted by Æschylos and
Sophokles. (Gladstone, Homer and the
Homeric Age, iii. 535). But no great
regret needs to be felt at giving up
an anomaly which would be strange
and perplexing in any literature, and
which is rendered doubly perplexing by

the history of Athenian thought and
feeling.
[1] Odyss. viii. 72, &c.
[2] Paley, Iliad of Homer, introduction,
xxx.
[3] History of Greek Literature, book ii.
ch. ii. § 4.
[4] Paley, Iliad of Homer, introd. xxvi.
[5] I avail myself without scruple of the
results of Mr. Paley's labours on a field
which is wholly his own—the evidence,
namely, that our Homer was not the
Homer of the great Attic tragedians. In
this portion of his task he has demolished
the verbal fallacy which lies at the root
of all the arguments of Mure and
Bunsen; and the whole burden of proof
lies on those who maintain them. 'As

thirty-five such references in Pindar, only about seven have a distinct reference to our present Iliad or Odyssey : '[1] and even in some of these the reference is very vague, while the lyric poet speaks of the madness of Aias, his midnight attack on the herds, and his suicide, as Homeric subjects. A line, perhaps two or three lines, in the Hesiodic Theogony and the Works and Days may point to our Homer; but of the Trojan legend generally ' very scant mention is made in the poets preceding Pindar and the Tragic writers.'[2] One of the three passages in Theognis cannot be referred to our Iliad, and a fragment of Simonides speaks of Homer ' as describing Meleager in terms not now occurring in the Iliad.'[3] Of the Homeric or Trojan subjects carved on the chest of Kypselos,[4] five are not in the Iliad, and some refer to versions wholly different from our Homeric story. Colonel Mure will have it that Tyrtaios was familiar with our Homer.[5] In the only passage which can be cited in proof of this assertion it is most difficult to discover even a distant allusion. Twice only does Herodotos name the

it is certain' says Mr. Paley 'that by the epics of *Homer* the ancients mean a great deal more than we understand by them—and in fact that they attributed to that vague and misty personage all the mass of ballad literature on the sieges of Troy and Thebes which, we can hardly be wrong in saying, was the accumulated product of the genius of rhapsodists extending over some four centuries at least—it is incumbent on those who' rely on the use of the name *Homer* in such writers as Pindar and Herodotos, to show that they meant by it the same as we do. If this cannot be shown, still more, if the contrary can be shown, the case of these apologists entirely fails.' The same verbal fallacy has led these apologists to urge that our Homer could not have succeeded the old Homer 'silently, almost fraudulently, and without protest.' To this difficulty Mr. Paley attributes very little weight, 'first, because Homer was a vague term that included all epic literature; secondly, because the remodelling and reducing any important part of that vast mass of Homeric literature would necessarily leave the stamp of the old authorship upon it, and so would remain "Homer," still : thirdly, because it

must have been open to individual rhapsodists to take any definite portion of the Trojan story, and to treat it in their own way. Yet every such part, however varied or combined, would still have been "Homer." The above objection, therefore, is based on a misconception as to what "Homer" meant in ancient times.' The discussion as to the materials on which our Homer, whoever he may have been, worked, is not affected by Mr. Paley's conclusions. He admits unreservedly that these materials 'were certainly existing ready for any poet who chose to give them a new treatment, or exhibit them in a more popular and dramatic form at a comparatively late date.'—*On the late Date and composite Character of our Iliad and Odyssey*, p. 8, &c.

[1] Paley, *Iliad of Homer*, introduction, xxvii.
[2] *Ib.* xxx.
[3] *Ib.* xxxi.
[4] Pausanias, v. 18, 19.
[5] *History of Greek Literature*, book ii. ch. ii. § 3. That this series of facts should be assumed on such scanty evidence or in the teeth of evidence to the contrary, is indeed astonishing.

Iliad; and although the former of these two passages may be set aside as ambiguous, in the second he distinctly rejects the Homeric authorship of the Kyprian verses on the ground that the latter speak of Paris as reaching Troy on the third day after leaving Sparta, while the Iliad describes his long wanderings to Sidon, Egypt and other places, for which in our Iliad we look in vain. The reason given by Kleisthenes for the stopping of the rhapsodists at Sikyôn Mr. Blakesley regards as 'quite inapplicable to the Iliad or the Odyssey.' Equally inconclusive are the few references in Thucydides for any evidence in favour of the identity of our Iliad and Odyssey with the Iliad and Odyssey of the age of Perikles. The references of Aristophanes are of the same kind, sometimes tending to prove that passages in our Iliad have been altered since his time, sometimes ascribing to Homer passages which we do not find in our texts.

The Homer of the Greek tragic poets.
The case, then, may be stated thus:—A vast number of incidents belonging to τὰ Τρωικά, not mentioned or barely noticed in our Iliad and Odyssey, were treated of in epic poems current in the days of the great Attic tragedians. All these epic poems, Colonel Mure emphatically asserts, were 'vastly inferior, both in design and execution, to their two prototypes.'[1] Nevertheless from this vastly inferior literature Æschylos, Sophokles, and Euripides 'drew so largely, that at least sixty of their known plays are taken directly from it, while only two are taken from the Iliad and Odyssey.'[2] We are left to wonder with Mr. Paley 'how it came to pass that the Greeks, in the best ages of their poetic genius, preferred to take their themes from the inferior and secondary, to the neglect of the superior and primary,' and 'that the authors of the Cypria, the Little Iliad, the Nosti, should have won all the credit, and left little or none for their great master and predecessor, Homer.' Our Iliad and Odyssey then (even if they were in existence), had not in the days of Æschylos and Sophokles the popularity which they have since attained; and the theories of Baron Bunsen,

[1] *History of Greek Literature*, b. ii. ch. ii. § 3.
[2] Paley, *Iliad*, introd. xxxvii.

Colonel Mure, and Mr. Gladstone fall to the ground. These poems did not 'regulate the mental developement of the Greeks,' nor were they 'the acknowledged standard of early national history, geography, and mythology.' The historical character of these poems being, therefore, definitely disproved, the time of their composition and the method of their transmission, although they remain subjects of great interest, become points of secondary importance. The knowledge of writing (if the fact be proved) even from an age earlier than that which has been assigned to the Homeric poets, will explain but very few of the difficulties which surround the question. A few words scratched on stone and wood furnish slender grounds indeed for assuming the existence of voluminous manuscripts during centuries preceding the dawn of contemporary history.[1]

The conclusion, put briefly and nakedly, is this—that if any real facts underlie the narrative of the Iliad and Odyssey, they are so completely buried beneath the mythical overgrowth as to make the task of separation impossible; that the legend of the Trojan war is unhistorical; that we have no grounds for asserting that Agamemnon, Achilleus, or any other of the actors in the tale were real persons; that the story of the return of the Herakleids is as mythical as that of the war of Troy; that the sequence of these myths throws no light on the time of the composition of our Iliad and Odyssey; that no historical knowledge can be gained from the legends of Hellenic colonisation in Asia Minor; that the mythical history of Greece exhibits a succession of movements from west to east, and from the east back to the west again; that these movements are for the purpose of recovering a stolen treasure or a rightful inheritance; that this heritage is the bright land where the sun sinks to rest after his journey through the heaven; that the stolen treasure is the light·of day carried off by the powers of darkness, and brought back again, after a hard battle, in the morning; that the materials of the Iliad and Odyssey are taken from the vast stores of mythical tradition common to all the Aryan nations; that these traditions can be traced

Results of the inquiry.

---

[1] Paley, *Iliad.* xli. &c. See Appendix A.

back to phrases indicating physical phenomena of whatever
kind; that these phrases furnish an inexhaustible supply of
themes for epic poetry; that the growth of a vast epical
literature was as inevitable as the multiplication of myths,
when the original meaning of the phrases which gave birth
to them was either in part or wholly forgotten; that the
substance of the Iliad and the Odyssey existed from an
indefinitely early time; that these poems were not composed
at once, and as a coherent whole; that they exercised little
influence on the mental developement of the Greek lyric and
tragic poets; and that their present form cannot be traced
to any age much earlier than that of Plato.[1] But these
conclusions give us far more than they take away. If the
fabric of the so-called Homeric history has been shattered,
its ruin must be laid to the charge of the Euemerists not
less than to the assaults of Comparative Mythologists. The
former have left us nothing but the barest outline of possible
incidents, for which no evidence can be adduced, and which
can have for us no interest. The latter, if they have dealt
rudely with some arbitrary assumptions and scattered some
dearly cherished but unreasonable fancies, have at least
made ample compensation. No charm which might have
attached to the human characters of Helen and Hektor,
Paris and Achilleus (had the Euemerists spared us the old
story of their lives),—no pathos which lay in the tale of
Sarpêdôn's early death or of the heart-piercing grief of
Priam can equal that infinitely higher charm which takes
its place, when we see in these legends the hidden thoughts
of our forefathers during those distant ages when they knew
nothing of an order of nature, and the fading twilight of
every evening marked the death of the toiling and short-
lived sun. We can well afford to part with the poor residuum of historical tradition which possibly underlies the
story of the expedition from Mykênai to Ilion, when we
find that the myth reveals to us a momentous chapter in the
history of the human mind, and tells us what in that olden
time men thought of God, of the world, and of themselves.[2]

[1] The limit may be assigned as B.C. 450 at the earliest.
[2] See Appendix B.

CHAPTER X.

THE CHARACTER OF GREEK DYNASTIC AND POPULAR LEGENDS IN RELATION TO THEIR TRIBAL AND NATIONAL NAMES.

IF the Homeric poets wrote as historians, they might well have prayed to be saved from their friends, had they foreseen the way in which their poems were to be treated by the modern Euemerists. After the hard blows dealt by these professed champions of Homeric unity and credibility, it is clear that nothing can restore to the stories of the Argonautic voyage, of the sieges of Ilion and Thebes, and the return of the Herakleids, any measure of their supposed historical character, unless some contemporary evidence can be forthcoming, apart from the poems which contain the mythical narratives of those events. But for such evidence we must look in vain; and the inquiry which has proved that if any real strife between mortal men lay at the root of the legends which relate the story of Achilleus or Sigurd, it must be a strife preceding the first separation of the Aryan tribes, would of itself suffice to take away all interest from the search. But the process of analysing and comparing the stories common to all the Aryan nations has exhibited to us a form of thought resulting in phrases which could not fail to become an inexhaustible source of mythical narratives. We have seen that from this fountain-head might flow a thousand streams, while they who drank of their waters might be quite unconscious of the spring from which they came. We have seen that the simple elements of which these stories were composed were, like the few notes of the musical scale,[1] capable of endless combination; that the polyonymy resulting from this early phase of language yielded a vast number

[1] Newman, *University Sermons*, p. 348.

of names for the same object, and that each of these names might become, and in most cases actually became, the names of anthropomorphosed gods or heroic men. Round each of these beings a number of mythical legends would, as we have seen, group themselves, and impart to each actor a marvellous individuality. Yet all these beings, at first glance so different, would be really the same ; and the keenest political rivalry and even animosity might be fed on the merest fancy.

If then the several Hellenic cities, like other Aryan folk, took pride in their own peculiar legends, and were obstinately convinced that these legends had an existence wholly independent of the traditions of other cities or states, this is only what we might expect. If, again, these stories, when resolved into their simplest forms, impress us with a feeling of something like monotonous repetition, we have here no cause for perplexity or surprise. The form of thought which attributed a conscious life to all sensible objects would find expression in phrases denoting all kinds of phenomena. It would exhibit no narrowness and no partiality ; but regarded as a whole, the phenomena of day and night and of the changing seasons would assume the form of great struggles, in which a bright hero strove for the mastery of the dark beings opposed to him, and achieved in the end a dearly bought victory. This hero would naturally be the favourite subject of national song in every country, and in this beneficent conqueror we have, it needs scarcely to be said, the sun.` The dynastic legends of the Greek cities precisely answer to this expectation. All without exception exhibit under forms the most varied that daily and yearly struggle between Indra and Vritra which assumed a moral aspect in the Iranian land.

The national story of the Argives is made up, we may now fairly say, of a solar myth, which is recounted at length in the adventures of Perseus, and repeated in the career of Herakles without the slightest consciousness that the two stories are but versions of one and the same myth. Perseus is the child of the Golden Shower, and of Danaê, Daphnê, Dahanâ, the dawn, and he is doomed, like other solar children, to be the slayer of the sire to whom he owes his life. His weapons are those of Apollôn and Hermes. The sword of Chrysâôr is in his hand, the golden sandals of the Nymphs are on his feet. His journey to the land of the Graiai, the dim twilight, is only another form of the journey of Herakles to the garden of the Hesperides. When from the home of the Graiai he went to the cave of the Gorgons, the story sprang from the mythical phrase, 'The Sun has gone from the twilight land to fight with the powers of darkness.' But night has a twofold meaning or aspect. There is the darkness which must yield to the morning light and die, and there is the absolute darkness which the sun can never penetrate. The former is the mortal Medousa, the latter her deathless sisters. The story ran that Medousa compared her own beauty with that of Athênê, but the starlit night in its solemn grandeur could be no rival for the radiant goddess on whom rested the full glory of Zeus and Phoibos. When from the Gorgon land Perseus wandered to the shores of Libya, the story introduced an adventure which recurs in a hundred forms. Andromeda, Ariadnê, Brynhild, Aslauga, Hesionê, Dêianeira, Philonoê, Medeia, Augê, Iokastê, were all won after the slaughter of monsters or serpents, while the triumphant return of Danaê with her son to Argos, after his toil is ended, is but the meeting of Herakles with Iolê, the return of the sun in the evening to the mother that bore him in the morning.

In the Theban legend the solar character of the hero is none the less apparent for the ethical tone which, as in the story of Crœsus and in the great trilogy of Æschylos, has converted the myth into something like a philosophy of life. When once the results of old mythical phrases were submitted to a moral criticism, the new turn so given to the tale could not fail to give birth to an entirely new narrative; but the earlier part of the legend exhibits the framework of many another tale of Aryan mythology. Oidipous is the son of Iokastê, whose name suggests those of Iolê, Iamos, or Iobates. Laios, like Akrisios, Priam, and Aleos, dreads his own child, exposes him on the rough hill side,[1] while his gloomy and

[1] As the tale of Paris went, on Ida. But the Sanskrit Idâ is the Earth, the wife of Dyaus; and so we have before us the mythical phrase, 'The sun at its birth rests on the earth or on the hill side.'

negative character is in complete accord with that of Hekabê or Lêtô. But the prophecy of Apollôn must be fulfilled. Oidipous, like Têlephos or Perseus, Romulus or Cyrus, grows up far away from his home, and like them, remarkable for strength, beauty, and vigour. The suspicion that he is not the child of his supposed mother, Meropê, sends him forth to Delphoi, and the homicide of Laios is the death of the parent of the sun, as the latter starts in his career. Then, like Perseus, Theseus, and Bellerophôn, Oidipous in his turn must destroy a monster which vexes the land of Kadmos; but with the strength of Herakles he unites the wisdom of Medeia and Asklepios, and the Sphinx, baffled by the solution of her riddle, leaps from the rock, and dies. This monster belongs, beyond doubt, to the class of which Python, Typhon, Vritra, Zohak, Fafnir, Cacus are examples. Few of these, however, represent precisely the same impressions. Fafnir is the dragon of winter, who guards the treasures of the earth within his pitiless folds. The Sphinx is the dark and lowering cloud, striking terror into the hearts of men and heightening the agonies of a time of drought, until Oidipous, who knows her mysterious speech—as the sun was said, in a still earlier age, to understand the mutterings of the grumbling thunder—unfolds her dark sayings, and drives her from her throne, just as the cloud, smitten by the sun, breaks into rain, and then vanishes away. His victory is won. The bright being has reached his goal, and the fair Iokastê becomes his bride.[1] This point marks the close of the original myth; but Iokastê, his wife, is also his mother, and the morality of Greeks could not recognise a form of speech in which the same person might at once be the son and the husband of another. The relations of anthropomorphous gods were no longer interchangeable, as they appear in Vedic Hymns. From the union of a mother with her son,

---

[1] This incident alone is enough to determine the origin of the myth. Oidipous has reached maturity before he leaves Corinth for Delphoi; and, due account being taken of the youthful looks of the Theban queen, a woman of Iokastê's years would scarcely be brought forward as a prize for a youth just entering into manhood. But Iokastê belongs to that class of mythical beings whose beauty time cannot touch. When the suitors are slain, Penelopê is as radiant as when Odysseus had left her twenty years before. Each morning the Dawn renews her everlasting youth. See Appendix C.

the moral sense of the Greek would turn with horror,[1] and unconscious of the real nature of the incident so related, he would look at once for an awful recompense from the sleepless Erinys of the murdered Laios. Iokastê dies in her marriage-chamber, and in something of the spirit of the old tale, Oidipous must tear out his own eyes, as the light of the setting sun is blotted out by the dark storm-cloud. Henceforth the story is the expression of Greek ethics, until in the last scene (in the company of Theseus, the solar hero of Attica) he goes forth to die amid the blaze of the lightning in the sacred grove of the Eumenides. The blinded Oidipous dies unseen; but in his last hours he has been cheered by the presence of Antigone, the fair and tender light which sheds its soft hue over the Eastern heaven as the sun sinks in death beneath the western waters. Throughout the tale, whether in the slaughter of his father, or in his marriage with Iokastê, Oidipous was but fulfilling his doom. These things must be so. Herakles must see Iolê in the evening, Odysseus must journey homeward, Bellerophôn must wander westward to the Aleian plain, Kephalos must meet his doom at the Leukadian cape, as surely as the sun, once risen, must go across the sky, and then sink down into his bed beneath the earth or sea. It was an iron fate from which there was no escaping, and this teaching of the outer world evoked the awful 'Aváγκη, the invincible necessity, which urges on the wretched Oidipous, and explains the origin of that theological belief which finds its mightiest expression in the dramas which tell us of the sin of Agamemnon and the vengeance of Klytaimnêstra.

The Megarian stories, like those of Attica, form a tangled

[1] The morality of Assyrians was not so easily shocked. The marriage of mothers with sons is one of the institutions ascribed to Semiramis; but in the myth of Semiramis we have precisely the same elements which we find in the stories of Cyrus, Romulus, Oidipous, Telephos, and others. Like them she is exposed in her infancy, saved by doves, and brought up by a shepherd. Like Iokastê, she is the wife of two husbands; and there is no reason why the legend should not have made her the mother as well as the wife of Ninos. Semiramis is simply the dawn goddess, the daughter of the fish-god Derketo, the lover of Tammuz, the counterpart of Aphroditê with the boy Adonis. We may therefore safely say that the Assyrian tradition of the marriage institutions of Semiramis is only another form of the myth which made Iokastê the wife and the mother of Oidipous, and with it we may compare the origin of the Hindu rite of Suttee. See *Dictionary of Literature, Science and Art,* s.v.

skein in which several threads of solar legend have been mingled. Minos is himself a son of Zeus, and the husband of Pasiphaê, whose name speaks of her at once as the daughter of Helios. The daughter of Nisos is smitten with the glorious beauty of his countenance, as is Echidna with that of Herakles; but the golden lock of her father, while it remains unshorn, is an invincible safeguard to the city against the assaults of the Cretan king. The love of Skylla is not thus to be disappointed. The lock is shorn; and the name of the maiden (as the rending monster) shows how well she has served the enemy of her father and her kinsfolk.

The Athenian story.
In the Athenian story the same elements of solar legend are conspicuous. The myth of Kephalos is reproduced in that of Theseus, as the career of the Argive Herakles repeats that of his ancestor Perseus. Like these, Theseus is a slayer of monsters, and more especially of robbers and evil-doers, while, like Herakles, he forsakes those whom he loves, and has many loves in many lands.[1] Armed with a sword (Sigurd's good sword Gram) welded of the same metal with the sword of Apollôn and the spear of Achilleus, he, like Skythes, in the tale of Echidna,[2] wins the inheritance of his fathers, and becomes a companion of Meleagros, whose life is bound up with the burning brand. His descent to Hades is indeed disastrous; but the mishap is repaired by another solar legend. It is Herakles who delivers the wooer of Persephonê.

The story of the Pelopids.
A still more transparent solar tale is brought before us in the myth of the hero who gave his name to the Peloponnesos; but it tells us not so much of the might and exploits of the being who represents the sun-god, as of his wealth and his wisdom and the fearful doom inflicted for his sin. The palace of the Phrygian king is but the golden house of Helios, from which Phaethôn went forth on his ill-starred journey. His wisdom is that keen insight into the counsels of Zeus which Phoibos cannot impart even to Hermes, the

---

[1] Bishop Thirlwall (*History of Greece*, vol. i. ch. v.) lays stress on the substantial identity of the legends of Theseus and Herakles. 'It was not without reason that Theseus was said to have given rise to the proverb *another* *Hercules*, for not only is there a strong resemblance between them in many particular features, but it also seems clear that Theseus was to Attica what Hercules was to the east of Greece.'

[2] Herodotos, iv. 9, 10.

messenger of the gods. His frequent converse with the king of gods and men is an image of the daily visit of Helios to the dizzy heights of heaven. The theft of nectar and ambrosia [1] finds its parallel in the stealing of the fire by Prometheus; and the gift thus bestowed on his people is but the wealth which the sun brings from the sky, and bestows lavishly on the children of men. The slaughter of Pelops, and the serving up of his limbs to Zeus at the banquet, is as horrible as the tale which relates the birth of Erichthonios,[2] but its meaning is as clear and as innocent. The genial warmth of the sun brings to light and life the fruits of the earth, which is his bride; his raging heat kills the very offspring in which he had delighted, and offers it up a scorched and withered sacrifice in the eyes of Zeus, the sky. The sentence passed upon him is in still closer accordance with the old mythical language. When Hermes first kindled a fire by rubbing together the dried branches of the forest, and slew one of the oxen of Phoibos in solemn sacrifice, he appeased not his hunger,[3] for the wind may kindle the fire, but it cannot eat of that which the fire devours. So, too, Tantalos may gaze on sparkling waters and golden fruits; but if he stoops to drink, or puts forth his hand to the laden branches, the water is dried up as by the scorching wind of the desert, and in the words of the poet,[4] only black mud and gaping clay remain in place of flowing streams, and the leaves wither away beneath the fierce glare of tropical noonday. In the rock which threatens to crush him, we see again only the Sphinx brooding over the devoted city, or the misshapen Polyphêmos hurling down huge crags on the ships of Odysseus—the unsightly offspring of the stormy sea, the huge cumulus cloud whose awful blackness oppresses both eye and heart as an omen of impending doom.

The Attic legend of Theseus is connected with the story of Ixiôn through his son Peirithoös, but this myth brings before us only the action of the sun under another phase. It belongs perhaps to the least attractive class of Hellenic stories; but its origin is as simple as that of the repulsive

---

[1] Pind. *Ol.* i. 100.
[2] Apollod. iii. 14, 6.
[3] *Hymn to Hermes,* 130–135.
[4] *Odyssey,* xi. 187.

legend of Erichthonios. The wheel of the sun is mentioned in many of the Vedic hymns, which speak of the battle waged by Dyaus, the heaven, to snatch it from the grasp of night. So Ixîôn loves Hêrê, the queen of the ether, the pure heaven, because Indra loves the Dawn and Phoibos longs for Daphnê. But he is also wedded to the mist, and becomes the father of the Kentaurs, perhaps the Sanskrit Gandharvas, the bright clouds in whose arms the sun reposes as he journeys through the sky. And so the tale went that in the clouds he saw the image of the lady Hêrê, and paid the penalty of his unlawful love. The idea of toil unwillingly borne, as by Herakles or Apollôn, again comes in; for the wheel of Ixîôn can never rest, any more than the sun can pause in his daily career. The legend is almost transparent throughout. As the wealth of Tantalos was the fruit which the genial sunshine calls up from the earth, the treasure-house of Ixîôn is the blazing orb of Helios, the abyss of consuming fire which devours the body of Hesioneus.[1] The darkness and gloom which follow the treacherous deed of Ixîôn represent a time of plague and drought, during which the hidden sun was thought to bow himself before the throne of Zeus. But even yet the doom pursues him. He has scarcely sought pardon for one offence before he suffers himself to be hurried into another. Hêrê, the queen whose placid majesty reflects the solemn stillness of the blue heaven, fills with a new love the heart which had once beaten only for Dia. Each day his love grows warmer, as the summer sun gains a greater power. But the time of vengeance is at hand. As he goes on his way, he sees a form as of Hêrê, reposing in the arms of the clouds; but when he draws nigh to embrace her she vanishes, like Daphnê from the gaze of Phoibos, or Eurydikê from that of Orpheus; and he shares the doom of the Phrygian Tantalos and his counterpart, the crafty Sisyphos, in the traditional stories of Corinth.

Connection
of these
stories
with the
tribal or
national
names.

In all these legends and tales of cities and states whose rivalry was not always friendly, we trace precisely the same elements. The Argives and Athenians each regarded their own traditions as of independent growth; we have seen that

---

[1] εἰς βόθρον πυρὸς μεστόν.—Diod. iv. 69.

their belief was groundless. Differences of names and of local colouring prevented their eyes from discerning the substantial identity of stories in which the very names, when they do not translate each other, have received their explanation from languages not known to Greeks or Romans. At once then we are driven to ask whether the same process which has explained the legends may not also throw light on the names of the cities or states themselves. If the former have been divested of all historical character, is it not possible that the latter may be really destitute of either historical or geographical value? The Ionians looked on the Dorians as on men of an antagonistic race; the Argives who fought with Agamemnon were arrayed against the Lykians who were ranged on the side of Hektor. But did their names in themselves betoken or warrant the feuds which had sprung up among them? The question is one in which it is impossible to do more than argue from the known to the unknown; and something is gained if facts which all would allow to be fairly ascertained justify the suspicion that the tribal or national names of the Aryan peoples have, in very few instances, any geographical significance, or furnish any grounds for drawing distinctions of blood between one tribe or clan and another. The few names belonging to the former class refer to the most prominent physical features of the country, or to the position of one part as distinguished from another. The Thrakians are plainly the inhabitants of a rough and rugged country. They are the Highlanders of the Greek regions, and may be ranged with the Albanians or dwellers among the Alps and hills; and their name falls into the same class with the names of certain Attic divisions, as of the Mesogaian and Diakrian tribes ascribed to the times of King Kranaos, and of the Pediaioi, Paraloi, and Hyperakrioi, the men of the plains, the sea-coast, and the hills.

But if some of the local tribes had names generally describing the nature of their position, the name of the whole Athenian people had no such geographical meaning. Their title can be explained only through the meaning of that of Athênê; and the process which has stripped of all historical value the traditions of the Argonautic expedition, of the tale of Troy, the Aiolic migrations, the Herakleid conquests, leaves the origin of this name, and of all similar titles, if there should be any such, a purely philological question. Few probably will be unwilling to allow that this question may be regarded as settled. The name Athênê, in its Doric form Athûnâ, is the name also of the Sanskrit Ahanâ and Dahanâ, the morning, and of the Greek Daphnê, who flies from the pursuit of the sun-god Phoibos.[1] With scarcely an exception, all the names by which the virgin goddess of the Akropolis was known point to this mythology of the Dawn. The morning flashes up in full splendour from the eastern sky; and the phrase not only grew up into the story that Athênê sprang fully armed from the head of Zeus (Dyaus, the sky), but was represented by many epithets of which her worshippers had forgotten the meaning. Her name Trito-geneia was referred by grammarians to an Aiolic word, trito, denoting a head; but the myth is in no way affected if the name is to be referred to a Vedic god of the waters and the air.[2] Athênê thus is but Aphroditê Anadyomenê, the dawn springing from the sky and the sea; and we see her at once as the Argive Akria, the Messenian Koryphasia, the Roman Capta, the goddess of the heights of heaven. The same idea is embodied in the name Kranaai, and in the eponymos Kranaos, who was invented to explain it. But the strength of the mythical tradition is shown most clearly in the feelings which centred in another epithet throughout probably the whole history of the Athenian people. It was hard for Athenians to turn a deaf ear to any one who spoke of them as the men of the bright and glistering city.[3] When the comic poet twitted his countrymen with taking pleasure in a

---

[1] Max Müller, *Lectures on the Science of Language*, second series, xi. The origin and meanings of the name Danaë must be treated separately.

[2] ' Athéné s'appelle aussi Τριτογένεια, c'est-à-dire la fille de Tritos. Ce dieu a disparu de la mythologie grecque: mais il se retrouve dans les Védas, où Trita règne sur les eaux et sur l'atmosphère. Son nom s'est conservé dans les mots grecs *Triton, Amphitrite, Tritopator*, (surnom des vents) et dans le nom du fleuve Triton qui entoure cette île enchantée où se passe l'enfance

de Bacchus. Quand le dieu *Tritos* cessa d'être connu, le mot Τριτογένεια devint une énigme, et les éoliens, qui dans leur dialecte appelaient τριτώ la tête, comme l'attestent le scoliaste d'Aristophane et Hésychius, n'hésitèrent pas à reconnaître dans Athéné la déesse sortie de la tête de Zeus.'—Bréal, *Hercule et Cacus*, 17.

[3] εἰ δέ τις ὑμᾶς ὑποθωπεύσας λιπαρὰς καλέσειεν 'Αθήνας, εὕρετο πᾶν ἂν διὰ τὰς λιπαρὰς ἀφυῶν τιμὴν περιάψας.
Arist. *Acharn.* 606.

name fit enough for marking the shining of fish preserved in oil, he was unconsciously going back to the root which has supplied a name for the most beautiful beings of his own mythology. According to the old Vedic phrase, the horses of the Sun and the fire alike glisten with oil or are covered with fat; and the root *har*, modified from *ghar*, is seen in the Sanskrit Harits, the Greek Charites, and the Latin Gratiæ.[1] The common origin of these names would be enough to show how Athens came to be so called, and why the epithet took so strong a hold on Athenian sentiment.

CHAP.
X.

But if the Athenian name thus proclaimed them simply the children of the morning or the dawn, another epithet to which they clung with a jealous tenacity carries us to the title which, as they supposed, marked a generic distinction between themselves and the Spartans.

The Ionians and Phenicians.

> Heretofore when the States' commissioners
> Came with an eye to bamboozle the town,
> Did they ever fail to address you
> As the men 'of the violet crown'?
> Straight at the word you were up in your seats.[2]

But to call the Athenians Iostephanoi was but to call them Ionians; and we cannot refuse to connect this name with the names of Iô, Iolê, Iolâos, Iobates, Iokastê, Iasôn, Iamos, and others—names which without exception belong to legends which are more or less transparent. In Iô, the mother of the sacred bull, the mother also of Perseus and of Herakles; in Iolê, the last comforter of the greatest of all the solar heroes; in Iokastê, the mother and the bride of Oidipous, we see the violet-tinted morning from which the sun is born, and who may be said either to fly from, or to be slain by, or wedded to her child. In Iolâos we have only a faint image of his kinsman Herakles; in Iobates we see the king of the far-off eastern land, at whose bidding Hipponoös goes forth to do battle with the monsters of darkness. Iasôn again is the husband of Medeia, the daughter of the Sun, endowed with the sun's mysterious wisdom and magic robe.[3] In the

---

[1] See p. 48, et seq.
[2] Arist. *Ach.* 602, translated by L. H. Rudd.
[3] The Greek explanation made Iasôn the healer; but there is nothing in the myth to suggest the notion. The powers of healing and destruction are exercised not by him but by Medeia; and the explanation is worth as much or as little as the attempts to account for such

story of Iamos, the violet crown of Athens has become a bed of violet flowers ; but Iamos is himself the child of the sungod Phoibos, and he receives his wisdom from the keensighted beings who draw the chariot of Medeia.[1] In the name Ionians we have, then, a word strictly denoting colour and nothing more ; and the colour is the tint which overspreads the sky before the rising of the sun. The word is thus identical in meaning with the name Phoinikê (Phenicia), and Phenicia is accordingly the purple or blood-red land, where Europê is born, and whence she is borne on the back of the snow-white bull westwards to Delphoi. The name is purely Greek, and exhibits its full meaning when taken along with that of Telephassa, the mother of the broad day, who dies in the far west weary with searching for her child. The same purple colour is embodied in Phoinix, the early teacher of Achilleus, who recites to the wayward chief the story of the short-lived hero whose life is bound up with the torch of day. No distinction of race is therefore denoted by the names whether of Ionians or Phenicians.

In historical Hellas the Argives were a people inhabiting about a fifth part of the Peloponnesos. If the Iliad is to be regarded as throwing any light on the conditions of an earlier time, the name Argos had a far more extensive application. It was a territory rather than a city or a state, and with the exception of the islands over which he ruled, it formed the whole of the dominion of Agamemnon. But the name itself was not confined to the Peloponnesos ; and whatever be the explanation to be given of it, it must be applicable to every extra-Peloponnesian Argos, and to the ship which carried the Achaian chieftains on the quest of the Golden Fleece. The word reappears in the title of Aphroditê Argynnis, and in Argennos the supposed favourite of

---

names as Odysseus and Oidipous. A similar confusion between *ios* an arrow, and *ios* poison, fastened on Herakles and Philoktetes the practice of using poisoned arrows (Max Müller, *Lectures*, second series, 292). It is, therefore, quite likely that the worship of Iaso, as the daughter of Asklepios, may be the result of the same forgetfulness of the meaning

of words which turned Lykaon into a wolf or Kallistô into a bear. Another form of the name appears in Iasion, the beloved of Dêmêtêr.

[1] When the word Dragon, which is only another form of Dorkas, the cleareyed gazelle, became the name for serpents, these mythical beings were necessarily transformed into snakes.

Agamemnon, and this epithet has been identified with the Sanskrit Arjunî, the brilliant, a name for the morning.[1] Here again, then, we have a name denoting brilliancy, and we see at once that Argos Panoptes, the guardian of Io, is with his thousand eyes only another image of St. Ursula and her eleven thousand maidens, or of Tara Bai in the folk-lore of southern India,[2] while the word itself carries us to the shining metal, the Greek argyros and the Latin argentum, silver. Whatever then the Argo may be, it is clearly the bright vessel in which the children of the sun go to seek the lost light of day, and in which they return possessed of the golden robe in the morning. It is in short, the Sanskrit archî, light, and arkâh, the sun himself;[3] and thus the process which has explained the name of the Argive people explains also that of the Arkadians, whose mythology runs riot in the equivocal uses of words all originally denoting brilliancy. The eponym Arkas, is like Argos, a son of Zeus, Kallistô being the mother of the former, Niobê of the latter. But in the story of Kallistô we have precisely that same confusion of thought which in India converted the seven shiners, or strewers of light, into seven sages, and in the West changed them into bears or waggons. The root, in short, furnished a name for stars, bears, and poets alike; and when its first meaning faded from the mind, the myth took the forms with which we are now familiar.[4] In the west, the old word arksha as a name for star became confused with the Greek arktos, the Latin Ursa, the name for the golden bear, (the names Argos and Ursula being thus etymologically the same), and the story went that Kallistô, the most brilliant of all the daughters of Zeus, was changed into a bear by Hêrê, as she changed Iô into a heifer. The version given by Hyginus brings before us another transformation; in it Arkas is the son of Lykaon, and Lykaon is

[1] Max Müller, Lectures on Language, second series, viii.
[2] See page 164.
[3] Max Müller, Lect. second series, 360. The same name, Professor Müller goes on to say, was bestowed independently on a hymn of praise, as gladdening the heart and brightening the countenances of the gods, and he adds, 'If the reason of the

independent bestowal of the same root on these two distinct ideas, sun and hymns, was forgotten, there was danger of mythology; and we actually find in India that a myth sprang up, and that hymns of praise were fabled to have proceeded from or to have originally been revealed by the sun.'
[4] Max Müller, Lect. second series, 303.

changed into a wolf for his impiety in offering human flesh as food to Zeus. The story is simply another version of the myth of Tantalos and Pelops, and the solar character of the one must be extended to the other. The confusion between Leukos, brilliant, and Lukos, a wolf was as natural and inevitable as between arksha and arktos, and the readiness with which the one name would suggest the other is shown in the passage where Æschylos makes the Theban maidens pray that the Lykian or bright god might become a very Lykeian or wolf to their enemies.[1]

We come to a class of names, the original significance of which is even less disguised. Unless we are prepared to maintain that Phoibos received his name Delios because he was born in Delos, we are compelled to account for the name of the island from the myth of the god for whom it is said to have furnished a birth-place. But this myth is so indisputably solar that all further discussion on the character of the legend becomes superfluous. The word itself denotes the kindling of the heaven which goes before the sunrise; and although it is possible that the coincidence between the local name and the myth may in any one given case be accidental, such a supposition becomes desperate when we find the same coincidence running through many myths in many countries. If the lord of light is born in Delos, he is born also in the Lykian land. Phoibos is Lykêgenês, light-born, not less than Delian: and through that far off-eastern land flows the golden stream of Xanthos, watering the realm in which Sarpêdôn and Glaukos bare rule. But Sarpêdôn is a name which has been traced to the same root with the names of Hermes and Helen, of Saramâ, Saranyû and Erinys, and it expresses the flushing of the heaven after dawn, as the name of his friend Glaukos also denotes the brightening light of Athênê Glaukôpis.[2] Another chieftain of this morn-

---

[1] Æsch. Sept. c. Thebas, 145.

[2] It is scarcely necessary to trace the roots through the several Greek forms λάω, λευκός, λεύσσω, λάμπω, γλήνη, and others, and the Latin lux, luceo, lumen, lucina, lucna, luna. The silent journey in which Hypnos and Thanatos, Sleep and Death, bear the dead body of Sarpê-dôn to his home, is but another incident stamping the myth with a distinctively solar character. They move through the dark hours, like the Achaian chieftain in search of the Golden Fleece, or like Helios himself in his golden cup: they reach Lykia early in the morning, and there were versions which brought Sar-pêdôn to life again when he reached the Lykian shore. The myth of Sarpêdôn

ing-land is Iobates, whose name, as we have seen, has the
same meaning as that of Phoinix; and Phenicians and
Lykians alike existed only in the terminology of the Greeks.
If we are to follow Herodotos,[1] the people of the country to
which he gave the name of Lykia, called themselves Termilai,
and the name of the Athenian Lykos the son of Pandion was
drawn in to explain the origin of the new title, as the name
of the Arkadian Lykâon might have been used, had the
Attic mythical genealogy failed to supply one. Thus Delians
and Lykians are also, like the Athenians and the Lucanians
of southern Italy, the people of the dawn land; but the versions of the myth are countless, and they all carry us back to
mythical phrases of the like kind. According to one story,
Artemis, like Phoibos, is born in Delos; according to another,
in Asteria the starland; in others Asteria and Ortygia are
other names for Delos itself. But the name Ortygia points
in Greek to the word Ortyx, a quail, and there was no lack
of myths to be localised, whether in the Egean island or in
the islet off the eastern shore of Sicily near to Syracuse.
In one Zeus changes Lêtô into a quail, from the same motive
which led him to transform Iô into a heifer: in another he
himself becomes a quail in order to approach the goddess, as
for the same reason he assumes the form of a golden shower
in the story of Danaê. In yet another, the children are
born in Asteria, and Lêtô takes them thence into Lykia,
where she vainly tries to bathe them in the fountain of
Melitê: but by the same confusion which produces the myth
of Lykâon and possibly all the modern superstitions of
Lykanthropy, wolves come to the aid of the goddess, and
carry her to the stream of Xanthos.[2] In all these legends
the only name which calls for any comment is that of
Ortygia, and Ortygia itself is only the dawn-land. 'The
quail in Sanskrit is called Vartikâ, i.e. the returning
bird, one of the first birds that return with the return of
spring.'[3] The name, it is obvious, might be applied to
the dawn, as naturally as the setting sun might become

thus resolves itself into that of Memnón,
and Memnón is the child of the dawn.
[1] I. 172.

[2] Jacobi, *Mythologie*, s. v. Lêtô.
[3] Max Müller, *Lectures*, second series,
506.

in the Sanskrit Bhekî and the frog-princess of the German tale.[1]

The myth of the Lykian Sarpêdôn has a close affinity with that of the Ethiopian Memnôn; and in the Ethiopians who fight at Troy we have another people for whom it becomes impossible to find a local earthly habitation. The story explains itself. The tears which Eôs sheds on the death of her child are morning dew. The men who follow him are, according to the Herodotean story, exempt from the ills of humanity; and their tables are always loaded with banquets which no labour of theirs has provided. It may amuse historians to regard this mysterious people as the invaders and conquerors of the so-called Chaldæan empire; but no historical inference can be drawn from any mention of them in the Iliad or Odyssey. The name itself is as purely Greek as are the names of the Phenicians and the Lykians, and any explanation given of it must also explain the names Aithon, Aithylla, Aithra, Aithrios, Aithousa. But when we have done this, we shall find the Ethiopians dwelling, not as Mr. Rawlinson believes, on the south coast both of Asia and Africa, and as divided by the Arabian Gulf into Eastern and Western, Asiatic and African,[2] but in the bright Aithêr, the ethereal home of Zeus himself, far above the murky air of our lower world.

There remain yet two names, which, according to Thucy-

[1] See page 165. The story of the Frog Prince is singularly significant. The dawn-maiden is here playing with a golden ball, which, like Endymion, plunges into the water. This ball can be brought to her again only by the Frog—the returning Sun. The Frog re-appears as a Toad in Grimm's story of the Iron Stove. In the Nix of the Mill-pond the man and his wife are changed into a toad and a frog, as the sun and the twilight fade beneath the waters. In the Man of Iron the golden ball with which the king's son is playing rolls, not into the water but into the cage in which the wild man (the Winter) is confined; the king's son here being Phoibos of the golden locks. In the story of the Old Griffin the ball takes the form of golden apples, which instantaneously restore the king's daughter to health, as the nymphs

exult when they look on the new born Apollôn. This ball is the red-hot egg which the bird drops in the story of the Ball of Crystal. The Frog reappears in other stories. In the legend of Briar Rose it is he who promises the queen that she shall have a daughter. In that of the Three Feathers, Dummling, whose exploits reveal him like Theseus as an-other Herakles, receives the beautiful carpet (of clouds—the web of Penelope) from the Frog who is now underground, in other words, after sundown. In the Faithful Beasts it is again the Frog who brings up from the water the wonderful stone (the orb of the Sun), the owner of which can wish himself in whatever place he desires to be.

[2] *Eastern Monarchies*, i. 60. In reply to Mr. Rawlinson it has been urged that the poet of the *Odyssey* could not

dides,[1] were applied in the time of the Homeric poets to the tribes afterwards known collectively as Hellenic. In Mr. Gladstone's judgment, the followers of Agamemnon were called Danaans in their military capacity, the name Argive being used as a geographical designation, while that of Achaians was confined to the ruling tribe.[2] How vague the name Argive is as a local term, we have already seen; and even if the other two names are used in these senses, we are obviously no nearer to their original meaning. The quantity of the first syllable is urged as a reason for not identifying the term Danaans with Ahanâ, Dahanâ, and Daphnê, names of the dawn. At the least, it must be admitted that the word must be taken along with the stories of Danaê the mother of Perseus, and of Danaos with his fifty daughters. Of these the former is throughout strictly solar.[3] If, however, Niebuhr be right, the one reason for not holding Danaê and Daphnê to be different forms of the same name loses its force, for in his judgment the word reappears in Italy under a form more closely allied to Daphnê than to Danaê, and the Latins who regarded themselves as if coming of the pure Trojan stock, bore precisely the same name with the enemies of Priam and of Hektor.[4] So unsubstantial, in all that relates to names, are the bases on which distinctions of race and political attractions and animosities have been made to depend, that we might well look with patience on the arguments by which Mr. Gladstone[5] seeks to connect the names of the Western Achaians and the Persian Achaimenidai, if the names were not adduced as the evidence of ethno-

---

possibly have meant what he is thus supposed to mean. 'Whether the explanations of comparative mythologists be right or wrong, it is certain that the poet cannot mean a people who were neither toward the rising nor the setting sun relatively to himself.'—*Edinburgh Review*, January 1867, p. 117.

[1] I. 3.
[2] *Homer and the Homeric Age*, vol. i. p. 346, &c.
[3] See page 227, &c.
[4] 'Dauni and Daunii are unquestionably the same, and the Daunii are clearly allied to the Tyrrhenian race. Danaê is said to have founded the Pelasgico-

Tyrrhenian Ardea, and on the other hand the father of Tyrrhenus (= Turnus) was, according to some, called Daunus and his mother Danaê. Daunus and Launus again are the same, *d* and *l* in Latin and in the so-called Æolic dialect being always exchanged for one another, as in δάκρυον and *lacryma*, *Ducetius* and *Leucetius*. Laura, Lavinia, and Lavinium are the same as the different names of the Latins, *Lavini, Lakini, Latini*, and all these names are identical with Danai.'—Niebuhr, *Lectures on Ancient History*, xxii.
[5] *Homer and the Homeric Age*, i. 559, &c.

logical affinity. Certainly it is not much more surprising that Persian and Hellenic tribes should bear the same name, than that the Hindu of the Vedic age and the Persian of our own day should both speak of themselves as Aryans.[1] But the Achaian name is too manifestly linked with that of Achilleus to allow any explanation to pass unchallenged which does not apply alike to both. It is enough to say that, so far as we may form a judgment, it must be placed in the class of tribal names which had originally the same meaning with those of Phenicians, Lykians, Delians, Arkadians, Athenians, and Ionians.[2]

The Hellênes and Aiolians.

We reach at last the great name which imparted something like a national character to the centrifugal tribes known to us as Greek: and at once it may be said that the name Hellênes was no more distinctive than that of Ionians or Dorians, Delians and Ortygians, Arkadians and Lykians. Under another form it expresses only the same idea of brightness, with a reservation which limits it to the brightness of the sun. Whether there be, as Mr. Gladstone supposes,[3] the same ethnical connection between the Hellenes of the West and the Eelliats of Persia, which, following the popular Argive tradition,[4] he assumes between the men of Argos as descended from Perseus and the people of the Eteo-Persian province of Fars, is a question with which we need not concern ourselves. Although the possibility of such a connection cannot be denied, the reality of it cannot be inferred from names which carry us into the regions of cloudland. But of the philological identity of the names Hellên, Hellas, Hellê, Helloi and Selloi,[5] Sellêcis, and

---

[1] With the Persians the name is employed as constituting with the correlative An-iran, or non-Aryans, an exhaustive division of mankind: but in this division the Persians alone are Aryans. Max Müller, _Lectures on Language_, first series, lecture vi.

[2] Professor Max Müller is inclined to think that Achilleus is the mortal solar hero Aharyu. According to Kumârila, Ahalyâ (in whose name the change from r to l begins) is the goddess of night; but 'Indra is called _ahalyâiai jârah_: it is most likely that she was meant for the dawn.' _Lectures_, second series, 502.

[3] The Persians of the Persians bear, Mr. Gladstone remarks, 'the name Eelliat, which at least presents a striking resemblance to that of the Helli. The aspirate would pass into the doubled _e_ like "HΛιος into ἠέλιος, or ἔδνα into ἐέδνα.'—_Homer and the Homeric Age_, i. 572

[4] _Ibid._ i. 557. Herod. vii. 61, 150.

[5] The reading of the text in _Il._ xvi. 234 is a matter of indifference. As the name Hellas points to the collective name Helloi, so the Sellêcis, _Il._ ii. 659, &c., points to the Selloi; and the change of the aspirate into _s_ is one of the commonest.

Hellôtis as a name of Athênê, or again of these names with CHAP. Helios, Eëlios, and the Latin Sol, there can be no question. X. Here then we have another group of names, every one of which resolves itself into the idea of solar brightness, for the root *sur*, to glitter, furnished the special Sanskrit name for the Sun whether male or female.[1] Hence, as we might expect, the mythical genealogy of the Hellênes plays throughout on the ideas of light and darkness. For Hellên himself is in one form of the legend the son of Deukalion and Pyrrha, names which connect themselves with such words as Polydeukes, Phoinix, and Ion; in another, he is the child of Zeus, the gleaming heaven, and Dorippê. Of his children one is the dusky Xouthos, another the flashing Aiolos, a name which must be traced seemingly to the same root with the Aithêr of Zeus and the Aithiopians (Ethiopians) of the Odyssey. The two sons of the dark Xouthos are the eponyms of the Ionian and Achaian clans; but Iôn shares his name with other violet-coloured mythical creations, and Achaios with Achilleus must, it would seem, be referred to the Vedic solar hero Aharyu. Thus, with the Delians, Lykians, and Ortygians, the Hellênes are, like the people of Khorassan, simply the children of the light and the sun, and the Hellespont marks their pathway.[2]

By this name all the tribes and clans who traced their descent from Hellên and Deukalion acknowledged the bonds of affinity which, as they supposed, connected them with each other. A strictly local or geographical name it never became. Wherever the Hellênes went, they carried Hellas with them. It might be scattered among the islands of the Egean; it might be fixed on the mainland between that sea and the Hadriatic; it might be transferred to the soil of Italy; but the dwelling-place of the children of the Sun retained everywhere the same name.[3] As Hellênes they

Greeks and Hesperians.

[1] Sûryâ is 'a female Sûrya, i.e. the Sun as a feminine, or, according to the commentator, the Dawn again under a different name. In the Rig-Veda, too, the Dawn is called the wife of Sûrya, and the Asvins are sometimes called the husbands of Sûryâ.'—Max Müller, *Lectures*, second series, xi.

[2] πόντος : πάτος = πένθος : πάθος =

βένθος : βάθος.—Max Müller, *Comparative Mythology*, 47. The word is thus the precise equivalent of Lykabas, the path of Light trodden by the Sun-god.

[3] Ἑλλὰς σποραδική, Ἑλλὰς συνεχής. With the Latins it was long before Southern Italy ceased to be commonly spoken of as Magna Græcia.

had a bond of union, which was the nearest Greek approach to the modern idea of nationality, and which in greater or less degree counteracted or softened the animosities of Dorians and Ionians, of Athenians and Spartans, of Argives and Achaians. And yet the name which thus served to link them together with some sort of friendly or even national feeling was a word of precisely the same meaning with the tribal or local names which were supposed to denote some real distinctions of blood. But this was not the title by which they were known in Western Europe. It never came into common use among the Latins, who spoke of them as Graii, and Græci or Greeks. Of any such people to the east of the Hadriatic the earliest notice is in the statement of Aristotle, that the people dwelling round the Thesprotian Dodona were called Graikoi before they were called Hellênes.[1] Following the path in which the names thus far examined assuredly lead us, we should expect to find in Western Hellas some names denoting the gloaming or doubtful light of eventide. As Perseus journeyed westward, he came to the land of the Graiai, or gray beings, before he reached the gloomy dwelling of the Gorgons. To the inhabitants of Thessaly, Epeiros was the gray land of the setting sun, and here accordingly we find the Graioi. But this name, it would seem, must have been accepted as a local name for the country to the west of mount Pindos, before the Latin tribes had any knowledge of their Eastern neighbours. The name Hesperia, which the Hellênes applied to Italy, the Latins never acknowledged for themselves; and with Virgil the use of it is due merely to the poet's fancy. Graians and Hesperians are thus alike the people of the dusky land, the Epeirot tribes acknowledging the name because it was applied to them by their immediate kinsfolk, the Italians ignoring it, or possibly not knowing it as a word belonging to another language.[2]

But if the Latin name has any connection with that of the Danaoi, it becomes at the least possible that other tribal

[1] Grote, *History of Greece*, part ii. ch. ii.

[2] Niebuhr remarks that in old Latin two names of nations were in use in every instance, one simple, as Graii, and one derivative, as Græci. *History of Rome*, i. 45.

names of the countries east of the Hadriatic may be found on the great Italian peninsula: and thus, following the law which modifies the Sanskrit *apa*, water, into the Greek Acheldôos, Acheron, and Axios, and the Latin aqua, we should expect that the name of the Achaians, if it reappeared at all, would undergo a similar change. Apulians and Æquians we do find; and it remains to be proved whether the coincidence be or be not accidental. That the same names should be used in common by tribes whose dialects are so closely akin as those of the Greeks and Latins, is assuredly not antecedently improbable: and thus some colour is furnished for the inferences of Niebuhr, who traces to these two forms a very large proportion of the tribal names of the Italian peninsula.[1] Such a name as that of the Rutulians forces on us a comparison with that of Argives, Arkadians, and Phenicians: and the mythology of Virgil points in the same direction.[2] Whether this identity be established or not, the instances already adduced suffice to show that, with scarcely an exception, the Greek tribal names are merely words denoting colour, and all pointing in the same direction of mythopœic or radical metaphor. That the same process should go on among all peoples speaking kindred dialects, is no more than we should expect; and the expectation will be fully justified. The English Baldringas are children of the Sun not less than the Hellenes, the Athenians, and the Lykians, and they still have their home at Baldringham. Another Teutonic Sun-god, the Eddic Tyr, the English Tiw, had his dwelling and his children at Tewing and Tewesley. The sons of Thunder and grinding War gave their names to

---

[1] It must be remembered that the Italian dialects exhibited differences as great as those which separated them from the Greek, or the Greek dialects from each other; and thus the Latin equivalents of Greek words would show changes analogous to the Greek equivalents of Latin words. Thus, in Niebuhr's judgment, the Latin form of the name of the Apulian or Opican people would be Æqui. Other forms of these names would be Opscus, Oscus, Ausones, Aurunci, Sabini, Savnis, Samnis, Iapygians. Niebuhr seems inclined to identify the names Æqui and Volsci through the intermediate forms Opicus, Opscus, Oscus, Olsus. *History of Rome*, vol. i. 'Ancient Italy.'

[2] We know that the name Tyrrhenus was not an Etruscan word, and hence there is perhaps some reason for connecting Tyrrhenus, Turnus, Τύῤῥος, Τύῤ-σος, turris, and for regarding the name as the equivalent of the Greek Iarissuioi. Turnus is a son of Danaus, and of Venilia (Venus) a sister of Amata. In the Æneid Juturna is his faithful sister; but the resemblance of the two names is probably the result of accident.

Thorington and Eormington. Nay, the very names of Yng and Isco, the two sons of Man the son of Tiw, are merely words denoting the ash tree, from which, according to both German and Hellenic notions, some of the human races had sprung.[1]

From all these names no further ethnological conclusion can be drawn than that all the nations and tribes speaking Aryan dialects are sprung from ancestors who once dwelt somewhere as a single people. As evidence for narrower distinctions they are worthless. Argives and Athenians, Ionians and Arkadians, may have regarded each other as aliens, but their names have all the same meaning; and all their legends of prehistoric migrations and conquests resolve themselves into the great journey and the mighty battle which is repeated every morning and evening through all the seasons of the rolling year. We can no longer look to movements of Aiolians, Argives, or Herakleids as throwing light on the distribution of the Hellenic tribes in historical times.[2] The facts of that distribution must be received as they are given to us by the most trustworthy contemporary historians : to reason back from history into the regions of myth is an occupation not more profitable than the attempt to fill a sieve with water.

[1] Yng is apparently the eponymos of Angeln and the English. Max Müller, *Lectures*, second series, x.

[2] On this point Professor Max Müller speaks with sufficient emphasis: 'It may be difficult to confess that with all the traditions of the early migrations of Cecrops and Danaus into Greece, with the Homeric poems of the Trojan war, and the genealogies of the ancient dynasties of Greece, we know nothing of Greek history before the Olympiads, and very little even then. . . . Even the traditions of the migrations of the Chichimecs, Colhuas, and Nahuas, which form the staple of all American antiquarians, are no better than the Greek traditions about Pelasgians, Æolians, and Ionians, and it would be a mere waste of time to construct out of such elements a systematic history, only to be destroyed again sooner or later by some Niebuhr, Grote, or Lewis.'—*Chips*, i. 331.

CHAPTER XI.

MYTHICAL PHRASES FURNISHING THE MATERIALS OF THE HOMERIC POEMS.

IF the history of Greek literature to the close of the Peloponnesian War shows that the poems to which we give the name of Homer did not constitute the Homer of the lyric, tragic, or comic poets, and that our Iliad and Odyssey were, in the precise form transmitted to us, either unknown to them, or (what is altogether improbable), unpopular if known, these conclusions, it must not be forgotten, are only negative. The most zealous Euemerists of the present day admit that ' the general scheme of the Iliad existed before the days of Homer;' the most advanced sceptics have never supposed that the later poets of the Iliad and the Odyssey invented the materials of which they have made use. It is even likely that large portions of our Iliad and Odyssey may have existed substantially in their present shape long before the days of Æschylos and Sophokles; and even if we say that these two poems were thrown into their final form not long before the time of Plato, we do but say that from the vast mass of Homeric literature the poets chose those portions which from their general tone of thought and feeling were most congenial to the sentiment of the age in which they lived, that from the stories so chosen they removed unpleasant roughnesses and archaisms, and kept as much in the background as they could the ruder and more savage features of the traditions followed by the great tragic poets.[1]

CHAP.
XI.

Extent of the old Homeric literature.

[1] Mr. Paley, in his paper on the comparatively late date of our Homeric poems, asserts distinctly that 'the remodelling and reducing any important part of' the 'vast mass of "Homeric" literature would necessarily leave the stamp of the old authorship upon it, and so it would remain "Homer" still.' Not only, therefore, are the objections groundless which urge ' that no historical

BOOK
I.

In short, as soon as we have dismissed all speculations on possible historical quarrels fought out on the shores of the Propontis, as soon as we allow that if the Homeric poems turn on any historical quarrel at all, that quarrel must be carried back to an age indefinitely preceding the first dispersion of the Aryan tribes, we are at once left free to account for the origin and the growth of Homeric materials; and the shutting up of all other pathways shows, that if the question is ever to be answered, it can be answered only by following the track of Comparative Mythology.

Extent of
Homeric
mytho-
logy.

But the evidence which disproves the assertion of Bunsen, that our Iliad is 'the sacred ground-work of lyrical poetry no less than of the drama,'[1] invalidates at the same time all those arguments from the silence of our Homeric poems, on which some recent writers have been disposed to lay much stress. These arguments at best cannot reach very far. The epithet which speaks of Zeus as a son of Kronos implies a knowledge of dynasties among the gods; and the weight of proof lies therefore with those who maintain that the framer of the Iliad had never heard the story of Prometheus. Another epithet implies the knowledge that Achilleus was to die young, even if we put aside the passage which speaks of his death in the Odyssey. The poet of our Iliad knew that Paris was called Alexandros; and it is impossible to show that he was unacquainted with the myths which professed to explain the origin of this name. He also knew that the whole expedition of the Achaians against Troy was but an incident in the epical history of Paris, for the very cause of the war is that Paris came and stole Helen from the house of Menelaos. He knew further, for he tells us plainly, that the inaction of Achilleus had its counterpart in the inaction of Paris; and if he tells us how, after his long fit of sullen anger, Achilleus came forth in all his old energy, he also knew that Paris was not to be always idle, and that from him Achilleus himself was to receive his death-wound.[2]   Nothing

evidence exists of any new Homer having superseded the old Homer,' but it follows that the poets would ' retain the general archaic type of the heroic manners and dialogue.'

[1] *God in History*, book iv. ch. viii.
[2] ἤματι τῷ ὅτε κέν σε Πάρις καὶ Φοῖβος Ἀπόλλων
ἐσθλὸν ἐόντ' ὀλέσωσιν ἐνὶ Σκαιῇσι
πύλῃσιν.   *Il.* xxii. 359.

less than the clearest proof that our Homer was the Homer
of Pindar, Æschylos, and Sophokles, can weaken the conclusion that our poems are compilations, made for a purpose,
from the vast existing mass of Homeric literature. If this
purpose was to supply, 'in a convenient and symmetrical
form, the most celebrated and most engrossing incidents of
the war,'[1] it is unreasonable to look to the Iliad for notices
of myths which lay beyond the region of the poet's immediate subject, and it clearly did not concern him to go through
the genealogies of the Hesiodic theogony even if he knew
them. His task was to exhibit a few incidents in the special
career of Paris on the one side and of Achilleus on the
other; and if he knew that these incidents were linked with
others of which he does not speak, it only remains to point
out resemblances which probably escaped his notice, and to
account for their occurrence. It is of the very essence of
mythology that the original signification of the names which
serve as the groundwork of its narratives should be only in
part remembered. The author of the hymn to Hermes had
at best only an intermittent consciousness that he was simply
relating the rivalry of the wind and the sun; but he knew
enough of the attributes of Hermeias to write a poem,
almost every line of which points to the mythical speech of
which the tale is a petrifaction. The author of the Iliad
may not have felt that Achilleus was but a reflection of
Tantalos and Ixion, Sisyphos and Lykaôn : but his language
throughout the poem harmonises strangely with the mythical
phrases which speak of the lord of day when he hides away
his face behind the clouds. He could not know that the
Northman, even then wandering in regions which for the
Achaian had no existence, was framing the tale which grew
up into the epic of the Volsungs and the Nibelungs, and that
in that tale Achilleus and his mother Thetis were represented by Sigurd and his mother Hjordis. With the cause
of the expedition to Troy he had no immediate concern. He
tells us, in passing, the cause of the war; but his theme is
the wrath of the great chieftain from Phthia, and he has
kept to that theme with wonderful fidelity, if not to the

[1] Paley, *On the late Date of our Iliad and Odyssey*, 8.

R 2

Greek nature, yet to the old mythical speech. For after the admission of critics opposed to the hypothesis of Wolf, that the fragments in which the Homeric text was handed down from remote antiquity 'were cast and recast, stitched together, unstitched again, handled by uncritical and unscrupulous compilers in every possible way,'[1] it is impossible to dispute the conclusion that those portions of the poem which relate exclusively to the independent exploits of the other chiefs were at some later time embodied into a poem which may conveniently be termed an Achilleis.[2] Nor, if it be necessary to account for this insertion, have we far to go for a reason. The theme chosen by the author of the Achilleis confined him to a period of comparative inaction. The valour of the Achaians could only be asserted by an independent poem which showed that they were not helpless[3] even without the aid of the great son of Peleus. It is not surprising that the two poems should, with others which fitted in with the general plan, have been gradually blended together.[4]

[1] Edinburgh Review, October, 1858, p. 603.

[2] The downfall of the Euemeristic or conservative hypotheses make it really unnecessary to examine the mode in which the several portions of the Iliad have been pieced together. It is enough to say that, when the whole narrative of the Iliad has been proved to be unhistorical, and when the narratives of later alleged events have also been shown to possess no historical value, the burden of proof rests with those who affirm, not with those who deny, the original unity of a poem which, it is admitted on all sides, was in existence before the use of writing became general or adequate to the production of long manuscripts. It may be added, however, that the arguments of Colonel Mure (History of Greek Literature, book ii. ch. xvi.) and Mr. Gladstone (Homer and the Homeric Age, 'Aoidos'), fail altogether to meet the objections urged by Mr. Grote against the original continuity of the poem in its present form. Mr. Grote's remarks (History of Greece, part i. ch. xxi.) on the embassy to Achilleus dispose conclusively of every attempt to maintain the unitarian

theory on the ground of a supposed moral consistency in the character of Achilleus, while it also shows that the writer of the Achilleis knew nothing of the first effort for reconciliation. See Muir, Sanskrit Texts, part iv. ch. ii. sect. 3, where the like reasons are urged for regarding certain passages in the Mahâbhârata as interpolations.

[3] Colonel Mure, strangely enough, sees in Il. ii.–vii. nothing but a catalogue of disasters, bringing misery and disgrace on the Argive hosts. Crit. Hist. Gr. Lit. vol. i. p. 256. Mr. Grote, far more truly, says that the great chiefs are 'in full force at the beginning of the eleventh book.'—History of Greece, part i. ch. xxi.

[4] It would seem that the chief error of Wolf and his followers was the attempt to fix the date of this combination, which they attributed to Peisistratos. The acknowledged antiquity of the materials led them naturally to throw back, as far as possible, their work of bringing them into their present shape. The question loses much of the factitious importance given to it by anti-Wolfian critics, when the unhistorical character of the whole narrative of the Iliad has

Thus was produced an epic as magnificent as it is complicated; but through all its intricacy may be traced the thread of the original myth : and the fact that it may be so traced becomes the more remarkable as we realise the extent to which the process of disintegration has been carried on. If the poem does not exhibit the systematised theogony of Hesiod, still Phoibos is in it a person distinct from Helios, Artemis, or Athênê. Hekabê is no longer identified with Selênê or Lêtô : Zeus is no longer one with Ouranos. Only a few signs remain of that interchangeable character which is so prominent in the gods of the earlier Vedic poems. And further, the Iliad, by the admission alike of those who uphold and of those who reject the Wolfian theory, necessarily exhibits the later elements which must spring up with the growth of a definite religion, and the developement of something like civil government. Still, on the Trojan shore, facing the island of Tenedos, the old tale is repeated, which assumes a gloomier form in the mythology of the North. The mighty Achilleus, over whose childhood had watched Phoinix (the purple cloud), is there to fight, but, like Bellerophon, as he insists emphatically, in no quarrel of his own.[1] A hard toil is before him, but, as with Herakles, the honour which he wins is not to be his own.[2] Like Herakles, again, and Perseus and Theseus, his limbs are strong, and his heart knows no fear. In place of the sword of Apollôn, the Chrysâôr, or the Teutonic Sigurd, he has the unerring spear which no mortal can wield but himself.[3] Still, like Herakles and Apollôn and Perseus and Bellerophôn, he is practically the servant of one on whom he looks down with a deserved contempt.[4] On him falls all the labour of war, but the spoil which he wins with his bow and spear must pass into the

been clearly shown on grounds quite unconnected with the time of their composition. The real facts of Greek literary history lead Mr. Paley to the conclusion ' that there is not one shadow or tittle of proof that the Homer which we have was the Homer that Peisistratos is said, whether truly or not, to have collected and introduced into Athens.' *The late Date of our Iliad and Odyssey*, 7.

[1] οὐ γὰρ ἐγὼ Τρώων ἕνεκ' ἤλυθον
αἰχμητάων
δεῦρο μαχησόμενος· ἐπεὶ οὔτι μοι
αἴτιοί εἰσιν.   *Iliad.* i. 153.
[2] τιμὴν ἀρνύμενοι Μενελάῳ, σοί τε,
κυνῶπα.   *Ib.* i. 159.
[3] τὸ μὲν οὐ δύνατ' ἄλλος 'Αχαιῶν
πάλλειν, ἀλλά μιν οἶος ἐπίστατο πῆλαι
'Αχιλλεύς.   *Ib.* xvi. 142.
[4] This contempt is fully expressed—
Il. i. 225–231.

hands of Agamemnon,[1] as those of Herakles fall to the lot of Eurystheus. Still he has his consolation. He is cheered by the love of Hippodameia[2] (the tamer of the horses of the Sun). But even Brisêis he must now give up, as Herakles was compelled to part from Iolê. At the very thought of losing her, his passion overleaps all barriers; but his rage is subdued by the touch of Athênê, the daughter of Zeus, the sky.[3] He must yield, but with Brisêis vanishes the light of his life, and he vows a solemn vow that henceforth in the war the Achaians shall look in vain for his aid.[4] He hangs up his sword and spear in his tent, takes off his glittering armour, and the Argive warriors see the face of the bright hero no more. Yet even the fierceness of his wrath cannot avail to keep entirely in the background another feature in which he resembles Herakles, Sigurd, Theseus, and Iasôn. Brisêis is gone, but Diomêdê, the daughter of Phorbas, supplies her place, as Oinônê gives way to Helen, and the wise Medeia to the daughter of the Argive Kreôn. But the mind of Achilleus remains unchanged. His wrath is terrible as the wrath of the angry sun, and he bids Thetis, his mother, go to the throne of Zeus, who dwells in the bright ether, and pray him to send such a storm as may well make the Achaians rate their king at his true value.[5] The darkness thickens, but at first the Achaians care not. Zeus alone knows and proclaims that the fortunes of the Argives themselves must remain under the cloud until Achilleus again goes forth to battle.[6] His words are soon accomplished. The knowledge that the great champion of the Argives no longer takes part in the war inspires the Trojans with fresh strength. The storm-clouds rise with greater volume when

[1] τὸ μὲν πλεῖον πολυάϊκος πολέμοιο χεῖρες ἐμαὶ διέπουσ'· ἀτὰρ ἤν ποτε δασμὸς ἵκηται, σοὶ τὸ γέρας πολὺ μεῖζον. *Il.* i. 167.

[2] Brisêis was to the Greek a mere patronymic. The father of Brisêis is the Vedic Brisaya. 'Destroy, Saraswati, the revilers of the gods, the offspring of the universal deluder, Brisaya.'— H. H. Wilson, *R. N. S.* iii. 515.

[3] It is at the least worthy of note that, while Brisêis comes from Lyrnessos,

Diomêdê, who takes her place, belongs to the south-western Lesbos. *Il.* ix. 658. So Oinônê lives on Ida, but Helen in the far west. Iolê is the daughter of Eurytos (another name of the class Eurygancia, &c.), in the eastern island of Euboia; Dêianeira lives in the western Kalydon.
[4] *Il.* i. 240.
[5] *Il.* i. 407–412.
[6] *Il.* viii. 477.

the light of the sun is blotted out of the sky. Still the great chiefs of the Argives stand forth in unabated confidence;[1] but Agamemnon, Odysseus, and Diomêdes are soon wounded in the fight, and the Achaians begin to realise their grievous loss. Their misery excites the compassion of Patroklos, in whom the character of Achilleus is reflected, as is that of Helios in Phaëthôn, or that of Odysseus in Telemachos.[2] Melted by the tears of his friend, Achilleus gives him his own armour, and bids him go forth to aid the Argives. But with this charge he joins a caution. Phaëthôn must not touch with his whip the horses of Helios.[3] Patroklos must not drive the chariot of Achilleus on any other path than that which has been pointed out to him.[4] But although Patroklos can wear the armour of Achilleus, he cannot wield his spear.[5] The sword and lance of Apollôn and Perseus, of Theseus and Artemis, may be touched by no other hands than their own. Patroklos is ready for the fight, and yoked to the car of Achilleus stand the immortal horses Xanthos and Balios (golden and speckled as a summer sky), which Podargê, the glistening-footed, bare to Zephyros, the strong west wind, near the shore of the Ocean stream.[6] The sun is breaking out for a moment through the mist. Like hungry wolves, the Myrmidons (the streaming rays) stand forth to arm themselves at the bidding of their chieftain.[7] For a time the strength of Achilleus nerves the arm of Patroklos, so that

[1] *Il.* ix. 55.

[2] Mr. Grote has remarked this. 'Patroklos has no substantive position; he is the attached friend and second of Achilleus, but nothing else.'—*History of Greece,* ii. 238. Colonel Mure, however, discerns in the contrast between the two strong evidence of Homer's 'knowledge of human nature.'—*Crit. Hist. Gr. Lit.* i. 285.

[3] These heavenly steeds of Achilleus and Indra are not less prominent in the myths of Northern Europe; and some of them are endowed with that gift of speech which Xanthos possesses as the golden or gleaming horse of the sun itself, while it is denied to Balios, the mottled or speckled steed which represents the sunlit clouds. Thus the horse of Skirnir speaks to its master in the Edda, and Gudrun, after the death of Sigurd, talks with Gran, the noble steed,

which may well mourn for the hero who took him from king Hiulprek's stall and rode on him through the flames when he went to recover the stolen treasures. This horse, Grimm remarks, appears in the Swedish and Danish folk-lore under the name Black, a word which, it can scarcely be necessary to say, may signify whiteness and light not less than gloom and darkness. The same power of speech belongs in the Servian legend to Scharatz, who speaks to Marko shortly before his death, as Xanthos warns Achilleus of his impending doom. For other instances see Grimm's *Deutsche Mythologie,* 365.

[4] μὴ σύ γ' ἄνευθεν ἐμεῖο λιλαίεσθαι πολεμίζειν. *Il.* xvi. 89.

[5] ἔγχος δ' οὐχ ἕλετ' οἶον ἀμύμονος Αἰακίδαο, κ.τ.λ. *Ib.* xvi. 140.

[6] *Ib.* xvi. 151.

[7] *Ib.* xvi. 156.

he can smite Sarpêdôn, the great chief of the Lykians, in whose veins runs the blood of Bellerophôn, and for whom the bitter tears of Zeus fall in big drops of rain from the sky.[1] But the transient splendour is soon dimmed. It was but the semblance of the sun looking out from the dark cloud; and Patroklos, therefore, meets his doom. But the poet recurs unconsciously to the old myth, and it is Apollôn who disarms Patroklos,[2] although it is Hektor who slays him. The immortal horses weep for his death and the fall of their charioteer Automedon, while Zeus mourns that ever he bestowed them as a gift on so mean and wretched a thing as man.[3] In the fearful struggle which follows for the body of Patroklos, the clouds are seen fighting a fierce battle over the sun, whose splendour they have for a time extinguished. The ragged and streaming vapours which rush across the sky have their counterpart in the throng of Trojans who fling themselves like hounds on the wounded boar.[4] But a fiercer storm is raging behind the dark veil. Beneath the ' black cloud of his sorrow ' the anguish of Achilleus is preparing an awful vengeance.[5] The beauty of his countenance is marred, but the nymphs rise from the sea to comfort him,[6] as folk still say, ' the sun drinks,' when the long rays stream slantwise from the clouds to the waters beneath. One desire alone fills his heart, the burning thirst for vengeance; but when Thetis warns him that the death of Hektor must soon be followed by his own,[7] his answer is that the destruction of his great enemy will be ample recompense for his own early doom. Even Herakles, the dearest of the sons of Zeus,

---

[1] αἱματοέσσας δὲ ψιάδας κατέχευεν
ἔραζε.   Il. xvi. 459.
[2] Il. xvi. 790, κ.τ.λ. This was a strict mythical necessity; yet Colonel Mure lays great stress on it as showing the cowardice and brutality of Hektor. Crit. Hist. vol. i. p. 281. The result of his method is, that he finds himself compelled on every occasion to vilify the Trojans for the exaltation of their enemies. In a less degree, Mr. Gladstone's criticism lies open to the same remark.
[3] Il. xvii. 444.
[4] Ib. xvii. 725.
[5] ὃς φάτο· τὸν δ᾽ ἄχεος νεφέλη ἐκάλυψε μέλαινα.   Ib. xviii. 22.

[6] Il. xviii. 36. These nymphs are only half anthropomorphised. Their names still express their own meaning.
[7] Ib. xviii. 96. The real nature of this myth becomes still more apparent when looked at through the bald statements of Apollodoros, iii. 13, 8. Troy, he says, cannot be taken without Achilleus : the sun alone can subdue the dark clouds. But Thetis knows that, after Troy is taken, Achilleus must die. The sun must set after his victory over the mists. So she disguises Achilleus in woman's garb, as the light clouds half veil the early risen sun.

had submitted to the same hard lot.[1] His mind is made up. He retains still the unerring spear. It remains only that he should wait for the glistening armour wrought on the anvil of the fire-god Hephaistos. But, although the hour of his vengeance is not yet come, his countenance still has its terrors, and the very sight of his form[2] fills the Trojans with dismay, as they hear his well-known war-cry. His work is in part done. The body of Patroklos is recovered as the sun goes down unwillingly into the stream of ocean.[3] Then follows the awful vow of Achilleus. There shall be a goodly mourning for Patroklos. The life-blood of twelve Trojans shall gush in twelve streams on the altar of sacrifice,[4] like the torn and crimsoned clouds which stream up into the purple heaven when the angry sun has sunk beneath the sea. But the old phrases, which spoke of Helios or Herakles as subject to death, still spoke of both as coming forth conquerors of the power which had seemed to subdue them; and, true to the ancient speech, the poet makes Thetis assure her son that no hurtful thing shall touch the body of Patroklos, and that, though it should lie untended the whole year round, his face should wear at its close a more glorious and touching beauty.[5] The end draws nigh. The very helmsmen leave the ships as they hear the cry of Achilleus calling them once again to battle.[6] His wrongs

---

[1] *Il.* xviii. 117.

[2] *Ib.* xviii. 205. Here the sun is not unclouded. So Achilleus has about his head a golden cloud (χρύσεον νέφος), and the glory streams from him like smoke going up to heaven. The rays of the sun are bursting from the cloud.

[3] *Il.* xviii. 240.

[4] *Ib.* xviii. 336.

[5] ἥνπερ γὰρ κῆταί γε τελεσφόρον εἰς
ἐνιαυτὸν,
αἰεὶ τῷδ' ἔσται χρὼς ἔμπεδος, ἢ καὶ
ἀρείων. *Il.* xix. 33.
This incorruptibility of the bodies of solar heroes is strikingly brought out in modern Hindu legends, which are, as we might expect, even more transparent than those of the Teutonic nations. Thus, when the destined husband of Panch Phul Ranee dies on the seventh hedge of spears, her father asks, 'How is it that he thus dazzles our eyes?' and the glory shines

round him even in the hours of darkness. It is the same with Chundun Rajah, whose tomb the people came from far and near to visit, 'and see the great miracle how the body of him who had been dead so many months remained perfect and undecayed.' So, too, the body of Sodewa Bai, the Hindu Cinderella or Rhodôpis, cannot decay, nor can the colour of her face change. 'A month afterwards, when her husband returned home, she looked as fair and lovely as on the night on which she died.'—Frere, *Old Deccan Days.* Both these beings die, or seem to die, because they are deprived of that in which their strength lies, as in the golden locks of Nisos, who becomes powerless as Samson when they are taken from his head; but over these bright beings death can have no real dominion, and they all rise to more than their former splendour.

[6] *Il.* xix. 44.

shall be redressed. Agamemnon, the king, will yield to him the maiden whom he had taken away, and with her shall come other maidens not less fair, and gifts of priceless beauty.[1] But, with a persistency which, except by a reference to the sources of the myth, is at best a dark riddle, Agamemnon asserts his own innocence. 'I am not guilty,' he said. 'The blame rests with Zeus and Moira (who fixes the lot of man), and Erinys, who wanders in the air.' So the old wrong is atoned. The gifts are placed before him. The fair maidens come forth from the tent, but, with a singular fidelity to the old legend, Brisêis comes last of all,[2] beautiful and pure as in the hour when he parted from her,[3] even as Oinônê in her unsullied loveliness appears by the side of the dying Paris, or Iolê by the pyre of Herakles. Then it is that Achilleus forgives the wrong done to him, but repeats the riddle which lurked in the words of Agamemnon. It was not anything in the son of Atreus that could really call forth his wrath. 'He could never, in his utter helplessness, have taken the maiden from me against my will; but so Zeus would have it, that the doom of many Achaians might be accomplished.'[4] So he bids them go and eat, and make ready for the fight; but when Agamemnon would have Achilleus himself feast with them, the answer is that the time for the banquet is not yet come. His friend lies unavenged, and of neither meat nor drink will he taste till his last fight is fought and won.[5] The same truthfulness to the old idea runs through the magnificent passage which tells of the arming of Achilleus. The helmets of the humbler warriors are like the cold snow-flakes which gather in the north.[6] But when Achilleus dons his armour, a glorious light flushes up to heaven, and the earth laughs at its dazzling radiance.[7]

---

[1] *Il.* xix. 140. This is the first submission made by Agamemnon in the *Achilléis*. It may be noted that here he not only acquits himself of guilt (86), but, in order to fix the blame on Zeus, recites a tale which is essentially a separate poem, and may have existed long before, or apart from, the *Ilias* or the *Achilléis*, as may have been the case with such lays as those of Phoinix, *Il.* ix. 529, and Demodokos. *Od.* viii. 266.

[2] ἔστ', ἀτὰρ ὀγδοάτην Βρισηΐδα καλλιπάρηον. *Il.* xix. 245.

[3] *Ib.* xix. 261.

[4] *Ib.* xix. 274.

[5] *Ib.* xix. 210.

[6] ὡς δ' ὅτε ταρφειαὶ νιφάδες Διὸς ἐκποτέονται ψυχραί, ὑπὸ ῥιπῆς αἰθρηγενέος βορέαο. *Ib.* xix. 358.

[7] αἴγλη δ' οὐρανὸν ἷκε, γέλασσε δὲ πᾶσα περὶ χθὼν χαλκοῦ ὑπὸ στεροπῆς. *Ib.* xix. 363.

His shield gleams like the blood-red moon, as it rises from
the sea.[1] His helmet glitters like a star, and each hair in
the plume glistens like burnished gold. When he tries the
armour to see whether it fits his limbs, it bears him like a
bird upon the wing.[2] Last of all, he takes down his spear,
which none but himself can handle, while Alkimos and
Automedon (the strong and the mighty) harness his immortal horses. As he mounts the chariot, he bids them bear
him safe through the battle, and not leave him to die as they
had left Patroklos. Then the horse Xanthos bows his head,
and warns him of the coming doom. Their force is not
abated. They can still run swifter than the swiftest wind,
and their will is only to save the lord whom they serve and
love. But the will of Zeus is stronger still, and Achilleus
too must die.[3] It is a kindly warning, and the hero takes it
in good part. ' I know,' he says, ' that I shall see my father
and my mother again no more ; but the work of vengeance
must be accomplished.' Then, before the great strife begins,
Zeus bids all the gods (the powers of heaven) take each his
side. He alone will look down serenely on the struggle as
it rages beneath him.[4] Many a Trojan warrior falls by the
spear of Achilleus, and the battle waxes fiercer, until all the
powers of heaven and earth seem mingled in one wild turmoil.
The river Skamandros is indignant that the dead body of
Lykâôn, the (bright) son of Priam, should be cast into its
waters, and complains to Achilleus that his course to the sea
is clogged by the blood which is poured into it.[5] But
Achilleus leaps fearlessly into the stream, and Skamandros
calls for aid to Simoeis. The two rivers swell, and Achilleus
is almost overborne.[6] It is a war of elements. The sun is
almost conquered by the raging rain. But another power
comes upon the scene, and the flood yields to Hephaistos,
the might of the fiery lightning.[7] Fiercer yet grows the

---

[1] *Il.* xix. 374.
[2] *Ib.* xix. 386.
[3] *Ib.* xix. 387–417.
[4] *Ib.* xx. 22. The sky itself, regarded as the pure ether in which Zeus dwells, far above the murky air breathed by mortal men (κελαινεφές, αἰθέρι ναίων),
cannot be conceived as taking part in the contest, although the clouds and lightnings, the winds and vapours, beneath it may.
[5] *Il.* xxi. 219.
[6] *Ib.* xxi. 325.
[7] *Ib.* xxi. 345.

strife. The gods themselves struggle wildly in the fray, while Zeus laughs at the sight.[1] Artemis falls, smitten by Hêrê, and her arrows (the sun's rays) are gathered up by Lêtô and carried to the throne of Zeus.[2] But through all the wild confusion of the strife Achilleus hastens surely to his victory. Before him stands his enemy; but the spell which guarded the life of Hektor is broken, for Phoibos has forsaken him.[3] In vain he hurls his spear at Achilleus, in vain he draws his sword. Still Achilleus cannot reach him through the armour of Patroklos,[4] and the death wound is given where an opening in the plates left his neck bare. The prayer of Hektor for mercy is dismissed with contempt, and, in his boundless rage, Achilleus tramples on the body,[5] as the blazing sun seems to trample on the darkness into which it is sinking.

The close of the Achilléis.

At this point, in the belief of Mr. Grote, the original Achilléis ended. 'The death of Hektor satisfies the exigencies of a coherent scheme, and we are not entitled to extend the oldest poem beyond the limit which such necessity prescribes.'[6] The force of the objection depends on the idea by which the poet, either consciously or unconsciously, was guided in his design. The sudden plunge of the sun into the darkness which he has for a moment dispelled would be well represented by an abrupt ending with the death of Hektor. The 'more merciful temper' which Achilleus displays in the last book would not only be necessary 'to create proper sympathy with his triumph,' but it would be strictly in accordance with the idea of the sun setting in a broad blaze of generous splendour after his victory over the black mists, even though these are again to close in fierce strife

---

[1]   ἐγέλασσε δέ οἱ φίλον ἦτορ
γηθοσύνῃ, ὅθ' ὁρᾶτο θεοὺς ἔριδι ξυνιόντας.   Il. xxi. 390.
The ether looks down in grim serenity on the wild battle in the air beneath.
[2] Il. xxi. 490-505.
[3] Ib. xxii. 213: λίπεν δέ ἑ Φοῖβος 'Απόλλων. Too much stress can scarcely be laid on these words. In the first place, they make the slaying of Hektor quite as much an act of butchery as Colonel Mure represents the death of

Patroklos to be on the part of Hektor. In the second place, they remove both incidents out of the reach of all ethical criticism.
[4] Il. xxii. 322.
[5] Ib. xxii. 395, κ.τ.λ. This is a trait of brutality scarcely to be explained by a reference to the manners of the heroic age. The mystery is solved when we compare it with the mythical language of the earlier Vedic hymns.
[6] History of Greece, vol. ii. p. 266.

when he is dead.[1] It is this transient gleam of more serene
splendour which is signified by the games over which Achilleus presides genially after the slaughter of the Trojan
captives, whose blood reddens the ground, just as the torn
streamers rush in crimsoned bands across the sky after a
storm. Yet it is not easy to suppose with Mr. Grote that
the Achillêis ended with the twenty-second book as it now
stands, for that book closes with the mourning of Andro-
machê for Hektor, which, even in the eyes of a Greek, would
hardly heighten the glory of the conqueror; and the author
of it certainly knew of the visit of Priam which is related in
the last book, for he makes the old man express his intention
of going to Achilleus when he first learns that his son is
dead.[2] But the feeling of the old solar myth is once more
brought out prominently in the case of Hektor. With the
aid of Apollôn he had been the great champion of his country.
The desertion of the sun-god left him at the mercy of his
enemy. But his body, like the body of Patroklos, must be
preserved from all corruption. The ravenous dogs and birds
are chased away by Aphroditê,[3] and Apollôn himself wraps
it in mist and covers it with a golden shield.[4] From the
Odyssey we learn that the idea underlying the story of the
death of Achilleus was that of an expiring blaze of splendour,
followed by the darkness of the storm. Over his body the
Achaians and Trojans struggle in mortal conflict, like the
clouds fighting over the dead sun; and only the might of
Zeus puts an end to the strife, for the winds alone can drive
away the clouds. Then the sea-nymphs rise, fair as the
skies of tranquil night, and wrap the form of the dead hero
in a spotless shroud.

Thus the whole Achillêis is a magnificent solar epic, telling
us of a sun rising in radiant majesty, soon hidden by the
clouds, yet abiding his time of vengeance, when from the
dark veil he breaks forth at last in more than his early
strength, scattering the mists and kindling the ragged clouds
which form his funeral pyre, nor caring whether his brief
splendour shall be succeeded by a darker battle as the vapours

The whole Achillêis is a magnifi-cent solar epic.

---

[1] *Odyssey*, xxiv. 41, 42.
[2] *Iliad*, xxii. 415.
[3] *Iliad*, xxiii. 185.
[4] *Ib.* xxiv. 20.

close again over his dying glory. The feeling of the old tale is scarcely weakened when the poet tells us of the great cairn which the mariner shall see from afar on the shore of the broad Hellespontos.[1]

If this then be the common groundwork of the Achilléis and the epics of Northern Europe, the arguments of Mr. Grote against the original continuity of the Iliad in its present form are indefinitely strengthened. The Trojan war itself becomes simply a scene in a long drama,[2] of the other acts of which the poet incidentally betrays his knowledge. The life of Achilleus runs in the same groove with that of Odysseus and Bellerophon ; the personality of Patroklos dimly reflects that of Achilleus, while the tale of Meleagros is simply an echo of the legend which, in its more expanded form and with heightened colours, relates the exploits of the son of Peleus.

With this groundwork, the original Achilléis may have ended with the twenty-second book of our Iliad, or have been extended to the twenty-fourth. Apart from considerations of style, there is nothing in the story to militate against either supposition. If it ended with the earlier book, the poet closed his narrative with the triumphant outburst of the sun from the clouds which had hidden his glory. The poet who added the last two books was inspired by the old phrases which spoke of a time of serene though short-lived splendour after the sun's great victory. But with this tale of the Achilléis, whatever may be its close, the books which relate the independent exploits of Agamemnon and his attendant chiefs cannot possibly be made to fit. They are the expression of an almost unconscious feeling that a son of Peleus and Thetis was a being not sufficiently akin to Achaians to satisfy the instincts of national pride and patriotism.[3] It is of

---

[1] *Od.* xxiv. 82.

[2] Much blame, perhaps not altogether undeserved, has been bestowed on the critics who formed the so-called epic cycle and sought to find the sequence of the several legends on which the poems included in that cycle were founded. So far as they sought an historical sequence, they were wrong. Yet their feeling that there was a sequence in these tales was not without foundation. But the sequence is one of phenomena, not of facts in human history.

[3] Both Colonel Mure and Mr. Gladstone search vigorously for every vestige of patriotism in the character of Achilleus. It is very hard to find any, and harder still to see any in the passages which they adduce. It does exist in Hektor, and the reason why it should exist in him is manifest.

course possible—in the opinion of Mr. Grote, it may be even probable—that the same poet who sang the wrath of Achilleus afterwards recounted the exploits of Odysseus, Aias, and Diomêdes. The question is, after all, not material. If Mr. Grote is right in thinking that the last two books are an addition,[1] then the closing scene, which exhibits Achilleus in his more genial aspect, existed as a distinct poem, and the final complement of this lay is found far apart in the closing book of the Odyssey. The perfect harmony of that picture of the hero's death with the spirit and language of the Achillêis may possibly be adduced as an argument for ascribing both Iliad and Odyssey to the same author; but it furnishes a much stronger warrant for asserting that more than one poet derived his inspiration from the mythical speech, which, even in the Greek heroic age, still retained more than half its life. Nay, in the Ilias itself, the legend of Meleagros, recited (it must be remembered) by the same Phoinix who guarded Achilleus in his earlier years, exhibits still more forcibly the method in which phrases but partially understood, and incidents which had each received a local colouring and name, were wrought into the tales, whether of the Kalydonian chieftain, or Perseus, or Achilleus. In times which even then were old, such phrases formed the common speech of the people, such incidents expressed the phenomena of their daily life; and this language was strictly the language of poetry, literally revelling in its boundless powers of creation and developement. In almost every word lay the germ of an epic poem or a romance.[2] It is the less wonderful, therefore, if each incident was embodied in a separate legend, or even reproduced in the independent tales of separate tribes. A

[1] *History of Greece*, ii. 266.

[2] I cannot refrain from quoting the words of Mr. Price, in his Introduction to Warton's *History of English Poetry*: 'To take one example out of many, the life of Perseus might be made to pass for the outline of an old romance, or the story of some genuine chevalier proux. Let the reader only remember the illegitimate but royal descent of the hero, his exposure to almost certain death in infancy, his providential escape, the hospitality of Dictys, the criminal artifices of Polydectes, the gallant vow by which the unsuspecting stranger hopes to lessen his obligation to the royal house of Seriphus, the consequences of that vow, the aid he receives from a god and goddess, the stratagem by which he gains a power over the monstrous daughter of Phorcys, &c. &c. &c.—let the reader only recall these circumstances to his memory, and he will instantly recognise the common details of early European romance.'—(P. 120.)

hundred Homers may well have lit their torch from this living fire.

Nor can we well shut our eyes to the fact that in the main story of the Odyssey the poet has set the same solar strain in another key. When Odysseus goes to Troy, he is simply a chieftain in the great host which went to recover the treasure taken from the West, like the Argonauts in their search for the Golden Fleece. But all these eastward expeditions are successful. The robber or seducer is despoiled of his prey, and the victors must journey back to their distant home. Thus, round the chieftain of each tribe would gather again all the ideas suggested by the ancient myths; and the light reflected from the glory of the great Phthiotic hero might well rest on the head of Odysseus as he turns to go from Ilion. Thus would begin a new career, not unlike that of Herakles or Perseus in all its essential features. Throughout the whole poem the one absorbing desire which fills the heart of Odysseus is to reach his home once more and see the wife whom, like most other mythical heroes, he had been obliged to leave in the spring-time of his career. There are grievous toils and many hindrances on his way, but nothing can turn him from his course. He has to fight, like Herakles and Perseus, Theseus and Bellerophôn, with more than mortal beings and more than earthly powers, but he has the strength which they had to overcome or to evade them. It is true that he conquers chiefly by strength of will and sagacity of mind; but this again is the phase which the idea of Helios, the great eye of day, as surveying and scanning everything, assumes in Medeia, Prometheus, Asklêpios, Oidipous, Iamos, and Melampous. The other phase, however, is not wanting. He, too, has a bow which none but he can wield,[1] and he wields it to terrible purpose, when, like Achilleus, after his time of disguise, he bursts on the astonished suitors, as the

[1] *Odyssey*, xxi. 405. κ. τ. λ. The phraseology of the poet here assumes, perhaps without his being fully aware of it, the same tone with the narrative which tells of the arming of Achilleus. Others have tried with all their might to bend the bow. Odysseus stretches it without the least effort (ἄτερ σπουδῆς), and the sound of the string is like the whizzing of a swallow in its flight. In an instant every heart is filled with dread, and every cheek turns pale (πᾶσι χρὼς ἐτράπετο), and, to complete the imagery, they hear at the same moment the crash of the thunder in the sky.

sun breaks from the stormcloud before he sinks to rest. So, again, in his westward wanderings (for this is the common path of the children of Zeus or Helios), he must encounter fearful dangers. It is no unclouded sky which looks down on him as he journeys towards rocky Ithaka. He has to fight with Kyklôpes and Laistrygonians; he has to shun the snares of the Seirens and the jaws of Skylla and Charybdis, as Perseus had to overcome the Gorgons, and Theseus to do battle with the Minotauros. Yet there are times of rest for him, as for Herakles and Bellerophôn. He yearns for the love of Penelopê, but his grief can be soothed for awhile by the affection of Kirkê and Kalypso, as Achilleus found solace in that of Diomêdê, and Herakles awhile in that of Dêianeira. Nay, wherever he goes, mortal kings and chiefs and undying goddesses seek to make him tarry by their side, as Menelaos sought to retain Paris in his home by the side of the Spartan Helen, and as Gunnar strove to win Sigurd to be the husband of his sister. So is it with Alkinoös; but, in spite of the loveliness and purity of Nausikaâ, Odysseus may not tarry in the happy land of the Phaiakians, even as he might not tarry in the palace of the wise Kirkê or the sparkling cave of the gentle Kalypso. At last he approaches his home; but he returns to it unknown and friendless. The sky is as dark as when Achilleus lay nursing his great wrath behind the veil of his sorrow. Still he too, like Achilleus, knows how to take vengeance on his enemies; and in stillness and silence he makes ready for the mortal conflict in which he knows that in the end he must be victorious. His foes are many and strong; and, like Patroklos against Hektor, Telemachos[1] can do but little against the suitors, in whom are reflected the Trojan enemies of the Achaians. But for him also, as for Achilleus, there is aid from the gods. Athênê, the daughter of the sky, cheers him on, and restores him to the glorious beauty of his youth, as Thetis clothed her child in the armour of Hephaistos, and Apollôn directed his spear against Hektor. Still in his ragged beggar's dress, like the sun behind the rent and tattered clouds, he appears in his own hall on the day of doom. The old bow is taken down

[1] Grote, *History of Greece*, vol. ii. p. 238.

from the wall, and none but he can be found to stretch
it. His enemies begin to fear that the chief has indeed
returned to his home, and they crouch in terror before the
stranger, as the Trojans quailed at the mere sight and war-
cry of Achilleus. But their cry for mercy falls as vain as
that of Lykâôn or of Hektor, who must die to aveuge the
dead Patroklos; for the doom of the suitors is come for the
wrongs which they had done to Penelopê. The fatal bow is
stretched. The arrows fly deadly and unerring as the spear
of Artemis, and the hall is bathed in blood. There is nothing
to stay his arm till all are dead. The sun-god is taking
vengeance on the clouds, and trampling them down in his
fury. The work is done; and Penelopê sees in Odysseus the
husband who had left her long ago to face his toils, like
Herakles and Perseus. But she will try him still. If indeed
he be the same, he will know his bridal chamber and the
cunningly carved couch which his own hands had wrought.
Iolê will try whether Herakles remembers the beautiful network of violet clouds which he spread as her couch in the
morning. The sun is setting in peace. Penelopê, fair as
Oinônê and as pure (for no touch of defilement must pass on
her, or on Iolê or Daphnê or Brisêis), is once again by his
side. The darkness is utterly scattered; the corpses of the
suitors and of the handmaidens who ministered to them
cumber the hall no more. A few flying vapours rush at
random across the sky, as the men of Ithaka raise a feeble
clamour in behalf of the slain chieftains. Soon these, too,
are gone. Penelopê and Odysseus are within their bridal
chamber. Oinônê has gone to rest with Paris by her side;
but there is no gloom in the house of Odysseus, and the hero
lives still, strong and beautiful as in the early days. The
battle is over. The one yearning of his heart has been fulfilled. The sun has laid him down to rest

In one unclouded blaze of living light.

But unless the marvellous resemblance (may it not be said,
the identity?) of the Greek, the Trojan[1] and the Teutonic

---

[1] The stories of Paris, Hektor,
Sarpêdôn, Memnôn are all subjects
which might be expanded into separate
epics. The extent to which solar
imagery is introduced into these tales
is very remarkable. Paris as the seducer

epics can be explained away, it follows that in Achilleus and in Paris, in Meleagros and Sigurd, in Ragnar Lodbrog and Theseus, in Telephos, Perseus, Kephalos, Herakles, Bellerophôn and Odysseus, we have pictures drawn from the same ideal as regarded under its several aspects. It mattered not which of these aspects the poet might choose for his theme. In each case he had much more than the framework of his story made ready to his hand. The departure of Achilleus from his own land to fight in a quarrel which was not his own—the transfer of the spoils won by him to a chief of meaner spirit than his own—his unerring spear and immortal horses—the robbery of Brisêis or Hippodameia—the fierce wrath of Achilleus which yet could leave room for the love of another in her place—the sullen inaction from which he refuses to be roused—the dismay of the Achaians and the exultation of the Trojans at his absence from the fight—the partial glory spread over the scene by the appearance of Patroklos, only to close in the deeper gloom which followed his overthrow—the fury of Achilleus behind the dark cloud of his sorrow—the sudden outburst of the hero, armed with his irresistible spear and clad in armour more dazzling than that which he had lost—the invincible might which deals death to Hektor and his comrades—the blood which streams from the human victims on his altar of sacrifice—his forgiveness of Agamemnon for that which Agamemnon of himself would have been powerless to do—

CHAP.
XI.
or the Odyssey belongs to the invention of the poet.

of Helen is indubitably the dark robber who steals away the treasure of light from the sky; but it is difficult to deny that Paris, as fighting for his country, or in the beneficence of his early career, has all the features of Persons, Oidipous and Telephos. The same blending of two different ideas runs through all the Aryan mythology, and is a necessary result when the myths of two or more different countries are brought together in the same narrative. In the great struggle between the Achaians and Trojans, Agamemnon and Achilleus are ranged on the side of Helen, or Saramâ, the dawn; and all the Trojan champions, from this point of view, are in league with the dark powers of night. But among these champions are Sarpêdôn, the great chief

of the Lykians, and Glaukos, his friend, who also comes from the golden stream of Xanthos, and Memnôn the son of Êôs, who leads the glittering band of the Aithiopians (Ethiopians). The names of these heroes are as transparent as the stories which have gathered round them. Sarpêdôn more particularly is a counterpart of Achilleus, destined to exhibit the same magnificent qualities, and doomed to the same early death, but more equable and beneficent and therefore also happier. It is the same with the Argives. As fighting against Paris, Agamemnon is the adversary of the dark powers: but to Achilleus he stands precisely in the relation of Eurystheus to Herakles, or of Laios to Oidipous, or of Akrisios to Perseus.

a 2

the warning of his own early death which he receives from the horse Xanthos—the battle of the gods, as they take part in the storm which rages in the heavens and on the earth—the swelling of the waters, their brief mastery over the hero, their conquest by fire—the generous splendour which follows the accomplishment of his vengeance—the sudden close of his brilliant but brief career—the fierce battle fought over his dead body—the beauty which cannot be marred or dimmed by death—are incidents which the poet might introduce or omit at will, but the spirit of which he was not free to alter. The character of Achilleus was no more his own creation than were the shifting scenes in the great drama of his life. The idea of his picture no more originated in himself than the idea of Sigurd in the mind of the more rugged poet of the north. The materials were not of his own making; and the words of Mr. Gladstone acquire a stronger meaning, though not the meaning which he designed to convey, when, insisting that there must be a foundation for the Homeric theology and for the chief incidents in the war of Troy, he said that poets may embellish, but cannot invent.[1] Their course was marked out for them, but the swiftness with

---

[1] Of the *Æneid* of Virgil it is unnecessary to say much. Epic poetry, composed in a time of highly artificial civilisation, stands on a wholly different ground from the true epic of a simpler age, the growth of generations from the myth-making talk of the people. The tradition which brought Æneas to Italy was not of Virgil's making, and in taking him for his hero he bound himself to give the sequel of a career which belonged in its earlier stages to Greek mythology. Hence we have naturally in the story of Æneas nothing more than one more version of the old mythical history. Æneas, like Odysseus, moves from east to west, seeking a home, as Phoibos on a like errand journeyed to Pytho. His visit to the shades may have been directly suggested by the Greek poems which Virgil had before him as his model; and these were assuredly not confined to our *Iliad* and *Odyssey*. But it must have been a genuine tradition which led Virgil to tell how he left Creusa, as Theseus deserted Ariadnê and Apollôn forsook

Korônis. So, again, the war with Turnus for the possession of Lavinia reflects the war at Troy for Helen and the contest in the *Odyssey* with the enemies who strive to win the rightful bride of Odysseus. In this war Æneas, like other solar heroes, is successful, and, like them, after his victory, which is followed by a time of tranquil happiness, he plunges into the Numician stream and is seen no more, as Kephalos and Bellerophôn sink to sleep in the western waters of the Leukadian gulf.

The same type reappears in Romulus, whose story Niebuhr supposed that Livy obtained from a great epic now lost (Cornewall Lewis, *Credibility of Early Roman History*, vol. i. ch. vi. sect. 5); and the key is found to this legendary narrative as well as to that of Cyrus, of Chandragupta, and of the progenitor of the Turks. All these tales repeat the exposure of the infant Oidipous, or Telephos, or Iamos, or Alexandros. The same myth is seen under another aspect in the legend of Servius Tullius.

which each ran his race depended on his own power. The genius of the Homeric poets was shown, not in the creation of their materials, but in the truthful and magnificent colouring which they threw over a legend which in weaker hands might exhibit but a tinsel glitter.

But if there is this affinity between the character of the Achaian and the Teutonic heroes, it follows that the character is neither strictly Achaian nor strictly Teutonic. It cannot be regarded as expressing the real morality either of the one or of the other. Any attempt to criticise these as genuine pictures of national character[1] must be followed by

The portraits of the greater chieftains and heroes are not true to national character.

[1] The wish to base his criticism on this foundation has led Mr. Gladstone to assume without evidence, that the cause of Achilleus was substantially that of right and justice, and that the apology made by Agamemnon in *Il.* xix. 67, is essentially different from the apology made in ix. 120. But, in the first place, it is difficult to see that 'justice is' more 'outraged in the person of Achilleus' (*Homer, &c.* vol. iii. p. 370), than it is in the person of Agamemnon. If the former is compelled to part with Briseïs, the latter has also been obliged to give up the daughter of Chryses, for whom, with a plainness of speech not used either by Achilleus or even by Paris in deserting Oinônê, he avows his preference over his wedded wife Klytaimnêstra (*Il.* i. 110). Moreover, the taking away of Briseïs is the sole act of Agamemnon, in which his counsellors and the people take no part. Yet Mr. Gladstone holds it to be a 'deadly wrong,' justifying Achilleus in visiting his wrath on an army which had nothing whatever to do with it. The truth is, that by an analysis of this kind we may prove that Achilleus was mad, but we can never show that his character was either common, or even known among the Achaians. We have no right to say that the sufferings of Agamemnon were not at the least equal to those of Achilleus, and we are surely treating him most unfairly if we say that his apology 'comes first in his faltering speech' given in *Il.* xix. 67. If there he says—

ἀψ ἐθέλω ἀρέσαι δόμεναίτ' ἀπερείσι' ἄποινα,

he had said precisely the same thing in *Il.* ix. 120, &c. and there also confesses that he had been infatuated. In

fact, Mr. Gladstone is furnishing conclusive evidence in proof of the assertion that the writer of the nineteenth book knew nothing of the ninth. But it is hard to yield a self-chosen position; and Mr. Gladstone therefore holds that the apology of the nineteenth book is a valid atonement, although it is, word for word, the same as that which is contained in the ninth. The very fact that Achilleus is so ready, and even eager, to visit on the whole army the sin of the individual Agamemnon, shows how utterly destitute his character is of real patriotism. If anything more were needed to exhibit the falsity of such critical methods, it would be furnished by Colonel Mure's remarks that the aim of Homer is not to show, with Mr. Gladstone, the justice of the cause of Achilleus, but to prove that both he and Agamemnon were utterly in the wrong (*Crit. Hist. Gr. Lit.* vol. i. p. 277). Both sides in his judgment are equally deserving of blame : the one must be punished, the other convinced of his folly. This is the result of taking Homer to be a moral philosopher or teacher who, to adopt Mr. Gladstone's favourite Horatian motto, tells us all about human life and duty much better than Chrysippos and Krantor. Indeed, there seems to be no limit to violent interpretations of the text of Homer, if any such hypothesis is to be entertained. It is Mr. Gladstone's belief that the last book of the *Iliad* was added to show that Achilleus 'must surrender the darling object of his desire, the wreaking of his vengeance on an inanimate corpse' (*Homer, &c.* iii. 395). His ambition might, perhaps, have been more dignified; but such as it was, it had surely been gratified

that feeling of repulsion which Mr. Dasent openly avows for the Greek mythology, and which he also feels in part for the Teutonic.[1] In either case, this moral indignation is thrown away. There was doubtless quite enough evil in the character of the Northman and the Greek; but it never would have assumed that aspect which is common to the heroes of their epic poetry. We look in vain in the pages of acknowledged contemporary writers for an instance of the same unbounded wrath arising from a cause which the Achaian would be rather disposed to treat too lightly, of an inaction which cares not though all around him die, of a bloody vengeance on meaner enemies when his great foe has been vanquished, of the awful sacrifice of human victims,—a sacrifice completely alien to the general character of the Achaians, so far as they are known to us historically. But every one of these characteristics is at once exhaustively explained, when they are compared with those of all the other great legendary heroes. The grave attempt to judge them by a reference to the ordinary standard of Greek, or rather of Christian and modern morality, has imparted to the criticism of Colonel Mure an air almost of burlesque. In his analysis of the Iliad, the motives which sway Achilleus are taken to pieces as seriously as if he were examining the conduct of Themistokles or Archidamos. It might be well to speak of the 'defective principles of heroic morality,'[2] of the sarcasms of Achilleus against Agamemnon in the first book as 'unwarranted at this stage of the discussion,'[3] of the 'respectful deference to the sovereign will of Agamemnon' as a duty 'inculcated by the poet' and 'scrupulously fulfilled by the other chiefs,'[4] if the poet were telling us of a

already. If he was not contented with tying the body to his chariot wheels and dragging it about till every feature was disfigured, what more did he want? The whole of this moral criticism of epical characters is altogether out of place; and such criticism can be applied least of all as a means of determining national character to the hero who (in order to beat Hektor, in every respect, as Mr. Gladstone asserts, his inferior) is made invulnerable like Baldur and Rustem in all parts but the heel, and, clad in armour wrought by He-

phaistos, wields a spear (guaranteed never to miss its mark) against an enemy who, acknowledging his inferiority, yet faces him from the high motive of patriotism and duty, and whom he is unable to overcome except by the aid of Athênê and after he has been deserted by Apollôn. Such a condition of things lies altogether beyond the range of Ethics.

[1] See page 62.
[2] Crit. Hist. Gr. Lit. vol. i. p. 275.
[3] Ib. p. 277.
[4] Ib. p. 275.

struggle not with gods and heroes, Amazons and Aithiopians, but carried on after the sober and prosy fashion of the Trojan war of Thucydides. Colonel Mure lays great stress on the 'ethic unity' with which the incidental references to the early death of Achilleus invest the whole poem, and he finds a deep 'knowledge of human nature' 'in the adaptation to each other of the characters of the hero and his friend,' where Mr. Grote sees little more than a reflection.[1] But his anxiety to exalt the character of Achilleus has led him, in one instance of no slight moment, to vilify unduly that of his antagonist. 'The proudest exploit of Hektor, his slaughter and spoliation of Patroklos, is so described as to be conspicuous only for its ferocity. The Greek hero, after being disabled by Apollôn, is mortally wounded by another Trojan, when Hektor steps in with the finishing blow, as his butcher rather than conqueror.'[2] The remark is simply disingenuous. The incidents of the slaughter of Patroklos by Hektor are essentially identical with incidents attending the death of Hektor by the hands of Achilleus, and where there is any difference, it lies in the additional ferocity and brutality of the latter. If it be to the disparagement of Hektor that he should have the aid of a god, the poet is not less careful in saying that Achilleus could not slay Hektor until Phoibos Apollôn had deserted him. But if Colonel Mure anxiously seeks out apologies for the wrath,[3] the inaction, and the furious revenge of the hero, his criticism utterly fails to explain the very incidents which seem most deeply to have impressed him. It does not explain why he should choose inaction as the particular mode of avenging himself against Agamemnon.[4] It does not show why during his absence 'the gods had, at his own request, decreed victory to Hektor, rout and slaughter to the Greeks,'[5] why in him 'no affection

---

[1] *History of Greece*, vol. ii. p. 238.
[2] *Crit. Hist. Gr. Lit.* vol. i. p. 282.
[3] *Ib.* p. 284.
[4] When Helios complains to Zeus (*Od.* xii. 383) of the slaughter of his sacred cattle by Eurylochos and his comrades, his threat is that if justice is not done to him, he will leave his place in heaven and go and shine among the dead. But Helios was to the poet the

actual dweller in the visible sun. He could not well apply such a phrase even to Phoibos, and with Achilleus, Odysseus, Perseus, Meleagros, and other heroes, the memory of the old phrases has been still further weakened; but the voluntary and sullen inaction of such heroes answers precisely to the hiding of Helios in the dark land of Hades.
[5] *Crit. Hist. Gr. Lit.* vol. i. p. 288.

amiable or the reverse' should 'exist but in overpowering excess,'—why he should be 'soothed by the fulfilment of his duties as mourner,' why the games should 'usher in an agreeable change,' or why 'we should part with Achilleus at the moment best calculated to exalt and purify our impression of his character.'[2] Still less does it explain why, before the final struggle, the gods should be let loose to take whichever side they might prefer. Colonel Mure seems to imply that they were all sent to take the part of the Trojans.[3] Mr. Grote, with a far keener discernment of the character of this part of the poem, insists that 'that which chiefly distinguishes these books is the direct, incessant, and manual intervention of the gods and goddesses, formally permitted by Zeus, and the repetition of vast and fantastic conceptions to which each superhuman agency gives occasion, not omitting the battle of Achilles against Skamander and Simoïs, and the burning up of these rivers by Hephæstus.' In his judgment this interference mars the poem and 'somewhat vulgarises' the gods.[4] But while he thinks that the poet has failed in a task where success was impossible, he has not explained why the poet should feel himself compelled to undertake it.

The character of Odysseus.
But if Mr. Gladstone strains every nerve to save the character of Achilleus, Colonel Mure is not less zealous in behalf of the chieftain of Ithaka. If Achilleus 'represents the grandeur of the heroic character as reflected in the very excess of its noblest attributes,' Odysseus, in his belief, represents its virtue, possessing as he does, in greater number and in higher degree than any other chief, the qualities which in that age constituted the accomplished king and citizen.'[5] The matter is brought to a plain issue. The Odyssey is 'a rich picture-gallery of human life as it existed in that age and country,'[6] and we are to see in Odysseus a favourable specimen of the manners and habits of his people. It is quite possible, by Colonel Mure's method, so to represent him. But if we speak of him as one whose 'habitual

[1] Crit. Hist. Gr. Lit. vol. i. p. 289.
[2] Ib. p. 291.
[3] Ib. p. 287.
[4] History of Greece, vol. ii. p. 264.
[5] Crit. Hist. Gr. Lit. vol. i. p. 391.
[6] Ib. p. 389.

prudence was modified, or even at times overcome, by his
thirst for glory, and by an eager pursuit of the marvellous,'[1]
—if we say that he never uttered an untruth or practised a
manœuvre for a base object,[2]—if we speak of him as incul-
cating in his adventures ' the duty incumbent on the most
vigorous minds not only to resist but to avoid temptation,'[3]
are we really speaking of the Odysseus of the Homeric poet?
If such a method may account for some features in his
character, will it in the least explain his character as bound
up with the whole structure of the poem? Will it not leave
the groundwork of the tale and its issue a greater mystery
than ever? Will it explain why Odysseus, like Herakles
and Philoktetês, should use poisoned arrows[4]—why, without
scruple, he should tell lies while he desires to remain un-
recognised, why he should never depart from the truth when
speaking in his own character—why he hesitates not to lurk
in ambush for an unarmed man[5] and stab him behind his
back and speak of the deed without shame—why he should
wish to pry into everything in heaven or on earth, or
in the dark land beneath the earth—why nothing less than
the slaughter of all his enemies will satiate a wrath not
much more reasonable than that of Achilleus? Still more
will it explain why Penelope weaves and unweaves her web,[6]

---

[1] *Crit. Hist. Gr. Lit.* vol. i. p. 393.
[2] *Ib.* p. 395.
[3] *Ib.* p. 403.
[4] *Odyssey*, i. 263. Dr. Thirlwall
(*History of Greece*, vol. i. p. 182) refers
to this passage as showing the ' manifest
disapprobation' of the poet. It is, at
the least, very faintly expressed. Zeus,
possibly as being above law, gives the
poison, and Athéné sees no harm in his
so doing.
[5] *Odyssey*, xiii. 260.
[6] The Dawn as weaving or spinning
is the subject of many Teutonic legends.
In the story of Rumpelstiltskin, the
poor miller has a daughter who can spin
straw into gold, and the sequel of the
tale makes her, of course, the king's
bride. The idea once suggested was
naturally applied also to the sun, who,
as weaving his robe of clouds, becomes
the Valiant Tailor who, in the story of
the Glass Coffin, finds the beautiful
maiden sleeping like the dead in her

glassy case (of ice), and whose touch at
once calls her back to life, as the prince's
kiss awakens Dornröschen. This glass
coffin answers to the hammer of Thor,
like which, when placed on the magic
stone, it rises thr ugh the floors to the
upper air; and the case, when opened,
expands into a magnificent castle. In
the story of the Spindle, the Shuttle, and
the Needle, these instruments of the
craft of Penelopê bring a wooer home
for the orphan maiden, who, like Cinderella, becomes the wife of the king. It
is almost unnecessary to say that in a
vast number of stories in which the
princesses are confessedly Dawn-maidens, they are known especially as the
weavers and weavers, like Penelopê,
of marks for their fathers or their brothers. Thus Snow White and Rosy
Red, in the story of the Twelve Wild
Ducks (Dasent), is always sewing at the
shirts for her twelve brothers (the
months), who have been thus trans-

—why, when Odysseus returns, she is restored by Athênê (the daughter of the Sky, the Dawn who makes the world young), to all her early loveliness,[1] while on him rests once more all the splendour of his ancient majesty,—why the nurse who recognises him should be Eurykleia,[2] and the maiden who reviles him should be Melantho,[3]—why his dog Argos, although forsaken and untended, still retains something of his noble qualities and at once recognises his old master[4]—why, when Penelopê wishes to speak with him on his return, she is charged to wait until the evening [5]—why, in his wanderings he should fight not so much with human enemies as with mighty beings and monsters of the earth and sea—why his long voyage and the time of gloomy disguise should be followed by a triumph so full of blood, ending with a picture of such serene repose ?

In truth, the character of Odysseus was not, in any greater degree than that of Achilleus, an original creation of the Homeric poet. In all its main features it came down ready to his hand. His wisdom is the wisdom of Athênê, and Prometheus, and Medeia, of Iamos and Asklêpios and Melampous: his craft is the craft of Hermes, his keen sagacity is the piercing eye of Helios or of Odin, and from Hermes comes the strange inquisitiveness which must pry into everything that he comes across in his path.[6] If he uses poisoned arrows, it is not because Achaian chieftains were in the habit of using them, but because the weapons

---

formed. The princess rescued by Short-shanks also sits and sews. In the story of the Best Wish, the instruments for performing her work are supplied by Boots, whose scissors, plied in the air, bring to light all kinds of beautiful shapes, as the clouds and the earth are lit up by the rising sun. Nor is the Doll in the Grass (Dasent) less expert, though the sark which she weaves and sews is ' so tiny tiny little.' Most or all of these stories have their counterpart in the German and Celtic folklore. The exploits of the Valiant Tailor of the German stories are repeated in the Gaelic story of Mac-a-Rusgaich (Campbell, ii. 307) which reproduces the Norse tale of Boots who ate a match with the Troll. (Dasent.)

[1] *Od.* xviii. 192.
[2] *Ib.* xvii. 31. In the name of her father Autolykos we have again the same word which gave rise to the story of Lykâôn, and to the meaning which Æschylos attached to the name of Phoibos Lykeios, or Lykêgenês, the child of light.
[3] *Ib.* xviii. 321. We see the process by which the force of the old mythical language was weakened and lost, when the poet speaks of Melantho as καλλιπάρῃος.
[4] *Ib.* xvii. 300.
[5] *Ib.* xvii. 582.
[6] This inquisitiveness is specially seen in the episodes of the Kyklops and the Seirens.

of Herakles were steeped in venom and the robe of Medeia
scorched the body of Glaukê: if he submits to be the lover of
Kirkê and Kalypso, it is because Achilleus solaced himself
with Diomêdê for the loss of Brisêis, and Herakles awhile
forgot his sorrows in the house of Dêianeira. If he can be
a secret stabber, it is not because the heroic ideal could stoop
to such baseness, but because Phoibos can smite secretly as
well as slay openly, and because it matters not whether the
victim be but one man or the fifty who fall by the spear of
Bellerophôn. If at the end he smites all his enemies, it is
not because they have committed an offence which, according
to the standard of the age, would deserve such punishment,
but because the wrath of Achilleus could be appeased only
by the blood of his enemies, as the blazing sun tramples on
the dark clouds beneath his feet. We may be well assured
that such as these were not the habits of the men who dwelt
at Tiryns or in Ithaka—that such as these were not the
characteristics of the chieftains who dwelt in Mykênai. But
if the character of Odysseus is not strictly Achaian, so, like
that of Achilleus, it is not, in strictness of speech, human.
Mr. Grote has truly said that the aim of the poet is not ethical
or didactic either in the Iliad or in the Odyssey;[1] and an
examination of the latter poem scatters to the winds all
fancies which see in Odysseus an image of the Christian
warrior fighting the good fight of faith, yet yearning for his
rest in heaven.[2] The ideal is indeed magnificent, and it
has never been more magnificently realised, but it is not
the ideal either of Christianity or even of humanity; it is
the life of the sun. At the outset of his return from the
east, Odysseus has to encounter superhuman foes; and
the discomfiture of the Kyklops rouses the wrath of the
sea-god Poseidôn, as the clouds rise from the waters and
curl round the rising sun. Still Zeus is on his side, and

[1] *History of Greece*, vol. ii. p. 278.
Horace draws but a feeble moral when
he says of the *Iliad*—
Quicquid delirant reges, plectuntur
Achivi. *Ep.* i. 2, 14.
But that this should be the case is perfectly explained by the growth of mythology. The wrath of beings like
Achilleus and Odysseus must be widespreading and indiscriminate. The
clouds and winds take no heed of man.
[2] For a minute working out of this
view see Isaac Williams, *Christian
Scholar*, p. 115.

Poseidôn himself shall not be able to cut short his course,[1] though all his comrades should fall by the way, as the morning clouds may be scattered before the noonday. But while he moves steadily towards his home, that home is dark and gloomy. From it the sun is still far distant, and only from time to time a faint reflected light is shed upon it as Telemachos strives to maintain the honour of his father's house.[2] So Penelopê remains quiet in her home. Forbidding forms crowd around her, but her purity remains unsullied. The web begun is never ended; the fairy tracery of cirri clouds is blotted out from the sky every night, and must be wrought again during the coming day. There are others too who have not forgotten the hero, and Eurykleia strives to retain Telemachos, when he would go forth to seek his father.[3] But he cannot stay. The slant rays vanish from the sky, and the house of Laertes is shadowed with deeper gloom. Meanwhile Odysseus is hastening on. For awhile he tarries with Kirkê and Kalypsô, and makes a longer sojourn in the house of Alkinoös, even as Sigurd abode long time in the house of Gunnar. The Phaiakian chieftain would have him stay for ever. His land is as fair

[1] The influence of Polyphêmos on the fortunes of Odysseus strangely perplexes Colonel Mure, who sees in it the chief defect of the *Odyssey*, as interfering with the 'retributive equity' which he fancies that he finds in the *Iliad*. 'No reader of taste or judgment,' he thinks, 'can fail to experience in its perusal a certain feeling of impatience, not only that the destinies of a blameless hero and an innocent woman, but that any important trains of events, should hinge on so offensive a mechanism as the blind affection of a mighty deity for so odious a monster as Polyphêmus.'— *Crit. Hist. Gr. Lit.* vol. ii. p. 151. The real question to be answered was how the mighty deity came to be the father of the odious monster. As, according to the myth, he was his father, there was nothing unnatural in attributing to Poseidôn the affection of a parent for his offspring. But, in truth, nothing could show more clearly than these words Colonel Mure's inability to enter fairly into the spirit of Greek mythology. It was simply impossible that the poet could make use of any other mechanism. The train of

events which he recounts is not the sequence of any human life, but the career of Phoibos and Daphnê, Perseus and Andromeda. In short, the Kyklops is the son of Poseidôn, originally a god of the air—in other words, the exhalations which form themselves into the hideous storm-clouds, through which the sun sometimes glares down like a huge eye in the midst of the black forehead of the giant. Mr. Kelly, therefore, mistakes the eye which really belongs to the sun for the Kyklops himself, when he says, 'The Greek mythology shows us a whole people of suns in the Cyclops, giants with one eye round as a wheel in their foreheads.' He is right in adding that 'they were akin to the heavenly giants, and dwelt with the Phæacians, the navigators of the cloud sea in the broad Hyperia, the upper land, i. e. heaven, until the legend transplanted them both to the Western horizon.'— *Indo-European Folk-lore*, p. 32.

[2] The merely secondary character of Telemachos has been already noticed, p. 247.

[3] *Od.* ii. 365.

as summer : but the sun may not tarry, and Odysseus cannot abide there, even with Nausikaâ. So he hastens home, sometimes showing his might, as the sun breaks · for a moment through a rift in the clouds; but the darkness is greatest when he lands on his own shores. He is surrounded by enemies and spies, and he takes refuge in craft and falsehood.[1] The darkness itself must aid him to win the victory, and Athênê takes all beauty from his face, and all brightness from his golden hair.[2] These ideas, with all the others which had come down to him as a fruitful heritage from the language of his remote forefathers, the Homeric poet might recombine or develope; but if he brought him to Ithaka under a cloud, he could not but say that Athênê took away his glory, while yet his dog Argos, the same hound who couches at the feet of Artemis or drives the herds of the sun to their pastures, knows his old master in all his squalid raiment, and dies for joy at seeing him.[3] When on his return Telemachos asks whether the bridal couch of Odysseus is covered with spiders' webs, he could not but say in reply that Penelopê still remained faithful to her early love;[4] and when Telemachos is once more to see his father, he could not but make Athênê restore him to more than his ancient beauty.[5] So the man of many toils and wanderings returns to his home,[6] only to find that his son is unable to rule his house,[7] as Phaëthôn and Patroklos were alike unable to guide the horses of Helios. Still Penelopê is fair as Artemis or Aphroditê,[8] although Melantho and Melanthios,[9] the black children of the crafty (Dolios) Night, strive to dash her life with gloom, and Odysseus stands a squalid beggar in his own hall.[10] Thenceforth the poet's path was still more distinctly marked. He must make the arm of Odysseus irresistible,[11] he must make Athênê aid him in storing up weapons for the conflict,[12] as

---

[1] *Odyss.* xiii. 255, κ.τ.λ.
[2] *Ibid.* xii. 431. The language adheres even more closely to the myth. His locks are actually destroyed,

ξανθὰς ἐκ κεφαλῆς ὅλεσσε τρίχας·

Those which she gave him when she restored his beauty would be strictly the new rays bursting from behind the clouds.

[3] *Odyss.* xvii. 327. [4] *Ibid.* xvi. 35.
[5] *Ibid.* xvi. 175.
[6] *Ibid.* i. 2; xvi. 205.
[7] *Ibid.* xvi. 256. [8] *Ibid.* xvii. 37.
[9] *Ibid.* xvii. 212; xviii. 320.
[10] *Ibid.* xvii. 363. [11] *Ibid.* xviii. 95.
[12] *Ibid.* xix. 33.

Thetis brought the armour of Hephaistos to Achilleus, and Hjordis that of Regin to Sigurd. He must make Penelopê tell how often she had woven and undone her web while he tarried so long away.[1] When Penelopê asks tidings of Odysseus, the poet could not but give an answer in which the flash of gold and blaze of purple carries us directly to the arming of Achilleus.[2] As Eurykleia, the old nurse, tends him at the bath, he must make her recognise the wound made by the wild boar,[3] who wrought the death of the fair Adonis, and tell how her foster-child came to be called Odysseus.[4] Then, as the day of doom is ushered in, he must relate how as the lightning flashed from the sky[5] the rumour went abroad that the chieftain was come again to his home. So Penelopê takes down the bow which Iphitos, the mighty, had given to Odysseus,[6] and bids the suitors stretch it; but they cannot, and there is no need that Telemachos should waste his strength now that his father has come home.[7] Then follows the awful tragedy. Zeus must thunder as the beggar seizes the bow.[8] The suitors begin to fall beneath the unerring arrows; but the victory is not to be won without a struggle. Telemachos has left the chamber door ajar and the enemy arm themselves with the weapons which they find there.[9] It is but another version of the battle which Achilleus fought with Skamandros and Simoeis in the war of elements; and as then the heart of Achilleus almost failed him, so wavers now the courage of Odysseus.[10] For a moment the dark clouds seem to be gaining mastery over

[1] *Od.* xix. 140. Penelopê is the weaver of the web (ἱστὸν) of cirri clouds. Mr. Kelly, summing up the general characteristics of Aryan mythology, says 'Light clouds were webs spun and woven by celestial women, who also drew water from the fountains on high and poured it down as rain. The yellow light gleaming through the clouds was their golden hair. A fast-scudding cloud was a horse flying from its pursuers. . . In all this and much more of the same kind, there was not yet an atom of that symbolism which has commonly been assumed as the starting-point of all mythology. The mythic animals, for example, were, for those who first gave them their names, no

mere images or figments of the mind. They were downright realities, for they were seen by men who were quick to see, and who had not yet learned to suspect any collusion between their eyes and their fancy.'—*Curiosities of Indo-European Tradition and Folk-lore*, p. 8.
[2] *Od.* xix. 225,
[3] *Ibid.* xix. 393.
[4] *Ibid.* xix. 201. The origin of this name, as of so many others, is wrongly accounted for. The same confusion was at work here, which changed Lykâon into a wolf, and Kallisto into a bear.
[5] *Od.* xx. 105.   [6] *Ibid.* xxi. 5.
[7] *Ibid.* xxi. 130.   [8] *Ibid.* xxi. 413.
[9] *Ibid.* xxii. 141.   [10] *Ibid.* xxii. 147.

the sun. But Athênê comes to his aid,[1] as before she had come to help Achilleus, and the arrows of the suitors are in vain aimed at the hero,[2] although Telemachos is wounded,[3] though not to the death, like Patroklos. Yet more, Athênê must show her Aigis,[4] dazzling as the face of the unclouded sun ; and when the victory is won, the corpses of the slain must be thrust away,[5] like the black vapours driven from the sky. Only for Melanthios he reserves the full measure of indignity which Achilleus wreaked on the body of the dead Hektor.[6] Then follows the recognition in which, under another form, Prokris again meets Kephalos, and Iolê once more rejoices the heart of Herakles. For a little while the brightness rests on Laertes, and the old man's limbs again grow strong; but the strength comes from Athênê.[7]

CHAP. XI.

Whatever light the progress of Comparative Mythology may hereafter throw on the growth of Aryan epic poetry, one conclusion, at the least, is forced upon us by this analysis, and Odysseus is found to be as much and as little an Achaian chieftain as Achilleus or Meleagros. The poems may remain a mine of wealth for all who seek to find in them pictures and manners of the social life of a pre-historic age ; but all the great chiefs are removed beyond a criticism, which starts with attributing to them the motives which influence mankind under any circumstances whatsoever.

The character of Odysseus not Achaian.

---

[1] *Odyss.* xxii. 205.   [2] *Ibid.* xxii. 257.   [3] *Ibid.* xxii. 277.   [4] *Ibid.* xxii. 297.
[5] *Ibid.* xxii. 460.   [6] *Ibid.* xxii. 475.   [7] *Ibid.* xxiv. 367.

CHAPTER XII.

MYTHICAL PHRASES AS FURNISHING MATERIALS FOR THE TEU-
TONIC EPIC POEMS, AND THE LEGENDS OF ARTHUR AND
ROLAND.

BOOK
I.

Points of
likeness
between
the Greek
and Teu-
tonic epics.

THE results obtained from an examination of Greek epic
poetry, so far as it has come down to us, have a direct and
important bearing on the mythology of northern Europe,
and on the estimate which we must take of it. Of the general
character of the Hellenic tribes we can form a notion more
or less exact from the evidence of contemporary documents,
as soon as we reach the historical age; but, whatever may
be its defects or its vices, we are fully justified in saying
that it is not the character of the great Achaian chieftains
as exhibited either in the Iliad or the Odyssey. We have
absolutely no warrant for the belief that the ancestors of
Perikles or Themistokles, within ten or even more generations,
were men who would approve the stabbing of enemies behind
their backs, the use of poisoned arrows, and the butchery of
captives deliberately set apart to grace the funeral sacrifices
of a slain chief. Nay, more, we shall look in vain in any
historical record for any portrait which will justify the belief
that the picture of Achilleus in the Iliad is the likeness
of an actual Achaian chieftain, while on any psychological
analysis we seem to be driven to the conclusion that the
character is one removed altogether from the bounds of
humanity. If the analysis already made of the character of
Odysseus and Achilleus shows that almost every feature is
traditional, and that the portraits, as a whole, are not of the
poet's making, that the wisdom and the falsehood, the truthfulness and the sullenness, whether of the one hero or the
other, were impressed upon each by a necessity which no

poet could resist, and that these conclusions are proved by
the evidence, overwhelming in its amount, which shows that
Achilleus and Odysseus are reflections of Perseus, Theseus,
Herakles, and these, again, of Phoibos and Helios, or of other
deities who share their attributes—if the whole story which
has gathered round the names of these great national heroes
resolves itself into the cloudland of heaven with its never
ceasing changes, we are at once justified in thinking that
the history of the Teutonic heroes may be of much the same
kind; and if on examining it we not only find this suspicion
borne out, but discern in it some of the most important
incidents and sequences which mark the Greek legends, the
conclusion is forced upon us that the Teutonic epics, like
the Hellenic, are the fruit of one and the same tree which
has spread its branches over all the Aryan lands, and that
the heroes of these epics no more exhibit the actual character
of Northmen and Germans than the portraits of the heroes
in the Iliad and Odyssey are pictures of actual Achaian chieftains. When we find further that the action in each case
turns on the possession of a beautiful woman and the treasures which make up her dowry, that this woman is in each
case seduced or betrayed, while the hero with his invincible
weapons is doomed to an early death after the same stormy
and vehement career, we see that we are dealing with materials which under different forms are essentially the same;
and our task becomes at each stage shorter and simpler.

Hence as we begin the story of Volsung (who is Diogenes
or the son of Odin, his father Rerir and his grandfather
Sigi being the only intermediate links), we suspect at once
that we are carried 'away from the world of mortal men,
when we find that he is one of those mysterious children
whose birth from a mother destined never to see them [1] por-
tends their future greatness and their early end; and as we
read further of the sword which is left for the strongest in

The Vol-
sung Tale.

[1] So in the Hindu popular story,
Vikramaditya (the child of Aditi, Kronos.
or the Dawn-land of the East), is the
son of Gandharba-sena. When his
sire died, his grandfather, the deity
Indra, resolved that 'the babe should
not be born, upon which his mother
stabbed herself. But the tragic event
duly happening during the ninth month,
Vikramaditya came into the world by
himself.'—Burton, *Tales of Indian
Devilry*, preface, p. xv.

the rooftree of Volsung's hall, no room is left for doubt that
we have before us the story of Theseus in another dress. The
one-eyed guest with the great striped cloak and broad flapping
hat, who buries the sword up to its hilt in the huge oak stem,[1]
is Odin, the lord of the air, who in Teutonic mythology is like
the Kyklops, one-eyed, as Indra Savitar is one-handed. But
Aigeus in the Argive story is but one of the many names of
Zeus Poseidôn, and as the husband of Aithra, the ether, he
also is lord of the air. In vain, when Odin has departed, do
Siggeir, the husband of Volsung's daughter Signy, and the
other guests at her marriage-feast, strive to draw the sword.
It remains motionless in the trunk until it is touched by
Sigmund,[2] the youngest and bravest of Volsung's sons—a
reproduction in part of Volsung himself, as Odysseus is of
Autolykos. To Sigmund's hand, as to Arthur, the sword
yields itself at once, without an effort. Theseus lifts the
huge stone beneath which Aigeus had placed his magic sword
and sandals. The weapon of the Greek story is the sword of
Chrysâôr; that of the Teutonic legend is the famous Gram,
the Excalibur of Arthur and the Durandal of Roland, and
Sigmund thus becomes, like Achilleus, the possessor of an
irresistible arm. In truth, the whole myth of Volsung and
his children is but a repetition, in all its phases, of that
great drama of Greek mythology which begins with the loss
of the golden fleece and ends with the return of the Herakleidai. This drama represents the course or history of the
sun in all its different aspects, as ever young or growing old,
as dying or immortal, as shooting with poisoned weapons or
as hating a lie like death, as conquering the powers of darkness or as smitten by their deadly weapons; and thus in the
defeat of Sigmund we have an incident belonging as strictly

[1] This tree grows through the roof of
the hall and spreads its branches far and
wide in the upper air. It is manifestly
the counterpart of Yggdrasil.
[2] The Sigmund of Beowulf and the
Volsung Tale bears a name which is an
epithet of Odin, the giver of victory.
He is drawn by Regin from the trunk
of a poplar tree, he is loved by the
Valkyrie Brynhild, and instructed by
the wise Gripir, as Achilleus and other
heroes are taught by Cheiron. He
wears the invisible helmet, and like
many or most mythical champions, can
be wounded only in one part of his
body. If again Fafnir, when dying by
his hand, tells him of the things which
shall happen hereafter, we must remember that the Pythian dragon guarded
the oracle of Delphi.—Grimm, Deutsche
Mythologie, 343.

to the solar myth as the victory of Achilleus over Hektor, or the slaughter of the Sphinx by Oidipous. It could not be otherwise. Odin and Phoibos live while Baldur and Asklepios die, but these rise again themselves or live in their children. So, too, there must be a struggle between Siggeir and Sigmund for the possession of Gram, for Siggeir stands to Sigmund in the relation of Polydektês to Perseus, or of Paris to Menelaos. But he is the dark being regarded for the present as the conqueror, and Sigmund and his ten brothers, the hours of the sunlit day, are taken and bound. The ten brothers are slain; Sigmund himself is saved by his sister Signy, and with his son Sinfiötli, now runs as a werewolf through the forest, the Lykeian or wolf-god wandering through the dark forest of the night—a dreary picture which the mythology of sunnier lands represented under the softer image of the sleeping Helios sailing in his golden cup from the western to the eastern ocean. But the beautiful Signy is no other than Penelopê, and Siggeir's followers are the suitors who eat up the substance of Sigmund, as they had deprived him of his armour. There remains therefore to be wrought again a vengeance like that of Odysseus: and when Sinfiötli is, like Telemachos, strong enough to help his father, the two, like the Ithakan chieftains, burn up Siggeir and all his followers, the mode in which they are slain pointing to the scorching heat of the sun not less clearly than the deadly arrows which stream from the bow of Odysseus. Sigmund now regains his heritage, and for him, as for Odysseus, there follows a time of serene repose. Like Nestor, who is exaggerated in Tithonos, he reaches a good old age: but as Odysseus must yet go through the valley of death, so Sigmund has to fight the old battle over again, and is slain in a war with the sons of King Hunding, in whom are reflected the followers of Siggeir. But Achilleus is slain only when Apollôn guides the spear of Paris; and so when Sigmund's hour is come, the one-eyed man with the flapping hat and the blue garment (of ether) is seen again. As he stretches out this spear, Sigmund strikes against it his good sword Gram, and the blade is shivered in twain. The hero at once knows that Odin stands before him, and prepares to die on the battle-field. But Iolê stood by the funeral pile of Herakles, and Sigmund dies in the arms of his young wife Hjordis, youthful as Daphnê or Arethousa, 'refusing all leechcraft and bowing his head to Odin's will,' as in the Trojan myth Paris cannot be healed even though Oinônê would gladly save him.

The Story of Sigurd.

So ends the first act of the great drama; but the wheel has only to make another turn, and bring back the same series of events with slight differences of names and colouring. Sigmund leaves Hjordis the mother of an unborn babe, the Phoibos who is the child of Lêtô, and of the Sun who sank yestereve beneath the western waters. This child, who receives the name of Sigurd, is born in the house of Hialprek, who is localised as King of Denmark, but who represents Laios or Akrisios in the Theban and Argive legends; and these, we need not say, are simply reflections of Vritra, the being who wraps all things in the veil of darkness. Sigurd himself is the favourite hero of northern tradition. Like Achilleus, he is the destined knight who succeeds where all others have failed before him. Troy cannot fall if the son of Peleus be absent; Fafnir cannot be slain, nor Brynhild rescued, except by the son of Sigmund. Physically, there is no difference between them. Both have the keen blue eyes, and golden locks, and invincible weapons of Phoibos and Athênê; on both alike rests the glory of a perfect beauty; and to both their weapons and their armour come from the god of fire. But in the Norse story there is a connection between Regin, the mysterious smith of King Hialprek, and the dragon Fafnir, which cannot be traced between Hephaistos and the Delphian Python, but which is fully explained by the differences of a northern and a mediterranean climate. In the Norse story, there is enmity between Fafnir and Regin, between the serpent who has coiled round the treasure of Brynhild (as the Panis hide the cows of Indra), and the faculties of life and growth represented by the dwarfs to whose race Regin belongs.[1] Regin,

---

[1] 'The dwarfs of Teutonic mythology are distinguished from its giants, because they do not, like the latter, represent the wild and lawless energies of nature, but the contrivance and wonderful properties present in the mineral and vegetable kingdoms, and shown in form and shape, in colour and growth, in

in short, is one of that class of beings who supply warmth
and vigour to all living things; Fafnir is the simple darkness
or cold, which is the mere negation of life and light. Hence
from Regin comes the bidding which charges Sigurd to slay
Fafnir; but the mode in which this enmity is said to have
been excited is singularly significant. In their wanderings,
Odin, Loki, and Hahnir, the gods of the glistening heavens,
come to a river where, nigh to a ford, an otter is eating a
salmon with its eyes shut. Loki, slaying the beast with a
stone, boasts that at one throw he has got both fish and flesh.
This is the first blow dealt by the lords of light to the powers
of cold and darkness: but the way is as yet by no means
open before them. Many a day has yet to pass, and many a
hero yet to fall, before the beautiful summer can be brought
out from the prison-house hedged in by its outwork of spears
or ice. The slain otter is a brother of Fafnir and Regin,
and a son of Reidmar, in whose house the three gods ask
shelter, showing at the same time their spoil. At Reidmar's
bidding his two surviving sons bind Loki, Odin, and Hahnir,
who are not set free until they promise to fill the otter's
skin with gold, and so to cover it that not a white hair shall
be seen—in other words, the powers of the bright heaven are
pledged to loosen the ice-fetters of the earth, and destroy
every sign of its long bondage. But the gold is the glistening treasure which has been taken away when Persephonê
was stolen from her mother Dêmêtêr and Brynhild left to
sleep within the walls of flame. Hence Loki must discharge
the office of Hermes when he goes to reclaim the maiden
from the rugged lord of Hades; and thus Odin sends Loki
to the dwelling of the dark elves, where he compels the
dwarf Andvari to give up the golden treasures which he had
hoarded in the stony caves, whose ice-like walls answer to
the dismal den of the Vedic Panis. One ring alone Andvari
seeks to keep. It is the source of all his wealth, and ring
after ring drops from it. He wishes, in other words, to keep

various hurtful or useful qualities.'
Bunsen (*God in History*, ii. 484),
rightly adds, ' The word must be a
simple Teutonic one, and we most likely
come on the traces of its primary signi-

ficance in our word *Zwerch*, as equivalent
to *quer*, wicked or cross, the intellectual
application of which has survived
in the English *queer*.'

his hold of the summer itself as represented by the symbol of the reproductive power in nature. The ring is the magic necklace of Harmonia and Eriphyle, the kestos of Aphroditê, the ship of Isis and Athênê, the Yoni of Vishnu, the Argo which bears within itself all the chieftains of the Achaian lands. Andvari prays in vain, but before he surrenders the ring, he lays on it a curse, which is to make it the bane of every man who owns it. It is, in short, to be the cause of more than one Trojan war,[1] the Helen who is to bring ruin to the hosts who seek to rescue her from thraldom. The beauty of the ring tempts Odin to keep it, but the gold he yields to Reidmar. It is, however, not enough to hide all the white hairs of the otter's skin. One yet remains visible, and this can be hidden only by the ring which Odin is thus compelled to lay upon it, as the ice cannot be wholly melted till the full warmth of summer has come back to the earth. Thus the three Æsir go free, but Loki lays again on the ring the curse of the dwarf Andvari. The working of this curse is seen first in the death of Reidmar, who is slain by Regin and Fafnir, because he refuses to share with them the gold which he had received from the Æsir. The same cause makes Regin and Fafnir enemies. Fafnir will not yield up the treasure, and taking a dragon's form he folds his coils around the golden heaps upon the glistening heath, as the Python imprisons the fertilising streams at Delphoi. Thus foiled, Regin beseeches Sigurd to smite the dragon; but even Sigurd cannot do this without a sword of sufficient temper. Regin forges two, but the blades of both are shivered at the first stroke. Sigurd exclaims bitterly that the weapons are untrue, like Regin and all his race,—a phrase which points with singular clearness to the difference between the subterranean fires and the life-giving rays of the sun, which alone can scatter the shades of night or conquer the winter's cold. It is clear that the victory cannot be won without the sword which Odin drove into the oak trunk, and which had been broken in the hands of Sigmund. But the

---

[1] This ring reappears with precisely the same qualities and consequences in many of the sagas of Northern Europe; and it is absurd to suppose that such a series of incidents was constantly recurring in actual history.

pieces remain in the keeping of Hjordis, the mother of Sigurd, and thus the wife of Sigmund plays here precisely the part of Thetis. In each case the weapons with which the hero is to win his victory come through the mother, and in each case they are forged or welded by the swarthy fire-god; but the Norse tale is even more true than the Homeric legend, for the sword which smites the darkness to-day is the same blade which the enemies of the sun yestereve snapped in twain. With the sword thus forged from the shattered pieces of Gram Regin bids Sigurd smite the Dragon: but the hero must first avenge his father's death, and King Hunding, his sons, and all his host are slain, like the suitors by the arrows of Odysseus, before Sigurd goes forth on his good steed Gran, which Odin had brought to him as Athênê brought Pegasos to Bellerophôn, to encounter the guardian of the earth's treasures. But no sooner is the Dragon slain than Regin in his turn feels the desire of vengeance for the very deed which he had urged Sigurd to do, and he insists that the hero shall bring him his brother's heart roasted. Then filling himself with Fafnir's blood, Regin lies down to sleep, and Sigurd, as he roasts the heart, wonders whether it be soft, and putting a portion to his lips, finds that he understands the voices of the birds, who, singing over his head, bid him eat it all and become the wisest of men, and then, cutting off Regin's head, take possession of all his gold. This is manifestly the legend of Iamos and Melampous, while the wisdom obtained by eating the heart of Fafnir has a further connection with the Python as the guardian of the Delphic oracle.[1]

[1] Grimm regards the words Python and Fafnir as standing to each other in the relation of Θήρ and φήρ. 'Die Erlegung des Drachen Fáfnir gemahnt an Πύθων, den Apollo besiegte, und wie Python das delfische Orakel hütete, weissagt der sterbende Fáfnir.'—*Deutsche Mythologie*, 345. In the lay of Beowulf this serpent or dragon appears under the name Grendel; and, in fact, the whole story of Sigurd is in that poem related substantially, although not with the same fulness of detail, of Sigmund the father of Beowulf, the Wælsing, who, having slain the worm, becomes the possessor of the ring hoard which he may enjoy at pleasure. Like the Norse Sigurd, Sigmund is 'of wanderers by far the greatest throughout the human race:' he is, in short, the Odysseus who wanders very far over many lands, after the fall of Ilion, which again answers to the slaying of the dragon. The Fitela of Beowulf is clearly the Sinfiötli of the Volsung tale. For some remarks on the comparative antiquity of these two legends see Ludlow, *Popular Epics of the Middle Ages*, i. 41. The substantial identity of the two myths renders the question of date of com-

With this exploit begins the career of Sigurd as Chrysâôr. As Achilleus is taught by Cheiron, so is Sigurd instructed by Gripir, the wise man, and thus in the fulness of wisdom and strength, with his golden hair flowing over his shoulders, and an eye whose glance dazzled all who faced it, he rides over the desolate heath, until he comes to the circle of flame within which sleeps the Valkyrie Brynhild.[1] No other horse but Gran can leap that wall of fire, no knight but Sigurd can guide him across that awful barrier: but at his touch the maiden is roused from the slumber which had lasted since Odin thrust the thorn of sleep or winter into her cloak, like the Rakshas' claw which threw the little sun-girl of the Hindu tale into her magic trance. At once she knows that before her stands the only man who never knew fear, the only man who should ever have her as his bride. But Brynhild also has the gift of marvellous wisdom, and as the Teutonic Alrune,[2] she reflects the knowledge of the Greek Athênê and the Latin Minerva. From her Sigurd receives all the runes, but these scarcely reveal to him so much of the future as had been laid bare for him in the prophecies of Gripir.[3] By the latter he had been told that

paratively little importance. The real point for consideration is that these stories are further identical with the sagas of the three Helgis, and of Baldur, and thus also with the myths of Adonis, Dionysos, Sarpêdón, Memnôn, and other gods and heroes of Hellenic tradition.

In one version, Fafnir predicts that Sigurd will die drowned. The prophecy is not fulfilled, but it points clearly to the myth of Endymion.—Ludlow, *Popular Epics*, i. 70.

[1] Brynhild, as we might suppose, reappears in many Teutonic stories. In the story of Strong Hans (Grimm), she is the chained maiden who is guarded by the dwarf (Andvari). When Hans (Sigurd) slays the dwarf, the chains immediately fall off her hands. In the story of the True Bride, the prince is as faithless as Sigurd, but the princess recovers him in the end with the happier lot of Penelopê. In the story of the Woodcutter's Child the Knight has to cut his way through the thorny hedges, as Sigurd has to ride through the flames. As the fearless

hero, Sigurd is the theme of the story of the 'Prince who was afraid of Nothing,' and whose fortunes are much like those of the deliverer of Brynhild.

[2] The Aurinia of Tacitus, *Germ.* 8.— Bunsen, *God in History*, ii. 454.

[3] With the runes he also receives a great deal of good advice, pointing precisely to those features in the myths of Phoibos, Helios, Hermes, and Herakles, which, when translated into the conditions of human morality, become faults or vices; Helios may burn his enemies without scruple or shame, but Sigurd must not do this, nor must he be, like Indra and Paris, γυναιμανής, nor a liar like Odysseus. The warnings which she adds are much of the same sort.

The winter sleep of Brynhild is travestied in the later story of Dietrich and Sigenot (Ludlow, *Popular Epics*, i. 263.) Dietrich is here the Sigurd or bright hero, who wears the helmet of Grein whom he has slain, and who is the nephew of the giant Sigenot. Sigenot now carries off Dietrich and shuts him up in a hollow

Brynhild (like Helen) would work him much woe: but Brynhild doubtless knew not, as Sigurd rode on to the hall of Giuki the Niflung, that her place was now to be taken by another, and that her own lot was to be that of Ariadnê, Aithra, or Oinônê. It is the old tale, repeated under a thousand different forms. The bright dawn who greeted the newly risen sun cannot be with him as he journeys through the heaven; and the bride whom he weds in her stead is nearer and more akin to the mists of evening or the cold of winter. Thus Gudrun, loving and beautiful as she is, is still the daughter of the Niflung, the child of the mist, and stands to Sigurd precisely in the relation of Dêianeira to Herakles, as the unwitting cause of her husband's ruin. But Brynhild yet lives, and Gunnar, who, like Hogni or Hagene, is a son of the Niflung and brother of Gudrun, seeks to have her as his wife. His desire can be satisfied only through Sigurd, who by the arts and philtres of Grimhild has been made to forget his first love and betroth himself to Gudrun. In vain Gunnar[1] strives to ride through the flames that encircle Brynhild, until at last, by the arts of Grimhild, Sigurd is made to change shapes and arms with Gunnar, and, mounting on Gran, to force Brynhild to yield. Thus Sigurd weds the Valkyrie in Gunnar's form, and lies down by her side with the unsheathed blade of Gram between them.[2] In the morning he gives to Brynhild the ring which

stone or tower, where, like Ragnar Lodbrog, he is attacked by many a strong worm or serpent—the snakes of night. One of his followers tries to raise him by a rope, which breaks, and Dietrich tells him that the wounds which he has received cannot be healed. Things, however, turn out better than he expects; but the one night which he spent in the house seemed to him as thirty years.

[1] 'Gunnar Gjukason seems to signify darkness, and thus we see that the awakening and budding spring is gone, carried away by Gunnar, like Proserpine by Pluto; like Sítá by Rávana. Gudrun, the daughter of Grimhild, and sometimes herself called Grimhild, whether the latter name meant summer (cf. Gharma in Sanskrit), or the earth and nature in the latter part of the

year, is a sister of the dark Gunnar, and though now married to the bright Sigurd, she belongs herself to the nebulous regions.'—Max Müller, *Chips*, ii. 110.

[2] This incident recurs in Grimm's story of the Two Brothers. In the Norse legend of the Big Bird Dan, who is no other than the Arabian Roc, the princess lays the bare sword between her and Ritter Red. Dr. Dasent adds many more instances, as the story of Hrólf and Ingegerd, of Tristan and Isolt, and he rightly insists that 'these mythical deep-rooted germs, throwing out fresh shoots from age to age in the popular literature of the race, are far more convincing proofs of the early existence of their traditions than any more external evidence.' — *Norse Tales*, introduction, cxlii. It is certainly

was under the double curse of Andvari and Loki, receiving from her another ring in return. This ring is necessarily connected with the catastrophe; but in the mode by which it is brought about, the Northern poets were left free to follow their fancy. In the Volsung tale, Gudrun and Brynhild are washing their hair in the same stream, when Brynhild says that no water from Gudrun's head shall fall upon her own, as her husband is braver than Gudrun's. When Gudrun replies that Sigurd, to whom she was wedded, had slain Fafnir and Regin and seized the hoard, Brynhild answers that Gunnar had done yet a braver deed in riding through the flames which surrounded her. A few words from Gudrun show her how things really are, and that the seeming Gunnar who had placed on her finger the ring won from the spoils of Andvari was really Sigurd who had transferred to Gudrun the ring which he had received from Brynhild. Thus her old love is re-awakened, only to be merged in the stinging sense of injustice which makes Oinônê in one version of the myth refuse to heal the wounded Paris, and leads Dêianeira to resolve on the death of Herakles. The three instances are precisely the same, although Oinônê is of the three the most gentle and the most merciful. But in all there is the consciousness of betrayal and the determination to punish it, and the feeling which animates them is reflected again in the hate of Helen for Paris after he has shut her up in Ilion. Thus Brynhild urges Gunnar to avenge her on Sigurd, like the evening twilight allying itself with the darkness of night to blot out the glory of the sun from the heavens. But Gunnar and his brothers cannot accomplish her will themselves: they have made a compact of friendship with Sigurd, and they must not break their oath. But Guttorm their half-brother is under no such covenant, and so this being, who represents the cold of winter, plunges a sword into the breast of Sigurd, who is sleeping in the arms of Gudrun. This weapon is the thorn which is fatal to the Persian Rustem and the gentle Surya Bai of modern Hindu folk-lore. But Sigurd is mighty even

worth noting that the incident is related also of Allah-ud-deen in the Arabian Nights' legend.

in death, and the blade Gram, hurled by his dying hand, cleaves Guttorm asunder, so that the upper part of his body fell out of the chamber, while the lower limbs remained in the room. The change which his death causes in the mind of Brynhild answers precisely to the pity which Oinône feels when her refusal to heal Paris has brought about his death. Like Helen, who hates herself, or is hated, for bringing ruin on ships, men, and cities, she bewails the doom which brought her into the world for everlasting damage and grief of soul to many men. Like Dêianeira, and Oinône, and Kleopatra, she feels that without the man whom she loves life is not worth living for, and thus she lies down to die on the funeral pile of Sigurd.

CHAP.
XII.

The sequel reproduces the same incidents under other names, and with different colours. As Sigurd, like Theseus and Herakles, first woos the Dawn, and thus has to dwell with the maiden who represents the broad and open day, so Gudrun, the loving companion of the Sun in his middle journey, has to mourn his early death, and in her widowhood to become the bride, first of the gloaming, then of the darkness. Between these there is a necessary enmity, but their hatred only serves the more thoroughly to avenge the death of Sigurd. Atli, the second husband of Gudrun, claims all the gold which Sigurd had won from the dragon, but which the chieftains of Niflheim had seized when he died. In fair fight he could never hope to match them; so Atli invites Hogni (Haugn or Hagen) and Gunnar to a feast, in which he overpowers them. Hogni's heart is then cut out, an incident which answers to the roasting of the heart of Fafnir; and as the latter is associated with the recovery of the golden treasure, so the former is connected with the subsequent loss which answers to the coming on of the night when the sun has reached the end of his glorious course. When Sigurd died, Gunnar and his brothers had thrown the hoard into the Rhine—the water which receives Endymiôn as he plunges into his dreamless sleep; and the secret of it is lost when they in their turn are cast into a pit full of snakes, all of whom, like Orpheus, Gunnar lulls to sleep by his harping, except one which flies at his heart, and kills him—a tale told

The Story of Gudrun.

over again in the transparent myth of Thora, Aslauga, and
Ragnar Lodbrog. Thus the beings who, though they might
be akin to the mist and cold of night, had made a covenant
of peace and friendship with Sigurd, are all gone, and to
Gudrun remains the task of avenging them. The story of
her vengeance is practically a repetition of the legend of
Medeia. Like the Kolchian woman, she slays the two sons
whom she had borne to Atli; but the ferocity of the Northern sentiment colours the sequel in which we see a sunset as
blood-red and stormy as that in which Herakles rose from
earth to the mansions of the undying gods. Gudrun makes
Atli eat the flesh and drink the blood of his sons; and then,
having slain him as he sleeps, by the aid of the son of her
brother Hogni, she sets fire to the hall, and consumes every
thing within it. The shades of evening or of autumn are
now fast closing in, and Gudrun, weary of her life, hastens
to the sea shore to end her woes by plunging into the deep.
But the waters carry her over to the land of King Jonakr,
who makes her his bride, and she now becomes the mother of
three sons, Saurli, Hamdir, and Erp, whose raven black hair
marks them as the children of clouds and darkness. Once more
the magic wheel revolves, and in the fortunes of Svanhild,
the daughter of Sigurd and Gunnar, we see the destiny of
the fateful Helen. Like her, Svanhild is the most beautiful of women, and Hermanric, the Gothic king, sends his
son Randver to woo her for him; but the young man is
advised by the treacherous Bikki to woo her for himself, and
he follows the counsel which chimes in only too well with
his own inclinations, as with those of Svanhild. Hermanric orders that his son shall be hanged. Presently he
receives a plucked hawk which Randver had sent to show
him the weakness of parents who deprive themselves of the
support of their children, and he gives orders to stop the
execution. The messenger comes too late, Randver is already
slain; and Svanhild is trampled to death by the steeds of
Hermanric's horsemen as she combs out her golden locks.
But Hermanric must pay the penalty for his ill-doing not
less than Sigurd or Atli. Gunnar's command goes forth to
her three Niflung sons, Saurli, Hamdir and Erp, to avenge

Svanhild; and thus, armed with helmets and cased in mail which no weapons can pierce, they take the way to the house of Hermanric. As they go, the Niflungs quarrel among themselves, and Saurli and Hamdir slay Erp, because he is his mother's darling.[1] But Hermanric, although he may be mutilated, cannot be slain. The two brothers cut off his hands and feet; but Erp is not there to smite off his head, and Hermanric has strength to call out to his men, who bind the Niflungs and stone them to death, by the advice of a one-eyed man who tells them that no steel can pierce their panoply. Here the one-eyed man is again the stranger who had left the sword in the oak tree of Volsung's hall, and the men of Hermanric answer to the Achaians in their struggle with the robbers of Ilion. It was time, however, that the tale should end, and it is brought to a close with the death of Gudrun, for no other reason probably than that the revolutions of the mythic wheel must be arrested some-where. The difference between the climates of northern and southern Europe is of itself enough to account for the more cheerful ending of the Hellenic story in the triumphant restoration of the Herakleidai.

The very fact that in all this story there is, as we have seen, scarcely an incident which we do not find in the tradi-tions of other Aryan nations or tribes, renders it impossible to judge of the character of Northmen or Germans from the legends themselves. It is possible, of course, and even likely

---

[1] The story of this murder has worked its way into the traditional history of Æthelstan and Godwine. At the least, it seems impossible to shut our eyes to the striking similarity of these stories; and as their non-historical character in the case of Æthelstan and Godwine has been placed beyond reach of questioning, we are the more justified in saying that the old myth has served as the founda-tion of the later legend. The Volsung story, in Dr. Dasent's words, runs as follows:—'As the three went along, the two asked Erp what help he would give them when they got to Hermanric. "Such as hand lends to foot," he said. "No help at all," they cried; and pass-ing from words to blows, and because their mother loved Erp best, they slew him. A little farther on Saurli stumbled and fell forward, but saved himself with one hand, and said, "Here hand helps foot; better were it that Erp lived." So they came on Hermanric as he slept, and Saurli hewed off his hands, and Hamdir his feet, but he awoke and called for his men. Then said Hamdir, "Were Erp alive, the head would be off, and he couldn't call out."' In the story of Æthelstan and of Godwine we have the same phrases about the hands and feet: in each case a brother is slain, and in each case the loss of this brother is sub-sequently felt as a source of weakness. For the several shapes assumed by the legend see Freeman, *Norman Conquest*, ii. 611–12.

that the poets or narrators have in each case thrown over
the characters and events of their tale a colouring borrowed
from the society of the time ; but that as portraits of actual
manners they are gross and impossible exaggerations we are
justified in concluding not only from the story itself, but from
the recurrence of the myth in many lands unchanged in its
essence, and even in its most prominent features. It is thrice
repeated in the legends of the three Helgis, who, it is scarcely
necessary to say, are mere reflections, the one of the others.
These are the holy ones, or saviours, who make whole or restore
life, like the Paicôn or Asklepios of Greek mythology.[1]

Of these Helgis, the first is called the son of Hiorvardur,
and he is loved by Swava, the daughter of King Eilimir.
But his brother Hedin makes a vow on the yule eve that
Swava shall be his wife, not the bride of Helgi. He has been
misled by the sorceress Hrimgerda, who seeks to make him
her own, as Kirkê and Kalypso use all their arts to detain
Odysseus; but the northern hero is more scrupulous than
the Ithakan chieftain, and he not only rejects her love, but
compels her to prophesy till the day dawns and her power is
at an end,—a sufficiently clear token of her nature.   Soon,
however, he repents him of the oath which the sorceress had
led him to take, and he confesses his guilt to Helgi, who,
foreboding his own death in the coming struggle with Alfur,
the son of Hrodmar, promises that when he is slain Swava
shall be Hedin's.   When he has received the death-wound,
he tells Swava of this promise; but she refuses to abide by it
or to have any other husband but Helgi, and Helgi in his
turn declares that though he must now die, he will come
back again when his death has been avenged. This is manifestly the avenging of Baldur, and Helgi is thus another form
of Adonis, or Memnôn, or Dionysos. The younger brother is
the waning autumn sun, who thinks to obtain his brother's
wife when the sun of summer has lost its power.

At the birth of the second Helgi, known as Hundingsbana,

[1] They are the Alcis mentioned by
Tacitus, *Germ.* 43, as worshipped by the
Naharvali, and as answering to the
Roman Castor and Pollux. They are
the Teutonic Dioskouroi or Asvins; and

for the loss of the aspirate in the name
as given by Tacitus, Bunsen cites the
analogous forms Irmin and Hermun,
Isco and Hisicion.—*God in History,* ii.
470.

the Nornas came and fixed the lot of the babe, like the
Moirai in the legend of Meleagros.[1]   When fifteen years
old, he slays King Hunding and his sons, and afterwards
wins the love of Sigrun, daughter of Hogni, who, like Swava,
is a Valkyrie and a sister of Bragi and Dag, the brilliant heaven and the day.   She promises Helgi that she will be his
wife if he will vanquish the sons of Granmar, the bearded
spirit, to one of whom she had been betrothed.   Thus again
we have the woman whom two heroes seek to obtain, the
Helen for whom Menelaos and Paris contend together. In the
battle which follows, Sigrun, as a Valkyrie, cheers him on,
and Dag alone is spared of all the sons of Granmar.   But
although Dag swears allegiance to the Volsungs, he yet treacherously stabs Helgi (another of the many forms of Baldur's
death), and tells Sigrun that he is dead.   The sequel,
although essentially the same, shows the working of a new
vein of thought.   Sigrun curses Dag as one who had broken
his oath, and refuses to live

> Unless a glory should break from the prince's grave,
> And Vigblar the horse should speed thither with him ;
> The gold-bridled steed becomes him whom I fain would embrace.

Her tears disturb the repose of Helgi in his grave, and he
rebukes her as making his wounds burst open afresh.   But
Sigrun is not to be scared or driven away.   She prepares a
common resting-place for him and for herself, a couch free
from all care, and enters of her own free will the land of the
dead.

> ' Nothing I now declare   Unlooked for,
> At Sefafiöll   Late or early,
> Since in a corpse's   Arms thou sleepest,
> Högni's fair daughter,   In a mound,
> And thou art living,   Daughter of kings.
>
>   Time 'tis for me to ride   On the reddening ways ;
> Let the pale horse   Tread the aerial path ;
> I toward the west must go   Over Vindhiälm's bridge,
> Ere Lulgofnir   Awakens heroes." [2]

The third Helgi, Haddingaheld, is but a reproduction of   The Third Helgi.

---

[1] He is also identified as Hermodhur,
Heermuth, the son of Odin, who is sent
to fetch up Baldur from the under
world and is thus the returning or conquering sun who comes back after the
winter solstice.—Bunsen, *God in History*, ii. 471.

[2] Second Lay of Helgi Hundingsbana, 46, 47.   This is the legend of Le-
nore, of which Bunsen says that ' Bürger
caught the soul of the story as it was on
the point of extinction, and lent it a new
and immortal life among the German
people.'—*God in History*, ii. 466.

the second Helgi, while Kara, the daughter of Halfdan, takes the place of Swava or Sigrun. In all these tales the heroes and the heroines stand in precisely the same relations to each other;[1] and thus, having seen that the myths of these heroes merely reproduce the legends of Baldur and of Sigurd the Volsung, we are prepared for the conclusion that the story of Siegfried, in the Lay of the Nibelungs, is only another form of the oft-repeated tale. For the most part the names are the same, as well as the incidents. The second Helgi is a son of Sigmund, his mother also being called Sigurlin; and so Sigurd of the Volsung and Siegfried of the Nibelung Saga are each the son of Sigmund. The slaying of Hunding by Helgi answers to the slaughter of Fafnir and Regin by Sigurd, Siegfried being also a dragon-slayer like Phoibos, or Oidipous, or Herakles. So too, as Sigurd first won the love of Brynhild and then marries Gudrun, for whose brother he finally wins Brynhild as a wife, so Siegfried in his turn marries Kriemhild, sister of the Burgundian Gunther, having wooed Brynhild for his brother-in-law. If, again, Brynhild causes the death of Sigurd, the man in whom she has garnered up her soul, so Siegfried is murdered at Brynhild's instigation. If in the Helgi Saga the son of Hogni bears the news of Helgi's death to Sigurd, so in the Volsung tale Hogni informs Gudrun of Sigurd's death, and in the Nibelung song Hagen brings to Kriemhild the tidings of the death of Siegfried. Like Swava and Sigrun, Brynhild kills herself that her body may be burnt with that of Sigurd; and as in the story of the Volsungs, Atli (who appears as the comrade of the first Helgi) gets possession of Gunnar and Hogni and has them put to death, so Kriemhild in the Nibelungenlied marries Etzel, who catches Gunther and his brothers in the same trap in which Gunnar and Hogni had been caught by Atli.[2]

---

[1] For a tabular view of these parallelisms see Bunsen, *ib.* 470, &c.

[2] On the historical residuum which may possibly be contained in the later forms of these myths it is really unnecessary to say anything. In Bunsen's words, 'The fundamental element common to them all is purely mythological, namely, the combat of the Sun-God, who is slain by his brother and avenged by a younger brother. . . . . This element constitutes the basis of the Sigurd Saga, and the substance of the Helgi Saga, with the exception of some later additions; it is the oldest form of the German myth of Herakles.'—*God in History*, ii. 474. Nevertheless, Bunsen thinks it worth while to make an attempt to determine the amount of historical matter wrapped up in it. He finds the

That the later forms into which the Volsung story has been thrown may contain some incidents which may be either truly told or else travestied from real history, it is impossible to deny. When at the best they who insist most on the historical character of these poems can but trace a name here and there, or perhaps see in the account of some fight a reference to some actual battle with which it has no likeness beyond the fact that men fought and were killed in both, as the fishes swim in the streams of Macedon and Monmouth, it seems useless to affirm it. When the motives are alike in all, when in each case there is a wealthily dowered maiden whose hoard is stolen, a robber who refuses to disclose the secret of the lost treasure, and bloody vengeance by those who lay claim to this wealth, when thousands are murdered in a single hall, and men lie down contentedly in flaming chambers floating in blood, treading out the falling brands in the gore and recruiting their strength by sucking the veins of the dead, we can scarcely regard it as a profitable task to search amidst such a mass of impossibilities the materials for a picture of society as existing whether amongst Northmen or amongst Greeks. That the colouring thrown over them is in part reflected from the manners of the age, there is no room to doubt; but when the groundwork of the story has been shown to be purely mythical, this fact will not carry us

name Atli or Etzel, and this represents the historical Attila, a conclusion which is strengthened by the mention of Bludi as the father of Attila, whereas history speaks of Bleda as his brother. He finds also Gunnar, the brother of Gudrun, and Gunther the king of the Burgundians. Beyond this, seemingly, it is impossible to advance. 'It is certainly difficult to make an expedition by Attila himself to the Rhine fit in with what we know of the history of these years. This, no more and no less, is the historical element in that great tragedy of the woes of the Nibelungs.'—*God in History*, ii. 478. If any can be satisfied with claiming for this belief a historical sanction on such evidence as this, it may perhaps be a pity to break in upon their self-complacence; but on the other side it may fairly be asserted that two or three names, with which not a single known historical event is associated, and of which the stories told cannot be reconciled with anything which comes down to us on genuine historical testimony, furnish a miserably insecure foundation for any historical inferences. If this is all that we learn from the popular tradition, can we be said to learn anything? In the one Bleda is the brother of Attila, in the other he is not: it seems rash, then, to speak of Bludi as a 'perfectly historical person.' To us they must remain mere names; and while we turn aside from the task of measuring the historical authority of these Sagas as a mere waste of time, we cannot on the same plea refuse consideration to evidence which may seem to trace such names as Atli, Bleda, and Gunnar to a time long preceding the days of Attila, Bludi, and Gunther.

far. We are confined to mere names or mere customs; and the attempt to advance further lands us in the region of guesswork. Thus to Mr. Kemble's assertion that Attila 'drew into his traditional history the exploits of others, and more particularly those of Chlodowic and his sons in the matter of the Burgundian kingdom,' and that this fact will be patent to any one who will look over the accounts of the Burgundian war in Gregory of Tours, Mr. Ludlow replies that the search yields only two names, Godegiselus namely, and Theudericus, answering to the Giselher and Dietrich of the Nibelungen Lay.[1] Nor do we gain much if we find Gundicar, the Burgundian king, as one of the sovereigns conquered by Attila, if the Atli of the Volsung story belonged to the myth long before the days of the Hunnish devastator. The name of the Bishop Pilgrim seems to be more genuinely historical; but even if he can be identified as a prelate who filled the see of Passau in the tenth century, we know no more about him from the poem than we learn of Hruodlandus from the myth of the Roland who fell at Roncesvalles.

Sigurd,
Siegfried,
and
Baldur.

The points of difference between the Norse and the German traditions are simply such as the comparison of one Greek myth with another would lead us to expect. Phoibos may be called the child of the darkness, as strictly as he may be said to be born in Delos or Ortygia. The offspring of Chrysâôr, the lord of the golden sword of day, is the three-headed Geryoneus; and Echidna, the throttling snake, who is united with Herakles, is the daughter of Kallirhoê, the fair-flowing stream of the ocean. Hence there is nothing surprising in the fact that in the one set of myths Sigurd fights with, or is slain by, the Niflungs, while in the other he is said to be a Niflung himself.[2] The real difference between the Teutonic and the Greek epics lies, not so much in the fact that a complex poem exhibits a being like Paris, sometimes in the garb of the Panis, sometimes with all the attributes of Helios, as in the greater compass of the northern poems. The Iliad relates the incidents only of a portion of a single year in the

[1] Ludlow, *Popular Epics of the Middle Ages*, i. 180.
[2] *Ibid.* i. 137.

Trojan war; the Nibelung lay adds two or three complete histories to the already completed history of Siegfried. The antiquity of these several portions of a poem, which by the confession of all has certainly been pieced together, is a question into which we need not enter. It is possible, as Mr. Ludlow thinks, that the portion which relates to Siegfried was added at a later time to explain the intense hatred of Kriemhild for her brothers, and that this may be the most modern addition to the Nibelungenlied; but it is not less certain that the myth of Siegfried is the myth of Baldur, and has existed in many shapes in every Aryan land. The Volsung story may represent the rougher songs of Norse sea-rovers, while the Nibelung song may introduce us to the more stately life and elaborate pageants of German kings and princes; but the heroes have changed simply their conditions, not their mind and temper, by crossing the sea or passing into another land. The doom of perpetual pilgrimage is laid on Perseus, Theseus, Bellerophôn, Herakles, Odysseus; and Sigurd and Siegfried are not more exempt from it.[1] In their golden locks and godlike countenances, in their flashing swords and unerring spears, there is no difference between them; and every additional point of likeness adds to the weight of proof that these epic poems represent neither the history nor the national character of Northmen, Greeks, or Germans. In each case the spirit of the tradition has been carefully preserved, but there is no servile adherence. In the Volsung story, Gudrun becomes the wife of Siegfried; in the Nibelung song, her mother Kriemhild takes her place. The Hogni of the

[1] This doom is brought out with singular clearness in the Gaelic story, where the Dame of the Fine Green Kirtle lays the Fair Grungach under her spell, that he shall not rest by night or by day (Ixîon, Sisiphos). '"Where thou takest thy breakfast that thou take not thy dinner, and where thou takest thy dinner that thou take not thy supper, in whatsoever place thou be, until thou findest out in what place I may be under the four brown quarters of the world." 'So it was in the morning of the morrow's day he went away without dog, without man, without calf, without child.

'He was going and going and journeying; there was blackening on his soles, and holes in his shoes; the black clouds of night coming, and the bright quiet clouds of the day going away, and without his finding a place of staying or rest for him.' He is, in short, the wandering Wuotan (Wegtam), Savitar, Odysseus, Bellerophôn, Phoibos, Dionysos, Herakles, Perseus, Sigurd, Indra, Oidipous, Theseus; and it is unnecessary to say that in the end he becomes the husband of the Dame of the Fine Green Kirtle, who is none other than Medeia with the magic robe of Helios. (Campbell, ii. 435).

former tale becomes in the latter the Hagen of Tronege, against whom Siegfried is warned when he desires to marry Kriemhild, the sister of Gunther, Gernot, and Giselher, and who recognises Siegfried as the slayer of the Niblungs, the conqueror of their magic sword, Balmung, and of all their treasures, and the possessor of the tarnkappe, or cape of darkness—all of them features with which the earlier legend has made us familiar. The story of Thetis or Dêmêtêr plunging Achilleus and Triptolemos into the bath of fire is here represented by the myth that Siegfried cannot be wounded, because he had bathed himself in the blood of a dragon whom he had slain—the Fafnir or Python of the Norse and Delphic legends.[1] At the first glance Kriemhild is filled with love for Siegfried, but the latter cannot see her until he has sojourned for a year in the country of King Gunther—a condition which answers to that under which Hades suffered Orpheus to lead away Eurydikê. Here, like Sigurd in the Volsung myth, Siegfried wins Brynhild for Gunther or Gunnar; but though there is here not the same complication, the narrative scarcely becomes on this account the more human. Like Perseus with the helmet of Hades, Siegfried can make himself invisible at will, and like Apollôn Delphinios, he pushes a ship through the sea—a myth in which we recognise also the Wish breeze.[2] Here also, as in the Norse story, the ring and girdle of Brynhild come through Siegfried into the possession of Kriemhild; and at this point the myth assumes a form which reminds us of the relations of

---

[1] Mr. Ludlow here remarks: 'The incidents differ greatly. Sigurd drinks the blood and learns mysteries; Sifrit bathes in it and becomes invulnerable.' The differences are simply such as must arise in myths developed independently from a common source. The essential part of it is the connection between the dragon and the power derived from it: and this connexion is manifest in the myths of Iamos, Medeia, and Phoibos.

[2] The power of the Fish Sun is strikingly shown in the German stories of the Gold Children and of the Fisherman and his Wife. In the former a poor man catches the Golden Fish which makes him the possessor of the palace of Helios, and bids the man divide him into six pieces; two to be given to his wife, two to his mare, and two to be put into the ground. The necessary consequence is that the woman has two golden children who, mounting on the two golden foals of the mare, represent the Asvins and the Dioskouroi, the pieces put into the ground producing two golden lilies on which the lives of the children depend. In the tale of the Fisherman and his Wife, the fish accomplishes the wishes of the woman, who chooses to become first a lady, then queen, then pope; but when she wishes to become the ruler of the universe, the flounder sends her back to her old hovel,—an incident reflecting the fall of Tantalos, Sisyphos, and Ixîon.

Herakles with Eurystheus. Like Hêrê in the Greek tale, Brynhild holds that Siegfried ought to do service to Gunther, as Herakles did to his lord, and thus urges him to summon Siegfried to Worms. The hero, who is found in the Niflung's castle on the Norwegian border, loads the messengers with treasures, and Hagen cannot suppress the longing that all this wealth may yet come into the hands of the Burgundians.[1] No sooner has Siegfried, with his father Sigmund and his wife Kriemhild, reached Worms, than Brynhild hastens to impress on Kriemhild that Siegfried is Gunther's man, and that, like Theseus to Minos, he must pay tribute. In deep anger Kriemhild resolves to insult her adversary, and when they go to church, she presses on before Brynhild, who bids her as a vassal stand back, and taunting her as having been won by Siegfried, shows him her girdle and ring as the evidence of her words. Gunther, urged by his wife, rebukes Siegfried for betraying the secret, but his anger is soon appeased. It is otherwise with Hogni, or Hagen, who here plays the part of Paris, by whose spear Achilleus is to fall. He sees his sister weeping, and, swearing to revenge her, spreads false tidings of the approach of an enemy, and when he knows that Siegfried is ready to set out against them, he asks Kriemhild how he may best insure her husband's safety. Not knowing to whom she spake, she tells him that when Siegfried bathed himself in the dragon's blood a broad linden leaf stuck between his shoulders, and there left him vulnerable, this place between the shoulders answering to the vulnerable heel of Achilleus. To make still more sure, Hagen asks Kriemhild to mark the spot, and the wife of the hero thus seals his doom. The narrative at this point becomes filled with all the tenderness and beauty of the Odyssey. Kriemhild is awakened to her folly in betraying Siegfried's secret to Hagen. Still, in vain she prays him not to go. He is the knight who knows no fear, and without fear he accompanies Hagen, doing marvellous things, until one day he

---

[1] These Burgundians in the later portion of the epic are often spoken of as Niblungs, as mythically they assuredly are. The fact evidently shows, in Mr. Ludlow's opinion, 'that the poem in its present state is put together out of two different legends.'—*Popular Epics of the Middle Ages*, i. 133. At the most, it would be but one of two versions of the legend.

asks Hagen why he has brought no wine to drink, when
Hagen offers to show him the way to a good spring. Siegfried hastens thither with him, and as he stoops to drink
Hagen shoots him through the back on the spot marked by
the silver cross. It is scarcely necessary to compare this with
the vast number of myths in which the death of the sun is
connected with water, whether of the ocean or the sea. In
the spirting out of Siegfried's blood on Hagen, in the wonderful stroke with which he almost smites his betrayer dead, in
the death wrestle which covers the flowers all around with
blood and gore, we have the chief features of the blood-stained
sunset which looms out in the legend of the death of Herakles.
The body of Siegfried, placed on a golden shield, is borne to
the chamber of Kriemhild, who feels, before she is told, that
it is the corpse of her murdered husband. ' This is Brynhild's
counsel,' she said, ' this is Hagen's deed ; ' and she swears to
avenge his death by a vengeance as fearful as that of Achilleus.
As Siegfried had spoken, so should Hagen assuredly rue the
day of his death hereafter. She gives orders to awaken
Siegfried's men and his father Sigmund ; but Sigmund has
not slept, for, like Peleus, he has felt that he should see his
son again no more. Then follows the burial of Siegfried,
when Gunther swears that no harm has come to the hero
either from himself or from his men : but the lie is given to
his words when the wounds bleed as Hagen passes before the
dead body. When all is over, Sigmund says that they must
return to their own land ; but Kriemhild is at last persuaded
to remain at Worms, where she sojourns for more than three
years in bitter grief, seeing neither Gunther nor Hagen.
The latter now makes Gernot press Kriemhild to have her
hoard brought from the Niblung land, and thus at length
gaining possession of it, he sinks it all in the Rhine. In
other words, Adonis is dead, and the women are left mourning
and wailing for him ; or the maiden is stolen away from
Dêmêtêr, and her wealth is carried to the house of Hades ;
or again, as in the Norse tale, the dwarf Andvari is keeping
watch over the treasures of Brynhild : and thus ends the
first of the series of mythical histories embodied in the
Nibelung Lay. Whether this portion of the great Teu-

tonic epic be, or be not, older than the parts which follow it, it is indubitably an integral narrative in itself, and by no means indispensable to the general plan of the poem, except in so far as it accounts for the implacable hatred of Kriemhild for her brothers.

The second part of the drama begins with the death of Helche, the wife of Etzel or Atli, who longs to marry Kriemhild, and who is restrained only by the recollection that he is a heathen while the widow of Siegfried is a Christian. This objection, however, is overruled by the whole council, who, with the one exception of Hagen, decide that Etzel shall marry Kriemhild. Hagen is opposed to it, because Siegfried swore that he should rue the day on which he touched him, and on account of the prophecy that if ever Kriemheld took the place of Helche, she would bring harm to the Burgundians, as Helen did to the fleet, the armies, and the cities of Hellas. But as the forsaken Ariadnê was wedded to Dionysos, so the messengers of Etzel tell Kriemhild that she shall be the lady of twelve rich crowns, and rule the lands of thirty princes. Kriemhild refuses to give an immediate answer; and the great struggle which goes on within her answers to the grief and sickness of soul which makes the mind of Helen oscillate between her affection for her husband Menelaos and the unhallowed fascinations of the Trojan Paris. So is brought about the second marriage of the bride of Siegfried, a marriage the sole interest of which lies in the means which it affords to her of avenging the death of Hagen's victim. This vengeance is now the one yearning of her heart, although outwardly she may be the contented wife of Etzel, just as Odysseus longed only to be once more at home with Penelopê even while he was compelled to sojourn in the house of Kirkê or the cave of Kalypsô; and if the parallel between Etzel and Paris is not close, yet it is closer than the likeness between the Etzel of the Niblungs' Lay and the Attila of history. The poet declares that her deadly wrath is roused by the reflection that at Hagen's instigation she has given herself to a heathen; but throughout it is clear that her heart and her thoughts are far away in the grave of the golden-haired youth who had wooed and won her in the beautiful spring-time, and that of Etzel she took heed only so far as it might suit her purpose to do so.   Her object now is to get Hagen into her power, and she sends messengers to Gunther bidding him bring all his best friends, whom Hagen can guide, as from his childhood he has known the way to the Huns' land.[1]   All are ready to go, except Hagen, and he is loth to put his foot into the trap which he sees that Kriemhild is setting for him; but he cannot bear the taunts of his brother Gunther, who tells him that if he feels guilty on the score of Siegfried's death he had better stay at home.   Still he advises that if they go they should go in force.   So Gunther sets out with three thousand men, Hagen, and Dankwart, his brother, and other chiefs with such as they can muster; and with them goes Volker, the renowned musician, who can fight as well as he can play.[2]   Hagen necessarily discerns evil omens as they journey on. The waters of the Danube are swollen, and as he searches along the banks for a ferryman, he seizes the wondrous apparel of two wise women who are bathing, one of whom promises that if he will give them their raiment, they will tell how he may journey to the Huns' land.   Floating like birds before him on the flood, they lure him with hopes of the great honours which are in store for him, and thus they recover their clothes—a myth which feebly reflects the beautiful legends of the Swan maidens and their knights.   No sooner, however, are they again clothed, than the wise woman who has not yet spoken tells him that her sister has lied, and that from the Huns' land not one shall return alive, except the king's chaplain.   To test her words, Hagen, as they are

---

[1] Mr. Ludlow here remarks that 'this is one of the passages which imply the legend contained in "Walther of Aquitaine," where Hagen is represented as a fellow hostage with Walthar at Etzel's court.'—*Popular Epics*, i. 130. It may be so; yet the phrase resolves itself into the simple statement that the Papis know their way to the land whence they steal the cattle of Indra.

[2] I must confine myself to those portions of the epic which call for a comparison with other legends, and which, taken together, show the amount of material which the poets of the Nibelung song, like those of the *Iliad* and *Odyssey*, found ready to their hand. The close agreement of the framework of the poem with that of the Volsung story and the legends of the Helgis, and the identity of all these with the myth of Baldur, has been already shown.   It is, therefore, quite unnecessary to give an abstract of the poem throughout, a task which has been performed already by many writers, and among them by Mr. Ludlow, *Popular Epics*, i.

crossing the river, throws the priest into the stream; but although he tries to push him down under the water, yet the chaplain, although unable to swim, is carried by Divine aid to the shore, and the doomed Burgundians go onwards to meet their fate.   In the house of Rudiger they receive a genial welcome; but when Rudiger's daughter approaches at his bidding to kiss Hagen, his countenance seemed to her so fearful that she would gladly have foregone the duty.   On their departure Rudiger loads them with gifts.   To Gernot he gives a sword which afterwards deals the death-blow to Rudiger himself, who resolves to accompany them; while Hagen receives the magnificent shield of Nuodung, whom Witege slew.   The ominous note is again sounded when Dietrich, who is sent to meet the Burgundians, tells Hagen that Kriemhild still weeps sore for the hero of the Niblung land; and Hagen can but say that her duty now is to Etzel, as Siegfried is buried and comes again no more.   It is the story of the Odyssey.   When Dietrich is asked how he knows the mind of Kriemhild, 'What shall I say?' he answers; 'every morning early I hear her, Etzel's wife, weep and wail full sadly to the God of heaven for strong Siegfried's body.'[1] It is the sorrow of Penelopê, who mourns for the absence of Odysseus during twenty weary years, though the suitors, like Etzel, are by her side, or though, as other versions went, she became a mother while the wise chief was far away fighting at Ilion or wandering over the wine-faced sea.

At length Hagen and Kriemhild stand face to face : but when the wife of Etzel asks what gifts he has brought, Hagen answers that one so wealthy needs no gifts.   The question is then put plainly, 'Where is the Niblungs' hoard? It was my own, as ye well know.'   Hagen answers that at his master's bidding it has been sunk in the Rhine, and there it must remain till the day of judgment.   But when Kriemhild tells the Burgundians that they must give up their arms before going into the hall, Hagen begs to be

The vengeance of Kriemhild.

---

[1] Compare the Gaelic story of the Rider of Orianaig (Campbell, iii. 18), where the dawn-maidens mourn because they have to marry the giant, but are rescued by the man who made the gold and silver cap, as Penelopê is delivered from her suitors by the man who wrought the bed in her bridal chamber.

excused. The honour is greater than he deserves, and he will himself be chamberman. Kriemhild sees that he has been warned, and learns to her grief and rage that the warning has come through Dietrich.[1] But the time for the avenging of Siegfried draws nigh. Etzel's men see Kriemhild weeping as through a window she looks down on Hagen and Volker, and when they assure her that the man who has called forth her tears shall pay for his offence with his blood, she bids them avenge her of Hagen, so that he may lose his life. Sixty men are ready to slay them, but Kriemhild says that so small a troop can never suffice to slay two heroes so powerful as Hagen and the still more mighty Volker who sits by his side,—words which at once show that we have before us no beings of human race, and that Hagen is akin to the Panis, while Volker is the whispering breeze or the strong wind of the night, whose harping, like that of Orpheus, few or none may withstand. Kriemhild herself goes down to them: but Hagen will not rise to greet her. On his knees she sees the gleaming sword which he had taken from Sigfried, the good blade Gram, which Odin left in the house of Volsung. The words which burst from her bespeak the grief of a Penelopê who nurses her sorrow in a harsher clime than that of Ithaka. She asks Hagen how he could venture into the lion's den, and who had sent for him to the Huns' country. To his reply that he had come only by constraint of the masters whose man he was, she rejoins by asking why he did the deed for which she bears hate to him. He has slain her beloved Siegfried, for whom if she weeps all her life long she could never weep enough. It is useless to deny the deed, and Hagen does not care to disown it. He tells the queen that he is in truth the man who slew Siegfried and has done to her great wrong; and the preparations for the last struggle go on with more speed and certainty. It is impossible not to think of the suitors in the house of Odysseus, although the bearing of Hagen and his men is altogether

---

[1] It is at this point that the passage is inserted which connects the Nibelungenlied with the story of Walthar of Aquitaine. It is of no further interest in our present inquiry than as showing the composite character of the great Teutonic epic.—Ludlow, *Popular Epics,* i. 146.

more dignified. The very weakening of the myth, which was too strong to allow the Homeric poet so to paint them, has enabled the Teutonic bard to ascribe to the slayers of Siegfried a character of real heroism. But here, as in the Odyssey, the scene of vengeance is the great hall; and we have to ask where the roof has ever been raised under which thousands have fought until scarcely one has been left to tell the tale of slaughter. In this hall the Burgundians are left to sleep on beds and couches covered with silks, ermine, and sable. But they are full of misgivings, and Hagen undertakes with Volker to keep watch before the door. Volker, the Phemios of the Odyssey, does more. With the soft and lulling tones of the harp of Hermes or of Pan, he lulls to sleep the sorrows of the men who are soon to die. Through all the house the sweet sounds find their way, until all the warriors are asleep; and then Volker takes his shield and goes out to guard his comrades against any sudden onslaught of the Huns. The tragedy begins on the morrow with the accidental slaying of a Hun by Volker at the jousts which follow the morning mass; and the fight grows hot when Dankwart smites off the head of Blödel, whom Kriemhild had sent to slay him because he was Hagen's brother. But Hagen survives to do the queen more mischief. Her son Ortlieb is being carried from table to table in the banqueting hall, and Hagen strikes off the boy's head which leaps into Kriemhild's lap. The hall runs with blood. Seven thousand bodies are flung down the steps; but Hagen is still unconquered, and Irinc who had charged himself with the office of Blödel, and succeeded in wounding him in the face, falls in his turn a victim to his zeal. A fresh thousand are poured in to avenge his death: the Burgundians slay them all, and then sit down to keep watch with the dead bodies as their seats. The tale goes on with increasing defiance of likelihood and possibility. Kriemhild and Etzel gather before the hall twenty-thousand men; but still the Burgundians maintain the strife deep into the night. When at length they ask for a truce, and Giselher tells his sister that he has never done her harm, her answer is that he is the brother of Siegfried's murderer, and therefore he and all must die unless they will yield up Hagen into her hands. This they refuse, and Kriemhild sets fire to the hall, an incident which occurs in other sagas, as those of Njal and Grettir. Drink there is none, unless it be human blood, which is gushing forth in rivers; but with this they slake their thirst and nerve their arms, while the burning rafters fall crashing around them, until the fire is extinguished in the horrid streams which gush from human bodies. Thousands have been slain within this fated hall; six hundred yet remain; the Huns attack them two to one. The fight is desperate. Rudiger, compelled to take part in it sorely against his will, is slain with his own sword by Gernot; and at length Volker the minstrel is killed by Hildebrand, who strives in vain to wound Hagen, for he is the master of Balmung, Siegfried's sword, the Gram of the Volsung story. Dietrich is at length more successful, and the slayer of Siegfried is at last brought bound into the presence of the woman who lives only to avenge him. . With him comes Gunther, the last of the Burgundian chiefs who is left alive. Once more, in this last dread hour, the story reverts to the ancient myth. Kriemhild places them apart, and then coming to Hagen, tells him that even now he may go free if he will yield up the treasure which he stole from Siegfried. Hagen's answer is that he cannot say where the hoard is as long as any of his masters remain alive. Kriemhild now takes to him the head of Gunther, the last of his liege lords, and Hagen prepares to die triumphantly. She has slain the last man who knew the secret besides himself, and from Hagen she shall never learn it. Frantic in her sorrow, Kriemhild cries that she will at least have the sword which her sweet love bore when the murderer smote him treacherously. She grasps it in her hand, she draws the blade from its sheath, she whirls it in the air, and the victory of Achilleus is accomplished. Hagen is slain like Hektor. Her heart's desire is attained. What matters it, if death is to follow her act of dread revenge, as Thetis told the chieftain of Phthia that his death must follow soon when he has slain Hektor? The night is not far off when the sun appears like a conqueror near the horizon after his long battle with the clouds. The sight of the dead Hagen rouses the grief of Etzel and the fury of Hildebrand who smites Kriemhild and hews her in pieces.

If we put aside the two or three names which may belong to persons of whose existence we have other evidence, the idea that this story of ferocious and impossible vengeance represents in any degree the history of the age of Attila becomes one of the wildest of dreams. Etzel himself is no more like the real Attila that the Alexandros of the Iliad is like the great son of the Macedonian Philip. The tale is, throughout, the story told, in every Aryan land, of the death of the short-lived sun, or the stealing of the dawn and her treasures, and of the vengeance which is taken for these deeds. It is but one of the many narratives of the great drama enacted before our eyes every year and every day, one of the many versions of the discomfiture of the thieves who seek to deceive the beautiful Saramâ. But if this great epic poem contains no history, it is remarkable as showing the extent to which the myth has been modified by the influence of Christianity and the growth of an historical sense in the treatment of national traditions. There is a certain awkwardness in the part played by Etzel, a part ludicrously unlike the action of the historical Attila; and the pitiable weakness or inconsistency which leads him throughout to favour the schemes of his wife, and then, when Hagen is slain, to mourn for him as the bravest and best of heroes, serves only to bring out more prominently the fact that it is Kriemhild who fights single-handed against all her enemies, and that she is in truth a Penelopê who trusts only to herself to deal with the ruffians who have dashed the cup of joy from her lips and stolen away her beautiful treasures. But the religious belief of the poets would not allow them to make use of any other method for bringing about the terrible issue. The bards who recounted the myths of the three Helgis would have brought back Siegfried from the grave, and added another to the heroes who represent the slain and risen gods, Baldur, Dionysos, and Adonis or Osiris. In no other way could Siegfried have been brought back to the aid of his wife, unless like Odysseus he had been represented is noteworthy chiefly as making the hero bear away both the bride and her hoard, and giving him a tranquil and a happy close to his troubled and stormy life. Here also we have the names of Gibicho, Gunther, Etzel: but the Sigurd of this version is Walthar, while the part of Brynhild is played by Hildegund, who declares her readiness to obey her lover's bidding, when he charges her, as the guardian of the treasure, to take out for him a helmet, a coat of mail, and a breastplate, and to fill two chests with Hunnish rings or money. Thus we have the same magic armour and weapons which we find in all such legends, while the war horse, appearing here under the name Lion, bears away the hero and his love. The king pursues with Hagen, who is by no means so doughty as in the Niblung Song, and who is not reassured when he finds Walthar performing a series of exploits which reproduce those of Herakles, Perseus, and Theseus. In the end he decides that he can have a chance of grappling successfully with Walthar only if he pretends to withdraw. His plan succeeds, and he is enabled to come up with Walthar as he is journeying on with Hildegund. In the fight which follows, Walthar smites off a portion of Hagen's armour, and brings Gunther to his knees with a stroke of his sword; but just as he is about to deal him the death-blow, Hagen interposes his helmeted head and the blade is shivered in pieces. Walthar in his impatience and anger throws away the hilt, and Hagen avails himself of the time to smite off Walthar's right hand, the right hand so fearful to princes and people. Here again it is the cap of darkness which is fatal to the gleaming sword, while the loss of Walthar's right hand carries us to the myth of Indra Savitar. The closing scene curiously reflects the death of Sigurd. With failing breath, Walthar deals a blow which strikes out Hagen's right eye; but whereas in the genuine myth Walthar's death ought here to follow, to be avenged afterwards by that of Hagen, here the two heroes, thus sorely bested, make up their quarrel, and Walthar bids Hildegund bring wine and offer the cup to Hagen, who will not drink first, because Walthar is the better man. In short, the story ends with an interchange of courtesies, which have an air of burlesque not unlike that which Euripides has thrown over the Herakles of his Alkêstis, and the bridal of Hildegund has all the joy and brightness which mark the reunion of Penelopê with Odysseus.[1]

[1] The later lay of Gudrun, of which Mr. Ludlow has given a summary, (*Popular Epics*, i. 193, &c.) has many of the features of the Nibelungen Lied and the story of Walthar of Aquitaine. It is scarcely necessary to note the endless modifications of myths, with which the poets of successive ages allowed themselves to deal as freely as they pleased; but we are fully justified in referring to the old myth incidents which are found in a hundred mythical traditions, but which never happen in the life of man. Thus, in the Lay of Gudrun, the child who is carried away to the griffin's or eagle's nest, whither three daughters of kings have been taken before, must remind us of the story of Surya Bai, although the child thus taken is Hagen, who grows up so mighty that he becomes celebrated as the Wayland of all kings, a title which sufficiently shows his real nature. Thus, although he is invested with all the splendour of the Trojan Paris, Hagen slays all the messengers sent by princes to sue for the hand of his beautiful daughter, nor can any succeed until Hettel comes—the mighty king at Hegelingen; a tale which merely repeats the story of Brynhild, Dornröschen, and all the enchanted maidens whom many suitors court to their own death. The wonderful ship which Hettel builds to fetch Hilda, capable of holding three thousand warriors, with its golden rudder and anchor of silver, is the counterpart of the Argo, which goes to bring back the wise and fair Medeia. The good knight Horant, at whose singing 'the beasts in the wood let their food stand, and the worms that should go in the grass, the fish that should swim in the wave, leave their purpose,' is the fiddler of the Nibelung Song, the Orpheus of the Hellenic legend. Of this feature in the story Mr. Ludlow says, 'The quaintly poetical incident of Horant's singing is perhaps the gem of the earlier portion,' a phrase to which objection can be taken only as it seems to look upon the incident as an original conception of the poets of the Gudrun Lay. From Mr. Ludlow's words no one would necessarily gather that the myth

is simply that of Orpheus and nothing more, while the old tradition is further marked by the words put into the mouth of Hilda, that she would willingly become king Hettel's wife, if Horant could sing to her every day at morn and even, like the breeze of the dawn and the twilight in the myth of Hermes. Here also we have the magic girdle of Brynhild, Harmonia, and Eriphyle, the Cestus of Freya and Aphroditê; while in the stealing of Hilda, who is no unwilling captive, and the fury of Hagen, as he sees the ship carry her away beyond the reach of pursuit, we have precisely the fury of Aiëtês and his vain chase after the Argo, which is bearing away Medeia. Here ends the first part of the tale; but it starts afresh and runs into greater complications after the birth of Ortwein and Gudrun, the son and daughter of Hettel and Hilda. Like her mother, Gudrun is carried away by Hartmut and his father, and a great struggle is the consequence. The Lay of King Rother (Ludlow, *ibid* i. 317), is in great part made up of the same materials. Here also we have the beautiful maiden whose suitors woo her to their own destruction—the wonderful ship which Rother builds to bring away the daughter of King Constantine of Constantinople; the sending of the messengers to the dungeon, where they remain until Rother comes to deliver them. But Rother, who wishes while on his expedition to be called Thiderich or Dietrich, is the splendid prince of the Cinderella story, and he obtains his wife by means of a gold and silver shoe which he alone is able to fit on her foot. But the princess is stolen away again from the home of king Rother, and brought back to Constantinople; and thus we have a repetition of the old story in another dress. It is unnecessary to say that although we hear much of Constantinople and Babylon, not a grain of genuine history is to be gleaned amidst this confused tangle of popular traditions and fancies. The form in which these myths are exhibited in the Danish ballads, agrees so closely with the general character of the Volsung and Nibelung legends, that

As we approach the later legends or romances, we find, as we might expect, a strange outgrowth of fancies often utterly incongruous, and phrases which show that the meaning of the old myths was fast fading from men's minds. Still we cannot fail to see that the stories, while they cannot by any process be reduced into harmony with the real history of any age, are built up with the materials which the bards of the Volsungs and the Nibelungs found ready to their hand. Thus in the story of Dietrich and Ecke, the latter, who plays a part something like that of Hagen or Paris, is exhibited in more lustrous colours than the Trojan Alexandros in the Iliad, although his nature and his doom are those of the Vedic Paṇis. Three knights, discoursing at Köln of brave warriors, give the palm to Dietrich of Bern, and Ecke who hears his praise swears that he must search through all lands till he finds him, and that Dietrich must slay him or lose all his praise. The incidents which follow are a strange travesty of the Volsung myth. Three queens hear the three knights talking, and the beautiful Seburk is immediately smitten with a love as vehement and lasting as that of Kriemhild in the Nibelung Song. Her one longing is to see Dietrich of Bern and to have him as her husband: but the means which she adopts to gain this end is to send Ecke in search of him, armed with a breastplate, which answers to the coat of mail wrought for Achilleus by Hephaistos. This breastplate had belonged to the Lombard king Otnit, to whom it had been a fatal possession, for as he slept before a stone wall (the wall of glass in the Hindu fairy tale) a worm found him and carried him into the hollow mountain—the tower in which Dietrich is confined, in the story of the giant Sigenot. This breastplate was recovered by Wolfdietrich of Greece, in whom it is hard not to see a reflection of the Lykeian god of Delos, the Lupercus of Latin mythology; and it is now given by Seburk to Ecke on the condition that if he finds Dietrich he will let him live. It is the Dawn pleading for the life of the Sun. ' Could I but see the hero, no greater boon could be bestowed upon me. His high name kills me.

it is unnecessary here to speak of them. Some remarks on the subject will be found in Mr. Ludlow's *Popular Epics*, i. 308, &c.

I know not what he hath done to me, that my heart so longs
after him.' It is the language of Selênê and Echo as they
look upon Endymiôn and Narkissos; and all that is said of
Dietrich recalls the picture of the youthful Herakles as given
in the apologue of Prodikos. He is the father of the afflicted;
what he wins he shares; all that is good he loves. Where-
ever he goes, Ecke hears the people recount the exploits and
dwell on the beauty and the goodness of Dietrich. Under a
linden tree he finds a wounded man, and looking at his
wounds, he cries out that he had never seen any so deep, and
that nothing remained whole to him under helmet or shield.
' No sword can have done this; it must be the wild thunder-
stroke from heaven.' Ecke is soon to see the hero who smote
down the wounded man; but no sooner is he confronted with
the valiant knight, than he forgets the part which he ought
to play if he means to appear as a messenger of Seburk and
to do her bidding. He now speaks in his own character, as
the Pani who bears an irrepressible hate for his adversary,
while Dietrich is as passive in the matter as Achilleus when
he declared that the Trojans had never done him any mischief. ' I will not strive with thee,' he says, ' thou hast done
me no harm; give my service to thy lady, and tell her I will
always be her knight.' But Ecke is bent only upon fighting,
and while he refuses to be the bearer of any message, he calls
Dietrich a coward and dares him to the contest. Nor can we
avoid noting that although Dietrich prays him to wait till
the sun shines if fight they must, Ecke by his intolerable
scoffs brings on the battle while it is yet night, and the strife
between the powers of light and darkness is carried on
amidst a storm of thunder and lightning until the day
breaks. Ecke then thinks that he has won the victory; but
just as he is boasting of his success, Dietrich is filled with
new strength, and when Ecke refuses to yield up his sword,
he runs him through. But he himself is sorely wounded,
and as he wanders on he finds a fair maiden sleeping by a
spring, as Daphnê, Arethousa, Melusina, and the nymphs are
all found near the running waters. The being whom Dietrich finds is gifted with the powers which Oinonê cannot or
will not exercise for the benefit of Paris. She heals him with

a wonderful salve, and tells him that she is a wise woman,
like Brynhild and Medeia, knowing the evil and the good,
and dwelling in a fair land beyond the sea. But the story
has been awkwardly put together, and of the fair Seburk we
hear no more. This, however, is but further evidence of the
mythical character of the materials with which the poets of
the early and middle ages for the most part had to deal.

The poem of the Great Rose Garden is a still more clumsy
travesty of the myth of the Phaiakian or Hyperborean
gardens. The birds are there, singing so sweetly that no
mournful heart could refuse to be solaced by them; but the
cold touch of the north is on the poet, and his seat under
the linden tree is covered with furs and samite, while the
wind which whispers through the branches comes from
bellows black as a coal. In this garden is waged the same
furious fight which fills Etzel's slaughter hall with blood in
the Nibelung Lay: but the battle assumes here a form so
horrible and so wantonly disgusting that we need only mark
the more modern vein of satire which has used the myth for
the purpose of pointing a jest against the monastic orders.
The monk Ilsan, who, putting aside his friar's cloak, stands
forth clad in impenetrable armour and wielding an unerring
sword, is Odysseus standing in beggar's garb among the
suitors; but the spirit of the ancient legend is gone, and
Ilsan appears on the whole in a character not much more
dignified than that of Friar Tuck in Ivanhoe.

The same wonderful armour is seen again in the beautiful
romance of Roland. How thoroughly devoid this romance is
of any materials of which the historian may make use, has
perhaps already been shown; that many incidents in the
legend may have been suggested by actual facts in the lifetime of Charles the Great, is an admission which may be
readily made. When Charles the Great is made to complain
on the death of Roland that now the Saxons, Bulgarians,
and many other nations, as those of Palermo and Africa, will
rebel against him, it is possible that the story may point to
some redoubtable leader whose loss left the empire vulnerable
in many quarters: but we do not learn this fact, if it be a
fact, from the romance, and the impenetrable disguise

which popular fancy has thrown over every incident makes the idea of verifying any of them an absurdity. Whatever may have been the cause of the war, Roland plays in it the part of Achilleus. The quarrel was none of his making, but he is ready to fight in his sovereign's cause; and the sword Durandal which he wields is manifestly the sword of Chrysâôr. When his strength is failing, a Saracen tries to wrest the blade from his hand, but with his ivory horn Roland strikes the infidel dead. The horn is split with the stroke, and all the crystal and gold fall from it. The night is at hand, but Roland raises himself on his feet, and strikes the recovered sword against a rock. 'Ha! Durandal,' he cries, 'how bright thou art and white! how thou shinest and flamest against the sun! Charles was in the vale of Mauricane when God from heaven commanded him by his angel that he should give thee to a captain; wherefore the gentle king, the great, did gird thee on me.'[1] This is the pedigree of no earthly weapon, and to the list of conquests wrought by it in the hands of Roland we may add the exploits of the good brands Excalibur, and Gram, and Balmung, and in short, the swords of all the Hellenic and Teutonic heroes. We are thus prepared for the issue when Alda (Hilda), to whom he has been betrothed, falls dead when she hears that Roland is slain. Kleopatra and Brynhild cannot survive Meleagros and Sigurd.[2]

The romance of Arthur.

As useless for all historical purposes, and as valuable to the comparative mythologist, is the magnificent romance of King Arthur. Probably in no other series of legends is there a more manifest recurrence of the same myth under different forms. The structure of the tale is simple enough. Arthur himself is simply a reproduction of Sigurd or Perseus. Round him are other brave knights, and these, not less than himself, must have their adventures; and thus Arthur and Balin answer respectively to Achilleus and Odysseus in the Achaian hosts. A new element is brought into the story with the Round Table, which forms part of the

---

[1] The address of Roland to his sword is more magniloquently given in the 'Chronicle of Turpin,' Ludlow, Ibid. i. 425.

[2] This is the story of Lord Nann and the Korrigan, Keightley, Fairy Mythology, 433.

dowry of Guinevere; and the institution of the Knights furnishes the starting-point for a series of exploits on the part of each knight, which are little more than a clog to the narrative, and may easily be detached from the main thread of it. They answer in fact to those books in our Iliad which relate the fortunes of the Achaian chieftains during the inaction of Achilleus. A third series of narratives, rising gradually to a strain of surpassing beauty and grandeur, begins with the manifestation of the Round Table in the form of the holy Grail; and the legend of the quest for the sacred vessel, while it is really an independent story, is in its essential features a mere repetition of some which have preceded it. In short, the original meaning of these myths had been completely forgotten by the mediæval romancers; but, like the Homeric poets, they have felt the irresistible spell, and have adhered to the traditional types with marvellous fidelity.

CHAP. XII.

Stripped thus of its adventitious matter, the poem assumes a form common to the traditions and folk-lore of all the Teutonic or even all the Aryan nations. Not only is the wonderful sword of Roland seen again in the first blade granted to King Arthur, but the story of the mode in which Arthur becomes master of it is precisely the story of the Teutonic Sigurd and the Greek Theseus. We might almost say with truth that there is not a single incident with which we are not familiar in the earlier legends. The fortunes of Igraine, Arthur's mother, are precisely those of Alkmênê, Uther playing the part of Zeus, while Gorlois takes the place of Amphitryon.[1] As soon as he is born, Arthur is wrapped in a cloth of gold, the same glittering raiment which in the Homeric hymn the nymphs wrap round the new-born Phoibos, and like the infant Cyrus, who is arrayed in the same splendid garb, is placed in the hands of a poor man whom the persons charged with him, like Harpagos, meet at the postern-gate of the castle. In his house the child grows like Cyrus

The birth and youth of Arthur.

<hr>

[1] The scene in which Sigurd personates Gunnar in order to win Brynhild for the latter is but slightly different from the story of Uther as told by Jeffrey of Monmouth or in the more detailed romance. This power of transformation is a special attribute of the gods of the heaven and the light, and as such is exercised by Phoibos the fish god, and Dionysos the lion and boar.

and Romulus and others, a model of human beauty, and like them he cannot long abide in his lowly station. Some one must be chosen king, and the trial is to be that which Odin appointed for the recovery of the sword Gram, which he had thrust up to the hilt in the great rooftree of Volsung's hall. ' There was seen in the churchyard, at the east end by the high altar, a great stone formed square, and in the midst thereof was like an anvil of steel a foot high, and therein stuck a fair sword naked by the point, and letters of gold were written about the sword that said thus, " Whoso pulleth out this sword out of this stone and anvil is rightwise born king of England." ' The incident by which Arthur's title is made known answers to the similar attempts made in Teutonic folk-lore to cheat Boots, the younger son, of his lawful inheritance. Sir Kay, leaving his sword at home, sends Arthur for it, and Arthur not being able to find it, draws the weapon imbedded in the stone as easily as Theseus performed the same exploit. Sir Kay, receiving it, forthwith claims the kingdom. Sir Ector, much doubting his tale, drives him to confess that it was Arthur who gave him the sword, and then bids Arthur replace it in the solid block. None now can draw it forth but Arthur, to whose touch it yields without force or pressure. Sir Ector then kneels to Arthur, who, supposing him to be his father, shrinks from the honour; but Ector, like the shepherds in the myths of Oidipous, Romulus, or Cyrus, replies, ' I was never your father nor of your blood, but I wote well ye are of an higher blood than I weened ye were.' But although like the play-mates of Cyrus, the knights scorn to be governed by a boy whom they hold to be baseborn, yet they are compelled to yield to the ordeal of the stone, and Arthur, being made king, forgives them all. The sword thus gained is in Arthur's first war so bright in his enemies' eyes that it gives light like thirty torches, as the glorious radiance flashes up to heaven when Achilleus dons his armour. But this weapon is not to be the blade with which Arthur is to perform his greatest exploits. Like the sword of Odin in the Volsung story, it is snapped in twain in the conflict with Pellinore; but it is of course brought back to him in the form of Excalibur, by a maiden who answers to Thetis or to Hjordis.[1] Arthur, riding with Merlin along a lake, becomes 'ware of an arm clothed in white samite that held a fair sword in the hand.' This is the fatal weapon, whose scabbard answers precisely to the panoply of Achilleus, for while he wears it Arthur cannot shed blood, even though he be wounded. Like all the other sons of Helios, Arthur has his enemies, and King Rience demands as a sign of homage the beard of Arthur, which gleams with the splendour of the golden locks or rays of Phoibos Akersekomes. The demand is refused, but in the mediæval romance there is room for others who reflect the glory of Arthur, while his own splendour is for the time obscured. At Camelot they see a maiden with a sword attached to her body, which Arthur himself cannot draw. In the knight Balin, who draws it, and who ' because he was poorly arrayed put him not far in the press,' we see not merely the humble Arthur who gives his sword to Sir Kay, but Odysseus, who in his beggar's dress shrinks from the brilliant throng which crowds his ancestral hall.[2]

On the significance of the Round Table we must speak elsewhere. It is enough for the present to note that it comes to Arthur with the bride whose dowry is to be to him as fatal as the treasures of the Argive Helen to Menelaos. In the warning of Merlin that Guinevere ' is not wholesome for him' we see that earlier conception of Helen in which the Attic tragedians differ so pointedly from the poets of the Iliad and the Odyssey. As Helen is to be the ruin of cities, of men, and of ships, so is Guinevere to bring misery on herself and on all around her. Dangers thicken round Arthur, and he is assailed by enemies as dangerous as Kirkê and Kalypso to Odysseus. The Fay Morgan seeks to steal Excalibur, and succeeds in getting the scabbard, which she throws into a lake, and Arthur now may both bleed and die.[3] At the

---

[1] 'The Manks hero, Olave of Norway, had a sword with a Celtic name, Macabuin.'—Campbell, *Tales of the West Highlands*, i. lxxii. It reappears as the sword Tirfing in the fairy tale. Keightley, *Fairy Mythology*, 73.

[2] The invisible knight who at this stage of the narrative smites Sir Herleus

wears the helmet of Hades, and his action is that of the Erinys who wanders in the air.

[3] Morgan has the power of transformation possessed by all the fish and water-gods, Proteus, Onues, Thetis, &c.

thereof were precious stones wrought with subtle letters of gold, which said, "Never shall man take me hence but he by whom I ought to hang; and he shall be the best knight of the world "'—bravery and goodness being thus made the prize instead of an earthly kingdom as in the case of Arthur. The king tells Lancelot that this sword ought to be his, but it is the prize which, like the princess for whom the unsuccessful suitors venture their bodies, brings ruin on those who fail to seize it. The hero who is to take it is revealed, when an old man coming in lifts up the cover that is on the Siege Perilous, and discloses the words, 'This is the siege of Sir Galahad the good knight.' The story of this peerless hero is introduced with an incident which is manifestly suggested by the narrative of Pentecost. As the Knights of the Round Table sat at supper in Camelot, 'they heard cracking and crying of thunder, that they thought the place should all-to rive. And in the midst of the blast entered a sunbeam more clear by seven times than ever they saw day, and all they were alighted by the grace of the Holy Ghost. Then began every knight to behold other; and each saw other by their seeming fairer than ever they saw afore. Then there entered into the hall the holy Grail covered with white samite, and there was none that might see it nor who bear it. And then was all the hall full filled with great odours, and every knight had such meat and drink as he best loved in the world.' The wonderful vessel is suddenly borne away, and the knights depart on a search which answers precisely to the quest of the Golden Fleece or the treasures of Helen the fair. The myth of the sword, already thrice given, is presented to us once more on board the ship Faith, on which there was 'a fair bed, and at the foot was a sword, fair and rich; and it was drawn out of the scabbard half a foot or more.' 'Wot ye well,' says a maiden to Sir Galahad, 'that the drawing of this sword is warned unto all men save unto you.' This ship is the same vessel which carries Helios round the stream of Ocean during the hours of darkness. In other words, it becomes the ship of the dead, the bark which carries the souls to the land of light which lies beyond the grave. This ship carries to the Spiritual

Place the body of Sir Percival's sister, who dies to save the lady of the castle by giving her a dish full of her own blood—a myth which reflects the story of Iphigeneia who dies that Helen, the lady of the castle of Menelaos, may be rescued, and of Polyxena, whose blood is shed that Achilleus may repose in the unseen land. From the quest of the Grail Lancelot comes back ennobled and exalted. Arthur longs for the return of the good knight Galahad, of Percival, and Bors; but the face of the purest of all men he may never see again. When at length the eyes of Galahad rest on the mystic vessel, he utters the Nunc Dimittis, and Joseph of Arimathæa says to him, 'Thou hast resembled me in two things; one is, that thou hast seen the San Greal, and the other is that thou art a clean maiden as I am.' Then follows the farewell of Galahad to his comrades, as he charges Sir Bors to salute his father Sir Lancelot and bid him remember this unstable world. 'And therewith he kneeled down before the table and made his prayers, and then suddenly his soul departed unto Jesus Christ. And a great multitude of angels bare his soul up to heaven that his two fellows might behold it; also they saw come down from heaven a hand, but they saw not the body, and then it came right to the vessel and took it and the spear,[1] and so bare it up into heaven. Sithence was there never a man so hardy as to say that he had seen the San Greal.'

The sequel which tells the story of the final fortunes of Lancelot and Guinevere presents perhaps the most wonderful instance of the degree to which a myth may be modified, and in this case the modifying influence is strictly and purely Christian. In the Trojan legend, Paris, who plays the part of Lancelot in the seduction of Helen, is invested with some of the qualities of Achilleus, and with many of the attributes of Phoibos; but Lancelot is Paris purified of his sensuality, his cruelty, and his cowardice. It is true that he estranges the love of Guinevere from her lord Arthur, and that even the sanctifying influence of the holy Grail, which makes him proof against the heart-rending sorrow of Elaine, cannot avail to repress his unconquerable affection

[1] See book ii., chap. ii., sect. 12.

for the brightest and the fairest of women. But although
the romance throughout speaks of it as his great sin, the
love is one which asks only for her heart as its recompence,
and enables him to say even at the last, that Guinevere is
worthy of the love of Arthur. But the same Christian
influence which makes Arthur slow to believe any evil of his
dear friend Lancelot, could not allow Guinevere to end her
days in peace with Arthur, as Helen returns to live and die
in the house of Menelaos. Like Paris, whom Menelaos admitted to an equally trustful friendship, Lancelot had done a
great wrong; and even when Arthur has closed his brief but
splendid career, Guinevere tells Lancelot that all love on
earth is over between them. Their lips may not meet even
in the last kiss which should seal the death-warrant of their
old affection. Arthur is gone. When he will come back
again, no man may tell; but Guinevere is more faithful now
to the word which she had pledged to him than she had
been while his glorious form rose pre-eminent among the
bravest knights of Christendom. Yet in spite of all that
Christian influence has done to modify and ennoble the
story, the myth required that Guinevere should be separated
from Lancelot, as Helen is torn away from Paris; and the
narrative presents us from time to time with touches which
vividly recall the old Greek and Teutonic myths. Thus Sir
Urre of Hungary has wounds which only Lancelot can heal,
as Oinônê alone can heal Paris; and the last battle with
Modred is begun when a knight draws his sword on an
adder that has stung him in the foot, like the snake which
bit Eurydikê. So again, Excalibur is, by the hands of the
reluctant Sir Bedivere, thrown into the lake from which it
had been drawn, as the light of Helios is quenched in the
waters from which he sprung in the morning; and the barge,
which had borne away the fair maid of Astolat and the
sister of Sir Percival, brings the three queens (seemingly the
weird sisters who have already been seen in another form) to
carry off the wounded Arthur.

But even at the last the story exhibits the influence of the
old myth. Neither Arthur himself nor any others think
that he is really dying. His own words are, 'I will unto

the vale of Avilion, to heal me of my grievous wound.'
There, in the shadowy valley in which Endymion sinks to
sleep, the thought of the renewed life in store for Memnôn
or Sarpêdôn or Adonis showed itself in the epitaph

'Hic jacet Arthurus, rex quondam rexque futurus.'

Guinevere
and Diar-
maid.

Of the story of Arthur and Guinevere, Mr. Campbell says
that, 'when stripped to the bones,' it 'is almost identical
with the love story of the history of the Feinne,' the tradition
embodied in the poems which bear the name of Ossian, with
not less justice perhaps than the Iliad and Odyssey bear the
name of Homer, and the Finnish epic Kalewala that of
Wäinämöinen. To Grainne, the wife of Fionn, Diarmaid
stands in the relation of Lancelot to Guinevere, or of Paris
to Helen. Guinevere loves Lancelot at first sight: Diarmaid, when first he meets Grainne, 'shows a spot on his
forehead, which no woman can see without loving him.' But
if Lancelot follows Guinevere willingly, Grainne compels
Diarmaid to run away with her. In the sequel the conduct
of Fionn precisely matches that of Arthur, and Diarmaid is
as fearless a knight as Lancelot—the conclusion being that
'here are the same traditions worked up into wholly different
stories, and differently put upon the stage, according to the
manners of the age in which romances are written, but the
people go on telling their own story in their own way.'[1]

Later
mediaeval
epics and
romances.

It is unnecessary to examine the poems or romances which
some writers are fond of arranging under sub-cycles of the
main cycle of the Carolingian epics. These epics Mr.
Ludlow[2] pronounces 'historical.' The sort of history con-

---

[1] Into the question of the authenti-
city of Macpherson's *Ossian* it is altogether unnecessary to enter. The
matter has been admirably and conclusively treated by Mr. Campbell in
the fourth volume of his *Tales of the
West Highlands*, and no one probably
would for an instant suppose that Macpherson invented the tradition—in other
words, the framework of the myth: and
with this only we are here concerned.
The story of Sir Bevis of Hampton, Mr.
Campbell remarks, reflects the same
mythology, iv. 267. I must content
myself with calling attention to Mr.
Campbell's very valuable section on the
Welsh stories, iv. 270–299. Taken as
a whole, they run precisely parallel to
the streams of German, Scandinavian,
and Hindu folk-lore, and bring Mr.
Campbell to the conclusion that they
are 'all founded upon incidents which
have been woven into popular tales
almost ever since men began to speak:
that they are Celtic only because Celts
are men, and only peculiarly Celtic because Celts are admitted by all to be a
very ancient offshoot from the common
root.'

[2] *Popular Epics of the Middle Ages*,
vol. ii. p. 13.

tained in them we may take at his own estimate of it. 'The
history of them is *popular* history, utterly unchronological,
attributing to one age or hero the events and deeds of quite
another.' In other words, it is a history from which, if we
had no other sources of evidence, we could not by any possibility learn anything. Possessing the genuine contemporary
history of the time, the critic has a clue which may here and
there furnish some guidance through the labyrinth; but it
is the genuine history which enables him in whatever measure to account for the perversions of the poems, not the
perversions which add a jot to our knowledge of the facts.
But it is more important to remember that these poems are
of a quite different class from the general epics of the Aryan
nations. They are the result of book-work, or, as Professor
Max Müller has expressed it, they are not organic; and to
the stories spun by men sitting down at their desks, and
mingling mythical or historical traditions at their will,
there is literally no end. Yet even in these poems it
is remarkable that some of the most prominent or momentous incidents belong to the common inheritance of the
Aryan nations. The story of Garin the Lorrainer repeats in
great part the story of Odysseus. Thierry's daughter, the
White Flower (Blanche Flor), is the Argive Helen. 'That
maiden,' says the poet, ' in an evil hour was born, for many
a worthy man shall yet die through her.' The death of Bego,
after the slaying of the boar, is the death of Achilleus after
the fall of Hektor. But whatever travesty of real history
there may be in parts of this poem, or in the epics of William
of Orange and Ogier the Dane, there is next to none in the
story of Bertha Largefoot, which simply reflects the myth of
Cinderella, Penelopê, Punchkin, and perhaps one or two
more.[1] In short, it is mere patchwork. As in the case of
Cinderella and Rhodôpis, the true queen is made known by
her feet;[2] the only difference being that with Bertha it is the

---

[1] Bertha is in name the Teutonic
goddess, who in another form appears
as Frau Holle or Holda, the benignant
earth, and who, like Penelopê, has marvellous skill in spinning.

[2] This myth occurs again in the
Gaelic story of 'The King who wished

to marry his Daughter.' Mr. Campbell
(*Tales of the West Highlands*, i. 227),
mentions other instances, and remarks
that 'those who hold that popular tales
are preserved in all countries and in all
languages alike, will hold that the
Italian, German, French, Norse, English,

great size of her feet which determines the issue, not their smallness. To coin a word, she is Eurypous, instead of Eurôpê; and there was a version which spoke of her as Queen Goosefoot, a personage over whom Mr. Ludlow thinks it impossible that a poet could become sentimental. Yet the goose-footed queen is simply a swan-maiden, one of the most beautiful creatures of Aryan mythology. Mr. Ludlow seldom or never speaks as if he knew that the substance of these later poems has been given again and again in earlier myths. Thus he does not pause to notice that in the 'sub-cycle of William of Orange,' Renouart, the king's son, who 'must keep the kitchen, make the fire, skim the meat,' while he should be heading a host of a hundred thousand men, is only the Teutonic Boots, grown bulky and clumsy, like the Herakles of the 'Alkêstis.' And yet these parallelisms must be noted, if the mythical or historical value of these romances is to be accurately measured. With the character of the men and women portrayed in the mediæval epics, Mr. Ludlow is seemingly much perplexed. The type especially which is seen in Brynhild, Gudrun, or Kriemhild, he regards as 'foreign to the truth of woman's nature.'[1] It is so, and it must be so; and it is better to avow it than to twist such stories as the legends of Helen and Achilleus in the desperate attempt to judge by human standards the inhabitants of the Cloudland.

The same materials will probably be found to have furnished the framework of at least the greater part of the Saga literature of Northern Europe. If here and there a name or an incident belonging to real history be introduced into them, this cannot of itself raise the story above the level of plausible fiction. Far too much, probably, has been said of these Sagas as a true picture of society and manners. That the writers would throw over their narrative a colouring borrowed from the ways and customs of their own time is certain; but the acts which they record are not proved to be deeds which were constantly or even rarely occurring, if

and Gaelic are all versions of the same story, and that it is as old as the common stock from which all these races sprang.' See also the story of

the 'Sharp Grey Sheep,' Campbell, ii. 289.
[1] *Popular Epics*, ii. 386.

they involve either a direct contradiction or a physical im- possibility. To say that all incidents involving such diffi- culties are to be at once rejected, while we are yet to give faith to the residue, is to lay ourselves as bondmen at the feet of Euêmeros and his followers, and to bid farewell to truth and honesty. Even in pictures of life and manners there is a certain limit beyond which we refuse to credit tales of cruelty, villainy, and treachery, when they are related of whole tribes who are not represented as mere savages and ruffians; and unless we are prepared to disregard these limits, the history of many of these Sagas becomes at once, as a whole, incredible, although some of the incidents recorded in them may have occurred.

This is especially the case with the Grettir Saga, for The which a high historical character has been claimed by the Grettir translators.[1] Yet the tale from beginning to end is full of Saga. impossibilities. In his early youth Grettir, being set by his father to watch his horses, gets on the back of one named Keingala, and drawing a sharp knife across her shoulders and then all along both sides of the back, flays off the whole strip from the flank to the loins. When Asmund next strokes the horse, the hide to his surprise comes off in his hands, the animal being seemingly very little the worse for the loss. After this impossible result of his exploit, Grettir, having lost a mealbag, finds Skeggi in the same predicament, and joins him in a common search. Skeggi comes across Grettir's bag and tries to hide it. When Grettir complains, Skeggi throws his axe at him and is slain in requital. It can scarcely be pretended that we are reading the true story of ' an interesting race of men near akin to ourselves,' when instead of a fair field and no favour we find that six men do not hesitate to fall upon one.[2] Thorfin, walking away from his boat with a leather bottle full of drink on his back, is assaulted from behind by Thorgeir, who thinks that he has slain him when he has only cut the bottle. He is jeered at next day for his blunder; but the act is no more blamed for its treachery than is the same base deed when Odysseus

[1] Eiríkr Magnússon and William Morris.
[2] Preface, pp. i. and 94.

boastingly relates it of himself. Thorgeir Bottle-jack is slain soon afterwards in a bloody fight over the carcass of a whale, in which half the population of the village seems to be slaughtered. Thorbiorn Oxmain thinks it a goodly exploit to knock at a man's door and then to thrust him through with a spear when he comes to open it. The same honourable champion, wishing to slay Grettir, discourses thus to his comrades :—

'I will go against him in front, and take thou heed how matters go betwixt us, for I will trust myself against any man, if I have one alone to meet; but do thou go behind him, and drive the axe into him with both hands atwixt his shoulders; thou needest not fear that he will do thee hurt, as his back will be turned to thee.'[1]

When at a later time Grettir had slain Thorir Redbeard, Thorir of Garth assails the solitary outlaw with eighty men. Grettir slays eighteen and wounds many more, and the rest take to flight.[2]

This last incident brings us to the main question. It is, of course, a sheer impossibility: and if, as such, it is to be regarded as lying beyond the pale of human history, we are at once driven to ask wherein lies the real value of a narrative in which such incidents form the staple of the story. The translators tell us that throughout the tale 'the Saga-man never relaxes his grasp of Grettir's character, that he is the same man from beginning to end, thrust this way and that by circumstances, but little altered by them; unlucky in all things, yet made strong to bear all ill-luck; scornful of the world, yet capable of enjoyment and determined to make the most of it; not deceived by men's specious ways, but disdaining to cry out because he must needs bear with them; scorning men, yet helping them when called on, and desirous of fame; prudent in theory, and wise in foreseeing the inevitable sequence of events, but reckless even beyond the recklessness of that time and people, and finally capable of inspiring in others strong affection and devotion to him in spite of his rugged self-sufficing temper.'[3] It is one thing if this is to be regarded as the portrait of a man who really lived and died on this earth, or as the picture of some in-

[1] P. 141.   [2] P. 169.   [3] P. xiv.

habitant of the Phaiakian cloudland. The translators raise a vital issue when they say that 'to us moderns the real interest in these records of a past state of life lies principally in seeing events true in the main treated vividly and dramatically by people who completely understood the manners, life, and above all the turn of mind of the actors in them.'[1] If we have any honest anxiety to ascertain facts, and if we are prepared to give credit to a narrative only when the facts have been so ascertained, then everything is involved in the question whether the events here related are true in the main or not. The genealogies given in the earlier part of the Saga agree, we are told, with those of the Landnáma-bók and of the other most trustworthy Sagas; yet such names tell us as much and as little as the names in the genealogy of the tale-maker Hekataios. A catalogue of names belonging to real persons cannot impart authority to a narrative of fictitious events, if they are fictitious; and when we have put aside these genealogies and the names of one or two kings, as of Olaf, Hacon, and Harold Fairhair, we have numbered all the historical elements in the book: nor is it necessary to say that some safeguard is wanted when we remember that the Carolingian romances take the great Karl to Jerusalem.

If then we have before us a story, some of the incidents of which are manifestly impossible or absurd, we are scarcely justified in accepting, on the mere authority of the Saga, other portions which involve no such difficulties. We have the alternative of rejecting the whole story without troubling ourselves to examine it further, or we may take it to pieces, reducing it to its constituent elements, and then seeing whether these elements are to be found in any other narratives. If this should be the case, the character of the narratives in which these common elements are seen will go far towards determining the credibility of the story. Clearly the latter course is the more philosophical and the more honest. That the translators had the clue in their own hands, is clear from the sentence in which, speaking of the events which followed Grettir's death, they tell us that 'the Saga-

Materials of the Saga.

[1] P. xiii.

man here has taken an incident, with little or no change, from the romance of Tristram and Iseult.'[1] If, as they think, the chapters in which this incident is related were added to the tale, and if this part of the story be substantially the same as that of a romance which is known to be mythical; if further, as they say, the whole Saga, 'has no doubt gone through the stages which mark the growth of the Sagas in general, that is, it was for long handed about from mouth to mouth until it took a definite shape in men's minds,'[2] a presumption, to say the least, is furnished that other incidents in the Saga may be found to be of a like nature.

If we take the sentences which tell us of Grettir's childhood, how he had scant love from his father who set him to watch his home-geese, how he was fair to look on, red-haired and much freckled, how he would do no work or spoilt all that he did; how, when placed on board a boat, he 'would move for nought, neither for baling, nor to do aught for the sail, nor to work at what he was bound to work at in the ship in even share with the other men, neither would he buy himself off from the work,'[3] how, when he does some great thing, the remark is 'we wotted not that thou wert a man of such powers as we have now proved thee,'[4] how he goes disguised to the wrestling match, and when Thorbiorn Angle pushes and tugs hard at him, moves not a whit but sits quiet, yet wins the victory,—we have before us the Goose-girl and the Boots of Teutonic story, the Boots who sits among the ashes in the 'irony of greatness,' biding his time, —the disguised Odysseus, patiently enduring the gibes of the suitors and the beggar Arnaios.

When the Saga tells us that on coming back from a Thing, 'Grettir lifted a stone which now lies there in the grass and is called Grettir's heave,' and how 'many men came up to see the stone and found it a great wonder that so young a man should heave aloft such a huge rock,' it relates a well-known legend in the myths of Theseus and of Sigurd in the Volsung tale. When Grettir is driven forth from his home without arms and his mother draws forth

[1] P. xii.   [2] P. xv.   [3] P. 41.   [4] P. 58.

from her cloak the fair sword which has gained many a day, we
see before us Thetis and Hjordis bestowing on their children
the magic weapons which reappear in the hands of Arthur
and of Roland. In the horrible smiting of the bearsarks,
who are shut up in a barn, we have the awful hall of
slaughter in the Odyssey and the Nibelung Lay. In the
marvellous story of the demon who is vainly assailed first by
Glam who becomes a demon himself, then by Thorgaut,
but is finally slain by Grettir, we see the common type of the
popular story in which the youngest son, or Boots, wins the
day, when his two brothers or comrades fail. In the beaks
of the ship which is so full of weather-wisdom that the one
whistles before a south wind and the other before a north
wind, we have a reminiscence of the divine Argo.[1] In the
errand on which, when his companions have no fire, Grettir
is sent to bring fire from a distant cliff, although ' his mind
bids him hope to get nought of good thereby,' we see the
myth of Prometheus and his recompense. The conflict of
Grettir and Snækoll is related in words so nearly resembling
those of the narrative of David's fight with Goliath, that
it is hard to resist the suspicion that we may have here an
instance of mere copying,[2] or that we have a travesty of the
story of Samson, as we read that ' on a day as Grettir lay
sleeping, the bonders came upon him, and when they saw
him they took counsel how they should take him at the
least cost of life, and settled so that ten men should leap on
him while some laid bonds on his feet; and thus they did,
and threw themselves on him; but Grettir broke forth so
mightily that they fell from off him.'[3] In his enormous
strength, in his fitful action, which is as often mischievous
as it is beneficent, in the lot which makes him a servant of
beings meaner than himself, which stirs up enemies against
him in men whom he has never injured, in the doom which
he foresees and which he has not the power, and indeed
takes no pains, to avert, he is the very counterpart of
Herakles and Achilleus. When he slays afresh Glam who
has been long dead, the demon tells him ' Hitherto thou
hast earned fame by thy deeds, but henceforth will wrongs

[1] P. 115.   [2] P. 123.   [3] P. 153.

and manslayings fall upon thee, and the most part of thy doings will turn to thy woe and illhap; an outlaw shalt thou be made, and ever shall it be thy lot to dwell alone abroad.' Henceforth he is 'the traveller,' who can know no rest, who seeks shelter of many great men; 'but something ever came to pass whereby none of them would harbour him.' This, however, is the doom of Indra and Savitar in many Vedic hymns, of Wuotan Wegtam in Teutonic mythology, of Sigurd, Perseus, Bellerophon, Oidipous, Odysseus, Phoibos, and Dionysos. These are all wanderers and outlaws like Grettir, and there is scarcely an incident in the life of Grettir which is not found in the legends of one or more of the mythical beings just named. The overthrow of the eighty assassins led on by Thorir of Garth is the defeat of the Lykian ambuscade by Bellerophontes. After this the wounded hero goes to a cave under Balljökul, where the daughter of Hallmund heals his wound, and treats him well. 'Grettir dwelt long there that summer,' like Odysseus in the cave of Kalypsô, or Tanhaüser in the Venusberg, or True Thomas in the coverts of Ercildoune; but we look to find him chafing, as these did, at the enforced rest. We turn over the page and we read, 'Now as the summer wore, Grettir yearned for the peopled country, to see his friends and kin.'[1] It is Odysseus longing to see Penelopê once more. But he is under a doom. As Olaf says, 'If ever a man has been cursed, of all men must thou have been.'[2] It is the curse which is laid on Ixîon and Sisyphos, and singularly enough his father Asmund says of his son, 'Methinks over much on a whirling wheel his life turns.'[3] Hence also he dreads the darkness like a child, for Herakles, Helios, and Achilleus can do nothing when the sun has gone down. Hence too, the old mother of Thorbiorn lays on him the fate 'that thou be left of all health, wealth, and good hap, all good heed and wisdom,' the very fate of which Achilleus complains again and again to Thetis in the very bitterness of his heart. If again Grettir has his brother Illugi in whom he has garnered up his soul, this is the story of Achilleus and Patroklos, of Peirithoös and Theseus, of

Herakles and Iphitos, of the Dioskouroi, and a host of others. Nineteen years he is an outlaw. 'Then said the lawman that no one should be longer in outlawing than twenty winters in all,' and so Grettir was set free, as Odysseus returns home in the twentieth year. The incident which led to the death of Grettir is simply the myth of Philoktêtês and of Rustem. The cutting off of Grettir's hand is an incident in the myth of Indra Savitar and of Walthar of Aquitaine. When again it is said of him that 'he is right-well ribbed about the chest, but few might think he would be so small of growth below,'[1] we cannot avoid a comparison with the story of Shortshanks in Grimm's collection, or of Odysseus who, when sitting, is far more majestic than Menelaos who, when standing, towers above him by head and shoulders.

In short, the Saga, as a whole, ceases practically to have any distinctive features, and even in the sequel which relates the story of Thorstein, Dromund, and Spes, the incident which the translators compare with the romance of Tristram is not the only point of likeness with other legends. The closing scenes in the lives of the two lovers precisely reproduce the last incidents in the myth of Lancelot and Guinevere. Of the avenging of Grettir by Thorstein we need only say that the same issue belongs to the stories of Sigurd and the Three Helgis, and that all these have their type and find their explanation in the avenging of Baldur.

CHAP.
XII.

The avenging of Grettir.

[1] P. 232.

BOOK II.

CHAPTER I.

THE ETHEREAL HEAVENS.

SECTION I.—DYAUS.

The ancient Vedic mythology exhibits in a state of fusion the elements which the Hellenic legends present to us in forms more or less crystallised; and precisely on this account it has for us an inestimable value as throwing light on the process by which the treasure-house of Aryan mythology was filled. The myths of Achilleus and Sigurd point clearly enough to the idea of the sun as doomed to an early death: but the Vedic hymns bring before us a people to whom the death of the sun is a present reality, for whom no analogy has suggested the idea of a continuous alternation of day and night, and who know not, as the fiery chariot of the sun sinks down in the west, whether they shall ever see again the bright face of him who was their friend.[1] All their utterances were thus the utterances of children who knew little of themselves and nothing of the world without them, and thus also they could not fail to apply to the same objects names denoting very different relations or characteristics. The heaven might be the father of the dawn, or he might be the child of the earth. The morning might be the parent of the sun, or she might be his sister, or his bride; and we should expect (as we find), that, if the names denoting these ideas came to be employed as names of deities, the characters and

---

[1] See p. 41, et seq.

powers of these gods would show a constant tendency to run into each other.

But the attribution to all sensible objects of a life as personal and conscious as their own would lead to the thought of one common source or origin of the life of all; and this source could be found only in the broad bright heaven which brooded over the wide earth and across which the sun made his daily journey to cheer the children of men. Thus Dyaus, the glistening ether,[1] became to the Hindu, as Zeus was to the Greek, a name for the supreme God; but although some mythical features entered gradually into the conception of this deity, the name retained its original significance too clearly to hold its ground in Hindu theology. Dyaus, like the Hellenic Ouranos and Kronos, must be displaced by his child, who at the first had brought out more prominently the supremacy of his father; and thus Indra became to the Hindu what Zeus was to the Hellenic tribes, while the Vedic Varuna retained in the east a spiritual character which Ouranos never acquired in the west.[2]

The Glistening Ether.

[1] Thus Dyaus, Zeus, Divus, Theos, Deus, Juno, Diana, Dianus or Janus, with many others, are outgrowths from the same root, dyu to shine. But in his *Introduction to Greek and Latin Etymology*, Mr. Peile, while fully allowing that the Sanskrit name Dyaus is represented by the Greek Zeus and by the Latin divus and deus, yet denies that there is any relation between the Latin *deus* and the Greek θεός. By the laws of phonetic change, he insists, the Latin *d* must answer to a Greek δ, as in δόμος, domus: hence some other root must be sought for θεός, perhaps ΘΕΣ, a secondary form of ΘΕ, the root of τίθημι, though this is rejected by Professor Curtius, *Gr. Et.* pp. 230, 404, in favour of a distinct root *thes* or *fes* (meaning to pray), which he traces in *festus* and in θέσασθαι. (Pind. *N.* v. 18.) I venture to think that too great a stress is here laid on laws which undoubtedly apply generally to the Aryan languages, but to which there are yet some instances of apparent and some even of real exception. The Greek δάκρυ is rightly represented by the English *tear*, while δάκος, the biting beast, reappears in its legitimate dress in the German Toggenburg; but in English we have not *t* as

in tear, but *dog*, while in Latin it is seen in 'tigris,' tiger, which approaches nearly to the English 'tyke' as a name for the dog. In the same way π in the Greek πατός ought to be represented by *f* in English; but it appears as ' path.' The connection of the two words can scarcely be doubted, for if Professor Curtius may give the equation πάτος: πόντος = πάθος: πίνθος = βάθος: βένθος, we may also add πάτος: πόντος = path: pond. Hence the fact that the Greek form of Dyaus is θεός, not δεός, scarcely warrants our severing the two words. If the Vedic adeva is the Greek ἄθεος, the relationship of θεός with the Latin 'deus' is established. In this conclusion I am following Professor Max Müller, *Lectures on Language*, second series, 425–455.

[2] Heaven and earth, it would seem, are in the earliest hymns alike self-existent; but Dr. Muir ('Principal Deities of the Rig Veda,' *Transactions of the Royal Society of Edinburgh*, vol. xxiii. part iii.) remarks that we are not told, as in the Hesiodic Theogony, which of the two is the older. 'On the contrary, one of the ancient poets seems to have been perplexed by the difficulty of this question, as at the beginning of

Dyu, then, in the land of the five streams was at once a name for the sky and a name for God, Dyaus pitâr, Dyaus the Father, answering to the Zeus Patêr of the Greeks and the Jupiter and Janus Pater of the Latins. As such, he was Visvakarman, the great architect of the universe, who knows all spheres and worlds,[1] janita (γενετήρ), the parent of all things, Prithivî, the broad earth, being the mother of his children.[2] As, again, with the Greeks Zeus is both the god of rain and the being to whom all who are in pain and sorrow address their prayer, so the Maruts or storms go about in dyu, the sky, while their worshippers on earth invoke the mercy of Dyaus, Prithivî, and Agni. But the Indian land under its scorching sun depends wholly on the bounty of the benignant rain god; and hence Indra, who is the child of Dyu, and who from Dyu receives his might, becomes more immediately the fertiliser of the earth and is regarded as more powerful than his father. But Dyu, although his greatness is obscured by that of his son, still wields the thunderbolt; and the original meaning of the name reappears in the myth which represents him as the father of the dawn who is invincible by all but Indra.

Thus Dyaus is to Prithivî what Ouranos is to Gaia in the Hesiodic theogony, the Greek myth differing from the former only in deciding that Gaia herself produced Ouranos to be coextensive with herself. The Hindu had not so far solved the difficulty; and the doubt expressed on this subject shows the peculiar attitude of the Indian mind to the problems of the sensible universe. The Greek was at once contented with answers suggested by the old mythical phrases, or by the phenomena which he might be describing. The Hindu, ever dwelling on the thought of an unseen world,

---

one of the hymns, (i. 185), he exclaims, "Which of you twain was the first, and which the last? How were they produced? Sages, who knows?" His power and wisdom are shown most of all in the creation or evocation of his son Indra. Thus of Indra it is said, "Thy father was the parent of a most heroic son: the maker of Indra, he who produced the celestial and invincible thunderer, was a most skilful workman."—R. V. iv. 17, 4. But it was

obvious that the abstract conception of Dyu as the father of Indra could not stand against the overwhelming weight of the myths which were continually springing up from phrases not originally antagonistic with the monotheistic belief or conviction.

[1] Muir, Principal Deities of R.V. 553.
[2] This name is not found in any Greek myth as the designation of a person; but it is represented by πλατεῖα, the feminine of πλατύς, broad.

strove to gain some insight into the nature of things, and to unlock secrets for which the material world could never furnish a key. Hence Dyu was for him sometimes the supreme God, sometimes the heaven which with the earth had been fashioned by the gods and strengthened with undecaying supports, and which trembled and bowed down in the presence of the deities. Sometimes he was the all-pervading spirit, sometimes a material and tangible firmament; and thus again the question arose of the origin of matter. Of his own ignorance the Hindu was perfectly conscious, and he had already begun to think that this ignorance extended even to the gods themselves. 'Who can tell whence this creation arose? The gods are subsequent to its production. Who then knows whence it sprung? He who in the highest heaven is its ruler, he knows, or perhaps not even he.'[1] So far as this question was answered at all, it was answered, as Dr. Muir has well remarked, by Greek and Hindu in the same way. In the Hesiodic theogony, Chaos, Gaia, and Tartaros are beings apparently self-existent; or at the least the scheme begins with Chaos, and no parents are assigned to Gaia and Tartaros, or to Eros, who immediately follows, and precedes the birth of Erebos and Nyx, of Aithêr and Hemera. The Hellenic poet had brought with him from his primeval home the tradition which he shared with the Hindu: but having given utterance to it, he bestowed no further thought upon it. With the latter the position of Kama, the representative of the Hesiodic Eros, determines the character of his philosophy. The desire (ὄρεξις), which in the Aristotelian Ethics must precede all moral action, is as essential to the divine as to the human mind, and thus Kama is the being through whom the world is fashioned, when as yet there existed only the one.[2] The Wish of Teutonic mythology answers more closely to the Hesiodic Eros than to the Vedic Kama. The Homeric poet knew that men always have a need of the gods;[3] but he was not, like the Hindu, always conscious of the need, always striving to know

---

[1] R. V. x. 129; Muir, ib. 553.
[2] Muir, ib. Max Müller, Sanskrit Literature, 559, et seq.

[3] πάντες θεῶν χατέουσ' ἄνθρωποι·
Od. iii. 48.

more of that mysterious power, always yearning for the time
when he should no more see through the glass darkly.

SECTION II.—VARUNA AND MITRA.

The solid
Heaven.
As Dyaus is the god of heaven in its dazzling purity and
brightness, so is Varuna also the heaven as serving, like the
Hellenic Ouranos, to veil or cover the earth. It is true that
in the Hesiodic theogony Ouranos is united with Gaia,
whereas it is not Varuna but Dyaus who in the Vedic
hymns is mentioned as having Prithivi for the mother of his
children. The difference is, perhaps, only in appearance.
Gaia is really wedded to Zeus not less than to Ouranos, if
Dêmêtêr be but Gaia viewed as the mother of all living
things. Varuna, then, as the solid heaven, which is spread
over the earth, is strictly a creation of mythical speech and
is embodied in a visible form. He sits on his throne, clothed
in golden armour, and along with Mitra dwells in a palace
which, like that of Helios, is supported by a thousand
columns, while his messengers stand around to do his bidding. But his mythical characteristics are in the Rig Veda
perpetually suggesting the idea of an unseen and almighty
Being who has made all things and upholds them by his
will. In many of the Vedic hymns we are carried altogether
out of the region of mythology, and we see only the man
communing directly with his Maker. In these hymns
Varuna, in the words of Dr. Muir, ' dwells in all worlds as
sovereign ; indeed, the three worlds are embraced within
him. The wind which resounds through the firmament is
his breath. He has placed the sun in the heaven, and
opened up a boundless path for it to traverse. He has hol-
lowed out the channels of the rivers. It is by his wise contrivance that, though all the rivers pour out their waters
into the sea, the sea is never filled. By his ordinance the
moon shines in the sky, and the stars which are visible by
night disappear on the approach of daylight. Neither the
birds flying in the air, nor the rivers in their sleepless flow,
can attain a knowledge of his power or his wrath. His spies
(or angels) behold both worlds. He himself has a thousand

eyes. He knows the flight of birds in the sky, the path of ships on the sea, the course of the far-sweeping wind, and perceives all the hidden things that have been or shall be done.'[1]

CHAP.
I.

All these are phrases which may be suggested directly by the phenomena of the heaven; but the chariot in which Varuṇa is borne over the earth,[2] is, like the eye of Zeus, lost in the purely spiritual thought of One who has no body and no passions, who, as seeing all things, sees also that which is evil, and who, as having nothing that is evil in himself, must punish and finally destroy it in the sinner. In some hymns, however, the two lines of thought seem to be blended strangely together; in other words, we see in them the process by which men rose from the lower conception to the higher. That sense of sin, which, as distinguished from the transgression of a positive law, can scarcely be said to have been present to the Greek mind, weighs heavy on the spirit of the Hindu, even while his conception of the Deity whom he addresses may be almost coarse in its familiarity. Varuṇa has received in the sacrifice the choice portions which please him most, and the worshipper may fairly demand that the question between them may be discussed reasonably as between friends.[3] But whatever may be said of the theory of the nature of sin, a pure monotheistic conviction is pre-eminently seen in the following prayer.

'Let me not yet, O Varuṇa, enter into the house of clay; have mercy, almighty, have mercy.

'If I go along trembling like a cloud driven by the wind, have mercy, almighty, have mercy.

'Through want of strength, thou strong and bright god,

Moral aspects of Varuṇa.

---

[1] *Principal Deities of R.V.* 558. In a passage from the Atharva Veda, quoted by Dr. Muir, *ibid.* and Professor Max Müller, *Chips,* i. 42, the same thought is worked out in language which is precisely reproduced in the 139th Psalm, and which also carries us to expressions and sentences in the Sermon on the Mount, and in other parts of the New Testament. The parallelism between the expressions of Aryan and Semitic monotheism is further traced out by M. Maury, *Croyances et Légendes*

de l'Antiquité:—'La Religion des Aryas.'

[2] This chariot 'shines with a golden radiance at the break of day, and at sunset assumes the colour of iron.'—Muir, *ib.* 557.

[3] Max Müller, *History of Sanskrit Literature,* 537. It is scarcely necessary to compare this language with the similar tone of familiar expostulation which runs through many of the Hebrew Psalms.

have I gone to the wrong shore: have mercy, almighty, have mercy.

'Thirst came upon the worshipper, though he stood in the midst of the waters: have mercy, almighty, have mercy.

'Whenever we men, O Varuna, commit an offence before the heavenly host, whenever we break thy law through thoughtlessness, have mercy, almighty, have mercy.' [1]

If the singular purity and unselfishness of the Hesiodic morality, as compared with that of the poems to which we give the name of Homer, suffice of themselves to prove the essential distinction between mythology and religion, these simple utterances of the Vedic poets show even more forcibly that the genuine belief in one almighty Being who is at once our Father, our Teacher, and our Judge, had its home first in the ancient Aryan land. It was a conviction to which they were guided by all that they saw or could apprehend of outward phenomena as well as by the irrepressible yearnings which stirred their hearts. For such yearnings and for such a consciousness in the Hebrew tribes we look in vain, before the Babylonish captivity. Among them we have at best only the warnings of a few isolated teachers, who saw things hidden from other eyes, and whose words, although they sounded in the ears of their countrymen like parables, would have conveyed a familiar meaning to the Aryans of northern India.[2] It matters little then whether Varuna be in these hymns mentioned almost invariably in conjunction with Mitra and sometimes with other gods. Like these, he is Âditya, Kronion, if Aditi be time; but the mythical notion

[1] Max Müller, *Hist.of Sansk.Lit.* 540.

[2] These words were written before the appearance of Professor Max Müller's article on Semitic Monotheism in his volumes of collected essays. Few probably will read that paper without feeling that on the main question very little room is left for doubt. Polytheism is to be found in both the Semitic and the Aryan races, but it was more ingrained in the former. The very interchangeableness of the attributes of the Vedic gods was, to a certain extent, a safeguard against any conscious and systematic polytheism. So long as this state of thought continued, Dyaus, Varuna, Indra, Vishnu, would be but many names for one and the same Being; but of course 'every new name threatened,' to use Professor Müller's words, 'to obscure more and more the primitive intuition of God.'—*Chips*, ii. 358. With the Jews the names under which they worshipped a multitude of gods were manifestly mere appellatives which never underwent any phonetic corruption, and thus the tendency to polytheism became the more inveterate. It is, however, scarcely necessary to say more than that 'if there had been in the Semitic race a truly monotheistic instinct, the history of those nations would become perfectly unintelligible.' —*Ib.* 365.

thus introduced sate so loosely on those who held it, that CHAP. their language ceased to show any sign of its influence in I. times of real anguish and sorrow.[1] It was enough that they could realise at once the righteousness of God, and His readiness to forgive those who disobeyed his laws so soon as they repented them of their sin.[2]

The process which converted the physical Varuṇa into a Aditi and spiritual God is carried to its extreme results in the concep-the Adi-tion of Aditi, 'the unbound, the unbounded,' or even, as being expressed by the negation of *diti*, a bond, 'the Absolute.' This indefinite term was naturally used to denote the source from which all life, even the life of the gods, springs; and thus Aditi, the Infinite, became the mother of all the gods. The fact is startling; but, in Professor Muller's words, 'the thoughts of primitive humanity were not only different from our thoughts, but different also from what we think their thoughts ought to have been. The poets of the Veda indulged freely in theogonic speculations without being frightened by any contradictions. They knew of Indra as the greatest of gods, they knew of Agni as the god of gods, they knew of Varuṇa as the ruler of all; but they were by no means startled at the idea, that their Indra had a mother, or that their Agni was born like a babe from the friction of two fire-sticks, or that Varuṇa and his brother Mitra were nursed in the lap of Aditi.' Hence Aditi was contrasted

[1] 'Every god is conceived as supreme, or at least as inferior to no other god, at the time that he is praised or invoked by the Vedic poets; and the feeling that the various deities are but different names, different conceptions of that incomprehensible Being which no thought can reach and no language express, is not yet quite extinct in the minds of some of the more thoughtful Rishis.'— Max Müller, *Lectures on Language*, second series, 412. It might be added that the interpretations of later theologians cannot be accounted for except by the fact that this conviction never became totally extinct. Even when the whole Hindu Pantheon has attained its final dimensions, the myths are so treated as to leave little doubt of the real meaning in the writer's mind. The outward respect paid to the popular legends thinly disguises that monotheistic conviction, which accounts for much that would otherwise be perplexing in the writings of Roman Catholic and other theologians.

[2] The distinction between the old Vedic theory of sin and the forms of belief still prevalent on the subject cannot always be very broadly drawn.

'I ask, O Varuṇa, wishing to know this my sin. I go to ask the wise. The Sages all tell me the same. Varuṇa it is who is angry with me.

'Was it an old sin, O Varuṇa, that thou wishest to destroy thy friend, who always praises thee? Tell me, thou unconquerable lord, and I will quickly turn to thee with praise freed from sin.

'Absolve us from the sins of our fathers and from those which we committed with our own bodies.'

with Diti, the unbounded with the definite, while it became
more and more a name for the distant east from which all
the bright gods seem to come, and for the boundless space
beyond the east, drawing a sharp distinction between 'what
is yonder, and what is here.' But the process could not be
stopped at this point. The gods had been called dáksha-
pitar, the fathers of strength, the mighty; and the same
equivocation which made Odysseus spring from Autolykos
converted the epithet Daksha into the father of the gods.
It followed that Aditi was sprung from Daksha, or Daksha
from Aditi, who also owed his existence to Bhu, being, and
the conclusion was reached that 'Not-being and Being are
in the higher heaven, in the birth-place of Daksha, in the
lap of Aditi.' But more especially Aditi became the mother
of the bright gods, of Varuna, Mitra, Aryaman, and, in fact,
of the seven Ádityas, although their names are not definitely
given in the hymns of the Rig Veda.[1] On the one side,
then, Diti was growing into 'a definite person, one of the
daughters of Daksha, the wife of Kasyapa, the mother of
the enemies of the gods, the Daityas' (such, Professor
Müller remarks, being 'the growth of legend, mythology,
and religion),' while on the other, Aditi herself was fast
becoming 'one of those deities, who would best remove
the bonds of sin or misery.' Thus the poet prays to Agni,—

' Whatever, O youthful god, we have committed against
thee, men as we are, whatever sin through thoughtlessness,
make us guiltless of Aditi, loosen the sins on all sides.'

All this, however, simply reproduces the Hesiodic theogony, in which Eros precedes Ouranos, to be represented
again in Himeros.

The phy-
sical and
spiritual
Varuna.
Some light is thrown on the relations of Varuna with
Mitra by the Hesiodic description of Ouranos as the lover of
the earth over which he broods each night;[2] and thus Va-

[1] Why the Ádityas should be seven
or eight in number, is a question of
which Professor Max Müller, whom here
I have simply to follow, admits the difficulty. The number seven, though a
sacred number, is not more sacred than
other numbers in the Rig Veda, and he
contents himself with suggesting ' the
seven days or tithis of the four parvanas
of the lunar month as a possible proto-
type of the Ádityas,' adding that 'this
might even explain the destruction of
the eighth Áditya, considering that the
eighth day of each parvan, owing to its
uncertainty, might be represented as
exposed to decay and destruction.'—Rig
Veda Sanhita, i. 241.
[2] Theog. 176.

runa, like Ouranos, is specially the veiling heaven whose presence is most felt at nightfall, when the sky seems to descend nearest to the earth, while Mitra, like Dyu and Zeus, represents the firmament glistening with the splendour of noon-day. But although the same root which furnished the names of Varuna and Ouranos yielded a name also for the evil power, first of physical, and afterwards of moral darkness, still the idea of Varuna has nothing in common with that of Vritra. His destructive nooses are prepared for the wicked only. They ensnare the man who speaks lies and pass by the man who speaks truth.[1] Like the Greek Poseidôn Pylaochos, he holds the unrighteous fast in prison : but it is as the punisher of iniquity which cannot be hidden from his piercing eye,[2] and not as the gloomy and inflexible Hades of the nether world. He is the omniscient Asura or spirit who props up the sky,[3] and this epithet may almost suffice to identify him with the Zendic Ahura who appears commonly in conjunction with Mithras, as Varuna is linked with Mitra.[4] From the simple germ thus afforded by mythical phrases which described the various changes of the heaven, sprung the metaphysical refinements of later Hindu philosophers, and the wild and cumbrous developements of later Hindu mythology. The true greatness of Varuna belongs to the earliest phase of Hindu thought. He is eclipsed first by Indra, and at length is overthrown by Krishna beneath the waters of the ocean.[5]

---

[1] *Atharva Veda*, iv. 16, 6. Muir, *Principal Deities of R. V.*, 558.

[2] ' King Varuna perceives all that is within and all that is beyond heaven and earth. The winkings of men's eyes are numbered by him.' Cf. ' the very hairs of your head are all numbered : '

πάντα ἰδὼν Διὸς ὀφθαλμὸς καὶ πάντα
νοήσας·   Hes. Op. et Dies, 265.
' The eyes of the Lord are in every place, beholding the evil and the good.'

[3] *R. V.* viii. 42, 1. Muir, *Sanskrit Texts*, part iv. chap. ii. sect. 2. The name Asura belongs to the same root with that of the Teutonic Asen, or Æsir.

[4] The reasons urged in support of this conclusion are given by Dr. Muir, *Principal Deities of R. V.* 556, as follows, (1) the name Asura, etymologi-cally identical with Ahura, is a common epithet of Varuna ; (2) the class of Indian gods called Adityas, of whom Varuna is the highest, bears a certain analogy to the Zendic Amshaspands, of whom Ahura-Mazdâo is the highest ; (3) a close connection exists between Varuna and Mitra, just as Ahura and Mithra are frequently associated in the Zendavesta, though the position of the two has otherwise become altered, and Mithra, who is not even reckoned among the Amshaspands, is placed between the two powers of good and evil. 'Zwischen Ormuzd (Licht) und Ariman (Finsterniss) steht Mithras mitten inne, heisst darum Mittler, μεσίτης, Plut. de Is.'—Nork, *Real Wörterbuch, s. v.* Mithrascult.

[5] Muir, *Sanskrit Texts*, part iv. ch. ii. section 5.

SECTION III.—INDRA.

BOOK
II.

The pri-
mary con-
ception of
Indra
purely
physical.

If Dyaus and Varuṇa were alike doomed to lose their ancient majesty, a brighter lot was in store for Indra ; and the picture which the oldest Vedic hymns present to us of this god has a special value as enabling us to determine the measure in which religion and mythology affected each other. That a moral or spiritual element may be discerned in some of the characteristics of this deity, is beyond question: that the whole idea of the god can be traced to the religious instinct of mankind, the boldest champions of the theory which ascribes the growth of all mythology to the direct action of religious impulse or revelation will scarcely venture to affirm. The true religious instinct must point to the absolute rule of one righteous God, and cannot itself originate the idea of many independent centres of action. If this instinct furnished the true germ of all mythology, then the mythology of the Iliad and Odyssey is far older than that of the Veda; in other words, the crystallised granite is older than the ingredients of which it is composed. In our Homeric poems, in the midst of abundant signs indicating the later growth of the notion, we have an acknowledged King of heaven, from whom all the Olympian gods derive their power, or whose will they are at least bound to perform, and who alone retains unimpaired his full characteristics as lord of the bright heaven. Although Phoibos still bears his unerring weapons, yet his arrows lie within the quiver until some wickedness of man compels him to draw them forth. The superhuman action of the Iliad and Odyssey, in short, has reference strictly to the deeds and fortunes of men ; the age of conflicts between the gods has almost passed away. The conspiracy of Hêrê, Poseidôn and Athênê to bind Zeus, is amongst the latest of those struggles which had culminated in the wars of the Titans, for when in the last great battle of Achilleus the gods turn against each other in the fray, there is still no thought of assailing the great King who sits in his serene ether far above the turmoil raging beneath him.[1]

[1] 'L'Olympe, dans Homère, ressemble à une monarchie établie de longue date, où chaque personnage a, par droit de naissance, son emploi, ses titres invari-

The true mythical action of the Achaian deities is thus intermittent. In the hymns of the Rig Veda it is continuous, and their action is but remotely concerned with human interests. Like the Hesiodic Zeus, they love the savour of burnt-offerings, and hasten to receive their share of the sacrifice: but as soon as the rites are over, they return to their own proper work as wielding the forces which are manifested in the changing heavens. The Vedic gods are thus, pre-eminently, transparent. Instead of one acknowledged king, each is lord in his own domain; each is addressed as the maker of all visible things, while their features and characteristics are in almost all cases interchangeable.[1] Dyaus and Indra, Varuṇa and Agni are each in his turn spoken of as knowing no superior, and the objects of their chief care are not the children of men, but the winds, the storms, the clouds, and the thunder, which are constantly rising in rebellion against them. No sooner is one conflict ended than another is begun, or rather the same conflict is repeated as the days and seasons come round. Whenever the rain is shut up in the clouds, the dark power is in revolt against Dyaus and Indra. In the rumblings of the thunder, while the drought still sucks out the life of the earth, are heard the mutterings of their hateful enemy. In the lightning flashes which precede the outburst of the pent-up waters are seen the irresistible spears of the god, who is attacking the throttling serpent in his den; and in the serene heaven which shone out when the deluging clouds had passed away, men beheld the face of the mighty deity

ables, et son rang dont il ne songe pas à se départir. Dans cette sorte de cour que les dieux tiennent autour de Jupiter, ils se sont dépouillés de leur caractère propre et de leur originalité native . . . Comme ces dignitaires des anciennes monarchies qui continuent à porter des titres depuis longtemps vides de sens, ils ont des surnoms dont ils semblent ignorer la valeur.'—Bréal, *Hercule et Cacus*, 81. The very fact that the mythical attributes of these gods become less and less defined, while their subordination to Zeus becomes more and more marked, is the strongest evidence of the mythological origin of the whole.
[1] Their names are, in short, mere

signs for one and the same conception. He who knows Brahma knows Prajâpati; they who know Brahma know Skambha, the supporter of the world, who, like Atlas, upholds the earth and sky, and who is 'all which has soul, which breathes and winks.' Again, this office of supporting the universe is fulfilled by Varuṇa, Indra, Savitri, and Vishṇu. So, too, Prajâpati is Mahâdeva, the great god, and Bhava (probably Phoibos) the supreme lord. He is also Daksha, and the year, the ender of all things, as the days bring the life of man to a close.— Muir, *Sanskrit Texts*, part iv. pp. 17, 18, 24, 49, 156, &c.

who was their friend. So completely does the older mythology of the Veda carry us away from the one idea which must be first awakened by the genuine religious instinct of mankind.

The Greek mythology not borrowed from the Vedic.

No stronger evidence than that which is furnished by this contrast could be adduced to show that in no single feature is the mythology of our Homeric poems borrowed from the people who betook themselves to the banks of the Indus and the Ganges. The Vedic Dyaus may in all essential features be reproduced in the Hellenic Zeus. Like Phoibos Chrysâôr, Indra may bear a lance or an arrow, which can never miss its mark: but in the one case we have a mere sketch, in the other a finished picture; and the differences in the character of the detail preclude all idea that for either Zeus or Hermes, Helen or Paris, Erinys or Achilleus, the Achaian poets were indebted to the Vedic Dyaus or Sarameya, to Pani or Saramâ, to Saranyû or Aharyu. To one common source they do indeed point; and the several stages of developement which mark the early mythologies of India and Hellas leave us in no doubt of the nature of the germ from which they spring.

Indra, a god of the bright heaven.

At once, then, we turn away from the cumbrous and complicated mythology of the later Vedic literature,[1] as from the uncouth outgrowths of the Orphic theogony we turn to the earlier phases in which the Greek epic and lyric poets exhibit their ancestral deities. We are not concerned with the later conflicts of Indra, which end in his being bound by Indragit,[2] while we have before us a series of songs which speak of him simply as the invincible god of the bright heaven. Yet, although there still remains a large difference between Indra and Apollôn, too great stress can scarcely be laid on the fact that as we trace the Vedic gods as far back as the Veda itself will carry us, the essential likeness between the Hindu and the Hellenic deities becomes more and more striking. If further we find that, when thus examined, their functions become, if the expression may be

[1] See the remarks quoted by Professor Max Müller from Professor Roth (Sanskrit Literature 60).

[2] A summary of the story of Indra and Indragit is given by Dr. Muir, Sanskrit Texts, iv. p. 422.

used, more and more atmospheric,—if they become the
powers which produce the sights of the changing sky,—if
their great wars are waged in regions far above the abodes of
men, the last blow is given to the theory which by the most
arbitrary of assumptions finds the root of all mythology in
the religious instincts of mankind.

In the Vedic Indra there is this further peculiarity, that, *Meaning of the name.*
although his name ceased, like that of Dyaus, to be chiefly
a name for the sky, and although the struggle in which he
is constantly engaged has indefinitely affected the faith of
Christendom, yet the deity himself has but little of a purely
moral or spiritual element in his character. It is true that
he is sometimes invoked as witnessing all the deeds of men
and thus as taking cognisance of their sins ; but the warfare
which he has to wage is purely a physical conflict, and it is
chiefly in the phrases by which his adversary is described,
that we find the germs of the dualistic creed which bears
the name of Zoroaster. Nowhere then, in the oldest monu-
ments of Hindu thought, is the real character of Indra lost
sight of. His home is in the bright heaven ; but, as his
name denotes,[1] he is specially the bringer of the most
precious of all boons to a thirsty and gaping land. He is
the giver of the rain which falls on the earth when the
tyranny of the scorching wind is overpast.

In vain is Indra assailed in his career by the same enemies *The might and majesty of Indra.*
which seek to destroy the infant Herakles. The Rakshasa
fares no better than the snakes.

'Vyansa, exulting and striking hard blows, smote thee,
Maghavan, upon the jaw; whereupon, being so smitten,
thou provedst the stronger and didst crush the head of the
slave with the thunderbolt.'[2]

Like Herakles and Phoibos again, he has to go in search
of lost or stolen cattle. With the conveying Maruts, 'the
traversers of places difficult of access,' he discovers the cows
hidden in their caves.

'Great is thy prowess, Indra, we are thine. Satisfy,

---

[1] 'Indra, a name peculiar to India, admits of but one etymology, i.e. it must be derived from the same root, whatever that may be, which in Sanskrit yielded *indu*, drop, sap.'—Max Müller, *Lectures on Language*, second series, 430.
[2] *Rig Veda Sanhita*, H. H. Wilson, vol. iii. p. 156.

Maghavan, the desires of thy worshipper. The vast heaven has acknowledged thy might; this earth has been bowed down through thy vigour.

'Thou, thunderer, hast shattered with thy bolt the broad and massive cloud into fragments, and hast sent down the waters that were confined in it, to flow at will: verily thou alone possessest all power.'[1]

So, again, addressing Indra as Parjanya the rain-bringer, the poet says,

'The winds blow strong, the lightnings flash, the plants spring up, the firmament dissolves; earth becomes fit for all creatures, when Parjanya fertilises the soil with showers.'[2]

'Master of tawny steeds, the remotest regions are not remote for thee.'[3]

'At the birth of thee who art resplendent, trembled the heaven and trembled the earth through fear of thy wrath: the mighty clouds were confined: they destroyed (the distress of drought), spreading the waters over the dry places.'[4]

Lastly, as the solar god, he is the Wanderer, like the Teutonic Wegtam, like Odysseus, Sigurd, Dionysos, Phoibos, Theseus, Bellerophôn, Oidipous, Herakles and Savitar.

'Wonderful Indra, wanderer at times, thou art verily the granter of our desires.'[5]

Indra then is the lord of the heaven, omnipotent and all-seeing: but so had been, or rather was, his father Dyu; and thus some epithets which in the west are reserved for Zeus are in the east transferred to Indra, and the Jupiter Stator of the Latins reappears as the Indra sthâtar of the Hindu.[6] The rain-bringer must be younger than the sky in which the clouds have their birthplace; but however sharply his personality may be defined, the meaning of the name is never forgotten. As the Maruts, or winds, are said

Indra the rain-bringer.

[1] R. V. Sanhita, H. H. Wilson, i. 154.
[2] Ib. ii. 373.   [3] Ib. iii. 37.
[4] Cf. Judges, v. 4.
[5] R. V. Sanhita, H. H. Wilson, vol. iii. p. 187.
[6] The Latins, it would seem, misunderstood the name, Livy, i. 12. 'Le mot sthâtar est ordinairement complété en Sanscrit par un génitif, tel que rathasya,

harînâm, ce qui détermine le véritable sens de cette épithète, qui signifie, celui qui se tient debout sur son char, sur ses coursiers. Quel est ce char? On ne peut douter qu'il ne soit question du soleil, qui est souvent représenté dans les Vedas comme une roue d'or roulant dans le firmament.'— Bréal, Hercule et Cacus, 103.

sometimes to course through Dyaus (the heaven), so the CHAP. clouds sometimes move in Indra (the sky). In all the phrases which describe this god, the local colouring arising from the climate of northern India may be plainly discerned. Although the Delian Phoibos soon belts his golden sword to his side, yet for sometime after his birth he lies in the white and spotless robe in which the nymphs had wrapped him. The Vedic Indra awakes sooner to the consciousness of his power, and as soon as he is born, the slayer of Vritra asks his mother, ' Who are they that are renowned as fierce warriors?'[1] Like the Hellenic Apollôn, he has golden locks and a quiver of irresistible arrows; but the arrows have a hundred points and are winged with a thousand feathers. In his hand he holds the golden whip which Phoibos gives to Hermes as the guardian of his cattle; and like Helios, he is borne across the heavens in a flaming chariot drawn by the tawny or glistening steeds called the Harits, whose name and whose brightness alone reappear in the Charites of the Hellenic land, but who still retain the form most familiar to the Hindu in the Xanthos and Balios who are yoked to the car of Achilleus. Like the streaming locks from the head of Phoibos, so the beard of Indra flashes like lightning, as he speeds on his journey through the heaven. As looking down on the wide earth spread beneath, he is possessed, like Apollôn, of an inscrutable wisdom. Like him also, he chases the Dawn, Dahanâ or Daphnê, of whom he is said to be sometimes the father, sometimes the son, and sometimes the husband; and as Phoibos causes the death of Daphnê, so Indra is said to shatter the chariot of Dahanâ.[2]

The prayers addressed to this god show that the chief idea associated with him was that of an irresistible material power. The Hindu, as he comes before the deity to whom he looks for his yearly harvest, assumes unconsciously the

Physical conflict between light and darkness.

---

[1] Muir, *Principal Deities of R. V.* 560.

[2] In this myth Dahanâ is regarded as hostile to Indra and as meditating mischief, a thought which might easily be suggested by the legends of Arethousa and Daphnê. Her shattered car reposes, however, on the banks of the Vipar (river or water), an incident which recalls the disappearance of Arethousa or Daphnê in the waters from which Aphroditè rises. H. H. Wilson, *R. V. Sanhita*, vol. ii. p. 178.

attitude of the Baal-worshipper of Syria.[1]   But the real
prayer of the heart is addressed to Varuṇa, as the Greek in
his hour of need prays always to Zeus.   The cry for mercy
from those who through thoughtlessness have broken the
law of God is never sent up to Indra, although, like Herakles, 'he engages in many conflicts for the good of man
with overwhelming power.'[2]   It was impossible that it
should be so, while the great work for which Indra might
be said to exist was the battle for life or death with the
hateful monster who imprisons the rain-clouds in his dun-
geons.   This battle is brought before us under a thousand
forms.   His great enemy Vritra, the hiding thief, is also
Ahi, the strangling snake, or Paṇi the marauder.

'Ahi has been prostrated beneath the feet of the waters
which the Vritra by his might had obstructed.'[3]

He appears again as Atri, a name which may perhaps be
the same as the Atli of the Volsung tale and the Etzel of
the Nibelung song.

'Thou, Indra, hast opened the cloud for the Angirasas:
thou hast shown the way to Atri who vexes his adversaries
by a hundred doors.'[4]

He is also Namuki (the Greek Amykos), and Sambara.

'Thou, Indra, with thy bolt didst slay afar off the deceiver
Namuki.'[5]

'Thou hast slain Sambara by thy resolute self.'[6]

---

[1] The power of Indra is the one
theme of the praise accorded to him in
R. V. vii. 32.   The worshipper calls on
him who holds the thunderbolt with
his arm, whom no one can check if he
wishes to give, who makes mortal men
obtain spoil in fighting, who is the
benefactor of everyone, whatever battles
there be, who is the rich of old and to
be called in every battle.   Max Müller,
Sanskrit Literature, 543.

'This contest with the clouds,' says
Professor H. H. Wilson (Introduction
to R. V. Sanhita, xxx.) 'seems to have
suggested to the authors of the Sûktas
the martial character of Indra on other
occasions, and he is especially described
as the god of battles, the giver of victory
to his worshippers, the destroyer of the
enemies of religious rites, the subverter
of the cities of the Asuras.'

The stanza known as the Hansavatí
Rich is noteworthy as exhibiting the
germs of more than one myth.   Indra
'is Hansa (the sun) dwelling in light:
Vasu (the wind) dwelling in the firmament: the invoker of the gods (Agni)
dwelling on the altar: the guest (of the
worshipper) dwelling in the house (as
the culinary fire): the dweller amongst
men (as consciousness): the dweller in
the most excellent (orb, the sun): the
dweller in truth, the dweller in the sky
(the air), born in the waters, in the
rays of light, in the verity (of manifestation), in the (Eastern) mountain, the
truth (itself).'—H. H. Wilson, R. V.
Sanhita, iii. 199.

[2] H. H. Wilson, R. V. Sanhita, i.
151.

[3] Ib. i. 87.   [4] Ib. i. 136.
[5] Ib. i. 147.   [6] Ib. i. 148.

'Verily thou hast made me, Indra, thy associate, when CHAP.
grinding the head of the slave Namuki like a sounding and I.
rolling cloud.'[1]

In the same way Indra is the slayer of Bala, of Chumuri,
Dhuni, Pipon, Sushna, and many others,[2] and against him
the strength of the Rakshasas is concentrated in vain, for
Indra scatters them 'with his friend the thunderbolt.' On
the issue of this conflict depends, it is true, the welfare
of all human creatures. The victory of Indra brings with
it wealth of corn and wine and oil, but the struggle and its
issue are alike external to the human spirit. In other words,
the religious instinct found little scope in the phrases which
described the offices of Indra, and most assuredly had nothing
to do with suggesting them. It was not on the soil of
Hindustan that the momentous physical struggle between
Indra and his enemy was to become a spiritual struggle of
still more fearful proportions.

The wife of Indra is Indrani, who alone of the goddesses The wife
who bear the names of the gods is associated with her of Indra.
husband. Like the rest, she has but a vague and shadowy
personality. But although the goddesses who are not thus
simply developed from the names of their consorts are far
more prominent, yet even these are spoken of in terms little
resembling the language addressed to the supreme god
under his many names. Ahanâ is a daughter of Dyaus,
and her might is great, but Indra is mightier still. Ushas
is hard to vanquish; but Indra shatters her chariot, while
Saranyû, the Harits, and the Rohits are rather beings who
do his will than deities possessed of any independent power.
In this respect a vast gulf separates the later from the early
mythology of the Hindus; and although Mahâdeva retains
a nominal supremacy, yet the popular mind dwells less on
the god than on the awful terrors of his wife, whether
known as Uma, Durga, or Kali.[3] In an inquiry designed
chiefly to bring out the points of resemblance and difference
between cognate mythological systems, we are not called
upon to enter the unwholesome labyrinth in which a morbid

[1] H. H. Wilson, *R. V. Sanhita*, i. 279.
[2] *Ib.* ii. 418, 419.   [3] Muir, *Principal Deities of R. V.* 577.

philosophy has bewildered and oppressed a race once more simple and perhaps more truthful in their faith than the forefathers of the Hellenic and even of the Teutonic nations. The more modern Hindu traditions may have an interest for the theologian or the philosopher, while the ingenious symbolical interpretations which make anything mean anything may be as noteworthy in the pages of Brahmanic commentators as in those of Chrysostom, Gregory, or Augustine. But they lead us away into a world of their own, where it becomes scarcely worth while to trace the faint vestiges of earlier thought which may be here and there discerned in the rank crop of cumbrous and repulsive fancies. Nor is there much profit in lists even of earlier deities in whom we have little more than a name or an epithet. If the earth is called Nishtigrî, we have only another word denoting Prithivî the wife of Dyaus. In Sarasvatî, the watery, we have, first, a name given to the river which with the Indus and the waters of the Penjab made up the seven streams of the ancient Hindu home, and then to a goddess who, as inspiring the hymns composed in her honour, became identified with Vach,[1] Voice, and was invoked as the muse of eloquence. As such, she is produced on the mountain-top, as Athênê Akria springs from the forehead of Zeus.[2] Much in the same way, Nirriti,[3] the western land, to which Yama had first crossed the rapid waters, became first the land of death, and afterwards a personification of evil. In Sraddhâ we have nothing more than a name for religious faith.[4]

Section IV.—BRAHMA.

If an examination of the Vedic theology tends to prove that it was wholly one of words and names, the impression is not weakened as we survey the ponderous fancies of later times. The fabric of Brahmanic sacerdotalism may have reached gigantic proportions, and may exhibit a wonderful ingenuity

---

[1] Gr. *ἔπος, εἴπειν, ἀκούειν,* Latin vox, vocare.

[2] Muir, *Sanskrit Texts,* part iv. p. 360, note.

[3] Max Müller, *Lectures on Language,* second series, 515. Is the name Nirriti

connected with that of the Ithakan Neritos and the Leukadian Nerikos?

[4] 'The Latin word credo, "I believe," is the same as the Sanskrit Sraddhâ.'— Max Müller, *Chips,* i. 42.

in the piecing together of its several parts, but it cannot be CHAP.
regarded as the result of a logical system. The properties of I.
Vishnu are those of Agni, Vayu, and Súrya; and as Agni is
all the deities, so also is Vishnu. The character of Brahma
is not less flexible. At first the word is but a name for the
self-existent principle, and the various mythical acts recorded
of him are not only susceptible of a spiritual or metaphysical
interpretation, but are actually so interpreted in all the Hindu
comments on the sacred literature of the country. As in the
Orphic theogony, the generation of Brahma begins sometimes
with the great mundane egg; but it is Brahma who therein
produces himself. The self-existent lord, 'desiring to produce various creatures from his own body, first, with a
thought, created the waters, and deposited in them a seed.
This seed became a golden egg, resplendent as the sun, in
which he himself was born as Brahma, the progenitor of all
worlds.'[1] He is the first god of a later Indian Trimúrtti;
but the threefold deity of Yaska is Agni, Vayu, and Súrya,
and thus Dr. Muir concludes that the conjunction of Brahma,
Vishnu, and Rudra (? Siva) was unknown to that ancient
commentator.[2] Even in the Mahâbhârata, Brahma is both
created and uncreated. In that poem Mahâdeva (μέγας θεός,
the great god), is the creator of Brahma, Vishnu, and Indra.
'From his right side he produced Brahma, the originator of
the worlds, and from his left side Vishnu, for the preservation of the universe, and when the end of the age had

<hr />

[1] Muir, *Sanskrit Texts*, part iv. p. 27.
[2] The three names given by Yaska
are with him mere names for one object.
'These deities,' he says, 'receive many
designations in consequence of their
greatness, or from the diversity of their
functions, as (the appellations of) hotri,
adhvaryu, brahman, and udgatri are
applied to one and the same person.'
The functions connected with these
names carry us back to the old mythical
phrases. 'Indra's function is to bestow
moisture, to slay Vritra; and all exer-
tions of force are the work of Indra.'
'The function of Áditya (the sun) is to
draw up moisture and to retain it by
his rays: and whatever is mysterious is
the work of Áditya.'—Muir, *Sanskrit*

Texts, part iv. pp. 134–6. To the objection that the Puranic mythology,
of which the Trimúrtti of Brahma,
Vishnu and Siva is a part, might have
grown up along with the Vedic, Dr.
Muir answers that 'if Yaska had been
cognisant of any other than the Vedic
mythology (at least, if he had attached
any authority to any other), he would
not have failed to make some reference
to the latter, and would have endea-
voured to blend and reconcile it with
the former. As we find no attempt of
the kind in his work, we must conclude
either that the Puranic mythology had
no existence in his day, or that he
regarded it as undeserving of any attention.'—*Ib.* 137.

BOOK
II.

Prajápati.

Visva-
karman.

arrived, the mighty god created Rudra.'[1] But Mahâdeva is
is identified by the poets of the Mahâbhârata with Rudra,
Siva, Agni, Sûrya, Varuṇa, the Asvins, and a host of other
deities, and, as the originator of all life, even assumes the
forms and functions of the Hellenic Priapos.[2] Mahâdeva,
again, is himself also the destroyer Siva, and like Vishṇu he
wields a dreadful bow made by Visvakarman. These bows
are used by the two gods in a terrible battle, the result
being that the bow of Mahâdeva is relaxed and Vishṇu is
esteemed the superior.[3] Elsewhere it is said that Brahma
and Mahâdeva are both sprung from Krishna, the one from
the lotus issuing from his navel, the other from his forehead,
like Dahanâ and Athênê from the head of Dyaus or Zeus.[4]

As Prajâpati, Brahma offers violence to his own daughter;
and from this myth of Indra and Ahalya a story is produced
much resembling that of the Hellenic Erichthonios.[5] He is
also a worshipper of the Linga, and acts as the charioteer of
Mahâdeva or of Rudra, who springs from his forehead (as he
does also from that of Krishna), glorious as the noon-day
sun.[6]

Like Brahma, Visvakarman, the Creator, is one of the
many names which may be applied to almost any of the
gods at the will of the worshipper. Wise and mighty in
act, Visvakarman orders all things, and men desire the attainment of good in the world where 'he, the One Being,
dwells beyond the seven Rishis.'[7] He is the maker of the
region Sutala, where by his will, as in the Greek Elysion,
' neither mental nor bodily pains, nor fatigue, nor weariness,
nor discomfiture, nor diseases afflict the inhabitants.'[8] He
is also the son of Bhuvana, the first of all beings who sprang
into existence from the earth.[9]

[1] Muir. *Sanskrit Texts*, pp. 156, 162.
[2] *Ib.* 160.　　[3] *Ib.* 146, 147.
[4] *Ib.* 193.　　[5] *Ib.* 39.
[6] *Ib.* 190. Athênê in like manner
springs fully armed from the head
of Zeus; but in the story of the
Vishṇu Purana (Muir, *ib.* 331), Rudra
is both sun and moon, as dividing his
body into two parts, male and female,
like the Greek Hermaphroditos. The
portions into which his male form is

further divided seem to point to the
month of the year which is represented
by Rudra himself, as by Aditi.
[7] Muir, *Sanskrit Texts*, part iv. p. 7.
[8] *Ib.* 129.
[9] The name Bhuvana itself is from
the same root with the Greek φύσις and
our own words Be and Being. It has
been urged with at least some plausibility that the Latin Consus is a name
of the same kind, and that it is not to

SECTION V.—ZEUS.

In the conception of the poets known to us by the name of Homer, the earth on which we tread is covered with a gross and thick air, through which course the clouds, and in which the winds work their will. Above this air rises the serene Aithêr or Ether, the abode of Zeus, never sullied by mists or vexed with storms. Here he dwells, surrounded by the gods of Olympos; but while these can visit the earth and take part in the quarrels of mortal men, Zeus alone may not descend for this purpose from the clear heaven whence he looks down on all that is being done beneath him. It is true that there are on the earth some whom he loves, and others whom he hates; and when his son Sarpêdôn is smitten by the spear of Patroklos, the tears of Zeus fall in large raindrops from the sky. But that which he wills must be done by others, and in their toils he can have no share. So when the hour for the battle between Achilleus and Hektor is come, Zeus tells the gods, the streams, and the nymphs, who sit around his throne, that they may go down and choose each his side, while for himself, though he cares for the mortals whose death-struggle is at hand, the sight of all that is done on the plains of Ilion will none the less gladden his eyes as he looks down from Olympos. When, after the conflict of Achilleus with the burning river, the gods turn their weapons on each other, the mind of Zeus remains unruffled, and he listens in silence to the charge brought against Hêrê by Lêtô, as she lays before his feet the arrows of her child Artemis.[1]

Thus for the poets of the Iliad and the Odyssey, Zeus, though he might be called the gatherer of the dark clouds,[2]

---

be referred to the verb Consulero. It is by no means likely that even the title of the Dii Consentes can be taken as indicating a divine council: and the coincidence is noteworthy between the Latin Consus and the Hindu Ganesa, the lord of life and of the reproductive powers of nature, the name reappearing in the Greek γένος and our *kin*. Hence it is that when Romulus is in need of women for his new city, it is to Consus that he makes his vows and prayers. The Consualia would thus precisely correspond with the Eleusinian festival of Dêmêtêr.

[1] *Il.* xxi. 388.

[2] Ζεὺς Αἰγίοχος. 'Le verbe grec ἀίσσω, qui signifie s'élancer, a fait d'une part le substantif αἴξ chèvre (à cause de la nature boudissante de l'animal), et de

was pre-eminently the lord of the bright heaven, and the thought most closely associated with the name was that of a serene and unchangeable splendour. As the heavy masses of vapour were cloven by the rays of the sun, the blue heaven was seen smiling on the havoc wrought by storms and tempest, itself undimmed by the years which devoured the generations of men. From the face of this heaven the morning sprang to scatter the shades of night. Beneath it the lightning flashed, the rain fell, the winds blew; but above them all shone still the light which can know no change.

The idea
of Zeus
suggested
by phy-
sical phe-
nomena. Without referring, therefore, to the legends of other nations, we are brought at once by the language even of our Homeric poets to that earliest form of thought in which words now used to denote spiritual conceptions conveyed only the impression left on the human mind by the phenomena of the outward world. As man awoke gradually to a conscious perception of the things around him, the sensation most comforting in the alternations of a day and night alike uncomprehended would be that of the pure and bright heaven which broods over the earth as the sun speeds on his journey across the sky. If, then, in the names which were afterwards used to denote the supreme God we have words which in all Aryan dialects convey this primary idea of brightness, a clear light is at once shed on the first stages in the mental and moral education of mankind. The profound splendour of the unclouded heaven must mark the abode of the Being who made and sustains all things; and thus names denoting at first only the sky became in the West as in the East names of God, the Zeus Patêr (the Father) of the Greeks corresponding to the Dyauspitar of the Hindu. If even in the Vedic hymns the most prominent deity is Indra, still Indra was himself worshipped as the god of the bright sky, and as

l'autre les mots καταῖξ, καταιγίς, tempête. De là une nouvelle série d'images et de fables où la chèvre joue le rôle principal. L'égide, avant d'être un bouclier fait en peau de chèvre, était le ciel au moment de l'orage; Jupiter αἰγίοχος était le dieu qui envoie la tempête (il faut entendre ἔχω dans son sens primitif veho): plus tard, on traduisit le dieu qui porte l'égide. Homère semble se souvenir de la première signification, quand il nous montre, au seul mouvement du bouclier, le tonnerre qui éclate, l'Ida qui se couvre de nuages, et les hommes frappés de terreur.'—Bréal, Hercule et Cacus, 116.

the son of the brilliant Dyu. As in the Hellenic land Kronos was displaced by Zeus, so in the country of the seven rivers, Dyu gave way to the lord of the wealth-bringing rain clouds. The process (even if we assign a very late origin to the mythical Kronos) was in both cases the same. The epithet could not become or be long retained as a personal name until its original meaning had been obscured or forgotten. The Greek had his Aêr, his Aithêr, and his Ouranos to express the visible heavens, and Zeus became to him more and more the personal God whose hand is seen in his works. In India the name Dyaus retained, as we have seen, its appellative force, and as a designation for the supreme God, was supplanted by the less significant Indra.

But in the West, as in the East, the original character of the god is in close accordance with the etymology of the word. The Athenians called on Zeus to rain on their land; the Latin poet spoke of the glistening heaven which by all is named Jove, while the phrases 'sub dio vivere,' 'sub Jove frigido,' and even 'malus Jupiter' remained common expressions in every day speech.[1]

The idea of brightness was, however, not the only one suggested by the sight of the clear heaven. If the sky beams with light, it is also spread as a covering over the earth which lies beneath it, and Zeus was thus Ouranion who spread his veil over his bride; but before he came to be spoken of as son of Kronos, the attribute had suggested the idea of a person, and the Western Ouranos corresponded with the Vedic Varuṇa. In this case the name remained more transparent in the West than in the East. The Vedic Varuṇa becomes the moral ruler of the universe, and the Father and friend of man; but in the Hellenic land the starry Ouranos is the son to whom Gaia gives birth in order that he may cover everything and be a steadfast seat for the blessed gods,[2] and we look in vain for the spiritual attributes which belong to Varuṇa in the hymns of the Rig Veda.

CHAP.
I.

The Latin Jupiter.

Zeus Ouranion.

[1] ὅσον, ὦ φίλε Ζεῦ, κατὰ τῆς ἀρούρας τῶν Ἀθηναίων.
Aspice hoc sublime candens quod invocant omnes Jovem.

The word ἔνδιος has the same transparent meaning.—Max Müller, Lectures on Language, second series, 434.
[2] Hesiod, Theog. 122.

BOOK
II.

The my-
thical and
spiritual
Zeus.

But the developement of a personal Zeus was followed necessarily by two results, which long continued astonishingly distinct the one from the other. The thought of Zeus as the one God and Father gave birth to a religion. The many names employed to denote the varying phases of the sky became each the germ of a myth, and every one of these myths, when translated into the conditions of human life, tended to degrade the idea of the god as much as the idea of his changeless perfection, rising more and more in the mind, tended to raise it. According to the latter, he would be the righteous Judge, seen by none, yet beholding all, looking down from heaven on the children of men to see if they will understand and seek after God, appointing to them a life of labour for their highest good, and finally recompensing to all men after their works. By the other process he would become all that names applied to outward phenomena must denote when used to signify the actions of a personal and conscious being. As in every land the dews of heaven fertilise the earth, Zeus must be the husband of many brides, the father of countless children in every country. As looking down on the havoc caused by drought or pestilence, storm or war, he would be a god of merciless indifference and disinterested cruelty. He must smile alike over the wealth of a teeming harvest or the withered fruits of a sun-scorched land. But the blighting of a spring-tide fair in its promise is his work, and he would thus become capricious as well as treacherous, while the interchangeable characteristics of the earliest gods would heighten still more the repulsive features of the anthropomorphised Zeus. If the old hymn had praised Aditi as 'mother, father, and son,' Zeus must become at once the brother and the husband, and his own daughters through many generations would become the mothers of his children. The transference of these phrases to the relations of human life has its necessary result in the fearful horrors of the tale of Oidipous and Iokastê.

That the two streams of religion and mythology ran on side by side, or rather that the same words are used to express two wholly different lines of thought, is abundantly

proved by Greek not less than by Hindu literature. The
result was that the same man might seem to speak two
languages, and perhaps delude himself into the notion that
under the name of Zeus he spoke of one person, and of one
person only. This would be the case especially with the
classes, which, although familiar, or because they were familiar, with the complicated mythical lore of their country,
might not care to analyse their own thoughts, or fairly to
face the difficulties involved in many or most of these ancient
stories. But there would be a lower class who, as being
perhaps practically ignorant of these narratives, would be
saved in great measure from this traditional influence.[1]
However imperfect his conceptions may have been, it is
certain that the swineherd Eumaios did not derive his
religious convictions from mythical phrases, when he told
Odysseus that God gives and withholds according to his
pleasure and in the plenitude of his power. Nor can too
great a stress be laid on the fact that, as the mythology
grew more complicated and more repulsive, ideas of morality
and religion became more reasonable and more pure. Nowhere is this conclusion so clearly forced upon us as in the
Hesiodic Works and Days. In this poem the teacher
who bids his friend to deal with all men after the rule of
righteousness which comes from Zeus,[2] who tells that justice
and truth shall in the end prevail,[3] and that they who do
evil to others inflict evil on themselves,[4] who is sure that
the eyes of God are in every place, that the way of evil is
broad and smooth, and the path of good rough and narrow
at the first, tells us also how Zeus bade the gods to make
Pandôra fair to look upon but all evil within, and laughed
at the thought of the miseries which should overtake mankind when all the evils should be let loose from her box,
while, to crush them utterly, hope should remain a prisoner

[1] 'What,' asks Professor Max Müller,
'did the swineherd Eumaios know of
the intricate Olympian theogony? Had
he ever heard the name of the Charites
or the Harpyias? Could he have told
who was the father of Aphroditê, who
were her husbands and her children?
I doubt it; and when Homer introduces
him to us, speaking of this life and the

higher powers that rule it, Eumaios
knows only of just gods, "who hate
cruel deeds, but honour justice and the
righteous works of men."'—*Lectures on
Language*, second series, 453.
[2] 35.
[3] 215.
[4] 263.

within it. So conscious apparently is the poet that the Zeus who thus cheats mankind is not the Zeus who commands them to do justice and mercy, that he can use the same name without a thought that he is dishonouring the just and holy God whom he reverences. It seems impossible to ignore a distinction without which the Hesiodic poem becomes unintelligible. With our Homeric poets the contrast is not so marked, simply because their thoughts were not so earnest and their hearts were not so wakened by the sterner experiences of human life. With these moral indifference would naturally find expression in confusion of language, and they might lead others to think, as they themselves may have fancied, that the Zeus to whom they prayed in moments of real anguish was the Zeus who laughed at the wretchedness and the ruin of mankind. Still less can it be said that the mythology of India choked the growth of a right faith. The Hindu might in his prayer employ the names of Varuṇa or Dyaus, but he knew well that these were only names for One whose nature, infinite and incomprehensible, yet corresponded with his own, and of whose aid he felt himself to stand in the deepest and most constant need.

The Zeus of the Tragic poets.

But if it be true generally that the Greek, especially in the prehistoric ages, 'was not aware that there were different tributaries which entered from different points into the central idea of Zeus,'[1] it was far otherwise with the few to whom a belief in the righteousness of God was no empty phrase but a profound and practical conviction. The fact that national and political institutions were intertwined inextricably with the old mythology, if they were not actually based upon it, only brought out its repulsive features more prominently before all who could not bring themselves to believe that the righteous God could issue to men immoral commands or himself do the things which he condemned in them. Whether the difficulties thus involved in the traditional creed should lead them to covert opposition or to open antagonism, would depend much on the temper and the circumstances of those who felt them. There are some

[1] Max Müller, *Lectures on Language*, second series, 442.

who, like Sophokles, are well content if they can express
their own convictions without assailing popular ideas; there
are others who, like Euripides, cannot rest until they bring
others to see inconsistencies which to themselves are palpable
and glaring. Yet it cannot be denied that the thoughts of
Sophokles are as true and high as those of the younger
poet. There is nothing in the latter more outspoken than
the words in which Sophokles tells us that the laws of
righteousness are established in heaven and that in them
God is great and cannot grow old. But where there is an
earnest yearning for truth, this happy condition of mind will
not probably last long. The thought of the mischief which
the popular creeds inflict on ordinary minds will lead them
openly to condemn a system which they might otherwise
treat with indifference or contempt; and to this sense we
may ascribe the protests of Xenophanes and Protagoras, of
Anaxagoras and Herakleitos, of Pindar and of Plato. The
controversy was brought to an issue, when Euripides said
plainly that if the gods are righteous, the stories of the poets
are wretched falsehoods, and that if they do the things which
the poets ascribe to them, then they are not gods at all: and
this issue was anticipated by the conviction of Æschylos that
Zeus was a mere name, one of many names, for the One true
God, which might serve to convey some faint notion and inadequate idea of his goodness and his greatness.

Hindu and Greek, then, alike worshipped the same God, *The name*
of whom they also spoke sometimes under other names. But *Zeus.*
these names were in no case borrowed the one from the other.
The analysis of language has proved that in some instances
Greeks, Latins, or Lithuanians have preserved older forms
than any which are exhibited in Sanskrit, while the variations in the incidents and local colouring of the myths carry
us back to one common source for all in the home of the yet
undivided Aryan tribes. The seed, however, could not ger-
minate while as yet there was no failure of memory; and if,
when the meaning of words was in part or wholly forgotten,
expressions not less graceful once than true became coarse
and mischievous, we may learn to curb our indignation when

[1] On this subject see further, Muir, *Sanskrit Texts*, part iv. p. 41.

we find that both the process and the result were alike in-evitable.

But the name Zeus is not confined to Greeks and Hindus. The Zeus Patêr of the former and the Dyaus-pitar of the latter represent the Jupiter of the Latins, and the Tuisco, Zio, Tyr and Tiw of the German nations. The etymological changes of the word are indeed almost numberless. The brightness of the heaven reappears in the Latin dies, the Sanskrit dyu, and our day: and from the same root spring the Greek Theos, the Latin Deus, and the Lithuanian Diewas. These changes have been fully traced by Professor Max Müller;[1] but we must here note that the Greek Zen, Zenos answers to the Latin Janus, Januspater; that Janus again, resolved into Dianus and Diana, carries us to the Greek digammated forms Δι ός, Δίϝα, and appears again in the word *divine*. With these may be taken the forms con-nected with Zeus by the transition of dy (Dyaus) into j (Jupiter, Janus, Juno), or dj, as in the Djovis of Oscan in-scriptions and the old Italian deity Vedjovis (Vejovis). Akin to all these is the Sanskrit deva, a word which like Dyaus denoted only splendour, but was afterwards as a name for the gods; but although it had thus acquired the general notion of deity, it was never applied to any but the bright gods who were the companions of Indra. The evil powers of night or darkness are Adeva, atheists, or enemies of the devas; and thus even on Indian soil we find the germ of that moral and spiritual meaning which was imported into a myth purely physical in its origin. While the adeva grew, like Asmo-deus,[2] into malignant demons, Vritra the cloud enemy of Indra was gradually passing into the evil god of Iranian theology. If the Diabolos of the New Testament, a word not found in the Septuagint, is to be referred to forms like Dyavan and Diovis, the name deva had lost in the West the meaning of brightness which it retained in the East,[3] though the evil spirit was still regarded as the prince of the powers of the air. The Teutonic devil is thus traced to that Iranian

---

[1] *Lectures on Language*, second series, 453. For Mr. Peile's remarks on the connection of Theos and Deus see note p. 327.

[2] Eshem-dev, aêshma-daêva, 'le démon de la concupiscence.'—Bréal, *Hercule et Cacus*, 135.

[3] Grimm, *Deutsche Mythologie*, 939.

source from which the Jews derived their later complicated demonology. That the term Diabolos, as applied to Satan, should be regarded as identical with the Greek word denoting a slanderer, is a confusion precisely similar to that which turned Lykâôn and his sons into wolves and the seven arkshas or shiners into bears.

If from the Greek conceptions of Zeus we separate all those which, springing from the idea of his relations to men as a Father, grew up into a moral and religious faith, the rest may all be traced to mythical phrases which describe the varying appearances of the heavens and the manifold influence of the atmosphere on the earth and its fruits. Of the countless names thus employed the most transparent would remain as attributes, while the greater number would be localised either as places or as persons. Hence would spring up distinctions between the Zeus of Arkadia, Dodona, Olympos and Crete, distinctions arising wholly from a forgetfulness of the original meaning of words, but fixed irrevocably by the real or apparent identity of the mythical epithets with any mythical names which had become geographical.[1] The sun as Endymiôn plunges into Latmos, the land of sleep; but the presence of the Latmian hill was a conclusive answer to any who might dare to call in question the veracity of the local legend. The old mythical speech had its Phainkian or cloudland geography. It had its Arkadia and Delos, the birthplace of the light, its Phoinikia and Ortygia, the purple land of the quail and the dawn, its bright Lykian regions with its golden stream of Xanthos, its Idâ or earth on which rest the rays of the newly risen sun, its Graian or Hesperian lands where the light dies out in the evening. Carrying with them the treasures of their common inheritance, the Aryan tribes could not fail to give to the hills and streams of their new homes the names which had once described only the morning, the heaven, or the sun. The lord of day sinks to sleep in the glowing west: and the tomb of Endymiôn could therefore be only in Elis. The god of the blue ether is throned in light: so also must the seat of the anthropomorphised Zeus be on some hill whose name, like

---

[1] See Book i. ch. x.

the Delos of Apollôn and the Athens of his virgin sister,
expresses the one idea of splendour; and thus he was made
to dwell on the summit of the Arkadian Lykaios and the
Olympian heights of Mysia and Thessaly. As the veil of
night is slowly withdrawn, the clear heaven is first seen in
the east, and thus Zeus must be born in Lyktos or in Diktê;
but the Cretan who could point to a Diktaian cave in his
own land clung tenaciously to the notion that the child who
was there nourished by Amaltheia was not the Zeus of
Arkadia and Olympos.

The story of his birth and exploits is to be gathered not
so much from the Iliad and Odyssey as from the Hesiodic
and Orphic theogonies; but unless we find manifest contradictions between the accounts which they set before us, it is
unsafe to infer that the poets whom we style Homeric were
unacquainted with details or incidents about which they are
silent, even if it be assumed that their poems in their present
shape are more ancient than those which bear the names of
Hesiod or Orpheus. That the theogony of the former was
far less complicated and retrospective than that of the latter,
there can scarcely be a doubt. The prison to which they
assign Kronos is proof that they looked on Zeus as one who
had not always been supreme in power; but the names with
which their theogony begins are not those of Chaos and
Gaia, but those of Têthys and Okeanos.[1] The struggle between Zeus and the Titans may be inferred from the fact
that Hêrê and Hephaistos speak of them as thrust away
under Tartaros;[2] but the Polyphêmos of the Odyssey who
feeds his flocks in broad pastures has nothing but his size
and his one eye in common with the Hesiodic Kyklôpes who
forge the thunderbolts of Zeus.[3]

[1] Il. xiv. 201.

[2] Ibid. 279.

[3] In the Gaelic story of Osgar, the
son of Oisein, the monster appears with
two eyes; but he is blinded, as in all
other forms of the myth, and for the
same reason.—Campbell, Tales of the
West Highlands, iii. 297. Still, it is
significant that 'not a bit of him was to
be seen but his eyes with blue-green
scales of hardening upon him,' the livid
garment of storm-cloud. But in another
legend we have the genuine Kyklops.

'There was seen nearing us
A big man upon one foot,
With his black, dusky black-skin mantle,
With his hammering tools and his steel
lathe.
'One shaggy eye in his forehead; . . . .
He set off like the wind of the spring-
time
Out to the dark mountains of the high
grounds.
He would take but a single leap
O'er each single cold glen of the desert.'
Campbell, ib. 392.

The lateness of many at least among the Hesiodic ideas seems to be manifested not so much in the allegorical elements introduced,[1] as in the transparent meaning of the names. Zeus and Hades, Phoibos and Lêtô already denoted the conflicting powers of light and darkness, of day and night; but these words had in great part lost their original force, and the poet who wished to frame a systematic theogony felt constrained to speak of Aithêr (ether) and Hêmera as children of Nyx and Erebos. In some important points the story of Ouranos is told over again in the myths of Kronos and Zeus. From Ouranos and Gaia, according to the Hesiodic theogony, spring Koios and Krios, Hyperiôn and Iapetos, the Kyklôpes and other monstrous beings, together with Rhea the mother of Zeus. All these Ouranos hid away in the secret places of Gaia who called on Kronos to avenge her wrongs and his own. From the blood of the mutilated Ouranos which fell on the broad sea was born the laughter-loving Aphroditê.[2] Thus the goddess of love and beauty is, like the Kyklôpes, older than the Father of gods and men; nor can anything show more clearly how thoroughly the mythology of the Aryan world was in conflict with its religion. Kronos and Rhea, then, became the parents of Hestia, Dêmêtêr, Hêrê and Hades; but these are all swallowed by Kronos, who knows that some day he will be dethroned by some child of his own. In grief of heart, Rhea, shortly before the birth of Zeus, betakes herself to Ouranos and Gaia, who send her to the Cretan Lyktos, and there Zeus, like Mithras and Krishna, was born in a cave which Apollodoros calls the cave of Diktê. A stone wrapped in swaddling-clothes was presented to Kronos, who, taking

All this explains itself. The hammering tools and steel lathe are the thunder and lightning; and the thundercloud strides across whole valleys at each step, and clings to the high grounds and the mountain sides.

[1] It is, in Professor Max Müller's belief, manifest allegory when the 'long hills,' 'the pleasant dwellings of the gods,' are reckoned among the children of Gaia.—*Chips*, ii. 66.

[2] This is probably the only meaning which the word φιλομμειδής conveyed to

the poets of the *Iliad* and *Odyssey*. But the whole mythology of Aphroditê renders it far more likely that we have here a confusion similar to that which turned Lykáôn into a wolf, and that the epithet was originally φιλομμηδής, not perhaps, as in the line (200) marked as spurious in the Hesiodic *Theogony*, ὅτι μηδέων ἐξεφαάνθη, but from the attributes which made her the vehement lover of Adonis. With this epithet we may compare that of Pallas (the Phallic) Athênê.

it for the new-born babe, swallowed it as he had swallowed the others. Deceived at length by Gaia, Kronos disgorged them all, the stone first and the living children afterwards.[1] The stone was set up by Zeus for a memorial in Pytho. But Zeus, when he became the husband of Mêtis, felt the same strange desire which had led Ouranos and Kronos to consume their children; and thus, by the advice again of Ouranos and Gaia, he swallowed Mêtis before she became the mother of Athênê. In these exaggerations of a late age we trace the same thought which made the Vedic poet speak of the Dawn as making men old, yet as ever young herself. The light of the heaven calls all things into life; but the heaven retains its unchangeable beauty while generations spring up on the earth and pass away. The children swallowed are thus produced again; and so the Heaven or the Dawn, regarded as Time, might be spoken of as relentless and cruel, and as rightly punished by their injured children.[2]

The war of the Titans. A hard fight now awaited Zeus, who, by delivering the children of Ouranos, had been armed for the struggle with thunder and lightning.[3] On his side against the Titans and the offspring of Kronos were ranged Kottos, Gyas, and Briareôs, who cast the Titans into Tartaros and there left them chained. The struggle itself is described in language which shows how little the poet cared about the subject. Thunders, lightning, and earthquake attest the majesty of

---

[1] With this myth Grimm's story of the Wolf and the Seven Little Goats presents a striking parallel. The wolf is here the night or the darkness which tries to swallow up the seven days of the week, and actually swallows six. The seventh, the youngest, escapes by hiding herself in the clockcase; in other words, the week is not quite run out, and before it comes to an end the mother of the goats unrips the wolf's stomach and places stones in it in place of the little goats who come trooping out, as the days of the week begin again to run their course.

[2] Kronos himself is indeed simply produced from the epithet Kronídês as applied to Zeus in a sense corresponding to the Hebrew phrase 'Ancient of Days.'

When this fact was forgotten, the word was regarded as meaning 'son of Kronos:' and then it became necessary to assign Kronos a place in the Theogony and provide him with a wife and children. See further, Max Müller, *Chips*, ii. 152. The name Mêtis is closely connected with Medeia, and denotes the wisdom which stands out with special clearness in the Latin Minerva. Thus the phrase would run that the Dawn was the daughter of Wisdom, but as the older myth spoke of the dawn as springing from the forehead of the sky, there was no help for the later mythopœists but to make Zeus swallow Mêtis.

[3] Hesiod, *Theog.* 504.

Zeus, by whose thunderbolts land and ocean arc wrapped in seething fire; the din of the conflict is as though the earth and the solid heavens were crashing together; and nine days would pass before a brazen anvil (Akmôn) let down from the earth could fathom the depths of Tartaros.[1] Above this gloomy prison-house are the roots of the earth and the barren sea, and there within walls and gates built by Poseidôn dwell the three sons of Ouranos who befriended Zeus in his hour of need.

Yet this struggle which, like that between Zeus and Typhôeus the latest-born child of Gaia and Tartaros, is related with so much pomp of high sounding but empty words, is the conflict which runs through all mythology and which, in its more human forms, has a singular and unfailing interest. It is the battle of Phoibos with the Pythian monster, of Indra with the throttling snake Vritra, of Sigurd with the dragon of the Glistening Heath, of Oidipous with the Sphinx, and in the earlier phase of the legend, of Achilleus and Agamemnôn with Paris.

Having related the story of Typhôeus, the Hesiodic Theogony recounts the loves of Zeus with Mêtis, Themis, Eurynomê, Dêmêtêr, Mnêmosynê, Lêtô, and with Hêrê, who in this scheme is the latest of his brides and has fallen far below the majesty with which she is invested in the Iliad and the Odyssey. Of these names some are the growth of a comparatively late age. The dawn-goddess of the far east is described as waking all men and receiving praise from every thinker; and the character here faintly attributed to her is brought out more clearly in the Hellenic Athênê, and finds its utmost developement in the Latin Minerva. Athênê, then, as the goddess of the morning, must have a mother with qualities corresponding to her own, and this

---

[1] This is indubitably the hammer of Thor, which is sunk eight rasks beneath the surface of the earth and which takes nine months to rise again to Asgard. In fact the Greek word translated by 'anvil' is etymologically identical with the Teutonic 'hammer.' 'Professor Curtius,' says Mr. Peile, 'seems to be right in combining the O. H. G. *hamar*, our *hammer*, with the Lithuanian akman and the Sk. açman, each of which means "a stone," and the latter also "a thunderbolt;" and with the Greek ἄκμων which commonly means an anvil, but which in Hesiod, *Theog.* 722, where he speaks of the χάλκεος ἄκμων οὐρανόθεν κατίων, can mean nothing but the thunderbolt.'—*Introduction to Greek and Latin Etymology*, 37.

parent was found in the Wisdom which is wedded to Zeus. To this class of invented names belong those of the Hôrai, or Hours, and their mother Themis; but the name of Eurynomê, the mother of the Charites, is more true to the original character of these beautiful maidens. The broad spreading light is the parent of the glistening beings who in the form of horses draw the chariot of Indra, and in the west are the maidens who attend on Aphroditê. But as the dawn may be regarded as springing from the face of the sky, so in another and an earlier myth Athênê springs armed from the forehead of Zeus, and the dark powers of night at once retreat before her. The same idea rendered it necessary to assign to Hêrê some offspring of her own unaided power whether in the person of Typhôeus,[1] or, as the Hesiodic theogony relates, of Hêphaistos also.

The twelve
Olympian
deities.
Thus the number of the kinsfolk and the children of Zeus is already large; but of the class of deities specially known at Athens in the days of Thucydides as the twelve Olympian gods neither our Homeric poems nor the Hesiodic theogony know anything. In the latter, Zeus and Poseidôn are the shakers of the earth and sea, while Hades dwells in the regions under the earth; but of a threefold partition of the Kosmos between the three Kronid brothers we have no formal mention. Of Poseidôn the Theogony tells us only that he built the walls within which Briareôs guards the Titans: nor is there any difference of rank between Arês and his sisters Hêbê and Eileithyia, or again between Dêmêtêr and Eurynomê. From the number of the so-called twelve, Hades is excluded; but in the Iliad and Odyssey he appears at will in the Olympian home of Zeus, and moves as an equal among the gods who are there assembled.

The in-
fancy of
Zeus.
The myth as related by Apollodoros has received some amplifications. The child Zeus in the Diktaian cave is nourished by the nymphs Adrasteia and Ida with the milk of Amaltheia, and the armed Kourêtes clash their shields and spears lest the cry of the babe should reach the ear of his

[1] 'Typhôeus, the whirlwind or Ty-phoon, has a hundred dragon or serpent heads, the long writhing strise of vapour which run before the hurricane-cloud. He belches fire, that is, lightnings issue from the clouds, and his roaring is like the howling of wild dogs.'—S. B. Gould, *The Were Wolf*, p. 174.

father Kronos. In the war with the Titans the Kyklôpes give to Zeus their thunder and lightning, to Hades the helmet which in the Iliad renders the wearer invisible, and to Poseidôn a trident. The struggle is followed by the casting of lots between the three Kronid brothers for the partition of the heaven above, of the earth beneath, and of the hidden regions under the earth. There was no need of any such method. The old mythical phrase rendered it impossible that any but Zeus could be the lord of the bright heaven. In other points also the account of the mythographer is at variance with that of the Hesiodic poet. According to the latter Aphroditê is the offspring of Ouranos; the former represents her as the child of Zeus and Diônê, and makes the scheme of things begin with Ouranos himself instead of Chaos.

That Zeus should be nursed by Ida is an incident for which we are at once prepared when in the Eastern myth we find that Idâ is a name of the earth, and that she is assigned as a wife to Dyaus. That he should have a sanctuary specially sacred on the Lykaian heights in Arkadia was, as we have seen, as indispensable as the birth of Phoibos in Delos. But the Arkadian legend is noteworthy as showing the fantastic forms which spring up in rank luxuriance from mythical phrases when either wholly or partially misunderstood. The blue heaven is seen first in the morning against the highest mountain tops, and on these the rays of the sun rest before they light up the regions beneath; and as it had been said that Zeus dwelt on high Olympos and that his palace was the first building which the sun ever saw, so in strict fidelity to the old phrases the Arkadians insisted that their own Lykosoura was the most ancient of all cities, and the first which Helios had ever beheld, and that Zeus had been nourished by the nymphs Theisoa, Neda, and Hagno on the Lykaian hill hard by the temple of our Lady (Despoina). Nay, as Pausanias tells us,[1] the hill was also called Olympos, and in it there was a spot named Kretea, and hence, as some would have it, here Zeus was born, and not in Crete, the island of the

[1] viii. 38, 1.

Egean sea. Cretans and Arkadians were doubtless alike sincere in their convictions; but, had they remembered the meaning of the words which they used, they would have known that Zeus had his Olympian and Lykaian hills, his Crete, his Diktê, his Arkadia, his Phoinikian home wherever the sun sent forth his long train of light[1] across the sky. But in the minds of Achaians and Hellenes the old phrase had associated with the abode of Zeus the idea of an ineffable splendour; and the tenacity with which they clung to this idea is singularly exhibited in the strange superstition which made the Lykeian sanctuary an object of wondering dread. As the Hebrew of old said that none might look on the face of God and live, so the Aryan held that the doom of death was on the man who dared to look on the unveiled splendour of Zeus. The Arkadian localised this faith in his Lykaian Temenos, and averred not only that all living things which might enter it would die within the year, but that not a single object within it ever cast a shadow. The idea, being once suggested, ran out into the wildest fancies, and the hunstman, who drew back at the inclosure when a hunted beast entered it, failed not to see that its body no longer cast a shadow after it had entered the charmed circle. The science of the geographer does but heighten his faith in the local tradition. When the sun is in the sign of the Crab, he knows that at the Ethiopian Syênê there are no shadows at midday; but the marvel was that in this Arkadian sanctuary there was never any shadow the whole year round. Pausanias admitted the fact as readily as the Royal Society set to work, it is said, to explain why a vessel of water with a fish in it was no heavier than it would have been without the fish: but he could not know that in the real Lykosoura there could be no shade, although this Lykosoura was not to be sought in Peloponnesos or in any land of human habitation. In the bright heaven, through which travels the unclouded sun, there can be no darkness at all.[2]

---

[1] Λυκόσουρα.

[2] When Pausanias, v. 7, 4, says that the Olympian temple was built by men of the golden race, he was simply saying that it was built, as it must necessarily be, by Lykians or men of light.

CHAP.
I.

Lykosoura
and Ly-
kâôn.

Lykan-
thropy.

But the word which supplied the name of the shadowless Lykaian sanctuary was confused in their mind with the name of the wolf, so called for the same reason which led the German to speak of the bear as Goldfuss: and at once it became necessary to show how the idea of wolves was linked with the fortunes of Lykâôn. This son of Pelasgos was the builder of Lykosoura, and he called Zeus Lykaios,[1] after his own name, instituting in his honour the Lykaian festival which answered to the Dawn festival in the city of the Athenians. But his wisdom, as Pausanias testifies, was not equal to that of his contemporary Kekrops, who felt that no living thing should be offered up to the Zeus whom he reverenced as the most high. The zeal of Lykâôn was more vehement, and the blood of an infant, or, as some said, of his own child, flowed on the altar of sacrifice. At once the human form of Lykâôn was changed into that of a wolf. It was the just recompense of his iniquity in a time when men were linked in a close intercourse with the gods; but to the grief of Pausanias the increasing wickedness of mankind had put an end to the age of miracles, and the true story of Lykâôn had been overlaid by miserable falsehoods, which affirmed that men turned into wolves at the Lyknian sacrifice were restored to their old shape after ten years, if they abstained from human flesh, but that, if they tasted it, then they remained wolves for ever.

We have here more than the germ of mediæval Lykan-thropy, and little more is needed to bring before us the Were-wolf or Vampire superstition in its full deformity. That superstition has been amongst the most fearful scourges of mankind; but here, as elsewhere, it is something to learn that a confusion between two words identical in sound, and springing from the same root, laid the foundations of this frightful delusion. The myth of Lykâôn is in this incident nothing more than a repetition of the story of Tantalos. His name is but one of a thousand epithets for the sun, who in times of drought offers up on the altar of Zeus (the heaven) the scorched and withered fruits which owed their life to his own vivifying heat; and for him, as for the

---

[1] Paus. viii. 2, 1.

BOOK
II.

Phrygian king, the sin and its punishment inevitably followed the translation of mythical phrases into the conditions of human life.

The Dodonnaian and Olympian Zeus.

Like the god of Arkadia, the Zeus of Dodona is nourished by nymphs, who in this instance are called Hyades, the bringers of moisture from the blue heights of heaven. That the Cretan story is but another version of the Arkadian, the identity of names alone sufficiently proves. The Lykaian hill had its Crete, and the Eleutherai, to which unintentional trespassers into the Temenos of Zeus were conveyed, reappears in the mythical geography of the Egean island.[1] But although Zeus must be wherever there is an Olympian city, yet the greatness of the Eleian Zeus overshadowed the majesty of the Zeus who abode in Crete, Lykosoura, or Dodona, when his temple at Olympia became the sanctuary of the great Panhellenic festival. But here, too, the local legend gives names with which the Cretan and Arkadian myths have already made us familiar. Here, too, it was said that Rhea entrusted the infant Zeus to the care of the Idaian Daktyloi.[2] If the name given to these mysterious beings be akin to the Diktê and Lyktos of the Cretan tale, to Artemis Diktynna and Diktys of Seriphos, we have in it only a general designation which applies to each of the Daktyloi, Heraklês, Paionios, Iasios and Idas. This Idas is but the counterpart of the nymph Ida, the companion of Adrasteia; and Ida, as we have seen, is but the earth, which may be regarded as either the nurse, or, as in the Vedic hymns, the bride of Zeus. The name of Herakles, like that of Hêrê, indicates simply the splendour of the risen sun, and in Iasios, as in Iasiôn, Iamos, Iolê and others, we have the violet tint with which the heaven is flushed in early morning. The olive branch, which Herakles made the prize of victory, itself came from the Hyperboreans, whence Achaia, the mother of the Zeus-born Achaians, journeyed to Dêlos.

Limits to the power of Zeus.

That the relations of Zeus to other mythical beings were very variously described, a comparison of our Hesiodic and Homeric narratives has already shown us. In the latter, he is the father not only of Aphroditê, who in the former is his

---

[1] Hesiod, *Theog.* 54.   [2] Paus. v. 7, 4.

sister, but of Arês and Hephaistos, who, according to another legend, were like Typhôeus the children of Hêrê only. In one story he is the father also of Phoibos, who in another is the son of Athênê. The power with which he is invested varies in like manner according to the point of view from which he is regarded. The Zeus who is the father of all living things, knows neither weakness, change, nor passion ; the Zeus who is the growth of mythical phrases, is beneficent or treacherous, just or capricious, pure or lustful, according to the character of the phenomena to be described. By himself he is styled all-powerful : but Hêrê too, as the sovereign queen of heaven, can know no higher authority, and thus they are represented as acting sometimes with and sometimes against each other. Nay, even Athênê, the maiden who stands by his side to do his will, is sometimes an accomplice with Hêrê and Poseidôn in plots to circumscribe his power. But although he can do much, he cannot arrest the course of the sun, he cannot lighten his toils for beings meaner than himself, he cannot avert the early doom which awaits him when his short career across the heaven is ended. Hence he can but bring up to Olympos from the dead the beautiful Memnôn for whom the tears of Eôs fall in dewdrops from the sky; he can but rescue the body of the brave Sarpêdôn, and give it to Phoibos to bathe in Simoeis, and to the powers of sleep and death to bear it to the glistening home which they cannot reach until the morning.[1] Heraklês may toil for Eurystheus and have no profit at all of his labour; but Zeus can only look down on his brave son until the flames ascend to heaven from his funeral pile on Oita. There is, in short, no one phrase which might be said to describe the varying aspects of the sky, which is not petrified into some myth characteristic of the Kronid Zeus; and the smile of the blue heaven, when all

[1] In some other respects the Homeric Zeus is greater than the Zeus of historical Hellas. The awful Atê whom the latter cannot turn aside, and who broods over a house until the penalty for the shedding of innocent blood has been fully paid is in the *Iliad* only the spirit of mischievous folly. So too, the Moirai, who, like Atê, had been only his ministers, become possessed, like the Norns, of an irresponsible authority, while finally the force of destiny attains its most overpowering proportions in the Anankê whom, according to the theology of Euripides, not even the father of gods and men is able to withstand or control.

the brightness of day bursts upon it, becomes the rapture of Zeus when Hêrê comes to him armed with the kestos (cestus) of Aphroditê, and the lulling spells of Hypnos.[1] Thus also the serene height in which Zeus dwells, and from which he cannot descend, explains his indifference and seeming immorality in the great conflict at Ilion. At the prayer of Thetis he may be induced to help the Trojans until Agamemnon has repaired the wrong done to Achilleus, or his inaction may be secured by the devices of Hêrê; but with Hêrê herself there can be no such uncertainty or vacillation. Her name is but one of many names for the sun, and she must take part steadily with the Argives and Danaans, the children of the Dawn. To her Paris, the seducer of the fair Helen, is strictly the evil Pani who tempts Saramâ to betray the trust reposed in her by Iudra; and hence she may employ without scruple the power of her beauty, aided by the magic girdle of Aphroditê, to turn the scale in favour of Agamemnon and his Achaian warriors.

But if Zeus cannot himself descend to the regions of the murky air, he has messengers who do his bidding. Foremost among these is Hermes, the god who flies on the breezes and the storm; but Iris of the flashing feet is more truly the minister who joins the ether to the lower atmosphere of the earth. Whatever be the origin of the name Iris, the word was used by the poets of the Iliad to denote not only the divine messenger, but the rainbow itself. Thus the dragons on the breastplate of Agamemnon are likened to the Irises which Zeus has set in the heavens as a marvel to mortal men;[2] and more plainly Iris is the purple arch or bow which Zeus stretches from one end of heaven to the other, to give warning of war or deadly drought.[3] She is a daughter of Thaumas and Elektra, the wonderful amber tints, and a sister of the Harpyiai, the rent and ragged clouds against which those tints are seen; and she would be the golden-winged messenger, not only because the rainbow can come and vanish with the speed of lightning, but because its arch seems to join the heaven and the earth, as a ladder by which the angels may descend and rise up again into their

---

[1] *Il.* xiv. 210, &c.   [2] *Ib.* xi. 27.   [3] *Ib.* xviii. 549.

home above. Hence the phrase was that the rainbow spread
its glorious path across the sky, whenever the gods wished
to send their messenger to do their bidding. In this office
Iris carries out the behests sometimes of Zeus, sometimes of
Hêrê or of Phoibos, while sometimes she comes of her own
free act. She is, in short, the counterpart of Hermes, whose
staff she bears in her hand.[1] If, again, in some myths she
may be spoken of as always a maiden, it may not less truly
be said that the winds love her exquisite tints, while the
earth lies enraptured at her feet; and this accordingly is the
tale which makes her the bride of Zephyros and the mother
of Eros, the darling of the gods. But the name of this
lovely being soon became a mere general title of messengers
or errand-carriers, and reappears in Iros the beggar of the
Odyssey, who resembles her in no other way.

Lastly, as seeing from his throne in heaven all that is
done on earth, Zeus must be the punisher of all iniquity.

But the judgments of a god, whose characteristics depend on
half-forgotten mythical phrases, or on words wholly misunderstood, will not be always equitable. The sentences
passed will have reference often to his mythical rights, while
they may be designed generally to redress wrongs between man
and man. The punishments of Tantalos and Ixîon, of Lykâôn
and Sisyphos are involved in the very idea of these beings.
The sun, who woos the dawn, yet drives her from him as he
rises in the sky. He loves the dew which his rays burn up;
and if he shine on the earth too fiercely, its harvests must
be withered. If his face approaches the stream too closely,
the water-courses will soon be beds of gaping slime. The
penalty paid by Tantalos is bound up with the phrases which
described the action of the sun, while that of Lykâôn sprung,
as we have seen, from a confusion between two words derived
from the same source. If, again, the sun, as rising into the
dizzy heights of heaven, might be said to gaze too boldly
on the bride of Zeus, his downward course is not less certain
than his ascent, and at midday he must revolve like Ixîon on
his blazing wheel; while the stone which Sisyphos has with
huge toil rolled to the mountain summit (the zenith) must

---

[1] 'Der weibliche Hermes.'—Preller, *Griechische Mythologie*, i. 390.

slip from his grasp and dash down again into the valley
below. Still more must Zeus punish the insults done to him
as lord of the fire-laden thunder clouds; and Promêtheus, as
teaching men how to kindle a flame and cheat the gods with
offerings of fat and bone, is an offender less easily pardoned
than chiefs who sacrifice their children on his. altars. In
this Promethean legend alone we seem to have a glimpse of
that future twilight of the gods which is so prominent a
characteristic of Northern mythology. But it is only in the
tragedy of Æschylos that the liberation of Promêtheus involves the humiliation of Zeus. In the summary of Apollodoros, it is mentioned only as one among the countless
exploits of Herakles; and we may owe to the mind of
Æschylos alone a notion which we are perhaps not justified
in connecting with the idea developed by the Northmen into
a common doom awaiting Odin and all the Æsir.

Section VI.—ODIN, WODEN, WUOTAN.

Character-
istics of
Teutonic
mytho-
logy.
The Teutonic belief in the twilight or final extinction of
the gods is of itself evidence that the mythology of the
German and Scandinavian nations belongs to an earlier form
of thought than that of the Hindu or the Greek.[1] The gods
of the latter are essentially free from decay and death.
They live for ever in Olympos, eating ambrosial food and
drinking the nectar of immortality, while in their veins flows
not mortal blood, but the imperishable ichor. Nor can it be
said that even the myth of Promêtheus points to any complete suppression of the present order of things. It does
but say that Zeus should be put down, and a more righteous
ruler set up in his place. But in the Teutonic legends
Odin himself falls and Thor dies, and the body of the

[1] Bunsen asserts this fact when he
says 'that the old Teutonic mythology
of Germany and Scandinavia does not
possess the grace of the Hellenic fictions.
The Muses and Graces have not smiled
on her birth as on that of her Greek
sister. Nor has she been reared under
the sunny skies of Ionia, but amid
constant strife with an austere clime
and rugged nature. Consequently this
mythology has not, like the former,
received such an organic elaboration as
to impart to it an undying influence
upon the course of human history.
Christianity did not blight it in its bloom,
but put an end to the progressive
decay that had begun before its buds
had come to their full flower.'—*God in
History*, ii. 405.

beautiful Baldur is consumed in the flames. In other words, these deities answer not to the Olympian gods, but to the mortal Herakles or Perseus or Asklêpios. But the links which connect the belief of the one race with that of the others may be traced readily enough. The Vedic gods, like the Hellenic, live for ever. The Soma inspires them with fresh vigour, as the soul of Zeus is refreshed and strengthened by heavenly banquets; but the draughts, which only add to their inherent force, give to the Teutonic deities a new lease of life.[1] Thus the Soma draught becomes in northern Europe the cup of honey mingled with the blood of Qvasir, the wisest of all beings, who during his life had gone about the world doing the work of Promêtheus for the wretched children of men. His wisdom, however, could not save him from the dwarfs Fialar and Galar, who, mingling his blood with honey, made a costly mead, the taste of which imparted the eloquence of the bard and the wisdom of the sage.[2] In other respects the Teutonic deities exhibit the closest likeness to the Greek. The rapidly acquired strength and might of Zeus, Phoibos, and Hermes simply express the brief period needed to fill the heaven with light, to give to the sun its scorching heat, to the wind its irresistible force; and the same idea is expressed by the myth of Vali, the son of Wuotan and Rind, who, when only a night old, comes with his hair untouched by a comb, like Phoibos Akersekomês, to take vengeance on Hödr for the death of Baldur, and again in the story of Magni, the son of Iarnsaxa, who, when three days old, rescued his father Thor as he lay crushed beneath the foot of the gigantic Hrungnir.[3] There is the same agreement in the size of their bodies and in the power of their voices. The roaring of the waves and the crash of the thunder are louder than any din of mortal warfare or the cries of any earthly monsters; and thus at once we have the gigantic size of Arês, and the roar of Poseidôn louder than the noise of a myriad warriors in close conflict. Thus, also, as Hêrê lays one hand on the earth and the other on the sea, so Thor drinks up no small part of the ocean with his horn which reaches from heaven to its surface—a ponderous

[1] Grimm, *Deutsche Mythologie*, 295. [2] *Ibid.* 855. [3] *Ibid.* 298.

image for the clouds or the rays of the sun as they drink from the sea. But neither the Greek nor the Teutonic deities have the monstrous forms of the four-armed Vishnu or the four-headed Brahma — these fearful combinations being confined to beings like Briareôs and Geryôn and the giants of northern mythology, unless an exception is to be made of the three-handed Hekatê, who, however, can scarcely be reckoned among the Olympian gods, and the four-armed Lakedaimonian Apollôn.[1] The two-headed Janus is a Latin deity. But if the Teutonic gods are never monstrous, they are sometimes maimed; and in the one-eyed Odin we have the idea which called the Hellenic Kyklops into existence; while in the one-handed Tyr we see Indra Savitar; and in the limping Loki, the lame Hephaistos. But whatever may be their office, these are all bright and radiant deities; Hel alone, like the rugged king of Hellenic mythology, has a dark and repulsive aspect.[2] The very expressions used in speaking of them are transparent. The flowing locks of the Wish-god and of Baldur are those of Zeus and Phoibos; the fair-haired Dêmêtêr of the Greek becomes the fair-haired Lif of the Teuton.[3] The power of Zeus is seen again in that of Thor, and the golden glory which surrounded the head of Phoibos or Asklêpios, and became the aureole of Christian saints, is not less a mark of the German deities, and appears on the head of Thor as a circlet of stars.[4]

Teutonic theogonies.
But when we turn to the theogony set forth in the Völuspa Saga, we can as little doubt that it marks a comparatively late stage of thought, as we can suppose that the Hesiodic theogony is older than the simple and transparent myths which tell us of Prokris or Tithônos or Endymiôn. The myth of Baldur, at least in its cruder forms, must be far more ancient than any classification resembling that of the Hesiodic ages. Such a classification we find in the relations of the Jötun or giants, who are conquered by Odin as the

[1] Grimm, *Deutsche Mythologie*, 298.
[2] Hel, the daughter of Loki, and sister of the wolf Fenris and the horrible worm or serpent, is half black and half human in appearance. Her dwelling is in Niflheim, far down in the depths of the earth, beneath the roots of Yggdrasil:

Grimm, *D. M.* 289. She is the hungry and insatiable goddess, the greedy Polydektês and Polydegmôn of Greek myths (Grimm, *ib.* 291), the black Kali of modern Hindu theology.
[3] Grimm, *ib.* 534.
[4] *Ib.* 300.

Titans are overthrown by Zeus; and this sequence forms part of a theogony which, like that of Hesiod, begins with chaos. From this chaos the earth emerged, made by the gods out of the blood and bones of the giant Ymir, whose name denotes the dead and barren sea. This being is sprung from the contact of the frozen with the heated waters, the former coming from Niflheim, the region of deadly cold at the northern end of the chaotic world, the latter from Muspelheim, the domain of the devouring fire. The Kosmos so called into existence is called the 'Bearer of God'—a phrase which finds its explanation in the world-tree Ygg-drasil, on which Odin himself hangs, like the Helenê Dendrítis of the Cretan legend :—

> I know that I hung On a wind-rocked tree
> Nine whole nights, With a spear wounded,
> And to Odin offered, Myself to myself,
> On that tree, Of which no one knows
> From what root it springs.[1]

This mighty tree, which in Odin's Rune Song becomes a veritable tree of knowledge, and whose roots are undermined by Hel or death and by the Hrimthursen or frost-giants, rises into Asgard, the highest heavens where the gods dwell, while men have their abode in Midgard, the middle garden or earth, embraced by its branches.

The giant Ymir was nourished by the four streams which flowed from the treasure of moisture, the cow Audhumla,[2] which belongs to Zoroastrian not less than to Teutonic mythology, and is there found with the meaning both of cow and earth.[3] This earth afforded salt, without which no life can be vigorous, and from Audhumla, as she fed on the salt of the blocks of ice, there came forth a perfect man, Buri, the fashioner of the world, whose son, Bor,[4] had as his wife Besla, or Bettla,[5] the daughter of the giant Bölthorn,

Genealogy of Odin.

---

[1] 'Odin's Rune Song,' Thorpe's *Translation of Sæmund's Edda*, p. 840. We may compare with the 'Bearer of God,' the names Atlas and Christophoros.

[2] This is the cow beneath whose udder the Dawn maiden hides herself in the Norse story of the Two Step-Sisters.—Dasent.

[3] Bunsen, *God in History*, ii. 483.

[4] The two names would answer to the active and passive meanings of the Greek φορος in compound words.

[5] Bunsen thinks that the original form of this name was Beidsla, a word perhaps denoting desire or longing, and thus answering to the Kama of Vedic and the Eros of the Hesiodic theogony, while it is reflected also in the Teutonic Wunsch or Wish.

BOOK
II.

the root or kernel of the earth.   From Buri proceeded apparently Odin himself, and also the race of the gods or Asas, the self-existent beings,[1] who dwell in Asgard or Aithêr, while the middle air, between the upper and under worlds, the ἀὴρ of the Greeks on which Zeus looks down, is Vanaheim, the home of the Vanen, or spirits of the breathing wind.[2]   To this race belong Freyr and Freya, the deities of beauty and love, ' the children of Mördur, the sea-god who dwells in the sea-city (Noatun), and whose spouse, Skadi (Elster?) is the daughter of the giant Thiassi, for he is indeed himself the shore.' [3]

Odin as the Creator of Man.

The idea of the composite nature of man must have preceded the rise of the myth which assigns the creation of the soul to Odin, of the mind to Hahnir, of the blood and outward complexion to Lodur.   This Hahnir is probably the same word as *hahn*, the cock, ' in its wider import the bird, the animal belonging to the air; ' [4] and thus possibly the framers of this theogony may have intended to set forth their belief that a Trinity, consisting of Ether, Air, and Fire, was concerned in the creation of man, Lodur being certainly fire, and in fact only another form of Loki, the shining god. But we approach the regions of pure mythology when we read that when Odur sets forth on his wanderings, his bride, the beautiful Freya,[5] sheds gold-gleaming tears—' an image of the bright gleams shooting across the rugged morning sky.' [6]   From these parents springs Hnossa, the jewel, the world under the aspect of beauty, while Frigga, as the wife of Odin, doubtless only another form of Odur, is the mother of Jörd, the earth, in the character of the nourishing Dêmêtêr.

The end of the Asas or Æsir.

But all this visible Kosmos is doomed to undergo a catastrophe, the results of which will be not its destruction but its renovation.   The whole world will be consumed by fire, kindled by Lodur, (*der Lodernde*, the glowing god), the Loki

---

[1] From the root *as*, to be; the word is thus simply another form of Weson.

[2] The original form of the word Asen connects it immediately with Atman as a name of Brahman, and the Latin animus, &c.—Bunsen, *God in History*, ii. 486.

[3] Bunsen, *God in History*, ii. 487.

[4] *Ibid.*

[5] For the several changes through which the names Freyr and Freya have passed, see Grimm, *D. M.* 276, &c.

[6] Bunsen, *God in History*, ii. 491.

who brought about the death of Baldur. The life or the reign of the Asas themselves will come to an end, but a new earth rising from this second chaos will resemble that of the golden age in the Hesiodic tradition. Of this Teutonic theogony we may say without the least misgiving that it exhibits not the slightest sign of any Christian influence. It would be almost as reasonable to trace such an influence in the Hesiodic poems, where, if we could get over the insurmountable difficulties of chronology, such an attempt might be made with far greater plausibility. Nor can we charge Bunsen with speaking too strongly, when he says that we must be brought to this negative conclusion, unless 'we are to set above facts a preconceived opinion, taken up at random on the slightest grounds, or indolently to decline scrutiny of those facts, or profound reflections on what they indicate.'[1]

The idea which the Aryans of India sought to express under the names Brahman and Atman, the Aryans of Europe strove to signify by the name Wuotan. That idea centred in the conception of Will as a power which brought all things into being and preserves them in it, of a will which followed man wherever he could go and from which there was no escape, which was present alike in the heavens above and in the depths beneath, an energy incessantly operating and making itself felt in the multiplication as well as in the sustaining of life. Obviously there was no one thing in the physical world which more vividly answered to such a conception than the wind, as the breath of the great Ether, the moving power which purifies the air. Thus the Hindu Brahman denoted originally the active and propulsive force in creation, and this conception was still more strictly set forth under the name Atman, the breath or spirit which becomes the atmosphere of the Greeks and the athem of the Germans. Atman is thus the breathing, in other words, the self-existent being,—the actual self of the universe ; and the meaning thus assigned to the word was so impressed upon the minds of the Aryans of India that no mythology ever grew up round it. In Professor Müller's words 'the

The name Wuotan.

---

[1] *God in History,* ii. 409.

idea of the Atman or self, like a pure crystal, was too transparent for poetry, and therefore was handed down to philosophy, which afterwards polished, and turned, and watched
it as the medium through which all is seen and in which all
is reflected and known.'[1] The conception of the Teutonic
Wuotan was at first not less exalted. Like Brahman and
Atman, it is the moving strength and power of creation, and
the word in Grimm's belief carries us to the Latin vad-cre,
to go or move, the Bavarian wueteln, to stir or grow. Thus
Grimm remarks that of Wuotan it may be said as Lucan says
of Jupiter—

Est quodcunque vides, quocunque moveris,

the pure spiritual deity. The word itself is therefore a par-
ticiple of the old verb watan, whose cognate forms vata, ôd,
account for the dialectical variations which converted it into
the Saxon Wuodan, Wodan, Woden, Odin, the Frisian Wêda,
the Norse Oðinn; and its meaning is in perfect analogy with
that of the Latin Minerva as connected with mens and the
Greek μένος, spirit or strength.[2] But the ideas thus expressed by the name were necessarily lost when the Christian
missionaries taught the people to look on Wuotan or Odin
as the archfiend ruling over troops of malignant demons;
nor is it improbable that the process may have begun at an
earlier period. The name is connected closely with the
German wuth, in which the notion of energy has been exaggerated into that of impulse uncontrolled by will. Such
a limitation of meaning was quite in harmony with the tendency of all the German tribes to identify energy with vehement strife, and thus Wuotan became essentially the armed
deity, the god of war and of battles, the father of victory.[3]
As such, he looks down on the earth from his heavenly home
through a window, sitting on his throne with Freya by his
side, as Hêrê sits by Zeus in Olympos. In the strange
story which is to account for the change which converted
the Winili into the Lombards, this attribute of Wuotan is

[1] Chips, &c. i. 71.
[2] Grimm, Deutsche Mythologie. 120.
[3] Sigfadr, Siegfater, Grimm, ib. 122.
Hence the phrases, Zu Oðinn fahren,
Oðinnsheim suchen, denoted simply

death. With the conversion to Christianity these expressions which spoke
of men as going home to Odin became
maledictions, consigning them to per-
dition.

connected with the rising of the sun, the great eye of day. As the giver of victory, the greatest of all blessings in Teutonic eyes, he was necessarily the giver of all other good things, like the Hermes of the Greeks with whose name his own is identical in meaning.[1] As such, he is Osci, Oski, the power of Wish or Will, so often exhibited in the mythology of northern Europe, the Wunsch to whom the poets of the thirteenth century [2] assign hands, eyes, knowledge, blood, with all the appetites and passions of humanity. This power of Wuotan is seen in the oska-stein, or wishing stone,[3] which the Irish localise in Blarney and which Grimm connects with the wishing-rod or staff of Hermes,[4] in the Oskmeyjar or Wishmaidens or Valkyries who guide to Valhalla all heroes slain in battle, and who are the wish or choice children of Wuotan, and more especially in the Oska-byrr, or Wish-wind, in which we recognise both in name and in the thing the ἴκμενος οὖρος of our Iliad.[5] It is this power doubtless which is denoted by the Sanskrit Kama, as the force which first brought the visible Kosmos into being,[6] and by the Eros of the Hesiodic theogony.

[1] This attribute of Wuotan, which Grimm discovers in the titles Gibicho, Kipicho, makes him δώτωρ ἐάων, i.e. Hermes, whose name denotes simply the motion of the air.

[2] For a long series of passages in which Wunsch is clearly both a power and a person, see Grimm, *D.M.* 126–8.

[3] The instruments of Wish generally run in triplets, as in the story of King Putraka (pp. 144, 159). In that of Cinderella, they are three nuts, containing each a splendid robe. In the story of The Pink, Wish assumes the Protean power of transformation; in that of Brother Lustig, it is a bag in which the possessor may see anything that he wishes to shut up in it, and by means of which he contrives, like the Master Smith, to find his way into heaven. In the tale of the Poor Man and the Rich Man, the three wishes which bring happiness here and hereafter to the former, bring only 'vexation, troubling, scolding, and the loss of a horse' upon the latter. In the story of the Faithful Beasts, it is a wonderful stone (the orb of the sun) which a fat old frog (the

Frog Prince or Fish Sun) brings up from the waters. In the tale of the Donkey Cabbages it is a wishing-cloak, and thus we are brought back to Solomon's carpet, which in the story of the Knapsack, the Hat, and the Horn, 'appears as a cloth, capable, like the Sangreal, of providing unlimited supplies of food and drink, and as a beautiful carpet in the story of the Three Feathers. In that of the Drummer, it is a ring in the hand of the Dawn Maiden, who becomes his bride. The three possessions of King Putraka are the three wishes which assume many forms in folk-lore.' Compare the story of the Best Wish with the wishes of the Master Smith in the *Norse Tales*. Dasent.

[4] Grimm, *D. M.* 131.

[5] There is really nothing to support the explanation which refers ἴκμενος to ἱκνέομαι. The word stands to Oski, or wish, precisely in the relation of ἴχω to ἴσχω, or ἐχυρός to ἰσχυρός.

[6] A translation of the very remarkable hymn in which this word occurs is given in Professor Max Müller's *History of Sanskrit Literature*, p. 561.

The single eye of Odin points beyond all doubt to the sun, the one eye which all day long looks down from heaven upon the earth. But when he was figured as an old man with a broad hood and a wide-flowing robe, the myth necessarily sprung up that he had lost an eye, a story which answers precisely to the myth of Indra Savitar, while it also throws further light, if any such were needed, on that of the Kyklôpes.[1] But as the sun is his eye, so his mantle is the vapour which like the cloud-gathering Zeus Odin wraps around himself, and thus becomes Hakolberend, the wearer of the veil, or Harbard, the bearded god. In his hand he bears the marvellous spear Gungnir, in which we see the lance of Phoibos or Artemis. By his side are the two wolves Gari and Freki, with whom he hunts down his victims, wolves like the Myrmidons whom Achilleus lets loose upon the Trojans, wolves like those from which Phoibos was supposed to derive his name Lykeios. On his shoulders sit the two ravens, Huginn and Muninn, who whisper into his ears all that they see or hear, as the serpents by their mysterious whisperings impart more than human wisdom to the infant Iamos.[2] They are the ravens who bring to Apollôn the tidings of the faithlessness of Korônis, as in the shape of a raven Aristeas tells the Metapontines that he followed Phoibos when he came to their country.[3]

As the bearded god, Odin becomes the giver of the rain, the Zeus Ombrios of the Greeks, the Jupiter Pluvius or flowing Jupiter of the Latins, as well as their Neptunus or

---

The first sentence shows the train of thought in the mind of the poet:

‘Darkness there was: and all at first was veiled
In gloom profound, an ocean without light:
The germ that still lay covered in the husk
Burst forth, one nature from the fervent heart;
Then first came love upon it.’

On this passage Professor H. H. Wilson remarks ‘The term “love” here appears to us to convey a notion too transcendental to have had a place in the conception of the original author. The word is Kama, which scarcely

indicates love in the sense in which it may here be understood, although not absolutely indefensible: but Kama means desire, wish, and it expresses here the wish, synonymous with the will, of the sole-existing Being to create.’—Edinburgh Review, Oct. 1860, p. 384.

[1] Thus in Saxo he is ‘grandævus altero orbus oculo,’ and again ‘Armipotens uno semper contentus ocello.’ The reason assigned by the myth is that he was obliged to leave one eye in pledge when he wished to drink at the well of Mimir.

[2] Grimm, D. M. 134, traces the names to hugr, thought, and munr, mind, as in Minerva, &c.

[3] Herod. iv. 15.

cloud-deity. As such, he is Hnikar, the Anglo-Saxon Nicor or water-god, whose offspring are the Nixies or water-sprites, as the Hellenic Naiads are the children of Zeus.[1] In this character he is the Biblindi, or drinker (the Latin bib-ere) of the Eddas. Like Phoibos again, or Asklêpios, he is the healer, who alone can restore strength and vigour to the maimed horses of Baldur; and as the Muses are the daughters of Zeus, so is Saga the daughter of Wuotan, the source of all poetry, the inspirer of all bards. In his hunts he rides the eight-footed horse Sleipnir, the white steed which bears him also through the thick of battle, like the rudderless and oarless ships which carry the Phaiakians across the blue seas of heaven.

Wuotan, the Allfather[2] and the Psychompompos, who takes all souls to himself when their earthly journey is done, has become for the nations of northern Europe a mere name; but the mark of his name he has impressed on many places. If our Wednesdays remind us of him, he has also left his relics in Onslew,[3] in the island Odinse, in Odinfors, Odenskülla and Wednesbury.

The close connection of the name Tyr with the several forms developed from the root dyu, to shine, would of itself lead us to expect that the word would remain practically a mere appellative for gods whose names might again betray a relation to the same root. Accordingly we meet with Sigtyr, the victorious god, as a name for Wuotan, and Reidartyr or Reidityr, the riding or driving Tyr, as a name for Thor. Nor can it be said that any real mythology has gathered round this word, for the Stauros which is specially connected with his name belongs rather to the region of symbolism than of mythology, although the conjunction of this emblem with the circle (the kestos of Aphroditê and the necklace of Harmonia and Eriphylê) is in itself a subject of some interest. Hence we should further be led to expect that the

[1] All these names come from the same root with the Sanskrit sna, the Greek νήχω, the Latin naro, to float or swim. With them we must link the common term 'Old Nick,' as a name for the devil.

[2] Professor Max Müller seems inclined to trace Christian influence in the description of Odin Allfadir as given, for instance, in the dialogue called Gylfi's Mocking.

[3] Othanslef, Othini reliquiæ. Grimm, D. M. 144, adds many other instances.

BOOK
II.
special emblem under which Tyr would be worshipped would be the sword : and to this fact Grimm traces the names, not only of the Saxons, but of the Cherusci as pointing to the old Cheru, Heru—a sword.

Section VII.—THUNDER, DONAR, THOR.

The name
Donar.
Englishmen may not unnaturally be tempted to think that our word Thunder is the older and more genuine form of the name given to the god who wields the lightnings, and that this name was chosen to express the loud crash which echoes across the heaven. Yet the word in its first meaning has no reference to noise and din. The root denotes simply extension as applied whether to sound or to any other objects, and from it we have the Greek and Latin words τείνω and *tendo*, to stretch, τόνος, tone, i.e. the stretching and vibration of chords, *tonitru*, thunder, as well as *tener* and *tenuis*, the Sanskrit *tanu*, answering to our *tender* and *thin*. Hence the dental letter which has led to the popular misconception of the word is found to be no essential part of it; and the same process which presents the English *tender* and the French *tendre* as an equivalent for the Latin *tener*, has with us substituted *thunder* for the Latin *tonitru*.[1] Thus the several forms Donar, Thunor, and perhaps Thor are really earlier than the shape which the word has assumed in our English dialect.

Thor the
Allfather.
As the lord of the lightning, the thunder, and the rain, Donar is as closely allied, and, indeed, as easily identified with Wuotan, as Vishnu with Indra, or Indra with Agni. But although most of their characteristics are as interchangeable as those of the Vedic gods generally, each has some features peculiar to himself. Thus, although Thor is sometimes said to move in a chariot like other deities, yet he is never represented as riding like Odin. He is essentially, like Vishnu, the walking or striding god, who moves amidst the lightnings like Hephaistos in his workshop of

[1] Professor Müller, having traced the connection between these words, adds 'The relations betwixt *tender, thin,* and *thunder* would be hard to be established, if the original conception of thunder had been its rumbling noise.'—*Lectures on Language,* first series, 350.

subterraneous fires. But in his power of penetrating and piercing the heavens or the earth, and in his ceaseless and irresistible energy, he is simply Wuotan in another form, and the conception of the deity has varied but little among the Aryan nations. The name itself is found in the name of the Gallic thunder-god Taranis, preserved to us by Lucan, and more nearly in its other form Tanarus, while the idea is expressed in the Jupiter Tonans of the Latins, and the Zeus Kerauneios of the Greeks. He is, in short, the great lord of heaven in his most awful manifestation, but he is, nevertheless, the maker and the father of mankind. Hence, like Odin, he is the Allfather, a title which Procopius tells us that the Slavonic nations gave only to the creator of the lightnings.[1] The deity thus worshipped was named Perkunas or Pehrkons by the Lithuanian tribes, and by the Slaves Perun, Piorun, and Peraun, a form which Grimm is inclined to connect with the Greek κέραυνος,[2] and more confidently with the Sanskrit Parjanya, a name of Indra as the bringer of the fertilising rain.[3] If, again, Sophokles speaks of Gê or Gaia as the mother of Zeus,[4] so is the earth the parent of Donar; and as Zeus and Wuotan are severally enthroned on Olympos and Wuotansberg, so has Thor or Donar his Donersperch, Thunresberg or Donnersberg, and Donnerskaute, while the oak, the special tree of the Thundering Jupiter of the Latins, is not less sacred to the Teutonic deity. Like Dyaus or Jupiter, Thor is bearded, but his beard is fiery red, like the lightnings which flash across the heaven.[5]

But his appearance varied with his functions, which were concerned with three things—the lightning flash, the thunderclap, and the thunderbolt. As using the first, he always

His triple functions.

[1] Grimm, *D. M.* 166.
[2] By a change analogous to that which makes the Latin sequor and equus answer to the Greek ἕπομαι and ἵππος.
[3] The connection of the name Perkunas with the Greek φόρκυν, φόρκυνος, seems scarcely less obvious, and the Hellenic deity has as much to do with water as the Vedic Parjanya. The name of the god Pikollos, who is associated

with Perkunas, has assumed a strange form in English folk-lore. In the Platt-Deutsch of Prussia it appears as Pùkkels =Puckle and Pickle: and thus he appears as a demon in the phrase 'pretty Pickle.'
[4] *Philokt.* 389.
[5] 'Rothbärtig, was auf die feurige Lufterscheinung des Blitzes bezogen werden muss.'—Grimm, *D. M.* 161.

walks or strides; as producing the thunderpeal, he is borne along in his chariot; as wielding the bolts, he is, like Wuotan, the armed god who hurls his irresistible weapons. These are sometimes called his spears and arrows; but more especially the thunderbolt is his hammer, the mighty club which, when hurled from his hand, comes back to him again after doing its deadly errand. As wielding this weapon, he is Miölnir or Tydeus, the pounder and crusher, the father of the Aloadai and the Molionids: but the word *hamar* meant not only a mallet, but a rock, and thus carries us to the weapons employed by the giants and the Titans.[1] When this hammer is stolen, Loki, in the Lay of Thrym, asks Freyja if she will lend him her feather-garment, that he may go and find it. With this dress Loki, as the god of light, flies to the abode of Thrym the giant, who has hidden the weapon in the depths of the earth, and will not give it up unless, like Hades, he has the maiden as his wife. When Loki returns to Asgard with this message, Freyja refuses to go.

> Then said Heimdall
> He well foresaw,
> ' Let us clothe Thor
> Let him have the famed
>
> ' Let by his side
> And woman's weeds
> But on his heart
> And a neat coif
>
> Of Æsir brightest,
> Like other Vanir,
> With bridal raiment,
> Brisinga necklace.
>
> Keys jingle,
> Fall down his knees;
> Place precious stones,
> Set on his head.'

He is now Dionysos, Achilleus, or Theseus in their woman-ly forms; and like Theseus, he speedily avenges himself on those who take liberties with him. Having come to Jötun-heim, he astonishes Thrym by devouring an ox and eight salmons, but the serving-maid lulls his fears.

> Then said Thrym,
> ' Bring the hammer in,
>
> The Thursar's lord,
> The Bride to consecrate:

---

[1] See note 6, p. 265. This hammer is said to have been stolen by a giant who hid it eight miles beneath the surface of the earth. In as many years it ascended into heaven again, accomplishing one mile in each year; and thus it was restored to Thor by Thrym, which however is only another name for thunder, and answers to Thrumketill, the proper name, as Thorketyll, Thurketil, answers to Thor. It is scarcely necessary to say that the thunder god has given his name to a vast number of places, the forms Donnersberg, Thorrsberg, and Torslunde representing the three varieties under which they may be classed. Our Thurs-day is an abbreviation of Thunresdäg; but we have to remember the identity of Thunor, Donar, and Thor. A long list of such names is given by Grimm, *D. M.* 169.

Lay Miölnir   On the maiden's knee,
Unite us with each other   By the hand of Vör.'
Laughed Hlórridi's   Soul in her breast,
When the fierce-hearted   His hammer recognised.
He first slew Thrym   The Thursar's lord,
And the Jötuns run   All crushed,
And so got Odin's son   His hammer back.'

SECTION VIII.—FRO.

In the oldest Teutonic mythology we find a god Fro or Friuja, which is worshipped as the lord of all created things. If we may judge from the name, the conception of this deity was probably far above the ideas formed of any of the Vedic or Olympian gods. If the word is connected with the modern German froh, it expresses an idea which is the very opposite of the Hebrew tendency to worship mere strength and power. For Fro is no harsh taskmaster, but the merciful and eternal god. He is, in short, the beneficence and long-suffering of nature. Fro is thus the power which imparts to human life all its strength and sweetness, and which consecrates all righteous efforts and sanctions all righteous motives. Nor can we doubt that Freya stands to Fro in precisely the relation of Liber and Libera in the cultus of Ceres, the connection between these deities being precisely that of Fro and Freya with the goddess whom Tacitus call Nerthus, the Teutonic Niördr. In this aspect Freya is the bringer of rain and sunshine for the fruits of the earth, while the worship of Fro runs parallel with that of Priapos. To this deity belongs the wonderful ship Skidbladnir, which can be folded up like a cloth,—in fact, a vessel much like the magic barks of the Phaiakians. But though this ship could carry all the Asas, yet these beings do not belong to their exalted race. They are Vanir, whose abode is in Vanaheim, as the Alfar or Elves live in Alfheim or Elfland and the Jotnar in Jötunheim.

Relations of Fro to Freya.

SECTION IX.—HEIMDALL, BRAGI, AND OEGIR.

The Hellenic Iris is represented by Heimdall in the mythology of northern Europe. This deity, who like Baldur

The Lord of Himinbiorg.

' *Lay of Thrym*, 16, 17, 31, 32. Thorpe's Translation of *Sæmund's Edda.*

is a white or light-giving god, is the guardian of the bridge
which joins heaven and earth (bif-rost, the waving resting-
place),[1] and his abode is in Himinbiorg, the hill of heaven,
the Latin Mons Cœlius, the first syllable of his name being,
like himin, only another form of himmel.   In other respects
he resembles Argos Panoptes.   Like him, he needs less sleep
than a bird; by night as by day he can see a hundred miles,
and so keen are his senses that he can hear the corn growing on the earth and the wool lengthening on the sheep's
back.[2]   As the watcher and warder of the gods, he carries
a horn, the point of which sticks in Niflheim at the root of
Yggdrasil; and it was easy to add that he rode a horse with
a golden mane and that his own teeth were of gold.   He
speaks of himself as the son of nine mothers, a phrase which
in Bunsen's opinion has nothing to do with the watches of
the night, and must be referred to the nine mythological
worlds of the Völuspa Saga, of which Niflheim is the ninth
and the lowest; and thus the myth would mean that ' the
sun-light is the common divine child of all these worlds.'[3]

Bragi, the
lord of
day.
Another god of the gleaming heaven is Bragi, the brilliant,
while, like Donar or Baldur, he is a son of Odin.   As the
god of poetry and eloquence, he is the guardian and patron
of bards and orators, and his name, like that of Vach or
Saga, passes from the signification of light to that of fluent
and honied speech.   Thus *bragr Karla* was simply an
eloquent man, and a further step degraded the name of *âsa
bragr*, the chief among the gods, and left it as an epithet of
vain boasters.

Oegir, the
sea-god.
The name of the god Oegir, with whom Bragi is sometimes associated in the Edda, has shared a similar fate.
Used first as a name for the sea, it has come to denote the
Ogres with which nurses frighten children.   If, as Grimm
supposes, the word belongs to the same root with the

[1] *Behende Ristätte*, Bunsen, *God in History*, ii. 412.
[2] These qualities reappear in the story of the Six Servants, Grimm. Of these, one has to keep a bandage over his eyes, for his sight is so keen that whatever he looks at splits in two; another can see all round the world: and a third can hear everything, even to the growing of the grass. These ministers of the solar hero are again seen in Grimm's story, How Six travelled through the World, and in the Gaelic tale of The King of Lochlin's Three Daughters, Campbell, *Tales of the West Highlands*, i. 238, 250.
[3] *God in History*, ii. 412, 490.

Gothic agas and ôg, the Anglo-Saxon ege, egesa, Old High German aki, eki, fear, dread, horror, the later meaning is quite in accordance with its original form. But however this may be, the word Oegir as a name for the sea carries us to the Greek stream which surrounds the earth. The phrase Sôl gengr î oeginn simply spoke of the sun going down into the sea, as Helios sinks into the ocean. The other forms Ogen, Ogyges, approach still more closely to the Teutonic Oegir. We find the idea of fear as attached to the name more fully developed when we come to the Oegishialmr, or helmet of dread, which the dragon Fafnir wears as he lies on the golden treasures, to strike terror into those who may dare to gaze on him, and again in the Eckesax or Uokesahs, the fearful sword tempered by the dwarfs in the Vilkina Saga,—weapons which, although there may be no affinity between the names, must remind us of the Aigis of Athênê and the helmet of Hades. Oegir's wife Ran is the mother of nine children, who become the eponymoi of fountains and streams.

CHAPTER II.

THE LIGHT.

SECTION I.—SÛRYA AND SAVITRI.

BOOK
II.

Sûrya, the
pervading
irresistible
luminary.

NEITHER Dyaus nor Varuna, Indra nor Agni, occupies that precise place which is filled by Helios in Greek mythology as the dweller in the globe of the sun, or·by Nereus as the actual inhabitant of the sea. This place in the Veda is reserved for Sûrya or Savitri, the former name being etymologically identical with that of Helios or Hêrê. Like Helios and Heimdall, Sûrya sees all things and hears all things, noting the good and evil deeds of men. Like Indra and Agni, he is sometimes independent, sometimes the servant of others; but he is never, like Dyaus, without a parent. His light is his own, and yet it has been given to him by Indra or by Soma, who is often spoken of as his father. He is the husband of the Dawn, but the Dawn is also his mother, as Iokastê is both mother and wife of Oidipous. In all such phrases it was impossible to lose sight of his real character. He is the most active of all the active gods, he is the third in the earlier trimûrtti in which he is associated with Agni and Vayu, he has measured the worlds with their undecaying supports, he is the divine leader of all the gods; but as such, he is still 'the pervading irresistible luminary.'[1] His chariot is drawn by seven mares, and he 'comes with them self-harnessed.' Like Ixiôn, Tantalos, and Sisyphos, he is the 'lord of all treasures.'[2] He is the eye of Mitra, Varuna and Agni.[3] Sometimes again he is 'without steeds, without stay, borne

---

[1] Muir, Sanskrit Texts, part iv. p. 96. R. V. viii. 90, 12.
[2] R. H. Wilson, R. V. i. 189.
[3] Ib. i. 304.

swift-moving and loud-sounding, he travels ascending higher and higher,[1] and when his daily course is run, he sinks, like Endymiôn or Kephalos, into the waters.

' I have beheld the permanent orb of the sun, your dwelling-place, concealed by water where (the hymns of the pious) liberate his steeds.'[2]

Savitar, the inspirer, from the root *su*, to drive or stimulate, is especially the glistening or golden god: he is golden-eyed, golden-tongued, and golden-handed; and in the later Brahmanic mythology such epithets might furnish a groundwork for strange and uncouth fancies. Thus the story, (which probably started as the myth of Midas and ended with the ass which poured out gold from its mouth on hearing the word Bricklebrit) went that once when Savitar cut off his hand at a sacrifice, the priests gave him instead a hand of gold; and in the same spirit the commentators interpreted the epithet as denoting not the splendour of the sun but the gold which he carried in his hand to lavish on his worshippers.[3] The Teutonic god Tyr is also said to have lost one hand; but the German story ran that Tyr placed his hand as a pledge in the mouth of the wolf and that the wolf bit it off.[4] In the latter tale we have an instance of that confusion of homonyms which converted Lykâôn into a wolf, Kallistô into a bear, and the Seven Arkshas into seven sages.

The one-handed Savitar.

The power and strength of Savitar are naturally represented as irresistible. Not even Indra, or Varuṇa, or any other being can resist his will; and the verse which is regarded as the holiest in the Veda is addressed to Savitar.[5] He is a Tithônos who waxes not old.

The power of Savitar.

---

[1] H. H. Wilson, *R. V.* ii. 91.
[2] Cf. Eurip. *Alk.* 591, ἀμφὶ δελίου κνεφαίαν ἱππόστασιν.
[3] Professor Max Müller, speaking of this myth, compares it with the German proverb, 'Morgenstunde hat Gold im Munde,' as enforcing the same moral with the prosaic English adage which promises health, wealth, and wisdom to those who go to sleep early and rise early. *Lectures*, second series, 378. There was another version of the myth of Savitar, which made him lose both his

hands. H. H. Wilson, *R. V.* i. 51.
[4] Compare the story of Nund of the Silver Hand (Fergusson, *Irish before the Conquest*) and Grimm's tale of the Handless Maiden, for whom the king, when he takes her as his wife, orders silver hands to be made. But she is taken from him, like Urvasi from Purúravas, and when, after grievous sufferings, she is restored to him, her hands have grown again as beautiful as ever.
[5] Muir, *Principal Deities of R. V.* p. 567.

'Shining forth, he rises from the lap of the Dawn, praised by singers; he, my god Savitar, stepped forth, who never misses the same place.

'He steps forth, the splendour of the sky, the wide-seeing, the far-shining, the shining wanderer; surely, enlivened by the sun, do men go to their tasks and do their work.'[1]

'May the golden-eyed Savitri come hither.

'May the golden-handed, life-bestowing, well-guarding, exhilarating, and affluent Savitri be present at the sacrifice.'

These phrases which seem to have no reference to the later myth, carry us to the myth of the one-eyed Odin, who like Savitar, is also Wegtam, or the wanderer, the broad heaven looking down on the earth with its one gleaming eye, the sun.[2] Like Indra, Varuna, and Vishnu, he is Skambha, the supporter.

'Savitri has established the earth by supports; Savitri has fixed the sky in unsupported space;[3] he has milked the atmosphere, restless (or noisy) as a horse; Savitri, the son of the waters, knows the place where the ocean, supported, issued forth.'[4]

SECTION II.—SOMA.

The ninth book of the Rig Veda consists wholly of hymns written in praise of Soma, who is lauded as the source of life and vigour, of mental power and bodily strength both to gods and men, the generator or parent of Agni, Sûrya, Indra, and Vishnu. Of the phrases employed in describing

[1] *R. V.* vii. 63.
[2] H. H. Wilson, *R. V. Sanhita*, i. 99.
[3] Dr. Muir points out the inconsistency of this phrase with the later mythology, which spoke of the earth as resting on the head of the serpent S'esha, or on other supports, and remarks that the Siddhantas, or scientific astronomical works of India, maintain that the earth is unsupported. In these it is said plainly that, 'if the earth were supported by any material substance or living creature, then that would require a second supporter, and for that second a third would be required. Here we have the absurdity of an interminable series. If the last of the series be sup-

posed to remain from its own inherent power, then why may not the same power be supposed to exist in the first —that is, in the earth?' Dr. Muir adds that Aryya Bhatta, one of the most ancient of Indian scientific astronomers, even maintained that the alternation of day and night is produced by the rotation of the earth on its own axis. *Sanskrit Texts*, part iv. p. 97. It is remarkable that the Copernican system should thus have been anticipated in the East, as by Aristarchos of Samos in the West, without making any impression on the thought of the age.
[4] *R. V.* x. 149, 1. Muir, *Sanskrit Texts*, part iv. p. 97.

the nature and functions of Soma, many relate exclusively to
the juice of the Soma plant, and to the process by which
that juice is converted into an intoxicating drink. These
phrases are often curiously blended with expressions which
speak of a god exalted higher even than Varuṇa or Indra,
while others show clearly that, like almost all other names
of Hindu mythology, Soma was a word which might be
applied alike to the gladdening power of wine and to the
life-giving force from which the sky and sun derive their
strength and brilliance. In the latter sense, Soma imparts
to Indra the power which enables him to overcome Vritra,
and, like Indra, is the conqueror of demons and the destroyer of cities. All things are in his hand, for Soma rules
over gods and men, and, like the other deities known as
Skambha, supports the heaven and earth in his hands. In
short, there are no powers attributed to Varuṇa, Indra, or
Vishṇu, which are not, if it be possible, exceeded by those
which are inherent in Soma. Yet Soma is also the drink of
the gods, the Olympian nectar, the beverage which gives immortality. Soma is Indu, the sap which flows for Indra—
the stream which is purity itself, and the cleanser of all defilement. In the symbolical interpretations of later times
Soma is a mere name, which may denote physical, moral, or
spiritual life, a name strictly of the one everlasting God.

'Soma purifies, [he who is] the generator of hymns, the
generator of the sky, the generator of the earth, the generator
of Agni, the generator of Sûrya, the generator of Indra, and
the generator of Vishṇu.' [1]

Soma is the Beatific Vision to which the pilgrims of this
earth aspire.

'Where there is eternal light, in the world where the sun

---

[1] The explanation of this verse given
in the Nirukta-parisishta shows that the
commentator was perfectly aware of the
real nature of the myth. 'Soma,' he
says, 'is the generator of hymns (or
thought), i.e. of those solar rays whose
function it is to reveal; of the sky, i.e.
of those solar rays whose function it is
to shine; of the earth, i.e. of those solar
rays whose function it is to spread; of
Agni, i.e. of those solar rays whose
function it is to move; of Sûrya, i.e. of
those solar rays whose function it is to
appropriate; of Indra, i.e. of those
solar rays whose function is sovereignty;
of Vishṇu, i.e. of those solar rays whose
function is diffusion.'—Muir, *Sanskrit
Texts*, part iv. p. 81. In these comments
all the deities disappear together, leaving
Soma as the representative of the one
great Cause of all things.

BOOK
II.

is placed, in that immortal imperishable world place me, O
Soma. . . .

'Where life is free, in the third heaven of heavens, where
the worlds are radiant, there make me immortal. . . .

'Where there is happiness and delight, where joy and
pleasure reside, where the desires of our desire are attained,
there make me immortal.' [1]

In some hymns of the Rig Veda, all creatures are said to
spring from the divine seed of Soma. All things are under
his control, and he is, like Varuna and other deities, the
divine sustainer (Skambha) of the world. He is an omniscient ocean, and his are the stars and the sun. He too,
like Indra, is the slayer of Vritra.

'This divine Soma, with Indra for its ally, crushed, as
soon as generated, Pani by force: thou, Soma, didst baffle
the devices and weapons of the malignant secreter of the
(stolen) wealth (the cattle).' [2]

But at once the poet recurs to metaphors suggested by the
process of preparing the Soma juice.

'In the filter, which is the support of the world, thou,
pure Soma, art purified for the gods. The Usijas first
gathered thee. In thee all these worlds are contained.' [3]

'The Soma flowed into the vessel for Indra, for Vishnu;
may it be honied for Vayu.' [4]

'Pouring forth streams, the Soma hastens to Indra, Vayu,
Varuna, the Maruts, and to Vishnu.' [5]

'Indu, do thou flow sweet to Indra, to Vishnu. Preserve
from sin the men who praise thee.' [6]

'Soma, Indu, purified, thou exhilaratest Varuna, thou
exhilaratest Mitra, thou exhilaratest Indra, thou exhilaratest
Vishnu, thou exhilaratest the troop of the Maruts, thou
exhilaratest the gods and the great Indra that they may be
merry.' [7]

When in the later mythology, Mahadeva had thrown the

[1] R. V. ix. 113, 7; Max Müller,
Chips, i. 47.
[2] H. H. Wilson, R. V. S. iii. 461.
[3] R. V. ix. 86; Muir, Sanskrit
Texts, part iv. p. 99.
[4] R. V. ix. 63, 3; Muir, Sanskrit
Texts, part iv. p. 80.

[5] R. V. ix. 65, 20; Muir, Sanskrit
Texts, part iv. p. 80.
[6] R. V. ix. 56, 4; Muir, Sanskrit
Texts, part iv. p. 80.
[7] R. V. ix. 90, 5; Muir, Sanskrit
Texts, part iv. p. 80.

older deities into the shade; Vishṇu, Soma, and Agni became different parts of his bow and arrow; ' for all the world,' we are told, 'is formed of Agni and Soma, and is said to be composed of Vishṇu, and Vishṇu is the soul of Maḥûdeva of boundless power.' [1] So with Uma, as divine knowledge, Soma, as the supreme spirit, falls into the ranks of correlative deities. [2]

With the change which came over later Hindu thought the popularity of Soma passed away; but the hymns of the Rig Veda suffice to show how great a charm the Soma drink had possessed for the people. It was to them life in health, strength in weakness, medicine in sickness, the restoration of youth in old age; and the vigour which it imparted to human beings was imparted with unstinting lavishness to the gods. The exultation of Indra is the exultation of Polyphemôs when he has drunk the wine given to him by Odysseus.

Powers of Soma.

Section III.—CORRELATIVE DEITIES.

A very slight acquaintance with the language of the Vedic hymns will suffice to show that the idea of any one deity rarely failed to suggest to the mind of the worshipper the idea of another god, whose attributes answered to, or were contrasted with, his own. The thought of Dyaus, the sky, was bound up with that of Prithivî, the earth, who was his bride; and their very names, blended into one word Dyava-prithivî, denoted their inseparable union. The idea of Varuṇa, the veiling heaven, brought up that of Mitra, the light-illumined sky.

Complementary deities.

The connection was forced upon them by the phenomena of the outward world. We cannot sever in our minds the thought of day from that of night, of morning from evening,

The dualism of Nature.

[1] Muir. *Sanskrit Texts,* part iv. p. 189. Uma is also the wife of Maḥâ-deva, *ib.* 227. For further details respecting Uma, see Muir, *ib.* p. 357, *et seq.* Of genuine mythology the story of Uma, if it can be called a story, exhibits very little. It has been drawn out to suit an idea, but the idea has not been suggested by the myth. 'Uma is divine knowledge; thou who existest with her, O Soma, supreme spirit, &c.' Hence her attributes are plastic enough, and thus she becomes identified with Ambika, the sister of Rudra, a being not much more clearly defined than Uma herself.

[2] Max Müller, *Lectures on Language,* second series, 486.

of light from darkness; and 'this palpable dualism of nature '[1] has left its most marked impression on the mythology of the Veda. The dawn and the gloaming, the summer and the winter may, it is obvious, be described as twins or as sisters, standing side by side or dwelling in the same house. Thus, not only are Dyava-prithivî, heaven and earth, described as twins, but Indra and Agni are spoken of in the dual as the two Indras, Indragni, not only ushasanakta, the dawn and the night, but ushasau, the two dawns,[2] and the two Varunas. Like Indragni again, the twin Asvins, or horse-men, are called Vritrahana, destroyers of Vritra.

Functions of the Asvins.
These Asvins have been made the subject of a somewhat lengthened controversy. Their features are not very definite, but in the oldest hymns they are worshipped with a peculiar reverence, as able not merely to heal sicknesses but to restore the aged to youth. Their relations to each other and to their worshippers are placed in a clearer light by a reference to Greek mythical phraseology. Speaking of these beings, the commentator Yaska says that their sphere is the heaven, and remarks that some regard them as heaven and earth, as day and night, or as sun and moon, while they who antici-pated the method of Euêmeros affirmed that they were two deified kings. But when he adds that their time is after midnight, whilst the break of day is yet delayed, all room for doubt seems taken away. The two Ahans, or Dawns, Day and Night, are born, it is said, when the Asvins yoke their horses to their car. The twins are born 'when the Night leaves her sister, the Dawn, when the dark one gives way to the bright.' After them comes Ushas, the Greek Eôs, who is followed first by Sûryâ, a feminine, or sister of Sûrya, the sun, then by Vrishakapayi, then by Saranyû,[3] and lastly by Savitar. They are *ihehajâte*, born here and there, either as appearing in the East and in the West, or as springing up on the earth and in the air; and this epithet may explain the alternate manifestations of the Dioskouroi, who stand to Helen in the same relation which the Asvins bear to Saramâ or Ushas.

[1] Max Müller, *Lectures on Language*, second series, 486.
[2] *Ib.* 487, 495.   [3] *Ib.* 492.

The Asvins are thus the conquerors of darkness, the lords
of light: ever youthful, swift as thought, and possessed, like
Indra, Agni, and Phoibos, of a profound wisdom. If the
poet needs to give them a father, he must assign them a
parent in the clear heaven, or say that they are the children
of Prajâpati, Tvashtar, or Savitar, names for the Creator.
Their mother must be the East or West, from which they
spring, regarded not as a place, but as the being who
imparts to them their mysterious life.[1] As ushering in the
healthful light of the sun, they are, like Asklêpios and his
children, healers and physicians, and their power of restoring
the aged to youth reappears in Medeia, the daughter of the
Sun. They are adored at morning and evening tide as
Rudrau, the terrible lords of wealth, and are thus identified
or connected with another deity who became of supreme
importance in the later Hindu mythology.[2] Like the Kourêtes and Telchines, like Proteus, Thetis, and the other fish-
gods, they have the power of changing their shape at will.

' The twin pair adopt various forms; one of them shines
brightly, the other is black; twin sisters are they, the one
black, the other white,'[3]—phrases which bring before us the
rivalry not only of the Dioskouroi, but of the Theban Eteokles
and Polyneikes, and perhaps the black and white eagles in
the Agamemnon of Æschylos.[4] Like Phoibos the healer,
and like Asklêpios and his sons Podaleirios and Machâôn,
the Asvins are ' physicians conversant with all medicaments.'[5]
In the Norse tale of Dapplegrim we have the Asvins in their
original form as horses; for when the lad, who, having won
on his wonderful steed the victories of Indra, Herakles, and
Bellerophôn, is told that he must produce its match or die,
complains to the horse that the task is not easy, ' for your
match is not to be found in the wide world,' the steed replies
that he has a match, although it is hard to get at him, for
he abides in Hell.

In Indra and in Agni, Mitra and Varuṇa, and in the
Asvins we have three sets of twins, Yaman, Gemini, each

[1] Max Müller, *Lectures on Language*,
second series, 498.
[2] Muir, *Sanskrit Texts*, part iv. ch. 3,
sect. 1, p. 265.

[3] H. H. Wilson, *R. V. S.* iii. 97.
[4] *Ib.* 103.
[5] *Ib.* 101.

being spoken of as Yama or Yami, the twin brother or the
twin sister. These Yaman are the children of Vivasvat, who is
wedded both to the morning and to the evening; and their
sister, the night, prays her brother to become her husband.
In this Yama we have probably the Hindu god of the dead,
whose two dogs with four eyes and wide nostrils go about
among men as his messengers. As both are children of Vivasvat, Professor Max Müller thinks it unnecessary to assume
that two Vivasvats were each the father of Yama. The twin
who represented the evening would naturally become the lord
or judge or guide of the departed. As from the East came all
life, so in the West lay the land of the dead, the Elysian
fields, the region of Sutala; and thither the sun hastens as
he sinks down from the heights of heaven. Thus 'Yama is
said to have crossed the rapid waters, to have shown the way
to many, to have first known the path on which our fathers
crossed over;[1] and the gulf is not wide which separates the
functions of the Psychopompos from those of Hades. Like
Varuna, Yama has his nooses, and he sends a bird as a token
to those who are about to die. But although a darker side
is not wanting to his character, Yama remains in the Veda
chiefly the god of the blessed in the paradise where he dwells
with Varuna. This Yama reappears in the Yima of the
Avesta, his father Vivasvat being reproduced as Vivanghvat;[2]
and in Yima we have an embodiment of the Hesiodic golden
age free from heat and cold, from sickness and death, an
image of the happy region to which Krishna consigns his
conquered enemy. In a grotesque myth of the later Yamen,
the death of men in youth as well as in old age is accounted
for by a mistake made by the herald of Yamen after the
latter had been restored to life by Siva who had put him to
death. While Yamen lay dead, mankind multiplied so that
the earth could scarcely contain them. Yamen on returning
to life sent his herald to summon at once all the old men, for
none others had ever been called away before. The herald,
getting drunk, proclaimed instead that henceforth all leaves,

---

[1] Max Müller, *Lectures*, second series, 515; Muir, *Principal Deities of R. V.* 575.
[2] Max Müller, *Lectures*, second series, 522.

fruits, and flowers, should fall to the ground, and thus men of all ages began to yield to the power of death.

The connection of Soma with Umá has been already noticed. Another couplet of deities is found in Soma and Súryâ, the daughter of Súrya the Sun; and here the twin Asvins stand by the side of Soma as the friends of the bride-groom. A later version, which says that, although Savitar had destined his daughter Súryâ to be the wife of Soma, she was nevertheless won by the Asvins,[1] repeats the story of Pelops and Hippodameia, which represents the maiden as becoming the prize of the hero who can overtake her in a foot race. So again, Arjuna, the Argennos of the myth of Agamemnon, stands to Krishna, who is represented as de-claring him to be his own half, in that dual relation which links Phaëthôn with Helios, Patroklos with Achilleus, Theseus with Peirithoös, Telemachos with Odysseus, and which is seen again in the stories of Pelias and Neleus, Romulus and Remus, Prometheus and Epimetheus, Hengest and Horsa, and in the Teutonic tales of the Two Brothers and of the Faithful John who guards his prince as carefully as the Lux-man of Hindu folk-lore guards Rama. This dualism we find again in the Hellenic Eros and Anteros, and still more plainly in the myth of Hermaphroditos.[2] The tale which describes Arjuna as receiving from Mahâdeva the Pasupata (or sceptre which guides the cows) under a strict charge not to use it rashly as it might destroy the whole world,[3] carries us to the ill-omened gifts which brought destruction to Phaëthôn and Patroklos. In the same way Rama is linked with his brother Laxmana, and one myth which regards Rama as a mortal hero speaks of both as wounded and rendered senseless by a cloud of serpents transformed into arrows.[4]

---

[1] Muir, *Contributions to a Knowledge of Vedic Theogony*, 3.

[2] This story is after all only a coun-terpart of the legends of Echo and Seléné, whose part is here played by the nymph of the well, Salmakis. Like Endymiôn and Narkissos, the youth rejects her love, until the nymph lays hands on him as Aphroditê does on Adonis.

[3] Muir, *Sanskrit Texts*, iv. 196, 225.

[4] *Ib.* 384. The modern version of the story has been already given, book i. ch. viii.

Section IV.—THE DAWN.

To the poets of all ages and countries the phenomena of morning and evening are full of pathos and sadness. The course of the day itself is but brief, and the career of the bright being who bears it across the heaven may be little more than a series of struggles with the vapours which strive to dim his splendours. All his life long he must toil for the benefit of the mean thing called man, and look on clear streams and luscious fruits without daring to quench his thirst or appease his hunger. He may be armed with invincible weapons; he may be the conqueror of all his enemies: but the doom is upon him; he must die in the flower of his age. Still there is for him a grief yet more bitter than this. Throughout almost the whole of his long journey he must go alone. The beautiful being who cheered him when his heart beat high and his limbs were fresh was parted from him almost as soon as he had found her, and there remains of her grace and loveliness only a consoling memory. He has hard toils before him, and there are grievous perils to be encountered. Still for him, as for the sons of men,

'Tis better to have loved and lost,
Than never to have loved at all.

But although he cannot go back to the bright land where he saw his early love, she may yet be restored to him when the hour of his death has come. The sight of that beautiful form, the tender glance of that loving countenance, will be more than a compensation for his long toil and his early death. He will die looking on her face. But in the meanwhile his heart is filled with an irrepressible yearning. He must hasten on until his eye has seen its desire, even though the shadow of death must immediately fall upon him. He may have been early severed from her; but she is his bride, pure and incorruptible, though the mightiest of the land seek to taint her faith and lead her aside into a new love. Her dwelling is his home, and to it he must hasten across the blue seas of heaven, although monsters may seek to scare him, and beautiful beings may beseech him to tarry awhile with them in their luxurious chambers.

Under this thin disguise we see at once the story of Odysseus and Penelopê; but this is, after all, one only of almost a thousand forms which the legends of Phoibos and Dionysos, of Perseus and Bellerophontes, may assume. The doom of the Dawn is as woeful as that of the Sun who has loved her. The glance of both is fatal. The Sun looks upon the tender dew, and under his rays the sparkling drops vanish away. The evening turns to gaze upon the setting sun, and the being on whom her life depends is snatched from her sight. They can remain together only on the condition that the one shall not see the form and face of the other; and so when, after the rising of the sun, the violet hues of morning faded from the sky, the phrase would run that Indra, or Phoibos, or Orpheus had fixed their eyes on Dahanâ, or Daphnê, or Eurydikê, and their love had passed away from them like the fleeting colours of a dream. But the myth itself might be developed in many ways. The disappearance or death of Daphnê, or Prokris, or Arethousa would mark the moment of the great catastrophe; but the disaster was only the interruption of a union which had been continued during the long hours of the night, and at once we have in this fact the suggestion of disguise. If the being whose glance scorched even the object of his love could keep her near him without doing her hurt, this could only be because he had shrouded his splendour in darkness, or because he had assumed some other form. Either he might hide his limbs behind the skin of a lion, as in Greek stories, or of a fox or a jackal in Hindu folk-lore, or he might himself assume their form. Such an idea would prompt the tale that the beautiful Dawn had been given by her father in marriage to a hideous monster; or that she, the youngest and loveliest of his daughters, had been frightened by her gloomy sisters, the earlier hours of the night, into the belief that she was wedded to a loathsome being. The natural growth of the story would frame the more minute details, that before this terrible union the mother of the Dawn was dead; that the beautiful maiden was sacrificed by a new bride, who took part with her elder sisters; and that, as she sought to verify their words, she discovered the beauty and majesty of her husband only to see it vanish from her sight. Then over the heart of the forsaken Dawn would come that irrepressible yearning which filled the soul of Odysseus. For her life would now have nothing worth living for but the hope that one day she should be reunited to him whom she had lost; and until she should so recover him, she could know no rest or peace. She must follow him through all lands, she must seek him at all costs and at every sacrifice. To the uttermost bounds of the earth, and far beyond the clouds which veil the distant mountains, beyond the mists which brood on the restless sea, she must journey on, buoyed up by the ever undying longing to see his face once more. There are fearful dangers to be encountered and overcome. She is surrounded by awful shapes, who blot out all brightness from the sky; but the powers of light are on her side. The beautiful clouds which sail on the pure ether will bear her up above the murky vapours, and carry her, as on swan's wings, across the mysterious vaults of heaven. Her heart is full of sadness; but the tenderness of her beauty is not lessened, and as she moves on her weary way, helpless creatures feel her kindness, and declare that their gratitude shall not end in words. She may be doomed to scale a mountain of ice, or remove heaps of enormous stones; but the winds are content to be her ministers, and their warm breath melts the ice, and drives away the massy storm-clouds. Still the malignant influence of one powerful enemy rests upon her, the influence of that witching sorceress who seeks to win for herself the love which Odysseus bears to Penelopê. But the tasks imposed upon her by her unpitying rival are at last accomplished; and as the clouds break away from the heaven, the Dawn, or the Eôs, who closes the day in our Homeric poems, sees before her the form of him whom she has sought with undaunted and untiring devotion.

The story of Urvasi.
In these simple phrases relating to a drama acted before us every day, we have the framework of a vast number of stories, some of which have furnished subjects for epic poems, while others have assumed strange and grotesque forms in the homely lore of popular tradition. One of the

simplest versions of the myth is found in the story of Urvasî,[1] although even here the artificial influence of a growing ceremonial system is manifest. The personification of Urvasî herself is as thin as that of Eôs or Selênê. Her name is often found in the Veda as a mere name for the morning, and in the plural number it is used to denote the dawns which passing over men bring them to old age and death. Urvasî is the bright flush of light overspreading the heaven before the sun rises, and is but another form of the many mythical beings of Greek mythology whose names take us back to the same idea or the same root. As the dawn in the Vedic hymns is called Urûkî, the far-going (Têlephassa, Têlephos), so is she also Urunsî, the wide-existing or widespreading; as are Eurôpê, Euryanassa, Euryphassa, and many more of the sisters of Athênê and Aphroditê. As such she is the mother of Vasishtha, the bright being, as Oidipous is the son of Iokastê; and although Vasishtha, like Oidipous, has become a mortal bard or sage, he is still the son of Mitra and Varuṇa, of night and day. Her lover, Purûravas, is the counterpart of the Hellenic Polydeukês;[2] but the continuance of her union with him depends on the condition that she never sees him unclothed. But the Gandharvas, impatient of her long sojourn among mortal men, resolved to bring her back to their bright home; and Purûravas is thus led unwittingly to disregard her warning. A ewe with two lambs was tied to her couch, and the Gandharvas stole one of them. 'Urvasî said, "They take away my darling, as if I lived in a land where there is no hero and no man." They stole the second, and she upbraided her husband again. Then Purûravas looked and said, "How can that be a land without heroes or men where I am?" And naked he sprang up; he thought it was too long to put on his dress. Then the Gandharvas sent a flash of lightning, and Urvasî saw her husband naked as by daylight. Then she vanished.

[1] Max Müller, *Chips, &c.* ii. 99, *et seq.*

[2] 'Though *rava* is generally used of sound, yet the root *ru*, which means originally to cry, is also applied to colour in the sense of a loud or crying colour. Besides, Purûravas calls himself Vasishtha, which, as we know, is a name of the sun; and if he is called Aida, the son of Idâ, the same name is elsewhere (*R. V.* iii. 29, 3) given to Agni, the Fire.'—Max Müller, *ib.* 101. This son of Idâ reappears perhaps as Idas, the father of Kleopatra.

BOOK.
II.

"I come back," she said, and went. Then he bewailed his vanished love in bitter grief.' Her promise to return was fulfilled, but for a moment only, at the Lotos-lake, and Purûravas in vain beseeches her to tarry longer. 'What shall I do with thy speech?' is the answer of Urvasî. 'I am gone like the first of the dawns. Purûravas, go home again. I am hard to be caught like the winds.' Her lover is in utter despair; but when he lies down to die, the heart of Urvasî was melted, and she bids him come to her on the last night of the year. For that night only he might be with her; but a son should be born to him.[1] On that day he went up to the golden seats, and there Urvasî told him that the Gandharvas would grant him one wish, and that he must make his choice. 'Choose thou for me,' he said; and she answered, 'Say to them, Let me be one of you.' So the Gandharvas initiated Purûravas into their mysteries, and he became one of the Gandharvas.

Germs of the story of Penelopê.

In the story thus related in the Brâhmana of the Yagur-Veda we have a maiden wedded to a being on whose form her eyes may not rest, although she dwells in his house; and the terms of the compact are broken practically by herself, for although it is Purûravas who springs up, still it is Urvasî who provokes him to do so. Finally, she is impelled so to tempt him by beings who wish to obtain her treasures; and thus the element of jealousy enters into the legend. These leading ideas, of a broken pledge or violated secret, of beings jealous of her purity and happiness, and of immediate separation to be followed by reunion in the end, furnish the groundwork of a large group of stories belonging chiefly to the common lore of the people. They resolve themselves into the yet more simple notion of brief union broken by an

---

[1] This child may be the first sun of the new year; but whether the myth bo taken of that or any other sunrise, it is equally true that the mother must vanish soon after her child has been born. Hence in the play of Kalidasa, after Urvasî has been reunited to her lover, she tells him,

When for your love I gladly left the courts
Of heaven, the monarch thus declared his will,

'Go and be happy with the prince, my friend:
But when he views the son that thou shalt bear him,
Then hitherward direct thy prompt return.
The fated term expires, and to console His father for my loss, he is restored. I may no longer tarry.'

See the analysis of this play by Professor Max Müller, 'Comparative Mythology,' *Chips*, ii. 126.

early parting and a long absence, and this notion is the germ of the Odyssey. In the very spring-time of their joy the chieftain of Ithaka is parted from his bride. While he is away, she has to undergo hard trial at the hands of men who seek rather her riches than herself; and even when the twenty years are over, and Odysseus sees Penelopê once more, the poet still speaks of a time soon coming when they must again be parted. Here also the myth of Purûravas is in close agreement with that of Odysseus, for he too must be again parted from his love. She who, ever young, yet making men old, can know neither age nor change, cannot avert the doom which falls alike on Phaëthôn, Memnôn, and Sarpêdôn, on Achilleus, Baldur, and Sigurd. But all have the same work to do; and if the dawn cannot save them from death, she can restore them to life, and thus through her they become immortal. Thus Purûravas, who was created especially to do battle with and to conquer the powers of darkness, addresses Urvasî as the immortal among the mortals; and says of himself that he, as the brightest sun, holds her who spreads the sky and fills the air with light. The very rite for the sake of which the Brahmans converted the simple myth into an institutional legend, points to the true nature of Purûravas. He can become immortal only by devising the mode of kindling fire by friction; and thus like Bhuranyu and Phorôneus, Hermes and Prometheus, he falls into the ranks of those who are the first to bestow the boon of fire on man. Nor is it without significance that in the play of Kalidasa Purûravas, when first he rescues Urvasî from the beings who have carried her away, has already a wife, who, seeing her husband wasting away with love for another, makes a vow to treat with kindness the object of his love, whoever she may be. Purûravas has not indeed for his first wife the love which Kephalos is said to bear to Prokris; but here Urvasî, who hesitates not to take her rival's place, is so far the exact counterpart of Eôs, while in the first wife we have all the self-devotion which marks the beautiful daughter of Hersê.

In most of these legends the meeting and the severance of these lovers take place by the side of the stream or

the water from which Aphroditê rises, and in which the
nymphs bathe the newly-born Apollôn. It is on the
river's bank that Eurydikê is bitten by the fatal snake,
and Orpheus is doomed to the same weary search as Purûravas, for the love which has been lost. On the heights
which overhang Peneios, Phoibos sees and chases the beautiful Daphnê, and into the blue stream the maiden plunges
when she almost feels the breath of her pursuer. So again
Arethousa commits herself to the waters as she flies from
the huntsman Alpheios, who wins her love only when they
meet again upon the shore of Ortygia, the dawn-land. The
Greek river is but the Teutonic Elbe, the running stream,
and in the huntsman of Mainalos we see only an image of
the sun as he rests on the waters in the morning or the
evening, in other words, the Frog-prince of the German
legend.[1] In the Sanskrit story Bhekî, the frog, is a maiden
who consents to marry a king on condition that he never
shows her a drop of water. ' One day being tired, she asked
the king for water ; the king forgot his promise, brought
water, and Bhekî disappeared.'[2] As in the story of Urvasî

[1] In the mythology of Assyria, Bhekî,
or the frog-sun is represented by the
fish-sun, who, as Berosus says, rose up
from the sea each morning, and plunged
into it every evening. Mr. Gould
remarks (Curious Myths, second series,
231) that ' his semipiscine form was an
expression of the idea, that half his time
was spent above ground, and half below
the waves.' This fish-god is, like the Aryan
Proteus, or Helios, the possessor of a mysterious wisdom of which, under certain
conditions, he will make human beings
partakers. As Oannes, or Dag-on, the
fish Ou, he is the great teacher of the
Babylonians, and his name is seen in
the Hebrew Bethuon (Bethaven), which
is translated by Bethshemesh, the house
of the Sun. He is horned as Mr.
Gould remarks, like all other sun and
moon deities, the moon goddess of the
Syrians being Derketo, Atergatis, the
mother of Semiramis, in whose story
again we have the elements of many
Aryan myths. See note 1, p. 223.
Like Cyrus and Romulus, Semiramis
is brought up by a shepherd, and
her beauty attracts the attention of a
general, whose name is, of course,

Onnes. But she is wooed also by
Ninos, and thereupon Onnes slays himself. After a life full of marvels she
wings her way to heaven in the form of
a dove, as Romulus vanishes in the
storm cloud, and Aineias disappears in
the waters of the Numician stream.
The fish-sun is seen in that portion of
the so-called Homeric hymn which
speaks of Apollôn as plunging into the
sea, and in the form of a dolphin
guiding the ship of the Kretan mariners
to Krisa. On coming out of the water,
he reassumes, like Proteus, a human
form. Mr. Gould states that, among
North American Indians, a story is told
that they were guided to their Western
home by a man or fish who kept close
to the boat, until it reached the American
coast.

[2] Max Müller, Chips, ii. 248. This
is the germ of the beautiful story of
Undine, as told by Fouqué. She, like
Daphnê, is the daughter of the stream ;
and the condition imposed upon her
husband is, that he is never to speak
angrily to her when on or near any
water. 'If you should, my kinsfolk
would regain their right over me. They

the husband is the actual delinquent, but he is hurried into the fatal act by the words of his wife. If instead of the promise not to show her water we substitute a pledge that the lover shall not look upon his bride while she is bathing, the myth remains essentially the same; and in this form we see at once the germ of the story of Melusina. If Mr. Gould is right in connecting this name with that of the Babylonian moon-goddess Mylitta, we have an instance of an imported title parallel to those of the Semitic Melkarth and Adonai, the Hellenised Melikertes and Adonis. Melusina is found by Count Raymund, as Daphnê is found by Apollôn, near running water, and like Bhekî or Urvasî, she readily consents to marry her human lover on the condition that he shall never attempt to see her on one day of each week. When at length the promise is broken, Raymund sees his beautiful wife in the water, the lower portion of her body being now in the form of a fish. But Melusina did not know that her husband had thus seen her, and, as in Fouqué's story of Undine, the catastrophe comes only when Raymund calls her a serpent and bids her depart from his house.[1]

would tear me from you in their fury, because they would conceive that one of their race was injured; and I should be compelled, as long as I lived, to dwell below in the crystal palaces and never dare ascend to you again; or should they send me up to you, that would be far worse still.' If he is false to her, she can reappear only to kiss him to death. Selênê can look upon Endymiôn only when he is just plunging into his dreamless sleep. The tale so exquisitely told by Fouqué was derived by him from the *Treatise of Elemental Spirits* by Theophrastus Paracelsus. The leading feature of his story is the acquisition of a human soul by Undine on her marriage with the knight Huldbrand. Mr. Gould cites a Canadian story of an Ottawa chief, who, whilst sitting by the water-side, sees arising from the flood a beautiful woman, who prays him to suffer her to live on earth, as she sought to win a human soul, and could do this only by marriage with a mortal. 'He consented and took her to his own house, where she was to him as a daughter. Seven years after, an Andirondak youth be-

held and loved her. He took her to wife, and she obtained that which she had desired, a human soul.'— *Curious Myths*, second series, 238. It is possible that this story may be an importation from Europe: but we may ask for some conclusive evidence of the fact, when we find the legend of Pandora's box among the Indians of Labrador. Jesuit missionaries may have imparted much to their converts, but it is not likely that they instructed their hearers in the mythical fancies of pagan Greeks.— Hinds, *Explorations in Labrador*, i. 61.

[1] For other versions and variations of this story see Gould, *Curious Myths*, 'Melusina.' The same myth is introduced by Sir Walter Scott in his romance of *Anne of Geierstein* (ch. xi.), whose mother's life depends on a brilliant opal which must not be touched with water. This gem, like many others, is sympathetic. It is, in short, the fatal brand of Meleagros. See also Scott, *Border Minstrelsy*, introduction to Ballad of Tamlane.

The idea of ugliness or unseemliness would naturally come to be connected

The idea, common to all these tales, of beings who though united in the closest love may not look upon each other, is but little modified in the story of Erôs and Psychê. The version given by Appuleius is commonly spoken of as an allegory. It deserves the name as much and as little as the Odyssey. Here, as in the tales already referred to, no liquid must come near the mysterious being to whom the love of the mortal husband or wife is given. The old phrase that the sun must die at the sight of water,[1] has retained its hold on the storytellers of all the Aryan nations; but the version of Appuleius assigns reasons where the earlier Sanskrit myth is content to relate incidents. If like Urvasî Psychê brings about her own punishment, she does so because she is under a doom laid on her by Venus. But Venus is Aphroditê Anadyomenê, the mother, the wife, or the child of the sun; and the notion that the love of the sun for another must excite her jealousy and anger was one which must sooner or later be imported into the myth. With its introduction the framework of the story was completed; and so the tale ran that Venus charged her son to fill Psychê with the madness which made Titania fall in love with the enchanted Bottom. But Psychê, the dawn with its soft breath, is so beautiful that Erôs (Amor, Cupido) falls in love with her himself and taking her to a secret cave (the cave of Diktê or of Lyktos), visits her as Purûravas comes to Urvasî. Stirred up by Venus, her sisters tell Psychê that she is wedded to a hideous monster, and at length her

with Bheki or the Frog. Hence the king's daughter in the German story of the Frog Prince shows no special fancy for the little creature which brings up for her the golden ball (the sun's orb) from the bottom of the well. The ugliness of Bheki serves to give point to the beautiful Gaelic legend of Nighean Righ Fo Thuinn, Campbell, *Tales of the West Highlands*, iii. 404. The maiden (Aphroditê) is not, indeed, here described as a frog; but she is a 'strange looking ugly creature' with her hair down to her heels, who in vain intreats Fionn and Oiscan (Finn and Ossian) to let her come to their fire. Diarmaid, who scruples not to say how hideous

he thinks her, is more merciful; but the Loathly Lady (for it is the same myth) becomes as exacting as the little Frog in Grimm's story. She has not been long at the fire when she insists on coming under Diarmid's plaid. He turns a fold of it between them; and presently he finds by his side 'the most beautiful woman that man ever saw.' She is the Dawn-maiden, and she raises for his dwelling that palace of the sun which the Arabian storyteller delights to describe in the tale of Allah-ud-deen. The same being appears as the 'foul wight' in Chaucer's tale of the Wife of Bath, Keightley. *Fairy Mythology*, 323.
[1] Max Müller, *Chips*, ii. 248.

curiosity is so roused that, taking a lamp, she gazes upon her lover and beholds before her the perfection of beauty. But a drop of oil falls from her lamp on the sleeping god, and the brief happiness of Psychê is ended. She is left desolate like Purûravas, and like him she must go in search of her lost love. Eôs has looked on Helios, and he has plunged beneath the sea. If she seek him, it must be through the weary hours of the night, amidst many perils and at the cost of vast labour. In every temple Psychê looks for her lover until at last she reaches the dwelling of Venus, under whose spell he lies like Odysseus in the home of Kirkê or Kalypsô. At her bidding she accomplishes some hard and degrading tasks, under which she must have died but for the love of Erôs, who, though invisible, still consoled and cheered her. By his aid she at last made her peace with Venus, and becoming immortal, was united with her lover for ever. Of all these incidents not one has been invented by Appuleius; and all that can be said is that he has weakened rather than strengthened the beauty of the myth by adapting it to the taste of a thoroughly artificial age. Having taken up a story which had not yet been brought within the charmed circle of epic or lyric poetry, he has received credit for an originality to which the familiar tale of Beauty and the Beast, with which it is substantially identical, may lay an equal claim.[1]

The idea which underlies these tales runs through a large class of legends, which carry us into almost every Aryan land and make the hypothesis of conscious borrowing or importation as perilous as we have seen it to be in the story

The search of the Dawn for the Sun.

---

[1] In Hindu folk-lore this is the story of Gandharba-sena. Of this being Captain Burton (*Tales of Indian Devilry*, preface xiii.) says that he 'is a quasi-historical personage who lived a century preceding the Christian era.' Even granting the fact, we have here only a name belonging to the same class with Roland, Arthur, Dietrich of Bern, or others for whom an historical existence has been claimed. The name clearly suggests a comparison with Gandharva Purûravas. The story of Gandharba-sena Captain Burton regards as the original of the Golden Ass of Appuleius.

The hypothesis is scarcely necessary, unless it is to be maintained that the whole folk-lore of Greece, Germany, Scandinavia, and other countries has been bodily imported from India. The story of Gandharba-sena is, however, the story of Midas, of the Irish Lavra Loingsech, and of the Little Ass in Grimm's collection; and it may be noted that the being transformed into an ass in the romance of Appuleius is Lucius of Corinth (Phoibos Lykeios). The story of Psychê is also told in the Gaelic Tale of the Daughter of the Skies.

of the Master Thief.   In almost all these legends the youngest and most beautiful of three (sometimes of twelve) daughters is married or given up to some unsightly being or monster, or to some one whom she is led to suppose hideous or repulsive.   In some instances, as in the common English nursery tale, the enchantment is ended when the maiden confesses her love for the disguised being in his unsightly shape : [1] in the version which Appuleius followed, the maiden has a lover who is marvellously beautiful, but whose beauty she has never seen.   In all cases, however, there are jealous sisters or a jealous mother who insist that the lover is hideous, and incite her to look upon him while he is asleep.   Thus goaded on, she disregards the warnings in each case given that such curiosity cannot be indulged without causing grievous disaster, and in each case the sleeping lover is awakened by a drop of oil or tallow from the torch or lamp in the maiden's hand, and instantly vanishes or is transformed, generally into a bird which tells her that she must wander in search of him through many weary years, and do the bidding of some harsh mistress into whose power her fatal curiosity has brought her.   In some versions, as in that of Appuleius, this mistress is the mother of the lost lover.[2]   Then follow the years of wandering and toil, which can be brought to an end only by the achievement of tasks, generally three in number, each utterly beyond human powers.   In these tasks the maiden is aided by brute creatures whom she has befriended in their moment of need, and who perform for her that which she could not possibly accomplish herself.   The completion of the ordeal is followed by the happy union of the maiden with her lover.

The Search
of the Sun
for the
Dawn.
It is scarcely necessary to say that there is perhaps no

[1] The converse of this incident is found in the legend of the Loathly Lady. See also Fouqué's *Sintram*.

[2] In Grimm's Story of the Twelve Brothers she is the mother of the king who marries the dawn-maiden, i.e. she is Venus.   She reappears as his second wife in the tales of The Little Brother and Sister, of the Six- Swans, who fly away like the children of Nephelé, and of Little Snow White.   The Little Brother and Sister (Phrixos and Hellé)

are seen again in the story of Hansel and Grethel.   These two come in the end to a pond (Hellespontos); but the maiden who represents Hellé is more fortunate than the daughter of Athamas. In the Gaelic story of The Chest, Campbell, ii. 4, she disguises herself as a gillie in order to search for her lost lover.   This story contains also the myth of the judgment of Portia in the *Merchant of Venice*, ib. 6, 13.

one feature in these stories which does not reappear in the tales told of Boots, or the youngest son, in his search for the enchanted princess who has been torn away from him, or whom after a long toil he is to win as his bride. It could not be otherwise, when the stories turn in the one case on the search of the dawn for the sun, in the other on the search of the sun for the dawn. As we might expect in popular tales, the images drawn from myths of the day and night are mingled with notions supplied by myths of summer and winter. The search is always in comparative gloom or in darkness.[1] Either it is Odysseus journeying homeward among grievous perils, clad in beggar's raiment, or it is Orpheus seeking Eurydikê in the awful regions of Hades. The toil or the battle which precedes the victory is common to all the traditions, whether epical or popular; but in the wildest forms of Aryan folk-lore the machinery of the most complicated tales can be broken up into its original parts. In northern countries especially, the powers of frost, snow, and cold, must be conquered before Phoibos can really win Daphnê, or Psychê recover Erôs. Hence there are mountains of glass (glaciers) to be scaled, huge castles of ice to be thrown down, or myriads of icebergs or boulders to be removed. In these tasks the youth or the maiden is aided by bears, wolves, or foxes, by ducks, swans, eagles, or by ants, the Myrmidons of Achilleus; but all these are names under which the old mythical language spoke of the clouds or the winds, or of the light which conquers the darkness. The bear appears in the myth of the seven shiners as well as in that of Arkas and Kallistô, the wolf in the stories of Phoibos Lykeios, of Lykâôn, and the Myrmidons. The clouds assume the forms of eagles and swans alike in Eastern or Western traditions. The eagles bear Sûrya Bai on their

---

[1] This search is well described in the Gaelic story of Nighean Righ Fo Thuinn, where the hero Diarmaid loses his wife, as Raymund of Toulouse is separated from Melusina, because he breaks the compact made with her. The search goes as in the other stories, but an odd turn is given to it at the end by making Diarmaid take a dislike to the maiden whom he rescues in the Realm Underwaves (where Herakles regains Alkêstis), and thus he leaves her to go to his own home. After all it is but Orpheus, who here abandons Eurydikê, instead of Eurydikê fading from the eyes of Orpheus. The one myth is as forcible and true as the other. Campbell, iii. 419.

wings through the heaven, and the swans, or white cirri clouds, are seen in all the stories which tell of Swan maidens and the knights who woo and win them.[1] These creatures, who are as devoted to the youth or the maiden as the Myrmidons are to Achilleus, speedily remove the mighty heaps of grain, stones, or ice, and leave the battle-ground clear for their joyous meeting. In the German story of the White Snake, the flesh of which, like the serpents of Iamos and the heart of Hogni in the Volsung tale, imparts to him who eats it a knowledge of the language of birds, the labour falls on the lover, while the maiden plays the part of Aphroditê in the legend of Psyché. The animals here befriended by the trusty servant, who is Erôs, or Boots, or Odysseus, or a thousand others, are fishes, ants, and ravens—names which carry us to the fish or frog sun, to the Myrmidons and the clouds; and the tasks are the recovery of a ring,[2] the picking-up of some bags of millet seed, and the finding of the apple of life (the sun's orb). The first is accomplished by the fishes, one of which, as in the story of Polykrates, brings the ring in its mouth, the second by the ants, and the third by the ravens.

Origin of these myths.
That these tales, of which the most familiar type for English children is that of Beauty and the Beast, have been borrowed directly from the apologue of Appuleius, no one probably will venture to maintain. With as little likelihood can it be said that they were suggested by the Vedic myth of Urvasî and Purûravas. Their relationship to the latter is precisely that of the Latin and Greek dialects to the ancient Sanskrit; and thus they must be placed in the class of organic myths. They spring up on all soils from the seed which the Aryan tribes carried away with them when they left their common home, and every variation may therefore be noted as exhibiting the power of growth inherent in the old mythical ideas. In few cases is there even a plausible ground for saying that any one tale is copied or consciously adopted from another; in none is there any necessity for the assumption. The Teutonic nurse was as little conscious

---

[1] See Appendix D.
[2] Compare also the Gaelic story of

Mac Iain Direach, Campbell, *Tales of the West Highlands*, ii. 359.

that the Frog Prince and Boots were one and the same person, as the grandams of the Punjâb were that Bheki was but another form of Urvasî. As an example of the measure in which the myth, retaining still the essential idea, may become modified, we may take the tale of the Soaring Lark.[1] In this story, the maiden knows that the being who, like Herakles with the lion's skin on his back, is during the day a lion is at night a man, but no ray of light must fall upon him while he is in his human shape. At her entreaty, however, he goes to the bridal feast of the elder sister, where a single ray of light streams in upon him through a chink in a door made of unseasoned wood, and the maiden entering the room finds a dove, which says that for seven years he must fly about in the world, but that at every seventh mile he will let fall a drop of blood and a feather, to guide her in her quest of him.[2] At last this guidance fails her, and she asks the sun and moon to tell her whither the dove had gone. As in the tale of Dêmêtêr and Persephonê, they are unable to say: but they give her a casket and an egg which may one day be of use. She then asks aid of the North Wind, who bears her over the world until she rescues her lover, who has resumed his lion's shape, from a caterpillar who is an enchanted princess. But the latter, when disenchanted, seizes on the maiden's lover, and bears him away. The maiden follows to the place in which she hears that the wedding is to be celebrated, and then opening the casket, finds a dress which glistens like the sun and which the princess seeks to buy. But it can be given only for flesh and blood, and the maiden demands access to the bridegroom's chamber as her recompense. During the first night her lover sleeps by force of a potion, but her voice sounds in his ears like the murmuring of the wind through the fir-trees. On the next day, learning the trick, he refuses the draught, and the maiden, availing

---

[1] Grimm. With these legends may be compared the story of Tulisa (a tale which in Professor Benfey's opinion is very ancient), obtained from a washerwoman at Benares, and published in the *Asiatic Journal.* See also the tales in

the *Pentameron of Basil,* 15, 19, 44; and Hahn's *Greek and Albanian Tales.* A complete analysis of the fable of Appuleius is given in Friedlaüter's *Sittengeschichte Roms.*

[2] Frere, *Deccan Tales,* 221.

herself of the gift bestowed by the moon, is reunited to him at last.[1]

The Norse tale 'East of the Sun and West of the Moon,' approaches more nearly to the form of Beauty and the Beast. A white bear (we are at once reminded of the process which converted the seven shiners into seven bears) taps at a poor man's window on a cold winter night, and promises him boundless wealth, on condition that he receives his daughter as his wife. The man is willing, but the maiden flatly says nay, until, overcome by the thought of her father's poverty, she agrees to live with the beast. The bear takes her to a palace in which the rooms gleam with silver and gold; but the being who comes to her at night is a beautiful youth who never allows her to see him. The woman who acts the part of Venus in this tale is the mother, not of the lover, but of the maiden, and as she could scarcely be represented as jealous of her daughter's happiness, we are told that, while suggesting the same doubts which brought Psyché to her trouble, she warned her child not to let a drop of oil fall on her husband while she stooped to look upon him. The sequel of the story presents no features materially different from that of the Soaring Lark, except that the oil dropped from the maiden's lamp is made to bring about the catastrophe. The prince is, of course, under the power of the sorceress, who wishes to marry him, like Odysseus in the house of Kirkê or the cave of Kalypsô; but when on the wedding morning he displays a fine shirt with three drops of tallow on it, and declares that he will marry only the woman who can wash them out, the Trolls, vainly attempting the task, see the prize snatched from their hand by the maiden whom they had despised as a stranger and a beggar.[2]

---

[1] In the German story of the Iron Stove (Grimm), the part of Erôs is played by a king's son, who is compelled by a witch to sit in a great iron stove which stood in a wood. This is manifestly a reversing of the myth of Brynhild, in which the flame surrounding the maiden on the Glistening Heath answers to the fiery stove in which the prince is imprisoned. In the tale of Strong Hans (Grimm), it is Psyché who is rescued from a tower or well in which she is confined like the Argive Danaê. In the legends of the True Bride and of the Drummer the maiden recovers her lover as in the story of the Soaring Lark. See also ch. viii. sect. 2 of this book.

[2] In the German story of Bearskin, the soldier is not turned into a beast, but is under compact with the evil one not to comb his hair or wash his face for seven years, but to wear a bear sark or cloak. In this disguise he compels

The myth passed into other forms. In every case the bonds of true love were severed; but the persons thus separated were sometimes brothers and sisters, sometimes parents and children. In the German story of the Twelve Brothers, the sister goes forth to search for the lost children in that great forest which reappears in almost all tales of Teutonic folk-lore, the forest of the night or the winter, in which the huntsman or the king's daughter, or the two babes, or Tanhaüser or True Thomas, the prince, the tailor, or the soldier, lose their way, to fall in every instance into the hands of witches, or robbers, or magicians, sometimes malignant, sometimes merciful and almost genial. It is perhaps no exaggeration to say that under this type of solar legend (for, as turning on the presence or the absence of light and warmth, these are all solar legends), four-fifths of the folk-lore of northern Europe may be ranged. The inhabitants of this dark forest are the Panis, by whom the wanderers are sometimes welcomed, sometimes slain. These wanderers, or stolen youths or maidens, can be recovered only through much suffering on the part of those who seek them. In the tales of the Twelve Brothers and the Six Swans, the sister must not utter a word for seven or for six years, an incident which, in the story of the Woodcutter's Child, is changed into loss of voice, inflicted as a punishment by the angel who has charged her not to look into the thirteenth door of the palace in the land of Happiness, or in other words, into the treasure-house of Ixiôn or Tantalos. But the appetite for mythical narratives was easily gratified. Incidents repeated a thousand times, with different names and slight differences in their sequence or arrangement, never palled upon it. If Psychê has hard tasks to perform before recovering Erôs, the Greek was as well content to listen to the story of the same tasks as they are performed by Erôs before he can recover Psychê. Thus the part of the latter in the legend of Appuleius is played by the former in the German stories of

the king to give him one of his daughters in marriage, and the youngest consents to be the victim, saying that a promise which has been made must be kept. The transformation is more complete in the story of Hans the Hedgehog, whose enchantment is brought to an end by burning his skin, as in the Deccan story of the enchanted rajah.

The spell of moon-light.

the White Snake and the Golden Bird, the Queen Bee, Strong Hans, the Drummer, and many others.[1]

The common element of all these stories is the separation of two lovers by the intervention of a third person, who is represented sometimes as the mother, more often as another lover of the youth whose heart is given to the maiden from whom he is to be parted. In the latter case, her great object is to prolong the separation for her own benefit; and we have at once the framework of the tales which relate the sojourn of Odysseus in the abodes of Kirkê and Kalypsô. Penelopê, like Psychê, is far away, and though Odysseus has not forgotten her and longs to be with her, still he cannot escape from his irksome bondage. While the time of slumber lasts, he must tarry with the beautiful women who seek to wean him from his early love. The myth is but the fruit of phrases which spoke of the sun as sojourning in the land of sleep, freed from all woes and cares,[2] and but dimly remembering the beautiful hues of morning under the magic charm of night. Thus in Kirkê and Kalypsô alike we have the moon-goddess beneath whose spell the sun may be said to slumber, and in the palace of the one and the flashing cave of the other we see the wonderful home of Tara Bai, the Star-maiden, the Ursula or Selênê of the modern Indian tale. Girt with her zone of stars, the beautiful being who can neither grow old nor die sings the lulling song whose witching power no mortal may withstand. If she seeks for sensuous enjoyment, still her desire is not for the brutal pleasures which turn men into swine;[3] but to see before her

---

[1] This myth reappears in a very thin disguise in the ballad of Erlinton, Scott's *Border Minstrelsy.* Here we have the forest, the maiden and her lover, while the robbers are a troop of knights headed by an old and grey-haired warrior, Winter himself. The knight, of course, fights with and slays all, except the grey-haired chief, who is suffered to go home to tell the tale; in other words, the mortal Medousa is slain, but the power of cold itself (her immortal sisters) cannot be destroyed. With this we may compare the death of Hellê while Phrixos lives on. So, too, the youngest child of Kronos is not

devoured, and the youngest goat in Grimm's story of the Wolf and the Seven Little Goats escapes the fate of the six others.

[2] Τὴν ὀδύνας ἀδαῆς ὕπνε δ' ἀλγέων.
Soph. *Phil.* 827.

[3] The turning of the companions of Odysseus into swine is only another form of the more common transformation into birds which the witches of Teutonic and Arabian folk-lore keep hung up in cages round their walls. Compare the story of Jorinde and Joringel (Grimm) with that of Punchkin in the *Deccan Tales,* and of the Two Sisters in the *Arabian Nights.*

the wise chief whose glory is in all lands is a happiness for which she is ready to sacrifice all her wealth and splendour. Still her abode is full of a strange mystery. Its magnificence is not the magnificence of the open sunshine, its pleasures are not the wholesome pleasures of the outer air. If then the sun tarries in her chambers, it is because ho is under a spell, because Selênê has cast her deep sleep upon Endymiôn, and Zeus has not yet sent Hermes to bid Kalypsô let Odysseus go. Thus in these Greek myths we have the germ and the groundwork of all those countless stories which speak of mortal men carried away from their homes to dwell with unseen beings beneath the earth. These beings are in each story headed by a beautiful queen, whose will it is impossible to resist. This power is prominent in the myth which tells us that Thomas the Rhymer was carried off in his youth to Fairyland, where he became possessed of vast and mysterious knowledge. At the end of seven years he was suffered to go back to the upper earth on condition of obeying the summons to return to Elfland whenever it might be given. The bidding came while Thomas was making merry with some friends in the Tower of Ercildoune. A hart and a hind, it was said, had come from the neighbouring forest and were slowly moving up the street of the village. Thomas immediately rose, left the house, and following the animals to the wood was never seen again.[1] The story of Thomas is substantially identical with Chaucer's Rhyme of Sir Thopas, in whom the beauty of the Fairy Queen excites the same desire which the sight of Helen awakened in the Athenian Peirithoös.[2] This fairy queen sometimes assumes the form of the Echidna who for a time made Herakles

[1] Scott, *Border Minstrelsy,* iv. 114. Mr. Gould, in his chapter on the Mountain of Venus, notices among other stories that of the Norse Helgi, Thorir's son, who is invited by Ingebjorg the Troll queen to come and live with her. His absence, however, is confined to three days, at the end of which he returns home laden with treasure. His second visit was extended over many years, and from this he returned blind. The story told by Gervase of Tilbury, the scene of which is the mountain of

Cavargum in Catalonia, is cited by Sir Walter Scott in his introduction to the Ballad of Tamlane, *Border Minstrelsy.*

[2] Mr. Price (introduction to Warton's *History of English Poetry,* 49) compares the journey of Thomas to Elfland, in the Scottish ballad, with Ælian's story (*Var. Hist.* iii. 18) respecting Anostos 'the bourne from which no traveller returns,' and remarks that the prophetic power acquired by the Rhymer during his sojourn with the Fairy Queen is no novel feature in the history of

sojourn in her dwelling: but the Tailor's son of Basle in the mediæval story had the courage neither of Herakles nor of Sir Gawain, and he was so terrified by the writhing of her tail that in spite of the beauty of her face he fled after giving her only two of the three kisses which she had bargained for.[1] Such a myth as this, it is obvious, would, if subjected to Christian influence, exhibit the fairy queen as a malignant demon who takes delight in corrupting the faith of true believers by plunging them into a horrible sensuality. Thus modified, the myth of Odysseus and Kalypsô appears as the story of Tanhaüser, whom Venus entices into her magic cave, within the Horselberg (Ercildoune) or mountain of Ursula. After a time the sensuous enjoyment of the place palls upon him as upon Odysseus, and he makes his escape to the earth with a weary load of sin upon his heart, for which he vainly seeks to obtain absolution.[2] At last he comes before pope Urban IV., who tells him that his pastoral staff will put forth leaves and blossoms sooner than God should pardon him. Tanhaüser has scarcely departed when the staff is seen to bloom; but it is too late. The minnesinger cannot be found, and he re-enters the Horselberg in despair, never to leave it again. Another modification, not less obvious and more in accordance with the spirit of the mediæval myth, would be that of mere sleep, and Endymiôn would thus become the

such fictions. 'In one of Plutarch's tracts, *De Defect. Orac.* 21, a certain Cleombrotus entertains the company with an account of an Eastern traveller whose character and fortunes are still more remarkable than those of the Scottish seer. Of this man we are told that he only appeared among his fellow mortals once a year. The rest of his time was spent in the society of nymphs and demons who had granted him an unusual share of personal beauty, had rendered him proof against disease, and supplied him with a fruit which was to satisfy his hunger, and of which he partook only once a month. He was, moreover, endowed with a miraculous gift of tongues; his conversation resembled a continuous flow of verse; his knowledge was universal, and an unusual visitation of prophetic fervour enabled him to unfold the hidden secrets of futurity.' This is practically the story of the Thrakian Zalmoxis, which Herodotos refuses to believe, iv. 94.

[1] Gould, *Curious Myths, &c.*, second series, 223.

[2] The same story is presented in the romance of Sir Launfal and the Fay Tryamour, who bestows on him the never-failing purse, and in the tale of Oberon and Huon of Bordeaux. This Oberon is the dwarf king Elberich of the Heldenbuch, who performs to Otnit the service discharged by Oberon to Huon. The story of Tanhaüser, again, is only another form of the legend of Ogier the Dane, who is Tithônos restored to a youth, which, like that of Meleagros, is to last as long as a brand which the fairy gives him remains unconsumed.—Keightley, *Fairy Mythology*, 34, et seq.

typo of other slumberers to whom a century was but as a
day. Among such is Epimenides, who while tending
sheep fell asleep one day in a cave, and did not wake until
more than fifty years had passed away. But Epimenides
was one of the Seven Sages, who reappear in the Seven
Manes of Leicester,[1] and in the Seven Champions of Christendom; and thus the idea of seven sleepers was at once
suggested. This idea finds expression in the remarkable
legend of the seven sleepers of Ephesus; and the number
seven is further traced by Mr. Gould through other mediæval
stories. 'Barbarossa changes his position every seven years.
Charlemagne starts in his chair at similar intervals. Olger
Dansk stamps his iron mace on the floor every seven years.'
To the number of these sleepers must be added Arthur who
slumbers in Avallon, waiting for the time when he shall
wake up to free Britain once more; Sebastian of Portugal;
the three Tells of Rütli; the priest of the Church of Hagia
Sophia, who bides the day when the Turk shall be driven
from Constantinople; and Boabdil, the last of the Moorish
kings of Spain, who lies spell-bound within the hill of the
Alhambra in a slumber broken only on the eve of St. John,[2]
who himself slumbers at Ephesus.

The same mystic number is found in the seven Rishis of
ancient Hindu traditions. These Rishis are the media or
instruments through which the divine Veda was imparted
to mankind. In its widest meaning the word was taken to
denote the priestly bards who conducted the worship of the
gods; but they are spoken of sometimes as the poets who
compose the songs and present them to the deities whom
they celebrate, and sometimes as the mere mouthpieces of
these gods. They are mortal, and yet they are united with
immortals, and are rivals of the gods. But although the idea
most promptly associated with them is that of wisdom, they
are sometimes mentioned in language which carries us back
to the etymological meaning of the name. With their true
hymns, we are told, they caused the dawn to arise and the

[1] Fergusson, *The Irish before the Conquest.*   *Alhambra,* 'Legend of the Two Discreet Statues.'
[2] Washington Irving, *Tales of the*

sun to shine for the afflicted Vayu and Manu.[1] The names
of the Rishis are variously given, Manu with Bhrigu,
Angiras and others, being sometimes reckoned among them :
but of the whole number seven attained a pre-eminent dignity. With Manu, according to one version, they entered
into the ark while the earth lay beneath the waters of the
flood, and therein abode with him until the vessel rested on
the peak called Naubandhana from the binding of the ship.
In the account of this flood the Brahmana story introduces a
fish which guides the ark as the Delphian Apollôn guides
the vessel of the Cretan mariners to Krisa.[2]

The Ark-
shas or
Shiners.
The main story connected with the Rishis has already
been noticed as the result of an equivocal word.[3] The notion
of making bright conveyed also the idea of gladdening and
cheering, and hence arkshah became a name not only for the
sun, but for a hymn or song of praise, and the makers or
singers of these hymns were naturally termed Rishis or
gladdeners. It was not less natural that, as the Rishis or
sages took a stronger hold on the imagination of the people,
the seven arkshas or stars should be converted into rishis,
and that the rishis should be said to have their abode in
them. Among the Western Aryans, as *lykos*, the glistening,
denoted the wolf, *arktos* became a name for the bear, and
stood to the Sanskrit riksha in the relation of the Greek
τέκτων, a carpenter, to takshan, and the Latin pectus, a
breast, to vakshas ;[4] and then the seven stars were necessarily converted into seven bears, while the sages whom
the Hindu placed in those shining orbs survived as the seven
wise men of Hellas, to reappear under different forms, as we
have already seen, elsewhere.

The Rishis
and Manu.
In the name of Manu, the friend of the Rishis, we have
simply and strictly *man*, as the measurer or the thinker.
The same root has also yielded names for the moon and the
month,[5] while in Europe, as in Asia, there arose the idea of

[1] *R. V.* viii. 76, 4, and 91, 1 ; Muir,
Sanskrit Texts, part iii. p. 119. During
this time of oppression and sorrow, it is
said that Vishnu thrice measured the
mundane regions for Manu. *R. V.* vi.
49, 13 ; Muir, *ib.* part iv. p. 71.

[2] Max Müller, *Sanskrit Literature*,
526.
[3] Book i. ch. iii.
[4] Max Müller, *Lectures on Language*,
second series, 361.
[5] Greek, μήν, μήνη : Latin, mensis.

a man of whom they spoke as the son of heaven and earth. CHAP.
II.
In India he was known as Manu Svayambhuva, the child of
Svayambhu, the self-existent, or, like the Hellenic Minos,
the son of Europê, the dawn, as Vaivasti, the worshipper or
child of Vivasvat, the sun, whose wife Saranyû, having borne
the twin Asvins, the steeds or horsemen, left in her place
another like herself, Savarna, who became the mother of
Manu.[1] But Manu is also not unfrequently called the son
of Dyaus or of Brahma, just as the German tribes spoke of
their ancestor Manu as the son of Tiw or Tuisco.

SECTION V.—DAWN GODDESSES.

The name Ushas reappears in the Greek Eôs, and Ushas, Ushas and Eôs.
like Eôs, is the goddess of the dawn or morning.[2] The
language addressed to her betokens a more distinct personality than that even of Varuna and Indra, because the worshipper in addressing her speaks always from the heart, and
his words are the manifest utterances of love. She is the
daughter of the heaven, who brings with her light and life
and joy; she drives away pain and anguish; she is the
image of undying youth, for day by day she appears in
unfading beauty, although they who look upon her grow
daily older and at last die.[3]

[1] Professor Max Müller, *Lectures on Language*, second series, 482, 509, thinks that Manu may have been called Savarni, as meaning the Manu of all colours, i.e. of all tribes or castes, while Savarna, the second wife of the sun, is simply the twilight in which he dies, just as the myth that Saranyû had left her twins behind, meant only that the Dawn had disappeared. The root *man* is taken also to denote 'backward thought, remembering and admonishing; whence the proper name Mentor, the adviser.' With this may be compared the name Juno Moneta : and thus Athênê, when she appears among the suitors before the great vengeance of Odysseus, is naturally said to assume the likeness of Mentor.

[2] The root US, to burn, appears as USH in Sanskrit. From this Ushas is formed without any vowel modification, 'The Græco-Italian people raised the vowel by regular process to *au*, and formed *ausos*, which received no further increase in Greek, but in Latin a secondary noun was formed from the primary one, that is *ausosa*. Now both Greeks and Italians, as is well known, disliked the sound *s* between two vowels: the Greeks generally dropped it, and so got *aὐ(σ)ώs*: the Latins changed it to *r*, and made *aurora*: the verb appears as *uro*.'—Peile, *Introduction to Greek and Latin Etymology*, xii. The Lithuanian form of the word is Ausera.

[3] Hence the decrepitude of some of the mythical beings beloved by the Dawn. This is the idea of the myth of Eôs and Tithonos, and it seems to be united with that of Odin, Savitri, or Odysseus the wanderers, in the story of the Wandering Jew. The myth is here, as we might expect, strangely distorted : but the Jew must wander on until the evening of the world is come.

'Ushas, nourishing all, comes daily like a matron, conducting all transient (creatures) to decay.'[1]

'The divine and ancient Ushas, born again and again and
bright with unchanging hues, wastes away the life of a
mortal, like the wife of a hunter cutting up the birds.'[2]

'How long is it that the dawns have risen? How long
will they rise?

'Those mortals who beheld the pristine Ushas dawning
have passed away: to us she is now visible, and they approach who will behold her in after times.'[3]

Like the Greek Athênê, she is pure and unsullied, the
image of truth and wisdom.

'Ushas, endowed with truth, who art the sister of Bhava,
the sister of Varuna, be thou hymned first of the gods.'

'Unimpeding divine rites, although wearing away the ages
of mankind, the Dawn shines the likeness of the mornings
that have passed, or that are to be for ever, the first of those
that are to come.'[4]

In all this, although it determines the source of later
myths beyond all possibility of question, there is little or no
mythology; and we have advanced scarcely more than half-
way on the road to a full-formed myth even when we read
that 'the night, her sister, prepares a birth-place for her
elder sister (the day), and having made it known to her
departs;'[5] that the night and dawn 'of various complexions,
repeatedly born but ever youthful, have traversed in their
revolutions alternately from a remote period earth and heaven
—night with her dark, dawn with her luminous limbs,'[6] or
that 'of all the sisters who have gone before a successor
daily follows the one that has preceded.'[7] It is this very
transparency of meaning which imparts value to almost
every expression of praise in the hymns addressed to her.

'She shines upon us like a young wife, rousing every
living being to go to his work. The fire had to be kindled
by men: she brought light by striking down darkness.

[1] H. H. Wilson, *R. V. Sanhita*, i. 129.
[2] *Ib.* i. 274.   [3] *Ib.* i. 298.
[4] *Ib.* ii. 8. 10.   [5] *Ib.* ii. 12.
[6] *Ib.* i. 169.
[7] *Ib.* ii. 12. The idea of Ushas as
bringing to an end the days which

spring from her is closely allied to the
myth of Kronos, and seems to lie at the
root of the many popular German and
Norse stories, in which the bride of the
king is accused of being a murderess
who destroys her own children.

'She rose up, spreading far and wide, and moving towards every one she grew in brightness, wearing her brilliant garment. The mother of the cows, the leader of the dogs, she shone gold-coloured, lovely to behold.

'She, the fortunate, who brings the eye of the god, who leads the white and lovely steed (of the sun), the Dawn was seen revealed by her rays, with brilliant treasures she follows every one.

'Thou, who art a blessing when thou art near, drive far away the unfriendly; make the pastures wide, give us safety. Remove the haters, bring treasures. Raise up wealth to the worshipper, thou mighty Dawn.

'Shine for us with thy best rays, thou bright Dawn, thou who lengthenest our life, thou the love of all, who givest us food, who givest us wealth in cows, horses, and chariots.' [1]

The hymns speak especially of the broad-spreading light of Ushas; and this flush of dawn suddenly passing across the heaven takes us at once to the many names of like meaning which belong to the Hellenic solar beings. She 'shines wide' (Urvasî), like Euryphassa and Eurydikê, like Euryganeia, Eurynomê, and Eurôpê. As the daughter of Dyaus, who chases away the darkness of the night, she goes before Indra, Savitar, and Sûrya. She reveals mysteries and opens the ends of heaven, where the Panis had hidden away the cows of which she is the mother. She tells the Angiras where they are to be found, and as she lightens the sky she is said to drive her own herds to their pastures. She is sent especially to awaken men; but she is charged to let the Panis (the dark powers) sleep. She is the beloved of all men and the darling of the god of love, Aniruddha, the resistless,[2] who thus receives the name Ushâpati, lord of the dawn; and finally, we have in Ushas the germ of the idea which found its most graceful expression in the Hellenic Athênê, and its most majestic developement in the Latin Minerva. The Sanskrit *budh* means both to wake and to know, and *vayuná* has the double meaning of light and knowledge, just as the notions of knowledge and of creative power are both expressed by the root *jan* and the English

Ushas the broad-spreading.

---

[1] *R. V.* vii. 77.   [2] ἔρως ἀνίκατε μάχαν.—Soph. *Ant.* 781.

can and *ken.* Hence Ushas is said to enable men to cross the frontier of darkness, and, as the seer, to give light far and wide. 'Waking every mortal to walk about, she receives praise from every thinker.' Thus, as the Day, she is the mother of the Divine Night, who reveals all her splendour after she has driven away her sister the Twilight.[1] Of the birth of Athênê fully armed from the head of Zeus, when cloven by the axe of Hephaistos, the poets of the Iliad and Odyssey say nothing; but the presence of the story in the Hesiodic Theogony is a conclusive argument against any inference which might be drawn from their silence, even if Ushas were not, as she actually is, spoken of in the Veda as sprung from the forehead of Dyaus, the sky.[2]

Ahanâ.
But Ushas is only one of many names for the light of early morning. As Ahanâ, she plays the part as well as bears the name of Athênê and of Daphnê. The word expresses the idea of burning light; and although it occurs only once in the Rig Veda,[3] the flexibility of the old mythology justifies us in attributing to Ahanâ all that is told us of Ushas or of Saramâ.[4] If then we apply to Dahanâ the phrases which spoke of Ushas as pursued by the Sun, who slays though he loves her, or as dying in his arms, we see at once an offshoot from the parent stem which in the West yielded the myths of Daphnê and of Prokris. Daphnê too is loved by Phoibos, and, like Ahanâ, she flies from his face until she takes refuge in the Peneian stream. But in some passages of the Veda the idea of her might remains too prominent to allow much room for that of love.

'This strong and manly deed also thou hast performed, O Indra, that thou struckest the daughter of Dyaus, a woman difficult to vanquish.

---

[1] The benignant aspect of night must be carefully borne in mind, as the germ of the myths of Asteria, Asterodia, Kalypsô, and other Fairy Queens. Under all these forms we have the νὺξ φιλία μεγάλων κόσμων κτεάτειρα of Æschylos. *Agam.* 356. As such, Night is invoked in the Veda to 'drive away the wolf and the thief, and carry her worshippers safely across' (to the light). —*R. V.* x. 127; Muir, *Sanskrit Texts,* part iv. p. 123.

[2] Max Müller, *Lectures on Language,* second series, 503.

[3] 'Ahanâ comes near to every house, she who makes every day to be known. 'Dyotana (the dawn), the active maiden, comes back for evermore: she enjoys always the first of all goods.'— *R. V.* i. 123, 4.

[4] 'Athênê, as far as letters go, would correspond to a Sanskrit Ahanâ, which is but a slightly differing variety of Ahanâ.'—Max Müller, *Lectures,* second series, 503.

'Yes, even the daughter of Dyaus, the magnified, the Dawn, thou, O Indra, a great hero, hast ground to pieces.

'The Dawn rushed off from her crushed car, fearing that Indra, the bull, might strike her.

'This her car lay there, well ground to pieces. She went far away.' [1]

More commonly, however, she is beloved by all the gods, and the Asvins bear her away triumphant in her chariot.

But it is to the phrases which speak of the dawn under the name of Saramâ, that we must look for the germ of the great epics of the western Aryans. It is indeed only the germ, and no fancy can be more thoroughly groundless than that which would regard the Hellenic representative of Saramâ as derived from the dawn-goddess of the Hindu. Identity of names and of attributes can prove nothing more than the affinity of legends, which, as differing not only in local colour but also in the form of thought, must point to some common source in a past yet more remote. Whatever may be the precise meaning of the name, whether Saramâ or Saranyû be taken to denote the storm-cloud or the morning, there is no doubt that the root of the word is *sar*, to creep or go, which we find in *serpent* as well as in the Greek Erinys and Sarpêdôn. In the Rig Veda, Saramâ is especially the guardian of the cows of Indra, and as his messenger she goes to the Panis, who have stolen them away. She, too, like Ushas, is said to be the first to spy out the cleft in the rock where the Panis, like Cacus, had hid the plundered cattle, and, like Herakles, she is the first to hear their lowings. Like Ushas also, she walks in a straight path: but when she comes to the stronghold of the Panis, a conference follows in which we see unmistakably the dawn peering about through the sky in search of the bright clouds, and restoring them in all their brilliance and beauty to the broad pastures of the heaven.

'The Panis said, "With what intention did Saramâ reach this place? for the way is far, and leads tortuously away. What was your wish with us? How was the night? How did you cross the waters of the Râsa?"

Saramâ

---

[1] *R. V.* iv. 30.

'*The Panis*: "What kind of man is Indra, O Saramâ, what is his look, he as whose messenger thou comest from afar? Let him come hither, and we will make friends with him, and then he may be the cowherd of our cows."

'*Saramá*: "I do not know that he is to be subdued, for it is he himself that subdues, he as whose messenger I came hither from afar. Deep streams do not overwhelm him; you, Panis, will lie prostrate, killed by Indra."

'*The Panis*: "Those cows, O Saramâ, which thou desirest, fly about the ends of the sky, O darling. Who would give them up to thee without fighting? for our weapons too are sharp."

'*Saramá*: "Though your words, O Panis, be unconquerable, though your wretched bodies be arrowproof, though the way to you be hard to go, Brihaspati will not bless you for either."

'*The Panis*: "That store, O Saramâ, is fastened to the rock, furnished with cows, horses, and treasures. Panis watch it who are good watchers; thou art come in vain to this bright place."

'*Saramá*: "Let the Rishis come here fired with Soma, Ahasŷa (Indra), and the ninefold Angiras: they will divide the stable of cows; then the Panis will vomit out this speech."

'*The Panis*: "Even thus, O Saramâ, thou art come hither, driven by the violence of the gods; let us make thee our sister, do not go away again; we will give thee part of the cows, O darling."

'*Saramá*: "I know nothing of brotherhood or sisterhood: Indra knows it, and the awful Angiras. They seemed to me anxious for their cows when I came: therefore get away from here, O Panis, far away.

"Go far away, Panis, far away; let the cows come out straight, the cows which Brihaspati found hid away, Soma, the stones, and the wise Rishis." '[1]

This hymn, seemingly so transparent in its meaning, becomes unintelligible if interpreted of any other being than

---

[1] Max Müller, *Lectures on Language*, second series, 465.

the Dawn in her struggle with the powers of darkness : and
hence it seems a superfluous task to show that all the essential
features of Ushas reappear in Saramå ; that like Ushas Saramå
is followed by Indra, and that walking first she reveals the
treasures which had been hidden away ; that both alike go
to the uttermost ends of heaven; that both break the strong-
holds of the Paṇis; both are the mothers and deliverers of
the cows; both drive forth their cattle to the pastures; both
walk in the right path and bestow wealth and blessings upon
men. Every phrase tells us of some change in the heaven
from the time when the sun sinks to sleep in the west to the
moment when his face is first seen again in the east. As
the light of evening dies away, the power of the darkness is
restored, and the Paṇis extinguish the bright-coloured clouds
which have looked down on the death of the Sun, or in other
words they steal the cows of Indra, the cattle which Phaethousa and Lampetiê feed in the rich pastures of Helios. During the weary hours of night they are shut up in the demon's
prison-house ; but at length the messenger of the day comes to
reclaim her children. With a faint flush she starts slowly
from the doors of the east. Her light, creeping along the
dark face of the sky, seems to ebb and flow like the sea-
tide ; and so might Saramå be said to hold parley with the
Paṇis who refuse to yield up their plunder. But the Dawn
is only the messenger of one far mightier than herself, and
if they will not yield to her, they shall feel the force of the
arm of Indra ; and the conference with the Paṇis, which
answers to the spreading of the Dawn, ends in their overthrow, as soon as Indra appears in his chariot—in other
words, when the Sun is risen.

In the Rig Veda, Saramå steadily refuses the bribes offered
to her by the Paṇis. Another turn was given to the tale
when the faithfulness of Saramå was represented as not invincible. Saramå, we are told in the Anukramanika, was
sent as the dog of the gods to seek for the strayed or stolen
herds, and when she espied them in the town of Vala, the
Paṇis strove to make her an accomplice in their theft. But
although she refused to divide the booty, she yet drank a
cup of milk which they gave her, and returning to Indra

denied that she had seen the cows. On this Indra kicked her, and the milk which she vomited up gave the lie to her words. Here, then, we have in its germ the faithlessness of the Spartan Helen, who in name as in her act is Saramâ,[1] and who speaks of herself as the dog-eyed or dog-faced, although by none else is the name ever applied to her. Thus the Greek carried away with him the root of the great Trojan epic from the time when he parted from his ancient kinsfolk, he to find his way to his bright Hellenic home, they to take up their abode in the land of the seven streams. For him, Helen and Paris, Brisêis and Achilleus were already in existence. For him Phoibos already dwelt in Delos, and Sarpêdôn ruled in the land of the golden river. So, again, it makes but little difference whether the Sarameya, sometimes but rarely mentioned in the Rig Veda, be definitely the son of Saramâ, or whether the word remained a mere epithet for any one of the gods who might denote the morning. The name itself is etymologically identical with that of Hermes; and the fact that he is addressed as the watchdog of the house[2] may have led to the notion which made him in later times the hound which served as the messenger of the gods, and which in the story of Prokris reappears at the feet of Artemis.[3]

Saranyû.   Another name from the same root which has furnished

---

[1] See Appendix F.

[2] Professor Müller notices that in a hymn of the seventh book of the *Rig Veda*, Vastoshpati, the lord of the house, a kind of Lar, is called Sarameya, and is certainly addressed as the watchdog of the house; and he adds that this deity would thus denote the 'peep of day conceived as a person, watching unseen at the doors of heaven during the night and giving his first bark in the morning.' The features of the deity thus conceived are brought out with sufficient clearness in the following verses:

'When thou, bright Sarameya, openest thy teeth, O red one, spears seem to glisten on thy jaws as thou swallowest. Sleep, sleep.
'Bark at the thief, Sarameya, or at the robber, O restless one. Now thou barkest at the worshippers of Indru.

Why dost thou distress us? Sleep sleep.'—*Lectures on Language*, second series, 473.

[3] This dog of the morning is prominent in the Norse tale of Bushy Bride. While the hero lies in a pit full of snakes (Helios in the land of the throttling serpent), a lovely lady (Ushas or Saramâ) comes into the palace kitchen—the connection, as with Boots or Cinderella among the ashes, lying in the fire of the hearth or oven—and asks the kitchen-maid for a brush. 'Then she brushed her hair, and as she brushed down dropped gold. A little dog was at her heel, and to him she said "Run out little Flo, and see if it will soon be day." This she said three times, and the third time that she sent the dog it was just about the time the dawn begins to peep.' The old myth could not be retained with greater fidelity.

those of Saramâ, Helen, Hermes, and Sarpêdôn, is found in
Saranyû (a feminine of Saranyu), in whom some discern the
dark and impetuous stormcloud.[1] The phrases employed
when the poet addresses her all seem to point in another
direction. Like Ushas, she is spoken of as the mare, and as
the mother of twins. The male Saranyu is in like manner
called a horse, and the goddess herself is the mother of the
twins Yama and Yami, and again of Nasatya and Dasra, the
twin Asvins or steeds, who represent the Dioskouroi. The
persons with whom this dualism connects her indicate at
once her real nature, and with Saranyu she takes her place
by the side of the two Ahans or Dawns, of Indrâ, the two
Indras, of Dyavâ, the double Dyaus, of Ushasau, the two
mornings, of Agnî, the two Agnis, of Varunâ, the two
Varunas.

But as Saramâ is Helen, so Saranyû is Erinys; and here
too the seed, which in the East sprang up only to wither
away, shot up in the West to a portentous growth. It was
certainly no Euphemism which spoke of the Erinyes as the
gentle beings or Eumenides, and there was no incongruity
in giving the name to the Dawn-mother Dêmêtêr.[2] Hence
in spite of all the failure of memory, and of the fearful character which Erinys had assumed, the poet who tells the
terrible tale of Oidipous could not but make him die in the
sacred grove of beings who, however awful to others, were
always benignant to him—in groves which to the storm-
tossed wanderer were the Hyperborean gardens into which
grief, and fear, and anguish could never enter. The change
which converted the beautiful Saranyû into the avenging
furies of Æschylos has excited the wonder of some who
hesitate on this account to believe that Erinys and Saranyû
can come to us from a common source. It is more than
probable that their scepticism arises from the notion that
comparative mythologists derive the Greek from the Sanskrit
deity. It is enough to say that they do not.

The change itself is one which could scarcely fail to be

Erinys.

The
Harpies.

---

[1] Roth, quoted by Professor Max
Müller, *ib.* 404. The name itself, as in
Hermes, Saramâ, and ὁρμή, may express
any motion, slow or rapid.

[2] Professor Max Müller seems to
see in Dêmêtêr, not the earth, but the
dawn-mother, Dyâvâ Mâtur, corresponding to Dyauspitar.—*Ib.* 517.

brought about. The Harpies, who in our Homeric poems
are the beautiful daughters of Thaumas and Elektra, appear
in the Æneid of Virgil as foul monsters, who do the work of
vultures. The Ara, or prayer of the longing heart,[1] became
more and more the curse which the weak uttered against
their tyrants. Indra and Phoibos, who, as the sun-gods, see
and hear all things, become almost more dreaded for their
destructive power, than loved for their beneficence. As
representing the day with its searching light, Varuṇa and
Indra are the avengers of all iniquity; and in this sense it
could not fail to be said of evil-doers that Saranyû would
find them out. The old phrase survives with its clearness
scarcely dimmed in the Hesiodic Theogony. Night there is
the mother of Strife (Eris), and of all the evils that come of
Strife;[2] but she is also the mother of righteous recompense
(Nemesis). In other words, the evil deeds done in the night
will receive their reward when brought to light in the day;
and thus, according to Æschylos the Erinyes also are
daughters of the Night, who, like the Drukhs, the Vedic
Atê, track out the sins of men. It was in truth impossible
that, the germ once given, its developements should fail to
be modified by time and place, by power of imagination and
failure of memory. The Atê of the Iliad is the spirit merely
of mischievous folly, and as such, she is hurled by Zeus from
Olympos, for postponing the birth of Herakles to that of
Eurystheus; the Atê of Æschylos is the sleepless doom
which broods over a house until the vengeance for the
shedding of innocent blood has been exacted to the uttermost farthing. There is nothing wonderful therefore in the
process which changed the lovely Saranyû of the Veda into
the awful goddesses[3] of Athens; and if the Erinys of the
Iliad is called hateful, yet she wanders in the air and hears
the summons addressed to her from the land of darkness.[4]
In the fact that at Athens there were statues only of two
Erinyes, we have perhaps a memory of that early dualism
which is so marked a feature in the mythology of the Veda.

Arjuni.
But if Eôs and Zeus remained to the Greeks what Ushas

---

[1] ἀρὴν ἐποιήσαντο παῖδα γενέσθαι.—
Herod. vi. 63.

[2] Hes. Theog. 226.

[3] σεμναὶ θεαί.

[4] Il. x. 571.

and Dyaus were to the Hindu, there were other names which seem to have been transplanted to Hellenic soil only to die. Among these is Argennos in whose honour Agamemnon is said to have built a temple to Aphroditê Argynnis on the banks of Kephîsos. The name in the West had no meaning: but in the Vedic Arjunî we have simply an epithet denoting the brilliance of the dawn, while in the later Hindu mythology, Arjuna comes before us as standing to Krishna in the relation of Luxman to Rama, of Phaëthôn to Helios, or of Patroklos to Achilleus.

The analysis of all these myths proves convincingly that for human thought in its earliest stages the danger lay not in the poverty of language, but in its superabundant wealth. The heaven, the sun, the dawn, the clouds, might be described by a thousand names, all truthfully and vividly denoting the thing spoken of in one of its countless aspects. But the characteristic features so marked were found in more than one object. If the sun shone brightly or moved rapidly, so did the horse. If the clouds gave nourishment to the thirsty earth, so did the cows bestow a gift scarcely less necessary for man. The words which told of the one would serve also to designate the other; and so in fact we find that they did. The cow received its name as the moving animal; the horse was named from its speed, asvan, or from its colour, harit, the glistening—rohit, the brown: and all these names were of necessity applied to the sun, the dawn, and the sky, first in their strictly etymological sense, but insensibly, and by an inevitable result, in the meaning to which usage gradually confined each word. Thus, when the name asvan was reserved especially for the horse, the sun, who had been hitherto called asvan simply as speeding through the sky, now himself became the steed who hurries across the broad heaven.[1] The impulse once given issued in an almost incredible wealth of metaphor. The horse as the bearer of burdens was called vahni;[2] but the flames also bore their burdens into the air, and the rays of the sun

The cows and horses of the Sun-gods.

---

[1] The process is completely analysed by Professor Max Müller, 'Comparative Mythology,' *Chips, &c.* ii. 132, &c.

[2] The root is found in the Latin *vehere*, the Greek ἔχειν, and in compound words as *cervix*, the neck, as carrying the head.

brought his light to man. Thus the flame of fire and the solar rays, being both alike vahni, became vehement and fiery horses. So, too, the morning and the evening, the gloaming and the dawn, became, as we have seen, twin steeds—the Asvins—joined together in a mysterious bond which made it impossible to draw a line between the approach of the one and the vanishing of the other. But this step taken rendered another step necessary. The glorious being whose light wakes a sleeping world to life must be enthroned in a burning chariot, of which the rays that stream across the heaven must be the gleaming steeds; and thus the sun who had himself been Hari, the flashing, now became Indra, or Sûrya, or Savitar, whose car was drawn by the glistening Harits. Where we say that 'the sun is rising,' or that 'he is high in the heaven,' they said, 'the sun has yoked his steeds for his journey,' or that 'his horses have borne his chariot to the house of Dyaus.' But how little the name Harit had lost its original meaning, is clear from the many terms which are used in describing them. The Vedic poet knew well the differences of meaning in the words which he uttered when he spoke of them as Harits, or Rohits, or Arushis; yet under each of these names was growing up a distinct personality, and thus the Harits, whose number is given sometimes as seven, sometimes as ten, become sisters who fly on beautiful wings.[1] But while even in India, the idea of loveliness was beginning to predominate over that of mere animal strength, among the Western Aryans the glistening Harits became the lovely Charites whom the Latins called the Gratiæ and we the Graces. Yet by the side of these fair creations of human thought, the root which yielded these names was discharging a more homely function: and the grease with which our wheels are rubbed is but another form of the names of Charis in the Iliad, and the Graces of Canova.

Arushi.
Arushi, however, is only the feminine form of arvan, a horse; and the masculine arusha is a common Vedic epithet for the sun. But this name is applied to him only at his rising. He is arusha, when 'Night goes away from her sister the

[1] Max Müller, *Chips, &c.* ii. 131.

dawn, and the dark one opens the path for the bright god.' But arusha is also a child. 'The seven sisters have nursed him, the joyful, the white one, as he was born, the Arusha with great might; as horses go to the foal that is born, so did the gods bring up his son when he was born.' [1] He has the eyes of a man, and he is also Saparnas, with beautiful wings. More evidence can scarcely be needed to show that in this picture we have the Hellenic god of love, the bright and winged Erôs. But further, as Professor Max Müller has noted in his exhaustive analysis of this myth, Arusha is called the young child of Dyaus, the child of heaven, the sun of strength. He is the first of the gods, as coming at the point of the days; and of his two daughters (the Snow-White and Rose-Red of German folk-lore), the one is clad in stars, the other is the wife of Svar, the sun. He moves swift as thought, longing for victory: he is the love or desire, Kama, of all men; and as irresistible in his strength, he is Ushâpati, lord of the dawn. With all these phrases the mythology of the Greeks is in thorough harmony. Although, according to later poets, Erôs is a son of Zeus and of Gaia, or Aphroditê, or Artemis, we may fairly assert that in the Hesiodic theogony, as in the Veda, he is 'the first of the gods,' for with Chaos, Gaia, and Tartaros, he makes up the number of self-existent deities. Still, although appearing thus in the awful silence of a formless universe, he is the most beautiful of all the gods, and he conquers the mind and will both of gods and of men. The transition was easy to the thought of Erôs, ever bright and fair as (like Yavishtha or Hephaistos) the youngest of the gods, as the companion of the Charites, as the child of the Charis Aphroditê : and this association of Erôs and Charis brings us back to Arusha and the glistening Harits, who bear him across the wide seas of heaven.[2]

[1] This is precisely the picture of the Muses nursing the infant Phoibos in the Homeric hymn. Max Müller, *ib.* 136.

[2] In his notes on the *Rig Veda Sanhita*, vol. i. p. 11, Professor Max Müller, noting the objections made to some of his interpretations of passages in which the word Arusha occurs, on the ground that in them the word is an epithet of Agni, Indra, or Sûrya, remarks that this objection would apply 'to many other names originally intended for these conceptions, but which, nevertheless, in the course of time, become independent names of independent deities.'

The brilliant steeds reappear in the myth of Medeia as the dragons who bear her mysterious chariot through the air. The name dragon, indeed, denotes simply any keen-sighted thing, and in its other form, Dorkas, is applied to a gazelle. We shall presently see that a sharp distinction is drawn between the serpent as an object of love and affection, and the snake which is regarded (whether as Ahi, Vritra, or Ahriman) with profound hatred. But the serpent-worship of the East and West is founded on the emblem of the Linga,[1] and belongs to a class of ideas altogether different from those which were awakened by the struggle of darkness against the light and the sun. This darkness is everywhere described as a snake or serpent : but the names applied to Ahi and Vritra do not imply keenness of sight, and the enemy of Indra and Phoibos becomes on Hellenic soil a dragon, only because the beast had there received this as its special name. The tradition, however, survived that the steeds of the sun were also Drakontes or keen-eyed things, and thus they not only draw the chariot of Medeia, but reveal to Iamos the knowledge of things to come. These snakes who nurse the infant prophet on the violet beds are the flashing-eyed messengers of morning, not the devouring serpents of darkness who seek to slay the new-born Herakles in his cradle.

As possessing this gift of the dragon-chariot bestowed on her by Helios, Medeia is emphatically the wise woman ; and in this myth we have probably the groundwork of those notions which were finally developed into the system of sorcery and witchcraft. The knowledge of Medeia came to her from the same superhuman source with the inspiration of the Pythian priestess of Delphoi ; the Latin witch derived her power from a secret compact with Hekatê. Christianity converted Phoibos and his sister into demons ; and at once the Canidias of the empire were regarded as trafficking with devils for the acquisition of unlawful powers. In the transition from the idea of a wisdom which, although not naturally attainable, might be conferred on some by the bright being whose eye pierces all space, to the notion of compacts made

[1] See Section XII. of this chapter.

between witches and the devil we have a developement or corruption in close analogy with that confusion between Leukos, bright, as a general epithet, and the same word Lukos, as a special name for the wolf, from which sprung first the myth of the transformation of Lykûôn, and then probably the wide-spread superstition of Lykanthropy.[1]

As the wise woman, Medeia is the child of the ocean nymph Idyia, or, in another version, of Hekatê (the female correlative of Hekatos or Phoibos), who is herself the daughter of Asteria, the starlit night. Her father is Aiêtês, the Kolchian king, but he is a son of Helios who leaves to him and his descendants the magic wreath and robe by which Medeia revenges herself on Glaukê.[2] This robe is, indeed, only another form of the golden fleece, the mantle of burnished cloud seen at sunrise and sunset. As such, it eats into the flesh not only of Glaukê, the fair daughter of the Corinthian Kreôn, but of Herakles himself, when his toils come to an end on mount Oita. Of her share in the victory of Iasôn at Aia, it is enough here to say that in the taming of the fire-breathing bulls, and in the discomfiture of the men sprung from the dragon's teeth, she plays the part of Ariadnê and receives Ariadnê's reward. Whether faithful or treacherous, the sun can never remain with his first love, and even Odysseus, whose one longing is to return to his home, is parted from Penelopê during the weary hours which pass between sunset and sunset. But before the time of her great sorrow comes, Medeia avenges the wrongs done to Iasôn long ago at Iolkos. During her sojourn there in the house of Pelias, she persuaded his daughters to cut up his body and boil his limbs in a cauldron, in the belief that he would thus be restored to youth.[3] Medeia purposely failed to pronounce the spell at the right time, and the limbs of Pelias were consumed by the fire. Then follows her escape with Iasôn in her dragon chariot to Corinth, where his love is trans-

CHAP. II.

The story of Medeia.

---

[1] See Appendix F.

[2] Eurip. *Med.* 957.

[3] With this may be compared the Norse story of the Master Smith, in whom we see another form of Hephaistos or Way- and. The incident of the cutting up of the body of Pelias occurs also in the German story of Brother Lustig. Medeia herself appears in benignant guise in the legend of the Goose-girl at the Well (the Dawn-maiden with her snow-white clouds).

ferred to Glaukê, after whose death Medeia, like Gudrun in the Volsung story, slays her own children—a crime closely resembling the slaughter of Pelops by Tantalos. Such are the chief features of the myth of Medeia, to which some added that she became the wife of Aigeus, the Athenian king, or of the Corinthian Sisyphos. Some, again, made her return with Iasôn to Kolchis, while others took her to Italy, and described her as acquiring the name Anguitia from her power of fascinating serpents. Finally, she is said to have been wedded to Achilleus in Elysion.

The myth of Prokris. The involuntary departure of the sun from the dawn or his capricious desertion of her is exhibited in the myths of a long series of maidens wooed and forsaken, whether by Phoibos himself or by heroes on whose head rests his light and majesty. With the story of Korônis the mother of Asklêpios the myth of Prokris is in close accordance. Her birthplace is Athens, the city of the Dawn, and her mother is Hersê, the Dew, while her own name denotes also simply the sparkling drops.[1] We are thus prepared for the myth which tells us that Kephalos, a Phokian chief, coming to Athens, won her love and plighted his faith to her. But Kephalos was loved also by Eôs, who sought to weaken his love for Prokris with a purpose so persistent that at last she induced him to make trial of her affection. He therefore deserts Prokris, to whom after a time he returns in disguise. When in this shape he has won her love, he reveals himself, and Prokris in an agony of grief and shame flies to Crete, where she obtains from Artemis the gift of a spear which shall never miss its mark and of a hound which can never fail to seize its prey.[2] With these

[1] Professor Max Müller, refers Prokris to the Sanskrit prush and prish, to sprinkle, used chiefly of raindrops. 'The same root in the Teutonic languages has taken the sense of "frost," and Bopp identifies prush with the O. H. G. frus, frigere. In Greek we must refer to the same root πρώξ, πρωκός, a dewdrop, and also Prokris, the dew. Thus the wife of Kephalos is only a repetition of Hersê, her mother—Hersê, dew, being derived from Sanskrit prish, to sprinkle.'—'Comparative My-

thology,' Chips, &c. ii. 87.
[2] In the myth of Ikaros, or Ikarios, this dog appears under the name Maira (the glistening), who helps Erigonê the daughter of Ikarios in her search for the body of her father, who has been slain by the peasants and thrown into the well Anygros (the parched). Her grief leads her to hang herself on a tree under which he was buried, a myth which suggests a comparison with that of Helenê Dendritis. Ikaros, the son of Daidalos, is only a reflection of Phaëthon.

gifts she returns to Kephalos, who after seeing her success in the chase longs to possess them. But they can be yielded only in return for his love, and thus Prokris brings home to him the wrong done to herself, and Eôs is for the time discomfited. But Prokris still fears the jealousy of Eôs and watches Kephalos as he goes forth to hunt, until, as one day she lurked among the thick bushes, the unerring dart of Artemis hurled by Kephalos brings the life of the gentle Prokris to an end. This myth explains itself. Kephalos is the head of the sun, and Kephalos loves Prokris,—in other words, the sun loves the dew. But Eôs also loves Kephalos, i.e. the dawn loves the sun, and thus at once we have the groundwork for her envy of Prokris. So again when we are told that, though Prokris breaks her faith, yet her love is still given to the same Kephalos, different though he may appear, we have here only a myth formed from phrases which told how the dew seems to reflect many suns which are yet the same sun. The gifts of Artemis are the rays which flash from each dewdrop, and which Prokris is described as being obliged to yield up to Kephalos, who slays her as unwittingly as Phoibos causes the death of Daphnê or Alpheios that of Arethousa. The spot where she dies is a thicket, in which the last dewdrops would linger before the approach of the midday heats.

The various incidents belonging to the life of Eôs are so transparent that the legend can scarcely be said to be a myth at all. Her name is, as we have seen, that of the Vedic dawn-goddess Ushas, and she is a daughter of Hyperion (the soaring sun) and of Euryphassa (the broad shining), and a sister of the sun and moon (Helios and Selênê). If Ovid calls her a child of Pallas, this is only saying again that she is the offspring of the dawn. Like Phoibos and Herakles, she has many loves; but from all she is daily parted. Every morning she leaves the couch of Tithônos,[1] and drawn by the gleaming steeds Lampos and Phaëthôn, rises into heaven to announce to the gods and to mortal men the coming of the sun. In the Odyssey she closes, as she began, the day. Her love, which is given to

---

[1] The lot of Tithônos is simply the reverse of that of Endymiôn.

Tithônos and Kephalos is granted also to Oriôn (the sun in
his character as the hunting and far-shooting god), whom
according to one version she conveys to Delos, the bright
land, but who in another is slain by the arrow of Artemis.
She also carries to the home of the gods the beautiful
Kleitos. Her children are born in many lands. As united
with Astraios, the starry, she is the mother of Zephyros,
Boreas, and Notos, the breezes or winds of morning, and
of Heôsphoros, the light-bringer. Another son of Eôs is
Phaëthôn, whom mythographers made the father of the luck-
less son of Helios, but who is really the same being with his
son. Finally, she is the mother of Memnôn, the chieftain
from the glistening land of the Aithiopians (Ethiopians),
who falls by the spear of Antilochos, and on whose death she
weeps tears of morning dew, and obtains from Zeus the
boon that he shall rise again to renewed and endless life.

Hébé and
Gany-
mêdê.
Another form of Eôs is the beautiful Hêbê, ever young,
on whom is bestowed without any drawback the youthful-
ness of the maimed Hêphaistos. She is the daughter necessarily of Zeus and Hêrê. Like the Vedic Ahanâ or Ushas
she can make the old young again, and she ministers to
the gods the life-giving nectar and ambrosia. But Hêbê,
though the bride of the deified Herakles, or the mother of
his children Alexiarês and Anikêtos, the invincible deliverers,
remains little more than a name. She is Ganymêdê, the
brilliant; and thus what Iris is to Hermes, that is Hêbê to
Ganymêdês, the lovely Trojan youth who is borne away on
the eagle's wing to the Olympian heaven, where he also
became the immortal cup-bearer of the gods. Thus in both
alike we see the morning light carried up into heaven on
the wings of the sunlit cloud. ·

The story
of Dido
and Anna.
The same story of unrequited love which has been embodied in the myths of Ariadnê and Medeia, of Selênê and
Echo, meets us again in the legends which the Latin poets
modified to suit their own traditions, or their prejudices and
fancies. But although Virgil has chosen to mix up the
story of Dido with that of Æneas (Aineias), he has introduced into it little or nothing which is not found in the
myth as related by Justin. In fact, the story of Aphroditê

or Daphnê is twice told in the life of Dido, for the Sichæus or Acerbas whose death she bewails is the Adonis who, like Sichæus, is slain by the dark being or power of night. As the Panis look greedily on the cattle of Indra, Pygmalion covets the vast treasures which Sichæus possesses with Tantalos, Sisyphos, Helen and Brynhild, or Ixîôn; and thus is the husband of Dido murdered, her first and, according to the version of Justin, her only love, and his wealth is in the hands of his destroyer. But the idea of dwelling with Pygmalion is as hateful to her as Paris became to the Helen whom he had stolen with her treasures. As faithful to the memory of her lost love as is Saramâ to Indra, Dido pretends to listen to the traitor, while she makes ready for flight. In her new home another suitor appears in the Libyan Hiarbas, who repeats the importunities of the Itha- kan suitors, until Dido, wearied out, promises to do as he wishes; but having made a huge pile for the offering of a hecatomb, she slays herself upon it, declaring that now she is going, as her people and the Libyans desired it, to her husband. The version of Virgil differs from this in little more than a name. Æneas is only another form of the bright being with whom Dido would willingly have dwelt for ever; but he is the sun-god who cannot pause to bestow on her his love, or who must hasten away after a brief mockery of gladness. In the former case, the myth answers to the legends of Adonis, Endymiôn, or Narkissos; in the latter the desertion of Dido is but the desertion of Prokris, Ariadnê, or Korônis; and the Tyrian Elissa dies, like Herakles, amid the flames of a fiery sunset. The same story is re- peated yet again in the myth of Anna, the sister of Dido, whom Latin tradition identified with the goddess Anna Perenna.[1] After her sister's death Anna follows Æneas to

[1] This name was naturally referred to the words *annus* and *perennis* by a people who had retained the mere name with- out its meaning. Hence the goddess became to the Latins the bestower of fruitful seasons; but the false etymology of the prayer, 'ut annaro perennaroque commode liceat,' happened to correspond with the original force of the name, if Anna Perenna be the Sanskrit Apna- purna, who is described by Paterson as 'of ruddy complexion, her robe of various colours, a crescent on her fore- head: She gives subsistence; who is bent by the weight of her full breasts, all good is united in her.' In short, she is a deity who, in Colebrooke's words 'fills with food, 'and is very similar to Lakshmi, or the goddess of abundance, although not the same deity.

Italy where, though she is kindly received by him, she finds
in Lavinia a Prokris, whom she, like Eôs, must regard with
deadly jealousy. But her arms are turned not upon her
rival but upon herself; and the second woman who has
lavished her affections on Æneas casts herself into the same
Numician stream in which Æneas afterwards disappears from
the sight of men. The same repetitions mark the story of
Æneas, who, although fighting (reluctantly, as some versions
have it,) on the side of the thief who steals Helen, is yet a
being like the Lykian Sarpêdôn or the Aithiopian Memnôn.
Like them, he is the child not of a mortal mother, but of the
brilliant goddess of the dawn, and in the Trojan army he
plays the part of Achilleus in the Achaian host. Like the
son of Thetis, he is the possessor of immortal horses, and
like him he is at feud with the king, for Priam fails to do
him honour, as Agamemnon heaps disgrace on Achilleus.
From the flames of the ruined Ilion he escapes bearing on
his shoulders his father Anchises, the aged man who, while
yet he had the youth and beauty of Tithônos, had been the
darling of Aphroditê. His wife Creusa (Kreiousa, a name
answering to that of Euryanassa, the wide-ruling, and being
simply the feminine form of Kreôn or Kreiôn), comes behind
him like the twilight following the sun who is hastening
on into the land of night. But the twilight must vanish
before the sun can be seen again, and Creusa dies or disappears, like Hellê,—the converse of the myth of Hêrô and
Leiandros (Leander). But Æneas like Herakles has other
loves before him; and the fortunes of Dido and Anna are
brought before us again in the legend of the Italian Lavinia.
She too is the bright Helen for whom kings and nations are
ready to fight and die; but although Æneas wins her, there
remain yet other dangers and other enemies, and in the
final strife with the Rutulians the dawn-child vanishes in
the stream of Numicius, as Arethousa and Daphnê plunge
into the waters from which Anadyomenê comes up in the
morning. The true feeling of the people who recounted

The title Apna, in which we see the
root ap (aqua), points to nourishment by
water, while the name Purna comes
apparently from the same stem with
the Latin pario, to produce. Nork,
Real-Wörterbuch, i. 89.

this myth is shown in the title which they accorded to him.
Henceforth he is Jupiter Indiges, the father from whom
they spring, and who bestows upon them all that makes life
worth living for.

The same story of disastrous love is presented under other Hêrô and
names in the legend of Leiandros (Leander), a myth which Leiandros.
exhibits the sun as plunging through the waters to reach the
beautiful morning, who holds out her gleaming light in the
east; for Hêrô (whose name is identical with that of Hêrê)
is the priestess of the dawn-goddess Aphroditê, and the road
which separates her lover from herself is the Hellespontos,
the Lykabas or path of light, the track of Hellê the dawn-
maiden. Hêrô, again, dwells in the eastern Lesbos, while
Leiandros has his home in Abydos. He is thus the Phoibos
Delphinios, the fish or frog-sun, who dies in the furious
storm; and through grief for her lost love Hêrô casts herself
into the waters, like Kephalos from the Leukadian cliff after
the death of Prokris.

Not less sad than that of Prokris or of Dido is the lot of The Brides
Iolê, Iokastê, Aithra, Augê, Danaê, or Ariadnê. In the first of the Sun.
two of these forsaken wives or desolate mothers we see the
violet tints of morning, which reappear in Iamos, Iolâos,
and Iasôn. From Herakles, Iolê is parted almost at the
moment when she meets him. Her beautiful form is seen
near his funeral pile, as the violet-tinted clouds may be seen
among the flaming vapours lit up in a blood-red sunset;
and as the blaze of the fire which consumes the body of
Herakles rises to the heavens, she is left alone in her sorrow
to vanish before the cheerless gloaming. The fate of Iokastê
had for the Greeks of the age of Perikles a more terrible
significance. She is not only the mother of Oidipous, but
his wife. As his mother, she had been tortured by seeing
her child torn from her arms, to be cast away on Mount
Kithairôn; and the shame of finding herself his wife after
his victory over the Sphinx drives her to end her misery
with her own hands.[1] According to the version of Hyginus,
the life of Aithra (the pure air), the mother of Theseus, had

---

[1] Iokastê is the wife of the gloomy   which the sun is born may be regarded as
Laios: in other words, the dawn from   the wife of the dark and cheerless night.

the same end. Long ago she had been loved by Bellerophôn ; but when he was driven from Corinth, she became the wife of the Athenian Aigeus, who left her with the infant Theseus at Troizen, having, like the father of Sigurd, placed his invincible weapons under a large stone, that his son might become possessed of them only when he had reached his full strength. Later still, the Dioskouroi, it is said, carried her away to Sparta, where she became the slave of Helen, and whence with Helen she was taken to Troy, to be brought back again through the prayers of her grandson Demophon. By the same hard fate, Augê, the (brilliant) daughter of Neaira, who, as the early morning, reappears as the mother of the nymphs Phaethousa and Lampetiê in the Odyssey, no sooner becomes the mother of Têlephos (the being who shines from far) than she is deprived of her child, who is exposed on Mount Parthenion. The story of Ariadnê exhibits much the same outlines. She is the daughter of Minos, the son of Zeus, and the all-brilliant Pasiphaê, who is the mother of the Minotauros, as the bright Hêrê is the mother of Typhâôn. In the slaughter of this monster she has a share corresponding to that of Medeia in the conquest of the bulls and the' dragon-sprung men ; like Medeia, she accompanies the conqueror, and like her she is deserted by him. Ariadnê then either slays herself, like Iokastê and Augê, Dido or Anna, or becomes the wife of Dionysos, who places her among the stars. In substance this is also the story of the Argive Danaê, who is shut up by her father Akrisios in a brazen dungeon,[1] which Zeus enters in the form of a golden shower, as the light of morning pierces the dark chambers of the night. She thus becomes the mother of Perseus ; but, as in the case of Oidipous, the oracle had foretold that if she had a son, he would become the slayer of her father Akrisios, and Akrisios, anxious like Laios to preserve his own life, placed Danaê and her child in a chest, as according to one version Oidipous also was placed and borne away to Brasiai. The story of her sojourn in the house of Polydektês at Scriphos, of his persecutions and the more benignant treatment of his brother Diktys, of her rescue on the return of her son, and her restor-

[1] The Iron Store of the German story. (Grimm.)

ation to her native land, belongs rather to the mythical history of Perseus. The myth of Andromeda, the beautiful daughter of the Aithiopian king Kepheus, is less gloomy; but although her woes seem to end with her deliverance from the dragon, she had up to that time had her full share of sorrow. Her mother Kassiopeia had, like Niobê, boasted that her child was more beautiful even than the daughters of Nereus, who prayed to Poseidôn to avenge the insult, as Lêtô called on Phoibos to requite the wrong done to her by Niobê. Poseidôn accordingly brought the waters of the sea over the land, and with them a sea-monster who, like the Sphinx or the Minotauros, can be satisfied only with human blood. The former fills the streets of Thebes with corpses; the latter exacts the yearly tribute of the dawn-children. But the solitary Andromeda, abandoned to the huge sea-dragon, takes a firmer hold on the popular imagination, and is reproduced in a thousand forms, from the women rescued by Oidipous and Theseus down to Una and her Red Cross Knight. All these deliverers are men unknown to fame; but they are all endowed with powers for which they who see them give them no credit, and they all exhibit the manly type of generous chivalry which finds its consummation in the pure Sir Galahad.

CHAP. II.

The same idea is the groundwork of the myth of the Arkadian Augê, the clear atmosphere of the land of light. Hence the local myth necessarily related that Herakles came to her whenever he visited Tegea, and thus she becomes the mother of one of the fatal children whose life begins and ends in disaster. No sooner is her son born than her father Aleos decrees her death and the exposure of the child. But Augê is saved to become the wife of the Mysian Teuthras, or, according to another version, to escape narrowly the fate of the Theban Iokastê, and in the end to be brought back to Tegea by her son Têlephos, as Perseus brings his mother back to Argos.

The Arkadian Augê.

The story of Eurôpê brings before us the dawn, not as fleeing from the pursuit of the sun, but as borne across the heaven by the lord of the pure ether. Zeus here, like Indra, himself assumes the form of a bull, and takes away the child

Eurôpê and the Bull.

as she plays with her brother in her Phenician home.[1] Almost every name in the myth tells its own tale, although we may perhaps have to put aside the names of Agênôr and Kadmos as merely Hellenised forms of the Semitic Kedem and Chnas. Eurôpê herself is simply the broad-spreading flush of dawn, which is seen first in the Phoinikia, or purple region of the morning, and whose name belongs to the same class with Eurykleia, Eurydikê, Euryganeia, and Euryphassa. She is the child of Têlephassa, the being whose light streams from afar;[2] and in her first loveliness she is lost to those who delight in her, when she is snatched away to her western exile. Then follows the long journey of Kadmos and Têlephassa, the weary search of the sun through the livelong day for his early lost sister or bride. There were obviously a thousand ways of treating the myth. They might recover her in the end, as Alpheios is reunited to Arethousa and Perseus comes again to Danaê; but as it might be said that they might behold her like hereafter, so the tale might run that the being who had delighted them with her beauty should be seen herself again no more. The myth of Eurôpê sets forth the latter notion. Têlephassa sinks down and dies far in the west on the plains of Thessaly, and Kadmos, journeying westward still, learns at Delphoi that he is to seek his sister no longer.

The myth of Althaia sets forth the dawn or morning as the mother of a child whose life is bound up with a burning brand. As soon as the brand is burnt out her son will die, according to the inexorable doom pronounced by the Moirai. This brand is the torch of day, which is extinguished when the sun sinks beneath the western horizon. From this con-

---

[1] This bull reappears in the Norse tale of Katie Wooden-cloak (Dasent), endowed with the powers of Wish. In its left ear is a cloth which, when spread out, furnishes abundant banquets for the dawn-maiden, who has been thrust out of her father's house; but when the stepmother says that she cannot rest until she has eaten the Dun Bull's flesh, the beast, hearing her, tells the dawn-maiden that, if she wills, he will carry her away. The pursuit of Katie on her bull is the chase of Iasôn by the angry Aiêtês, not the loving search of Kadmos and Têlephassa; and the bull has to go through fearful conflicts with the Trolls, before the happy end is brought about by means of a golden slipper as in the stories of Cinderella and Sodewa Bai.

[2] Pindar (Pyth. iv.) speaks of Eurôpê as a daughter of Tityos, a gigantic being, who is slain by the swift arrow of Artemis, and condemned to a like penalty with Ixîon, Sisyphos, Tantalos, and Prometheus.

ccption of the sun's course sprung the idea that his mother
kept him alive by snatching the log from the fire. But
although Meleagros is, like Phoibos and Achilleus, invincible
and invulnerable, the words of the Moirai must be accomplished; and as the mother of the sun may be either the
dark night or the nourishing dawn (Althaia), so the wife of
Oineus has her kinsfolk among the dark beings; and when
these are slain by Meleagros, she thrusts the brand again
into the fire, and the life of her brilliant child smoulders
away. But his death brings with it the death alike of his
mother and his bride, for the tints of the dawn or the
gloaming cannot linger long after the sun is down. The
names introduced into this myth are found for the most part
in a host of other stories. She is the daughter of Eury-
themis, a reflection of Európê or Euryganeia, and a sister of
Leda, the mother of the brilliant Dioskouroi; and among
her own children is Dêianeira, whose union with Herakles is
fatal to the hero.[1] Of Kleopatra, the beautiful wife of
Meleagros, there is little more to say than that she is,
like Daphnê and Arethousa, a child of the waters, the
Euênos being her father, and that, like Oinônê and Brynhild, she dies of grief when the chequered life of the being
whom she loves has been brought to an end.

Section VI.—ATHÉNÉ.

The name Athénê is practically a transliteration of the
Vedic Ahanâ, the morning, which in a cognate form appears
as Dahanâ, the Greek Daphnê.[2] The myths which have
clustered round this greatest of Hellenic dawn-goddesses
differ indefinitely in detail, but all may manifestly be traced
back to the same source, and resolved into the same mythical
phrases. She is pre-eminently the child of the waters, she
springs from the forehead of the sky, and remains fresh,
pure, and undefiled for ever. In her origin the virgin deity

*The ori-
ginal idea
of Athénê
purely
physical.*

---

[1] Dêianeira is the last of the many
brides of Herakles, and belongs in truth,
rather to the darkness than the light,
and as sending to him the fatal garment,
may be regarded as rather the colleague

or bride of the enemy of the day: and
thus her name is Dâsyanari, the wife of
the fiend. *Chips, &c.* ii. 89. 234.
[2] See note 4, p. 418.

BOOK
II.

of the Athenian Akropolis was strictly physical; but the notion of the being who wakes up the world after the darkness of night might soon pass into that of wisdom, the connection between light and knowledge (the φῶς and γιῶσις of the Fourth Gospel) being of the closest kind. Thus, in one of the Vedic hymns we have already had the phrase that the dawn as waking every mortal to walk about receives praise from every thinker. But as being sprung from the forehead of the sky, she may be expected to know the secrets of heaven; and thus we have in Athênê a being who, like Phoibos, is filled with all the wisdom of Zeus. In the earlier form of the myth neither the Vedic Ahanâ nor the Hellenic Athênê has any mother. In the Rig Veda, 'Ushas, the dawn, sprung from the head of Dyu, the mûrddhadivah, the East, the forehead of the sky.'[1]

Athênê
Tritoge-
neia.

But if Athênê is Zeus-born, the poet, when he tells us this, speaks of her as Tritogeneia, the child of Tritos.[2] It is strange that this god, whose name differs so slightly from that of the water-god Triton, should have so far disappeared from the memory of the Greeks as to leave them at a loss to account for the epithet except by connecting it with places bearing a similar name, as among others the Libyan lake Tritonis, and the Boiotian stream Triton, on whose banks, as on those of the Attic stream, towns sprung up called Athênai and Eleusis.[3] In short, every stream so named became a birthplace for Athênê, although the meaning of the old phrase was not lost, until an attempt was made, by referring the myth to the alleged Eolic word for a head, to resolve it into the story of her springing from the head of Zeus. But the fact that in the Veda Trita rules over the water and the air, establishes the identity of Trito or Tritos, the father of

---

[1] Max Müller, *ib.* 'Homer knows of no mother of Athênê, nor does the Veda mention a name for the mother of the dawn, though her parents are spoken of in the dual.'

[2] Hes. *Theog.* 924.

[3] This connection of the dawn with water runs through almost every legend which turns on the phenomena of morning. Thus in the Norse tale of Katie Wooden-cloak the dawn-maiden, while working humbly like Cinderella in the kitchen, asks permission to take up water for the prince, who will receive no service from one so mean-looking. Next day she appears at the palace on a splendid steed, and to his question whence she comes, her reply is 'I'm from Bath;' the next day she is from Towel-land, the third day from Comb-land, the comb being that with which the dawn-maidens always comb their golden locks by the water-side.

Athênê, not only with that deity, but with Triton, Amphi- tritê, and the Tritopatores or lords of the winds.[1] The theory which, from the supposed Libyan birthplace of Athênê, infers a relation between Egyptian and Hellenic mythology calls for no notice.

The Hesiodic Theogony assigns Mêtis (a name akin to that of the wise Medeia) as a mother to Athênê; but this story is reconciled with the other myth by saying, that by the counsel of Ouranos and Gaia Zeus swallowed Mêtis before her child was born. In the saying of Pindar, that Hephaistos at her birth split the forehead of Zeus with a brazen axe, we see the sudden stream of light shooting up in the morning sky, which it seems to cleave; and in the golden shower which falls at her birth, we have only a repetition of the mode in which Danaê became the mother of Perseus.[2] When Apollodoros and others say that the forehead of Zeus was cloven by Prometheus or Hermes, we have only to remember that these are both spoken of (together with the Argive Phorôneus) as the first givers of the boon of fire to mankind.[3]

As springing from the forehead of Zeus, Athênê was known as Koryphasia in Messênê, as Akria in Argos, while Minerva

Birth of Athênê.

Parentage of Athênê.

[1] M. Bréal, who traces this identity, *Hercule et Cacus*, 17, cites the words of Suid s, 'τριτοπάτορες· Δήμων ἐν τῇ 'Ατθίδι φησὶν ἀνέμους εἶναι τοὺς Τριτοπάτορας.' It is said of Indra that 'animated by the sacrificial food, he broke through the defences of Vala, as did Trita through the coverings of the well.'— H. H. Wilson, *R. V. S.* vol. i. p. 141. Professor Wilson here remarks that 'Ekata, Dwita, and Trita [the first, second, and third] were three men produced in water, by Agni, for the purpose of removing or rubbing off the reliques of an oblation of clarified butter. The Scholiast . . . says that Agui threw the cinders of the burnt-offering into the water, whence successively arose Ekata, Dwita, and Trita, who, as elsewhere appears, were therefore called Aptyas or sons of water.' Noticing Dr. Roth's opinion that Trita is the same name as Thraêtana (Feridun), he says that the identity of Trita and Traitana remains to be established. It is, at the least, not disproved by the story which he

cites as setting it aside. This story is that 'the slaves of Dirghotamas, when he was old and blind, became insubordinate, and attempted to destroy him, first by throwing him into the fire, whence he was saved by the Asvins, then into water, whence he was extricated by the same divinities; upon which Traitana, one of the slaves, wounded him on the head, breast, and arms, and then inflicted like injuries on himself, of which he perished.' This story becomes clear throughout when compared with the myth of Eôs, who, like the slaves of Dirghotama, shut up the decrepit Tithônos. The other incidents of the tale carry us to the fiery death of Herakles, and to Endymiôn plunging into the waters which are soon lost to sight in the darkness which comes on after sunset.

[2] Pind. *Olymp.* vii. 65.

[3] Apollod. i. 3, 5. The myth which makes Hephaistos himself her father speaks only of the burst of flaming light from which the day seems to be born.

was called Capta (capita) at Rome.[1] But there were also traditions which spoke of her as a child not of Zeus, but of the giant Pallas,[2] who attempts to violate her purity, and is therefore slain by her. Here we have the dawn regarded as springing from the night, and the night as seeking to mar or to destroy his offspring. It is, in·short, the myth which makes Laios, Akrisios, and Astyages hate their children, who are in their turn doomed to slay their sires, as Athênê slays the monster Pallas. The legend which makes her a daughter of Poseidôn is merely a statement that the morning is born from the waters. But as with the dawn there comes generally the morning breeze (Sarameya, Hermeias, Hermes, the child of Saramâ) with its sweet and soothing tones, so when, by the aid of Athênê, Perseus has slain the dark Gorgon, Athênê is said, like Hermes, to have invented the flute in order to imitate the plaintive sounds in which the Gorgon sisters mourned the slain Medousa.[3]

Athênê
mother of
Phoibos
and Lych-
nos. But pure and undefiled though the dawn may be, she is yet followed by the sun, who may therefore be regarded as her offspring; and thus Phoibos Apollôn was sometimes called a son of Hephaistos and Athênê, while another version expressed the same idea by making them the parents of Lychnos (the brilliant), another Phaëthôn.[4] As the dawn-goddess, she can keep men young, or make them old. She rouses them to fresh vigour from healthful sleep, or as the days come round she brings them at last to old age and death. From her come the beauty and strength, the golden locks and piercing glances of Achilleus and Odysseus. But when for the accomplishment of the great work it becomes needful that Odysseus shall enter his own house as a toil-worn beggar, it is Athênê who dims the brightness of his eye, and wraps him in squalid raiment,[5] and again she

---

[1] Max Müller, *Lectures on Language*, second series, 503.
[2] This name is manifestly only another form of Phallos.
[3] Pind. *Pyth.* xii. 36.
[4] Athênê also brings up and nourishes Erechtheus, and lodges him in her own temple. On this Mr. Grote, *History of*

Greece, i. 75, remarks, ' It was altogether impossible to make Erechtheus the son of Athênê: the type of the goddess forbade it.' Rather, it was forbidden only by the form which the idea of Athênê assumed in the minds of the Athenians ; and the reason is obvious.
[5] *Od.* xiii. 430. See vol. i. p. 160.

restores his former majesty when once more he is to meet his son Telemachos.[1] So, again, she preserves to Penelopê all the loveliness of her youth, and presents her to Odysseus as beautiful as when he left her twenty years ago, when the Achaian hosts set out for Ilion, while she restores Laertes also to something of his ancient vigour.[2]

Of the vast number of names by which she was known and worshipped, the earliest probably, and certainly the most common, denote simply the light. She is especially the goddess of the grey or gleaming face, Glaukôpis. She is Optiletis, Oxyderkes, Ophthalmitis, the being of keen eyes and piercing vision; but these epithets might, it is plain, be made to bear a moral or intellectual meaning; and thus a starting point would be furnished for the endless series of names which described her as full of wisdom and counsel, as enforcing order and justice, as promoting the tillage of the earth, and as fostering all science and all art. Thus the epithets Akria and Akraia, which can be rightly interpreted only after a comparison with her other names, Koryphasia and Capta, might be taken to denote her protection of cities and fortresses, while her name Ageleia, as the driver of the clouds whom Saramâ leads forth to their pastures, might be regarded as denoting her care for those who till the soil or keep herds. But her physical character is never kept out of sight. She is the goddess especially of the Athenians, and of the dawn city which received her name after the contest in which she produced the olive against the horse created by Poseidôn, for so it was decreed by Zeus that the city should be called after the deity who should confer the greatest boon on man, and the sentence was that the olive, as the emblem of peace, was better than the horse, whose chief use was for war. But the city so named after her was emphatically the glistening city (λιπαραὶ 'Αθῆναι), although the epithet it seems was so little applicable to it in its outward aspect that the Athenians of the historical ages prized it with a jealous earnestness, and were ready to grant any prayer made by people who addressed them as citizens of brilliant Athens.

---

[1] *Od.* xvi. 172.　　　[2] *Ib.* xxiv. 368.

She is, however, the guardian not of Athenians only but
of all the solar heroes; in her Bellerophontes, Achilleus,
Herakles and Perseus, Odysseus and Diomêdes, find their
unfailing friend and comforter. From her come all wealth
and prosperity, and accordingly we find the special emblems
of wealth and fertility intimately associated with her worship. Her sacred serpent was fed on the Akropolis, and
yearly in her great procession the sacred ship, covered with
the peplos woven by Athenian maidens, was carried to her
shrine.[1] In one of the so-called Orphic hymns, she is said
to be both male and female, and thus to remain unwedded.
Doubtless the dawn may be regarded as of spotless purity
and unfading loveliness, and this idea might give rise to
images of transcendent holiness and majesty; but she may be
thought of also not only as giving birth to children, but as
being sensible to passion, and we are not justified in leaving
out of sight those myths which present Athênê in this light.
On the one hand, according to one story, she blinds Teiresias
because he had looked upon her unclothed form (a myth
closely akin to that of the dazzling treasures of Ixîôn, which
no man might look upon and live), and shrinks with loathing
from Hephaistos when he seeks to lay hands upon her. On
the other, the myth of Prometheus exhibits her as aiding
him in his theft of fire against the will of Zeus, while one
version represents her as so acting from feelings not of
friendship but of love. In general, however, the harmony
between the dawn and the sky from which it springs, in
other words, between Zeus and Athênê, is undisturbed; and
thus when Zeus is determined to take vengeance for the
deceit put upon him by Prometheus, Athênê lends herself as
a willing accomplice in his scheme. She is to teach Pandora
the skilful use of the loom, while Aphroditê is to adorn her
with all the enticements of physical beauty, and Hermes is
to give her a crafty and thievish mind and temper.[3] But
even in the Iliad where she is generally represented as being

[1] See section xii. of this chapter.
[2] xxxii.
[3] Hes. Op. et Dies. 60, et seq. The
statement in line 72 that Athênê placed
the girdle on Pandora and made her
beautiful may be regarded as another
version of the myth. It is certainly not
in accordance with line 65.

in perfect accord with the will of Zeus, she engages, as we have seen, in an abortive conspiracy to bind Zeus, in which she is the accomplice of Hêrê and Poseidôn.[1]

In all her essential attributes, the Hellenic Athênê is represented by the Latin Minerva, a name which Professor Max Müller connects with mens, the Greek μένος, and the Sanskrit manas, mind, and compares it with mane, the morning, Mânia, an old name of the mother of the Lares, and the verb manare as applied especially to the sun, while Matuta and other kindred words denote the dawn.[2] Whatever may be the connection between Minerva and Matuta, we can scarcely fail to see the affinity of the name with the verb promenervare, used in the Carmen Saliare as an equivalent to the kindred moneo, to admonish. The Latin Minerva, as embodying a purely intellectual idea, is thus a being even more majestic than the Hellenic Athênê; and to so intellectual a conception we should scarcely expect that many fables would attach themselves. Hence the Latin Minerva can scarcely be said to have any mythology. Like Ceres she stands alone in incommunicable sanctity and in unfathomable wisdom.

[1] Il. i. 400.

[2] Lectures on Language, second series, 505. To the same root, probably, must be referred the epithet moneta, applied to Juno as the guardian of the mint on the Capitoline hill. See also note i., p. 115.

APPENDICES.

———◦◦◦———

APPENDIX A.—Page 217.

The Antiquity of written Poems.

It is impossible not to see that ages must have intervened between the invention of writing, or rather as we should term it of scratching, and the preservation of long poems in manuscript. It is much more reasonable to suppose that greater facilities for writing would lead rather to the rise of contemporary chroniclers than to the practice of writing down poems, which would lose half or all their value in the eyes of rhapsodists if put upon paper.

It seems scarcely necessary to treat seriously the arguments or rather the dicta by which M. Barthélemy St.-Hilaire (*L'Iliade d'Homère traduite en vers Français*), holds himself to have proved not only that our *Iliad* is one poem, and that therefore there was only one Homer, but that it was from the first a written poem. The authority of M. de St.-Hilaire is deservedly great; but it must, nevertheless, be repeated that the question is one wholly of evidence, and that the answer must be given in accordance with that evidence and without regard to sentiment, prejudice, or any supposed powers of literary divination acquired by long study. From a rapid survey of the *Iliad*, which omits all that is to be set on the other side, M. St.-Hilaire infers that the unity of the poem is demonstrated, and asserts that this unity must be regarded as an incontestable fact, and that any one who does not admit this postulate can only make false steps if he ventures to speak about Homer (introduction, xxx). His opponents appeal to the evidence of facts: M. St.-Hilaire, in that strain of exaggerated eulogy which is the bane of conservative criticism, addresses himself to our feelings: 'A mon sens, il suffit d'un coup d'œil même rapide sur l'Iliade, pour sentir immédiatement que c'est là une impossibilité. Quoi! Cette œuvre, prodigieuse plus encore dans son ensemble que dans ses détails, a été faite au hasard, dans la durée de plusieurs siècles, par quinze ou vingt poëtes différents, qui ne se sont pas connus, qui ne se sont pas concertés,

et qui, sous le feu d'une égale inspiration, ont pu produire des fragments, réunis plus tard en un merveilleux édifice, d'une harmonie,
d'une proportion, d'une symétrie, d'une solidité sans pareilles!
Quoi! C'est là expliquer la composition de l'Iliade! C'est se
rendre compte en critique, c'est-à-dire en juge éclairé et compétent
de ce chef-d'œuvre, dont la beauté ne peut épuiser ni l'admiration
de la foule ni celle des philosophes!' (introduction, xxxiv). On
arguments of much the same weight as these M. St.-Hilaire rests
his conclusion that the *Iliad* and *Odyssey* were poems not merely
composed, but written down on a soft material, by a single poet.
Every story about Lykourgos, Solon, or other legislators is taken
as indubitable fact; and the priority of Laios to Proitos furnishes
evidence precisely the same in kind with the priority of William the
Conqueror to Henry I. The times of Bellerophôn are certainly
historical, and Bellerophôn lived two generations before the Trojan
war. But letters were written in his days: and therefore letters
were in use in the time of the poet who wrote about him and the
Trojan war. The question turning on the phrase σήματα λυγρά,
'the woful signs,' is barely noticed. It must have been an alpha-
betical writing, for the other supposition would ascribe to painting
a perfection which it had not attained (intr. xlvi). The difficulty
has probably been rarely felt in savage life. But again, writing was
familiar to the heroes of the Trojan war, for they mark the lots
which they throw into a helmet (*Iliad*, v. 171, et seq.) M. St-
Hilaire's conclusion may well take away our breath: 'Chacun des
guerriers trace sa marque: on agite toutes ces marques dans le
casque d'Agamemnon, et Nestor, qui les secoua, tire celle d'Ajax,
fils de Télamon, que toute l'armée désirait. On montre la marque
favorisée du sort à chacun des concurrents. Aucun ne la reconnaît:
mais quand elle arrive à celui qui l'avait écrite ou tracée, aussitôt
Ajax, plein de joie, déclare qu'elle est la sienne. . . Qu'est-ce au
juste que cette marque? Il n'est pas aisé de le dire avec précision.
Mais comme Homère se sert du même mot qui, pour la missive du
Proetus, a paru signifier l'écriture, tout porte à croire qu'ici encore
c'est bien de l'écriture qu'il s'agit, et non d'une marque quelconque
où aucun signe graphique n'eût été tracé' (introd. xlviii). As
bearing on the main question of an *Iliad* written from the first, an
argument resting on a word scratched by ten or a dozen men would
be worthless. There can, however, be no sort of doubt that in a
writing age each man would have inscribed his own name, and that
the drawer would at once have named the man who had been
chosen. In this case the herald has to carry the lot about the
camp, as each hero failed, not to read (for it has never been pretended that γιγνώσκειν can be used in this sense) but to recognise

his particular mark. It would be impossible for the poet to show more clearly that the marks were not letters or words, but mere arbitrary signs. This is literally the whole of the evidence adduced from our Homeric poems, on which M. St.-Hilaire rests his conclusions that those poems were from the first written compositions. It becomes a superfluous task to follow M. St.-Hilaire through his remarks on the alleged abundance of writing materials in the Homeric age, or on the libraries of Osymandyas and Peisistratos. The real question is not whether poems were written centuries before the time of Herodotus, but whether the Greeks had any written literature before the Persian wars. Mr. Paley has expressed his conviction that no such literature existed in the times of Pindar, and the subject has been further examined by Mr. Fennell, in a paper on the 'First Ages of a written Greek Literature,' *Transactions of the Cambridge Philosophical Society*, 1868.

APPENDIX B.—Page 218.

The Historical Value of ' Homer.'

Since this chapter was written, Mr. Gladstone has published his ' Juventus Mundi,' in which he states his present convictions with regard to the authorship and historical credibility of our Iliad and Odyssey, which alone he regards as the poems of Homer. These convictions are substantially what they were ten years ago, but the discussion has really advanced beyond the point at which Mr. Gladstone leaves it; and the only reason for repeating objections to arguments which might well be left to themselves, is the weight which in the opinion of some they may receive from his name and authority. Instead of noting the result of recent Homeric criticism, whether conservative or destructive, Mr. Gladstone has chosen the simpler and easier task of asserting that to himself his old conclusions on the subject of Homer are thoroughly satisfactory. Homer is still with him undoubtedly an historical person, and the Iliad and Odyssey are emphatically historical poems. The poet was born, he thinks, before or during the Trojan war, and was probably familiar with those who had fought in it. These conjectures or convictions are supported by a series of propositions which certainly prove his point if they are suffered to pass unchallenged, but of most of which it must be said that they are mere assertion or hypothesis for which no evidence whatever is adduced.

The ambiguity of much of Mr. Gladstone's language introduces a further element of difficulty into the discussion. When, for instance

ho says that, 'A cardinal argument for placing the date of the poet
near that of his subject is, that he describes manners from first to last
with the easy, natural, and intimate knowledge of a contemporary
observer,' there is a sense in which the most sceptical critics will
agree with him. No one doubts that the Homeric poet (or poets)
threw over his (or their) narrative a colour borrowed from the
society in which he (or they) lived. Here there was every motive
for the poet to be truthful, none to depart from the truth ; and
the exactness with which all customs of peace and war, of arts
and games, of public and private life were reproduced in the poem,
would inevitably impart an air of reality to the events related,
whatever these might be. This is probably true of the genuine epic
poetry of all nations ; but for the historical character of the incidents
which they relate, it obviously proves nothing. The society of the
age in which the poet lives may be described with indefinite
accuracy, though the house which he builds may be raised on sand.
In this sense certainly 'it cannot be too strongly affirmed that the
song of Homer is historic song,' or even that he has 'told us more
about the world and its inhabitants at his own epoch than any
historian that ever lived.'—(P. 7.) But unless, with Mr. Gladstone,
we are prepared to infer facts from the 'tone and feeling' of a poet,
or from his knowledge of human nature generally and of his own
countrymen in particular, we are bound to say plainly that we
speak only of his pictures of life and manners. This limitation will
not satisfy Mr. Gladstone. With him the 'subject' of Homer is
not so much the picture of society existing in his own time as the
war of which he relates some of the most important incidents.
Here then we are brought face to face with the question of facts ;
and it is, to say the least, most unfortunate that Mr. Gladstone
has not told us plainly and candidly what the 'chief persons
and events' are with regard to which we are to look upon
'Homer' as 'historical.' Mr. Blackie has done this; and we have
seen how the confidence with which he first enunciates the result
of his analysis is modified until the supposed substance vanishes
into thin air, and how, after asserting in one place that there
was one real war, and a real quarrel between Achilleus and Agamemnon, he admits in another not only that there may have been
no Paris and no Helen, but that it makes no difference to the
history if Agamemnon and Achilleus never met at all and were
'distinct captains of two separate armaments' (see p. 185). What
would Mr. Gladstone think of an English history which should tell
us that it made no difference to the essential character of the narrative whether we suppose that Laud and Strafford were joint con-
spirators against the liberties of England, or the leaders in two

several attempts made in successive centuries? We must be pardoned if we refuse altogether to admit the historical character of narratives to which the champions of their veracity obviously give no real credit. Mr. Gladstone leads us through a region of mists, in which he would have us follow paths not pointed out to us by our best historical guides. Thus his first reason for accepting as historical the chief events of our Iliad and Odyssey is that 'It is the chief business of the poet or bard, as such, in early times, to record facts, while he records them in the forms of beauty supplied by his art.'

If we write with the sole aim and hope of discovering the truth, if truth and truth alone is our single object, we are bound to refuse any leap which must be taken in the dark. Mr. Gladstone's reason is a mere assumption. Why are we to believe that the recording of facts was the business of the poet in early times, until we know what their ideas of a fact were, and, indeed, until we have proved what is here merely asserted? Against Mr. Gladstone's dogmatic assertion we may set the conclusion of Mr. Grote, that the early poets and bards dealt with 'the entire intellectual stock of the age to which they belonged,' and that the value of this was measured by its power of satisfying that 'craving for adventure and appetite for the marvellous which has in modern times become the province of fiction proper' (*History of Greece*, part i. ch. xvi.), as well as the deliberate judgment of Bishop Thirlwall that 'the kind of history for which Homer invoked the aid of the Muses was not chiefly valued as a recital of real events,' and that 'if in detached passages the poet sometimes appears to be relating with the naked simplicity of truth, we cannot ascribe any higher authority to those episodes than to the rest of the poem.' How completely Bishop Thirlwall sweeps away the whole 'Homeric' narrative of the Trojan war, we have seen already, p. 197.

On Mr. Gladstone's second reason that the truthful recording of events is especially the business 'of the bard who lives near the events which he professes to sing,' it is unnecessary to say more than that Thucydides denies as positively as Mr. Gladstone affirms, that Homer lived near to the Trojan war (p. 198). Mr. Gladstone's fourth reason (the third is a mere inference from the first and second), is that the poems were always viewed as historical by the Greeks. This assertion is practically identical with the opinions of Colonel Mure and Baron Bunsen, which we have been already compelled to reject as not only resting on no evidence, but as being altogether opposed to such evidence as we possess (p. 213). This summary of evidence I had published in the Fortnightly Review for May 1, 1867; and I must maintain with all earnestness that it was

the duty of every Homeric critic who deals with this portion of the
subject to examine and accept or refute the evidence of the facts
thus alleged. The mere statement of an opinion ought to carry no
more weight on one side than on another; but Mr. Paley took his
stand wholly on facts, which proved, or seemed to prove, that the
Greek lyric, tragic, and comic poets either knew nothing or next to
nothing of our Iliad and Odyssey, or, if they did, deliberately preferred to them certain other poems to which they resorted for their
materials. (He further stated, that Greek art, down to a time later
than that of Perikles, exhibits precisely the same phenomena.) In
either case the assertions of Mr. Gladstone, Colonel Mure, and
Baron Bunsen fall to the ground; and for such assertions a hearing
cannot reasonably be expected, until this evidence has been met and
refuted. Mr. Gladstone not only takes no notice of it, but apparently even contradicts himself, for, having stated that from the
earliest times we find these poems holding continuously (the word
is necessary, if the opinion is to have any force) a position of honour
and authority among the Greeks paralleled in no other literature,
he asserts that 'the antiquity of the present text is not over-
thrown by the fact that the later poets in many instances have
followed other forms of legend in regard to the Troica, for they
would necessarily consult the state of popular feeling from time to
time; and tradition, which as to religion altered so greatly after the
time of Homer, would, as to facts and persons, as it is evident, vary
materially according to the sympathies of blood and otherwise at
different periods of Greek history' (p. 19). Even if we concede
(and it is not necessary that we should concede) that this may
possibly account for the choice of the later poets in a very few
instances, perhaps five or six, Mr. Gladstone's admission is in complete conflict with the position of unparalleled honour and authority
which he attributes to our Iliad and Odyssey throughout the historical ages. But no political sympathies or antipathies could render
necessary that systematic degradation of characters like Odysseus,
Aias, Hektor, to say nothing of Helen, to account for which Mr.
Gladstone felt himself driven to devise a theory in his Homeric
Studies (vol. iii. p. 555). Nor can they explain the phenomena of
Greek literature already adduced (p. 214). Mr. Gladstone is com-
pelled to admit that Thucydides speaks of the Hymn to Apollôn as
Homeric, and that '' doubtless he represents a tradition of his day.'
But these hymns are, in Mr. Gladstone's opinion, very inferior to
'Homer,' and, therefore, Thucydides and his contemporaries were
mistaken; and thus the unparalleled honour and authority of our
Iliad and Odyssey are modified into the statement that no other
poems were regarded as Homeric 'by the general and unhesitating

opinion of the Greeks.' We do not know enough of this general opinion to warrant any very positive statements with regard to it; but until it can be proved that the lyric and tragic poets were acquainted with our Iliad and Odyssey, it can scarcely be affirmed that the general opinion of the Greeks regarded those poems as Homeric at all. But, further, what is the actual evidence that the poems to which alone Mr. Gladstone will give the name of Homer, were 'always viewed as historical by the Greeks'? All that Herodotos and Thucydides leave of the story is the solitary fact of a war which lasted ten years; but if they reject its motive and incidents, the hinges on which the whole action turns together with all the action itself, in what sense can it be said that they regarded the Homeric tale of Troy as historical? The fact is, that neither of these great historians could receive that tangled skein of marvels, miracles, and prodigies, which are inextricably intertwined in the supernatural machinery of these mythical tales. Hence they summarily rejected the whole, having thus 'judged on its own grounds' Homer's 'intermixture of supernatural agency with human events,' although Mr. Gladstone insists that this intermixture 'cannot by the laws of historical criticism be held of itself to overthrow his general credit' (p. 9). Mr. Gladstone does not tell us what are the laws of historical criticism; but his conception of them appears to differ widely from that of Bishop Thirlwall, whose judgment I have more than once been obliged to cite.

It is scarcely an exaggeration to say that all the reasons adduced by Mr. Gladstone for regarding the Iliad and Odyssey as narratives of real events are of the same shadowy and intangible kind. We are told that the singular correspondence of the genealogies in these poems strongly attests the historical trustworthiness of Homer. But although the lowest links may possibly, in any given case, represent real persons, these lists all run up to some god or deified hero; and Mr. Grote has long since asked by what method we are to determine the point at which history ends and fable begins in the links between the real Hekataios and his divine progenitor (*History of Greece*, part i. ch. iv.). In the same spirit the prophecy of Poseidôn (p. 4) is taken as proving, not that a family calling themselves Aineiadai were reigning in Troas at the time when this portion of the Iliad (p. 92) was composed or recited, but that the then ruling chief was the actual grandson of the child of Anchises and of Aphroditê, who visibly interferes to rescue her son on the field of battle. Mr. Gladstone assures us that 'Homer often introduces curious legends of genealogy, and in a manner which is palpably inopportune for the purposes of poetry, and which is, on the other hand, fully accounted for by the historic aim.' It is enough to say that these episodes and digressions may be as legitimately used to prove the composite character of the poems as to uphold their historical authority.

Of the personality of Homer, and the purity or preservation of our Homeric text, I need here say but little. On the former Mr. Gladstone admits that 'nothing is known of his person' (p. 2), nothing of the time of his birth, or his place of abode, or of any event in his life (p. 6). The most determined of the separatists could scarcely desire a thicker darkness; but to the historical critic, these, as we have already seen (p. 174 *et seq.*), are points of supreme indifference. Of the text Mr. Gladstone still thinks that 'we may, as a general rule, proceed to handle it with a reasonable confidence that the ground is firm under our feet,' in spite of the evidence adduced by Mr. Paley for questioning that it was known to the great lyric and tragic poets of Hellas. Its integrity was guaranteed by 'the intense love of the song of Homer felt by every Greek' (p. 23), although the evidence is unfortunately scanty on which to rest the conclusion that their Homer was our Homer, neither less nor more.

In short, after an interval of more than ten years, during which the phase of the controversy has been wholly changed, Mr. Gladstone has simply repeated the confession of his old Homeric faith. Doubtless, his appeal is not to the credulity, but to the judgment of his countrymen, and if I say that his criticism as little upholds the historical character of our Homeric poems as that of Mr. Blackie, I do so because the evidence of facts seems to me to preclude any other conclusion.

APPENDIX C.—Page 222.

The Myth of Oidipous.

A vigorous attempt to overthrow M. Bréal's explanation of the myth of Oidipous, *Le mythe d'Œdipe*, 1863, and so to bring discredit on the method and results of Comparative Mythology, has been made by M. Comparetti, *Edipo e la mitologia comparata*, Pisa, 1867. His chief argument seems to be the composite nature of this myth (as of others), which compels him to regard the episode of the Sphinx as a mere formula and in no way an essential part of the legend, and to conclude that at the first this incident had nothing to do with the story of Oidipous. In proof of this assertion, he lays stress on the silence of the Homeric poet (*Odyssey*, xi. 270) on this subject, while speaking of the woeful fortunes of Epikastê (Iokastê), and again of the Hesiodic poet (*Works and Days*, 163) when referring to the feuds of the sons of Oidipous about their father's treasures (whether these be sheep or apples). To this argument M. Bréal in his answer to M. Comparetti, *Révue critique d'Histoire et de Litterature,* Jan. 22, 1870, replies that in the Hesiodic Theogony the Phix (Sphinx) is expressly mentioned as inflicting deadly woes on the Kadmeians, and thus the connexion of the Sphinx with the mythical history of Thebes is established beyond question. He adds that if so capital an incident be left out of the story of Oidipous, any other myth may be pared down to the Euemeristic level of plausible fiction. At the same time there is a sense in which M. Comparetti's remark that this episode might be replaced by any other tale of prowess is perfectly true. There is no reason why Oidipous should not be the slayer of Geryon or Echidna or Chimaira, or why the Sphinx should not fall by the sword of Hipponoös, the slayer of Belleros. The assortment of exploits from which we may make choice is large, but they are all equally mythical and equally transparent in their meaning.

Having disposed of the Sphinx, M. Comparetti, with the usual assurance of Euemerists, asserts that Oidipous is a purely human person, in the story of whose life we shall look in vain for the marvellous adventures which usually grace the traditions of the gods or demigods. Here the answer is obvious, and M. Bréal joins issue on the plain fact that the whole story is full of marvels from the moment of his birth. His infancy is that of Perseus, Cyrus, Romulus, or Semiramis, his grave in the gardens of the Merciful Beings represents the treasures of the Nibelungs ; and even if we get rid of the Sphinx, his victory over the fox of Teumessos, an exploit of the same kind, still remains.

M. Comparetti's reason for thus banishing the Sphinx from the story is, that he may thus exhibit the myth as designedly setting forth the horrors of incest, and so as being purely didactic in its first intention. But he adheres to this conclusion not much more consistently than Mr. Blackie to his historical residuum in the Iliad. Iokastê is not the only wife assigned to Oidipous, and M. Comparetti hastens to say that the other wives were a later invention, and were introduced to take away the feeling of disgust excited by the idea of the incest. This plea M. Bréal rightly dismisses in very few words : ' Si tout le récit, comme le suppose M. Comparetti, est destiné à produire une impression morale, un changement de cette nature (et les autres femmes d'Œdipe sont déjà mentionées dans l'Œdipodie) va contre l'intention du narrateur.'

Having demolished the Sphinx, M. Comparetti goes on to say that, far from blinding himself and departing into exile, Oidipous, according to the oldest form of the legend, continued to reign at

Thebes. But on this supposition, the idea of a moral intention is still more completely shut out. What sort of Nemesis is it that would allow the doer of such things to go unpunished ?

With the failure of the attempt to reduce the myth to a caput mortuum of historical facts the question is carried back into the province of Comparative Mythology, and M. Bréal rightly urges that the problem to be solved is the recurrence of the incidents, or as M. Comparetti styles them, the formulæ which characterise the myth of Oidipous, in the stories of other Aryan nations during times which altogether preclude the idea of any borrowing or artificial adaptation of popular stories.

APPENDIX D.—Page 406.

Swan-Maidens.

Many of these myths have been gathered together in the Chapters on Swan Maidens and the Knight of the Swan, by Mr. Baring Gould (*Curious Myths*, second series), who follows them also into the mythology of the Turanian tribes. The coincidences thus pointed out call for the same consideration which should be given to the traditions of American native tribes when they exhibit any striking features in common with those of Aryan races. Some of these traditions, which resemble the myths of Pandora, Pyrrha and the dolphin or fish god, have been already referred to. But it would be as dangerous to assume that myths circulating among Turanian tribes have been imported by them through intercourse with Aryan nations, as to assume that these American traditions are the result of Jesuit teaching. Of the substantial identity of the Turanian myths cited by Mr. Gould with the stories belonging to Germany and India there can be no question. In a Samojed story, a man, finding seven maidens swimming on a lake, takes up from the bank the Swan's dress belonging to one of them, and refuses to yield it up except on the condition that she becomes his wife and gets for him the hearts of seven brothers which are hung up by them every night on their tent pegs. When she brings them, he dashes all but one on the ground, and as each falls, the brother to whom it belongs dies. When the eldest whose heart has not been broken awakes and begs to have it restored, the Samojed says that he must first bring back to life his mother who had been killed by him. The man then bids him go to the place where the dead lie, and there he should find a purse in which is his mother's soul. 'Shake the purse over the dead woman's bones, and she will come to life.' The Samojed, having thus recovered his mother, dashes the remaining heart on the ground, and the last of the seven dies. This is the groundwork of the story of Punchkin, and of the Giant who had no Heart in his Body (book i. chap. viii.). The difficulty in finding the magician's heart is here transferred to the discovery of the purse containing the murdered woman's soul.

Mr. Gould adds that among the Minussinian Tartars the swan-maidens assume loathsome as well as beautiful forms, and appear in fact, like the Hellenic Harpyiai, the black storm-clouds which sweep furiously across the sky, the swan-shaped daughters of Phorkys (Æsch. *Prom. V.* 795). In the hymn addressed to Delos by Kallimachos the Muses are still nymphs or watermaidens, the Apsaras (apa, water, and sar, to go), which have acquired a faint personality in the Veda (Max Müller, *Chips*, ii. 202), and can scarcely be distinguished from the swans which attend upon them.

κύκνοι δὲ θεοῦ μέλποντες ἀοιδοί
Μηόνιον Πακτωλὸν ἐκυκ\ώσαντο λιπόντες
ἑβδομάκις περὶ Δῆλον, ἐπήεισαν δὲ λοχείη
μουσάων ὄρνιθες, δειδότατοι πετεηνῶν. 249–252.

The same phrases which spoke of clouds as swans have given birth to the myths of Kyknos transformed into a swan by Phoibos, and of Leda wooed by Zeus in the guise of a white swan (a white mist answering to the golden shower in the legend of Danaê). Mr. Gould, having cited among other northern tales that in which Völund, or Wayland the Smith, wins as his wife the maiden Angelburga, whose dress of dove's feathers he had stolen as she was bathing, thinks that to such beings we must trace back the angels with flowing white robes and large pinions, which Christendom has derived immediately from the later Greek and Roman representations of Victory. In his chapter on the Knight of the Swan, Mr. Gould has brought together some mediæval versions of the myth which Southey has versified in his ballad of Rudiger. These versions turn on the main incident in the stories of Urvasî and Psychê. The bride must never ask her husband's name; and the old suggestion that the lover is in reality a monster is travestied into the remark of the Duchess of Cleves: ' This Lohengrin (the Purûravas of the tale) may be a strong man and a Christian; but who knows whence he has sprung ? ' These words awaken the curiosity of the Duchess of Brabant, who pays the penalty of Psychê. Lohengrin accordingly leaves to his children his horn and his sword, and to his wife the ring which had been given to him by his mother, and departs never to return. The story of Matabruno in the romance of Helias, the Knight of the Swan, is that of many jealous stepmothers who seek the death of the light-children (Gould, *ibid.* 315; Frere,

Deccan Days, 59).   This Helias becomes Duke of Bouillon, and his
daughter is the mother of the heroic Godfrey.   So pertinaciously
do the old fables of nymphs and harpies and Erinyes keep their hold
on the annals of an historical age.

From the image of the Swan to that of the Phaiakian ship, which
needs neither rudder nor sail, the transition is obvious and easy.
On such a ship Odysseus is borne to his home, and in such a vessel
Scild, the son of Sceaf (the skiff) is carried to the coast of Scandia
where he becomes king. 'In Beowulf it is added that Scild
reigned long, and when he saw that he was about to die, he bade
his men lay him fully armed in a boat, and thrust him out to sea.
. . . And the same is told of Baldur.'—Gould, *ibid.* 336.   The incident is repeated in the case of Elaine and Arthur.

APPENDIX E.—Page 422.

The Name Helenê.

I am indebted to Professor Max Müller for the following note.
'The only objection which might be made by those who are not
acquainted with the latest researches on the so-called digamma is
that ἰλίνα is among those words, which, according to the testimony
of Greek and Latin grammarians, had an initial digamma (cf. Tryph.
παθ. λεξ. § 11 ; Priscianus, i. p. 21, xiii. p. 574; Ahrens, *De Gr. Ling.
Dialectis*, lib. i. pp. 30, 31).   Now because the so-called digamma
(the F, the old vau, the Latin F) corresponds in most cases to a
Sanskrit and Latin V, it has become the fashion to use digamma
as almost synonymous with the labial semi-vowel *v* in Greek.
Benfey, however, in his article on ἑκάτερος (in Kuhn's 'Zeitschrift
für vergleichende Sprachforschung,' viii. 331,) pointed out that
what is generally, though not correctly, called digamma in Greek,
represents at least three different letters in the cognate languages,
v, s, y.   These three letters became evanescent in later Greek ; and
when either on the evidence of the Homeric metre, or on the
evidence of grammarians, or even on the evidence of inscriptions,
certain Greek words are said to have had an initial digamma, we
must be prepared to find, corresponding to this so-called digamma,
not only the *v*, but also the *s*, and *y*, in Sanskrit and Latin.   Greek
scholars are apt to put F, whereas the metre proves the former
presence of some one initial consonant.   When however we find
Fεξ, the F here represents a lost *s*, as proved by the Latin *sex*,
Sanskrit *shat*.   When we find in Homer θεὸς ὥς, the ος is lengthened
because ὥς had an initial *y*, as proved by the Sanskrit *yat*.   In

the same manner, the fact that grammarians quote Ϝελένα, nay, even the occurrence of Ϝελένα in ancient inscriptions, would by no means prove that Helenê was originally Velena, and was derived from the root *svar*, but only that Helenê might in the cognate languages begin with *v*, *s*, or *y*. The statement of Priscianus, 'Sciendum tamen quòd hoc ipsum (digamma) Æoles quidem ubique loco aspirationis ponebant, effugientes spiritus asperitatem,' is more correct than was at one time supposed even by comparative grammarians; and as the asper in Greek commonly represents an original *s* or *y*, the Æolic digamma became the exponent of *s* and *y*, as well as of the *v* for which it stood originally.'

APPENDIX F.—Page 429.

Lykanthropy.

I am speaking, of course, of the special form of the superstition, not of enormities of which depraved appetites and unbridled passions may have made men guilty. The question to be answered is, whence came the notions that men were changed into wolves, bears, and birds, and not into lions, fishes, or reptiles; and to this question Comparative Mythology seems to me to furnish a complete answer; nor can I disavow my belief that this loathsome vampire superstition was in the first instance purely the result of the verbal equivocation which, as we have seen, has furnished so fruitful a source of myths. I cannot, in the face of this evidence, believe that the choice of the wolf or the bear as the form to be assumed by the patient is 'a mere matter of taste,' as Mr. Gould says in a work which will be most regretted by those who most value his volumes on the myths of the middle ages. Whether there be, as Mr. Gould maintains, 'an innate craving for blood in certain natures,' is a point which little concerns us here, although we might suppose that if such an impulse be according to the hypothesis innate (i. e. placed there by God himself), the impulse could not be wrong, and that hence such persons were not fit subjects for punishment. But the evidence for the case breaks down, and much of the evidence adduced by Mr. Gould is really no evidence at all. Thus he tells us that, 'as every one knows, Jupiter changed himself into a bull, Hecuba became a bitch, Actæon a stag, the comrades of Ulysses were transformed into swine, and the daughters of Prœtus fled through the fields, believing themselves to be cows, and would not allow any one to come near them lest they should be caught and yoked.'—'Werewolf,' p. 12. These myths belong to a different class. The persons so transformed neither did nor attempted to do any harm; but the peculiar mischievous form of lykanthropy is found developed with sufficient clearness in the pages of Pausanias. Hence we may dismiss the story told by Augustine of the old woman who turned men into asses, or of the golden ass of Appuleius; and the tale related by Mr. Gould of the Bjorn (bear) who 'loves the Carle's daughter,' and taking her into a cave tells her that 'by day he is a beast, by night a man,' *ib.* 24, is only a clumsy version of Beauty and the Beast, of Erôs and Psychê. Mr. Gould's faith is large. He gives credit to 'the unanimous testimony of the old Norse historians that the berserk rage was extinguished by baptism, and as Christianity advanced, the number of the berserkers decreased,' *ib.* 40. The stories of bearsarks have probably as much and as little truth as the story of the frenzy of Herakles, the madness of the one and the rage of the other being the same thing; and the unanimous testimony of the Norse historians is worth as much and as little as the convictions of Glanvil and Hale on the reality of witchcraft. Such a canon of evidence would compel us to receive the whole Catholic hagiology as veritable history. That Mr. Gould should have thought it necessary to give the loathsome details of the story of the Maréchal de Retz, which is simply the myth of Ph..aris, is the more to be deplored, as this man according to the tale never supposed himself to be either a wolf or a brute of any other sort. The account of the woman who single-handed and unaided kills six hundred and fifty girls to bathe in their blood brings before us a series of exploits worthy of a Herakles; and the story of Mr. J. Holloway of the Bank of England is simply an impudent repetition of the myth of Hermotimos of Klazomenai.

END OF THE FIRST VOLUME.

R. BOMBAY BIBLIOTECA

LONDON: PRINTED BY
SPOTTISWOODE AND CO., NEW-STREET SQUARE
AND PARLIAMENT STREET

www.ingramcontent.com/pod-product-compliance
Lightning Source LLC
Chambersburg PA
CBHW052344110726
47901CB00005B/1351

* 9 7 8 3 7 4 2 8 5 1 0 4 8 *